Against the walnut brown of her coarse, home-dyed kirtle her hair was a lone flash of sunlight on a dreary cloudy day. She wore a scattering of freckles across her cheekbones, sown by the spring sun; in a good year they would be brought to full glory by Lammas Day. Her green eyes were dappled with gold, like a sunlit glade, and they were full of life and reflected sorrow and unquenchable warmth.

Aldyth had lived most of her twenty-two years nestled beneath the wing of her godmother, Sirona, the village healer and wisewoman. From this vantage point, she saw more than her share of suffering, but Sirona had taught her to be strong as well as compassionate. The healer had raised Aldyth from infancy to follow her craft. She was well suited to her occupation, for even as a child her quick, bright mind had acted like a sponge, absorbing everything that Sirona could teach her.

Kingdom Come

Naomi and Deborah Baltuck

CORONET BOOKS
Hodder and Stoughton

First published in the United States of America by Viking/Penguin
First published in Great Britain in 1998 by Hodder and Stoughton
First published in paperback in 1998 by Hodder and Stoughton
A division of Hodder Headline PLC

A Coronet Paperback

10 9 8 7 6 5 4 3 2 1

A CIP catalogue record is available
from the British Library

ISBN 0 340 71742 4

Printed and bound in Great Britain by
Mackays of Chatham PLC, Chatham, Kent

Hodder and Stoughton
A division of Hodder Headline PLC
338 Euston Road
London NW1 3BH

For our mother, Eleanor

FROM THE *ANGLO-SAXON CHRONICLES*,
1066 A.D.

. . .then Duke William sailed from Normandy into Pevensey, on the eve of Michaelmas. As soon as his men were fit for service, they constructed a castle at Hastings. When King Harold was informed of this, he gathered together a great host, and came to oppose him at the gray apple tree, and William came upon him unexpectedly before his army was set in order. Nevertheless the king fought against him most resolutely with those men who wished to stand by him, and there was great slaughter on both sides. King Harold was slain, and Leofwine, his brother, and Earl Garth, his brother, and many good men.

. . . they gave William the Conqueror hostages and swore oaths of fealty, and he promised to be a gracious lord to the English. Nevertheless, in the meantime, his armies harried everywhere they came . . . and imposed a very heavy tax on the country . . . they built castles far and wide throughout the land, oppressing the unhappy people, and things went ever from bad to worse. When God wills may the end be good.

PROLOGUE

The Blood Month
November 1067

'Our Father, who art in Heaven, hallowed be Thy name, Thy kingdom come, Thy will be done on earth as it is in Heaven.' Young Gandulf paused in his silent prayer to rein in his restless horse. From across the harvest-stubbled fields the boy watched with no expression as his father's Norman army destroyed a way of life. The Saxons defended themselves from within their timber stronghold with its huge oaken gate, but Gandulf's father had sent soldiers to the forest to fell an oak. Now the repetitive boom of oak upon oak carried far across the vale, mingled with the crash of approaching thunder.

At first light the Normans had struck like a plague of hornets, fiercely and without warning. Gandulf tried to blot out the images in his mind, of the defenders flinging hot coals and boiling water on the swarm attempting to raise siege ladders against the palisade walls. He had seen it all before, the frantic bloodied fingers casting down cobblestones wrenched from the mud of the bailey and hurling water jugs and clay beer mugs that broke into cutting shards on helmed heads.

The screech of wood echoing down the steep bluff like a banshee's keening wail scattered the boy's ugly visions, only to flood his mind with crueler images, for that was a signal that the great gate on the far side of the fortress had splintered and given way. He knew from the triumphant war cries that the Normans were mobbing the breach in the timber enclosure surrounding the Saxon lord Aethelstan's hall. Once again he took up his desperate prayer: 'And forgive us our trespasses . . .'

Soot-blackened smoke rose up to merge with the descending thunderheads, and as dusk fell, long red streamers of searing light shot skyward and flames licked up through thatched roofs. The pale gold fields beneath Castle Hill took on the uncanny green-gray that foretold a storm of epic proportions.

The boy's bodyguards, a hard-bitten lot, shifted restlessly in their saddles, muttering bitterly. With the fighting done, the looting, pillaging, and division of spoils would follow. Yet they were duty-bound to watch their lord's worthless heir. Gandulf shrank from the resentment in their sullen eyes.

The boy was only seven, young to be taken on such a dangerous campaign, the sacking and occupation of the ancient West Saxon settlement of Sceapterbyrig, overlooking the Blackmore Vale, but his father hoped to harden the boy into a warrior. Aware of the soldiers' scorn, the boy urged his horse to a more comfortable distance from his guard as they bickered over a nearly empty wine flask, a poor substitute for the spoils being sparred over across the vale. So Gandulf alone saw the rope lowered down the palisade wall with the straw basket tied to it. He alone watched as a dusky shadow at the base of the wall rose up from the weeds. Like a wraith, the shadow seized the basket and melted back into the dusk, but the boy kept silent.

The dying sun slipped down through the lowering clouds like a drowning man, staining the narrow ribbon of clear sky at the horizon blood red. At last came the signal the guard had been watching for and the boy had been dreading. From the rampart a Norman waved a torch; the day was theirs. The captain of the guard dashed the flask to the ground and spurred his war mount across the open field toward the burning settlement. Without a backward glance at their young charge, the others followed. Reluctantly, the warlord's son trailed after.

In the time it took the Normans to cross the deserted fields and rush the hill to the fort, the light had faded. As they guided their horses through the ruined gateway of the fortress and into the bailey, the latecomers were met by shouts of recognition and taunting jests from their comrades in arms, but the boy heard only the groans of the dying. It took all Gandulf's strength to keep his horse from shying, for unlike the seasoned destriers bred for war, his mount was unused to the sights and smells of battle, the rubble, and the corpses, both Saxon and Norman, that littered the blood-soaked ground.

A scattering of shouts drew Gandulf's gaze; his small party, duty forgotten, spurred their mounts across the bailey to take part in the last of the bloodletting. By the light of the burning buildings the boy watched the lady of the hall as she sat cradling the head of her husband, Aethelstan, who lay where he had fallen guarding the retreat into the refuge of the keep. Gandulf leaned forward in the saddle and watched as Aethelstan's wife held her dying lord, whispering into his ear. His father's warriors, the taste of blood still on their tongues, left off jeering and fell silent, as if straining to catch her words. But no sound could be heard above the cracking of the tattered Saxon standard in the wind.

The harsh bellowing of Gandulf's father, Lord Ralf fitzGerald, shattered the moment. 'I told you idiots to clear the way to the keep. Why is that carrion blocking the door?'

Lord Ralf strode up and seized Aethelstan's leg to pull him roughly to one side but leaped back when he saw the glint of firelight reflected on steel. The lady had drawn a dagger from her belt and clearly meant to use it. Lord Ralf drew back, as startled as if the rushes had risen off the ground against him and come to life. Then he smirked and said in Saxon, 'Do you expect to hold off a Norman army with a jeweled table knife?'

'It has sliced the flesh of swine before,' she spat, 'and 'twill do so again if need be.'

Before Lord Ralf could respond, from the lips of the dying man came a ragged sigh, like the sound of a soul escaping. The lady bent closer to hear him wheeze, 'Brave girl.' His eyes glazed over, and he gave one last slight shudder.

Gandulf's father, cursing in his cups, had often repeated, 'Scratch a Saxon and find a swineherd,' but the dignity of the Saxon lord's death belied his father's words. Gandulf was impressed by Aethelstan's final gesture, yet more so by the woman's, for she must live to face the conqueror. She closed her husband's eyes, smoothed the damp hair from his bloody brow, and gently laid his head upon the ground. Then, rising, she met the conquering Norman's eyes. Touching her bloodstained

3

fingertips to her lips, she said quietly, 'There is that of my husband you can never take from me.' Her eyes shot blue lightning to rival the dazzling flashes that seared the skies, her cheeks blazed scarlet, and her honey-gold hair, fallen loose from her veil, lashed about in the rising winds like the tail of a furious cat. 'Let's get on with it,' she said briskly.

'By God's loins,' said the warlord with an appraising glance, 'I could use a woman like you. You might do worse than become mistress of a conquering Norman baron.'

Her eyes widened in what Gandulf took for fear; he realized his mistake when she curled her lip in disgust and spat on the ground at his father's feet. Gandulf was certain she could not know whom she addressed. His father did not need her consent to do as he pleased with her; if he were to cut her down or take her, no one would lift an eyebrow except in raucous amusement. Gandulf had seen his father do far worse on this campaign.

Lord Ralf's mouth pulled into a sour grin as he announced, 'She goes first to the man who can bring me her dagger. Then you shall each have your turn, but not before we tie her lord's stinking corpse behind a wild horse and turn the hounds loose on him.'

By now a ragged group of survivors, mostly women and children, had been herded into the confines of the stable yard. Their whimpering died away as the horror of their lady's fate penetrated their fear-numbed minds. Gandulf saw several cross themselves.

The breathless silence in the courtyard was broken by a bloodcurdling war cry. 'For King Harold and Lord Aethelstan!' came the shrill scream. A small figure darted out from the crowd and charged Lord Ralf. It was only a towheaded blur until the warlord caught hold of a thin wrist and wrenched a little boy, writhing and kicking, off the ground. In the child's hand was a grown man's dirk.

'Ha!' snorted the Norman. 'The pup would bite with his father's teeth!' With a viselike grip, he squeezed until the child's fingers fell open and the weapon dropped to the ground.

'I hate you!' he shrieked, tears of fury washing tracks down his sooty cheeks. 'You killed my lord. You killed my king.'

4

He lashed out with a fresh barrage of kicks. 'You killed my *mother!*'

Amused, Lord Ralf held the child at arm's length until he was spent. 'Look at this savage whelp, racing headlong into the jaws of the lion to avenge his dam.'

Gandulf's stomach soured. He knew that his father spoke not to his soldiers nor to the Saxon prisoners, but to him alone. Lord Ralf whirled about sharply to glare at his son. Grabbing fistfuls of the waif's tunic, he took two steps in Gandulf's direction and heaved him through the air toward Gandulf. Gandulf's startled horse screamed and reared up, nearly throwing the Norman boy out of the saddle. Amid a shower of curses, some of the Norman soldiers dodged its flailing hooves, while others grabbed for the flying reins. In the confusion, the Saxon boy scrambled to his feet and sprinted toward a break in the wall. Several archers raised arrow to bowstring, while foot soldiers dashed after the fugitive like hounds at the hunt.

'Let him go!' barked Lord Ralf. As the fleeing prisoner slipped through the breach, he nodded approvingly and muttered, 'Would that I had such a whelp.'

Gandulf, still clutching at the pommel of his saddle, felt the color rise in his cheeks and swallowed his tears. He wished to God that he were as wild and brave as the Saxon boy so that his father might love him. But he was not and would never be, and he knew that his father never would.

Lord Ralf smirked to see that his dart had hit its mark, then turned back to the Saxon lady. 'As for you, madam, perhaps I shall be magnanimous after all.'

Ralf fitzGerald's fits and furies were as unpredictable as they were intense and could be cast off as lightly as they were assumed. The Saxon boy would never know, thought Gandulf, that he had saved the life of his liege lady with his flamboyant display.

Drawing his dirk, Lord Ralf began to clean the dried blood from beneath his fingernails. He looked up and inquired idly, 'Madam, where are your children?'

She lifted her chin, but the colour drained from her cheeks. Gandulf should have known his father would not let her escape so lightly; he had merely changed tactics to prick out the chink in her armor. The Norman warlord turned to the Saxon prisoners. 'Produce the brats!' he demanded. They shuffled their feet in determined silence. 'We'll find them soon enough!' he roared. 'Better now than after we've had it out of your hides!'

Angry winds rushing over the stockade walls sucked up the stubborn silence of the Saxon prisoners and carried it into the turbulent darkness. Proud and grieving, the lady shed tears for the first time – not tears of pain, thought Gandulf, but of gratitude.

Lord Ralf growled almost inaudibly and commanded, 'Fetch me the priest.'

Within minutes a mild man with straw-gold hair was dragged before them, his cassock stained with soot and blood, his hands still clutching a small cruet of holy water.

'Please, my Lord,' he implored, 'the dying must receive their extreme unction.'

'Oh, a saint,' Lord Ralf sneered. 'You think to keep them out of Hell, but will they do as much for you?' With a startling swiftness, he seized the priest's forelock in one hand, whirled him about to face the crowd, and raised his dirk to the man's throat. His mocking tone became a chilling snarl as he said coldly over the unresisting priest's shoulder, 'The Saxon whelps, or the priest dies.'

With only the slightest flick of the blade, the Norman slit a gash from the priest's ear to just under his chin. Children whimpered, and several of the women began to wail. The priest closed his eyes and quietly began to whisper the Lord's Prayer.

A plump, redheaded woman stumbled forward. Wringing her filthy apron, she stammered, 'Our lord and lady were only lately married and had as yet but one child. 'Twas only a girl, your worship, just a babe in arms, and a sickly one at that.'

The priest, crimson streams running down his neck and soaking the front of his robe, opened his eyes. 'Margaret speaks the truth,' he said hoarsely. 'Yesterday the child died of a fever in her mother's arms.'

Lord Ralf yanked the cleric's head back by the hair. 'Swear this is so, Priest.'

'I swear . . . By Saint Mary of Egypt's kirtle I buried the child myself.'

Lord Ralf released his hold, and the priest fell in a crumpled heap at his feet. Stepping around the cleric, the Norman said, 'So much the better. I'll have no loose strings and no pretenders, no helpless cubs to grow into snarling wolves.' To the Saxon lady, he said coldly, 'Madam, you will find that my bed would have been warmer than the dark halls of the abbey.' Then he turned to the huddled prisoners standing amid the rubble. He had to shout to be heard over the wailing of the wind as the storm broke out in all its fury. 'Hear this now, and pass it on to those in hiding. The pope has sent me to enforce God's will. Today is Judgment Day, and this is Kingdom Come. From this day forth, these lands belong to King William, and you are mine.'

With an electrifying crash a bolt of lightning seared the sky and struck the pole that flew the tattered rags of the Saxon standard; the banner burst into flame, and the pole exploded into a shower of splinters. The heavens split open, and, like a passionate outpouring of hopeless tears, the rain came spilling down.

'So long as a maiden pure watches over the Crystal Spring, these waters shall flow cold and clear.'

CHAPTER ONE

The Harvest Month
August 1086

'Aldyth! Sirona! Are you there?'

An urgency in the voice sped Aldyth through the morning chill to her door. When she swung it open, the dank smell of fish identified her caller even before the red-faced youth stepped over the threshold.

'Oscar, what's amiss?' she asked. 'Should you not be at the ponds by now?'

''Tis my grandmother Winifred.'

'She's not taken a turn for the worse?' asked Aldyth anxiously, reaching instinctively for her withy basket of potions and simples.

''Tisn't that,' he said quickly, 'but today the women must go up to the hall and spin for Lord Ralf. She's not well enough to make the walk, and Father Edmund's donkey is gone missing again.'

Aldyth laughed, and then, in answer to the flustered lad's look of surprise, she explained, 'So Father Edmund told me this morning, as did Wulfstan the Reeve, when he learned of Winifred's predicament, as well and Mildburh and Judith and Edith on their way up to the hall. The dust never settled from the procession of callers on Winifred's behalf. Don't worry, Oscar. Sirona has already gone up the hill to speak for your grandmother.'

'But Aldyth,' he fretted, 'Lord Ralf said he'd put her off her toft if it happened again.'

'It didn't happen last time, Oscar, and Sirona won't let it happen this time, either.'

9

The lad allowed himself a faint smile. 'Well, then, I'll be off to the stews.' As Oscar Fisher stepped outside, he added, 'I'd like to see the sparks fly when Sirona gets there.'

'Be just as glad,' admonished Aldyth, 'you are not so close as to catch the heat.'

He guffawed at her jest and set off to put in his day's work at the abbey fishponds.

'Poor lad,' thought Aldyth, 'the wool of his tunic is worn thin for this cool weather.' She shifted her gaze from the shabby fisher lad and looked upward through the drizzle to Castle Hill, shrouded in low-hanging mist like a corpse left unburied for a score of years. It had been twenty years since the conquest, and the wooden stockade atop the hill had long since been rebuilt; the scars that would not heal were those of the spirit. Aldyth recalled the Jews who had followed Moses in the wilderness for forty years, until the last of the slave-born souls had returned to God, because the Lord their God had decreed that only the freeborn might enter the Promised Land. Perhaps when the last vanquished Saxon died, Aldyth mused, leaving only slave-born subjects like poor Oscar Fisher for the Normans to rule, there might be peace in England.

Aldyth slipped the handle of her basket over her arm and stepped out into the drizzle to make her way among the huddle of huts that formed the little village of Enmore Green. The mud on the path squished up between her toes with each step of her bare feet. Her shawl slipped unnoticed from her head, and her long honey-gold tresses tumbled carelessly down her back. Against the walnut brown of her coarse, home-dyed kirtle her hair was a lone flash of sunlight on a dreary cloudy day. She wore a scattering of freckles across her cheekbones, sown by the spring sun; in a good year they would be brought to full glory by Lammas Day. Her green eyes were dappled with gold, like a sunlit glade, and they were full of life and reflected sorrow and unquenchable warmth.

Aldyth had lived most of her twenty-two years nestled beneath the wing of her godmother, Sirona, the village healer and wisewoman. From this vantage point, she saw more than her share of suffering, but Sirona had taught her to be strong as well as compassionate. The healer had raised Aldyth from infancy to follow her craft. She was well suited to her occupation, for even as a child her quick, bright mind had acted like a sponge, absorbing everything that Sirona could teach her.

Aldyth knew every shrub, every herb, every tree and its powers. She knew that a sip of milk each day would prevent the growth of small stones in the kidneys and that a meal of liver would cure the weakening of the eyes that occurred at winter's end. She knew how to stanch bleeding and how to ease a fever, how to set a broken limb and how to birth a child. But most of all, Sirona had taught her to love the Great Mother, in whichever guise she took, be it Modron the Little Mother, Sula of the Underworld, or Gefion the Giver, and to respect the gift of the Goddess, the Crystal Spring.

Aldyth was there to give her people their first and last baths. As every child was born, it was bathed in the waters of the Crystal Spring, its first baptism, before even the priest's birth rites. As the deceased was bathed and laid out, the chrismal oil of extreme unction was washed off with the waters of the Crystal Spring. So it was that every soul in Enmore Green began and ended life as a follower of the Goddess, and Aldyth embraced her responsibilities as shepherdess of the Lady's flock.

'Less satisfying ways there are to earn your bread,' said her godmother.

Even as Aldyth had grown in the sheltering shadow of Sirona, so did Enmore Green nestle beneath the great sandstone outcropping chosen in ancient times by great King Alfred as the site for Sceapterbyrig. Most Normans did not concern themselves with the language of the conquered natives, and the many-voweled name was difficult to pronounce, so they simply called the town 'Scafton.' Three miles of walls encircled the city, and the settlement boasted a population of nearly two thousand, rivaling all but the very biggest towns in England. It had fourteen inns, a dozen churches, and a thriving public market. On the site of the wooden Saxon fort that had crowned the bluff overlooking the Blackmore Vale, foundations were being laid for one of the hundreds of Norman stone castles that were mushrooming up throughout England.

Yet the town's dominant force was the Abbey of Saint Mary and Saint Edward, commonly known as Scafton Abbey.

Scafton's abbey was one of the largest and wealthiest, home to nuns from the noblest and most powerful families in all of England and Normandy. The abbey, like the town, had been founded more than two hundred years before by King Alfred the Great. Now, in its ascendancy, great stone additions were being erected and more than thirty nuns prayed and worshiped within its walls of yellow stone.

The nuns were not allowed to give communion, take confessions, or say mass. These essential offices were fulfilled by the abbey's chaplain, Father Fulk. But if Father Fulk resided at the abbey, Abbess Eulalia presided. Father Fulk had already been an old man when he had first instructed Eulalia as her father's chaplain in Normandy. Soon after her fellow nuns had elected her abbess, she had sent for the old cleric and appointed him resident priest. Father Fulk considered himself fortunate to have come into an easy retirement, while the nuns considered themselves fortunate to be able to carry on their affairs without the interference of an officious priest, for he had spent most of the last twelve years in his chamber over the chapel tippling and dozing by the fire.

Upon taking office, Abbess Eulalia had put the abbey's affairs into order. She dismissed, without fear or favor, the slothful and incompetent, from the seneschal of her largest manor to the lowliest scullion, and she began laying the foundations for a great new Norman abbey. It was an expensive undertaking, and even her efficient management of the abbey and its properties would not have sufficed to pay for the construction. 'The life's blood of the abbey,' Abbess Eulalia would say, 'lies in Enmore Green.'

Enmore Green was much the same as any other little village in the Blackmore Vale, with one exception: the Crystal Spring. Scafton had no source of water. The Saxon hilltop had been chosen as a fortress site for its commanding defensive capabilities, for the sandstone outcrop rose high above the rolling hills of Dorsetshire, but its porous stone would hold no water. All the water on Castle Hill was supplied by the Crystal Spring in Enmore Green.

Under most circumstances, the Norman conquerors took what they wanted. But this was a delicate situation, for the spring was on land owned by Scafton Abbey. The legitimacy of Duke William's claim to the throne of England, dearly bought, rested on his cooperation with the Church. This prevented any rough dealings with the good ladies of Scafton Abbey, lest they run back to Rome with complaints to the pope. So when a conflict of interest arose and quarrels ensued, those on Castle Hill drank beer.

The grateful abbess called the springwater 'Enmore pennies' because of the income it brought to the abbey, but it conferred other benefits as well. According to local legend, the waters had mystical curative powers. The Norman conquerors scoffed at the superstitious locals but could not deny that many citizens of Scafton and Enmore Green lived to see their grandchildren or even their great-grandchildren, and they were glad to have a healthy workforce when it came time to put hand to plow.

'But the power of the Crystal Spring cannot mend all ills,' thought Aldyth ruefully, 'and it would seem that even the Goddess cannot coax the sun from behind the clouds nor make the crops grow in this cold and damp.' Aldyth made her way to old Elviva's to check on her asthma, which seemed to wax as her rheumatism waned. The old woman lived in her own small hut on the same toft as her son and daughter-in-law. They did their best to provide for her, but both had to spend most of their time in the fields.

Aldyth paused a moment outside Elviva's door, called out a greeting to announce herself, and stepped inside. It was dark and smoky within and no wonder that the old woman was afflicted with asthma. Elviva was huddled on her straw pallet by the fire.

'Good morning, old mother,' said Aldyth.

'Aldyth Lightfoot,' replied the old woman, looking up guiltily but burrowing down deeper into her blanket.

'Sirona has sent a fresh egg for me to boil for you this morning.' It was a rare treat, but Sirona had taken to sending an egg whenever she could spare one, 'to give Elviva a reason for getting out of bed in the morning,' she explained. 'Even an ass is offered a carrot at the end of the day, and Elviva has already pulled her fair share of the load.'

Aldyth, bending down to take the old woman's arm, said,

'Let me help you up. I've brought some freshly gathered thyme to sweeten your wash water.'

'You coddle me so,' said Elviva.

'No more than you deserve, old mother.' Aldyth put the egg on to boil and set an infusion of comfrey, wild cucumber, and dandelion root on to steep. 'While we are waiting, let me comb your hair.'

The old widow had had no intention of stirring from her bed, but somehow she found herself sitting at the table breathing in the steam of the infusion, while Aldyth stood behind combing and braiding her hair. 'My breath gets shorter all the time,' Elviva complained. 'Sometimes I can feel the Mara's hands choking the life out of me.'

'Even were it true that troll women roved through the night, the Little Mother would never allow them to plague the unwary in their sleep,' said Aldyth. ''Tis this weather, old mother, that worsens your ailment. Pray to the Lady for a drier summer next year.'

'And a better harvest,' added Elviva. 'I've not seen such an ill-omened year since the Great Maned Star lit up the skies just before I lost my man, Edgar, at Hastings.'

Hardly a family had not lost a husband, a brother, a father, and their overlord to the Normans. Most men had lost their freedom and every woman had, nor was there a Saxon child in England who did not understand that it was born of a beaten race. Almost twenty years had passed, but never a visit went by that Elviva did not bring up Hastings and Edgar.

Aldyth could not treat the old woman's sorrow, but she had learned that Elviva would as soon worry about someone else's problems as her own. 'Have you seen Bertha's new baby?' asked Aldyth. ''Tis a boy; they're going to call him Edmund.'

Elviva blanched. ''Tis bad luck to speak the child's name aloud before the christening.' Crossing herself, she mused, 'Maybe I'll call on Bertha today. Perhaps I could hold the baby while Bertha sleeps.' Smiling to herself, she said, 'It has been too long since I've held a newborn. God grant the next be my own grandchild.'

'I shouldn't wonder if you were to have a grandchild

very soon to hang on your skirts and lift up your spirits,' ventured Aldyth.

'My boy Wulfric married a good girl,' said Elviva. 'Some say Edith is addled; it runs in her family, for you know that her father is Edwin MoonCatcher. But she takes good care of Wulfric and her heart is in the right place, bless her.' Elviva leaned forward and confided, 'I only hope she's not barren. Married two years and no child yet.'

Aldyth was not concerned about Edith's fertility; she had been secretly providing her friend with herbs to prevent a pregnancy, just until the newly-weds could settle in. Edith was hoping to conceive the following spring; summer babies were healthier because there were more fresh foods in the mother's diet to nourish a baby growing in the womb. But Aldyth kept this in the strictest confidence; not even Wulfric knew, and certainly not the Church. Sirona had explained, 'Women must make commonsense choices that bullheaded males and an unbending Church would never condone. Some things are best left unsaid.'

Aldyth finished setting Elviva's house in order. 'Remember to keep your bedding aired and dry. Drink plenty of comfrey, and use dill and garlic in your cooking.'

'I do that,' said Elviva.

'Yes, I know,' said Aldyth, smiling faintly. She gave Elviva a quick peck on the cheek and hurried on her way, relieved to escape the garlic-tainted air of the hut.

It was only a short walk to the cottage of Alcuin HardHead. Alcuin's son Leofwine, barely twelve, had been working in the fields since he could toddle, carrying water, bundling straw, and scaring away greedy cows. He'd been proud to take part in his first harvest as a man, but late in the day his scythe had slipped and cut a slice out of his calf.

Alcuin and Eanfled's cottage reminded Aldyth of a blanket alive with fleas, for Leofwine was the oldest of six and the place was always crawling with grubby urchins, milling, fighting, tugging on their mother's apron strings, and vying for her notice. Nine months to the day after Eanfled and Alcuin had wed, Leofwine had been born. Since then, before one had been weaned, the next was begun. At wit's end and fearful of damnation, Eanfled had come to Sirona for a potion to end her relentless childbearing. Sirona had set her fears of hellfire to rest by saying 'God himself had only one.' Eanfled knew then that she had borne her last child and had only to worry about feeding those already hatched.

As Aldyth applied a fresh poultice to Leofwine's leg, she glanced up at his face for signs of pain lest she tie the bandages too tightly. What she saw concerned her more than mere pain: lines of worry that should mark no young boy's face. Leofwine took no notice of Aldyth, for his eyes were on his father's hands, which Alcuin was wringing nervously.

'Don't fret, Leofwine,' said Aldyth as she rose to go. 'If you must sit out this year's harvest, next year you'll be leading the reapers in the field.'

Alcuin followed her out and caught up with her at the gate of their little toft. Speaking in low tones, he asked, 'Is the lad going to be all right, Aldyth?'

''Tis a deep wound, but it seems clean. By the Lady's grace, he will live.'

'But will he have use of his leg? He alone is old enough to help with the harvest.'

'Not with this year's harvest.' With a note of warning, Aldyth added, 'Too soon on his feet, and the leg will never be sound. Don't worry about your harvest obligations to Lord Ralf, for the villagers will come to your aid. Do as I say now, and Leofwine will be fit again in time for spring planting.'

This was no small worry, for the dues exacted by the Normans from their serfs were heavy. In Saxon society a dispute over what was owed to a lord might have ended up in negotiation and the lightening of duties. If a Saxon freeman was unhappy with the decision, he was entitled to find satisfaction elsewhere. Alcuin and Leofwine would have been freemen in his father's time, but now they were only serfs, little better than slaves: tied to the land like a dog on a rope. Everyone had his place in the new order; everyone was somebody's man. Alcuin belonged to Lord Ralf, Lord Ralf answered to the earl of Gillingham, and the earl of Gillingham had sworn life, limb, and fealty to King William. King William alone answered only to God – and the pope, if it suited him.

These thoughts scattered like chaff in the wind as Aldyth took the muddy wattle-and-hedge-lined path to the hut of Bertha Tofter and Agilbert MoonCatcher, to measure the progress of their firstborn. They were as mismatched as a mastiff and a terrier. At fourteen, Bertha was a small girl. Agilbert, barely grown, was like a great gangling puppy not yet used to handling his massive bulk. Both orphaned, they had come into their tiny holdings quite young. They had made for themselves a new family that had proved to be at once a joy and a refuge. The lad, in his desire to coddle his pregnant child bride, had carried her to church like a doll and followed her about with a cloth to throw over her head that she might not lay eye upon a hare in the brush, for it was common knowledge that Bertha's harelip had been caused by her mother's sighting of a hare.

Sirona had warned that the birthing would be like trying to pull a bear through a fox's den. But the baby had come early, which Sirona pronounced a blessing in this case, as the child was already big enough to thrive. Even so, the birthing had been difficult, with too much bleeding and too long a labor. The moment the baby had emerged, the exhausted mother had anxiously looked him over. The father's vigilance had paid off.

'He's perfect,' said Bertha for the hundredth time, smiling up at Agilbert while Aldyth dandled the baby and tickled the palms of his tiny hands, noting with her healer's eye that the little fingers curled and flexed as a healthy baby's should.

'A boy on the first try,' boasted the proud father, 'and a strong, healthy one at that.'

'When the hen lays an egg, the rooster cackles,' murmured Aldyth, winking at Bertha as she returned the swaddled infant to its mother.

'Aye,' Bertha replied, winking at Aldyth. 'There would be no baby boys were there not foolish girls to bear them.'

'You're still bleeding, and that's to be expected,' Aldyth added quickly, noting the anxious look that flashed across Agilbert's face. 'I've applied a poultice of Saint-John's-wort and grape leaves to stanch the bleeding, and I've brewed you some rose hips and ragwort to thicken your blood. Have you any honey?'

'Very little,' admitted Bertha.

'I'll have Father Edmund send you some. Drink the brew sweetened with honey. But rest now. I'll look in on you tomorrow, little sister.' To the father, she added, 'I'm leaving more herbs for the infusion, and be sure to give her plenty of caudle and springwater.'

Agilbert accepted Aldyth's orders with a deference that would have scandalized the Normans; but Saxons were accustomed to respecting the rights and position of women. According to Saxon law, a murderer had had to pay as much wergild, or blood money, for the death of a woman as for that of a man. A woman had been as likely as her brother to inherit property from her father or mother, and the protection of these rights had been written into Saxon law. 'Outrageous!' King William had growled. 'No wonder their women are plagued with pride. We shall put an end to that!' The status of Saxon women had been reduced to that of Norman women – lower, in fact, for they were the conquered race. They had become pawns in King William's rearrangement of the political chessboard. It had become legal to wed a woman against her will, and Saxon heiresses had been parceled out as rewards to knights who had supported William's fight for the English throne. Saxon noblewomen had been dragged to church to wed the butchers who had slaughtered their husbands, brothers, and fathers.

As she stepped out of the hut, Aldyth's eyes were caught by movement on Castle Hill. Even in rain that would have driven any freeman into the shelter of thatch and fire, those poor serfs were forced to cart stones and heavy baskets of dirt up to the motte rising at the top of the steep bluff. William was famous for his castle building by the infamous means of using impressed Saxon labor. The Norman conquerors were devoid of artistic accomplishments, but they were excellent military strategists, on the cutting edge when it came to war. Aldyth shuddered and pulled her damp shawl about her shoulders, as though it might keep out those chilling thoughts.

The squealing and snuffling of a wandering pig offered welcome distraction. Since the pigs and cows of the village were not fenced in, they had to be fenced out. Every hut, with its garden and its apple tree and plum tree, was enclosed in a wattle fence. As Aldyth approached the low end of the village, she saw that Father Edmund had repaired the fence surrounding the tiny churchyard of Saint Wulfstan's. 'It wouldn't do,' he had explained, 'for someone to find a cow eating the flowers off his mother's grave.'

But the fence of the toft next to the little stone church sagged drunkenly. Chickens ran through gaps in the fence, and pigs had worn paths from the gaps to the garden. This was the enclosure surrounding Father Edmund's own holding. The old priest meant to mend his own fence too, but something always came up to prevent it. This week his attention was focused on Bertha's baby, Leofwine's accident, mending the churchyard fence, and finding someone to milk Winifred's cow while she recovered from a chill. The following week would be the baptism of the new child, visits to Leofwine as he convalesced, and enlisting volunteers to take the lad's place in his father's field.

It was past noon when Aldyth stepped up to Father Edmund's gate to find the old man picking caterpillars off his cabbages. A wave of tenderness washed over Aldyth as she watched him gently remove the pests and drop them on the far side of the fence. He saw Aldyth and his sweet, tired mouth broke into a broad smile of welcome. He was somewhere over fifty, with a shock of snow-white hair naturally tonsured by time. The puckered red scar that ran from ear to throat was so familiar to Aldyth that she scarcely noticed it anymore. The kindly gaze of his faded blue eyes masked a shrewd grasp of human nature. Although Father Edmund firmly believed in the adage that one can catch more flies with honey than with vinegar, he had never put it to the test, for he had not a dram of vinegar in him. 'Bless you, daughter. What news of Bertha and her child?'

'Bertha's child will be hale and hearty enough for christening this Sunday, Father, but you won't be if you don't get in out of this wet.'

Father Edmund looked up and blinked into the rain. 'Quite so,' he said with a chuckle. 'Have you time to come in? We could see what is waiting for us in the pot.'

Aldyth smiled and gave him her arm. As they entered, there

was a scramble of chickens about their feet, and the smell of wet feathers and musty earth assaulted their nostrils. When the clucking subsided, Aldyth heard a wet snuffling from a dark corner.

'Hello, Gregory,' she called.

''Tis too damp for him outside today,' said Father Edmund protectively. 'His rheumatism is acting up. He wandered home this morning, and he was stiff in the knees.'

Aldyth patted the graying muzzle of the scrawny donkey tethered in the corner. 'Well, Gregory, let me see what I have in my basket for you.' She held out a fragrant bunch of feverfew, which Gregory gathered in with big soft lips. 'I thought you'd like that,' she said. Aldyth explained to the priest, ''Twill take the ache from his joints.' She gave the donkey one last tug on the ear. 'Gregory, you've had a bite to eat. 'Tis our turn now.'

Father Edmund served up a thin, warm broth that tasted of cabbage and onion and only faintly of the thrice-boiled beef bone that languished in the bottom of the pot. Aldyth settled onto the hard wooden bench by the fire and warmed her face in the steam rising from the bowl. 'So you'll have a new godson next Sunday,' she observed.

Father Edmund's eyes were lost in smile wrinkles that accompanied his proud grin. He already had quite a collection of godchildren, and he took his duties as godfather quite seriously. There were now two generations of Edmunds in the village. There was Elviva's son, who had married into Long Cross, and Alcuin HardHead had had a brother Edmund, who had been gored to death by an ox, which had been hanged as punishment, and they had all eaten beef at his funeral. Father Edmund had stood godfather to one of Alcuin's large brood, and Mildburh Miller's youngest was also named after his priestly godfather. Even Judith Alcester had a daughter Edmunda. The priest loved them all as if he had borne them himself, though he had never experienced parenthood of the flesh.

Father Edmund had married into Enmore Green from the neighboring parish of Alcester when he took Aelfgyth DoeEyes to wife. Except for her long-lashed eyes, she had been homely as a hedgehog and as thin as a broom handle. But she was as sweet-tempered as he, and together they had muddled along, living each day in joy. Their idyll had been cut short when she had died giving birth to their only child, which was stillborn.

Some of the more radical clergy had claimed that the tragedy was God's vengeance, for Father Edmund had rejected the Church's draconian new doctrine requiring celibacy for priests, but Father Edmund had offered no apologies. 'Saint Peter himself had been married and was a better man for it. Aelfgyth was my helpmeet, my soul mate, my love,' he had told Aldyth and Sirona in a rare moment of reminiscence. 'I'll not marry again,' he had said, 'but not because of threats by Church fanatics or strange new doctrines. 'Tis rather because I am one who can give his heart but once.'

'You say you can give your your heart but once,' Sirona had gently contradicted him, 'but I see you tossing it to the children in the streets.'

Aldyth looked up to see Father Edmund feeding a crust to a chicken at his feet. She smiled, then sighed; her rounds had gone smoothly enough, but something nagged at her.

'Daughter,' asked the old priest, 'what troubles you?'

Somehow his question crystalized her concern. ''Tis Leofwine, Father.'

'Is the leg not mending properly?'

'The leg will heal, given rest, but the lad seems sick at heart. As you know, he's the oldest of Alcuin and Eanfled's brood, always an eager helper, and he had hoped to prove himself this harvest. Now he feels he is only a burden to his family.'

'Distraction,' Father Edmund said quickly. 'That's what the lad needs.' The old man knit his brow in thought, absentmindedly shooing a chicken off the table. Quite suddenly, his face brightened. 'I shall teach the boy to read! If he is an apt learner, he could keep the parish records for me. A clerk can earn a very good living, with a limp or no.'

'That would be just the thing to lift his spirits,' agreed Aldyth. As so often happened, she had brought the priest a problem and he had provided a solution. She and Father Edmund were both shepherds of the same flock, and though each ministered in a different fashion, they had come to respect and even to depend upon each other. Father Edmund was more interested in hearts and souls than in catechism. If he, like Pope

Gregory the Great, was aware of the pagan roots and veiled meanings of so many of the holy days and rituals, he was willing to accept them with a thin Christian veneer.

Aldyth walked back up the hill into the village. Like a snake, the rising motte on Castle Hill drew her gaze. According to the elders, many changes had taken place since the conquest. Even aside from the poor harvest this year, matters were worse than they had been for some time. Conquest had only made the Conqueror hungry for more war, more territory, more conquest. King William's wars on the continent had so depleted the store of treasure bled from the English that he could not afford to send troops back across the channel from Normandy to defend the English coast from the present threat of invasion by the Danes. Not trusting the English to fight against their Danish cousins, William had deemed it necessary to raise another army of mercenaries to fight that war while his Norman army was engaged on the mainland. But mercenaries would have to be paid. So last Christmas King William had decreed that a new tax roll be drawn up, listing in detail the worth and possessions of every household, from the greatest castle to the meanest hovel. The Normans made certain that every last pig was counted that it might be taxed or confiscated. After an inquest had been held in every village in England, at which the possessions of each man were inventoried, spies were dispatched and informers sought out to report any possible withholding. Now no Englishman dared meet his neighbor's eye; those who had hidden even a penny were afraid the guilt would show in their faces, and the innocent feared people would think they were counting their neighbors' chickens. King William had finally robbed the Saxons of their last treasure: their oneness in the face of a tyrant's oppression.

Lost in her grim thoughts, Aldyth came to her own hut hardly knowing how she had gotten there. Like the others in the village, it was made of wattle and daub, sheets of woven sticks plastered over with mud. The roof too was wattle, covered with thatch. It was nearly impossible to know night from day in the windowless, unventilated hut. Aside from the wash of dim light that streamed through the doorway, there was only the flickering light of the hearth fire, which burned day and night in the center of the hut. For most families, the close conditions were made even closer, for living space was commonly shared with the livestock. But Aldyth's situation was more comfortable than most; she shared her quarters only with her godmother, their milk cow, Godiva, and their chickens.

Wooden planks pegged to the rafter poles under the thatch served as shelves to hold pottery jars filled with syrups, salves, and ointments. Other shelves held neatly folded rags, ready to be used as bandages. On one shelf was Aldyth's spare kirtle, moved to the shelves on the far wall after the time Sirona had mistaken it for a rag and nearly ripped it into bandages. The gown shared its spot with the wooden clogs Aldyth wore in the winter and the spare cloak that served as an extra blanket when the weather turned. Straw ropes hung crisscross from the rafters, festooned with bunches of herbs hanging upside down to dry, and the fragrance of the herbs filled the tiny cottage, pleasantly masking the ever-present odor of smoke, damp earth, and wet feathers.

Aldyth heard the cackle of excited hens even before stepping inside. As her eyes grew used to the dark, she saw Sirona crouched over her little red hens as they pecked at a scattering of grain on the floor. This was not unusual; the wisewoman's hens were the fattest in the village, for she took readings for omens by casting down grain and observing the manner in which the hens received it. Unusual was the clucking noise the seeress herself began to make.

Sirona watched the hens, but Aldyth was watching her godmother. The wisewoman was a small woman, once slender but now lean with age. It was said that in Sirona's youth, she had been a wild beauty, although there was no one alive who could confirm this, for there was not an elder in the village who could remember a time when Sirona had not been old; some said she had grown out of the land with the hills. Yet with age Sirona had become regally handsome, the fine bones of her face taking on a feeling of quiet strength and endurance, like craggy granite. Her long silver hair hung loose, unconfined by her kerchief, which lay about her shoulders like a shawl. Remarkably – some said it was magic – not one of her teeth had been lost or pulled. And out of this age-old face peered hawklike eyes as black as polished obsidian, gleaming with a kindly irony. She was loved by the villagers and feared by the Normans, for she was known to have the power to heal or to harm. In this age of footpads and fugitives, Aldyth walked freely, for everyone knew she was under the crone's protection.

Aldyth placed her hand in Sirona's outstretched palm, listening, wide-eyed, as the seeress whispered, 'Wave upon wave crashed over our beaches. At last I see the End of the Beginning.'

Aldyth was impressed and a little frightened by her godmother's earnest and somber demeanor. 'What does this mean, Sirona?'

Cupping Aldyth's chin gently in her hand, the old woman peered into her godchild's green eyes. 'Do you remember years ago, child, when I told you that you must be patient, that your destiny was yet to come?'

Aldyth nodded.

'Your name, Aldyth, means "ancient prophecy," and the time has come for you to fulfill the ancient prophecy for which you are named. May we both be wise and strong enough for this day, for the stars have completed their dance, the Great Mother has aligned the spheres, the spectators have stepped into play. In other words,' said Sirona wryly, 'the pot has come to a boil.'

Sirona often said things that Aldyth could not comprehend. But never had they been accompanied by such a sense of forboding. Aldyth looked questioningly at her godmother.

Sirona shrugged. 'Never mind, child. In the fullness of time, you will understand.' Abruptly she said, 'I've a stock of valerian for your basket. Stop by the old hermit's with some syrup for his lung fever, and go by way of the Crystal Spring to say a prayer for Ethelred. Step quickly, so you can be home before the bells toll curfew.'

Curfew, meaning 'cover fire,' was a word introduced by the Normans. To prevent the plotting of the English by night, King William had ordered that in every city and village of England, every Saxon must bank his fire, blow out his candle, and, unless he wished to sit in the dark, go to bed. To be caught out after curfew was punishable by heavy fines or worse, for the penalty might depend upon the whim of the local authorities.

Hugh fitzGrip, the sheriff of Dorset, found this an easy way to squeeze a few pence out of the peasants; if he suspected that the people of a certain village were getting careless, he would send his deputies to keep a watch upon its folk to catch them burning a late candle or hurrying home from a wedding feast after hours and then pocket the resulting fine.

'I'll leave right away, Godmother,' said Aldyth, tucking the bunch of dried herbs into her basket. She had gotten as far as the threshold when Sirona called out, 'Remember, my child, everything happens for a reason, and the Lady Modron watches over us.'

Their hut lay at the very edge of the green, created by the meeting of many paths and cut through by the main road to Scafton. The Crystal Fountain lay on the edge of the green beneath the steep bluff that was crowned by Castle Hill. Stretching high into the sky, the huge twisted limbs of an ancient oak tree overhung the fountain like sheltering arms. It was said that the murmuring voices of elves could be heard among its leaves. Its gnarled branches were adorned with little strips of rags, each representing a wish made in hope that the Fairy Folk might grant it. Father Odo, the priest who ministered to the Norman garrison, paid regular visits to this altar of pagan worship. In a rage, he would tear the rags from its branches, but the next time he passed by, there were always enough strips impudently wagging their tails at him to arouse his fury once again. He dared not destroy the tree itself, for it was an important landmark, visible from as far away as Glastonbury Tor across the Blackmore Vale. And besides, it was whispered that Father Odo actually feared the vengeance of the Fairy Folk.

Scafton was a hub of commerce and culture; travelers were no nine days' wonder, let alone the talk of a lifetime, as in some villages. The path the fountain overlooked was a main thoroughfare, leading from the gates of Scafton down steep Tout Hill to Sherbourne and the world beyond. Peddlers and tinkers, farmers and shepherds on their way to market stopped for a sip of sweet water at the Crystal Spring. Knights and stewards who held land of Lord Ralf fitzGerald and came to renew fealty stopped to water their horses. There were pilgrims who had come to kiss Saint Edward the Martyr's bones and messengers to and from Abbess Eulalia. There were even those who had heard of the Crystal Spring and came to say a prayer to the Goddess and drink of the healing waters. Most travelers who stopped to drink of the fountain, however, were unaware of its significance. The fountain was no chalice of silver or gold but only a mean stone trough, simple and of the earth, for the worth of it lay not in the vessel but in its contents.

The damp, misty day was not darkening so much as fading unnoticed into dusk. By the time Aldyth knelt beside the fountain, most travelers were bedded for the night and the villagers huddled beside their hearthfires. Except for the burbling of the little brook that carried off the waters of the spring, the silence was complete.

Then came an unnatural stirring of the willow that grew so lushly along its banks. As Aldyth knelt in prayer, the undergrowth rustled. As she put down the offering of sky-blue asters she had plucked from the hazel hedgerow on her way to the fountain, grimy fingers parted several branches in the willow brush. From out of the greenery darted an ill-kempt man, looking hagridden and dressed in filthy rags. Stealthily he crept up behind the kneeling girl. She turned just as he was upon her and gasped as he seized her wrists and brought his face down to stare desperately into hers.

CHAPTER TWO

'Aldyth Lightfoot?' asked the stranger hoarsely, with something in his voice that spoke of the wet and reedy fenlands rather than Aldyth's own rolling chalk hills.

'Ethelred?'

He nodded with obvious relief.

'What are you doing?' Aldyth jerked her wrists free and nervously glanced around to determine whether anyone had observed their meeting in the twilight. Rising quickly and lifting her shawl over her hair, Aldyth snatched up her basket and herded him into the woods like a dainty sheepdog driving a bull. Under cover of the trees, she rebuked him gently: 'You must show more caution than to step out into the open like this.'

Ethelred assumed the posture of a chastened puppy and followed her into the thickening woods of alder, hazel, oak, and holly. The path was indistinguishable from those followed by cattle wandering loose through the woods in search of forage. The twilight deepened, and in the gloom the trees melted into an indistinct mass. He asked in a low whisper, 'How far to the next hide? I've had no rest since Sarum.'

''Tis six miles, but they go quickly,' she replied. 'You must be weary.'

'Weary indeed. I never thought the day would come when I'd be slinking out of England like a thief in the night. I haven't slept for two days, haven't eaten for three.'

Aldyth reached into her basket and handed him a chunk of coarse brown bread and a bit of hard cheese. 'Eat now. Even the trees have ears. We can talk later.'

They made their journey in silence, but the black forest was far from silent. A whisper of movement in the brush was the passing of a fox. A sudden rattle of branches to one side betrayed nothing more threatening than the position of a startled hedgehog. The scent of crushed bracken beneath their feet lost its comforting familiarity in the dead of night, but Aldyth had learned to discount the magnified terrors on these runs, for she understood the effects of stretched nerves upon the senses.

Indistinct tufts of gray cloud scudded across the black sky but could not blot out the starlight. Judging from the swing of the stars in the sky, Aldyth knew they were making good speed. At last they came to a large clearing in the woods of Cranborne Chase. Although Cranborne Chase, the private hunting ground of the earl of Gillingham, was small compared to the huge tracts of forest seized by the king for his personal use, it would take more than one man's lifetime to hunt it all.

On the far side of the clearing, cool shades of dusky purple and blue were turned to black against the stark orange splinters of light escaping through the cracks in the walls of the hermit's hovel. Ethelred glimpsed what appeared to be a figure looming in the darkness. As he jumped sideways, stifling a shout, he nearly knocked Aldyth over. Choking back her own cry, Aldyth spun around to discover the cause of his alarm.

Catching her breath, she whispered, ''Tis only a beehive on a stump.'

Ethelred peered at the blur of straw he had taken for a face in the dark. He shook his head at his foolishness, and they ventured out of the sheltered woods and into the open.

Aldyth suddenly realized that in the excitement of the upset, she had forgotten to warn Ethelred. She halted abruptly and began, 'Don't be alarmed—' It was too late; a startling cacophony of trumpeting sent Ethelred grabbing at Aldyth's arm and Aldyth clutching reflexively at the pendant that hung on a leather cord around her neck.

The pendant was only a baby's plaything, a tiny ivory wand made to fit an infant's grip, with three silver bells dangling from its end, but it was the only gift she had from parents she had no memory of. The wand was inscribed with words that Aldyth had often studied but could not read, for she had no knowledge of letters. She knew only that this was the single link she had with her blood kin, carried by her own tiny hand from another life in which she must have been pampered and loved.

Aldyth allowed the rush of nervous energy to escape in one long breath. The loud bugling was just the noisy stirring of the hermit's grumpy, territorial geese, but no matter how many times she had walked this path, she would never get used to it.

'I'm sorry,' she said, blushing in the dark. 'I meant to warn you.'

They crossed the grassy clearing and approached the hermit's door, an untanned hide stretched over a wooden frame. Aldyth knocked gently, swung the door open on its leather hinges, and motioned for Ethelred to follow. The hut was half the size of Sirona's. A straw pallet competed for space with a table, two crude benches, and a stool. In one dark corner was a scattered pile of straw for twisting into rope. In another, neatly stacked, were baskets fashioned from the same straw rope. Placed upside down on a tree stump, they would serve as beehives, like the one they had just passed. On the central hearth, embers burned low but warm. Steam rose from a wooden tankard on the table, but there was no trace of the hermit. The eerie silence drummed in their ears.

'Where is he?' asked Ethelred, his eyes darting about nervously.

'He'll be here,' Aldyth assured him. 'I'll brew you some valerian while we wait.'

A deep voice called from the doorway, 'A dancing hare lives longer than a basking lizard.' A tall, broad-shouldered man ducked under the lintel. 'Welcome,' he said.

Every time Aldyth saw him, she was taken aback to find him as impossibly handsome as she remembered him. His long sun-gold hair and azure eyes were not unusual among those of Saxon blood, but on Bedwyn they were striking. His muscular body moved with an easy grace. He spoke with a deep voice and a commanding air. Many Saxons sported mustaches, but Bedwyn was clean-shaven; too vain, Aldyth suspected, to cover up the perfection of his face. His only flaw, if it could be called that, was the too-strong set of his chin, which suggested a stubborn streak that Aldyth was already well-acquainted with. He was a magnificent creature, and there was no doubt that Bedwyn was as conscious of his good looks as Aldyth was innocent of her own.

'Bedwyn, greet Ethelred of Ely. He's been two nights and a day coming from Sarum.'

'So you are Ethelred,' said Bedwyn, clasping the man's shoulders warmly. 'Aldyth, tonight you have bumped shoulders with one of the stalwart men to serve with the Wake.'

Aldyth gasped. Her eyes widened. 'Hereward himself?'

'Aye,' replied Ethelred, making no effort to hide the bitterness in his voice. 'I was one of his captains before he turned his back on the cause after the fall of Ely.'

Ely, in the bleak and impenetrable fenlands of East Anglia, had been the seat of the last organized Saxon resistance. For two years the occupying Normans had trembled in their beds and traveled only in force, fearing Hereward's armed bands of Saxon rebels, marauding Danes, and outlawed renegades that harried the Norman occupation of the fenland. They had become a humiliating thorn in King William's side. A lengthy siege, Normandy's best military engineers, and the whole of the Norman army could not bring them down or flush them out. It was the treacherous betrayal by a cowardly abbot that had brought about Ely's fall a full six years after the Great Battle of Hastings. After Ely was lost, its leader, Hereward the Wake, had gone into hiding. Eventually, he had made his peace with King William, married a Norman, and received his family's holdings back. But many of Hereward's followers were less pragmatic. Refusing to capitulate, they had scattered and remained in hiding in wood, fen, and heath.

'I've heard rumors of your coming,' said Bedwyn, ushering Ethelred toward a bench.

'And I've heard whispers of the hermit of the Blackmore Vale, but little did I expect to meet you,' replied Ethelred.

'Let you wash the dust of the road off your lips with a mug of ale. Then you must tell us how you have fared on your journey.'

Bedwyn lifted a wooden mug from a peg in the wall and

dipped it into a bucket in the corner. 'Aldyth?' he offered, holding up a second mug.

She nodded and he dipped that one, too. As Bedwyn handed it to Aldyth, their fingers brushed, and the mere touch of his skin against hers roused such a primal response that it startled her. Bedwyn smiled knowingly as he met her eyes. Feeling her cheeks grow hot, she looked away, irritated and embarrassed.

Ethelred filled the awkward silence. 'I don't know how swiftly news travels, but I bring ill tidings. They've scorched the coast from the Wash to the Isle of Wight.'

Aldyth gasped.

'What, so soon?' exclaimed Bedwyn. 'We'd heard the Danes were coming, but we didn't know they'd already landed!'

'No, 'tis the Norman dogs!' Ethelred cried hotly. 'They're sacking their own coast on the chance of a Danish landing.'

'God damn their souls to Hell! I knew the Bastard didn't trust Englishmen to defend the English coast,' fumed Bedwyn, 'and that he'd brought in mercenaries because he feared we'd prefer a Danish tyrant to a Norman one. But to force us to give up our grain to pay for his troops when there is not enough to feed ourselves—'

'—and then to turn his dogs loose on the English—' interjected Ethelred.

'—to bite the hand that feeds them,' finished Aldyth quietly.

Bedwyn growled, 'They say this latest tax inquest is so thorough that God will be using it to make judgments on Doomsday.'

'God would never be so petty,' said Aldyth.

'That's not all,' continued Ethelred. 'I've spoken with Edward Shepherd—'

'Take care, Ethelred,' cautioned Aldyth. 'I know only the hide before us and the hide behind us. Anything more would endanger lives needlessly.'

'This has bearing upon every hide along the Starlit Path in every shire of England. A fortnight ago, the Normans smoked old Aeschwine OneTooth out of his hide in Ditchling, and Thane Siward Ericsson's eldest son, who was holed up there on his way to the coast.'

Aldyth stifled a sob rising in her throat.

Bedwyn sucked in his breath. 'Damn those carrion-sucking dogs!'

Aldyth's and Bedwyn's eyes met. 'Were they taken alive?' he asked somberly.

'Old OneTooth had a hidden dagger. He slew the thane's son and then himself before the Normans could take them. As far as we know, the secret of the next hide is safe.'

'By King Harold's bones, I shall slay a Norman for each of them!' raged Bedwyn.

'Now, more than ever, we must do nothing to draw suspicion,' said Aldyth quietly. Yet in spite of her reasonable counsel, her heart was pounding and she felt tiny beads of sweat forming on her upper lip. What if the king's spies were able to infiltrate the network that served to spirit Saxon fugitives to safety? Sirona and Bedwyn, two of the people Aldyth held most dear, were deeply involved in its operation. Then there were those like Father Edmund and Mother Rowena the widow of Lord Aethelstan and now the infirmarian at the abbey, who remained in willful ignorance but supported their efforts in any way possible. They, too, could be implicated. Would the villagers of Enmore Green be penalized? It was common practice for the Normans to punish an entire community simply for failing to police and inform upon their neighbors' activities. And that was a completely blameless village. How many times had one of Aldyth's neighbors come out of her way to mention, as if engaged in idle gossip, the sudden appearance of suspicious characters or indeed any stranger at all? Aldyth had come to rely upon their support. Had she selfishly endangered her friends?

Aldyth tried to shake off these disturbing thoughts but could not escape them, for when she turned back to the conversation, the men were engaged in the same vein of dark speculation. Stilling her shaking hands by gripping her basket handle, she rose to leave.

'Won't you break bread with us before you go?' asked Bedwyn.

Aldyth shook her head. ''Tis a long walk home.' Turning to Ethelred, she said, 'May the Lady guide you on your journey.'

Bedwyn excused himself to his guest with an apologetic nod in Aldyth's direction, then took a clay jar off a shelf and followed her into the night. The moon had risen and the low clouds dispersed, flooding the clearing with silver. Their eyes, adjusted to the warm-hued darkness of Bedwyn's hut, were dazzled by the monochrome brilliance of the night. From a few feet away came the sound of a startled hare leaping for cover. Its passage disturbed the damp grass, sending its summery fragrance floating past. How detached this natural world was from human concerns.

'A pot of honey, Aldyth,' said Bedwyn, placing it in her hands. ''Tis a good time of year for the bees; you can taste the honeysuckle on your tongue.'

'Thank you, Bedwyn,' she said, tucking it into her basket. ''Tis just the thing for Bertha. She has had her baby, a boy, and could use it to recover her strength.'

He smiled grimly. 'One more lusty little Saxon. Slap Agilbert on the back for me.'

Aldyth blurted, 'Will they find us, do you think?'

He gripped her shoulders firmly, looking down into her uplifted face. 'Never forget,' he said vehemently, 'that those who guide others along the Starlit Path would prefer, like old OneTooth, to take the swan's path rather than betray their countrymen.'

Aldyth nodded and glanced up at the moon in an effort to keep an anxious tear from brimming over. Cupping her trembling chin in his big hand, Bedwyn turned her face back toward his. The tear spilled over, and, with a gentle swipe of his callused thumb, Bedwyn brushed it away. Reflexively he fingered a tendril of hair that had escaped from her kerchief. The moment their eyes met, Bedwyn's half-formed words of reassurance were forgotten. Deftly she placed her hands in his to deflect his embrace.

'One kiss, Aldyth, to speed you on your way.'

As always, Aldyth thought with a sigh, Bedwyn had managed to destroy a tender moment with an earthy impulse. 'No, no, and ever no. How many times must I say it?'

'As many as you please,' he countered with a grin, 'so long as you say "yes" just once. Look at me, Aldyth; you've reduced me to begging.'

'You'll not starve,' she replied coolly. She had heard rumors

33

of a handsome Saxon, probably a fugitive in hiding, recently seen slipping into Elcomb Croft for a roll in the hay with one of the milkmaids.

Bedwyn laughed heartily but denied nothing. Pulling free of his hands, Aldyth backed out of his reach. 'You forget yourself, Bedwyn.'

'Would that you could as well, Mouse,' he quipped.

'Can no man keep his thoughts above the waist? Go tend to your company.' With a swirl of skirts around her bare calves, she started off. Feeling his eyes still upon her, she turned and called softly, 'And Bedwyn, take care.' Then she darted across the silvered glade and melted into the deeply shadowed woods.

As Aldyth wove her way home through moonlight and shadows, Bedwyn haunted her thoughts. She had no doubt that he cared for her in his bluff, hearty way. But if just once she said 'yes,' what then?

Bedwyn was of good blood, but that counted for very little in these unsettled times. He was also a poaching, womanizing, liegeless felon. No one who had lived his life could have escaped unscathed. Bedwyn had told her that his father, Torstin of High Hutton, had been a thane and a follower of Earl Morkere in Yorkshire. Torstin had been wounded during King Harold's stand against the Danes at Stamford Bridge, Saxon England's final victory. The battle at Hastings had followed so quickly that Bedwyn's father hadn't even had word of it until it was all over and Saxon England was no more. When Torstin had learned that London had opened its gates to William and accepted him as king, he had reluctantly sworn fealty to him, but in the following months, he had been outraged by William's high-handedness. 'This is the way an invader, not the rightful king, treats his subjects,' he had complained bitterly. 'If only I had died by Harold's side in that last proud hour!'

When Torstin had laid a petition of formal protest before the king, he had been thrown into prison and his lands confiscated to be given as booty to more loyal or less scrupulous servants of the king. Bedwyn, his younger sister, Hilde, and his mother had been thrown out into the night with no more than the clothes on their backs. One day they had been wealthy landowners; the next, fugitive beggars whose privilege and property were in the hands of foreigners speaking an alien tongue.

Bedwyn's mother, Dorset born, had married out of the shire. Lady Rowena, her cousin, still made her home in Dorset. Throughout England fugitives were streaming to the West Country. Bedwyn's mother, with her son and daughter in tow, had followed the ragged mob. They had slept in ditches and begged for their bread. Like so many others, Hilde had died along the way, with the cold November frost on her ragged kirtle. They had buried her tiny body in a hedgerow and, without a penny for a prayer, had left her there with the last of their false hopes. At last, footsore and heartsick, they had reached Sceapterbyrig in the Blackmore Vale. Bedwyn and his mother had been received by their kinswoman, Lady Rowena, with tears and embraces and made welcome by her husband, Thane Aethelstan.

A week later the Normans had stormed Aethelstan's gate. Bedwyn's mother had been killed and his newfound family swept away. After a futile attempt at revenge, Bedwyn had escaped from under the nose of Lord Ralf fitzGerald. It must have been the Goddess, thought Aldyth, who had led Bedwyn to the Crystal Spring, for there he had been befriended by a woman who had come to the fountain to draw its healing waters. She was the wife of a Saxon rebel turned forest outlaw. At last the boy had found refuge with Saxon fugitives living in the depths of Cranborne Chase in the Blackmore Vale.

Throughout England, there were raggle-taggle bands of Saxon outlaws hiding in the forests, magnets for fugitives from William's tyrannies. Within a few years, William had crushed even the least outward signs of rebellion; but still the Saxons had waited for a hero to rise up and lead them to deliverance. It was a known fact that at the battle at Hastings, King Harold had been so mutilated that his handfast wife, Edith SwanNeck, had had to be called in to identify the body, which she had done by marks that only a lover would know. Even now, thought Aldyth, rumors still circulated that the bones buried beneath the cold cairn of stones overlooking the Narrow Sea were not his, that someday King Harold would return to take back England and deliver the English from the Normans.

It had not happened. Eventually, the Saxons in hiding had realized they had forfeited their place and position even among the conquered and had no choice but to stay on in hiding. Fugitives were passed from band to band and shire to shire, to find anonymity at the far end of the country or escape by sea. Over the years this haphazard practice had been refined into a well-organized system. The king's highway traveled along a road cut out of the forest, but the outlaws had a road system that led through the trees and under the bushes. This secret network of trails traveled by night was called the Starlit Path, and its guides were the backbone of Saxon resistance.

And Bedwyn was one of its leaders. Aldyth was irked at both Bedwyn and herself for indulging in futile cat-and-mouse games. Even if she had wanted to say 'yes' to Bedwyn, she would have been fearful of becoming just one more of his conquests. But first and foremost, Aldyth knew in her heart that it was not her destiny.

When Aldyth had been in the first bloom of womanhood, Eldred the miller's boy had come courting. He was handsome and good-hearted, and the attention had been flattering. But Sirona had told her bluntly that Eldred was not for her, that no one in the village was for her; that Aldyth must set aside her desires and await her destiny. She had waited and waited.

Aldyth's childhood playmates were long since married and the mothers of thriving broods. Goda was already widowed and remarried. Mildburh, four years wed to Eldred Miller, Aldyth's own rejected suitor, was the mother of three. Even Edith, who had come late into bloom, was two years wed to old Elviva's son and hoping to conceive a child within the year. Not only had Aldyth long since reached marriageable age, but she had no widow's portion to improve her prospects and no offspring to prove her fertility.

Over the years, Aldyth had come to realize that Sirona was saving her for something far more important. Although no one had told her, she realized that it must be, it had to be that she was being groomed as the next Maiden of the Fountain, Keeper of the Crystal Spring. But everyone knew that the Maiden of the Fountain must remain just that − a maiden, pure and chaste.

Aldyth was proud to be chosen and determined to do what

was right. But whenever she saw two young people coming back from the fields with the smile of a shared secret on their faces, picking straw out of each other's hair, or whenever she held another woman's baby in her arms, she ached for what she knew could never be.

CHAPTER THREE

Aldyth was always on edge when returning from a run, although old Elviva's snoring was usually the loudest sound she heard when she came back to the sleeping village. Out of the gloom, a huge shadow loomed menacingly, but Aldyth recognized it as Sula's Stump, the charred trunk of a tree struck down by the fiery hand of the Goddess, that marked the outermost edge of Enmore Green. It was sacred to Sula and said to be haunted by Her imps, who guarded the village from thieves and goblins and even the Night Mara. Aldyth had just turned her thoughts from goblins to her warm bed when, from the darkness, a small black shadow leapt up at her. Only the discipline she had acquired as a guide on the Starlit Path silenced the shriek that arose from her throat.

'Aldyth, where have you been?'

Recognizing his voice, Aldyth hissed, 'Aelfric! Don't do that!'

'No time to scold,' he said, grabbing her sleeve and pulling her along the path toward the village. Panic shot out to her fingertips at the urgency in the boy's voice. 'It was the king's tax men,' he explained on the run. 'They banged Garth up good – said he'd hidden his cow at the inquest. They seized the beast, set the house afire before they left, and promised to serve up the same sauce to anyone else holding out on the king.'

As they stepped out from the thinning fringe of the woods, Aldyth's senses were assaulted by an orange glow, like that of a Midsummer bonfire, and the sound of weeping, moaning, a babble of confusion. 'My Lady!' she exclaimed. 'Was Garth the only one?'

'Not by a long shot,' gasped the boy, without breaking step. 'Talk is the king's spies snitched on Agilbert for hiding a pig. They broke his crown when he denied it.'

'Oh, my Lady!' Over the sound of her footfalls, Aldyth heard the crackling of fire. The thatched roofs of the village reflected its glow. Some people gaped as flames engulfed the hut of Garth KnockKnees and Hildegarde Brewer, others frantically laid sodden blankets over the wattle fencing to keep the fire from spreading to neighboring tofts. Hildegarde's wailing could be heard like the eerie screech of a banshee. Aldyth's first thought was fear for Sirona, yet her footsteps led her to where she sensed was the greater need. That, after all, was where she would most likely find her godmother.

Now it was Aldyth who dragged Aelfric along as she dashed toward the hut of Bertha and Agilbert, breathlessly questioning him as they ran. 'Where's Sirona?'

'With Elviva. The old woman had a fit, and Sirona was afraid her heart had burst.'

''Tis stuck!' cried Aldyth, pushing against the door. They squeezed through to discover Agilbert's unconscious body blocking the way. Aldyth cried out at the sight of so much blood, an ominous black in the dim firelight. The wailing of the baby added an uncanny effect, yet Aldyth knew instinctively that she heard fear, not pain, in his cry.

''Tis not all Agilbert's blood,' came a trembling voice. Edith MoonCatcher looked up from the shadows. 'When they clubbed Agilbert, Bertha tried to shield him. One flung her against the wall; she's been bleeding ever since.' Aldyth's dark-adjusted eyes made out the small figure at Edith's knees. 'Thank the Lady you're here, Aldyth,' said Edith.

'Quickly tell me, Edith, how long has it been?'

'Ten, maybe twelve Pater Nosters since.'

'Help me move her onto her pallet. Aelfric, fetch me water from the Crystal Spring – and you'd better find Father Edmund.' He was only a boy, but he understood that the priest's presence would be needed to give Bertha her last rites. He nodded gravely and scrambled through the wreckage toward the door. Aldyth covered Bertha with every scrap of blanket she could scrounge and prayed that she would not lapse into the deep chill.

Edith wiped the blood from Agilbert's forehead and moved aside for Aldyth to bandage it. 'Let's get him onto his pallet,' said Aldyth, placing her hands under his arms while Edith seized his ankles. After a short struggle, they settled on moving him out of the doorway. 'This will have to do for now,' said Aldyth. 'He's as big a bear.'

She hurried over to Bertha and lifted the blanket to apply a pad of rags to soak up the flow of blood from between Bertha's legs. Bertha stirred, then feebly tried to rise. 'Be still, little sister,' urged Aldyth, 'to slow the bleeding.'

'My child,' mumbled Bertha. With a start, Aldyth realized that the baby's cries still rent the air; Aldyth had been so intent upon her ministrations that she had ceased to hear them. At a nod from Aldyth, Edith darted over to the baby and scooped him up. Calmed by her warmth, his crying trailed off to a fretful whine as he nuzzled vainly for a meal.

There was nothing more to be done until Aelfric returned with the healing water to brew a blood-thickening potion for Bertha and a poultice for Agilbert. To be ready for that moment, Aldyth sorted through the little bunches and pouches of dried herbs in her basket, using her sense of smell rather than sight in the dim light.

'Bertha,' said Aldyth, smoothing the girl's brow, 'I'm taking the baby to Mildburh to suckle.' The new mother turned her face to the wall. Aldyth squeezed her hand. 'Be strong, little sister; your baby needs you. Edith, will you stay until I return?'

Edith nodded, biting her lip.

'I won't be long,' Aldyth promised. 'When Aelfric returns, you may go to Elviva.'

Cradling the baby in her arms, Aldyth stepped over its unconscious father and out the door. There was purpose in her stride as she approached the crowd milling about the remains of Garth and Hildegarde's house. The walls had collapsed, and embers throbbed on its floor. The cry of 'Aldyth!' rose up like a wave and washed over the villagers. Parting like the Red Sea, they regrouped around the young healer. A hush of silent

41

expectation descended, except for the keening of Hildegarde. Her husband sat slumped on the ground, his head in his hands. Their youngest daughter, Helga, rocked in the arms of her grown sister Goda, stared at the ruins of her home, clutching the single shoe that she had rescued from the flames.

'Hildegarde, take hold of yourself,' admonished Aldyth. 'The children are frightened enough as it is.' Lifting the baby to her shoulder, Aldyth gave Hildegarde a quick hug with her free arm and said, 'Goda, take your parents and sister home and give them some hot ale. Whose child is that crying? Go comfort him.' Addressing the uncertain crowd, she reminded them all, 'They've taken nothing that cannot be replaced. Everyone go home, and thank the Lady Modron for watching over us. Morning is wiser than night. Tomorrow we will see what needs to be done. But, Mildburh,' she called, 'a word, if you please.' A buxom young woman came forward carrying a child of her own. 'Could you give this little one suck and bring him back to Bertha when he's fed?'

Mildburh took the baby with her free arm, clucking and shaking her head. 'Poor little mite. We were lucky at the mill; they only scared the girls and bloodied Eldred's nose.'

'Thank the Lady,' called Aldyth over her shoulder, already hastening back to Bertha. She found Edith gone and Aelfric putting the water on to boil. Agilbert, still unconscious, had been resettled onto his straw pallet. Father Edmund sat beside Bertha, his lips moving in silent prayer while he bathed her forehead with a damp cloth.

At Aldyth's entrance, the priest rose. 'She has had the last rites, daughter. Perhaps you can give her something to help her sleep.' Wringing out the wet cloth, he said sadly, 'They swept through every hut and home, like an evil wind . . .'

'Yes, Father, I know.'

''Tis God's mercy you're here; Sirona thought you might not return before dawn. I must hurry off. I just got word that while the king's vandals sacked Judith's home, their armed escort fell upon her daughter Christine, who was bringing home the milk from the meadow. The child was crazed with fear, and we don't know exactly what happened. If you can spare me—'

'Christine? That poor innocent! Go, Father. I'd come too,

42

but I daren't leave Bertha. Give the child an infusion of this.' Aldyth drew a small bunch of dried herbs from her basket. ''Tis lavender and chamomile to calm her. Lace it with some good strong mead.'

Aelfric hopped up to follow, but the priest said, 'You'd best stay here and assist Aldyth, young man.'

'I can use you, Aelfric,' said Aldyth, seizing him by the collar before he could slip out the door. 'Go fetch back the baby from Mildburh; Bertha will need him tonight.'

Aldyth, preoccupied with dosing and nursing, was glad to have Aelfric to call upon. In the chill of the night, she sent him out to beg firewood from the neighbors. He returned promptly with a huge armload of fuel, and Aldyth knew better than to ask questions.

Aelfric was a rare bird, having managed to slip through the cracks in the new feudal system. In a country where everyone answered to a higher authority, Aelfric was no man's man. It was ten summers since he had been left hanging by his swaddling bands on the ancient oak by the Crystal Spring. Unwanted children might be left in church doorways or at the abbey gates, but a child placed by the Crystal Spring was no mere foundling; it was believed by its parents to be a changeling, left by the Fairies in place of their own stolen child, and that if the Fairies saw the baby at the fountain, they would take it back and return the stolen one. The scrawny infant had hung there from dawn till nightfall, quietly gazing about with curious eyes. Even his silence was eerie and seemed to confirm the villagers' fears. At dusk, Sirona had claimed him. 'The Fairies have had their chance,' she had said. 'I'm not about to give the wolves a turn.'

The wisewoman had named him Aelfric, meaning 'Fairy Prince,' and Father Edmund had offered to give him a good home as soon as he was weaned, a good Christian upbringing, and, if he proved to be a quick learner, the opportunity to train for the priesthood. The boy proved to be exceptionally bright, but to Father Edmund's dismay, he simply would not be domesticated. When Aelfric was no more than six summers old, he had taken to sleeping in plowsheds and hayricks. There was always a spot for him at Sirona's hearth, but only on the coldest nights of the year would he avail himself of it.

Waifs like Aelfric seldom survived their first harsh winter or famine, even if they managed to escape the vigilance of the local authorities, whose laws were merciless. Aelfric, however, had not only survived but flourished. He knew everybody's business, often before they did. Having no possessions of his own, he had little regard for the laws of property, but he never pinched an egg without rearranging the nest to cover his tracks. Most important, it was common knowledge that he was not only Fairy spawn but under Sirona's protection as well. Besides, he was at the heart of every disturbance, in the eye of every storm, as was Aldyth, who inevitably snatched him by the collar and put him to good use. There was not a family in Enmore Green who did not have cause to be grateful for some service rendered by Aelfric, however reluctantly. And no one had ever actually caught him milking their cows in the meadow or stealing the apples from their tree.

As the first light came streaking through the cracks, Aldyth knew she could do no more. After a fitful night, both Bertha and Agilbert were finally sleeping soundly. Aelfric was curled up with the baby asleep in his arms. Aldyth tucked the blanket around him and thought how humiliated he would be were anyone to catch him like that.

Aldyth glanced about; she had tried to tidy the mess, to wash away all signs of violence. But the clean straw Aelfric had scrounged up for Bertha to lie in was already soaked through. Somewhere she would have to find a wet nurse, for Bertha would go off her milk as a result of her injuries. Aldyth sighed, too weary to weep. As she threw the soiled straw onto the fire and bundled up bloodied rags to be washed and used again, Aldyth considered the long-range implications of this crisis. Bertha was needed to support Agilbert's obligations to Lord Ralf, who would expect a goose at Michaelmas, hens, eggs, and loaves of bread at Christmas, and a hen and eggs at Easter. And Agilbert would be in no condition to reap the harvest, as poor as it was this year.

Aldyth stepped out into the new dawn, her back sore from bending, her eyes stinging from the effects of smoke and fatigue.

The stink of wet ash and burned timber assaulted her nostrils; the rain hissed as it fell upon the smoking ruins of Garth and Hildegarde's home. Up on Castle Hill, the Normans had already begun cracking their whips upon the backs of their Saxon slaves. Workers were hauling heavy stones up the steep slope of the motte. Curses spewed by the Norman taskmasters, undamped by the rising wisps of early morning mist, spilled down the hill as in a scene out of Hell from one of Father Odo's sermons. 'Those poor souls should be working their own fields,' she thought bitterly.

Across the green a movement caught her eye. Half a dozen bedraggled Saxons were being herded off toward the wood beyond the fields, probably to one of Lord Ralf's coppices to cut saplings for scaffolding. Aldyth recognized Wulfric Edgarson and Agilbert's cousin Thurgood. Then her jaw dropped when she noticed Garth among the work crew. 'How could they drag him away from his family at a time like this?' she fumed. ''Tis too much to bear!' she cried aloud. 'I won't stand for it!'

Before Aldyth knew what she was doing, before she could stop herself, she had dashed her bundle of rags to the ground and was storming up Tout Hill to Sceapterbyrig. By the Goddess, she was going to have it out with Lord Ralf himself, once and for all.

CHAPTER FOUR

Fueled by her fury, Aldyth made the fifteen-minute trip up to Castle Hill in a heated ten. Even the steep walk could not take the edge off her anger. Apprentices scurrying about on their masters' errands leapt aside, wide-eyed, as she raged by. Aldyth arrived at the old wooden bailey, whose gate stood wide open. A sleepy-eyed sentry, enmeshed in chain mail and armed with a spear, raised a hand to signal a halt.

'Out of my way, Gilbert!' she snapped.

The Norman flinched, not at her words but at her icy tone. Aldyth was a familiar figure at the stronghold, for she was sometimes called to attend a difficult birth or to care for the Saxon servants' ills, but she had always been gentle and pleasant, calling even the Normans by name. Startled, Gilbert stepped back and stared dumbly after her.

Having breached the fortress walls, Aldyth scanned the courtyard for her quarry, never slackening her speed. Her eyes swept over the storage house and past the brew house, obviously deserted. Lord Ralf was nowhere near the stable, as was evidenced by the sluggish pace of the grooms. The open-sided smith's shed held no one but an apprentice, stacking charcoal for the day's work ahead. Barely glancing at the darkened chapel, Aldyth assumed that it was empty; at any rate, Lord Ralf would not be there.

As she shot a glance back toward the far side of the bailey, Aldyth crashed into a wall of flesh and went tumbling to the ground in a tangle of limbs. Stunned by the impact, the wind knocked out of her, Aldyth gave her head a shake to stop its spinning and raised herself to discover that she was intertwined with a tall, prostrate man who was still fumbling for his sword. When their eyes met, his eyebrows shot up in first surprise, then annoyance. Realizing that this was no armed assailant, he dropped his hands.

Blushing furiously, Aldyth scrambled to her feet. She had thought she knew everyone on Castle Hill, but this man was a stranger to her. She took in the Norman dress and dark Norman coloring of the man as he stiffly picked himself up and brushed the mud and bits of straw from his clothing. Once standing, Aldyth saw that he was a head taller than she, and she was taller than average. He gained mastery of his irritation and withdrew into cool detachment as he reached down and plucked a piece of straw from her hair.

She slapped his hand away and shot him a furious look.

'You're obviously not here to pay your respects,' he remarked in Norman French.

Aldyth could speak Norman French well enough to make herself understood, but it was in her native tongue that she replied curtly, 'I have business with Lord Ralf.'

He replied in fair Saxon, 'You'd best cool off first; he's got a terrible temper.'

'Mine is worse,' she growled.

Shrugging indifferently, he led the way toward the great hall. As Aldyth followed him across the bailey, she was mildly surprised that his hair was not shaved in a half circle from ear to ear, in the unbecoming style of the Normans, nor was it grown long in the Saxon fashion; it was somewhere in between, in the Parisian mode she recalled seeing on a French minstrel on his way to entertain at Lord Ralf's table the previous winter.

He was not a traveling minstrel, for his attire was too austere. A messenger from the king's court? She recalled the features of his clean-shaven face, the high cheekbones, the dark brown eyes flecked with copper. Even with his aquiline nose, obviously once broken, he was not unattractive. It was that air of reserve that was so forbidding.

Aldyth's strength abated as curiosity displaced her anger. But she found fuel to stoke the flames of her fury when she was forced to scramble to keep up. He strode along heedlessly, arrogantly, loping up the flight of stone stairs leading to the outside entrance of the hall. Aldyth, exhausted from her furious climb up Tout Hill, panted in the effort to keep up with his pace. On the top step, the Norman halted in midstride and spun about so abruptly that they collided. She would have fallen backward down the stone stairs had his hands not shot out and gripped her upper arms. Instinctively her breath caught in her lungs as she clutched at him frantically, grabbing handfuls of his tunic. Then time froze.

Muscles, tightened in readiness for a fall, relaxed, and she let out a relieved sigh. Closing her eyes, she took a moment to let the wild pounding of her heart lessen. When it continued to hammer, she realized with a start that it was not her heart she heard but his, that her head was pressed against his chest. Mortified, she sprang away only to find him tightening his grip to pull her roughly back against him. About to protest, she recalled where she was and saw that he had prevented another tumble down the stairs.

More contritely, Aldyth met his eyes; they were impenetrable, set in features of stone. She parted her lips to speak, but no words came. She felt a tingling in the pit of her stomach, and the unwelcome blush crept back into her cheeks. Surely this, she thought, must be what it was like to be trapped in a Fairy ring, for she could neither move out of his arms nor tear her eyes away from his. It was he who finally spoke.

In a voice oddly gentle, he said, 'I forgot to ask: How shall I announce you?'

Nervously she cleared her throat, and her voice rose from a whisper to a squeak. 'They call me Aldyth Lightfoot.' The ridiculous croaking of her name aloud broke the spell. Abruptly she stepped out of his arms and moved one stair down. 'I am beholden.'

He shrugged dismissively and was halfway across the great hall by the time she recovered herself. Aldyth hurried after him as he approached the hearth, where Lord Ralf sat breaking his fast on a chunk of white bread and a goblet of watered wine.

Aldyth had seen Lord Ralf at the manor court and from across the bailey, and it was not an uncommon sight to see him trampling the peasants' crops as he led the hunt across their fields, but this was the closest she had ever been to him. All of the villagers who held land of him had been required to kneel down before him, placing their hands between his to pledge their fealty, but Aldyth was just a woman, a landless peasant and of no great consequence to him, so that distasteful duty had never been required of her.

Lord Ralf was no taller than Aldyth, though he must have weighed twice what she did. But beneath that paunch of his, he was solid and muscular, not to be mistaken in any way for a soft man. Nor was he a noble man by nature or even by birth. He had come upon his station, a barony, with all its rank and privilege, through the fortunes of war, for he had followed William's banner thirty-odd years on both sides of the Narrow Sea. But neither silken tunics nor title and rank could disguise his vicious nature. The lines on his face were worn into a permanent sneer, and there was a predatory cruelty in his eyes. For once, Aldyth felt only relief that she could never marry. Most Norman lords could be bought off when it came to the right of the First Night, but it was common knowledge that Lord Ralf had taken sadistic pleasure in violating those Saxon maidens subject to his power on their wedding nights, though he had not exercised that right for several years.

Aldyth suddenly felt fearful. She had allowed herself to be driven up the hill by her own storm of emotions and, with their dissipation, found herself cast onto a hostile shore. Her instinct was to run, but it was too late and she had only herself to blame.

'My Lord,' said her Norman escort, 'there is a Mistress Aldyth Lightfoot with a petition to bring to your attention.'

Ralf fitzGerald farted loudly and scowled at the young man. 'You aren't enough of a nuisance to me, Gandulf, but that you must bring others in to annoy me?' Ralf turned to Aldyth, who made a token curtsy. Taking in her rags and bare feet at a glance, he grunted. 'Who in the name of God's blood do you think you are, wench, to take up my time?'

Aldyth's throat went dry, but she forced herself to speak. 'I am called Aldyth Lightfoot, and I am apprenticed to my godmother, Sirona, the healer of Enmore Green.'

Lord Ralf's face grew hard. 'Healer! Don't you mean witch?

I've already granted the old hag's crony a reprieve on her workday. What have you come begging for now?'

Since taking possession of his fief, he had had occasion to clash with Sirona more than once. After he had violated Mildburh Miller with exceptional cruelty on her wedding night four years before, Sirona had strongly suggested to Lord Ralf that he forgo the lord's right of the First Night from then on. Lord Ralf had laughed in her face, but on the next First Night, he had suffered from an affliction of the bedchamber, curbing his amorous exploits and causing him great humiliation. Suspecting a curse but unwilling to trust such a delicate matter to a messenger, he had ridden out the next morning intending to confront Sirona. He had met her on the path, and the look she had given him was a knowing one.

'My Lord,' she had said with a crooked smile, 'were you coming to see me?'

For the first time in his life, Lord Ralf had lost his nerve. Affecting not to see the crone, he had ridden past and not returned to the garrison until late that evening. Lord Ralf had no fear of wolves, brigands, or armored knights, but the magic arts could not be beaten back with a sword, and that was the chink in his armor. Even indirectly, Lord Ralf had no wish to antagonize the seeress. 'Make it quick,' he snapped to Aldyth.

'My Lord,' said Aldyth with nervous haste, 'last night the king's tax assessors, on pretext of a petty search for a few pennies and a stray pig, laid waste to Enmore Green.'

Even as she spoke, Aldyth perceived a shift in her lord's mood: he was appraising her as he would a brood mare. She recognized the lust in his stare, and the hairs on the back of her neck rose as she waited interminable seconds for his reply. At last he snorted, then rose and turned to walk away. ''Tis no business of mine. I have no control over the king's men.'

He was leaving. Aldyth was infuriated at his callous disinterest. Her outrage drove the fear from her heart and she kept pace with him, refusing to be dismissed. 'But you have the king's ear,' she countered. 'Could you not use your influence? 'Tis in your best interest to make right these wrongs.'

'Is it in my best interest to guard each peasant's pigpen?'

'I would not expect you to keep watch over their livestock

but over their livelihoods, for by their livings, you have yours. If Agilbert dies with his crown broken by the king's men, who will harvest your crops for you? And with even their plow lost when Garth and Hildegarde were burned out last night, how can you expect them to till your fields?'

Lord Ralf turned on his heel to face her; his ferocity drove her back three steps. 'What are you suggesting?' he barked. 'Do you expect me to bear these losses myself?'

'They are but small to you and great to them,' she replied, quavering. Forcing herself to meet his eye, she said, 'My Lord, release Agilbert and the Brewers from their obligations this harvest, and by spring they will be able to meet them in full.'

His lips thinned in irritation. Glaring at Aldyth, Lord Ralf reached into his purse and took out a few coins. Disdainfully he cast them into the straw on the floor. 'This is all the charity they will get from me; there will be no lightening of obligations. And by God, if you come pestering me again, I swear I'll have you stripped and whipped through the streets of Scafton.' He dashed the last drops of his wine among the rushes, tossed his cup to the quaking page who attended him, and snapped to the young Norman, 'Gandulf, see this wench out the gate and get me the name of the guard who allowed her in.'

'Yes, Father,' Gandulf replied.

Lord Ralf stalked off, his angry footsteps thundering down the hall. Aldyth's mouth dropped open; this tall, lean, soft-spoken Gandulf could not have sprung from the loins of that fleshy, harsh-voiced tyrant, yet she had clearly heard him address him as 'Father.'

''Tis nothing to me,' thought Aldyth as she dropped to her knees to pick through the straw for silver pennies. She opened her hand and stifled a gasp when she saw the gleam of gold in her palm. Lord Ralf must have inadvertently tossed out a French louis d'or, thinking it was silver. For an instant she stared in amazement, then clutched it in a suddenly sweaty palm. She raised her eyes to see Gandulf intently observing her. Both she and Gandulf knew that Lord Ralf had had no intention of giving her a gold coin; it was more money than a peasant might save in a lifetime. She waited tensely for him to call back his father. But the Norman's solemn expression melted into an ironic smile.

'Your father is a very generous man,' Aldyth commented dryly.

'And you must be a sorceress to have wheedled even a penny out of the old miser.'

Taking her cue from his frank informality, she chided, 'You might have told me he was your father.'

Taken aback by her direct manner, highly inappropriate for one of her station, Gandulf grew serious. 'You were lucky this time, Mistress Aldyth. Don't presume upon your luck. Best not come again. Now I'll see you to the gate.'

Aldyth was halfway down Tout Hill before she began to tremble. She had had no reason to expect any satisfaction from Lord Ralf, let alone a fistful of gold. More than ever, Aldyth felt the protective eye of the Goddess upon her. And somehow she sensed that the morning's events had been momentous in a way she could not yet comprehend.

The dew was still wet beneath the hedges when Aldyth came to her own threshold. Father Edmund and Sirona were sitting at the table, each holding a steaming mug. Godiva, Sirona's little red milk cow, had slipped loose from her halter and was peering over Sirona's shoulder to see if there were anything worthwhile on the table. Father Edmund looked up to see Aldyth in the doorway. 'Aldyth!' he exclaimed in relief, rising to greet her.

'I told you she would turn up, Edmund,' said Sirona.

'Where have you been?' the priest went on. 'They found only a bundle of bloodied rags outside Bertha's toft. After what happened to Christine . . .'

'Did you find out what happened?' asked Aldyth anxiously.

To dispel her concern, the priest hastily replied, 'The Normans' intentions were far from honorable, but one took pity on the child and shamed the others out of their wicked deed.'

'They'll find their way to Hell through one door or another,' said the more pragmatic Sirona, 'but the Lady be thanked, 'twas not at Christine's expense.'

'Oh, yes,' agreed Father Edmund, resettling himself at the table. 'Last night's work was the Devil's own, and they'll have the Devil to pay. But old Elviva has offered to keep the Brewers for the winter. The quarters will be cramped, and Hildegarde, bless her, confessed that it is difficult to feel grateful for a shelter so steeped in garlic.'

'Bravery and kindness come easier when the blood runs hot,' said Sirona, 'but 'tis the days ahead that will prove most trying, for 'tis in the wake of a crisis, when needs tend to linger and worry, that there is no disguising the stuff we are made of. But we will weather this storm, as we have so many before.' Earnestly the wisewoman said to Aldyth, 'We have much to be thankful for in Enmore Green, for life is not lived so gently elsewhere. People like Lord Ralf are driven by ugly passions you could not begin to fathom, yet here under the wing of the Goddess, Father Edmund is taking confessions from a goodwife whose worst sin is an imagined inability to be sufficiently grateful.'

'Is it by grace of the Crystal Spring that we live such sheltered lives?' asked Aldyth.

'Nay, child. The spring is our reward for living according to the Lady's precepts.'

'Are there no others like our Crystal Spring?'

'In the time of the small dark people who grew out of the land, there was a spring, a well, a lake, a tree in every village as a sign of the Goddess's favor. As people turned away from Her, both the people and the gifts lost their power and their virtue. There are yet other springs that bless, and there are groves in which may be found a healing peace. But they are few and far between, for a clouded spring cannot heal, nor is there shelter to be found in a felled tree.'

'How can the people destroy the Earth Mother's gifts?' asked Aldyth in dismay.

'Ignorance, like knowledge, can be taught. Cruelty, like kindness, is learned. Wickedness prefers darkness to light, but even in the darkness the Goddess shines. We must look for the starlight, but it is there, my child. It is always there.'

'And never forget, the light takes many forms,' added Father Edmund. 'Do not forget to be grateful for the sun. The glory of God is not less of a blessing.'

''Tis true the divine light takes many forms—' conceded Sirona.

'—as good Saint Gregory reminded us,' said Father Edmund, attempting to have the last word.

'Dear Edmund,' said the crone, fondly needling him, 'you forget that all men are born of women, and the son of God is no exception. The Lady guides Her people as a mother does her children. Your God exacts obedience through fear. Why do people choose the light that will blind them, rather than the gentle light that will guide them on their path?'

Before the priest could reply, the wisewoman patted his hand and shook her head. 'Nay, old friend. One can't hold back a windstorm with one's apron, nor Kingdom Come. I only wish that all men of the cloth had half your heart.' To Aldyth, she said, 'I've seen to Bertha. You did well, child. Now she is in our Lady Modron's hands.'

'The villagers have pledged to assist Bertha and Agilbert and Garth and Hildegarde too,' added Father Edmund. 'Judith has promised a portion of her cow's milk for the babe, for she has never forgotten their kindness to her when she was widowed. And while Mildburh has her own child to suckle, she will assist as much as she is able.'

''Tis hard for a nursing woman to keep enough milk flowing to suckle even one, especially in a year of famine,' cautioned Sirona.

'True,' agreed the priest, 'though 'twould be a pity if we could not raise him on mother's milk.'

With a broad grin on her face, Aldyth clapped her handful of coins down on the table. 'Then we shall buy him a wet nurse!' She beamed at the look of astonishment on both their faces. 'Well?' she said after a dramatic pause. 'Aren't you going to ask me?'

'Have you sold your soul to the Devil? No one else around here has that kind of money,' said Sirona.

'You're closer than you think, Sirona. I got it from Lord Ralf.' In a tumble of words Aldyth told them everything, concluding, 'I don't know how I could've been so bold.'

'It must have been a divine inspiration, child,' said Sirona with a crooked smile, 'but pray to the Lady it doesn't happen again.'

Father Edmund frowned. 'Ralf fitzGerald is a dangerous

man. You must not trifle with him, Aldyth. Even with his own flesh and blood, he is ruthless. You know full well that he imprisoned his wife in the abbey and banished his son to live under the harsh rule of the monks of Saint Denis in Paris. 'Twas only recently, when the lad was beginning to make a name for himself as a scholar, that his father sent an armed escort to claim him back. He vows to make a proper lord of his only heir, though it should kill the lad, and I've no doubt he means it.'

'If Lord Ralf had really wanted to make a proper nobleman of him, he would have sent him to serve at William's court, instead of hiding him away in a monastery,' said Aldyth.

'I think it was as much to punish as to train him, but now it seems Lord Ralf has given up hope of begetting himself another heir, even a bastard.'

'We have enough chagrin to go around without bringing more worries down from Castle Hill,' thought Aldyth bleakly. Her eyes burned, and she pressed her palms over them. Her long day and sleepless night had finally caught up with her.

'Aldyth,' said Sirona frankly, 'your feet are crusted with mud, your kirtle is stained with blood, and you've circles under your eyes. You look like Job in the dung heap.'

'I suppose I should have tidied up before calling upon Lord Ralf,' admitted Aldyth. 'I didn't even think of it.'

'You never do,' said her godmother fondly.

'No wonder Gilbert looked so frightened when he saw me coming.'

''Tis good to strike a little fear into their hearts. Or perhaps it was pity,' chuckled Sirona. 'Never mind. Wash up and come eat.'

'I will later,' Aldyth promised. 'I'm too tired to eat just now.' She tucked the coins up into the secret hidey-hole in the thatch. 'I'll change the gold into silver pennies at the abbey the first chance I get.'

There was a bucket of fresh springwater in the corner. Aldyth knew that Sirona had fetched it back from the spring especially for her, for one of the burdens of Sirona's power was that she must drink only free-flowing water, fresh from the heart of the earth.

Aldyth drank deeply, splashed the cold water over her face, collapsed onto her straw pallet, and covered herself with her winter cloak, which also served as her blanket. She had burrowed in and was dozing off when she felt hot, wet breath on her neck. 'Godiva!' Laughing, Aldyth gave the little cow a scratch, then pushed her away. 'You want me to think you came for a kiss, but I know you really want to eat the bed out from under me.'

'Godiva,' called Sirona, patting the table. 'Come over here, and I'll pull your ears.'

The surefooted little cow threaded her way around the table and sidled up to Sirona, who put her arm around her neck. 'Aldyth has earned her rest today,' she decreed.

Aldyth settled in once again, half listening as Sirona said to Father Edmund, 'I think I'll stew a chicken and send it over to Bertha.'

'I can spare a chicken as well as you, Sirona. Let me.'

'Nay, I've a fine flock of them: the fattest in Enmore Green and Sceapterbyrig, too,' stated the crone unequivocally. Their friendly rivalry in regard to their chickens was the jest of the village.

'I can't argue,' said the priest, 'but I'll send some eggs; my hens are better layers.'

'So you say,' teased Sirona.

'If I could only keep that scamp Aelfric out of my hens' nests, I could prove it, too,' the priest added with a chortle.

Aldyth drifted off to the comforting sound of their voices. One hand pillowing her cheek, the other holding the treasured keepsake she wore around her neck, Aldyth whispered a silent prayer of thanksgiving to the Goddess. ''Tis a good life I lead,' she thought drowsily, 'if a strange one.' Was it only last night that she had been looking up into Bedwyn's blue eyes by moonlight? But the last picture to drift through her mind as the fog of sleep overcame her was the sardonic smile in the fathomless eyes of the Norman lordling as he picked a piece of straw from her hair.

CHAPTER FIVE

The sound of a cock's crow jerked Aldyth back into the nightmare world of reality. Since Bertha's recovery had faltered, the luxury of a warm bed and a good night's sleep was the stuff of dreams for Aldyth. Snapping awake, she found herself sitting on the cold floor beside Bertha's straw pallet, holding the young girl's icy hand. The fever had broken, and at last Bertha slept. But Aldyth knew better than to believe the worst was over. When she roused herself and struggled to her feet, she was so stiff that the act of rising made her bones ache. At her movement, Agilbert scrambled to his feet and blocked her path to the door. His eyes were rubbed swollen, and Aldyth knew that he had not slept that night, that he had been watching, waiting for her to stir. She braced herself for what she knew was coming.

'Aldyth,' implored Agilbert, 'how is she? Is the fever gone?'

'Not gone, but it has waned.'

'Then she'll get well again?'

Patiently Aldyth said yet again, 'I'm sorry, Agilbert, but nothing is certain. Please let me give you something to help you sleep. You can't keep driving yourself this way.'

He looked at her in shock. 'What if she should wake and need me? After she's well again, there will plenty of time to sleep.'

Aldyth stood on tiptoe and gave him a peck on the cheek. 'I'll see you tonight,' she promised and began to plod wearily home. Had it only been a week last Sunday that little Edmund had been christened? Late that night Agilbert had rattled their door like a big bear, wild-eyed and desperate. Aldyth had remained calm, remembering that Sirona had had to sedate him during the birthing, yet she also noted her godmother's purposeful reaction to his summons; Sirona had been awaiting this call. They had accompanied him home, where his wife lay shivering in a restless state of fevered sleep. They had applied a poultice of cucumber, raw onion, pear seeds, and garlic to combat festering of the womb and given her infusions of nightshade root and willow bark for fever. And, of course, water from the Crystal Spring to drink and cool her brow. By dawn the fever had subsided. But the next night Agilbert had come to fetch them back.

Every evening Aldyth returned to keep watch over Bertha, and every morning Agilbert tried to pry promises of recovery from her, promises she could not give. Each day Aldyth's sense of dread increased as she anticipated the coming night's desolate vigil. As Aldyth stumbled in her door, she blurted out to Sirona, 'There must be something we haven't tried. We're too tired; we're just not thinking straight.'

Sirona looked up at Aldyth over her spinning. 'Once you have done all that you can do, you can only hope for the best and wait for the outcome,' replied the old healer.

'You know what the outcome will be, don't you?' insisted Aldyth.

'Only the Mother knows,' said Sirona gently.

'She's going to die, isn't she?' Aldyth crossed the room to kneel before her godmother. Fiercely she cried, 'Bertha is only a child herself; I was there at her birthing! Why not take someone who has already lived?' Hot tears spilled down her cheeks as she protested, 'How could the Goddess be so cruel?'

'Aldyth,' began Sirona, setting her spinning aside, 'people are born to live, and they are born to die. You must accept this without judgment if you are to remain a healer.'

'But it's so hard!' Aldyth cried.

'I know, my dear,' said Sirona, wiping a tear from Aldyth's cheek. She drew Aldyth's head down to rest in her lap, stroked her hair, and whispered, ''Tis very hard.'

That night, when morning seemed an eternity away but it had

been night-time forever, Bertha stirred. It was very dark, and the embers in the hearth had died to a red filigree. Aldyth, dozing in her blanket, roused herself and found a wet rag to wash the girl's face.

'Little Edmund?' asked Bertha weakly.

'I'll fetch him for you,' whispered Aldyth, rising to take the baby from the arms of his sleeping father. She met with an unexpected resistance as, even in his sleep, Agilbert tightened his hold upon the child. Aldyth waited a few seconds and tried again, leaving her own body-warmed blanket in his arms instead.

Bertha sighed as Aldyth placed the baby on her chest. 'And Bert?'

'Asleep,' replied Aldyth. 'Shall I wake him?'

'No, poor lad, let him sleep.' The ringing silence drew out, and Aldyth assumed that Bertha had drifted back to sleep, until she whispered, 'I don't worry about the baby. You and Father Edmund and Sirona will watch out for him.' Cutting off Aldyth's protest, Bertha continued. ''Tis Bert. He hasn't the sense to come in out of the rain.'

'How few of us do here in Enmore Green!'

'Aye, but Bert would hang out the shirts to bleach in it. Find him a good wife, Aldyth. One who is gentle but able to manage him, for he can be stubborn as a hungry pig.'

'You know we take care of our own here, little sister.'

Bertha, too weak to nod, whispered, 'Yes, I know.'

At dawn Sirona came to relieve her goddaughter. Outside the hut, the healers consulted in low voices. 'Still she hangs on by a thread,' said Aldyth.

'Not a thread but a heartstring,' answered the old woman. Looking up at the pale sky, Sirona said, 'She'll take her leave tonight with the setting of the sun.'

The abbey bells proclaimed the midmorning mass as Aldyth left to fetch rags from the abbey almoner to use as bandages. On her way, she stopped at the Crystal Spring to say a prayer for Bertha. Rising, she looked up into the branches of the Wishing Tree. Father Odo had stripped its branches the week before, but it was already decked with fresh, clean strips of cloth and even a few bits of ribbon. Aldyth wondered how many were for

Bertha. She thought she recognized the hem of Mildburh's old onion-skin-gold kirtle, and the walnut-brown strip that flapped back among the shadows surely came from the winter cloak of old Edwin MoonCatcher. How could the elves ignore such an outpouring, even if the Goddess were to turn Her back? Impulsively Aldyth bent down. Using the little digging knife she carried in her basket, she cut a strip from the hem of her own kirtle and wove her prayer among those already hanging in the branches of the Wishing Tree. 'For Bertha,' she whispered to the elves.

On her way to the abbey, Aldyth passed Father Edmund in the company of a handful of sweaty men. They were returning from harvesting Agilbert's crops for him, now that their own were all in. Usually the harvesting of the final strand of grain was a matter of rejoicing, with the last sheaf dressed as the Corn Maiden and carried home with boisterous song and celebration. This year's celebration was decidedly muted. The dispirited harvesters brought back the Corn Maiden, merely a sheaf of wheat wrapped in a cloak rather than an elaborately woven figure costumed and groomed. As Aldyth passed by, Alcuin HardHead called halfheartedly, 'Ho for the harvest.'

'Ho for the Corn Maiden,' came Aldyth's subdued reply.

When she got to the abbey, Aldyth knew she should probably ask Mother Rowena for a shroud for Bertha, but she could not bear to, lest she hurry the dying girl into it. More than ever, Aldyth realized how much she depended upon Mother Rowena, the abbey infirmarian. Both healers, they often traded herbs and tricks of their trade. But their relationship was not merely professional. To everyone else in the village, Aldyth gave aid and comfort. Even with Sirona, Aldyth felt she must be first and foremost a healer. The abbey was the one place she knew to which she herself could turn for consolation, and Mother Rowena was the one person who could provide it.

Aldyth stopped at the northeast gate of the city to catch her breath after the climb up Tout Hill. She stepped aside to let traffic pass, and a peasant with a sack of squealing piglets jostled on by, nearly colliding with a wagon carrying barrels of water up from the Crystal Spring. His backward leap nearly knocked over a tattered one-legged beggar. The beggar had hardly regained his balance again before continuing his monotone mumble: 'I was at Hastings. I was at Hastings.' A Saxon merchant dropped a penny into his bowl, and Aldyth handed the beggar an apple from her basket, which he bit into greedily and with profuse thanks. She smiled her welcome, then looked up at the centuries-old inscription engraved in stone above the city gate. Although Aldyth could not read, every Saxon thereabouts knew what it said: 'This city was founded by King Alfred in the eighth year of his reign in 880.'

Aldyth thought about good King Alfred, who had driven out the Danes. 'Who will drive out the Normans?' she wondered grimly. A rider approached and sidled up to the wall. Aldyth glanced up to see that it was Gandulf fitzGerald, dressed in a tunic of dark green worsted astride a little bay mare. She blushed to have him catch her carrying on this strange conversation with herself. Pretending not to notice him, she turned her back and intently scanned the letters of the inscription until he should move on. Among the cries of the street vendors and the rattle of a passing oxcart, Aldyth discerned the clop of horses' hooves passing through the gate. She turned to hurry on her way but found Gandulf still there, studying her as intently as she had been studying the inscription.

Taking a new tack, she met his eye boldly. To her surprise, he quickly shifted his gaze, almost nervously, to where her eyes had been focused. Squinting as he tried to decipher the weathered lettering, he remarked, ''Tis very difficult to read.'

'Every Saxon knows what it says,' replied Aldyth coolly, and she told him.

'He actually founded Scafton in the ninth year of his reign, not the eighth.'

'It's just a date to you, isn't it?' remarked Aldyth bitterly. 'For you Normans, the history of England begins in the year 1066.' With that she stepped into the eddying stream of humanity and strode off indignantly. She circled around the block to let her temper cool. As she walked, she chided herself for her rudeness. 'He meant no harm; he was only making conversation. I'll be more gracious the next time,' she promised herself. But walking past ruined buildings still piled with the rubble of destruction from the Norman sacking of the city, she found it difficult to banish bitter thoughts.

Aldyth focused instead on the abbey. Built on the crest of the outcrop overlooking Alcester to the south, its ancient walls stood high above the little thatched houses and shops of the town like a mother hen standing over her chicks. Before the conquest it had been a retreat for the devout and the last refuge of unwed Saxon maidens and inconsolable Saxon widows. After the conquest, it had become a prison for the Saxon elite and a dumping ground for unwanted Norman noblewomen. Walls of the local yellow sandstone were rising to replace the wooden ones, and Aldyth was cheered to think that for all eternity the abbey would serve in its one constant role as protector of the poor and nurse to the sick.

The porteress, Sister Arlette, was a stout, plain woman with three chins straining against the confines of her wimple and one long dark eyebrow shading both eyes like a thatched roof shared by two houses. A notorious but good-hearted gossip, she was perfectly suited for her job, for she kept careful track of the comings and goings at the abbey. Sister Arlette treated Aldyth to a recital of the day's news and waved her on, saying, 'Mother Rowena will be making her morning rounds in the infirmary.'

The infirmary, set on the south side of the abbey for sun and warmth, was a long hall built like the nave of a church, but with its altar on the side wall, so that when mass was celebrated it could be seen from the row of beds along the opposite wall. Unlike in most infirmaries, there was only one patient to a bed, and most of the beds were unoccupied.

Mother Rowena was chatting with Sister Rinalda, whose knees would no longer carry her up and down the steps from the chapel to the dorter, where most of the nuns slept. Occasionally, when the hours dragged by too drearily, the infirmarian sent for Sister Arlette that she might enthrall her charges with spirited accounts of abbey life. Sister Arlette, grateful for a fresh and appreciative audience, was always happy to comply.

Abbess Eulalia, however, frowned upon the spreading of malicious gossip. Once she had happened upon one of Sister Arlette's performances in the infirmary. The nuns had fallen into alarmed silence at her appearance. Eulalia's dark eyes, set deep in her thin face, had scanned the quaking congregation of nuns. She had broken the silence to commend them, straight-faced, for their worthy efforts to discuss and broaden their understanding of philosophy, religion, and current events. She had then given a curt nod of her head and taken her leave. As soon as she was gone, the nuns had broken out into a sibilant storm of relieved whispers – except for Sister Arlette, who for the first time in her life was struck dumb.

The memory made Aldyth smile. Mother Rowena looked up to see her enter, and the nun's face also lit up in a warm smile. She excused herself to Sister Rinalda and glided across the floor with outstretched arms, her veil billowing out behind like a sheet in the breeze. Aldyth never doubted Sirona's affection for her, but nowhere did she know such tender love as Mother Rowena rained upon her. 'Mother, can we talk privately?'

'Of course, child,' said the infirmarian. 'Come with me to the still-room.' Aldyth was ushered into a small dark room off the infirmary, where Mother Rowena mixed her poultices and brewed her remedies. Jars of salves lined the walls, and bunches of fragrant dried herbs hung from ropes strung across the ceiling like clotheslines.

'Sit down, my dear,' said the nun, pushing the clutter on the top of a bench to one end.

The two women sat side by side, Aldyth's basket resting on her lap. She peeled back the kerchief laid over its contents and placed several bunches of woodland herbs into Mother Rowena's lap. 'Bindweed, dog rose, ragwort, and wild raspberry.'

Mother Rowena sniffed each aromatic bundle with appreciation. 'Lovely,' she said, then set them in her lap, content to wait for Aldyth to speak.

Lining the bottom of the basket lay the other half of the large kerchief. One corner was securely knotted into a tiny bundle. Aldyth peered out the stillroom door. Certain that they were not being observed, she untied the knot and produced her gold coin.

'My Lord, child, where did you get that?' whispered Mother Rowena.

With a look of mock seriousness, Aldyth replied, ''Twas a miracle, Mother.'

'A miracle! What manner of miracle?'

'Given freely to pay for the damage done by King William's men – and from the purse of Lord Ralf, no less.'

'Given freely by Lord Ralf, who can squeeze blood from a turnip! That is a miracle, indeed!' The two women broke into girlish laughter.

'But tell,' insisted Mother Rowena, 'how came he to give this gift?'

As soon as Aldyth began to relate her experience, she regretted it.

'Aldyth,' said Mother Rowena in dismay, 'Lord Ralf is a wicked man; you must never draw his attention to yourself, however just a cause you wish to champion. Sirona is better able to fight those battles and less likely to draw a lecherous eye. Promise me you'll stay away from the stronghold.'

'If ever I can avoid it, I will,' Aldyth promised.

Knowing that she must be content with this half promise, Mother Rowena sighed and tucked the gold coin into her sleeve. 'I shall change it for silver before you go home today. But first tell me how Enmore Green fares.'

When they spoke of the upset in the village, Mother Rowena remarked ruefully, 'Even within these cloistered walls, where the sword and the stick are banished, ill winds rattle our roof tiles. Last week Father Fulk took to his bed with the gout, so Father Odo came to take confession in his place. Sister Aethelswith and Sister Priscilla both had to confess that they had raised their voices in anger.'

Aldyth knew that Mother Rowena was being charitable, for she had already heard Sister Arlette's version of the story. According to the porteress, Sister Aethelswith had felt the king's men had been unnecessarily cruel and had attacked King William on the same charge. Sister Priscilla, whose viewpoint was decidedly Norman, had accused the Saxon nun of treason. To finish the affair, Father Odo had stormed in with a vengeance and laid a penance upon Sister Aethelswith that would have absolved a murderer.

'Father Edmund says,' commented Aldyth, 'that Father Odo

justifies William's harsh rule by saying that a shepherd must drive his flock by whatever means.'

'You've been talking to Sister Arlette, haven't you?' A smile fleeted across the older woman's face, then quickly faded. 'King William is no shepherd,' she said quietly. 'I met him at King Edward's court, and I saw it in his eyes; the man is a wolf.'

'You met King William?' asked Aldyth, awed at the nun's brush with greatness.

'Well, he wasn't a king then, just the shabby duke of a war-tangled duchy, with greed and ambition burning in his soul.'

'Like Lord Ralf,' remarked Aldyth.

'Yes,' agreed Mother Rowena, 'but much more shrewd and efficient in his malice.'

'Did you know King Harold as well?'

'Oh, yes,' said Mother Rowena, her eyes suddenly growing misty. 'My husband held his land of Harold, and he was a good lord. Harold was no shepherd but a beacon. He was a peacemaker, the Land Father, and he led his people through reason and with love.' Mother Rowena had to stop, for her voice faltered. 'Forgive me,' she continued, giving Aldyth's hands a warm squeeze. ''Tis just that your world is so different from the one I grew up in. What can God possibly have had in mind when He allowed a handful of power-hungry foreigners and their mercenaries to obliterate a prosperous, peace-loving people?'

The nun was asking the same questions of her God that Aldyth had been asking of the Goddess only the day before. No matter who one prayed to, Aldyth suspected that these were questions that could never be answered, at least in this life.

'Don't look so worried, Aldyth. I do not brood upon these thoughts. 'Tis only when I think of you . . .'

Aldyth shrugged. 'When I hear of the golden years before the conquest, 'tis like one of the stories Sirona tells of the elfin folk; another world, like the land beneath the sea. My life is here and now, and it is full of purpose. What is more important than that?'

'Aye, child, there is nothing more important. The sun shines as warmly as ever it did, the sky is just as blue, and if the nightingale's song is tinged with sadness, she sings just as sweetly.'

Reluctantly they rose to return each to her own world. 'But first,' said Mother Rowena, 'I'll change your coin while you collect your rags. Then go to the garden and gather what herbs you need. I'll meet you there.'

The herb garden was in one corner of the abbey's walled garden, separated from the kitchen garden by a low hedge of lavender. On the other side of the hedge, a novice weeded a row of parsnips, her lips moving in silent prayer. Aldyth had just finished picking several sprigs of tender rosemary, which never grew very well in Sirona's exposed toft, when Mother Rowena rejoined her. The infirmarian placed a rag-wrapped bundle the size of a small egg into Aldyth's hand and watched her tuck it beneath the collection of bunched herbs in her basket. Aldyth picked up the sack of rags and was rising to leave when Gandulf fitzGerald strolled into the garden arm in arm with Sister Emma, Lord Ralf's discarded wife. Aldyth dropped to her knees, ostensibly to gather a sprig of thyme. Mother Rowena noticed the color rising in her cheeks and followed her eyes to the newest arrivals. 'Are you sure you've told me everything you wanted to tell me, dear?'

'Yes,' replied Aldyth too quickly, drawing a skeptical look from her mentor. Furtively, the two women watched as Gandulf and his mother seated themselves beside the espaliered apricot tree on the warm south wall of the garden. Sister Emma smiled as he took her hand and kissed it, and then mother and son fell into conversation.

Mother Rowena had unconsciously crouched down beside Aldyth. After a moment of shamefaced peeping, she whispered in a conspiratorial tone, 'In the fifteen years she has been here, I never once saw her smile. Now see how her face shines in his company.'

'That's Lord Ralf's son, Gandulf,' whispered Aldyth.

'Yes, I know. He comes to see her nearly every day, now that he's back from Paris.' Mother Rowena turned abruptly to Aldyth and said solemnly, 'There is no greater joy than to be with your own child. Some day I pray you will know mother love.'

Aldyth recalled how Mother Rowena's only child had died of a fever at the age of two, just before the fall of Sceapterbyrig. Not satisfied with Father Edmund's sworn oath that her child was dead, and not wishing for the babe to become a symbol of Saxon resistance, Lord Ralf had forced Father Edmund to lead them to a small unmarked grave and insisted the body be disinterred. It was indeed the decomposing body of a girl child, which the warlord had ordered carried away; no one had ever discovered its fate.

Until that moment, it had not occurred to Aldyth that Sister Emma was not only Ralf fitzGerald's cast-off wife but also Gandulf's mother. Gandulf resembled his mother no more than he did his father, except in complexion. She was short and thin, a mousy-looking thing, not especially pretty nor even ugly enough to be interesting.

Soon after Lord Ralf had taken possession of these lands, he had sent to Normandy for his wife. It was no secret that he despised her as much as he did their child, but he had not given up hope of begetting another heir. He took pleasure in his wife's humiliation as he paraded his whores and amorous conquests before her, and her meek acceptance of this outrageous behavior galled him further. Finally, in a drunken fit of temper, he had banished Gandulf to a monastery and forced Lady Emma to take the veil. At the time, the talk all over Sceapterbyrig was that he had told her that he would as soon bed a sheep as her, and that a sheep would look better in a dress. Aldyth's heart went out to her . . . and to Gandulf.

As if he had heard her thoughts, Gandulf looked up suddenly and met her eyes over the low hedgerow. Humiliated, she wanted to crawl under the garden bench, but it was too late. Gandulf apparently excused himself to his mother, then rose. Skirting the lavender hedge, he came walking across the garden directly toward them. Embarrassed at being caught peeping over a hedgerow, Aldyth mumbled to Mother Rowena, 'I must run now.'

Quickly she fled from the garden, leaving the blushing infirmarian to make excuses.

CHAPTER SIX

September 1086

'Aldyth Lightfoot! Fetch your arse over here!'

Mildburh Miller was completely devoid of polish, yet the fabric she was made of, interwoven with earthy humor and good intentions, was always worn inside out. Mildburh was nursing a baby on a bench outside the mill door. Sharing the bench were Judith Alcester and Edith MoonCatcher, who both sat spinning.

'Mildburh!' chided Edith. 'Come now, Aldyth, and give your feet a rest.'

Aldyth was on her way home from gathering herbs, her basket heaped with agrimony, which, picked this late in the year, could be made into a deep yellow dye. She had just trudged up the path that ran along the millpond's spillway. In Enmore Green, nothing went to waste; after man and beast had drunk their fill at the Goddess's well and water carriers had hauled away all they could use or sell, the overflow replenished the abbey's north fishpond, a shallow lake at the foot of Castle Hill. The runoff from the fishpond powered the mill, then formed a brook that spilled into the vale to water the crops.

Mildburh and Edith made a place for Aldyth on the bench they shared with Judith. Judith had married into Enmore Green from Alcester, but Edith and Mildburh had been Aldyth's childhood playmates. As they had grown older, their lives had taken different directions, and they no longer giggled together over a handsome lad's wink, but shared experience and affection bound the three women as closely as ever.

The stone mill was set into the hill so that its upper story was level with the pond, the runoff of which turned its huge wheel. Aldyth saw Eldred Miller dumping a load of grain into the hopper to grind. Then he came out to converse with the men seated on the other bench as they waited for their grain to be ground. Garth KnockKnees sat carving a ladle to replace one lost in the fire. Agilbert held Mildburh's baby, and Agilbert's great-uncle Edwin MoonCatcher presided. Old Edwin's hands were too palsied to engage in useful labor, but they were not idle, for he used them profusely to punctuate his conversation.

As Eldred went back inside to see to his work, the discreet swat on the rump that his wife delivered him did not go unnoticed by Aldyth. She smiled and thought, ''Tis little wonder they have three children after only four years of marriage.'

Eldred and the mill: this might have been her life, thought Aldyth, had she accepted his suit. Eldred was a good provider, a faithful husband, and still good-looking, though thinning on top and thickening in the middle. He was also a good businessman, honest, and generous as he could afford to be. He came out with a sack of flour and handed it to Judith. 'I just had the millstone recut,' he told her. 'Your bread should rise higher, please God.' She nodded and, tucking her spinning into her apron, shouldered the sack.

'This must be the end of last year's grain,' ventured Eldred.

'Aye,' she replied ruefully, 'and this year's puny crop won't last until Lady Day.'

'Yes,' called Edwin MoonCatcher from his seat on the other side of the doorway. ''Twas a hard summer, and the coming winter will be hard as well.' Mildburh's boy, Edmund, still in Agilbert's arms, watched the old man's gesticulating finger with quick eyes. The child snatched at the finger so swiftly that Agilbert, taken off guard, nearly dropped him. the baby screeched with delight as Agilbert lurched forward and back again in a quick recovery. Agilbert shook his head; by now he should have expected this, for every day at noon he walked down from the village with his son, Edmund, to mind Mildburh's Edmund while she served as wet nurse to his own.

People were already calling Mildburh's son 'Big Edmund' to distinguish him from the village's newest Edmund. The milk brothers were an odd pair. Big Edmund was loud, scrawny, and fearless, while Little Edmund was quiet, complacent, and quite an armload. Six-week-old Little Edmund was already as big as one-year-old Big Edmund.

Little Edmund's mother, Bertha, had gone with the sun, just as Sirona had foreseen. 'Agilbert's candle has never burnt too brightly,' said Sirona, 'but when Bertha goes, he'll be snuffed out entirely if we don't watch him.' She had also had the foresight to have a handful of able-bodied men within call to restrain the grief-maddened widower from charging up Castle Hill for revenge. Aside from their heartfelt concern for the lad, they knew that were a Saxon to murder a Norman, his entire village would be punished.

The waters of the Crystal Spring had not been able to save Bertha, nor had they had the power to spare Agilbert his frenzy of despair. At Bertha's burial, Agilbert had thrown himself into her grave and, bellowing like a maddened bull, had clung to the tiny shrouded figure at the bottom. Even if his friends could have lifted Agilbert's bulk out of the grave, no one had dared try to pry the dainty corpse from his grasping fingers. Sirona had snatched the baby from Aldyth's arms and carried him to the edge of the pit. When he realized what she was doing, Father Edmund had shaken his head pleadingly and stretched out his hands for his godson. Unheeding, Sirona had lowered Little Edmund into the grave by his swaddling clothes and called down, 'Here, take this one too. You might as well all go together.'

The wild cries had gradually quieted to sobs. Then only Agilbert's hoarse panting had echoed up from below. Little Edmund, still hanging in midair like a plump spider on a web, had watched his father placidly. At last Agilbert had climbed out of his wife's grave, accepted the baby from Sirona, and carried it back to his cold, empty hut. Since then, he had stumbled through his days in grim silence, like a sleep-walker, with the baby slung over his back in his dead wife's shawl. Father Edmund paid daily visits to be certain the baby was well tended. He could find no fault in Agilbert's care of the baby, but no joy either. It was the pig that would save him.

''Twill be a harsh winter, indeed,' reiterated Edwin, 'for my sow has never been wrong. In good times she has never had fewer than six, but now she has given birth to only four, and one of them is a runt, with a harelip at that! Well, good things come out of bad,' he conceded, 'for we'll sup on roast suckling pig one day soon.'

Old MoonCatcher did not even notice the widening of his great-nephew's eyes until the hulking lad turned around and seized his sleeve so suddenly that the frail old man was nearly pulled off the bench. 'I must have that pig!' cried Agilbert.

'What?' The old man could hardly credit his ears, for Agilbert had not spoken a word since the death of his runty, harelipped young wife.

'What will you take for the pig?' insisted Agilbert. 'You must not eat her!'

'What will you offer?' asked Edwin. ''Tis not every day I get a taste of suckling pig.'

'I haven't much set aside,' Agilbert admitted. 'Would you take two kirtles, and one of them nearly new?'

'Are you talking of Bertha's tiny kirtles?' asked the old man, frowning. 'What would I do with them? Your great-aunt Mildred is fatter than an abbot.'

'I could use the kirtles,' said Garth. 'Since the fire, my daughter Helga is forced to wear a borrowed kirtle or go naked. But I have nothing to trade for them.'

The three men sat looking dumbly at one another until the laughter of the women drew their indignant gaze. 'What are you laughing at?' demanded Edwin.

''Tis not the MoonCatcher blood,' said Edith to her friends in a voice meant to carry, 'because I'm a MoonCatcher too, and Garth hasn't a drop of it in his veins.'

''Tis a chronic condition,' said Aldyth sadly, 'and Sirona says there's no cure for it.'

Exasperated, Garth said irritably, 'What are you women talking about?'

Judith laughed and started up the path with her flour. She

74

stopped in front of the men's bench just long enough to say, 'What else? Men, of course.'

Mildburh declared magnanimously, 'They can't help it if they were born that way.' Turning toward the men, she suggested, 'Edwin, if you give Agilbert the pig, Garth can have the kirtles for Helga, and his wife, Hildegarde, can brew you up some ale.'

'But our brewing bowls were lost with everything else,' moaned Garth.

'Then go up to the abbey and borrow Mother Rowena's, addlepate.'

Edwin cackled gleefully at the simplicity of her solution. 'But never think for a moment,' he assured her, 'that we wouldn't have thought of it ourselves.'

'Not before the pig had died of old age,' said Mildburh, winking at the other women.

Ignoring her friendly dig, Edwin turned to his great-nephew and said, 'Take the runt, Bertie.' Spitting into his palm, he shook hands with the other two men to seal the bargain. 'I'll toast you and your harelipped pig with Hildegarde Brewer's beer.'

Once the deal was closed, Agilbert would not even allow the old man to wait until his grain was ground but hurried him home to collect the pig. 'And they say *I'm* daft!' Edwin called over his shoulder to the appreciative laughter of the spectators.

Aldyth smiled to herself. Life was never dull in Enmore Green. There was a scattering of nearby villages that all held land of Lord Ralf fitzGerald, each one with its own character. The villagers of Long Cross, just beyond the shadow of the great stone outcrop, had a reputation for being dull, steady, and staid. They would all find their way to Heaven, not because of any inherent virtue but simply because the ruts on the straight and narrow road they trod did not interest the broad and winding road to Hell. The villagers of Alcester, at the foot of the bluff on the south side, were at once grasping and self-righteous. In Alcester they enjoyed the hellfire-and-brimstone preaching of their sour-faced priest, but the collection plate was always empty at the end of the service. And the entire village of Enmore Green was said to be moon-touched. It was said that its inhabitants danced with Fairies by starlight and tried to catch the moon for a lantern. At any rate, on May Eve the girls of Long Cross were all home by midnight, their virtue still intact. The girls of Alcester stayed out late on May Eve and came home decked with flowers plucked in Enmore Green. As for the folk of Enmore Green, they were likely to go amaying whenever the fancy struck them. Who wouldn't choose Enmore Green?

After returning from the mill, Aldyth spent the afternoon boiling goose grease, while Sirona prepared the ingredients that would transform the grease into healing salves. But just before sunset, Sirona handed Aldyth her basket and said, 'Go to the fountain, child, and say a prayer for Hereward. Then take the hermit one of Godiva's cheeses.'

Another run. Aldyth's heart began to pound; she would see Bedwyn that night. Eagerly she picked up her shawl and set off. The fountain was deserted; all was quiet, except for the burbling of the spring and the chirping of the swallows at their dusk feeding. Aldyth was kneeling in prayer when she heard a traveler approach. She looked up to see a well-dressed man, not tall but burly, his red-gold hair streaked with gray. He filled the dipper and drank. Over the rim, their eyes met. Aldyth was startled to note that one of his eyes was gray and one blue: the mark of the Fairies. He nodded and moved on.

Aldyth left a posy of sweet-smelling feverfew as an offering to the Goddess, then took the familiar path among the lowering branches of the hawthorn trees. The stranger was quick and silent. She did not hear him coming up behind her, although she knew he must be there. The red-headed stranger with the elfin eyes fell into an easy gait behind her.

'Hereward,' she stated simply.

'Aldyth Lightfoot,' he replied.

Not a twig snapped beneath his feet; only the sounds of the forest could be heard, and then, off in the distance, the tolling of the bells for curfew. This runner was not driven to mindless chatter, nor did he look to her for reassurance. The darkness deepened until they blended with the gloom to become just two more shadows in the forest. As they approached Bedwyn's clearing, she warned, 'The hermit keeps a flock of noisy geese.'

Before the honking subsided, Hereward, dagger drawn,

pulled Aldyth back into the shadows. 'Let us be certain that it is our arrival that they announce,' he whispered. But the geese recognized Aldyth and soon returned to their nests.

'Geese make good sentries,' the runner commented. At Bedwyn's door he held up his hand in silent warning to halt Aldyth. Drawing his sword, he stepped inside, keeping his back to the wall. Aldyth followed, wondering at the extraordinary caution he displayed.

As soon as she offered her runner the customary cup of valerian, Bedwyn entered.

'Bedwyn, I bring you Hereward.' She realized that she had not asked the man from whence he had come. But as soon as Bedwyn met the stranger's eyes, he knew.

'My God,' said Bedwyn slowly, holding out his hand, which Hereward clasped firmly. 'Hereward of Bourne? The Wake himself?'

Aldyth's eyes grew wide. Hereward the Wake! What could possibly have been important enough to bring this living legend out of comfortable retirement to walk the Starlit Path once again? Aldyth suddenly felt like a mouse in the company of lions. If she had thought her legs and tongue would obey her, she would have stammered her farewell and left. Overawed, she could only stand there gaping.

'God's Mercy, Hereward!' exclaimed Bedwyn. 'Are you on the run?'

'Nay, I bring word, Bedwyn, to you and all the others who walk the Path.'

'Sit down, man,' said Bedwyn, gesturing to a bench. It was then that Bedwyn noticed Aldyth, still standing with a stupefied look on her face. Putting his hand on her shoulder, he ushered her to a seat. Aldyth sensed Bedwyn's agitation as he filled three mugs and placed bread and cheese on the table before them. Bedwyn then sat down beside Aldyth, stating bluntly and without ceremony, 'You shouldn't be here.'

Bedwyn had never met Hereward of Bourne, but there was not a Saxon in England who had not heard of Hereward's heroic stand at Ely, and there was not a guide on the Starlit Path who did not know that its very existence was due, in part, to the leadership of Hereward the Wake. Long before Ely's fall,

Hereward had developed a web of contacts that had served to guide rebels and fugitives into the fenland stronghold. He had shaped that motley mob of beaten rebels into the daring bands of marauders that had kept William out of the fens for six long years after the conquest. And after the fall of Ely, Hereward had been one of the key men to regroup the survivors in order to get them out of the fens and safely away from William's vengeance. King William had admired and respected Hereward, even in defeat, and he had courted his erstwhile adversary extravagantly, offering such generous terms as to outrage Hereward's former foes. Though the Wake had eventually made his peace with William, there were Saxons as well as Normans who despised him for coming to terms with the king.

'There are many who would relish seeing you proved a traitor,' warned Bedwyn.

'I'm here on pilgrimage to see the bones of Saint Edward the Martyr,' replied Hereward in mock innocence. 'So what if I pay a call on an old friend?'

Bedwyn shook his head dubiously. 'What is this news that brings you calling on the Hermit of the Blackmore Vale?'

'Last month King William called a great meeting in Sarum, that his followers might swear their oaths of fealty yet again. As you have obviously heard, Bedwyn,' said Hereward sourly, 'though William has forgiven me, his toadies never will. They try to undermine my position by bearing malicious tales to the king. While these tales are baseless, I am no longer taken into William's confidence. However, I am certain that last month's meeting was of greater significance than it would seem.'

'How so?'

'William is getting old. He's fat and weary. He has never had cause to question the loyalty of those who followed him across the channel, for he has rewarded them well. But the sons of his most faithful followers are grumbling and talking behind their hands, and soon they'll be thumbing their noses at him.'

'What has this to do with us and our work?'

'The king is setting his house in order and sweeping the rats out of the storerooms.'

'Including the Saxon rats that come out by starlight?' asked Bedwyn grimly.

'Just so,' came Hereward's unwelcome reply.

Bedwyn clenched his jaw and glanced across the table to observe Aldyth's reaction; he broke off a chunk of bread and set it before her, a gesture she found oddly touching, though her stomach churned and she could not think of eating.

'And what broom will he use to sweep away these rats?' asked Bedwyn.

'No broom, but one rat to lead in the cats.'

'Damn the Bastard!' Bedwyn pounded his fist on the table. 'Are we betrayed?'

'Alas, I cannot say,' replied Hereward glumly. 'I know only that William vows to sup on the fattest rats by Midsummer next. They are trying desperately to infiltrate. The spies who follow the tax men through every village have orders to watch for rats as well as stray pigs, and not all the king's spies are Norman. If just once a guide lets a runner through who can point a finger, they could take down the whole chain, link by link.'

Bedwyn leapt to his feet and began to pace like a nervous cat. He stopped and demanded, 'How can we protect ourselves?'

'There is only one way,' said Hereward. 'Disperse while you still can.'

Bedwyn looked at him through narrowed eyes. 'How do I know you are not the first cat come into the nest?'

''Tis a fair question,' acknowledged Hereward, 'and no secret I've made my bed, aye, and sleep with the enemy. But damn you if you don't think I grieve for every drop of Saxon blood spilled yesterday or today, and if I can prevent a bloodbath tomorrow, I shall.' Hereward sprang up and grasped Bedwyn by the shoulders. 'We can gloat at William as the new generation of snot-nosed conquerors whimpers to be tossed a bone, but the same thing is happening to us. Our own guides grow old, and youngsters who have never tasted freedom are unwilling to die for something they cannot fathom.'

Shrugging off Hereward's grasp as he would have wished to shrug off his ill tidings, Bedwyn turned away. His eyes fell upon Aldyth, whose lips trembled as she fought for composure. He stepped behind her and placed his hands upon her shoulders. Turning back toward Hereward, he asked quietly, 'Do you expect us simply to walk away?'

'I'm suggesting you run. Have you heard that the link at Sutton Wick is broken? Though the Normans don't know it, when they took the eyes of Oswald FourOx for poaching, they broke our chain yet again. And no one has stepped forward to take his place. Farther north there are guides who have been forced to flee on what is left of the Starlit Path, becoming the tail of the snake that swallows itself.'

'That is to the north,' cried Bedwyn fiercely. 'My territory leads to the sea, and the chain to the sea lies unbroken.'

'A bridge that burns from the middle can bear no weight.'

Bedwyn dropped down heavily beside Aldyth. Their hands met and clasped, conducting currents of comfort between them. 'What are the others doing?' he asked sullenly.

'Some have gone to Byzantium to join the Varangian Guard. Others fight alongside Normans in Sicily under Robert. Some go to Denmark, where they have kin; still others to Russ, where Harold Godwinson's daughter Gytha is queen.'

Bedwyn shook his head, too sick at heart to speak.

'Bedwyn, you're of noble blood, are you not? If you were to swear fealty,' ventured Hereward, 'I could speak to William about having your lands restored.'

'I would never swear fealty to a Norman, nor could I stomach calling a Norman "lord"!' Bedwyn snapped. Immediately he regretted his words. Meeting Hereward's eyes, he said sincerely, 'I'm glad you've made your peace. God knows you deserve it.'

Hereward's shoulders slumped. 'There are times when I would leave it all behind. I've a cousin in Denmark who tells of a new world beyond Iceland, beyond even Greenland. There lies a clean land for a fresh start, but I'm too old for that, and I've lived in exile before; I'll not leave England again. But you, Bedwyn, you're young enough to begin anew. Or are you still waiting for Harold's bones to rise? 'Tis not going to happen, and nothing short of that will stir a fire in these youngsters' guts. Believe me, I've tried. They just want to be left alone, by William and by me.'

Bedwyn sat in sullen silence.

'Will you at least think about what I've said?'

'Aye, I'll think about that,' said Bedwyn grudgingly, 'and

nothing else. But what of you? Now that you've delivered your message, will you go home to Bourne?'

'Not yet. I intend to carry the warning north along the relicts of the Path.'

'You'll surely be recognized,' warned Bedwyn. 'Let me go. I know all the guides and hides along the way. Besides, you've much to lose and I've very little.'

'I've less to lose than you suppose,' replied Hereward wearily. 'Call it a pilgrimage, if you like, but I wish to walk the Starlit Path one last time. I'll go north, and you, Bedwyn, can send warning southward to the sea.'

It struck Aldyth that Hereward carried himself like a man shriven for battle and expecting to die, and it made her flesh creep.

'Very well,' agreed Bedwyn, 'but you'll be safer in the hide north of here.' He pushed bread and cheese toward his guest. 'Eat before we go.' Bedwyn rose and pulled Aldyth to her feet. Picking up her basket, he led her outside into the moonlight.

'Will I ever see you again?' asked Aldyth.

Hugging her warmly, he promised, 'I'll never leave without saying good-bye, Mouse, but I need time to think this through. Tell Sirona what you have heard tonight, and show more caution about whom you guide.'

Hereward stepped outside and said, 'Remember me to Sirona, Aldyth.' A smile lit up his features like a flash of lightning. 'And tell her the old dog has had his day.' Hereward clasped Aldyth's hand and leaned forward to give her the kiss of peace.

'You make a Saxon proud of her race,' she said breathlessly. 'May the Lady keep you.'

Bedwyn handed Aldyth her basket, pulled her shawl up over her hair, then brushed his lips against her forehead. 'God bless you,' he whispered.

As she watched them melt into the darkness, Aldyth thought, 'Hereward's story is that of all England, and poor obstinate Bedwyn is the exception.'

Losing the Path would end the only adventure in her life, her tenuous connection to the world outside Enmore

Green and beyond. And she would lose Bedwyn as well, for if the Starlit Path were dissolved, what would hold him here? Not his bees. Not his geese. Not even the milkmaid in Elcomb Croft.

CHAPTER SEVEN

October 1086

'However fiercely you glower, you cannot stop the rain,' said Sirona.

Aldyth peered out at the endless drizzle of icy rain, her spinning idle in her hands.

''Tis cold outside and warm by the hearth,' Sirona said, 'but it won't be for long if you don't close the door.' Then, more gently: 'What ails you, child?'

As the dark, cold nights closed in, Aldyth had begun to feel a new restlessness. It itched and gnawed at her from the inside out. She had never been wildly happy, but she had always found contentment and fulfillment in her life. Aldyth could not have put her feelings into words even had she wished to share them, so she sat by the fire and tried to apply herself to her spinning. But her fingers slowed their deft twisting of the wool and her thoughts began to drift, as always, to the same subject. It had been weeks since her tender parting with Bedwyn, on the night she had guided Hereward to him. In spite of the growing danger, she found herself wishing that a runner would appear, providing an excuse to make the journey. Yet that was also one of her greatest fears.

'If a stranger comes seeking our aid,' Aldyth had asked Sirona when she told her godmother of Hereward's warning, 'how can we know he is trustworthy?'

'That we do not know,' Sirona replied somberly. 'But anyone coming to the well has thrown himself upon the mercy of the Goddess; we cannot turn our backs on such a one.'

With the Starlit Path in the forefront of Aldyth's mind, so

too was Bedwyn. Aldyth remembered the first time they had met. She had been in her eighth summer when Sirona had first taken her to the outlaws' forest camp, deep in the heart of Cranborne Chase. The band had consisted of a score of men and a few widows who had been turned out.

Young Aldyth had gone to help with a difficult birthing. The expectant mother was Seaxburh MoonCatcher, whom Aldyth had known when she had lived in Enmore Green. Seaxburh's husband, Osfrith, had been a freeman, but after fighting at Hastings and watching his father and two uncles die there, he had limped home to find himself reduced to a slave in serf's clothing, whose surliness was inflamed by the losses he was having his nose rubbed into. The breaking point had come in a petty quarrel with Lord Ralf's steward, William CloseFist, over the Christmas payment of eggs, and had culminated when Osfrith had knocked the Norman into a ditch. The price for his rashness, his right hand, had been higher than he was willing to pay. He had run home to collect his pregnant young wife, then headed for the wilds. In a hasty parting, Osfrith had given his brother, Agilbert the Elder, his tiny holding with his blessing. 'Pray for us,' he had said, and they were gone.

It was the dead of winter, but Osfrith and Seaxburh had heard of an outlaw band living within the chase and were determined to join them. Lost and starving, the runaways had wandered in the depths of the forest, certain that the stories of the outlaws living in the chase were just wild tales. Only after they had lain down in the snow to die had they found themselves surrounded by the very will-o'-the-wisps they had been seeking.

Nothing had been heard of them until that spring when, late one night, Osfrith had crept into Enmore Green to consult its wisewoman. His wife's baby was due and overdue, and Osfrith told Sirona anxiously, 'Seaxburh is big as a barn and close as a keep.'

'Can you hear a heartbeat?' whispered Sirona.

'Aye, like a drum.'

'I'll gather my things.'

The moon was out, but its light barely shone through the canopy of branches overhead. They had followed Osfrith deep into the woods of Cranborne Chase. He had taken well to his new life, for he was surefooted even in the dark. Aldyth estimated that they had come eight miles, or perhaps less, when they at last reached their destination.

The placement of the camp was ingenious. Those ancient woods were so heavily forested that it was said a squirrel could travel from one end of the chase to the other without ever touching foot to the ground. In the thick of those woods, in a dip at the top of a hill, the outlaws had made their home. Until Sirona and Aldyth walked over the edge of the last rise, it was undetectable. From the crest of the rise, they saw a faint light that turned out to be a shaded lantern. The lantern bearer, watching for their arrival, led them into a natural depression. By the dim light, Aldyth could barely discern a cluster of small mounds of brush, the makeshift roofs of shelters dug into the hillside. Only then did she notice the faint smell of wood fires, thin wisps of smoke rising up to be caught and dissipated in the heavy canopy of leaves overhead.

Osfrith led the old healer and her apprentice to a little hut set deep into the chalky hillside, like an earthen cave. By the low flame of a rushlight, they could see Seaxburh, pale and drawn, lying on a pallet of bracken, her unveiled hair hanging loose and lank with sweat. 'Sirona,' she said, her face set in a strained smile, 'I'm so glad you came.'

Sirona knelt and embraced her. She was encouraged to see that Seaxburh had lost that hungry look so common to the Saxon serf; there was meat on her bones, and it was obvious that she had been living well on the king's deer. The wisewoman felt Seaxburh's belly with knowing hands, then pressed her ear close, listening for a heartbeat.

'The womb is working to push the child out,' she said at last. 'Is the water broken?'

'Aye,' replied Osfrith. 'Since midday yesterday.'

'Seaxburh,' said the crone, 'there's a healthy baby in there, waiting to turn her face toward the warm spring sun, but she needs help. I'm going to give you spurred rye to strengthen the labor. Osfrith, have you any warm ale to mix it with?'

'No, but we have elderberry wine. Would that do?'

'Very nicely, I should think.'

85

Once the simple was given, it was only a matter of time. Leaving the women to catch up on gossip, Aldyth went outside and leaned against the trunk of a tree. She was startled by a boy, fifteen or sixteen she guessed, who appeared out of thin air and plopped himself down beside her. 'How's the birthing going?' he asked.

Stunned by his sudden appearance and awed by the boy's beauty, she was dumbstruck.

'What's the matter, Mouse? Cat got your tongue?' he teased.

Aldyth, shy under any circumstances, blushed and stammered an unintelligible answer. When the lad realized he was not going to get any information out of the skinny, flat-chested girl, he ruffled her hair, playfully tweaked her nose, and sauntered off.

Over the next few years, on her rare trips to the encampment, Aldyth watched for the sun-haired boy with the sapphire eyes. If she saw him, it was across the camp, roughhousing with the other lads as they went off to poach the king's deer or Lord Ralf's pigs.

Then one night, when Aldyth was twelve, she woke to a tap on their door. Sirona let in a pretty woman dressed in a shabby kirtle. They spoke in quiet whispers, and then Sirona hastily packed a basket. She gave Aldyth a gentle shake and said, 'Rise up and go to the fountain to fetch a skin of fresh water. I'll be back soon.'

'Where are you going?' Aldyth asked sleepily.

'To the smith's for a pair of pincers. We've another long night ahead of us, child.'

The stranger led Sirona and Aldyth through the dark woods, a trip weighted by the tension in the air. At last they reached the hollow-topped hill and descended to the outlaws' camp. Their guide called into one of the huts, 'We're here.'

'Thanks be to the Lady!' came a woman's voice from within. A stooping figure emerged from the low doorway, then straightened to greet them.

'Seaxburh,' said Sirona, 'how is he?'

'That is for you to discover; he'll admit to no frailty. We'll wait without, for there is little enough room for the two of you. Call if you need anything.'

'Fetch me a pot to boil our springwater in, a cup, and some wine,' said Sirona.

They entered a very small structure of wattle and daub dimly lit by a rushlight. Lying within was Bedwyn, now grown to his full height, though not quite grown out of the gangliness of youth. His leg was wrapped in bloody rags, and the splintered end of a broken arrow protruded from his thigh. At Aldyth's look of alarm, he flashed her a wry smile and said, 'Look what the cat dragged in. Hello, Mouse.'

His cheeks were flushed, sweat-soaked strands of golden hair were plastered to his forehead, and there was an unnatural brightness in his eyes. 'Fever,' said Sirona. 'We'll need the willow bark.' The crone unwrapped his leg. 'Where did you pick this up, lad?'

Bedwyn smiled weakly. ''Twas a gift.'

'Aye, from one of the king's foresters, I'll wager,' said Sirona. 'Caught poaching?'

'Stuck like a pig, but not caught,' he boasted. 'The bloody fool didn't know he hit me.'

'Just who played the bloody fool is still open to question,' observed Sirona acidly, 'but in a minute, lad, you'll get a chance to back up your bluster.'

Seaxburh returned with a skin of wine and a pot to boil the spring-water in. Sirona washed the pincers with wine, poured more wine into the cup, and laced it with poppy. 'Give him some of this,' she said, handing the cup to Aldyth.

As Aldyth raised him to drink, Bedwyn met her eyes over the rim of the cup. She felt it down to the pit of her stomach, as he had intended. She realized that he was appraising her budding figure, the new swell of curves at her hips and breasts. She blushed, uncertain whether she felt flattered or frightened.

When Bedwyn's eyes had become poppy-glazed, Sirona said, 'Aldyth, sit on his chest.'

'I need no restraint,' he said groggily. 'Besides, she'd be blocking my view.'

Sirona gave him an ironic half smile. 'Suit yourself. Aldyth, get behind this young peacock and prop him up so he can enjoy the show.'

Aldyth scrambled around behind him, and Bedwyn leaned

back against her. As she clasped her hands across his chest, he reached up and lightly rested his hands upon her wrists. Aldyth was prepared to pin his arms from behind; she had seen grown men scream and struggle for lesser wounds, and Sirona needed him to lie still. When Sirona first probed the flesh with her fingers to assess the wound, Bedwyn took a sharp breath and stiffened. The crone looked up at him and asked, 'Do you want this quick or clean?'

'Make it clean,' he said between clenched teeth.

The healer nodded approvingly and applied the pincers. Immediately beads of sweat appeared on Bedwyn's brow and his breath came in hoarse gasps. When Sirona found the iron arrowhead, she gripped the barbs with the pincers. First she had to push the arrow deeper into the wound to release the flesh from the barbs; then she applied all her strength to flatten the barbs against the shaft of the arrow.

With the painful deepening and sudden jarring of the arrow, Bedwyn groaned and tightened his grip on Aldyth's wrists. He shuddered as Sirona pulled the arrow out, ripping through muscle and scraping against bone. At last the old woman triumphantly held up the bloody arrow stump, then quickly stanched the wound with wild grape leaves, pressing down hard to make a tourniquet. Bedwyn relaxed into Aldyth's arms.

'I'll have that for a keepsake,' he said weakly to Sirona, nodding toward the bloody arrowhead that she had tossed aside.

'And you'll have another keepsake on your leg,' said the wisewoman.

He winked at Aldyth. 'A good scar impresses the lasses, but will the leg mend sound?'

'Chances are it will.'

Sirona stitched the wound closed and applied another poultice. 'You bore it well, lad. Now try to sleep, and I shall do the same, for I've been up the last two nights nursing a poxy child. I'll thank you the next time to call for me at a decent hour. Aldyth, I'll be at Seaxburh's if you need me. Watch the fever, and see that he sleeps soundly.'

But Bedwyn's pain was too great to allow for sleep. Aldyth gave him another measure of the poppy-laced wine. Then Bedwyn settled back with his head in her lap. He made drunk talk that night, his tongue loosened by the drugged wine. He told her of his father and his lost fortune, of seeing King Harold in York as a young boy, and how he hoped that someday Harold would return and lead them all to victory. Even half drunk and racked with pain, Bedwyn had an intensity, a contagious optimism that fascinated her. Glancing up at her, he mumbled, 'Look at you, Mouse. You're all grown up.' He frowned at the bruise that ringed her wrist like a bracelet, took her hand, and asked, 'What's this?'

'You had rather a tight grip when the arrow came out,' she said. ''Twill fade.'

'I never meant to hurt you, Mouse.' He gave her a playful kiss on the inside of her wrist, then chuckled as she blushed furiously and snatched back her hand.

'Drink,' she told him, lifting the wine cup to his lips, and at last he slept.

The next morning, the same woman who had summoned them woke Bedwyn with a warm kiss, which he returned eagerly. Aldyth was crushed, but what else had she expected? Even at twelve she had been old enough to understand that there could never be anything between the two of them. At twenty-two she knew the gulf was just as great and growing wider.

Men! Why couldn't she keep her thoughts free of them? Aldyth tossed aside her spinning, snatched up a stack of wooden bowls, and slammed one down under each drip in the leaky thatch. Her godmother raised an eyebrow at Aldyth's vehemence but said nothing. For once Sirona was wrong, thought Aldyth. It was not the rain that made her glower. Had she fallen in love with Bedwyn? She had never fallen in love before; she had no idea what it felt like or how it affected one. But if this was love, she thought grumpily, she did not need it.

One chilly, leaden afternoon, Aldyth hastily made her way through the sodden grass of the common, heading toward the forest. Mud and cowpats squelched beneath her wooden clogs. So absorbed was she in scanning the ground to avoid the filth that it did not at first register that Gandulf fitzGerald, astride the bay mare he always rode, had drawn up beside her. Perversely, she pretended not to notice him and quickened her step. He urged on the mare to match Aldyth's pace and waited for her to speak. When it became clear to him that she had no intention of doing so, Gandulf broke down and inquired in her language, 'Mistress Aldyth, have you lost something?'

Abruptly she turned on him and said curtly, 'No. One of the villagers has a fever; probably an obstruction in her bowels. I need chicory, and I need it now.'

'But chicory grows in every hedgerow hereabouts,' Gandulf pointed out.

'The chicory that grows hereabouts is harsh and bitter. I gather mine elsewhere,' Aldyth replied flatly. She knew the Normans scorned the Saxon peasants as pagan elf worshipers and had no wish to disclose her conviction that chicory gathered from the Fairy hill had greater curative powers. ''Tis late in the season for chicory and late in the day for idle chatter, so if you'll excuse me—'

'But perhaps I can be of some assistance to you,' he suggested.

'Have you some chicory on your person?'

'No,' he admitted.

'Well, then . . .' And she continued on her way at a brisk pace.

Gandulf sat upon his horse, trying to understand how the conversation had gotten off on such a bad foot or why he should even care. She had obviously not learned humility since her last trip up Castle Hill, nor was he so fond of rejection that he was willing to seek it out from an insolent Saxon wench. Yet even while he was drawing this conclusion, his eyes followed her springy step and his foot urged his mount forward. When he had caught up to Aldyth, he saw her stiffen and stubbornly refuse to look up from the ground.

'She's ignoring me!' he thought incredulously, as he reined in his mount to match her pace. He did not know whether to turn around and go home or laugh aloud at her childish effrontery. At last he said, 'Come up and ride pillion; I'll help you find your chicory.'

Aldyth heaved a weary sigh. The last time they had met, at the city gate, she had been extremely rude, but it had obviously not had a lasting effect. She stopped and looked up at him warily, weighing his possible motives against the obvious benefits of this arrangement.

'I promise to behave myself,' he quipped, reaching out his hand to her.

She stared at the proffered hand, then tried to peer through his eyes and into his mind; it was like trying to read a book without knowing her letters. She shrugged and took his hand, saying curtly, 'I do this only for the sake of Winifred.'

Aldyth placed her foot in the stirrup and Gandulf gave a heave, swinging her up onto the mare in a tangle of skirts. She flushed crimson as she dropped his hand and hastily pulled her skirts back down. It annoyed her to see the shadow of amusement on his face as he watched over his shoulder. 'What are you looking at?' she snapped.

He shrugged.

'This was not supposed to be a sightseeing expedition,' she scolded. 'If you would be so good, there is a Fairy hill just east of Melbury Abbas, where the chicory grows sweet and strong. Follow the road to Melbury Abbas, but turn off on the path to Zig-Zag Hill.'

'Hold tight, Mistress Aldyth.' She was still looking for a handhold when he reached back and took her wrists, pulling her arms around his waist. He clucked softly, the bay gave a forward lurch, and Aldyth, startled, tightened her grip. She was irked to hear him chuckle, and she wondered if he had done it on purpose. Reminding herself that he was doing her a favor, Aldyth admonished herself for her rudeness and even decided to be more gracious this time. But she changed her mind when she realized that the road would take them directly through Alcester. The sight of her riding pillion behind the Norman lordling would surely set the gossips' tongues to wagging.

'There are several Fairy hills in that area,' said Gandulf, breaking into her thoughts.

That was true. Aldyth had never dreamed that he might know these parts as well as she, and she was surprised to find herself feeling protective, even jealous, of her territory.

''Tis the one scarred by the grass fire,' she replied coolly.

At first Aldyth found the ride bumpy and uncomfortable,

especially when they rode past Alcuin and Wulfric plowing one of Lord Ralf's fields. But when the outlying fields of Enmore Green and Alcester had been left behind, she relaxed and fell into the rhythm of the horse. They spoke little, but once, when they flushed a pair of pheasants out of the bracken, Gandulf turned sideways, caught her eye, and pointed so that she could follow their flight. Without thinking, Aldyth responded with a nod and a smile.

She was soon to regret her warm response, which he might have considered encouragement on her part. A Saxon serf was especially vulnerable in the hands of a Norman noble, and she had knowingly placed herself in his power. At the foot of Zig-Zag Hill, Gandulf drew to an abrupt halt. Why was he stopping here, in the middle of nowhere? Aldyth wondered in alarm. It was still some way to the Fairy hill, there was not a soul within shouting distance, and there was no one who knew where she had gone. She was thankful then that her departure had been witnessed by Alcuin and Wulfric; at least they would know in which direction she had been carried off, and by whom.

Gandulf dismounted. Aldyth's palms grew cold, and she slipped her hand into her apron pocket to finger her digging knife nervously. Almost as an afterthought, Gandulf explained, ''Tis a very steep ride. I would lighten the horse's burden.' He must have wondered at the broad smile she gave in answer, but he returned it without comment.

Utterly relieved, Aldyth said, 'I'll get down, too.'

'Yours is but a featherweight. Stay where you are.' He made fond clucking noises to the mare and led her up the steep switchbacked path to the top of Zig-Zag Hill. The path then leveled out and ran along the top of a ridge. This was the ancient roadway of the small dark people who had lived there when the land was still so heavily forested that only on the high chalky ridgeways was it dry and bare enough to travel easily. Even now, the ridge protruded from the wooded bottomlands like a sandbar in a creek. On either side they could look down and see the hilly woods of Dorsetshire stretched out below. Behind, they could see Sceapterbyrig off in the distance. Ahead, just beneath the crest of the ridge to the north, there were three circular mounds, and, although she could not see it, Aldyth knew that farther down the slope and to the south a fourth mound rose.

The lordling, acquainted with the superstitious dread that caused most people to avoid the ancient mounds, asked teasingly, 'Aren't you afraid to risk the wrath of the Fairies by clambering about on their rooftop? Or are you so light of foot that they don't mind?'

'I am no more afraid to frequent this place than you are to stroll through the churchyard in Sceapterbyrig. These barrows are the last resting place of the small dark folk who lived here before the Welsh drove them out, before the Saxons drove out the Welsh, and they will rest here long after we Saxons are gone. The Normans, too, for that matter,' she added, giving him an insinuating sideways glance. Refusing to be baited, he gave a little tug on the bridle and turned toward the fire-swept barrow.

At the barrow, he dropped the reins. But when he reached up to lift Aldyth down, she reflexively recoiled from his touch. She caught herself, but it was too late, for Gandulf flinched as if she had struck him. For an instant, the two of them cringed back from each other, frozen. Aldyth understood then that this man had no evil on his mind. She knew too that if she did not mend the moment immediately, it might never be mended. Leaning down from her perch, she held out her arms as she might to a shy deer. Forced into a response, he stepped forward and took her by the waist. Lifting her from the saddle, Gandulf held her gingerly, as if she might melt at his touch, then set her down quickly and released her. But before she stepped away to a distance more comfortable to both of them, she met his eyes and smiled warmly. 'Thank you,' she said simply. The gratitude she sensed was pitiful. For a word of kindness? More likely for pretending not to have noticed the raw emotion he had tried so hard to hide.

Turning to the business at hand, Aldyth hurried toward a patch of disturbed ground, all holes and root-bound lumps of soil. She scanned the barrow for the stalks of chicory. Finally she said in dismay, 'This is where it should be. Little blue flowers on a spindly green stalk. Someone or something has cleared the lot of them. I pray it was a wild beast; no

Saxon gatherer would take the whole stand and leave none to replenish itself.'

'What does chicory like?' Gandulf asked. 'Sun? Open fields? Might we find it on one of the other barrows?'

'There used to be a small stand of it on the little south barrow,' recalled Aldyth.

'Very well,' said Gandulf, 'lead the way.' He took up the horse's lead and followed her over the top of the ridge and another quarter mile down the other side.

'Gandulf, look!' she cried. 'Chicory! And 'tis undisturbed!' In her excitement, she dragged him along by the hand, while fishing her bronze knife out of her apron pocket.

'Where?' asked Gandulf, scanning the frost-browned foliage at their feet. 'I thought you said there would be little blue flowers.'

She pointed to a stand of broken stalks, brown and dried. Suddenly solemn, she knelt before them and gazed down at the withered herbs.

'Will these not serve?' asked Gandulf.

'They shall serve,' she whispered.

'What then?' he asked. 'Is something amiss?'

'I was just thinking,' she mused, 'how like a Saxon is this wilted flower: victim of a cruel tyrant, winter, but its roots run deep and there is life in them yet.' Looking up at Gandulf, she explained, ''Tis the roots we need, my Lord.' Then she began to dig.

He stood watching her. Her hair defied confinement and had slipped from beneath her veil in all its honey-colored glory. Whether it was the wind or her excitement, the rising color in her cheeks made her green eyes sparkle a vibrant emerald. Gandulf marveled at her emotions, which played across her being like the weather that crossed the downs, sometimes shot through with sunlight, sometimes overrun by thunder and raging winds, sometimes uplifted to a gentle glittering shower backlit by a rainbow. He was awed at how she accepted them, opened herself to both pain and pleasure without reserve. He knew well that he himself merely read life like a book, always at one remove, reserving to himself the right to close the book whenever the plot struck too close

94

to the heart. Gandulf drew his dagger, knelt beside her, and began to dig.

On the return journey, Aldyth knew that magic had been wrought on the Fairy hill. If only for a short time, the two of them had broken through the barriers of class and race. But she also knew that their friendship could not survive beyond the Fairy hill, that their paths must soon diverge. When they reached the crossroads, she told him, 'Set me down here, please.' One path led directly to the city gate; the other wound around the town wall and down the hill into Enmore Green. ''Tis but a short distance for you from here, Gandulf, but the road to the garrison from my village is a long and winding one.'

'Nothing I have waiting for me is so pressing that I cannot see you home. The darkness is nearly upon us, and at night these roads teem with vagabonds and fugitives.'

'Like Aelfric and Bedwyn,' Aldyth thought ironically. 'Gandulf,' she said, 'I'll be open with you. I'd rather not give the gossips of Enmore Green any more grist for their mills. What are they to think if they see me riding pillion behind the son of Lord Ralf?'

'I'll be open with you, Aldyth,' he countered. 'The gossips of Alcester have probably already gotten word to the gossips of Enmore Green, who are even now peeking around their doors for a glimpse of the spectacle. I'll have no more argument.'

Resignedly, Aldyth directed him to Winifred's dwelling, a mean thatched hut on the main way through the village. Gandulf dismounted and held out his arms to Aldyth. He must have sensed the change as well, for this time there was no flinching, no shying, as he lifted her down from the saddle. His hands lingered about her waist slightly longer than necessary. 'Just long enough,' thought Aldyth, 'to give everyone in the village a good look and to call over their cousins from Long Cross, too.'

'I've seen an old woman sitting outside this door spinning. So her name is Winifred? I hope the chicory helps,' said Gandulf, trying to draw out the moment.

'By the Lady's grace, it will,' replied Aldyth. 'Good night, my Lord, and thank you.'

'And I would like to hear how the old woman gets on.'

'You'll be the first to know.'

'If you ever need assistance gathering your herbs, I go riding nearly every day—'

'Thank you, and good night!' she said with a laugh. If there was any doubt in Gandulf's mind that she was trying to be rid of him, it was dispelled when she took him by the arms, turned him toward his horse, and gave him a little push. As he watched her disappear into the doorway of Winifred's tiny dwelling, it struck Gandulf that the Saxon peasant girl had just dismissed him like a young boy smitten with calf love. It was not that he was in love; far from it. In any Norman court she would be considered unfashionably tall, and the freckles on her cheeks would be the bane of any noblewoman's life, but there had been beauties enough in Paris, and none had captured his interest. He had never met a woman who could make him forget himself the way he had that day. Most despised him because he was not cut from the same virile cloth as his father or fawned on him because he was heir to his father's fiefdom; then it was he who despised them.

'God in Heaven!' he cried aloud at a sudden memory. This maid had made him forget not only himself but the rest of the world as well. It was the night of the feast in honor of the earl of Gillingham, his father's liege lord, and he was already late. 'Saint Denis, you who lost your head,' he groaned, 'prithee save me from losing mine.'

Mud and gravel flew as Gandulf galloped into the bailey, lit by torches to greet guests. Leaping from the saddle, he hastily handed the reins to the groom posted to receive visitors' mounts and hurried to the horse trough to clean the dirt from his fingernails. Protocol demanded his punctual presence at the high table in deference to any guest, but especially one of such high rank and their liege lord as well. What excuse could he possibly make to justify such a breach of etiquette? Gandulf did not dislike the earl of Gillingham, and it would be neither courteous nor prudent to offend him. As for Lord Ralf, Gandulf had long since given up hope of pleasing or even appeasing his father.

It had not always been so. As Gandulf dried his hands on the seat of his tunic and hurried up to dinner, he recalled the events of the day that had convinced him once and for all of the futility of his efforts. He had been twelve years old, an awkward, gangly boy, on his way to sit with his mother in the solar, for they found solace in each other's company. But as he approached, Gandulf had heard his father's voice raised in anger, followed by the soft pleading of his mother. He knew it would not be long before his father would be raging and his mother weeping. He was tempted to flee, to remain in hiding until it was all over, but concern for his mother outweighed his fear of his father. He hovered in the hallway, too shaken to act, whether by running or intervening.

'I own you, I paid for you!' shouted his father.

'When have I ever disobeyed you?' his mother cried.

'Are you not using witchcraft to stop up your womb? I shall have another heir!'

''Tis not true! I swear it! Did I not already give you a son?'

'You call that a son? He should be a page at court by now. By the end of next year, he should become a squire, but he hasn't the guts for it. If I hadn't seen him naked, I'd have thought him a woman.'

Gandulf was horrified that he had brought his father's wrath down upon his mother. Guiltily he recalled the times when he had ducked out of sword practice or when, instead of riding at the quintain, he had stolen away with a book hidden in the folds of his cloak.

The sound of a blow being struck and the pained cry of his mother galvanized him into action. Gandulf charged through the doorway to find his father standing over his mother, a handful of her hair in one fist and the other poised to strike another blow.

'No!' he shouted, striking Lord Ralf's hands away. All three of them were so shocked at Gandulf's effrontery that they were stunned into motionless silence.

'Gandulf,' whispered his mother in hushed terror, her voice breaking the spell.

'Why, you little worm,' growled his father, 'I'll break your neck!'

'Mother, leave us,' Gandulf urged.

'Get out of my way!' roared his father.

'Mother, hurry!' Gandulf pleaded. But Lady Emma, paralyzed by fear, was forced to watch as her husband struck a blow that sent Gandulf flying across the room with a bloodied, broken nose. Lord Ralf stormed after him and hauled the boy up by the collar.

In a rare display of passion his mother threw herself at her husband's knees. 'Please,' she begged, 'leave him be! You'll kill him!'

Several servants had heard the commotion and came running. By then Lord Ralf's rage had died down, and he glowered in disgust at the bleeding boy and the tearful woman clinging to his knees. 'You're both pathetic,' he snarled. 'Get them out of my sight,' he spat to the cowering servants. 'Tomorrow he goes to the monks at Saint Denis.'

'Please, my lord,' wept Lady Emma, 'let me keep the boy at home. With him gone, there will be nothing for me here.'

'Very well,' said her husband coldly, 'I shall send you away as well.'

'He is your only heir,' she sobbed.

'I can get another one,' he said, sneering.

'Any heir you could hope to beget would be a bastard,' she objected.

'Does not a bastard rule all of England and Normandy?'

So Gandulf had gone into exile. His years at the monastery had been peaceful, if lonely, and tranquil, if dull. He had never been happy among the monks, but he had reached a state of acceptance and had even considered taking vows. But when the armed escort had come unannounced to reclaim him, it was not in Gandulf's nature to resist; in any case, resistance had never proved useful before. Though Gandulf had returned to Scafton, he had ceased to try to live up to his father's expectations. Nevertheless, it was unfortunate that he could not have seen Aldyth home and still arrived on time, he thought once again.

Not only had the trenchers been set, but the first course had already been carried around the high table. The earl of Gillingham and Lord Ralf had made their choices from among half a dozen dishes, which now circulated among the guests at the lower table. Although the butler hovered attentively, awaiting the call for more wine, servers no longer swarmed to and from the pantry carrying platters of food. The tables buzzed with the clanking cups and hum of conversation, while a minstrel's lute lent gaiety to the festivities.

Gandulf knelt before Gillingham at the high table. Lord Gillingham had also been a follower of William's at Hastings. He was now distinguished, gray-haired, and, unlike Ralf fitzGerald, mellowed by time. Lord Gillingham held out his hands, greasy with drippings of roast swan, and Gandulf placed his own between them in homage.

'I hope it was a pretty wench,' chuckled Lord Gillingham.

Lord Ralf snorted derisively. 'He still doesn't know he has left the monastery.'

'Forgive me, my Lord Gillingham,' said Gandulf, ignoring his father's dart. 'I set off for a short ride through Enmore Green, but somehow I found myself in Melbury Abbas.'

'Doubtless his mind was on Aristotle. I wonder he's here at all,' groused his father.

'We were young once ourselves, Ralf,' said the earl indulgently.

Gandulf was making a mental note to light a candle for Saint Denis when a servant hurried over bearing a jug of wine. In the earl's honor, the cooks had prepared roast swan, eel pie, and, as a special treat, whole roasted skylarks, thrushes, and wrens. Gandulf had arrived too late to partake of the special delicacies, but there were fresh venison, lamb-and-apple pie, hare stewed in ale, and salt fish to pile onto his trencher.

Also seated at the high table was the sheriff of Dorset, Hugh fitzGrip. FitzGrip was a tall, wiry man with vulpine eyes and long, grasping fingers. He always dressed in the richest fabrics and the latest fashions. If a minstrel came through wearing a silk undertunic embroidered with silver, at his next public appearance fitzGrip would be sporting a silk undertunic embroidered with gold. Gandulf had even heard the kitchen maids whisper that fitzGrip dyed his hair.

FitzGrip had come over as a common adventurer to fight for William at Hastings. The gamble had paid off, for he had been granted the office of sheriff, which was doubly rewarding;

not only did he receive a stipend for his duties, but he was in a position to wring bribes out of everyone in the shire. Lord Ralf's peasants feared him as much as they feared their own master. While Lord Ralf was prone to angry outbursts and violent rages, fitzGrip used anger only when it furthered his interests or increased his profits. And he always furthered his interests and increased his profits.

'And why shouldn't William exact another tax from them?' asked Lord Ralf, resuming the conversation interrupted by Gandulf's arrival. 'Did he not fight and bleed for the right? Did not we all? And it isn't as if he is using the proceeds on fripperies.'

'True enough,' declared fitzGrip, the jeweled rings on his fingers glittering as they caught the torchlight. 'He's defending their pigsty, is he not?'

Gandulf looked up from his plate. Usually he ate his dinner without attending to the table talk, then excused himself as soon as politely possible. That night, however, it occurred to him that they were discussing Aldyth and her people. 'How much,' Gandulf wondered aloud, 'do you suppose it would cost to buy the loyalty of the English? A great deal less than the king is paying for his mercenaries, bodyguards, and tasters, nor would he have to be afraid to turn his back to a crowd to take a piss.'

Both Lord Gillingham's and Lord Ralf's eyes widened in surprise, and fitzGrip's eyes narrowed speculatively as Gandulf, unmindful of their reaction, helped himself to more venison.

In the pantry at the far end of the great hall, several assistant servers came back with empty platters and handed them to the scullion. Even among the servants there was a rigid hierarchy of power. The servers were all Norman men, and they waited by the dais for their assistants to bring them plates laden with the next course. Their assistants, young boys and Saxon women, scurried about the pantry, preparing to serve the next course and tossing off orders to the scullions. The only person the scullions had to bully was the turnspit, that unfortunate child whose job it was to sit by the fire turning the meat.

One of the Saxon maidservants commented sourly, 'They're talking taxes again.'

'And what do we get for our money?' asked the maid called Wulfwynn. 'A fine show: Hugh fitzGrip preening himself and parading about the county like a scarlet peacock.'

'Hush your idle tongues,' scolded Margaret, the big-bosomed cook's assistant, eavesdropping as she supervised the preparations. Once Lord Aethelstan's head cook, she had been displaced by a Norman chef. Margaret was now officially only third in command, but everyone knew who was really in charge. Hurriedly arranging sweet cakes on a platter destined for the high table, Margaret glanced up to see Aelfric, like a small island in the rapids, sitting so still that his presence went unnoticed in the flurry. She scanned the pantry for hostile faces, but the boy had attracted no attention. Her relief was covered by a stern veneer. 'Shoo, lad! You've no business here.'

Margaret seized Aelfric's collar in one plump hand and ushered him none too gently toward the door. But with her other hand, she placed several sweet cakes into his upturned grubby palms as she gave him a final push out. Clucking her tongue, she began rearranging the platter so that the purloined treats would not be missed.

A Saxon maid who had been scouring dirty pots watched Margaret with amusement. 'What are you gawking at, Aeliva?' scolded Margaret. 'You've pots enough to keep you busy until dawn and firewood to fetch, not to mention that the day watch will be trooping in here any minute for a bite to eat, and they'll want it hot.'

'I don't know why you're always so concerned with the comfort of the Norman guards,' grumbled Aeliva, picking up a sling to fetch wood.

'On their good comfort rests your own, my girl. If they're ill humored, you'll feel the flat of their hand. Or mine,' Margaret added. It was an idle threat for, unlike Robert the head cook, who shouted out orders and used a wooden spoon to enforce them, Margaret never raised a hand to the kitchen help – not that she was not tempted. From the doorway she assessed the progress of the meat, then hurried servers bearing platters laden with pasties and sweetmeats. If she were lucky, she thought, the Norman guards would not arrive until the second course had been served; that would allow her time to feed them and send them on their way before the next course was called for. Amid the bustle of servants coming and going, Margaret saw Gandulf help himself to a handful of dried fruit from a passing tray, then slip discreetly from his place at the high table. The cook smiled to herself, thinking that he and Aelfric must both have been out on Saint John's Eve gathering the fern dust that renders invisibility, for they could both disappear at will.

Gandulf met her eye as he threaded his way through the crowd toward the servants' entrance between the pantry and buttery, and he nodded in passing. He had gone but a few steps farther when he stopped abruptly, as though something had just occurred to him. 'Margaret,' he said, 'do you know an old woman named Winifred in Enmore Green?'

'Aye, my Lord. She is a distant kinswoman.'

'I might have known,' he said, repressing a smile. 'You Saxons keep such careful track of your relations that I'd wager you could could trace your ancestry back to Eve.' For miles around, nearly everyone was claimed as distant kin, for the Saxons valued family so much that even sixth cousins were acknowledged and favored. It helped to keep the peace, for a Saxon would go a long way to avoid raising hand or voice toward a kinsman.

''Tis not how far back you can go that counts, my Lord,' said Margaret. 'A Saxon values her great-grandmother as the tie to her third cousins. You Normans care only for your dead ancestors, and not for the net and spread of the living. But what of Winifred?'

'She's doing poorly. Could you make up a basket to send her?'

Margaret had planned on sending a sickbed gift but began to revise upward her estimate of what she might give. Gandulf was halfway down the passage before she could call, ''Tis kind of you, my Lord.' He shrugged off her thanks and made his escape.

CHAPTER EIGHT

'Not again!' Peeking from her doorway, Aldyth spied Gandulf watering his horse at the fountain and stamped her foot; it was not the first time that week she had had to postpone fetching water to avoid him. She slammed the door with such force that it bounced back open. Irritably she set down her jug and took up the broom.

Sirona had gone out the night before to gather herbs by the full of the moon and was tying them in tidy bundles to hang from the rafters to dry. She looked up at Aldyth and glanced out the door at the well. 'This floor has been swept as clean as a new-washed pot this week,' she said, chortling. 'There's nary a crumb left for the hens anymore.'

Aldyth blushed. 'You know very well that Lord Ralf's son is loitering about the well again.' Leaning on her broom, Aldyth frowned as she watched him through the partly open door. Gandulf kicked awkwardly at the dirt, looked about one more time, then mounted up and rode away. Only then did Aldyth pick up her jug and start toward the fountain, vaguely annoyed at the sound of Sirona's teasing laughter, which trailed after her.

Later that day, having caught up on chores and finished her rounds, Aldyth was free to escape. Towering oak trees reached up to form an undersky of browns and yellows. Damp leaves had matted into cold, wet layers that would kill the undergrowth and make for poor grazing over the winter. Sirona, like Edwin, had foretold that the coming winter would be a harsh one. The wild geese had already fled; it was believed that the big birds burrowed into the mud of the fens to sleep until spring. The squirrels' coats were very thick, and pigs herded into the woods to forage on acorns and beechnuts returned later than usual, which Sirona attributed to their instinct to build up fat for a harsh winter. Besides, she said, she could feel it in her bones and smell it in the air.

But Aldyth didn't let that spoil the moment. She spent the afternoon gathering filberts and kindling from a hazel copse north of Long Cross and thinking of Gandulf fitzGerald. As young girls Aldyth and Mildburh had dreamed of being swept away by some admiring lord to a Fairy-tale castle, where they would be fed on dainties and dressed in miniver. Aldyth would never presume that that was what Gandulf had in mind. But if it was, the reality would be far more sordid than a young girl's dream, for without hope of marriage, it would be merely selling oneself body and soul for creature comforts.

Aldyth discovered a gnarled old crab apple tree, heavy with ripe fruit. A little sour, she thought, tasting one, but she filled her basket and even her apron. What they didn't roast over the next week would keep well over the winter.

Aldyth ran into Aelfric on her way home. Aelfric never appeared by chance. ''Tis a knowing look you wear,' she said warily, 'like the cat that ate the cream.'

'And you look like the sow that ate the crab apples,' he quipped.

Aldyth aimed a playful whack at the side of his head, which he easily ducked, as she had known he would. He reached into her basket and helped himself to as many crab apples as he could hold. 'Where'd you find them?' he asked, his mouth already full.

'And you talk about sows, piglet!' She directed him to the crab apple tree, knowing that he, too, was squirreling away his winter stores. As he hurried off, he called over his shoulder, 'By the way, Aldyth, if you don't get down to the spring, the Norman lordling will have his horse drink it dry.'

Aldyth frowned, wondering again what he wanted of her. All men seemed to want one of two things, and since she had no property, she could only suspect the other. Squaring her shoulders, she approached the well. She knew the exact instant he noticed her, because he straightened up nervously and she could see him taking a mental inventory: his hose were not bagging, his cloak draped well, his hair was combed.

'Good day, Mistress Aldyth,' Gandulf said, too quickly.

'And good day to you, my Lord. What brings you down from Castle Hill?'

'Cathedra was under the weather, so I brought her down to try your healing waters.'

'I hear she's been taking the waters for some time,' said Aldyth dryly.

'I have had occasion,' he admitted sheepishly, 'to ride through Enmore Green since the chicory harvest; I've not seen Winifred outside her cottage.'

'She is still recovering her strength, my Lord.'

'I'll have Margaret send her a chicken and some of her calf's foot jelly.'

''Tis very kind of you.'

There was an awkward pause. 'That's it?' thought Aldyth in annoyance. 'He's squandered his mornings and made a pest of himself for this?'

Gandulf cleared his throat as if to speak but seemed to change his mind. With a shrug, he turned to mount his horse.

Noticing that he was limping, Aldyth said, 'It appears that Cathedra is fitter than you, my Lord.'

'We took a fall yesterday.'

'Your horse's ills are better cared for than your own,' Aldyth remarked. 'Were it broken, you'd not be walking on it. 'Tis probably just a sprain. Soak the ankle in hot water drawn from the Crystal Spring to wash away the ache.'

'Our leech tells me 'tis only primitive belief that gives the springwater its power,' observed Gandulf. His detached tone recalled to Aldyth's mind the years he had spent in academic training at the monastery.

'Sirona tells me a man named Jesus said the same thing about his own healings, but I suppose your leech is pleased to take credit for the exceptional health on Castle Hill.'

'Well said,' replied Gandulf thoughtfully.

Aldyth, impressed by his generous response to her jibe, approached the bay mare and set down her basket to give it a pat. Uninvited, the mare nosed her way into Aldyth's laden apron and snatched up a crab apple.

'I just picked those, you scamp!' Aldyth held another one out on her palm. 'Here, Cathedra, since you've already left your tooth marks in it, you might as well have this one, too.' As the apple disappeared between soft wet lips, Aldyth mused, 'An unusual name, Cathedra. Most horses are called something like "Swiftfoot" or "Brownie." What does it mean?'

'Cathedra is the throne of power on which a ruler sits,' replied Gandulf, patting the mare's neck fondly. 'Her saddle is my throne.' He looked off to the misty wooded hills, and his voice assumed a surprising expressiveness. 'When we take to the hills, 'tis as though I'm riding on the back of the north wind. No one to care for or answer to . . .'

'Nor anyone else's expectations to live up to,' added Aldyth emphatically. 'I feel that way, too, when I'm out gathering my herbs in the hills.'

The emotions Gandulf carefully hoarded spilled out. 'Yes!' he said with an intensity she had not seen before. 'With the wind on my face and the fortress walls far behind me, I'm east of the sun and west of the moon and captain of my own fate.' He stopped suddenly, cleared his throat nervously, then looked off to one side. With no warning, all signs of emotion were locked away; a portcullis had come clanging down between the keep of his heart and the outside world. His change of manner was as marked as if he had already taken his leave. He mounted Cathedra, threw Aldyth a quick nod of farewell, and rode off.

''Tis too late,' Aldyth thought. 'He can't take it back.' How sad to have to don one's armor, instead of doffing it, to go home. Like the stronghold on the hill, it must have taken years to build such walls as he had raised around himself. 'Well, I don't need another sad soul to take care of,' she told herself. 'Let him go to his leech for that.'

Yet over the next few days, while gathering herbs, milking Godiva, or weeding her garden, Aldyth found her thoughts drawn to Gandulf and his extraordinary disclosure. Her stolen glimpse into the soul behind those dark Norman eyes haunted her. One night, as she kept vigil at the bedside of a fevered child, thoughts of Gandulf kept her company. A soft sigh from the child drew Aldyth's attention. She felt the small brow and found it cool and damp with sweat; the fever had broken. Aldyth crooned comfort to the child, who snuggled back into a healing sleep.

'Thank you, my Lady,' whispered Aldyth. It would need only time and rest to make the child whole. Most of those she cared for had simple problems that grew like weeds and could be easily cut back. They required only a better harvest next year, a few more pigs, or an infusion of lavender. But Gandulf's pain was twining like a vine around his heart, its roots deep in his past. What was it about the Norman that frightened her? She had never turned away from pain before, and Gandulf's suffering could be no worse than Agilbert's, yet she had room in her heart for him. She had always let her emotions carry her along, but since meeting Gandulf, she had found herself continually at odds with her feelings: denying them, misunderstanding them, trying to expunge them. In comparison to Gandulf, Bedwyn seemed incredibly wholesome. Life was so simple for Bedwyn; there was black and there was white, good and evil. She envied his certitude.

Whenever she thought of either man, Aldyth felt longing tighten her belly and tug at her heart. Sensing the girl's inward struggle, Sirona sent her up to the abbey. Aldyth told Mother Rowena, 'Sirona says I've become so gloomy that if I didn't come see you for a purgative, she'd make me sleep with Godiva.'

Mother Rowena laughed. 'If she said that, then the little red cow might indeed be a warmer bedmate.' Taking Aldyth's hands, she squeezed them gently and said, 'Come, child, I've just the restorative you need.' Mother Rowena guided her into the stillroom. The soothing smells of the herbs and the gentle bubble of the potions simmering in their pots were comforting. Mother Rowena sat her down. 'Try this,' she said, opening a little wooden box and removing a cloth-wrapped bundle. Within was a grainy lump the color of topaz. She watched curiously as Mother Rowena took from its sheath the tiny knife she wore at her belt and chipped off a piece. Smiling, Mother Rowena handed her a chunk the size of a hazelnut. She looked up questioningly. 'The physic books recommend it for melancholy,' said the nun. 'Go ahead, bite into it.' Gingerly, Aldyth gave it a crunch. 'Now hold it on your tongue and suck,' instructed Mother Rowena. Aldyth obeyed, and her mouth was filled with subtle sweetness.

'Is it magic?' asked Aldyth in amazement.

'No, my dear. 'Tis a rare preparation brought all the way from the Holy Land by the Venetians. It's called "sugar candy".'

Mother Rowena picked up a wooden comb from the table and sat beside Aldyth, who put her head into the infirmarian's lap. This was all part of a cherished ritual shared between the two, for the nun always said, 'Untangling the hair untangles the thoughts.' Drifting in a dreamlike state, Aldyth could view her cares with detachment. There were many, but of all the burdens she bore, the one that loomed largest, to her chagrin, was chastity. Intimacy with a man was frightening, yet she longed for the comfort of a mate, the joy of children. 'Why can't I resign myself to my lot?' she agonized mutely.

She thought about the nun whose fingers ran gently through her hair. Mother Rowena had lived Aldyth's dream, only to see it wrenched away. She had lost not only her loved ones but the freedom to love again when Lord Ralf had forced her to take the veil. There were worse things than chastity, mused Aldyth, thinking of the man who had driven both Rowena and Emma to the sanctuary of the abbey. But Rowena had caused good to come from evil, even as the muck of the stable makes the grain grow. 'I shall do the same,' Aldyth decided. Impulsively, she kissed Mother Rowena's hand and held it to her cheek.

'Is there something you would like to talk about, my dear?' asked the nun gently.

'No, thank you, Mother. I feel better already.'

It was a false alarm. Sirona and Aldyth had been called up to the garrison to deliver a baby of Jehanne, the wife of Roland, one of the Norman guards. Jehanne had been seeing the Norman midwife, but complications had made it prudent to call on the expertise of the Saxon healers. Aldyth had no more to show for the trip than the dark circles under her eyes and the gratitude of the exhausted parents-to-be. When it had become clear that the baby had no intention of putting in an appearance, Sirona had left Aldyth to minister to the still expectant mother.

This was Aldyth's education: accompanying Sirona, learning and practicing under her godmother's watchful eye. The aged healer could impart her knowledge of potions and procedures at any time, but only by watching her mentor practice her craft could Aldyth understand the curative power of a touch or a word. As they were expecting a summons to a small hut in Alcester, where Sirona had predicted the birth of twins, the old healer left Jehanne in Aldyth's competent hands.

'Don't be discouraged, Jehanne,' Aldyth told her. 'A child long in the womb stays long in the home. Think only of the joy to come, while I brew you some soothing lavender.'

'I look forward to that joy more than you can know, Mistress Aldyth, for I never thought to conceive. Roland and I have been married these four years and we'd had no luck, but I learned the secret from Father Odo.'

'Father Odo?' asked Aldyth curiously. 'Did he give you a special prayer to say?'

Jehanne blushed.

'Please tell me, so that others with the same difficulty might benefit.'

Jehanne considered, then leaned forward and whispered into Aldyth's ear, 'When I confessed my sins to Father Odo, he said, "Come, come, that can't be all. Have you done this? Have you done that?" Then he said, "Have you lain with your husband in the manner of a dog and its bitch?" "Oh, no, Father!" I said. "Are you sure?" he asked. Then he told me how it was done. I was shocked! I asked Roland if he'd heard of such a thing, and he said that he had, but it was a sin.' Jehanne blushed again and concluded, 'We tried it, and the next month when my bleeding did not come, we knew a child was on the way.'

Aldyth guffawed. 'Jehanne! You should ask Father Odo to stand godfather!'

Before heading down the hill to Enmore Green, Aldyth stopped by the pantry to ask Margaret to send some honeyed wine to Jehanne. Clucking like a mother hen, Margaret herded Aldyth toward a bench by the fire. 'If I didn't know better, I'd say you'd spent the night in a rocky field.' Aldyth straightened her kirtle and drew her shawl up over her disheveled hair. The big woman, who had lived through both birth and battle, smiled fondly. 'Never think I meant to chide you, child. But I'll not let you leave before you've had a bite to eat.' Margaret thrust a goblet of wine into one of Aldyth's hands and a chunk of honeyed white bread into the other, and Aldyth could not refuse such an unaccustomed pleasure.

On the same bench sat Wulfwynn, peeling parsnips for pasties. Aldyth, thankful that the maid seemed too sleepy to converse, gladly ate her breakfast in silence while Margaret bustled about preparing for the day's work. As Aldyth was licking the honey from her fingers, she heard a voice that made her stomach tighten.

'Good morning, Margaret,' Gandulf called from the pantry door. 'What have you to break my fast?' Aldyth froze. She had no wish for Gandulf to find her breakfasting in the pantry like a beggar, but from behind he mistook her for a servant, and she was grateful that Margaret's teasing had driven her to cover her unruly tresses.

'Good day to you, lad,' Margaret replied. 'I've just mixed some honeyed wine for poor Jehanne, who was up all night in a false labor. Help yourself to some of that.'

'Poor woman,' said Gandulf. 'Is that not the second time this week?'

'The child is putting off its work,' Margaret chuckled. 'As soon as it is born, it will be gathering eggs and fetching.'

Hugh fitzGrip and Father Odo pushed past Gandulf.

'Woman,' interrupted fitzGrip, 'we are on our way to Fontmell Magna. Pack some victuals and be quick about it.'

'Go ahead, Margaret,' said Gandulf lightly. 'I'm in no hurry.' Margaret, smiling gratefully, hastened to serve the sheriff and the priest.

The two men discussed their errand. 'And after we seize the slut, will you be returning with me to Scafton or shall I bring my own escort?' inquired Father Odo.

'I shan't return with you. I'll be delivering this one myself,' said fitzGrip with a grin. 'The archbishop has taken a personal interest in purging the clergy of this particular sin and will surely be generous in rewarding my zeal.'

'What dastardly crime inspires such fervor?' inquired Gandulf facetiously.

They shot each other a look of annoyance at this unwelcome intrusion, but having been addressed directly, they could no longer ignore Gandulf. Father Odo explained curtly, 'A priest's whore is being claimed by the archbishop of Salisbury.' With spiteful relish, he added, 'She can scrub away the filth of marriage as she scrubs the episcopal floors.'

'Are you saying her crime is to be the wedded wife of a priest?' asked Gandulf. 'Don't you think slavery excessive punishment? You cannot deny it is the custom of the land.'

'Not for long,' sneered Father Odo. 'And no punishment is excessive. All women are whores and sluts, the offspring of Eve and tools of the Devil.'

Margaret returned, red-faced and harried, and handed each man a bundle and a leather wine flask. With no word of thanks, Father Odo snatched the provisions. As he turned to leave, the priest glared at Gandulf and, irritated anew by the lordling's uncropped head of hair, snapped, 'Why don't you get a haircut?' Then the officious pair stalked off to take on the day's task, each man anticipating his part with pleasure.

Margaret said bleakly, 'Surely such hard hearts could not have been born of woman.'

'Not everyone in the Church feels that way,' said Gandulf, 'but unfortunately they are a powerful minority, and many are high up in the ranks.'

'Did not the Good Lord Himself tell us to be fruitful and multiply?' asked Margaret.

'Ironic, isn't it, that anyone who adheres to the command of God is branded a heretic? When I was a youth in Paris, there was a synod of the Church; the pope ordered bishops, abbots, and clerics to discard Church-blessed marriages and take a vow of celibacy.'

'How could they expect God-fearing men to cast off their wives and children? Are they not God's lambs as well?'

'Most do not accept this ruling, Margaret. The issue of

mandatory celibacy of the clergy caused the recent break between the Western Church and the Eastern Church. When Abbot Galter of Saint Martin demanded that priests cast out their wives and children, they beat him, spat upon him, and cast the abbot out onto the streets instead. That same year at Rouen in Normandy, the archbishop was stoned by a crowd of indignant clerics.'

'It would seem that the Normans are harder on us than on their own clerics.'

'Alas, Margaret, it would seem so.'

Wulfwynn interjected, 'Sister Aethelswith says any excuse will do. Pilgrims tell her that even the lowliest Saxon priests are being removed and replaced by Normans.' Aldyth was shocked at her outspokeness and even more surprised by Gandulf's frank reply.

''Tis an ugly business, conquest, but another matter entirely from this business of Church-blessed misogyny. That, at least, is just a passing obsession that cannot last. A small minority of bitter old men cannot possibly convert their personal perversions into official Church policy.' With that Gandulf slugged down his wine and took the bundle of victuals that Margaret handed him. 'Thank you,' he said and was gone.

When his footsteps had receded, Margaret plopped down beside Aldyth. 'He's changed,' said the cook. 'When he first arrived, his nose was out of joint if it wasn't buried in a book. Lord Ralf was resigned to his heir's lack of interest in politics, war, or even affairs of state, and he nearly wet himself the first day Gandulf chose to sit in on his father's court.' She chuckled. 'But the lad seems to do everything in his own time and way. Last week his father was ready to take off the hand of Thurstan of Alcester for sloth in rendering his payment. Wasn't it Gandulf who convinced him that if he took the hand, it would be the last payment he ever squeezed out of the poor fellow! Lord Ralf decided that sometimes mercy is profitable, and he settled for a flogging and double the dues.'

Aldyth made a mental note to send a penny to Thurstan, thanked Margaret, and hurried on her way. She wanted to discuss with Sirona the implications of fitzGrip and Odo's disturbing conversation: heady stuff that made her mind reel. Or was it the wine that warmed her from the inside on the frosty walk home from Castle Hill?

CHAPTER NINE

'Aelfric!' Aldyth gestured wildly in a desperate attempt to capture the boy's attention through the bustle of the market. On her way to the abbey, Aldyth had been admiring the colorful ribbons dancing on the mercer's rack when she had caught sight of Aelfric. She could tell that he was scouting for a meal, and she knew he was not above pinching an apple or an onion. The penalty for theft was to lose the offending hand, and Aldyth was in constant fear that one day the lad's luck would run out and he would be caught stealing.

'Aelfric!' she called again, but he had vanished into the crowd. She was darting into Abbey Street to collar him when an angry shout drew her attention. She looked up to find herself directly in the path of an oncoming tanner's cart. Cursing, the driver tried to rein in his oxen. Aldyth leapt backward, but her foot came down on something softer than a street cobble, and she lost her balance. Her fall was broken, though not prevented, by her impact with an unfortunate bystander, and Aldyth knew without looking that it was Gandulf fitzGerald.

He lay stunned and sprawled on the cobbles. Aldyth leapt to her feet and stammered an apology. When she bent down to help him up, he waved her away.

'We've got to get you out from under foot,' she insisted. Disregarding his feeble protestations, she pulled him out of the traffic and sat him up against the wall of the nearest shop. Aldyth noted the blood matting his dark hair and trickling down his neck. 'Gandulf, you're hurt!'

His hand moved to the back of his head. Wincing, he

muttered, 'I must have hit it on the cobbles.' Aldyth was speechless with contrition, but he said, 'Aren't we a couple of gawking fools, with our heads in the clouds rather than minding our feet?'

Aldth knelt beside Gandulf and reached into her basket for a small skin of springwater to wash the wound and a wad of cobweb to stanch the bleeding. Brushing aside a lock of dark hair from his forehead, she placed one hand there as a brace, then with the other hand pressed the cobweb against the wound.

Gandulf knew it was not the blow to the head but the feel of her hands in his hair that made him dizzy. He tried to recapture the feel of her long legs entwined in his but felt his blood rising and quickly shifted the tenor of his thoughts. Closing his eyes, he concentrated instead on the sweet scent of rosemary that clung to her hair.

Aldyth felt him shudder, and for a moment she feared she was hurting him. But he seemed to relax, and she decided that it had just been the sudden pressure on the wound. Beggars and tinkers, peddlers and pilgrims walked by with scarcely a glance. But she noted only the fragrance of woodruff. Aldyth wondered if Gandulf used a perfume as Hugh fitzGrip did; more likely, she decided, it was the aroma of the herbs strewn in the chest where his clothing was kept. At that moment, Aldyth knew she would never again pluck a sprig of woodruff, nor catch the scent of it on a breeze, without thinking of Gandulf.

Turning his head, Gandulf met her eyes. Caught unaware, she felt her cheeks flush. He broke into an unexpected smile. 'We seem to be making a habit of this,' he quipped.

'It looks to have stopped bleeding,' she stammered. Then she occupied herself in picking the cobwebs from his hair. 'How do you feel?'

'None the worse for the wear, but tell me: Why do they call you "Lightfoot?"' His teasing smile waxed into quiet laughter. Aldyth had never heard Gandulf laugh; it was a gentle, kindly sound, and soon her own laughter mingled with his.

'Where were you off to in such a hurry, Aldyth?'

'I was going to visit Mother Rowena at the abbey.'

'That was my destination. May I have the pleasure of your company?'

'If you dare,' she said. 'Honestly, Gandulf, I don't usually go knocking people onto their backsides. Doubtless 'tis a sign that we should keep to our own paths.'

'Or that we were meant to come together,' he said slyly. ''Tis not so great a coincidence, as our daily paths carry us to both to the abbey, nor one to be regretted.'

When Gandulf stood up, he reeled slightly and reached for the wall to steady himself.

'Not too fast,' said Aldyth, taking his arm. 'Best let the blind lead the lame, my Lord.'

'I'll be fine shortly,' he replied, but nevertheless he rested his hand on her shoulder. A few steps later, Aldyth realized that his arm had eased around her shoulders and that her own arm had slipped down around his waist. She suspected that Gandulf was enjoying himself too much, and she knew that she was. 'So are the town gossips,' she thought, for there were bound to be some waggle-tongues watching. To endow the moment with a shred of respectability, she asked, 'Are you going to visit your mother?'

'Yes, I try to see her as often as possible.'

'She is fortunate to have such a good son.'

'I wish there were more I could do for her,' he said ruefully.

'Mother Rowena says there is no greater joy than to be with your own child.'

'And where is your mother, Aldyth?'

Reflexively, Aldyth reached for the pendant she wore around her neck but stopped herself short. 'I never knew my mother,' she said flatly, hoping to close the subject.

Gandulf felt her stiffen. With anyone else, his instinct would have been to draw back, but his growing obsession with this girl drove him on; he felt compelled to probe. After an awkward pause, he asked, almost apologetically, 'Are you a foundling, then?'

The two of them left the crowded market and walked on past rubble-strewn sites on which had stood houses destroyed by the Normans. Chickens perched on remnants of stone walls — most of the loose stone had been salvaged by survivors for repair or rebuilding — and pigs rooted among the weeds overgrowing the ruins.

'I was raised by my godmother,' Aldyth replied curtly. 'I don't know who my parents were. I know only that they were good Saxons who loved their kind and that I lost them both when your father sacked Sceapterbyrig.'

The sting of her words hit him like a slap across the face. Aldyth had demonstrated indisputably that, even had they been of equal station in life, they were born enemies. Gandulf let go of her shoulders. They approached the looming wall of the abbey in strained silence, and at the gate they went their separate ways.

'This is oil of cloves,' said Mother Rowena to Aldyth as she applied it to the aching gums of Sister Matilde. ''Tis used for deadening pain, especially that of toothache.'

The hours Aldyth spent helping the nun were enough to put the unpleasant encounter out of her mind for a while. There was much to learn from observing the abbey infirmarian that Sirona could not teach her. Aldyth helped Mother Rowena bathe Sister Rinalda and watched her brew an infusion for Father Fulk's gout. Mother Rowena had greater expertise than the village healer in the use of imported ingredients, spices and tender herbs, for the abbey could afford to pay the price necessary to procure them.

When Aldyth stepped out of the infirmary later that day, the clouds were lowering. Her own gloom returned, and with it came a feeling of foreboding. She brooded over her exchange with Gandulf, but it was not only Gandulf that bothered her, she told herself. Perhaps the darkness of her mood was apprehension. Sirona had hinted that the Starlit Path might assert its claim on her at any time. Aldyth dreaded the call. Just yesterday Mildburh had told her of two strange men who had loitered about the well for hours. Perhaps they had merely stopped to rest, but Aldyth's instinct suggested otherwise.

As she left the cloister, Aldyth's heart jumped; across the courtyard Sister Arlette hovered over a Saxon townswoman with a wailing baby in her arms, a sobbing child pulling on her skirts, and a Norman guard at her back. Aldyth recognized the woman as Gytha, wife of John Baker, for she had helped to deliver the baby in Gytha's arms.

The guard turned; it was Gilbert, the sentry who had admitted her to the fortress in August, on the day she had confronted Lord Ralf. Aldyth wondered what trouble she had brought upon Gilbert that day, and she hoped that Lord Ralf had been lenient. In any case, it was too late to run, for Gilbert beckoned to her. Aldyth prepared a belated apology, but Gilbert cut her off. Awkwardly, he said in Norman, 'Mistress Aldyth, 'tis not right, the sound of weeping within these holy walls, but I know not how to quiet them.'

'Why do they weep, Gilbert?' she asked in halting Norman.

Slowly, that she might better understand, he said, 'Father Odo brought them here. Their marriage is incestuous; they share a great-grandparent.'

'That's ridiculous!' exclaimed Aldyth. In Saxon she expounded to Sister Arlette, 'if the Normans kept as careful track of their bloodlines as we do, half their marriages would be counted incestuous as well. Even King William's marriage is no more legitimate, and for the same reason. They enforce the law only when it suits them.'

Gilbert could not understand her words but could guess at their meaning. Noting his discomfort, Aldyth said in her awkward Norman French, ''Tis none of your doing, Gilbert. But what's to become of them?'

'Father Odo is speaking with the abbess at this moment. She will decide if they should be sent to the archbishop at Salisbury or if the case should be dismissed.'

Aldyth knew that if Gytha were sent to the archbishop, the marriage would be declared annulled, the woman a whore, and her children bastards. She put an arm around the goodwife. 'Gytha,' she said, with more confidence than she felt, 'the abbess is a woman of great goodness and common sense. She will decide the outcome of your case fairly.'

With red-rimmed eyes, Gytha Baker looked up at Aldyth, grateful for a reassuring word. 'John and I had the Church's blessing.' She burst into fresh weeping and moaned, 'If Father Odo has his way, half of the children in our parish will be hapless bastards.'

Aldyth picked up the little girl wailing at her mother's knee. 'Hush, child. All will be well.' From her pocket, she took a tiny piece of precious sugar candy, which the infirmarian had sent home with her. She popped it into the child's mouth, and the sound of crying was soon replaced by one of contented sucking.

A door into the courtyard opened. Father Odo, red-faced and fuming, stormed past them and out the gate. Sister Aethelswith followed on his heels, wearing a look of thinly suppressed triumph. She told Gilbert, 'The abbess wishes you to see this goodwife home.'

Gilbert's relief was pitiful to see. Aldyth smiled and handed the child over to him, along with a small handful of the raisins Mother Rowena had traded her for the wild herbs she had brought. 'These will guarantee a quiet trip, Gilbert.'

It was late when Aldyth got home, and all the darker because of the thickening clouds. She had hardly arrived before Sirona sat her down for a bowl of hot soup, then sent her off again. 'Step softly, my little doe,' warned her godmother, 'and while you are at the fountain, say a prayer for Gorm.'

It had been a long time since Aldyth had walked the Path. She had always enjoyed the excitement she felt while guiding a runner. But now there was too much excitement. Even the prospect of seeing Bedwyn was overshadowed by her fear. Word had it that a hide in Much Wenlock, two weeks' journey to the north, had been raided. Its guides, the twin brothers Willibald and Willibrord Weaver, had been taken alive. Before being carted off to William's tower in London, they had been forced to witness the retribution they had brought upon their village: homes had been burnt, fruit trees felled, and precious plow oxen slaughtered. As the Weavers were twins, for easier identification, Willibald's left hand and Willibrord's right one had been taken. There would be no more weaving for the brothers, but they would not need their looms in the tower. Aldyth could only imagine the fate that awaited them there, and she prayed to the Goddess to take them swiftly, for their sakes as well as for the sakes of those they might betray. After Much Wenlock's ruin, Aldyth's neighbors cast no stones in her direction, but they began to observe and obey the curfew and forest laws punctiliously, and they now watched their own backs as well as hers.

Sunset slipped by unnoticed as Aldyth made her way to the fountain. The wishing rags tied to the branches of the tree fluttered like fidgeting fingers; even the ancient oak seemed jittery. As she knelt beside the well, a hollow-eyed man slipped, wraithlike, from behind the tree. 'Aldyth Lightfoot?' he whispered uneasily.

He was so nervous that the mere sight of him made Aldyth edgy. The two eyed each other warily before Aldyth asked, 'For whose soul do you pray tonight?'

'Tonight I pray for Gorm, who needs all the help he can get,' came his pinched reply.

'Follow me,' she said, quickly scanning the green before leading him down the path through the willow copse that fed off the stream. The forest was alive that night, the sharp, frosty wind probing with icy fingers at the patches on their garments. A sudden gust set a willow branch whipping across Aldyth's face, and she jumped at the sting of it. From behind, she heard Gorm mutter a frantic oath. She turned to see him start like a flushed deer and dive off the path into the undergrowth at the foot of the willows. In panic, Aldyth scrambled after him. They lay panting in a pile of resettling leaves, two sets of ears and eyes straining for any sign of a hostile presence.

At last Aldyth ventured a whisper into Gorm's ear. 'What did you see?'

'Nothing,' he replied sharply. 'I thought you had seen something.'

''Twas only a willow branch striking my face.' Disgusted with herself, she grumbled, 'We're both too skittish tonight. We can't let our nerves get the best of us.'

She stepped back onto the path, feeling the crackle in the air that precedes a thunderstorm. Running through her mind was one of the old stories that Brihtnot the Poacher told when he was in his cups. 'All the trees are alive,' Brihtnot would say, 'and each has a nature of its own. The elder bleeds when cut, the kindly elm grieves the loss of a companion, and the wicked oak hates the woodcutter who cuts down its fellow; the woodsmen say that in an oak copse, formed from the root children of fallen oaks, you had best watch your footing, lest the roots reach up to trip you. Above all,' he had said ominously, 'be wary of the shallow-rooted willow, for 'twill step out of the ground and follow the unwary traveler. Like a huge twisted goblin in the night, it is betrayed only by the rustling of its leaves.' Aldyth shivered as she sloshed through the toe-numbing muck, and she wondered if the slap of the willow had been no accident. She spent the rest of the journey looking back over her shoulder, which set Gorm to looking over his.

The storm moved in, and the air changed from sharp and frosty to raw and damp. Branches slashed at their faces in the rising wind, dead leaves hurled themselves at their feet like yapping lapdogs. The first raindrop to strike Aldyth's face felt like a pebble hurled from a slingshot. A low grumble of thunder swelled into an angry roar that shook the ground. Both travelers froze, then wordlessly quickened their pace. Only a few drops fell before the rolling clouds vanished, curtained in sheets of rain. In an instant, Aldyth was wet to the bone, and icy rivulets ran down her neck. Her dripping kirtle clung to her legs and dragged at the bracken, tripping her as she splashed down the path.

When at last she stepped into Bedwyn's clearing, the thunder and lightning leaping at her senses both dazzled and deafened her. The noisy clatter of Bedwyn's geese was drowned by the wail of the wind. Aldyth waded through the wet grass with Gorm stumbling close behind. She threw herself against the door, nearly tripping on the doorsill as she entered. Gorm followed her into an empty hut, the eye of the storm. Though the wind rattled the door and tore at the thatch, a well-fed fire burned at the hearth, while the draft from a hundred cracks in the walls fanned the flames.

A hard, callused hand clamped over Aldyth's mouth. The hand was wet and slippery, and she clawed desperately with one hand to tear it away, while groping with the other for the bronze digging tool at her belt. Where was Gorm? she thought frantically. Why wasn't he helping her? Aldyth struggled for air while her wiry assailant pulled her hard against him and ripped the knife from her hand. Gorm's voice hissed into her ear, 'By God's wounds, if I am to die, you shall die with me.'

Aldyth saw stars burst before her eyes as darkness descended. Her last conscious thought was awareness of a cold-bladed knife held to her throat. Then, in the raw wet chaos, Aldyth felt strong arms holding her tightly. 'Gandulf,' she mumbled. But Lord Ralf's harsh voice assaulted her. 'Be damned to Hell, you bitch!' She whimpered and shrank back into Gandulf's arms – or was it Bedwyn's? Bedwyn was tugging at her clothing, trying to undress her. She struggled against him. Then somehow Sirona's voice came to her from the blackness. 'Peace, child,' she whispered. And Aldyth slipped into merciful oblivion.

CHAPTER TEN

It was the sunlight coming through chinks in the walls that woke Aldyth. She felt warm and comfortable and, for a moment, thought she was still dreaming. A hand gently stroked her hair. 'Sirona,' she murmured. Forcing herself to focus, she found herself staring into a pair of deep blue eyes. 'Bedwyn!' she cried, trying to sit up.

'Lie down, my girl; not too fast,' he said, gently pulling her back down into his lap.

'What are you doing here?' she asked.

'I live here.'

'Oh . . . then what am I doing here?' she said in alarm. She sat up to discover that she was naked beneath the blanket. Quickly she shrank back and pulled the ragged cover up to her chin. Glancing frantically around, she saw her kirtle and undershift draped over the benches by the fire to dry.

Bedwyn laughed at her look of dismay. 'Don't worry, Mouse, your wildest dreams have not come true.' Her eyes swept the dark interior of his hut and stopped at the sight of Gorm, his gaze concentrated upon her. She drew back into Bedwyn's arms, and he gave her a reassuring hug. ''Tis all right, Mouse; he's minding his manners.'

One side of Gorm's face was bruised, the eye swollen shut. When Aldyth met Gorm's good eye, he stammered, 'I'm so sorry, mistress. I arrived at the fountain two days ago to discover that the king's men had gotten there first, and I knew them for the ones who had smoked out the Weaver brothers in Much Wenlock; you must have heard of it, but I was there to watch it happen. Had I arrived an hour earlier, I'd have been dragged to William's tower along with them. When they had gone, their mother, who was expecting me, sought me out. In spite of the risk, she thought it wiser to pass me on to the next hide than to leave me hanging about the village, which had suffered enough already. I passed through Sarum safely enough, but when I arrived in Enmore Green, those same two men were waiting for me. They must have sent their prisoners on to London and returned to pick up the scent, for they were the ones; I'd know the scar-face anywhere.'

'It took courage to stay the course and keep watch at the well,' said Aldyth.

Gorm shrugged. 'I'd have run if I could, but there was nowhere to go, nothing to do but wait, and all the while I was sure the rumbling of my stomach would give me away. Then, coming through the woods with you, I felt the king's spies lurking behind every tree. When we came into an empty hut, I was sure I'd been betrayed. If Bedwyn hadn't stopped me . . .' Gorm reached up and gingerly touched the bruised side of his face.

With sudden alarm, Aldyth exclaimed, 'Sirona! She'll wonder where I've been all night!' She tried to rise, but Bedwyn drew her back down again.

'Easy, Mouse. She was here last night. She said she'd had a bad feeling about you and arrived soon after I did. When Sirona saw what Gorm had done to you, she was ready to give him a worse drubbing than I already had. She gave you something to help you sleep, Mouse, and thought it best we didn't move you.' Nodding toward the bucket of water in the corner, he said, 'We'll step outside, and you can wash up and get dressed . . . unless, of course,' he added with a sly grin, 'you'd like some help.'

'Thank you, I think I can manage.'

'Steady Aldyth. Always safe and sorry.'

'Don't flatter yourself,' she retorted.

He laughed again and gave her a light kiss on the forehead. On his way out he added, 'Let me know when you're ready, Mouse, and I'll get you something to break your fast.'

After the men had cleared out, Aldyth rose, feeling shakier

than she would have admitted. In a panic, her hands shot up to her neck. She sighed with relief; her ivory keepsake was still there. Sirona had told her never to allow anyone to see it and had suggested she keep it tucked in the hidey-hole in their thatch. But Aldyth felt the comfort it gave her was worth the risk; Sirona had reluctantly agreed that she might wear it hidden beneath her kirtle. When Aldyth had first understood, as a young girl, that she wore the key to her past around her neck, she had begged Sirona to tell her who she was. But Sirona had said it was too dangerous to do so and could only promise that one day all would be revealed. By the mere possession of such a valuable object, Aldyth knew her father must have been either a thane or a thief. She wished she had the courage to show her pendant to Mother Rowena, who knew her letters and could tell her what it said. She dreamed of returning to the land of her birth to search for her family. But she could never leave the Crystal Spring. Aldyth could only hope that if Bedwyn had seen the wand the night before, he had paid no mind in the confusion.

She dressed quickly, splashed some cold water onto her face, combed her hair with her fingers, and pulled her veil over her head. As she opened the door to call the men in, she was cut short by the sight of Bedwyn, stripped to the waist and shivering in the crisp October air as he took his morning wash. Aldyth watched him dry himself on a thin scrap of towel, and she wondered if he ever thought of those times in his childhood when he had stepped out of a hot tub to be dried by servants with fine white linen. He glanced up to see her watching him and flashed her a quick smile. She returned it, knowing that it would never occur to Bedwyn that she was doing anything other than admiring him. Of course she did admire him, but not so much for his physical beauty, she told herself primly, as for the grace with which he had accepted his fall from fortune. Aldyth knew so many bitter old men – and bitter young ones – and who could blame them? But Bedwyn was able to take whatever life offered and skim the cream, no matter how thin or sour the milk. If he could not be a Saxon thane exercising his ancient privilege, then he would be a leader of Saxons in this underground world of starlight and intrigue.

By the time she had filled three wooden mugs with weak ale, the men had returned. Bedwyn set the table with coarse brown bread and hard cheese. He and Aldyth seated themselves on the crude benches, but Gorm hung back.

''Tis quite all right, Gorm,' said Aldyth, noting his reluctance to join them. 'All is forgiven. But beware,' she added teasingly, with a nod in Bedwyn's direction, 'if you make any sudden moves, I'll set my watchdog on you.'

'Watch your words, Aldyth,' warned Bedwyn. 'I just might follow you home.'

The talk was light and breezy; Aldyth actually felt cheerful by the time they finished breakfast. 'I do have things to do this morning,' she said, pushing away from the table.

'If you must go now, Aldyth,' said Bedwyn, 'then let me walk with you for a bit, just to be sure that you're steady enough on your feet.'

'I feel fine, Bedwyn. Tend to your company,' she said with a nod in Gorm's direction.

'After last night, Gorm would not grudge you an escort.'

'As you wish,' she conceded, but she could not help feeling pleased.

A bright, bracing blue sky blanketed the treetops as they walked in silence down the path, listening to lark song overhead. The wet leaves squelched underfoot, giving the air a wholesome, earthy odor. Today the forest seemed a place of kindness and light, a different world entirely from last night's nightmare world of menace and storm.

Aldyth broke the silence. 'Bedwyn,' she said shyly, 'I didn't want to make Gorm feel any worse than he already does, but now I can thank you for coming to my aid last night.'

Bedwyn shook his head and somberly shrugged off her thanks.

'If you hadn't come in—'

'Aldyth,' blurted Bedwyn, grasping her by the arm to look into her face, 'I was never so frightened in all my life as when I came in to find him holding your own knife to your throat. It was all I could do to keep from killing him.'

'It looks as though you nearly did,' she said, surprised at his vehemence.

Taking her hand, Bedwyn continued down the path, but with none of his usual swagger. It occurred to her that they should be reviewing strategies, discussing options and contingencies in the face of their increasing danger, but she was too caught up in the physical joy of his warm, friendly touch.

Why did he have to ruin it? They had come to the edge of a bright glade, where sunbeams broke through the trees like columns of gold filtering down from Heaven. The grass, bleached by frost, glittered like icy fire, and the warmth of the morning sun conjured up wisps of mist like rising smoke. Bedwyn, who had been walking more and more slowly, drew to a halt. 'Aldyth,' he began, taking her hands. The velvet tone of his voice made her shiver. 'Aldyth,' he repeated awkwardly.

Aldyth sensed that his next words would be unwelcome, and she could not bear the tension. Impulsively, she reached up and tweaked his nose. 'Bedwyn, Bedwyn, yourself!' she cried. Whirling, she raced down the path toward home, her nervous elfin laughter trailing behind. Bedwyn frowned and stared after her, then took it as a challenge. When Aldyth looked back and saw Bedwyn giving chase, she cried out with a mixture of alarm and excitement and ducked off the path with a new burst of speed. She could hear Bedwyn crashing through the woods like a charging boar, his hearty laughter echoing through the trees. She stumbled, and by the time she regained her footing, Bedwyn was upon her. She darted behind a big oak, ducking and dodging, as Bedwyn reached around the trunk to snatch at her. His hand shot out and wrapped around her wrist.

'You vixen.' He laughed and pinned her against the tree between his arms. 'You would have me think that yours was a heart of stone, but it can strike sparks, I see.'

The two of them stood panting, laughing, catching their breath. Aldyth sensed what was coming; it was her own curiosity as much as his arms that held her in her place. His sapphire eyes glittered with excitement. His face was so close that she could see the golden stubble on his chin glinting in the sunlight. Aldyth wanted to feel it against her cheek, the warmth of his breath against her face. 'By the Lady,' she thought, her heart pounding, 'he is handsome.'

Bedywn leaned forward, and, as Aldyth opened her mouth

to say something sensible, he covered it with a kiss. She lifted her hands to his shoulders to push him away, but he took her hands and placed them around his neck. Still enveloped in his kiss, she closed her eyes and allowed her natural instincts to take over.

'Aldyth,' he whispered, 'I have never wanted a woman the way I want you.'

''Tis only because you know you can't have me,' she replied, pulling back.

'I've often wondered if that was true, but last night I knew it was much more than that.' He brushed aside any possible argument with his lips and pulled her against his broad chest. She felt his heart ponding against hers and her liver, the seat of passion, rise as she had not known possible. When she felt Bedwyn's hips pinning hers against the tree, she knew he was as aroused as she.

A sudden crashing in the brush nearby shook her free of his spell and startled Bedwyn enough to loosen his hold on her. Quickly Aldyth wriggled free of his grasp and fled to a safer distance. ''Tis only a deer or a boar,' he pleaded, trying to coax her back. 'Don't go, Aldyth.' But she was already making good her escape.

'I'm sorry, Bedwyn, I can't,' she called over her shoulder. 'Go home!' Aldyth hurried homeward without looking back, but she was relieved to hear his loud, good-natured laugh ringing out in the forest, and she knew that he would not pursue her.

It was a clear autumn morning, and Gandulf had had Cathedra saddled, then ridden off to drink in the day. He had long since passed the last hamlets and fields, and there in the brilliant depths of Cranborne Chase, he let his mind shoot back to Abbey Street and his encounter with the incomprehensible Aldyth. Why couldn't he have let things stand? She was probably suspicious of all men, especially a Norman overlord, and she had every reason to be. She had a wary innocence that made Gandulf suspect she was a virgin. 'Shall I steal her maidenhead when I cannot marry her?' he brooded. 'She would never give it to me willingly. I have imbued a few chance meetings with importance far beyond their actual significance; there is nothing between us,' he told himself bitterly.

He dwelt upon this grim thought, then brightened. 'But there could be. Plato teaches another kind of love, not born of carnal desire. 'Twould not be my first choice, yet it might be enough . . .' Scarcely aware of his surroundings or the distance he had traveled, he mused, 'Aldyth is a fragile flower and must not be willfully plucked.'

Suddenly his contemplation was split by a series of shrieks. Instantly alert, he pulled Cathedra to a halt and stared out of the dark woods into the brilliant light of a sunny glade. As clearly as if it had been set on a stage, he could see a mad and merry chase through the wood. This was no cry of distress, as he had feared, but a shriek of delight. One glance at the flying honey-gold hair told him more than he wanted to know. He realized that if he moved, he would be seen, so he remained an unwilling witness to what followed. He watched as a big Saxon caught Aldyth up against a tree.

Gandulf's stomach lurched, his fingernails dug into his palms, and he broke into a sweat, waiting tensely for her response. 'She'll spurn him, and I'll rescue her,' he thought fiercely. His hand moved to the hilt of his sword. Then the Saxon pulled Aldyth roughly into his arms, kissed her passionately – and she gave herself to him. Gandulf swallowed a cry, and looked away. He spurred Cathedra into a run and gave her the reins, not caring where she took him as long as it was far, far away.

CHAPTER ELEVEN

The Blood Month
November 1086

A loud pounding at the door made Aldyth sit up with a start.
Sirona too was instantly brought to the alert by the desperate
cries without. In the darkness they recognized the voice as
Wulfric's. 'It must be Elviva!' whispered Aldyth to Sirona.

Everyone had some ailment or complaint, and Aldyth spent
her days ministering to people who needed above all a good
meal and a dry bed, neither of which she could supply. The
harvest of that cold, wet summer was one of woe. The hay had
rotted in the fields in June, the wheat had rotted in the fields in
August. With winter upon them, only the carrion crows could
expect a bountiful harvest. The pick of the apples, the harvest
of haws, the gathering of wild nuts and berries that usually
filled everyone's larder had been scant as well. It could only
mean famine by March. Hungry children could not understand
why their mothers had food stored and would not give it to
them. There was not a villager who had begun the cold season
with more than half his usual harvest. People could keep their
worries at bay during the busy daylight hours, but at night
their fears gnawed away at their peace of mind, just as the
mice scurrying about the rafters gnawed away at their precious
stores. Midnight house calls had become common occurrences
for Sirona and Aldyth.

'Sirona! Do you hear me?' Wulfric burst in and cried, ''Tis
Edith! She needs you!'

The two healers were already pulling on their clothing.
Baskets in hand, they followed Wulfric next door to find Edith,
whey-faced and clutching her middle. Old Elviva sat beside her,

wiping her forehead with a cloth. Edith groaned, and Wulfric knelt beside her and took her hands.

'Feel how cold she is!' he cried. Drawing back the blanket that covered her, he revealed the blood-soaked straw of her bedding. 'It's been like this since the bells tolled curfew. She says 'tis only her monthly bleeding, but I've never seen it like this before.'

Edith let out another cry and doubled over. Sirona met Aldyth's eyes for an instant, passing a wordless message to her apprentice. Aldyth nodded imperceptibly and said to Elviva, 'This is women's work, old mother. Could you not take Wulfric home with you and brew him some lavender to calm his nerves?'

Grateful for a task she could carry out, Elviva took the little bunch of dried blossoms that Aldyth offered. 'Come, Son, and leave them to their work.'

Wulfric's pleading gaze returned to Edith.

'Do what your mother tells you,' she told him, nodding toward the door.

Wulfric nodded. 'May the Lady keep you, love,' he whispered.

When they had gone, Aldyth peeled back the blanket so that Sirona could examine their patient. Edith stiffened and cried out.

'She's passing clots,' Aldyth noted anxiously.

The young healer folded a cloth compress to soak up the blood and handed it to Sirona, then began brewing ragwort to thicken the blood and spurred rye to aid the womb in expelling the miscarried child.

'Edith,' said Sirona gently, applying the compress, 'did you stop taking the herbs?'

Edith nodded, her face pinched with pain.

'But why?' asked the old woman in puzzlement. 'You knew what a hungry winter this would be. I thought you were going to wait until the spring.'

Edith burst into tears. 'I was afraid to wait,' she wailed.

'Afraid of what, daughter?'

''Tis Mother Elviva,' sobbed Edith. 'I wanted to give her something to live for, to get her through the winter.'

Sirona's expression softened. 'Elviva is fortunate to have such a foolish, loving daughter. She will love you the more for your loss.'

Sirona undressed Edith and applied warm, wet cloths to her belly. Then she bathed her, pausing with each cramp of Edith's convulsing muscles as her womb rejected the failed attempt at new life. And with each spasm, a fist-sized clot of blood mingled with crushed hope forced its way out into the cold, dark night.

'It burns!' said Edith through clenched teeth. 'Oh, it hurts!'

'Aye, child,' said Sirona tenderly as she lifted a cup of poppied wine to Edith's lips. 'Drink now. 'Twill help the pain in your belly. If only I'd a cure for your aching heart.'

That was an ominous beginning for the Blood Month. It was during the Blood Month that all the livestock were slaughtered so they would not have to be fed through the winter, save those that would be needed as draft animals or for breeding. The few held over would be bled to make puddings. Even the most beloved pet lamb was turned into meat when forage grew scarce in the autumn, but this year there was an exception, for Agilbert refused to part with his pig. When his cousin Wulfstan the Reeve had strongly suggested that the pig was not worth the feed it would take to keep it over the winter, Agilbert had patiently explained that the pig he called Bertha housed the spirit of his young wife. 'Were I to kill the pig, I wouldn't know where to look for her when she came back the next time. Even were I to find her again, God forbid, she might come back as an ass, and I could never afford to feed her. Or a chicken, and they make me sneeze.' Wulfstan left Agilbert and his pig in peace; in the coming days, people would need their dreams and fancies to feed on.

Aldyth's waking hours belonged to others, but she too clung to her dreams. Gandulf was as civil as he had ever been, but more distant. There had been no more 'chance' meetings at the fountain or the abbey. She could only surmise that on that day in Abbey Street, the very day when she had realized how drawn she was to his strange, quiet ways, she had finally managed to push him so far away that he had found it easier not to come back. Spilt milk, water under the bridge, and all for the best, she told herself. A harmless friendship with the Norman lordling was more ridiculous to contemplate than a heated romance with Bedwyn. Naturally, her thoughts slipped back to Bedwyn and fed upon their last encounter. She relived those moments each night before slipping into an exhausted sleep, to escape from her damp dreary world and into one of sunshine and gaiety. 'What a waste of time,' she scolded herself, 'to weigh one against the other, when I know full well I can have neither!'

One icy morning Aldyth woke to find the light within the hut extraordinarily bright. Sirona was stirring the fire against the chill. Wrapping herself in the body-warmed cloak she had slept in, Aldyth peeked outside and gasped. The world was reborn into purity and brilliance with the first snow.

'How lovely!' exclaimed Aldyth. 'There are no more dark corners.'

'Yes, and no more forage for the beasts, either,' added Sirona. 'But the gifts of the Goddess do not come in a single handful. She has thrown a coverlet over the winter wheat to keep it safe until spring, and in Her wisdom, She has made the snow beautiful as well as useful, so that we may enjoy as we endure. Go out, my child, and enjoy.'

Aldyth did not need to be told twice. 'The mice have been at the bread again,' she observed as she brushed mouse droppings off the table and bit into a crust. She broke through a thin coat of ice to fill a mug from the water bucket. 'At least we have a bountiful harvest of mice,' she joked, 'and they are eating better than the rest of us.'

'Consider it an investment,' said Sirona, 'for we'll be eating mouse by February.'

Aldyth, wrapping her feet in woolly mullein leaves and rags for warmth, refused to let Sirona's grim jest cast a shadow over this snowbright world. Pulling on the blanket she used for a winter cloak, she stepped out into a dazzling fairyland and listened in delight to the crisp squeak of snow beneath her clogs. Scattered snowflakes drifted erratically out of the sky. As she walked past the abbey fishpond, it looked to be robed in black silk edged with ermine, for the snow-covered ice crept out to cover the dark water. Aldyth's bone skates hung from the rafters, and she hoped that the mice had not nibbled them beyond using, for it would not be long until the pond was frozen solid.

She looked forward to the breathtaking view she and Mother Rowena would share from the walls of the abbey. The road up to Castle Hill was deserted. Even the streets of the town were silent. Then a blow between the shoulder blades sent Aldyth reeling. She whirled to face her attacker. A flash of movement disappeared into a doorway. Aldyth waited breathlessly, and at last she saw a pair of laughing blue eyes cautiously peek out.

'Aelfric, you imp!' Before she could finish her scolding, he had darted into the open far enough to let fly another missile. He was wearing straw tied about his feet, and Aldyth wondered how he had managed to guard the precious straw from hungry goats. But as always he fared better than most, for the boy had a natural talent for survival.

His snowball missed her. 'Hah!' she crowed. 'You do well enough slinking about doorways and striking from behind, but face to face you put on a poor show, Aelfric!'

Aldyth launched a series of snowballs, moving closer with each volley. Their laughter echoed as she gave chase, slipping and sliding along through the deserted byways and alleys. As Aelfric ducked into Abbey Street, Aldyth launched a deadly missile; it flew arrow-straight to its target and made its mark on his ice-crusted rump. She trumpeted a shriek of triumph, then turned and ran in the opposite direction, knowing that retaliation was inevitable. Giggling at her own cleverness, Aldyth scooped snow into her apron before vanishing into one of the deeper doorways on Abbey Street. Trying to keep her panting laughter inaudible, she listened for the footsteps of her urchin adversary.

The crunch of footsteps in the snow warned of his approach. Aldyth leapt out with a bloodcurdling cry, flipping the contents of her apron into the face of – a well-dressed man. 'I'm so sorry!' she cried, clumsily brushing the snow from his hooded cloak. 'I thought you were someone else.'

'A friend of yours?' he asked ironically, and Gandulf pulled down his hood to scoop the snow out from under his collar.

Even in her shabby kirtle with a stable blanket for a cloak, she dazzled him. Escaping tendrils of golden hair vined about her cheeks. Her eyes, framed by eyelashes spangled with melted snow, glittered green as emeralds against the rosy blush of her cheeks. He was drawn to her untamed spirit, touched by the innocence in her play as she traded snowballs with a street urchin. He thought of the Saxon he had seen sporting with her in the woods and wished he could believe there had been the same innocence to their play. That stolen glimpse of forest frolic had plagued his thoughts by day and haunted his dreams by night. He had to avert his eyes to blot out the vision.

'He can't even bear to look at me,' Aldyth thought in dismay. 'What can I have done to offend him so?' Tears welled up in her eyes and began to freeze. She blinked them back and looked down at her feet to distance herself. She saw them through his eyes, wrapped in old rags, and for the first time in her memory, she felt ashamed of her station in life.

Gandulf chuckled softly. 'Cheer up, Mistress Aldyth. There is still enough snow on the ground for a few more snowballs.' The teasing tone went out of his voice. 'Aldyth, your face is grown so thin. Have things gone that hard with you this winter?'

'Surely you know how it is, Gandulf. After your father took his share, there was nothing left to set aside. I fare better than most.'

'Margaret has orders to feed anyone who comes up to the hall.'

''Tis a long walk for a bowl of broth; many haven't the strength to make the trip.'

'I see,' he said slowly. He wanted to pull her into the warmth of his cloak and hold her until, thawing, she melted into his arms. He scooped up some snow, shaped it into a snowball, and placed it in her hands, saying. 'Take care as you pass John Baker's house. I saw a ragamuffin stockpiling snowballs in his doorway.' He bowed and took his leave.

Later that afternoon Aldyth was drying her cloak before the fire so that it would not be frozen when she had to sleep in it. The door flew open, and Father Edmund burst in, too excited to knock. 'You'll never believe our good fortune!' he cried happily. 'A cartload of provisions was sent down from Castle

Hill for me to distribute to the needy and the hungry – in other words, all of us!' He dropped a sack of wheat by the door, then handed Sirona a skin of wine. 'To be doled out medicinally,' he explained.

'From Lord Ralf?' Sirona asked in astonishment.

'It did seem odd,' replied the priest. 'Lord Ralf's name was never actually mentioned, and the carter did suggest that we not make merry too openly. I suspect that we have a friend on Castle Hill, but it doesn't pay to ask questions. We can only thank God; He will apply our thanks to the account of our benefactor's treasures in heaven.'

'Why put God to the trouble of keeping accounts when Aldyth can thank our patron directly?' quipped Aelfric, driven by the cold to Sirona's hearth for the night.

'Does Aldyth know something about this?' asked Father Edmund.

'If she doesn't, she ought to,' teased Aelfric, 'for I saw the Norman lordling romancing her on Abbey Street today.'

Aldyth was too busy shooting darts at the ungrateful brat to notice the look of speculation that Sirona directed toward her goddaughter.

CHAPTER TWELVE

The Holy Month
December 1086

It was a bitter Christmas Eve. The soft, snowy world had become one of icy jagged edges, cutting cold, and slashing winds. Aldyth carried a precious portion of mulled wine to Elviva, hoping that it would strengthen her. Approaching Elviva's hut, Aldyth saw Father Edmund leaving. As he pulled the door shut, someone within pulled it back open a crack. 'Until she finds her way home, Father,' came Mildburh's tremulous voice.

'She's gone, then,' said Aldyth, dreading the old priest's confirmation.

'Yes, but Edgar came for her, for we heard her call out to him at the very last.'

'Who will help Edith attend to her?'

'Mildburh has offered, and perhaps you could ask Sirona to help lay out the body.'

'Of course, Father. Shall I let people know that the gathering will be here tonight?'

Father Edmund nodded tiredly.

'How hard it is to lose the hundredth lamb,' Aldyth said.

Father Edmund swallowed hard and nodded before hurrying off to tend to the rest of his flock. Inside, Edith was rocking her newly orphaned husband in her arms. At the sight of Aldyth she wailed, 'Oh, Aldyth, I wanted to give her a grandchild.'

Aldyth put her arms around them both. 'I am so sorry,' she said, 'but someday you will, and she will know.' Aldyth went to Elviva's bedside, where Mildburh kept vigil, and handed her the wine. 'Here, Mildburh. Wulfric and Edith could both use a drop of this. I'll go tell Sirona.' She knelt and kissed the old woman's cold cheek. 'Safe journey, old mother,' she whispered. Stepping from the muffled gloom of the firelit room and back into the wild night, Aldyth told herself it was the force of the wind that made her eyes water, and she went home to inform Sirona of Elviva's passing.

The beginning of Advent had brought another gift of food from Castle Hill, and Aldyth had hoped to lift Elviva's spirits with the unaccustomed treats, but eggs, bread, and hens were owed to Lord Ralf at Christmastide, so most of the fare sent down from the garrison made its way back up the hill as Lord Ralf's due.

From their cold, dark hovels at the foot of the hill, the suffering poor watched the steady stream of well-dressed travelers ride past on well-fed horses. They were attending the festivities, which would last from Advent to Epiphany. Every night, starving wretches would line up in the bailey, hoping to be asked to partake of the seasonal charity. Once, when Aldyth had been fetched to the garrison to treat Jehanne's baby, she had seen them waiting for a handout like half-starved mongrels, listening to the strains of lute and harp, the sound of laughter from within. It seemed a reenactment of the stone carvings in the abbey church, depicting the people in Heaven rejoicing while the damned in Hell were forced to listen to their merriment from below.

Returning home from Elviva's, Aldyth opened the door, but a sudden gust snatched it away and sent it banging against the wall of the house; daubed mud, brittle with cold, dropped off in chunks. She forced it closed against the wind and tied it shut. When she turned, she saw Sirona gazing at her with an odd detachment.

'So Elviva has finally gone,' stated Sirona flatly. 'She could have had a few more years if she hadn't decided it wasn't worth the struggle.'

Aldyth could not bring herself to reply. She felt the loss of a friend and could not help but blame herself for losing a patient. Could she have said something to change Elviva's mind? But Aldyth could never confess those feelings to Sirona, for the wisewoman would only chide her for taking too much upon herself. Aldyth felt she would never find the balance between caring and detachment necessary to becoming a good healer.

'The gathering will be at Wulfric's tonight, of course. Please let people know of the change in plans,' said Sirona. Gesturing at a concoction steaming in a pot, she continued, 'I must apply this poultice to Edwin's chilblains while it's hot. Then there will be the laying out to do.'

Aldyth nodded, pulled up the hood of her shabby cloak, and stepped back into the wintry night. It was only a five-minute walk from one end of the village to the other, but passing along the sorrowful tidings was exhausting, for Aldyth bore the heavy burden of grief on her shoulders, and though she shared the sorrow, her own load did not lessen. That done, she must make the trip to the abbey to beg a shroud to bury Elviva in. A visit with Mother Rowena, who would surely understand her grief, would make the trip worthwhile.

Stolidly placing one foot before the other, Aldyth forced herself to begin the trudge, with the wind tearing at her ragged cloak and pulling at the tangled tresses that had escaped from beneath her shawl. Unconsciously Aldyth paced herself, walking fast enough to keep her blood moving but not so fast as to exhaust herself, for her blood was as thin as the cowhide soup that Father Edmund had shared with them the night before. Aldyth ignored the icy pellets whipping against her face as she considered when and where and how they could bury Elviva with the ground frozen hard as rock.

The wind swept the snow into frozen ruts and hoofprints. Though wooden clogs protected the soles of Aldyth's feet, the sharp edges of ice shards from the frozen puddles slashed at the rags wrapped about her ankles. Leaning into the wind, she pushed onward, looking forward to the shelter of the city gate. But as she stepped between the deep walls of the sheltered archway, the sudden stillness caught her by surprise. Without the driving wind to hold her up, she lurched forward. Her reflexes numbed, she fell hard on her breastbone and lay stunned from the force of her fall. With a groan, she sat up. Her chest ached, her palms were scraped raw, and she wondered if she had sprained some fingers. Through the numbing cold, she felt her cheek and nose begin to sting. She put a hand to her face and found it bloodied. She forced herself back onto her unsteady feet. 'In this cold,' she thought morbidly, 'Elviva will keep better than I will.'

Steeling herself, she plunged headlong back into the wind. A cold blast stabbed her to the marrow, and for an instant the temptation to go home was almost irresistible. Even through her mental fog, she knew she should have turned back long ago. 'But I needed a moment alone,' she thought. Long-hoarded tears spilled over, freezing before they hit the ground. 'What's wrong with me?' she asked herself. 'Death is a part of life; Elviva was old and ready to go. Why, then, do I weep?' Suddenly Aldyth knew that it was not just for Edith and her shattered hope, not just for Wulfric who had lost his mother. 'I am crying for all the orphans of the cold, harsh world. I am crying,' she admitted, 'for myself.' Aldyth abandoned herself to her aching loneliness on the bitter walk up Abbey Street, but her sobs were lost in the wailing of the storm. Her pace slowed to a halt, and she buried her face in her hands, long past the point where she could fight back the storm of emotion that assailed her as fiercely from within as the elements did from without. But the street was deserted, for it was too early for mass goers and no one but a fool would be out in this weather to witness her ravening grief.

The fool was on horseback. He could not hear her over the wind, and neither saw the other with their hoods pulled up against the storm. Bursting out of the darkness, a dim hulk of horseflesh reared up, its flailing hooves looming overhead, its frightened scream piercing the air. Muscles numb with cold and fear, somehow Aldyth scrambled crabwise on all fours into the doorway of one of the houses lining the narrow street. Once the horseman got the frantic beast under control, he leapt out of the saddle to see if the fool who had spooked his horse was injured.

It was probably some drunken sot who had started celebrating early, thought Gandulf. He had to fight the impulse to keep riding, for if it really was a drunk, leaving him to sleep it off in the snow would mean certain death. So Gandulf knelt beside the trembling shadow huddled against the wall and asked, 'Are you hurt?' Spotting the blood in the snow at the miserable creature's feet, he thought bitterly, 'I'll not get out of this in a hurry.' He leaned forward and, over the whistle of the wind, asked, 'Where are you hurt?'

The dull-witted peasant made no answer. Reaching out, Gandulf lifted the ragged cloak to assess injuries. He hardly recognized her, she was so thin and pale; blood ran down from her nose and the side of her face, and there was a glazed look in her eyes.

'Good God, Aldyth!' he cried, running his hands along her limbs to feel for broken bones. 'Where were you struck?'

'I wasn't,' she answered dully.

'Are you sure? The blood on your face . . .'

'A fall at the gate,' she mumbled. 'No fault of yours.'

'Good God!' he repeated, scooping her up into his arms.

'What are you doing?' cried Aldyth, waking from her stupor. 'Where are you taking me?'

'To the abbey, of course.'

'No, no, you mustn't. They'll never let me go home tonight.'

'And so they ought not,' she replied firmly.

'But I must.' She pushed away and struggled to free herself.

'Don't be foolish, Aldyth! We've got to get you out of the weather.'

'Put me down at once,' she ordered fiercely, 'or I'll call the night watch.'

He only tightened his hold. 'Not even the rats are out on the streets tonight. I'm taking you to the abbey; you need to be tended to.'

'You don't understand, Gandulf,' she pleaded. ''Tis the Christmas gathering and Elviva's wake.' Fresh tears ran down her wind-bitten cheeks.

Gandulf's stern resolve was overcome by her tears like a snowflake that melts into the ocean as it meets a rising wave. He paused uncertainly. 'Was she dear to you?'

'Aye, very dear.'

With a sigh of resignation, Gandulf lifted her into the saddle, tore off his cloak, and wrapped it about her. With a grim set to his face, he climbed up behind Aldyth, settled her into his lap, and turned Cathedra down the hill toward Enmore Green.

★   ★   ★

As they approached the healers' toft, shreds of argument flew toward them on the wind. Gandulf saw the old woman he knew to be Aldyth's godmother haranguing a little red cow, which was stubbornly refusing to go out into the storm. Seeing Gandulf, Sirona loosed the cow. 'Never mind, Godiva. She's found her own way home,' said Sirona.

Gandulf was already lifting Aldyth from the saddle when the old woman pointed the way inside. 'Sit her before you by the fire,' she directed, waving him toward the hearth and hastily pulling Godiva back into the warmth of the hut.

As Gandulf settled Aldyth back onto his lap, Sirona knelt before her godchild and pried the cold, stiff cloak out of her frozen fingers, opening it to the warmth of the fire. 'Give her some of this,' she said, handing Gandulf a mug of steaming liquid. 'I've had it waiting for her this last half hour. 'Twill warm her from within.'

Aldyth said indistinctly, 'You needn't make such a fuss.'

Gandulf cut her off by lifting the mug to her chapped lips. 'Hush, now, and drink.'

Sirona removed the bloodied rags that bound the girl's feet, ladled warm water into a bucket, then lowered Aldyth's feet into it. Aldyth jumped as her toes met the water, and again as her feet thawed enough to feel the sting of the ice cuts on her ankles.

'We know there's nothing wrong with you,' said Sirona, pulling her goddaughter's feet back into the water, 'but a little cosseting never hurt anyone.'

'What about her face?' Gandulf asked doubtfully.

'What's wrong with my face?' Aldyth demanded irritably.

'That's the next order of business,' replied the old healer.

While Gandulf lifted the mug of hot ale to Aldyth's lips, Sirona began washing the scrapes on her cheek. Gandulf felt Aldyth cringe in pain, but he took it as a good sign. All the way down the hill she had sat listlessly in his arms. Any reaction was better than that deathlike stillness, a sad contrast to the vitality he remembered from their trip to the Fairy hill or, he thought bitterly, the enthusiasm she had displayed during her romp with the Saxon. He reminded himself of his vow to remain uninvolved with this peasant girl and wondered at the mischance that had brought them together again.

When Aldyth finished the ale, Gandulf set the mug aside. Considering his vow of renunciation temporarily in abeyance during this state of emergency, he reached around her waist to take her hands, meaning to rub some warmth into them, but she hastily withdrew them. Persisting, Gandulf gently took hold of them and turned them palm upward. He was appalled to find them crusted with blood and dirt.

'What have you done to your hands?' More insistently he demanded, 'Aldyth, what were you doing out there?'

'What does it matter?' she answered testily. 'Thank you for bringing me home, Gandulf. Sirona will take care of me now.'

'Not so fast. We're not done with you yet,' Sirona told him rather unceremoniously.

Gandulf laughed, more out of relief than anything. He was not ready to be sent away.

'And just what *were* you doing out there, Aldyth?' echoed Sirona.

Ignoring her godmother, Aldyth stole a glance at Gandulf, found his eyes upon her, blushed, and looked away.

'She might yet feel something for me,' he thought, himself blushing at the ease with which he had abandoned his vow.

'You're looking none too festive tonight, Aldyth,' said her godmother. 'But then again you're wearing the colors of the season; green around the gills and red around the eyes.'

'Don't mince words with me, Sirona. How do I really look?'

Gandulf laughed again at the teasing give-and-take between the two women.

Sirona took one of Aldyth's hands from Gandulf. 'Wiggle your fingers if you can, child. Now the other hand. Good, nothing broken. I expect we'll see some blood blisters on those fingertips – unless your blood is too thin to pool.' She applied some salve to the cuts, then wrapped Aldyth's hands in rags.

There was a loud knocking on the door. When Sirona opened it, a blast of wintry wind forced its way inside. Gandulf reached around Aldyth and pulled his cloak, now fire-warmed and damp with melted snow, more closely about her to keep off the draft. Aelfric peered past Sirona at Aldyth. The worry vanished from the boy's face when he saw that she was in no great danger.

Aelfric snorted. 'Father Edmund sent me. But I'll tell him things are . . . well in hand.'

Sirona guffawed. 'Get you gone, scamp, and tell him that we'll be along soon.' To Aldyth, 'Up with you, girl.' Gandulf, enjoying this glimpse into Aldyth's private life, was reluctant to release her until Sirona added, 'And get you out of that draggled kirtle.' Sirona took Aldyth's other kirtle down from the shelf. 'You can't go to the gathering like this, or they'll think you tried to catch a ride home on the Black Horse.'

'The Black Horse?' inquired Gandulf.

'A wicked spirit,' she explained. 'Late at night it takes the form of a gentle pony. Foolish the one who thinks to get an easy ride home, for it will swell into a fierce red-eyed stallion and rush into the nearest bog. 'Tis no pagan foolery, Aethling,' she warned, addressing him by the Saxon title for a nobleman. 'Take note and beware.' Gandulf shuddered and wondered if she were truly a witch, as his father believed.

Sirona handed the kirtle to Aldyth, who signaled her reluctance to undress by casting a sideways glance at Gandulf. 'You're so thin now,' teased Sirona, 'he'll see right through you!' But she took the cloak from Aldyth's shoulders and used it as a screen.

Gandulf averted his eyes, but not his thoughts, when he heard her dress fall to the floor. It was a patched rag, the only kirtle she had, he supposed, aside from the one she was changing into. He wished he could bring a new one as a Christmas gift, but he knew she would never wear it.

'There, now. You'll do,' said Sirona, brushing Aldyth's tangled hair. 'But you're not steady enough to walk, and I can't carry you.' Sirona sized up Gandulf, then said with mock formality, 'My Lord, you are invited to the Christmas gathering tonight.'

'Sirona, no,' said Aldyth quickly. 'The Normans will have festivities of their own for which Gandulf's presence will surely be required.'

'Don't be silly,' said Gandulf. 'Of course I'll come.'

For the wake, Elviva's body had been moved from her tiny hut into Wulfric's more spacious one, but even his home swarmed like an ants' nest. There must have been three dozen people crowded into the cottage, along with the makeshift bier the old widow's body had been lovingly laid out upon. There were rose-cheeked maidens, apple-cheeked matrons, and white-haired grandmothers; stripling youths, towering men, and doddering grandfathers. As the lordling stepped inside, carrying Aldyth in his arms, they were met with mixed looks: hostility at the Norman intrusion, curiosity, but above all concern for Aldyth. Gandulf's eyes sought the big blond Saxon, but he was not present.

Beside Elviva's bier sat Wulfric, and next to him sat his older brother, Edmund, who had married into Long Cross. Edmund was broader of shoulder and thinner on top, but the family resemblance was enhanced by the grief-ravaged eyes. In the remaining space men stood shoulder to shoulder against the wall, matrons crowded together on borrowed benches, young girls sat with squirming babies on their laps, and everywhere there were urchins peering from behind skirts, between legs, from over the edge of the loft. It reminded Gandulf of an overcrowded henhouse – except for the silence that fell over the crowd as he entered – and he suddenly felt like the fox in the henhouse.

But Sirona stated simply, 'Lord Gandulf will be sharing in the evening's festivities.'

Gandulf carried Aldyth to the bench that awaited them by the fire but declined to sit himself, choosing to stand near the wall by the door. At Sirona's signal, Father Edmund blessed the company and the evening began. Edith dished pottage from the cauldron over the fire. The first bowl was passed from hand to hand through the crowd, until at last it reached Gandulf. The company waited, as was the custom, for the honored guest to open the feast. He looked at the watery gray mess of pottage, and his stomach churned. Smiling weakly, he took a sip, lifted it in salute, and nodded approvingly, but privately he noted that it was not fit for pigs. 'Pass your bowls,' called Edith, and she began dishing up pottage. The slop was greedily lapped up with much slurping and burping.

'Do I taste onion in this?' Alcuin asked.

'I'm surprised it was on your tongue long enough to taste,' remarked his wife, Eanfled.

'I brought the onion,' said Mildburh demurely. 'I was saving it for today.'

'Sweet Baby Jesus,' thought Gandulf. 'This, then, is their Christmas *feast*.'

When everyone had eaten, Father Edmund rose. 'We are not truly dead until we are forgotten,' he began, and he told of his own sorrow at the death of his young wife, Aelfgyth DoeEyes. 'My faith was tested. But a simple goodwife put the love of God back into my heart, for Elviva had brought with her a mourning gift. 'Twas a loaf of bread and a warm blanket. The bread, the staff of life, put me to mind that I had others yet to live for. The blanket transformed my grief from a life-choking Mara to the common lot of humankind, for, having herself been widowed, she understood how cold my bed would be. As she placed her gifts in my hands, Elviva told me, "The doe-eyed lass shall wait and watch over you until you may both go home together. My Edgar waits for me, and when I feel especially alone, he talks to me in my dreams."' The priest's eyes swept the crowd. 'God bless her; she was right. But I think I'd have died of a broken heart had I not the hope Elviva gave me to cling to that night. We will miss Elviva, but she has left us many blankets. I take her words to heart, and I pray you all to remember them tonight.'

The company huddled beneath Wulfric's roof as under one great communal blanket, and one story led to another until nearly everyone had shared some remembrance.

'Mother Elviva's last words,' said Edith, 'were to remind Wulfric to fix the leak in the thatch before he let her cottage. May I face death with as much grace.'

'And she bore her widowhood well, too,' said Judith.

'Why shouldn't she?' shouted Edwin MoonCatcher. 'She never let Edgar go.' Ripples of gentle laughter washed across the room.

'She was the wiser,' observed Sirona, 'for wasn't Edgar there to guide her home?'

'And she will be here for us when we need her,' added

Aldyth. 'When Wulfric and Edith celebrate the birth of their babies, she will be here. At every wake and wedding, she will be here. At Midsummer and All Saints', she will be here. And when it is time for us to take the swan's path, she will be here to guide us home.'

Throughout the evening, Gandulf had been attuned to Aldyth's every movement. From across the room he had watched the swell of her chest before each soft sigh, had heard the fall of each teardrop she had shed, had felt the warmth of each sweet smile. Now he watched the crowd watching Aldyth as she spoke. He could tell by the way they attended to her that Aldyth was more than a midwife; she was a keystone of their community, raising their hopes and guiding them through good example. They had none of the fear of her that he had felt for his teacher, Father Odo, nor even the affectionate awe with which they seemed to regard Sirona. The wisewoman had an aura of mystery that made her seem otherworldly, but Aldyth was definitely of this world. Like moths at a flame, children hovered around her. Youngsters squeezed through the crowd to sit at her feet, and one little poppet had found his way into her lap. Gandulf smiled as yet another came to lean against her knees. As naturally as breathing, Aldyth put a bandaged hand around the child's shoulders and pulled her close.

As Father Edmund closed with a blessing, Gandulf thought to himself, 'This is not orthodox Church doctrine, but how much gentler and more forgiving it is.' He regarded the priest, and he had a haunting sensation that they had met before. 'Surely this country priest has never been to Paris, and I am certain that we have not spoken.' Then Father Edmund turned toward the other side of the room, and the old man's face caught the firelight. With a jolt, Gandulf saw the puckered red scar that stretched from the priest's ear to his throat, and he was assaulted by memories of a day more than twenty years before, the day his father had sacked Scafton. He had often thought of the priest whose throat his father had cut, but with the certainty that he had died that day. When Gandulf had been a boy and life had been difficult, he had sometimes remembered the nameless priest's courageous stoicism and had tried to live up to his example. He wished that he could tell the old man

151

of his influence on a young boy, but the man he had become could not.

After Father Edmund had closed, Wulfric stood and announced. 'To honor my mother's memory, I will extend her hospitality to Garth and Hildegarde; let them stay in her house until they can rebuild their own in the spring. And,' he added, meeting the eyes of the destitute couple, 'I promise to patch the roof.' There was a ripple of quiet mirth, followed by murmurs of approval at Wulfric's generosity to the homeless couple.

A tiny voice from the loft called out, 'Tell us a story, Sirona.' The call was taken up from all corners. An expectant hush descended as the wisewoman rose and held up her bony hands. In the silence, someone's stomach rumbled with unappeased hunger. Sirona smiled wryly. 'I cannot fill your bellies with a story, but let us now fill our hearts.'

She was slight of frame, yet conveyed the impression of height and power. When she spoke, the years melted away like snow from a holly tree, and she became as timeless as the tales she told. ''Tis Mothers' Eve, the opening between time and eternity. Tonight we honor Modron as the Great Mother of All and Mary as the Mother of God. Tonight Modron is all mothers and all mothers are Modron. Those who can, honor your mothers here and now. Those who must, go honor them where they lie in the churchyard.'

'Elviva chose a good day to take her leave, for between the end of the old year and the beginning of the new, time and eternity mingle. On our holy days, Lammas, Samhain, Beltain, the dead walk the earth and the living may descend to the land of Sula. Tonight marks the rending of a crack in time. Next week, when the Goddess is reborn as the new year's sun, all souls, living and dead, must return to their own sphere. Use this time, my beloved, to make peace among yourselves and to pay your debts or forgive them as you can. Welcome your loved ones, living or dead, and speak with them in your dreams.'

Father Edmund added vehemently, 'And do you not forget this is a holy time. Those who return are loving spirits and not the demons of Hell. They do not come to do mischief, and neither should you. Last year, as we all know, the mischief making got out of hand. I want no doors tied shut, no ice-water drenchings, nor any of the cruder jests played out.' Father Edmund spoke, as usual, with an ineffectual attempt at admonitory sternness and then, truer to his own nature, swept the crowd with a beseeching look. The priest made deliberate eye contact with those roisterers he suspected to have been chiefly responsible for last year's havoc, and with Aelfric in particular.

'You know who you are,' said Sirona with a crooked smile. 'And so will I,' she added. 'But now, my beloved, as this is a time for remembering,' she continued, 'there is a story I would have you hear . . .' She went on to tell of the first people, the small dark ones, and how they had grown up from the land and built the great stone ring that anchored the seasons and echoed the magic dance of sun and stars. Then had come her own people, the hot-blooded Celts, who had joined bloodlines with the Old Ones.

'We Welsh left our mark as well, for we cleared the land and laid out the tiny fields. We raised the Bokerly Dyke, which failed to keep the Romans out. The Romans flashed over the land like wildfire and were gone, but we could not fend off you Saxons. Then the Danes slipped in like tares among the wheat and strengthened the mix. And on the hill stands the towering gate of Sceapterbyrig, built by that great Saxon, Alfred. Yet it could not keep out the crashing wave of Normans. Even now, the Normans build a motte on which to raise a stone castle, but no castle shall ever stand there,' pronounced the seeress, boldly meeting Gandulf's fixed copper stare with her own deep, knowing eyes. Filling the room with a solemn spell of prophecy, the wisewoman proclaimed, 'From the small dark folk to the fair-haired Celts to the husky Saxons to the bellicose Normans, our roots are sunk into this land. Like trees in the forest, we are all children of one mother; our roots shall entwine, and we shall stand shoulder to shoulder in the storm.'

'But Sirona,' protested Alcuin, 'are we Saxons not over-shadowed? The Normans choke the life out of us like weeds in the wheat.'

'It would appear that the Normans have conquered the English, but they are here to serve the English and the Lady, for the sake of the land.'

'They serve themselves!' argued Garth.

'Aye,' added Agilbert bitterly, 'and we serve them.' Gandulf was startled to notice that the burly youth was balancing a baby on one knee and a pig on the other.

'No gift is given without sacrifice,' responded Sirona. 'Stand together, my children; be hard when you must and gentle when you can. This I swear to you, by all the powers of the fountain: we will conquer. We will absorb the Normans as we did the Saxons and the Danes. Like a steel blade, the English will suffer the fire and come out stronger; but for now, it will require the strength of endurance.' Sirona's voice burned with a fervor that belied her years, urging 'Hold fast to your faith, for you will need it in the fire.'

Like everyone else in the hut, Gandulf was mesmerized by the seeress's passion. The tolling of the abbey bells, summoning worshipers to midnight mass, broke the silence. For the second time since his return to Scafton, Gandulf had completely forgotten himself, shed the burdens of his past, and lived only for the moment. His first escape, he recalled, had been when Aldyth had taken him to the Fairy hills. This time, the Fairy hills had been brought to him on the wings of a story, as once again Aldyth shared her world with him. Hers was a world of poverty and suffering, but at its heart were a warmth and a wealth that drew him like a beggar to a feast. If the hovel had seemed an overcrowded henhouse, his father's great hall now seemed like a cold, dark bear's cave.

Father Edmund excused himself to prepare Saint Wulfstan's for the Christmas Eve service. Gandulf would have stayed for mass, but he had to hasten to the austere abbey chapel, his original destination before being waylaid, to attend mass with his mother.

Little groups of two and three hurried home to drop off their bowls before the service. Gandulf approached Aldyth to bid her good night and Good Yule. She was surrounded by well-wishers, and he realized that whomever Aldyth chose to share her life with would have to share her with the entire population of Enmore Green. As the crowd parted to make way for him, he finally understood how Aldyth had felt that day in Alcester, when she had feared setting the gossips' tongues to wagging.

'May I see you to church, Aldyth?' he offered stiffly, forgetting his duty to his mother as speedily as he had discarded his vows to himself.

'Thank you, my Lord, but you've done too much already.'

'In that case,' he said, showing neither the disappointment nor the relief he felt, 'Good Yule, Mistress Aldyth.' He bowed and went to offer his condolences to Wulfric and Edith before taking his leave.

Aldyth had had to bite her tongue to keep from accepting his offer of escort. But after his recent coolness toward her, she was certain that he had made the offer only out of courtesy. Later that night she focused on Father Edmund's service, using it as a makeshift defense against thoughts of Gandulf and the turn of events that had pulled him briefly back into her life. She watched the jiggling of the willow basket resting on the altar. At the end of the mass, Father Edmund held up the little basket and said, 'May God bless our Christmas wren, holiest of birds. May she fly over our woods and fields and spread the blessing throughout.' He took off the lid and tilted the basket gently sideways, and a little brown bird flew out. It circled overhead, as if to lay its blessing upon them all, then flew straight out through the small window over the altar, causing a stir of pleased whispering among the congregation.

'May old Elviva find her way as easily,' prayed Aldyth.

As the crowd stirred in preparation to leave, Aldyth caught a scent that jarred her senses and jerked her thoughts quickly back to earth. Among the accustomed smells of dank stone, unwashed humanity, wet wool, and smoking tallow candles drifted the sweet scent of woodruff. 'Gandulf!' she thought. She looked eagerly over her shoulder into the faces of her puzzled neighbors, but the lordling was nowhere to be seen. Aldyth blushed and quickly turned her eyes back toward the front of the church. Only then did she realize she was still wearing his sweetly scented cloak.

CHAPTER THIRTEEN

Gandulf looked down at the pasty on his plate, its crust a glossy gold from the egg yolk it had been brushed with before baking. 'That was a well-traveled egg,' he thought ironically, 'for it has been all the way to Enmore Green and back again.' Gandulf had always taken the Christmas revels for granted, yet now they seemed decadent.

Christmas on Castle Hill was lavish. The tables were arranged in a 'U' shape, with feasters seated upon the outside, and spread with three layers of linen, the topmost a festive red. Swags of cedar interwoven with red-berried holly were hung from the walls and draped over the rafters. Feasters loaded their trenchers with glazed ham, dried fruits, custards, venison pasties, and marchpane. The butler ensured a steady supply of drink, with the best wines reserved for the high table, lesser wines for those above the saltcellars, and ale for those seated below. Torches shed light on the great company, and beeswax candles brightened the high table. The shuffling of the servers' feet through freshly laid rushes was drowned out by the lilting strains of lute, viol, and trumpet. A boy whose sweet soprano voice still soared like an angel's sang Yuletide carols.

The roasted boar's head, a baked apple in its mouth and a wreath of yew crowning it, was paraded about the hall. Minstrels followed singing the 'Boar's Head Carol' until the boar's head was presented to the high table. As they toasted the poor dumb beast, Gandulf calculated that the fare served at this one feast would have fed Enmore Green until the spring.

Suddenly Father Odo sprang to his feet to intercept a

small cloaked figure heading toward the door of the hall. The priest jerked back the hood to expose an ashen-faced serving girl carrying a large cloth-covered basket.

'Thou shalt not steal!' he cried shrilly, his words cutting through the clatter of rattling dishes. The music of the lute and viol stopped, and for a second the trumpet trailed raggedly on. All eyes turned to drink in the unfolding drama. 'What have you pillaged from the kitchen of your lord?' demanded the priest.

She was just a child, too terrified to speak. When Father Odo struck the basket from her hands, spilling its contents into the rushes, Gandulf leapt to his feet to stride furiously down the length of the hall.

''Tis just trenchers from the last course,' stammered the girl.

'Just trenchers!' Father Odo dumped the table scraps onto the floor and began rooting among them for stolen valuables. 'How many spoons are missing? And what of the gold coin that disappeared from Lord Ralf's purse last Lammastide after you first came?'

The ravenous dogs scrambled and dived among the rushes for the scattered trenchers. In their frenzy, the hounds knocked the girl to the floor and snapped at her gravy-smeared cloak. She screamed in panic, and Gandulf broke into a run. The priest hauled the girl up by the collar. 'For the good of your soul, confess!' he demanded. He slapped her face, and she fell to her knees, weeping into her hands.

'Have you gone mad?' demanded Gandulf, pushing past the indignant priest to kneel before the girl cowering among the rushes. He pulled the girl's trembling hands away from her face to reveal the red imprint of Father Odo's palm upon her cheek.

There was confused silence until the onlookers realized that this was the next act of the farce just beginning; Lord Ralf's effete son was rescuing the silly child. Raucous laughter thundered through the hall. By now even the kitchen help had crowded in to watch. This was better than any of the planned entertainment; even the Christmas mystery play, saved for the height of the revels, would pale in comparison.

His father's grating voice pierced the tumult. 'Is she your whore, you sly cur? I might have known your monk's act was a sham. The secret is out; he prefers lamb to mutton.' Hoots and catcalls followed his father's crude jest. Gandulf was revolted; the girl could not have been more than eight or ten years old and was as sexless as a stick doll.

''Twas food for my family,' she sobbed, 'and the dogs have eaten it.'

'Wait here, lass,' he said, seizing her empty basket. ''Tis easily mended.' Silently, in a rage, he went to the sideboard, snatched up a ham, a venison pasty, and a stuffed capon, and pitched them into the basket. He picked up a whole plate of pastries and dainties and tipped them in as well, to be joined by a bowl of dried figs and cracked roasted almonds.

'Margaret, a clean cloth!' he barked. The cook produced a linen towel and held the corners to form a bowl. Into it he dumped rolls, white bread manchets, and braided loaves of dill bread. Tying the lot into a bulging bundle, Gandulf called for his cloak. A page hurried over with the cloak, which the lordling wrapped around the girl's shoulders.

'Lamb over mutton! Lamb over mutton!' came the lewd chorus.

'Norbert,' called Gandulf to the closest groom, 'ready my mount.'

'He'll have quite a ride tonight!' shouted fitzGrip, launching another wave of rude laughter. Turning his back on the bawdy company, Gandulf tossed the cloth-bundled bread to the dumbstruck page and led the little serving girl by the elbow out the door and into the night. Relieving the shivering page of the bundle, Gandulf told him, 'Go back inside where 'tis warm, William. The horse will be here soon enough.' When the lad had gone, Gandulf turned to the girl and asked, 'What is your name, child?'

'Helga, your lordship.'

'I'll see you home tonight, Helga.'

'Please, your lordship, if you don't mind, I'd rather walk.'

'With this heavy basket? You could never manage . . .' He looked on in bewilderment as the girl's face knotted up

159

with fear, sending fresh tears down her cheeks. 'What's this, Helga? There's no more need for tears.'

'I'm too young . . . please, my Lord, just let me go.'

With a sickening jolt Gandulf realized that she thought the rude jests in the hall were based in fact. 'Helga, I don't molest children.'

The revulsion in Gandulf's voice convinced her; her obvious relief left him speechless. He wondered how she could have imagined it of him, then conceded that many at his father's table would gladly have done what he had been accused of and found it no blot upon their conscience. He himself, had simply refused to dwell upon such ugliness before.

Norbert approached, leading his horse. Gandulf hooked the cloth bundle onto the pommel, mounted, then had the groom lift up the child, whom he settled onto his lap.

'Can you manage the basket, Helga? 'Tis quite large.'

'Oh, yes, my Lord,' she said. Norbert handed up the basket and she clutched it, resting the bulk of it on the pommel.

'Where do you call home?'

'Enmore Green, my lord. As you go out the gate, 'tis a left down Tout Hill.'

'I know the way, child.'

They rode for a short while in silence before Gandulf spoke softly, as he might to gentle a spooked horse. 'Whose child are you?'

'My father is Garth KnockKnees, and my mother is Hildegarde Brewer.'

'Does she brew up a good ale?'

'Aye, my Lord,' answered Helga, forgetting to be afraid. 'They come from as far as Long Cross for a taste of it, or they did. Our house burned down last summer, and her brewing bowls with it. I got a place on the hill, making one less mouth for them to feed.'

'You have brothers and sisters?'

'Two living. My sister, Goda, has one toddler, one at the breast, and two underfoot. My brother, Guthred, is apprenticed to the smith in town. My parents were staying with old Elviva, but with her gone, they'll have to move, for they can't afford to lease the cottage.'

'You'll find your parents' situation improved, Helga, but they'll tell you about that.'

Looking up into his face, she said earnestly, 'I swear to you, sir, I wasn't stealing. Someone's pinching the spoons, but 'tis not me, and that coin gone missing at Lammas—'

Gandulf's stomach heaved, for he suddenly realized that he himself had seen the coin go astray when his father had unwittingly tossed it to Aldyth. Were this fact to come out, she would surely lose her hand for theft, simply for taking what had been given.

'—and Margaret said I could have those trenchers, with her blessing.'

'Yes, of course, Helga.'

Her tension eased while his own heightened; what if his father made the same connection between Aldyth and the missing coin? They slipped into a silence broken only by the crunch of snow under hooves and the noisy breathing of the little mare. The path led among the dark deserted houses of Enmore Green. Gandulf hesitated, unwilling to leave Helga alone but no more eager to return to the hall with her than she would be to go.

'I wonder where the gathering is tonight?' he mused. He reined in his horse and they listened; the shrill strains of a pipe carried clearly in the chill night air.

'That will be Lufe Piper,' stated Helga. Gandulf nodded and followed the cheery piping down the hill from the green to a larger hut at the edge of the village. It was brightly lit despite the curfew, for even Sheriff fitzGrip's deputies would be unlikely to leave the blazing Yule log long enough to police the outlying villages in such bitter cold.

'This is Father Edmund's house,' said Helga. Gandulf dismounted and lifted her down. Arms laden, he followed her up the path. She knocked, and the door opened onto a huge gathering of humanity crammed into an impossibly small space. The cheerful greeting that met her died down abruptly when Gandulf stepped in behind. Hovering uncertainly in the doorway, he recognized many faces from the night before. Sirona sat in the place of honor, with Aldyth at her side. Aldyth looked much recovered, although her hands were still wrapped and one side of her face bore the scrapes and bruises of the previous night's calamity. Her dismay at his appearance did not escape him. Once again he scanned the crowd for her Saxon, but the man was nowhere to be seen.

'Baby!' Hildegarde cried joyfully, holding out her arms.

Helga wriggled through the crowd to embrace her mother. 'Good Yule, Mama!'

'Aye, poppet, now it is,' crooned Hildegarde, hugging her child close.

Gandulf, engrossed in their reunion, looked up to find that all eyes had turned to him. He still held the basket and the huge bundle. While he wondered how best to deliver the parcels and slip away, Sirona called out, 'Get in or get out, but shut the door!'

Awkwardly, he stepped in to hand Helga her basket. Somebody slammed the door shut, the crowd closed in, and his retreat was blocked. There was nowhere to go but forward.

'Father Edmund,' said Gandulf, 'you'll know what to do with this.' His face grew hot as he stepped through the crowd toward the priest, bumping people's heads with his bundle, sending them dodging and ducking. Meanwhile, Helga had handed her basket to her mother, who was stunned by the abundance of luxuries she had only heard of.

'Bones of the martyr!' cried Hildegarde. 'Helga, how came you by these riches?'

'My Lord Gandulf gave them to me,' replied the child, beaming. Her mother shot a wary look toward Gandulf, and his cheeks burned. Helga explained, 'He saved me, Mama.'

Hildegarde softened upon hearing Helga's story. 'Bless you, Lord Gandulf.' Without hesitation, Hildegarde announced, 'As you have all shared with us in our hour of need, we share with you in our good fortune. Father Edmund, I put this in your hands.'

Murmurs of speculation rose as Hildegarde relinquished the basket. Hand over hand, it moved across the sea of humanity in a buzz of excitement as people leaned over their neighbors' shoulders and craned their necks to glimpse into the passing basket of plenty.

The crowd opened a narrow passage, and Gandulf was shepherded to where Aldyth and Sirona sat. Like magic, a spot had appeared between the two women. Gandulf looked longingly to the safety of the door, then back to the bench. With a jerk of her head, Sirona indicated that he was to sit. He felt Aldyth stiffen as he squeezed in beside her.

Father Edmund made little bundles to go around. 'Pass your bowls,' he called.

'What manner of food is this?' asked Leofwine, holding up a marchpane-stuffed prune. The volume trebled as they traded a taste of this for a taste of that. Even had they not been half starved, sampling such delicacies would be a tale to tell their grandchildren.

'It doesn't take much to make a big splash in a little pond, eh, my Lord?' said Sirona, licking her fingers after finishing a custard tart.

'I had no idea,' Gandulf replied frankly, adding, 'But there's no glory in being the biggest frog in a small pond.'

'No glory, perhaps, but a great deal of gratitude.'

'If he were any closer,' thought Aldyth, 'he'd be in my lap.' The scent of woodruff bombarded her senses, even over the heady aroma of spiced sweetmeats. Too nervous to eat, she divided her portion among the hollow-cheeked children at her skirts. Like baby birds, they opened their mouths to be fed a tidbit each in turn.

'I'm glad I didn't bring her a kirtle,' thought Gandulf glumly, 'for she won't touch even a pastry that came by my hands.'

As they sat side by side, it gradually dawned upon Gandulf that the child in Aldyth's lap had divided and multiplied, for there were several now clinging to her skirts, as well as the one in her lap and another who had wedged itself in between them. Instead of becoming a buffer between the two, the child acted as a conductor of heat.

Big Edmund, Mildburh's youngest, crawled across the floor toward Gandulf, attracted by the glint of his silver belt buckle. The toddler pulled himself up the length of

Gandulf's tunic and pushed his way between the lordling's knees to grab hold of his belt. Gandulf's first reaction was alarm; then his dark eyes gleamed indulgently, and he lifted the child into his lap. When Big Edmund crowed gleefully, a look of pleasure came over Gandulf's face. As the baby settled in and began to tread a nest in his lord's lap with his little heels, Aldyth whispered, 'I'll take him.'

'The child seems content where he is,' replied Gandulf, pleased to have found a friend in this crowd of strangers.

'Another waif for your collection,' Aldyth observed with a smile.

'At least,' thought Gandulf ruefully, 'she's not leaning away from me anymore.'

A commotion arose when half the population of Enmore Green became hopelessly tangled as they strove to make way for a red-faced woman. Mildburh Miller's slow progress ground to a halt midway across the room. 'Oh, my Lord,' she stammered, 'he's but a babe and knows no better. Give him to Aldyth, and she'll pass the lad back to me.'

'He's snugger than a lapdog,' Gandulf assured her. 'I'm well pleased to have him, if you're content to leave him.'

Once again Gandulf borrowed their warmth as those simple folk sang carols of the season and, though there would be no Yule log for them, relished the companionship of a hearthfire and the stories told by its light. Father Edmund was not so riveting a storyteller as Sirona, but he gave a fine telling of 'The Christmas Cherries.' Even so, concentration was difficult, for Gandulf sat much closer to Aldyth than he had the night before. Again he searched for Aldyth's Saxon and wondered who the man was. If he were courting Aldyth properly, he would be here tonight, Gandulf thought critically. 'Can he be an outlaw?' he asked himself and concluded with conviction that it must be so. Gandulf felt fiercely protective and, though he knew he had no right, possessive.

Gandulf stayed until the fire began to die and people began to nod off. At last no one was forthcoming with a story to end the lull, and the evening was over. 'Aldyth,' whispered Gandulf, so as not to wake Big Edmund, asleep in his arms, 'do you feel better today?'

'Aye, my Lord.'

'I would be glad to carry you home tonight.'

'Thank you, but 'tis not necessary. I'm sure I look much worse than I feel.'

'There is nothing wrong with the way you look,' he said quickly, standing to leave. He had no wish to overstay his welcome or become a pest and thereby the laughingstock of the village. Neither did he want them to think he had nothing better to do with his time, even if it was true. Aldyth held out her arms to him, and Gandulf's heart leapt until he perceived that she was only trying to collect Big Edmund. Aldyth reached for the sleeping toddler but caught up the sleeves of Gandulf's tunic as well. She was afraid to let go for fear of dropping the child, so Gandulf attempted to take him back. To his horror, he found that he was grasping not just the child but a soft and yielding portion of Aldyth's bosom. Their eyes met in shock, and he jumped back so abruptly that he would have dropped the baby on his head had Aldyth not leapt forward to catch him. Gandulf blushed hotly, stammered out an apology, and quickly took his leave of her. Aldyth caught the knowing eye of Aelfric, who was observing from the loft. The lad grinned at her and made a suggestive gesture that brought an angry flush to her cheek.

Although Gandulf's foremost thought was to escape, protocol demanded that he bid his host good night. He thanked Father Edmund for his hospitality, then bowed to Sirona.

'Good Yule, my Lord,' she bade him. 'Tomorrow we will gather at our place.' He saw Aldyth cast a withering glance at her godmother as the crone said, 'You are welcome.'

'If my duties permit,' said Gandulf, although he had no intention of returning.

Aldyth forced herself to cross over to where the three of them stood. Lightly she quipped. 'Gandulf will run out of damsels in distress and cloaks too before the twelve days of Christmas are over. I see Helga left with your cloak, and I've another one of yours at home. Wait a moment, and I'll send Aelfric to fetch it.'

''Tis a gift,' Gandulf said, bowing slightly. 'Tell Helga that she may keep the other as well, for the dogs have made a fine piece of work out of hers.'

Gandulf shivered as he made his way home. He knew he would be teased mercilessly when he came slinking into the great hall in the middle of the night without his cloak. Most of all, he dreaded facing his father. Gandulf prayed to Saint Denis that they would all be lying in a drunken stupor, the incident with Helga forgotten when they awoke with splitting headaches, but he also knew that was too much to expect. If he ever again rode out to Enmore Green, they would believe it was to bed a child whose virtue they were convinced he had already tossed into the gutter. Besides, he was afraid of making a fool of himself over a ragged peasant girl. During the days he occupied himself with learning the responsibilities of running a barony, and when necessary he could ride out his frustration in the fields, but at night there was no escaping the loneliness.

'No,' Gandulf decided. 'I will never go back there. Not tomorrow. Not ever.'

CHAPTER FOURTEEN

Gandulf stood shivering in the dark outside the door of the tiny hut. All day he had mulled over Sirona's invitation and imagined himself beside Aldyth and her swarm of urchins. Despite his discomfort the night before, the gathering had lifted his spirits in the same way that romping with a litter of puppies always did. He recalled his first visit to her home on Christmas Eve, only two nights before. He liked the spicy, earthy scent of the herbs hanging from the rafters; it reminded him of Aldyth. Shifting stiffly from foot to foot, he listened to the piping from within, hauntingly lovely and new to his ears, calling to him like the song of a siren.

Late in the day, he had tried to loosen the pull this place had on him by going out riding. But first he had made off with a smoke ham, several loaves of bread, and a cheese. He had envisioned himself presenting this Christmas repast to the first hungry peasants he should meet. But as he stood outside the healers' hut holding the bag, he had to admit that he had known all along which hungry peasants he had meant to feed.

Yet now that he was within spitting distance, his courage gave way. How long he had been in this state of vacillation he could not even guess, but his feet were numb and his fingers freezing. He did know that he would be disgusted at his cowardice should he turn back and at his weakness should he go forward. He finally chose private Hell over public humiliation and whirled around to take his leave so abruptly that his sack swung about and nearly bowled over a latecomer who had just come up behind him. She gave a startled gasp, and, had not Gandulf's free hand shot out to catch her, she would have tumbled into the snow. 'Oh, my Lord, forgive me,' stammered the old woman.

'Winifred?'

'Aye, my Lord,' said the tiny woman, astonished that he should know her by name.

''Twas my fault. Forgive me for startling you,' he apologized.

'I am late to the gathering,' she explained nervously. 'I was plagued with headache and wasn't going to come, but it raises my spirits so . . .' It occurred to Gandulf that she must be wondering what business had brought him here. A dozen lame excuses ran through his mind. The truth, he decided, was easier if no less absurd than an obvious lie.

'I hardly know myself whether I was coming or going,' he said, taking her elbow.

When they stepped inside, there was a collective guffaw; the peasants had been placing bets as to whether Gandulf might put in an appearance. Gandulf located Aldyth, seated next to her mentor and garlanded with children. Their eyes met across the room, and he smiled sheepishly at the hint of laughter in her face as she nodded in greeting.

Sirona's voice cut through the trailing laughter as she cracked, 'Is this today's fair damsel? What desperate straits did you find her in? I see you still have your cloak.'

Winifred's delighted cackle set the crowd off again. Being the butt of jest was not so bad, for Gandulf sensed no malice, and half a smile from Aldyth made up for it. ''Twas remiss of me,' he responded. With a grand gesture, he removed his cloak and placed it about the old woman's bent shoulders. Winifred slapped her knee and laughed herself breathless, but when she tried to return the cloak, Gandulf said, 'A gift of the season, old mother. Father,' he said, handing the priest the victuals, 'I put this in your charge.'

By the time the latecomers were settled, the sound of chewing filled the hut as slices of bread and cheese and ham circulated. Big Edmund, wasting no time, crawled into

Gandulf's lap to tug at the cloak pin that hung useless at his shoulder. Gandulf called to Mildburh, 'I no longer have my cloak; may I borrow the lad for warmth?'

'For as long as you can keep him, my Lord,' she replied. 'He squirms like an eel.'

'He has neglected to introduce himself; what name does this little Viking go by?'

'That scapegrace is Edmund, Eldred Miller's son, my Lord. We call him Big Edmund to keep him straight from all the other Edmunds,' explained Mildburh.

Gandulf held up the scrawny boy and observed, 'He strikes me as small for such a big name. Perhaps you should call him Little Edmund.'

'We have one of those, too,' said Mildburh.

Agilbert obligingly held up his son. To do so, he released his grip on the small brown pig occupying the other knee. 'Bertha!' he scolded as the squealing pig bounded over the hearthfire and landed at Sirona's feet to beg for the last bite of her bread crust.

Smiling, Sirona tossed it to the pig. ''Tis only fair that Bertha have a share too.'

'Begging your pardon, Lord,' Agilbert apologized, 'but Bertha hasn't the manners she had when she wore clothes.'

'The pig wore clothes?'

'Well, she wasn't a pig then,' explained Agilbert.

'Ah,' said Gandulf, nodding his head. The stories about Enmore Green were all true, he thought to himself; they were all moon-touched. 'Then what was she?' he ventured.

'My wife,' said Agilbert.

'Pay no mind, my Lord. He's one of Edwin MoonCatcher's brood,' explained Eldred.

'Edwin MoonCatcher? There's a story in that name, I'll wager,' said Gandulf. 'Is there one here who can tell it to me?'

'Edwin!' they chanted in chorus. A cracked voice harrumphed, and Gandulf regarded the shriveled old man who said defensively, 'I hadn't seen six summers, my Lord, but you know how a name will stick.' MoonCatcher shrugged.

'You've been living in Paris, I hear. They say Paris has a king and a cathedral and a market every day of the year. I've heard 'tis so big that you might live there a lifetime and never lay eye upon all your neighbors. But in Enmore Green everybody knows everybody else from cradle to grave. You need do but one foolish thing to be remembered by it forever.'

'You cannot leave it at that,' said Gandulf over the chuckles of the crowd.

The anticipation was palpable as everyone waited with pleasure for Gandulf's reaction to a well-loved story. Of course Edwin would tell his story, as he had told it a hundred times before. 'As I said,' continued Edwin, 'I wasn't yet six, and the older lads, passing the time beneath the Wishing Tree beside the Crystal Spring, convinced me that the moon was tangled in the branches of the oak. I thought what a fine lantern it would make if I could fetch it down, but high as I climbed, I could get no closer. The older lads grew fearful and tried to call me back, but I refused to come down without it. I was in the topmost limbs when I reached out for the moon. The next thing I knew, I was bouncing from branch to branch, and the tree wasn't the only one with a broken limb!' He paused for the old punch line to be sufficiently appreciated. 'I didn't succeed in catching the moon, but no one could convince me that I hadn't shaken it loose from the branches. Sirona did what she could, but 'twas a bad break and it healed askew.'

Gandulf gave a start and looked at the old healer. She could not be so ancient as to have tended Edwin as a child; age must have muddled the old man's memory.

'When I was young,' continued Edwin, 'it didn't keep me from dancing, but as I aged the leg stiffened. Before I could rue my misfortune there came Stamford Bridge and King Harold's call to arms. All three of my brothers marched to Yorkshire to fight the Danes, but my crooked leg prevented me. And Mildred and I have raised my brother's children as well as our own, for those not lost at Stamford fell at Hastings. So you see, 'twas the Goddess who set the moon in the tree to tempt a foolish young boy!'

'Mildred and Edwin can be proud of their brood of

MoonCatchers,' said Sirona. 'Edith and Seaxburh, Agilbert the Elder, Wulfstan the Reeve, and even Thurgood GiantKiller, who has not yet been arrested.'

A voice called out. 'The last man Thurgood killed still keeps pigs in Swithin Field!'

People laughed at the good-natured jab, but Thurgood puffed up his chest and bragged, 'Mayhap, but he crosses to the other side of the lane when he sees me coming.'

'Who else has a name with a tale that hangs thereby?' asked Gandulf.

'Who doesn't?' said one. 'I'm Eldred Miller, for I run the mill. A dull tale soon told.'

'And I am Hildegarde Brewer, your lordship,' said Hildegarde, 'and when the new crop of barley comes in, you shall have a taste of my best ale.'

'I understand,' said Gandulf, 'that you brew up a good one.'

Hildegarde blushed and said, 'This is my daughter, Goda Weaver; two of her babes are lapdogs to Aldyth Lightfoot tonight, and the two oldest are up in the loft.' Raising her voice she said, 'Bid your lord a good Yule, lads!'

Two voices called from among the giggling swarm in the rafters. 'Good Yule, my Lord!'

'That's the way,' beamed their proud grandmother. 'Of course, you know Helga, my youngest. And here is my husband, Garth KnockKnees. He married over from Alcester.'

''Tis a good place to be from,' said Garth, drawing snickers.

'No one marries *into* Alcester,' explained Judith Alcester. 'I married over from there too. My first husband and I met amaying one year. When he died, I stayed on.'

'I'm Godwin Swineherd,' said the rosy-cheeked fellow next to Judith. 'I'm glad Judith stayed for she's a good wife, and brought a good girl with her. This is Christine Smithsdaughter,' he said, pointing to Judith's daughter by her first husband, 'and here is Edmunda,' he added, holding up the toddler in his lap, 'my morning gift to Judith!'

There were water carriers and quarrymen, charcoal burners and their ginger-haired children, and Alcuin HardHead, who had survived a blow from a Norman mace at Hastings. It had taken eight years for his brains to unscramble, and then he had taken Eanfled to wife. They had six children, the oldest being Leofwine Clerk, who was learning his letters from Father Edmund.

'I am Oscar Fisher and grandson to your lady,' said a lad, slyly winking at Winifred.

Winifred cackled and announced proudly, 'Oscar tends the fish at the stews.'

Next to Oscar sat a couple who had not the gaunt look of the villagers. When it came to their turn, there was a pause. Gandulf prompted, 'Who are you, and what do you do?'

After the slightest hesitation, the man said, 'I am Osfrith, uncle to Agilbert PigWife and nephew to Edwin MoonCatcher.' Then he added cheerfully, 'And I am an outlaw.'

At this admission, Gandulf found himself struck as dumb as everyone else in the room. Recovering quickly, he responded, 'Well, I hear it is a good living.'

'There are hazards,' Osfrith conceded, 'but the food is good and I'm my own master. Here is my wife and accomplice, Seaxburh MoonCatcher. You know her sister, Edith.'

'Did you reach for the moon as well, Edith?' asked Gandulf.

'She sings to it,' volunteered Mildburh fondly. 'She was raised by her grandfather Edwin, and 'tis in her blood, you see.'

Wulfric stood next to the bench on which Edith sat. Gandulf knew that he must miss his mother, Elviva amid the festivities, but he was not immune to the pull of happy memories. 'Edith stole my heart when I saw her dancing by moonlight in the Fairy ring,' he said.

Edith pulled Wulfric onto her lap for a kiss that drew wolf whistles. Eager to shift the focus from herself, she teased, 'Grimbald Shepherd, we've not heard from you.'

In the silence that followed, Gandulf's eye fell upon a big silver-haired man leaning against the back wall, the color rising in his leathery cheeks. At his feet was a little black dog, also silvered with age. Grimbald sighed. 'I mind the sheep of Enmore Green.'

'Aye,' said Edith, 'but your name doesn't tell your whole story or we would call you Grimbald ElfShot.' Edith turned to Gandulf and said, 'If I have danced round the Fairy ring, my lord, Grimbald has danced with the Fairies themselves.'

The silence that came over the company forced Grimbald to speak. 'I beg pardon,' said the old man. 'I'm not much of a talker, though the sheep don't mind.' The old shepherd cleared his throat and reluctantly cracked open his word hoard. 'Nowadays, the sheep must return to the lord's sheepfold each night, that he might have benefit of their droppings for his fields. But years ago, I would drive the flock to the downs. Months would pass, and I'd not lay eye upon another soul. I had only Baldwin here,' he said, setting his dog's tail thumping happily in recognition of his name, 'and the sheep and the Fairies for company.'

'It must have been lonely,' said Gandulf. To his surprise, the crowd hooted.

'Not so lonely,' said Edith with a wink.

'Like me, the Fairies say little; we got on well,' agreed Grimbald. 'I took one to wife. She gave me two children. Sabrina stays with the Fairies, but my son, Bran, chose to live among the Saxons and took Edwina LongBraid to wife.'

Heads turned to a middle-aged woman, her plait of gray-streaked hair hanging down past her waist. Grimbald shot her a look of gratitude when she took up his story. 'I'm Edwina LongBraid, your Lordship, and Grimbald is my father by marriage. On the day Grimbald's boy, Bran, fell at Hastings, our son, Lufe, was born to him in Enmore Green.' She pointed to a slight, dark-haired young man with a black-and-white pup at his feet. But Lufe turned sullenly away, refusing to meet Gandulf's eye.

'Forgive him, my Lord; he has small chance to practice manners, for Lufe is a shepherd as well, with only his grandfather and the sheep for company. If his grandfather says little, Lufe rarely speaks at all,' said his mother.

'Because he's tongue-tied,' came a child's voice from the loft.

The color rose in Lufe's cheeks as he retorted, 'M-m-mind your own b-business!'

'Lufe lets his music speak for him,' said Gandulf. 'Would that all men were so well spoken.' The Norman suspected that there was more than a stutter behind the lad's reticence, for he sensed in Lufe a very personal resentment toward himself.

Gandulf perceived a strong resemblance among the villagers, due to centuries of inbreeding, he suspected. It brought to mind the neighborhood cats of Paris, where it was clear when one stepped from one tomcat's territory to another by the color of the kittens underfoot. There were more blue eyes than gray, more big-boned men and tall women. But there were exceptions: Lufe with his small frame and dark coloring, Eafa AtWood with red hair and freckles, the charcoal burners with their ginger coloring, and Sirona. Gandulf could only guess what color Sirona's silver hair had been, but her eyes were as black as ebony. And then there was Aldyth, with her honey-gold hair, her emerald eyes flecked with gold, and her unusually delicate features. He realized he was staring at Aldyth only when she looked up and met his eyes. He longed to ask her for her story but knew better than to make that mistake twice. People followed his intense gaze across the room, and Mildburh said quietly, 'Everyone knows Aldyth Lightfoot.'

As Aldyth and Sirona got into bed that night, the old woman said, 'That was a good party, famine or no. The gatherings are well attended this year.'

'Yes,' agreed Aldyth, ''Tis good to see them laughing again.'

'People come to see the aethling; he is more amusing than a dancing bear.'

'A dancing bear doesn't bring supper,' observed Aldyth. ''Tis a pity he receives such cold comfort at home that he must warm himself at the hearths of Enmore Green.'

'Were it otherwise, we would all be going to bed hungry tonight.' Sirona paused. 'Talking of cold comfort, Aldyth, I've never known you to meet an open hand with a cold shoulder. Has he offended you in some way? Or is it a lovers' spat?' she teased.

'Oh, Sirona,' said Aldyth in exasperation, 'what would you

have me say? He is good and kind, but he cares no more for me than he does for Winifred or Helga, and they've the cloaks to prove it. Even if he did, it wouldn't be seemly to encourage it.'

It occurred to Aldyth that Sirona must sense her feelings for the lordling and fear that they might hinder her future role as Keeper of the Crystal Spring. 'Rest easy, Godmother,' Aldyth assured her. 'There's nothing between us, nor shall there ever be.'

Before Sirona could reply, there came the sound of furtive scratching at the door. Often they were awakened by the loud knockings of the villagers, but this was a more guarded summons. Aldyth rose, glad for an end to the strained conversation. Warily, she opened the door a crack. Against the dim gray of the starlit snow, she saw the silhouette of a tall, broad-shouldered man on the doorstep. 'Are you alone?' he whispered.

'Bedwyn! Quickly, come in.'

Bedwyn stooped to pick up a big bundle at his feet and slipped inside.

Sirona bent an ear to listen for outside noises. Aldyth stirred the fire and felt her curiosity rise with the flames; Bedwyn rarely came down from the hills.

'I backtracked and circled round; I wasn't followed,' he told them. 'We need to talk.' By firelight, Bedwyn took a haunch of venison from his fur bundle. 'I've been hunting.'

'Bedwyn, you've been poaching,' said Aldyth reproachfully.

'Call it what you like; I've brought dinner.'

'You know the penalty for poaching,' said Sirona coldly. 'We could be put to death.'

Unruffled, Bedwyn replied, 'Then you must eat up the evidence, for I've brought only enough to fill you. I'd heard you were hungry, and I've been starving for good company.'

Aldyth looked pleadingly at Sirona, and the crone relented. 'Refresh yourself, then. Your heart was in the right place, though your judgment be lacking.'

Grinning, Bedwyn drew several solid chunks of wood

from his bundle, a welcome gift since firewood had grown scarce, and Aldyth marveled at his nerve, for he was the only person she knew who was not intimidated by Sirona; even Aldyth herself sometimes was, and even Father Edmund found her mysterious ways fearsome at times. Yet there was a grudging respect between Sirona and Bedwyn, for they had been partners in crime for many years, ever since Sirona had removed the arrow from Bedwyn's thigh.

Years ago, Sirona and Aldyth had returned to the outlaws' camp on the pretense of reexamining Bedwyn's wound. Never before had they approached the encampment without a summons, and as they neared the camp, Osfrith Outlaw, the night watch, stepped out.

'Sirona!' he had said. 'I'm glad to see you but surprised all the same.'

'I've come to call on the Golden Cockerel.'

'You must mean Bedwyn,' chortled Osfrith. He led them into the encampment, stopping before a small thatched hut dug into the hillside. Osfrith gave a whack to the deerhide door flap, with the flat of his hand, and from within came a woman's surprised squeak. Winking, Osfrith said, 'Better he should come out than that we should surprise him.' Then he called, 'Leave off your wenching, Bedwyn. You've got visitors.'

Bedwyn emerged wearing only his knee-length tunic, for he had not taken the time to put on his linen breeches. He was slightly embarrassed when he recognized his callers but recovered quickly and grinned at Aldyth. 'Hello, Mouse. Nice night for a walk.'

'Apparently you're feeling better than you were the last time we saw you,' remarked Sirona. 'Is there somewhere we could talk?'

'My hut is free,' said Bedwyn. He led them to his own place and ushered them in. He gave the embers a stir and served them each a cup of elderberry wine.

'The leg is healing well?' asked Sirona.

'Aye, thanks to you,' he replied, 'but that's not what you came to talk to me about.'

'That is one reason. 'Twas an ugly wound; I see you still walk with a limp.'

Bedwyn frowned. 'Not for long,' he said. 'Each day is a little better.'

'I'll just have a look at it and take out the stitches,' said the old healer.

'I took them out myself,' he said, 'for I didn't want the skin to heal over them.'

Sirona smiled wryly. 'You always know best, don't you?' She lifted his tunic and examined the wound. 'You do heal quickly,' she admitted. 'Is it stiff?'

'Nay.'

'I'll wager not,' she cracked. 'Your nightly exercise must keep the muscles limber.'

Bedwyn laughed heartily. He and Sirona often rubbed each other the wrong way, but he appreciated her earthy humor. 'Now tell me what really brings you here, Sirona.'

Sirona grew grave. 'There has been an increase in the number of our lord's sheep and pigs gone missing. And last week, some Norman merchants were robbed on the highway to Gillingham. With the heightened seriousness of each crime, there is a higher price to pay, and the perpetrators are seldom the ones to pay it.'

Bedwyn bristled. 'We didn't think they'd miss the livestock.'

'You didn't think at all,' retorted Sirona, 'and I don't even want to hear your excuse for waylaying the Normans. You must cease these acts of violence.'

Bedwyn fumed, 'Must I stand by while the Normans ravage the land and ruin us all?'

'The other young men follow you naturally; you were born to lead, but with this wild behavior you lead them toward disaster. I admire your spirit, but you lack discipline and purpose. Stay this course, and you will come to a bad end, with your eyes gouged out for nothing better than poaching – unless the next arrow is truer to its mark. And what will you have accomplished with your life?' She glanced at him sharply and stated boldly, 'I think I have a good life's work for you, Bedwyn, if you've a mind.'

'What manner of work might this be?' he asked sullenly.

''Tis just as dangerous as highway robbery, though lacking,

perhaps, the glory. Yet 'tis meet work for a stouthearted Saxon.'

'Tell me more,' he said.

So Sirona had enlisted Bedwyn as a guide upon the Starlit Path some ten years before. He had settled into an abandoned hermit's hut deep in Cranborne Chase to keep bees and geese, and the legend of the Hermit of the Blackmore Vale was given a new lease on life. In the guise of a religious recluse, Bedwyn had the perfect cover for his secret life. He quickly rose to the top, for he was the one to walk the extra mile, carry the heavier load, and take the greater risk, if necessary or simply for the thrill of it. He inspired courage and loyalty in others and proved to be as useful as Sirona had hoped. He had even learned to temper his hot blood with discretion once he had something to lose.

'Pull your pot over, Mouse,' said Bedwyn, warming his hands by their fire. Bedwyn cut up the poached venison into small chunks and tossed them into the pot to boil. While Aldyth brought out salt bought from the peddlers who packed it in from the drying pans on the coast, Sirona served up a thin, sour ale. Bedwyn tasted it and made a face.

'Pitiful thin ale,' said Sirona unapologetically. 'How do you weather the famine?'

'I'm not wanting for meat, but I've been drinking Adam's ale these last few weeks.'

'We'll all be drinking water after Epiphany,' said Aldyth with a rueful smile.

'Do you get enough to eat?' he asked.

'Enmore Green has fared better than most of the villages hereabout,' replied Sirona.

'So I've heard,' said Bedwyn dryly. 'Give me your cups.' He drew a skin flask from his bundle and filled the cups. Handing them back, he grinned and recited, 'I am a golden treasure, pirated from wood and vale. Wings bear me in the buzzing air and a sweet basket is my home. Along comes a man who bathes me; I become the sapper of strength. I fell the young, ravage the old, and rob fools of their strength. Who am I?'

'Sweet mead!' exclaimed Aldyth, sniffing the fragrance of jewel-bright honey. She sipped slowly, savoring every drop. 'Bedwyn, how came you by this golden treasure?'

He beamed at her pleasure. 'The honey is mostly gone, but I've been saving this for tonight.' He launched into a bawdy story he had heard from Brihtnot the Poacher and told it so well that even Sirona had to smile. The night wore on, the mead worked its magic, and the conversation degenerated into a thinly disguised courtship dance. 'I've a new riddle for you to sharpen your wits on,' he challenged Aldyth.

'Go on,' she replied.

His sapphire eyes sparkled with mischief as he complied. '"Something hiding rises up, swelling and growing. The bold peasant girl seizes that boneless wonder with her hands; the earl's daughter covers it with a cloth."'

Whether due to the mead or his disarming frankness, Aldyth guffawed. Quickly regaining her composure, she chided, 'Bedwyn! Is that all you can ever think of?'

''Tis just bread dough!' he said in injured innocence. 'What did *you* think it was?'

When the leaping flames shrank into embers, Sirona said wryly, 'If you're not going to be in by curfew, Bedwyn, you might at least be out before it lifts.'

'Very well,' he agreed. 'But first we must speak of more serious matters. I didn't wish to darken the mood, but you must know that the men who followed Gorm to the fountain have returned. I suspect they've gotten a fresh lead; let us hope 'twas not at the expense of our friends in the tower. Aldyth,' he said soberly, ''tis too dangerous to guide anyone along the Path at present. If a runner comes through, let him wait at the spring; come fetch me, and I'll act as his guide.' Turning to the crone, he added, 'Don't let her be stubborn about this, Sirona. There's no need to take foolish risks. I'll know if the runner is true or traitorous. If he is false, I'll get rid of him before he can do further harm.'

Sirona nodded in reluctant agreement. Satisfied, Bedwyn began to pack up the evidence of his visit. Sirona presented him a basket filled with a few of their carefully hoarded crab apples, then crawled under her blanket, leaving Aldyth to see him off.

At the door, Bedwyn wrapped the squirrel fur coverlet, in which he had borne his gifts, around Aldyth's shoulders. 'Good Yule, Mouse,' he whispered in the dark. 'Would that it were I keeping you warm each night.' Frowning, he said, 'I've heard the Norman lordling is sniffing about the village. I've also heard he has set his sights on you.'

'Don't be ridiculous, Bedwyn. He can hardly bear to sit next to me.'

'Then what is he after?'

'He's not like the other Normans.'

Bedwyn's hackles rose. 'Is there anything between the two of you?'

'Could you really think that of me?'

''Tis not my mind but my jealous heart speaking. Swear this is so and set the matter to rest once and for all.'

'I swear this is so,' said Aldyth. It was true enough, and she determined to put Gandulf out of her mind once and for all.

Bedwyn pulled the fur more snugly around her shoulders. 'I'll never forget that day last fall, Mouse. Many a cold night the taste of your lips, like sun-warmed honey, has come back to haunt me.' He hesitated. 'Aldyth, you do feel anything for me?'

'Bedwyn, how could you think that I have no feelings for you? Of course I do, but—'

Before she could finish, his lips covered hers. 'Such a sweet kiss,' he whispered, 'and 'tis not the honey mead that makes it so.'

'Bedwyn . . .'

But he placed his finger on her lips. 'Say no more, Aldyth. You have told me what I came to hear.' Pulling her hard against him, Bedwyn kissed Aldyth with a passion that made their forest tryst look like child's play, then slipped into the predawn gloom.

Aldyth felt a throbbing within that she knew must be her liver rising with the animal passion he had roused in her. She stumbled into bed, her senses reeling. Beside her in the dark, she could feel Sirona's bristling curiosity. 'Don't worry, Godmother,' said Aldyth breathlessly, 'I know he is not for me.'

CHAPTER FIFTEEN

New Year's Eve 1086

Gandulf, a sackful of leftovers in each hand, jumped guiltily at the sound of footsteps as he skulked about the pantry like a thief. He had no wish to explain himself to anyone when he could not himself understand how he had come to this sorry state. Margaret, fiercely brandishing an iron ladle in one hand and a flickering torch in the other, leapt into the doorway with astonishing agility for one of her bulk and hissed, 'If you be on lawful business, show your face. Elsewise you'll sup on iron!'

Gandulf was startled into laughter. Then it was Margaret's turn to laugh at the sight of her lord's son, caught pilfering after hours like a naughty scullion.

Stifling a smile, she said, 'I thought you were our spoon thief.'

'I know this looks strange—' he began.

'Not another word,' she chuckled. 'I know all about it.'

'You do?' he asked in dismay. 'Does everyone?'

'If you mean Lord Ralf, he thinks you're out whoring and says 'tis better to pay in table scraps than to waste good coin on wenching.'

After leaving the abbey that night, Gandulf had stopped to raid the pantry on his way to Enmore Green. Ever since the first time, on Christmas Eve, one way or another Gandulf had found himself attending the gatherings and had finally given himself up to the impulse. Word had spread among the peasants that he was coming nightly and always brought something to throw into the pot. He was soon feeding half of

Enmore Green and even a few Alcestermen who had invited themselves over for a free meal. No home was big enough to house the gatherings, so Father Edmund had opened the church.

Most Saxons would not have dared flout the curfew so blatantly. With such large gatherings, discretion was no longer possible. But if Gandulf's attendance attracted crowds, it lent legitimacy to the affairs and protected them from raids by the sheriff.

Gandulf thanked Margaret for her discretion, then slipped out of the bustling hall, ignored by the drunken revelers. Gandulf had asked Norbert to saddle Cathedra, but when he got to the stable, he was mildly surprised to find Aelfric holding the mare's reins.

'What are you doing here, Aelfric?' he asked the boy.

'I told Norbert to return to the feast. I thought you'd need help with the extra load.'

'Extra load? What are you talking about?'

'Didn't you agree to be our First Footer?' asked Aelfric.

Gandulf began to suspect that the office was of more than an honorary nature. 'Yes,' he admitted. 'Does this entail more than being the first one to set foot inside the house after the New Year comes in?'

'Didn't anyone mention it?' asked Aelfric innocently. ''Tis unlucky for the First Footer to come empty-handed. He brings a loaf of bread, a bit of fuel, and a sip of ale to ensure plenty, warmth, and merriment in the new year. I came to help you carry it all.'

'Or to be sure I brought enough to suit you,' suggested Gandulf tartly as he led the mare into the bailey. 'Wait here; I'll see if I can scare up a few loaves of good fortune.'

The chapel bells had just tolled midnight when Gandulf returned with several skins of ale, a bundle of brushwood for fuel, and a large pannier of white bread. Aelfric was nowhere in sight, and the horse was tied to a ring in the wall. Annoyed, Gandulf was loading his pillaged provisions when Aelfric slipped up behind him like a ghost out of the darkness. Even as the boy appeared, there arose a howl of fury from the chapel.

Gandulf's head jerked around. 'What's that?' he exclaimed in alarm.

'I think someone must have put dog shit covered with burning leaves on the chapel porch,' postulated Aelfric, 'but I can't be sure from this distance.'

Gandulf raised an eyebrow. 'High time we were on our way, I would say.'

A cry of disgust echoed across the bailey.

'Father Odo must've tried to stamp it out,' speculated Aelfric.

Gandulf quickly mounted up and, grabbing Aelfric by the collar, slung the boy over his lap like a sack of meal. Once they had escaped, Gandulf lifted the lad into a sitting position. Aelfric tugged at his ragged tunic and combed his mop of sandy hair with his fingers. Listening critically to the curses echoing from above, he asked, 'Is that Latin?'

'Yes, but don't listen,' chuckled Gandulf. 'You know far too much as it is; in how many languages must you be able to curse fluently?'

The lad grinned, then asked, 'Why were you so late? Everyone will be waiting.'

'I was visiting my mother at the abbey, if it's any business of yours.' Gandulf had been attending the earlier nones service with Sister Emma, that his evenings might be free to spend in Enmore Green. But that night he had helped her usher in the New Year and delivered the traditional New Year's gift of gloves. Her vows of poverty precluded elaborate decoration, silken embroidery, or gold braid. Instead he had spent his money on kidskin gloves lined with sable, austere in appearance but luxurious to the touch.

'They're so dear!' his mother had exclaimed. Then, noticing that he was wearing his workaday cloak, she had demanded, 'Did you sell your cloak to buy these?'

'No, Mother,' Gandulf had assured her, leaning down to kiss her forehead.

Not to be put off, she had remarked, 'This week you have worn your three best cloaks, one after the other. And today you have on the cloak you wear only about the stables.'

'If you must know,' he had admitted, 'I've been playing Saint Martin.'

'You cut your cloak in two and gave half to a beggar?'

'I went one better. Instead of half a cloak, I've left three of them with one peasant or another in Enmore Green.'

'I heard about the little girl,' she had said, smiling fondly. 'You have a generous nature, dear boy. But take care that Ralf doesn't notice; he might begrudge the charity.'

Gandulf had taken her hand and drawn her over to a bench by the fire, joking, 'He has been amply repaid with amusement at my expense. Now tell me, do the gloves fit?'

Gandulf had never seen his mother so happy. It did not occur to him that it was because he himself was more cheerful; in fact, this was the closest he had ever come to happiness – in his waking hours. By day, Gandulf had a sense of belonging, at least peripherally, that he had never known before. But his nights were Hell, for he was tormented by phantoms of suppressed desire. There was no privacy for anyone in the household, save Lord Ralf, who slept in the solar. After the trestle tables were taken down, Gandulf would lie awake on his pallet in the great hall, trying not to listen to the moans of bed joy from those men who sported with their whores beneath the blankets. Sometimes he would wake in a sweat, his loins aching with unspilled seed or worse. The night before, he had lain awake till cock-crow, paying the price of exhaustion for lack of sleep yet having had none of love's rewards to carry him through the day.

'Have you done this before?' asked Aelfric, breaking into his thoughts.

'Done what?' asked Gandulf guiltily.

'Played the part of First Footer, of course.'

'No,' he replied. 'At Saint Denis, we just went to church and prayed for a good year.'

'I'll wager this works better.'

'At the very least, I'm sure 'tis more entertaining.'

'Whatever you do,' Aelfric instructed, 'say not a word before wishing all within a good new year. Take care not to stumble, for 'tis bad luck. The right foot goes in first, and always enter through the front door; if there's a back door, take it when you leave.'

'Is that all?' asked Gandulf.

'If I think of anything else, I'll let you know,' Aelfric assured him.

A group of men and boys awaited them on the green. There were Alcuin HardHead and Agilbert PigWife, Leofwine Clerk, Edwin MoonCatcher, Goldwin Swineherd, Wulfric Edgarson, and Garth KnockKnees, as well as half a dozen boys Gandulf couldn't put a name to. They shook his hand and he bade them a good New Year; then they started off toward the first house.

Suddenly Wulfric stopped dead in his tracks and asked gravely, 'You're not flat-footed?'

'No,' Gandulf replied in surprise. 'Why?'

''Tis a requirement of the station that you have a good high arch,' Wulfric replied.

'My wife assures me that he is tall, dark, and good-looking enough,' said Godwin.

'Mine, too,' Garth volunteered.

'He looks to have remembered not to wear black or mourning clothes,' observed Edwin, 'although his cloak is a bit shabby – for an aethling, that is. Will he do?'

'He will have to do,' said Wulfric soberly, 'so long as his eyebrows haven't grown together in the middle since last night.'

At this point Gandulf realized that they were ribbing him and said sternly, 'I might just stumble through the doorway of the next one who opens his mouth.'

The men broke into a hearty laugh, and several slapped him on the back. Wulfric held up a basket of brown bread broken into minuscule chunks and a jug of sour ale. 'Now that's settled,' he said, cheerfully disregarding the lordling's threats, 'off we go!'

'No need for that rough fare,' said Aelfric, waving a loaf of Gandulf's white bread. 'The First Footer brought his own.'

'In that case,' said Wulfric, 'my house first!'

Gandulf paused at the doorway of Wulfric's hut to be certain that he started their new year off on the right foot.

Then he stepped in and bade Edith a good new year, filled her cup with ale, put a twig upon her fire, and set a loaf of fine white bread in her hand.

'Oh, my Lord, a Happy New Year to you, too!' she beamed. They all shook Edith's hand and toasted her health. Then, as there was only one door to the tiny hut, they departed the same way they had come. The others carried Gandulf's bundles and followed him from house to house, from handshake to handshake, from toast to toast, growing noisier and merrier as the night wore on. In the distance another boisterous mob of First Footers circulated. Once there was a splash and a flurry of cries as some drunken First Footer with the other group fell into a pond and was fished out with a great deal of buffoonery.

The night was far gone, and so were the revelers, by the time they approached Aldyth and Sirona's toft. The two women could hear them coming and had, in fact, been able to follow their progress throughout the night without so much as bending an ear. 'Hullo!' came a chorus of greetings from outside. 'We're here! Will you let us in?'

Aldyth opened the door, and her eyes widened. She had heard that Gandulf was to play First Footer but had never expected to see him at her doorstep with his cloak half slung over his shoulder and a silly grin on his face. Sirona cracked, 'I hope this isn't the first house on your route, or you'll be crawling into the last one. Remember to put your right hand in first over the threshold!' Everyone laughed but Gandulf, who was abashed. Sirona assured him, 'You're holding up well enough, lad. Wulfric was our First Footer last year, and this far into the evening he was being carried into the houses feet first.'

Sirona and Aldyth stepped aside. Wulfric, grinning, gave Gandulf a push. Gandulf shot him a foolish grin, then stepped over the threshhold with the slow, cautious care of a man who knows he is drunk. But as he met Aldyth's eyes to deliver the blessing, he thought of all that he wished for her in the coming year. He wanted to build her a warm dry home, to dress her in fine gowns, warm stockings, and fur cloaks, to shower her with golden chains and jeweled brooches. He wanted to hold her, protect her, love her . . .

There was a long pause as the others waited silently; it would be bad luck to say a word before the First Footer had spoken his blessing. But the First Footer stood staring at Aldyth as though elf shot. Finally Aelfric elbowed Gandulf in the ribs.

Gandulf started, and Wulfric quickly clapped his hand over his lordling's mouth to prevent the blurting out of some ill-omened utterance. Gandulf blushed hotly and nodded. Taking an instant to compose himself, he said quietly, 'I wish you both a Happy New Year's Day and the best of everything throughout the year.' The others, drunk as they were, were impressed by the solemnity with which he placed the twig upon the fire and the bread into Aldyth's hand. They looked on curiously as Gandulf filled the women's cups, raised his own cup in salute, and whispered, 'May God be with you.'

He shook their hands and there came the obligatory round of handshakes and toasting, but it was as if someone had placed a wet blanket over all their shoulders. As Aldyth watched them depart, she wondered aloud, 'Why do I always have this baleful effect upon him?'

'You tell me,' replied Sirona, 'for he seems to have the same effect upon you.'

Gandulf was still glum when he arrived at the great hall, where by now the mummers' play was finished and the trestles were cleared. A few people were still sitting quietly in corners or by the fire finishing off the last pitchers of wine, but most were snoring drunkenly in their blankets. Gandulf relinquished all hope for the new year as he too wrapped himself in his cloak and subsided into the chorus of drunken snoring.

'Another merry night,' said Edith, linking her arm with Aldyth's.

'Did you see what the lordling put in the pot tonight?' asked Wulfric. 'A whole ham and a half-dozen onions!'

'And cabbage, too,' added Edith. 'I didn't think to taste cabbage until next summer.'

They were walking up the hill from church. Moonlight glittered on snow, lighting up the winding lane. It was the eleventh night of Christmas and the eve of Twelfth Night.

'Tomorrow is the last night of Christmas,' Aelfric reminded them. 'There will be no more hams or cabbage unless somebody speaks up and invites the aethling to come again.'

The next morning everyone attended a special Epiphany mass. That afternoon, before the Twelfth Night gathering, villagers bundled up to wassail the apple trees. From toft to toft they toasted the trees, admonishing them to fruit heavily and leaving among the branches of each a crust of ale-soaked bread. But when the crowd gathered at Saint Wulfstan's on Twelfth Night, they were dispirited; it had not occurred to Aelfric alone that this was the last decent meal they would have for a long time. But Wulfric stood up and announced, 'We have been having too good a time to let it end. You are all invited to our place tomorrow night for stone soup. You too, my Lord Gandulf.'

'And bring a ham!' piped up Aelfric from the loft.

'Thereby is revealed the secret of my popularity,' said Gandulf, drawing affectionate chuckles. Unlike Aldyth, most had stopped pondering why Gandulf came and simply enjoyed his company and his gifts. Gandulf was the babies' second choice if Aldyth's lap was taken, but there was no longer a spillover from one to the other, for they sat on opposite sides of the room and the children were forced to choose. Aldyth's eyes were still drawn to Gandulf, but she likened it to looking directly into the sun, knowing full well it could only cause harm, and she tried not to succumb to the impulse.

The energy was low, and a lull threatened to drag on until Aelfric called out, '*You* tell a story, Gandulf.' A chorus of little voices chimed in: 'A story, Gandulf! A story!'

Heads turned, and Gandulf squirmed. The Norman lordling looked about for a champion to absolve him or step forward in his place, but no one seemed inclined to rescue him.

Gandulf finally decided that he could not embarrass himself any more by speaking than he could by remaining the silent focus of all eyes. 'Very well,' he capitulated and recited,

'"There was a crow sat on a clod. Now my story's over. Isn't that odd?"'

'Give us a real story!' came the indignant cry.

Gandulf frowned, drumming his fingers on his knee. But after a moment, he smiled slyly and began, 'Reynard the fox came upon a crow in a tree. In the crow's beak was a chunk of cheese. "Dear crow," said Reynard, "your voice is the sweetest in the forest. Grant me the boon of a song." The fox flattered and the crow preened until finally he opened his beak to squawk out a sour song. The cheese fell into the waiting jaws of the fox, who said, "Silly crow, never believe the blandishment of a flatterer, especially if you have no talent." Just as you have all flattered me into singing,' Gandulf concluded.

'Aye,' said Sirona, 'but you had already dropped your cheese.'

The villagers roared with laughter and stamped their feet. Not one of them, not Aldyth nor even Sirona, suspected that amid the merriment their Lord Gandulf was thanking God in Heaven and all the saints above for guiding his feet down the hill to Enmore Green. So it was that Christmas came to an end.

'Bless these plows, dear Lord,' prayed Father Edmund, 'and have mercy in this time of need, when everything is in short supply—'

'Except work,' quipped Aelfric.

'How would you know?' asked Wulfric, aiming a playful swat at the boy.

It was Plow Monday, the first Monday after Twelfth Night, and Father Edmund was blessing the plows in a ceremony to mark the beginning of winter plowing and the new year's work cycle. From that day on, in good weather, the men would plow the mud in the fields. On rainy days they would report to Lord Ralf's steward to thresh and winnow their lord's grain in his great barn. On days of hard frost they would be called upon to cut and haul logs from the forest, to use for the framework of Lord Ralf's castle.

The manor court, or court leet, always began the day after the last day of Christmas. Most days, it was presided over by William CloseFist, Lord Ralf's steward. Once in a while, Lord Ralf came to assure himself that CloseFist carried on his business to his satisfaction. On the first day, a hall mote met within Lord Ralf's great hall. Every man who was of age was required to attend to pay suit to Lord Ralf. Also present were those women involved in cases to be tried before him. The Alcester court always met first, taking at least three days because so many of the contentious folk of that village brought suit against their neighbors. Long Cross never took more than a day, and then it was Enmore Green's turn. Half a day was all Enmore Green ever required, for there were fewer encroachments between neighbors. In warm weather, Enmore Green's court leet took place under the ancient oak by the Crystal Spring, but since winter still gripped the land and the lord's own hall was so near, they all walked up the hill.

The hall was crowded and noisy. At the high table sat the high-ranking officials, including Father Odo, who played watchdog upon the populace, seeing that no incestuous marriages were contracted or cases of legerwite – unlawful fornication – went unpunished. Sir Godfroi Le Breton, a second son from a minor Breton estate and one of Lord Ralf's hired swords, was there with his wife, Agnes. They sat on Ralf's right, while Gandulf sat on his left, as was expected. Sir Godfroi, nodding in Gandulf's direction, sneered, 'Since when has "the monk" taken an interest in the court leet?'

Lord Ralf snorted. 'Since the whelp has taken to slumming among the peasants.'

The shrill laughter of the knight's wife cut through the noisy hall. Ignoring the remark, Gandulf scanned the crowd for Aldyth's Saxon. He could tell himself that he attended the court session in support of his friends, but he had also attended the Alcester and Long Cross leets, hoping to locate the elusive Saxon. He spied Aldyth amid the crowd, bending to pick up Little Edmund. Her hair slipped from its shawl and fell over her face. Little Edmund laughed and caught it with his dimpled hands. She laughed, too tickling his nose with a loose tendril, then hugging the fortunate child to her breast.

When the requests for permission to marry came up, Gandulf was relieved that Aldyth was not among the petitioners. Then those who owed a heriot, or death tax, were called upon. Wulfric Edgarson and his older brother, Edmund of Long Cross, stepped forward to pledge Elviva's heriot, the lord's choice of her best beast. Lord Ralf was also entitled to the second-best beast, Wulfric's entry fee into the landholding system. Wulfric was then granted seisen, legal occupancy, and was required to swear fealty to Lord Ralf.

There were no cases of default for work owed to the lord. Gandulf knew that if a villager from Enmore Green was unable to fulfill his obligations, a substitute would be found. Moon-touched or no, Enmore Green showed a solidarity that put the other villages to shame. Gandulf was just thinking that the one thing he would not hear in the court of Enmore Green was the common suit of slander, when up stepped Garth KnockKnees.

'Master William,' said Garth timidly, 'I wish to lay a complaint of slander.'

'And who is this charge against?' asked the steward.

Garth nervously looked back over his shoulder at Sirona, who nodded encouragement. He said, 'I would like to lay a complaint of slander against Father Odo, for that he charged my daughter Helga with theft and struck her in public.'

An intake of breath among the spectators expressed outrage among the Normans and dread among the Saxons. William CloseFist looked uncertainly at Lord Ralf, expecting an outburst of rage. But Ralf guffawed and gave the knock-kneed peasant an appraising look. He was always partial to a man who showed backbone, even if it was a man whose back he meant to break. Gandulf heaved a sigh of relief; his father was as unpredictable as a rutting bull and on occasion surprised him with an unexpected show of good humor.

But Father Odo jumped to his feet. 'How dare you! I'll have you flogged for this!'

'Then he might charge you with battery as well,' quipped Gandulf.

Normans and Saxons alike exploded into laughter, and the tension was broken. Lord Ralf said disgustedly, 'Sit down, Odo. Turnabout is fair play. You have three weeks to find witnesses on both sides. This matter will be heard at the next court leet.'

Gandulf admired Garth's nerve. Helga had lost her situation as a serving girl in her lord's hall thanks to the priest, so she had no position at risk, and it might mean as much as sixpence and a new cloak were the priest required to pay damages. Helga had a good case and a surfeit of witnesses, but Gandulf doubted that any would testify in the face of Father Odo's wrath – perhaps Margaret, he speculated, but the priest would make her life hell forever after. Gandulf would have to step forward on Helga's behalf, though he rued the thought of it. It would assuredly revive the tasteless jests and rumors about his involvement with the girl. He wondered if Sirona was doing this to test him. Frowning, he scanned the crowd. Sirona's black eyes were waiting for him. She smiled over the heads of her neighbors, and Gandulf grudgingly saluted her.

When the court leet was dismissed, people gathered in groups to marvel over the day's developments. Sirona, Aldyth, and Garth squeezed through the buzzing crowds, dodging stares and questions as they made their way out of the hall. At the doorway, Father Odo, lying in wait, stepped directly into her path. His eyes burned with hatred as he snarled, 'You've gone too far this time, witch. It will cost you dearly!'

Sirona coolly met his eye and stepped around him as she would a pig in her path.

Aldyth rushed up to her toft, expecting to find the house cold and empty, though guests would be arriving any minute. She was puzzled to see firelight through the cracks, for she knew Sirona was at Alcuin and Eanfled's, where the winter fever had struck. The old healer had been summoned from the field, and Aldyth had been required to make up her time, for Lord Ralf made no allowances for illness. There had been no time to change plans for the gathering at the healers' home that night. Aldyth entered to find Mildburh stirring the fire and

Edith arranging the benches to accommodate the expected crowd. 'How good of you!' said Aldyth gratefully, hanging her cloak on a peg. 'How did you know I'd be late?'

'Just a guess,' explained Edith, 'after Alcuin came looking for you and Sirona and said they'd been puking all night. So when our plowing was done, I sent Wulfric home to warm his bones and stole Mildburh away from her family to come and help me.'

Aldyth nodded. 'As soon as I finished in the fields, I went to relieve Sirona, but she said I oughtn't expose myself to the sickness. She says she never gets sick because she can stare down the onfliers before they light.' All knew disease was borne by winged creatures too tiny to be seen that hovered about the ill, looking for a new home.

'I wonder if Lord Gandulf will come down with his stories while onfliers plague the village,' fretted Mildburh. 'The children are counting on a tale from him.'

'The Normans don't believe in onfliers,' said Aldyth. 'They think that disease is a visitation from God as punishment for their sins or the result of breathing foul air.'

'Then everyone in Alcester should be dead by now,' cracked Mildburh.

People had gone back to their workaday lives, and the Alcestermen could no longer spare the time to make the walk to Enmore Green. The gatherings still attracted the hungry, although Gandulf's offerings grew leaner, for they were more likely to be missed once the feasting of the holidays was over. Most who came took their leave soon after the food was gone and, exhausted after a day behind the plow, crawled home to bed. Those who remained could not afford to be idle and brought their spinning or whittling.

Aldyth preferred the more intimate gatherings. Each night they convened at a different home, so that everyone in turn might sleep in a crowdwarmed house. At the heart of the little group were the folk nearest to blood kin that Aldyth had. And inevitably, there was Gandulf. Aldyth wondered how he had managed to worm his way into her innermost circle, but his transformation was magical to behold.

Gandulf had lived in the great city of Paris and had been

educated by the monks of Saint Denis. His readings, from the pinch-lipped writings of Saint Augustine to the raunchy comedies of Plautus, had been broadening, even if his lifestyle had not. In Lord Ralf's court, Gandulf had heard the stories, poems, and ballads of traveling minstrels and raconteurs. He had analyzed the tales as literature and intellectualized them as history and philosophy, but unconsciously he had also embraced them as distraction, comfort, and escape into a world where fools triumph and love reigns supreme.

Gandulf had always preferred solitude to society. Talk of war or hawking bored him, but he was not comfortable discussing anything closer to his heart. Yet without discussing politics, defending his religion, or baring his soul, he had somehow forged a bridge between himself and this simple company of illiterate Saxon peasants.

Gandulf's fables were requested night after night. Each evening it took one less twist of the arm to pry a story from him. One day he realized that he was actually looking forward to the storytelling. His days, spent at Lord Ralf's elbow learning his father's duties and routines, went more quickly as he prepared in his mind the stories he planned to share. When his hoard of fables was exhausted, Gandulf recited the 'Song of Roland' and other chansons de geste, epic poems of chivalry and heroics. At last he had something to say that others deemed worth listening to, even if they were only uncultured peasants. In fact, Gandulf decided, he preferred uncultured peasants.

As for those peasants, their stories warmed the cold, dark nights and made the winter tolerable. The ancient traditions strengthened their ties to the past, gave them hope for the future, and helped them understand their connection to the land and to one another. They listened to the same stories again and again, for they never grew stale; their stories told them who they were. Gandulf's tales were fresh: no substitute for their own, but an exciting peek into the world of chivalry and romance.

One night, after exhausting his repertoire of heroic tales and poetry, Gandulf came to the gathering with a cloth-wrapped bundle. The ragged peasants had opened their world to him, and now Gandulf shyly invited them to share the best of his world. They looked on in curious silence as he unwrapped a thick, yellowed book. Except for Father Edmund and Leofwine, Gandulf was the only one present who knew his letters. He apologized, telling his friends that he knew no more tales by heart, but if they were not averse, he could read to them from a book. Books, to those unschooled peasants, were for churchmen and kings. Except for the priest's Bible, they were as likely to run across a spiral-horned unicorn as a book. The quilled markings on the pages were no less mysterious to them than the carvings on the ancient stones of the Fairy Folk, and they prepared to witness something no less marvelous, the alchemy of words conjured up before their eyes.

'These are the legends of King Arthur,' Gandulf said. 'I brought them from France.'

'Yes,' said Sirona, 'but they traveled there from here, for they are the stories of my people, the ancient Welsh.'

''Tis why I chose them,' Gandulf told her. Reverently he unclasped the leather-bound book. ''Twill be a bit choppy, for I'll be translating from the Latin as I go.'

Fuel had grown so scarce that even the twists of straw used by the peasants for light had become hoarded and precious. So by the light of the tallow candle that Gandulf had brought, he began to read. He read until the dim hovel with filled with the echo of clashing swords and the glitter of courtly pageantry, until his listeners' hearts were filled with awe, until the candle flame guttered out and darkness closed in.

CHAPTER SIXTEEN

February 1087

Aldyth was up to her knees in mud, clearing out the ditch bordering her toft, when she saw Mildburh rushing across the green. Mildburh halted on the bridge crossing the ditch, but even after recovering her breath, she seemed hesitant to speak.

Aldyth, glad for an excuse to lay her shovel aside, jested, 'Don't tell me you came in such a hurry just to watch me sling mud.'

''Tis not your mud slinging that concerns me, Aldyth,' replied Mildburh heatedly. 'Where is Sirona? She should hear this, too.'

But Sirona was off reading omens. Lord Ralf, for reasons of his own, had forbidden the Norman priest to bring charges against Sirona in his court leet, so Father Odo had tried to convince the abbess to press charges of witchcraft against the wisewoman. When she pointed out that official Church doctrine did not recognize the actuality of witchcraft, the priest had insisted upon speaking to Father Fulk. But Father Fulk had referred him back to the abbess, reminding him that Dame Eulalia was the elected head of the abbey and he was merely its chaplain. Although Father Odo's mission had accomplished nothing, the abbess had been concerned enough about his meddling to mention it to Mother Rowena, who had sent directly for Sirona. The wisewoman had laughed it off, saying 'Odo will be too busy plotting his revenge upon Eulalia and Father Fulk to bother with me.' But Aldyth suspected that her godmother was more worried than she would admit, for once again their hens were growing fat as Sirona used their feeding habits to scry the future.

'Sirona's not here, Mildburh,' said Aldyth, 'but tell me, and I'll pass it on.'

Mildburh nodded. 'Aldyth, you must know what's being said. Swein Miller of Alcester told Eldred that Father Rannulf called you a whore before the whole congregation!'

'But, Mildburh!' stammered Aldyth. 'How can he say such a thing?'

'Everyone knows 'tis not true,' consoled Mildburh, 'but that never stopped an Alcester tongue from wagging.'

Aldyth sputtered helplessly, first in disbelief and then in outrage. 'What can I do?'

'Go to Father Edmund right away. Father Odo is looking for any excuse; I fear he'll strike at Sirona through you, even charge you with legerwite at the next court leet.'

'Well, if he does,' Aldyth growled, 'he'll have to pay me as well as Helga for slander!'

Aldyth threw down the shovel, climbed out of the ditch, and stormed down the hill toward Father Edmund's. Tears of fury and humiliation stung her eyes. Such ugly, mean-spirited rumors! It was no secret that since Christmas the villagers had been getting one decent meal a day, thanks to Gandulf, and that the Alcestermen assumed it was because Gandulf was keeping a woman in Enmore Green. But she would not be falsely accused!

Forgetting to knock, Aldyth burst into Father Edmund's hut wild-eyed, mud-spattered, and panting. The priest had been going over Leofwine's letters with him; the startled pair leapt up, and Leofwine dropped his wax tablet and stylus on the floor.

'Aldyth!' exclaimed the priest. 'Whatever is the matter?'

'Mildburh says that Eldred told her that Swein Miller said that Father Rannulf is calling me a whore!'

For an instant Father Edmund was at a loss for words. Then he said, 'Leofwine, perhaps we should continue our lesson after dinner.' When he had gone, Father Edmund led Aldyth gently by the elbow to a seat and gave her a mug of thin ale.

'How could he do it?' she fumed. 'I serve his village as faithfully as any other.'

Father Edmund knew that it was no coincidence that Father Rannulf had been sent by the bishop of Salisbury to replace the Saxon priest, Father Thurstan. One by one Saxons were being weeded out of the Church hierarchy. He wondered if the Norman priest were trying to force him into a conflict that the bishop would mediate; if so, the settlement was a foregone conclusion. But to Aldyth he said, ''Tis sour grapes, child; every village should have a patron like ours.' He went to Gregory's corner, picked up the saddle, and said before stepping out, 'Wait here and finish your ale, daughter, and I'll go to Alcester and put a stop to this slander.' Aldyth heard him calling the little donkey, but only a moment later he returned. 'He seems to have gone missing again,' Father Edmund apologized as he dropped the saddle by the door. 'I'll go afoot.'

Aldyth sat in the priest's hut with only his chickens for company and gulped down the ale simply to occupy her otherwise clenched fists. She slammed down the empty mug, sending chickens scattering to the far corners, and bitterly she thought of Gandulf. She could not ask him to stay away; he had become community property, and it was not for her to say. Besides, he had done nothing to encourage such rumors, and she was certain that she had not. Groaning, she put her head down on the table and thought dismally, 'Unless you count hungry looks and stolen glances, in which case we're both guilty.'

It was Margaret who pulled Gandulf aside. 'I thought it only fitting that you know . . .'

Gandulf's first reaction was concern for Aldyth's reputation, though he would gladly have paid any price for the rumors to be true. Next came annoyance, for he detested conflict and was irritated that he would have to demand a retraction and an apology.

That morning, even as Mildburh spoke to Aldyth, Gandulf was on his way to Alcester to call upon Father Rannulf. The baron's son had seemed a safe target, not only because he was reputed to be spineless and unlikely to retaliate but also because everyone knew that Gandulf's own father would be more likely to delight in his son's discomfort than to take up his case. Though surprised by Gandulf's visit, the sour-faced priest stood his ground, blustering that power and position did not place one above the commandments of God.

Gandulf replied coolly, 'I have not broken any commandments as yet, but if you continue to slander that innocent virgin in Enmore Green, I shall be more than willing to break the Sixth Commandment.'

The priest's face blanched. 'Thou shalt not kill?'

'That's the one,' said Gandulf.

But even if Father Rannulf left off his pompous preaching, people would talk. For Aldyth's sake, Gandulf resigned himself to forgoing the gatherings. Then he weakened. 'As I already have prepared my story,' he rationalized, 'I'll go one last time.'

The Miller's house, down by the millpond, was a favorite place to meet as those attending need not bring their own stools, for Mildburh always brought over the benches from the mill. Gandulf arrived with a sack of bread and cheese over his shoulder and a book under his arm. His welcome was warm but muted. Father Edmund had one godson in his lap and another playing at his feet, and Agilbert's lap was occupied by his pig. Edith and Wulfric, Edwin and Mildred were seated on benches, while Leofwine Clerk knelt to coax more heat from the fire. Sirona sat beside Aldyth, her hand resting lightly on the girl's. With a wistful grin, Aelfric kicked an empty stool in invitation to Gandulf.

'They all know this is good-bye,' thought Gandulf glumly. Handing his sack to Mildburh, he sat down. Huddled about the hearth, they broke bread with none of the usual banter or playful teasing of Gandulf about his Norman accent and shabby cloak.

Sirona asked, 'My Lord, would you think it forward of me to scry your future?'

'That's never stopped you from having your way before, Sirona,' said Gandulf dryly.

'You take your medicine with a good will, lad. Give me your hand.'

She took his outstretched hand, but it was into his eyes the seeress peered, not at his palm. Placing her free hand over his heart, she said, 'I sense a burden here. You feel you must bear it alone, for it is your wish to spare your friends.'

''Tis God's truth,' he said. 'You have all heard the gossip. I only came tonight to bid you farewell.' Dejectedly he added, 'I will miss you.'

''Twould be for the best,' concurred Sirona, 'but no one could find fault were you to stop by and pay your respects to Father Edmund or consult an old healer now and again.'

'Don't trouble yourself about the rumors, my son,' added Father Edmund. 'I spoke to Father Rannulf today; he was quite agreeable when I suggested he temper his sermons.'

Gandulf smiled thinly and thanked the good priest for his efforts.

'You have shortened many a long, cold night with your tales,' Sirona told him.

'And it wasn't just the tales,' added Wulfric. ''Twas the company as well.'

'Yes,' said Edwin with a chuckle, 'Wulfric will miss having a new butt for all his old pranks.'

Leofwine rose and, with solemn dignity, knelt before Gandulf to place his hands between the Norman's. 'My Lord Gandulf,' he said quietly, 'I am your man.'

Gandulf stared down at the boy. Moved beyond words, he raised him to his feet. When he found his voice, he said gravely, 'I shall try to live up to the honor you pay me.'

'I think,' said Father Edmund, 'I speak for everyone when I say that you have earned our gratitude and our respect. In our hearts, we are all your men, my Lord.'

No one knew how to move past the gravity of the moment until Sirona asked, 'Will you bestow upon us one last tale that we can hold in our hearts to remember this night by?'

Gandulf nodded. With a brand from the fire he lit the candle he had brought and opened his book. He stared blankly at its yellowed pages, then abruptly blew out the candle and closed the book. 'I thought to read to you from the *Iliad*,' he explained, 'but another story comes to mind.' Gazing into the embers, he began, 'Hearken to me, good men, wives, and maidens, and I will tell you a tale of times long past . . .' So opened the tale of Tristan and Iseult. Tristan was born of true but forbidden love. His very name meant sorrow, for upon his birth his mother had died of grief at the loss of his father, lately fallen in battle. Fate carried the lad home to his people, though he deemed himself at his homecoming a stranger in a strange land. Against his will, he fell in love with Iseult, the daughter of his most hated foe and a woman destined for another. Theirs was a timeless story of doomed passion and star-crossed love. At the end, when the two lovers lay dead in their tombs, ivy was planted over Tristan's grave and a rose tree over Iseult's. 'And so,' concluded Gandulf quietly, 'even in death, the two reached out to each other and wove branch and root so closely that no man thereafter might separate them.'

When Gandulf looked up from the fire, it was like waking from a dream. He was touched to see hardly a dry eye amongst the gathering; even the children were caught in the web of words he had woven. But the tears streamed down Aldyth's cheeks unchecked.

Gandulf continued to send food whenever he could, but it came by messenger. The gatherings continued on for a while, but a pall had been cast over them. The days lengthened, the work of the fields became more demanding, and one cold night near the end of February, the tight-knit group acknowledged that it was time to go back to their own hearth fires. As they dispersed, each family making its way to its own dark hut, the healers heard the crunch of footsteps from behind. They looked back to see Eafa Atwood, wrapped in a shawl against the cutting wind. Aldyth wondered how long she had been standing in the snow watching the flicker of firelight through the cracks in the walls.

'May I speak with you, please?' she asked them.

'Of course, daughter,' said the wisewoman. 'Come home with us and warm yourself.'

Eafa, a solitary soul, had never come to them before. Her father had died at Hastings, and her mother had died three years before, leaving Eafa, her only child, the toft at the edge of the woods. Eafa was Aldyth's age, past her first bloom, but uncommonly handsome, with flaming red hair. Several men had been fascinated by her unusual beauty and challenged by her solitary nature, but Eafa had kept her maidenhead.

Once Sirona had her settled by the fire, Eafa told them, 'I always thought myself so sensible. I was waiting for what I wanted, and what I thought I wanted was Osgot.'

Osgot was the only son of a widow living on the same toft in Alcester, he managing the croft for her. Osgot had two cows and good business sense. His mother also owned two cows and kept chickens. Osgot was a devoted son, and Eafa thought he would also be a good father, but she would have felt better had he taken her home to meet his mother.

'We decided to marry, but Osgot wanted to break it to his mother gently, for she'd a jealous heart. So we pledged our troth and celebrated a handfast marriage in secret.'

'Then you are already husband and wife,' observed Sirona.

'So I thought,' said Eafa bitterly. 'But last month, when I told Osgot I was with child, he said he couldn't support a wife and a baby and urged me to put a stop to it.'

'He wanted you to use an abortifacient?' asked Aldyth in amazement.

'I refused, of course. I thought he needed only time to grow used to the idea, but he stayed away. When Osgot came last night, I thought all would be well. But he berated me for disregarding his wishes and said that as he and I were the only two witnesses to our marriage, no one could prove that we had ever been wed. I don't know what to do; I will be showing soon.' Eafa closed her eyes and said softly, 'I have shamed myself.'

'Not for conceiving a child in love,' said Aldyth firmly.

'Perhaps not, but for allowing myself to be so easily deceived!' came Eafa's hot reply.

'Tell us what we can do,' said Sirona. 'Do you need public acknowledgment from the man? Do you want to keep the child? Do you want us to find it a good home?'

Eafa rubbed her eyes with the heels of her hands. 'I don't know,' she said wearily, crossing her arms on the table and burying her face in them. 'Osgot will never acknowledge the marriage. He is well connected, and I am an orphan; 'twill be his word again mine.' Looking up, Eafa said, 'Of only one thing am I certain; I want to keep the child.'

'Fear not,' said Sirona. 'Father Edmund will facilitate the matter at Saint Wulfstan's.'

'Trial by ordeal?' asked Eafa, quavering.

'Justice will be served,' said the old woman grimly. 'Aldyth, see Eafa home. I will speak to Father Edmund. 'Tis late, but he will still be warming his feet by the fire.'

When Aldyth returned, the fire was banked and Sirona snug in bed. As Aldyth spread her cloak over their pallet and crawled in, Sirona told her, ''Tis all set for next Sunday.'

'I'm sure Eafa is telling the truth,' said Aldyth. 'Edward Forester, the cowherd from Long Cross, and Osgot were both courting her. Then it was just Osgot. He married her to rid himself of the competition. If he had never intended to honor those vows, Eafa was an excellent choice. She keeps to herself, lives far from the prying eyes of gossips, and would be unlikely to speak out against him publicly or make an appeal at the court leet.'

'She'll find that an appeal to us serves her better,' said her godmother dryly.

The sound of Sirona's steady breathing and the muffled cluck of a dreaming chicken acted as a backdrop for Aldyth's thoughts. She missed Godiva's homey snuffling. They had run out of fodder and had fed the poor starving beast all the thatch from the roof they could spare. Unable to bring herself to slaughter the little cow, Sirona had blessed her and set her free to fend for herself through the last lean months of winter.

As Aldyth pondered Eafa's plight, a disturbing thought occurred to her: Was Bedwyn any different from Osgot? He had taken his pleasure with many a maid, and surely more than one dandled a fatherless blue-eyed child on her knee. At least, Aldyth conceded, Bedwyn made no promises that he did not intend to honor, and, as far as Aldyth knew, he had never promised marriage to any woman. 'Then why are they so willing to fall into his arms?' she wondered. But she already knew the answer to that question.

The next week there was another trial of interest to everyone in Lord Ralf's demesne, and to the archbishop of Salisbury as well. At the year's second court leet, Helga and Garth had gone with Sirona to settle their case against Father Odo. As foreseen, Margaret alone had been willing to testify for Helga, but Gandulf could not have his accomplice's activities scrutinized too closely; she was the one who saved table scraps, stretched the handouts, and covered Gandulf's tracks so that food stores traveling down the hill were not missed. So Gandulf was there too, prepared to speak out for Helga in Margaret's stead.

Those present expected to see the plaintiffs forced to defend themselves against a countercharge of false suit. But Father Odo had sent his essoin, an excuse for nonattendance in court, and had been granted a delay of one session of the court leet. Everyone went home both relieved and disappointed. According to the law, Father Odo was allowed two further essoins and could absent himself a total of eight times altogether by using various excuses and legal ploys. In the meantime, the priest had seen that Garth would not be hired at the quarry or be granted license to gather building materials in Lord Ralf's woods. By one means or another, Father Odo could delay the trial for as long as six months, and by that time a peasant like Garth, who lived from hand to mouth, would be a ruined man – unless he had a patron or patroness. Therefore the Norman priest was infuriated to learn that Father Edmund had arranged with Abbess Eulalia for Garth to work in the abbey stews and be paid with building materials from the abbey's woodlands. In so doing, Father Edmund had moved himself to the top of Father Odo's list of enemies, just behind Sirona; nor had the abbess done herself any political favor.

The following Sunday Osgot was summoned to Saint Wulfstan's to answer the charges put against him. After mass, Father Edmund invited people to witness the ordeal by which

God would judge the dispute. Not a soul left the church, all choosing to brave the chill for the sake of the spectacle and to support a fellow villager. Osgot stood by his mother, who had come to look upon the slut who would steal him from her. A lifetime of habit had molded the old woman's features into a perpetual frown, which she directed at Eafa.

'She's lying,' Osgot announced. 'No one can bear witness that I ever touched her.'

'God will bear witness,' said Father Edmund. 'The candles will decide this matter.'

Trial by candle flame was not an uncommon means of rendering judgment, and it was much tidier and more congenial than ordeal by hot iron or cold water. Two candles were set side by side upon the altar and lit simultaneously by the two disputants, then left to burn. The first candle flame to flicker out would be that of the guilty party.

Both Eafa and Osgot stood in stiff silence, while below people speculated on the outcome or caught up on gossip. Eafa, watching her candle, moved her lips in silent prayer, but Osgot stared defiantly at any who dared meet his eye.

A baby cried, and its mother gave it her breast to quiet it. Wondering if it was a sign from God, people watched the young mother, and the sound of the baby's sucking filled the church. On the hill, the abbey bells tolled the passing of time. At last the mother gave her baby a gentle thumping on the back; its eyes widened with the force of its belch, then closed in sleepy satisfaction. All other eyes shifted back to the candles. A gasp rose up, for while Eafa's candle burned brightly, Osgot's was little more than a puddle of melted wax. It flared to a great height, spat noisily, and then guttered out. God had spoken.

'The judgment has gone against you, my son,' said Father Edmund. 'You must acknowledge the marriage or pay the usual forfeit of three cows, whichever she chooses.'

Osgot turned to Eafa. ''Twas my mother's fault, Eafa,' he pleaded. 'She threatened to disinherit me if I acknowledge you. Let's forgive and forget; we'll start over.'

'I'll have the cows,' Eafa said flatly. 'They'll be more faithful friends to me.'

'I have only two cows,' Ósgot complained. 'I'd have to sell everything to buy a third.'

'Tell that to your mother,' said Eafa coldly, stalking out of the church.

Aldyth sighed as she watched Eafa walk alone down the path. 'She'll have a hard time of it,' she said to Sirona, 'but with three cows she'll have milk and cheese, and maybe even some calves in the spring. It has all worked out for the best.'

'Of course it has,' said Sirona with a smug smile. 'I provided the candles.'

That night the dreams began. They started simply with the sound of dripping water, the smell of damp, stale earth. Then Aldyth was drowning, choking, groping for a handhold in that chill, fetid darkness. Her throat muscles constricted in panic when she heard a voice screaming out, and then she realized it was her own.

CHAPTER SEVENTEEN

March 1087

Half the hall awoke in a start. Soldiers went tumbling for their weapons, and pages, still half asleep, peered across the dimly lit hall with their blankets clutched to their chins. Gandulf too sat up, drenched in a cold sweat and squinting into the darkness with the rest of them. It took a moment for the fact to penetrate that it had been he who had screamed aloud and awakened not only himself but half the garrison with his bloodcurdling cry. With this humiliating realization, he discreetly settled back onto his pallet, pulled his blanket over his head, and feigned the sound sleep that always seemed to escape him. At last he drifted back into a restless doze.

He woke to find people stepping over him, some still discussing the night's alarm, trying to name the culprit or interpret the omen. He had slept late, as always when he had the nightmare. Each time was worse than the one before; as far as he knew, this was the first time he had cried out. He prayed it would be the last; life was hard enough without the mockery he would face should anyone discover who the midnight banshee was. This nightmare was worse than the hungry dreams he had been plagued with all winter; at least he understood those. He could not discuss the dreams, not even with his mother; how could he describe the terror, the moldering darkness, being unable to move or even breathe?

He went to the pantry to wash. William CloseFist, breaking his fast beside the fire, was engaged in an animated discussion with Father Odo. 'I figure,' said William, 'that the best beast would be that randy old ram who seems to sire all the lambs in that flock.'

Gandulf's attention was caught; this could only mean a death tax.

'Isn't he past his prime?' asked Father Odo. 'You'd better take a younger beast.'

'I've been trying to buy that ram from Grimbald for years, but now, by God, I shall have it!' crowed William triumphantly.

It had to be Grimbald Shepherd of Enmore Green. Gandulf had liked the old man with his Fairy wife and his faithful dog. Some weeks before, during lambing season, Gandulf had ridden by the lambing pen. The lambing shed was only a thatched roof and a back wall partitioned into birthing pens, each occupied by a swollen-bellied ewe or a contented mother and nursing lamb. Gandulf had watched Grimbald at his work and felt impelled by common courtesy to speak with him. Rather, to speak *at* him, for pulling words out of the old man was like rooting up the stumps of freshly felled trees, yet Grimbald's goodwill had been apparent. Gandulf had marvelled at the old man's tenderness toward the lambs; it could not have been greater had they been children. But he treated his dog, Baldwin, as if he were his firstborn. The dog understood what his master wanted of him and carried out his commands before the shepherd could put them into words. Though the little black dog's muzzle was silver with age and his gait was stiff, he worked as much for the joy of it as to show his devotion to his friend and master.

Grimbald had shared his meal of coarse brown bread, and Gandulf had provided the wine. It was satisfying to the Norman to be able to share silence companionably, rather than stiffly, with his usual discomfort. As they passed the wineskin back and forth, they sat on the height of the downs looking across the vale at Scafton. The abbey's church spire rose up in the distance from the wintry morning mist. The dog, as silent as his master, kept the sheep bunched using only gentle nudges to guide the flighty beasts.

Then Grimbald pointed to the big ram. 'I don't even have to tell you about this one; everyone knows ShakeTail. He's the one William CloseFist has his eye on, for he's fathered half the lambs in the vale. And that little ewe,' he said, 'is HedgeHopper. She's mine or she'd have been in the stew pot long ago, for there's not a hedge in the Blackmore Vale she hasn't breached, and she always takes a few of the others with her.' Pointing to another ewe, he said, 'That is Modron, the Little Mother. She gives me twins every year, and most of them have twins too.' After a pause, he concluded, ''Tis a good flock.'

The old man was done talking; the two of them sat and watched his charges foraging through the shallow crust of windblown snow. Footsteps crunching in the snow drew their attention; it was Lufe Piper and his dog. The dog growled at Gandulf, who had only to look at Lufe to know that it was merely giving voice to his master's feelings of ill will.

'Aethling, stay,' said Grimbald sharply. For a moment, Gandulf thought Grimbald was addressing him, until the old shepherd said, 'The dog is young and knows not his friends.' The remark was as much a rebuke to his grandson as an apology to Gandulf. But Gandulf, embarrassed and uncomfortable, made his excuses and took his leave.

Now the old man was dead, and it seemed important to Gandulf to pay his respects. He rode to the home of Edwina LongBraid, Grimbald Shepherd's daughter-in-law, to offer condolences. He took food – a smoke ham and a wheel of cheese – as was the custom at a wake, for friends would be calling and they would need to be fed. He was warmly greeted at Edwina's door by Mildburh, who relieved him of his gifts and ushered him through the mob of mourners. He nodded to Eldred and dodged the grasping hand of Big Edmund, perched on his father's shoulder. The MoonCatchers were all there. Gandulf saw Wulfric, his wife's comforting arm around his shoulders. At first he was surprised to see him so affected, until he realized that a few of the tears Wulfric shed must be for his mother. Gandulf could not imagine life without his own mother. He had never truly loved anyone but her until now. 'How pathetic a creature I am,' he thought with detached contempt. He knew too that there would be very few attending his own wake but for the funeral feast, and there were very few wakes he would attend but for his own sense of duty. Or at least that had been so until Aldyth had drawn him into her circle. 'God bless her!' he thought fervently, looking around the room at all his friends.

He felt a wave of rosemary-scented warmth and turned to see Aldyth herself, surrounded by a ring of youngsters. Like Baldwin, she kept them bunched with gentle looks and tender pats. When their eyes met, Gandulf's throat went dry. He had not seen her for a month, but he knew at once he had deluded himself into believing his interest had waned.

Edwina's red-rimmed eyes widened in surprise at seeing him. Gandulf longed to tell Edwina how much his visit with Grimbald had meant to him and how it grieved him that there could be no more. But his cheeks grow hot under Lufe's hostile stare. Instead, Gandulf bowed stiffly and said, 'My condolences, Edwina.'

'Thank you, my Lord,' she murmured, sniffing and blotting her eyes with her apron. Edwina had lost her plump curves, and her skin was the sallow yellow of one recovering from the winter fever. She led Gandulf to where Grimbald was laid out on four benches. Even cleaned up and in his Sunday best, Grimbald looked out of place indoors. The tuft of wool clutched in his hand would at once identify him to Saint Peter, explaining his absence from church, for a shepherd must say his prayers on the downs. That was where Gandulf preferred to remember him, with the blush of the wind upon his leathery cheeks, silvery hair ruffled by the breeze, and beads of dew glittering on the shoulders of his cloak.

Softly whining beneath the benches, Baldwin dejectedly rested his head on his front paws. 'Poor fellow; you're lost here, aren't you?' asked Gandulf. He let the dog sniff his hand before scratching his ears. The dog's tail thumped weakly on the floor, for Baldwin recognized Gandulf as his master's friend. 'What will become of him?' Gandulf asked Edwina.

'He'll live with me, though God knows how I'll manage to feed him. He's too old to work, and in any case they usually pine away once their masters are gone.' Gandulf promised himself that though Baldwin might die of a broken heart, he would not starve.

Father Edmund took the lordling's hands. 'We've missed you, my son.'

'And I have missed you all, Father,' said Gandulf.

''Tis close in here, and many wait outside to pay respects. Might I impose upon you?'

'If there is anything I can do . . .' said Gandulf.

The priest smiled warmly. 'Mayhap a story or two . . . ?'

Gandulf was ushered to Father Edmund's house and seated on a stool in the corner vacated by Gregory, the priest's donkey. It was a somber crowd, for they had all lost a grandfather, a friend, or a neighbor. They sat expectant, if subdued, but pleased to see Gandulf.

'By Saint Denis,' thought Gandulf, 'I'm glad I came.'

He looked on fondly as Father Edmund greeted guests with a heartiness that warmed the house. Leofwine arrived first with a swarm of siblings, followed by the Millers. Helga gazed up adoringly at Gandulf, Wulfric and Edith stood along the back wall, and Agilbert seated himself on a bench, Little Edmund on his knee, while Bertha, less inclined to sit and listen, squirmed between his feet. One of the last to come was Aelfric, still chewing a crust from the funeral feast, a sad occasion but a free meal. Gandulf was about to begin when the door creaked open. Would it be Aldyth?

Edwin MoonCatcher sidled in, asking sheepishly, 'Have I missed anything?'

Trying not to look deflated, Gandulf welcomed the old man and began, 'If I had known I was to be telling stories, I would have come better prepared.'

'We want stories, not apologies!' called Wulfric.

'Quite right,' conceded Gandulf.

He swept the room with a steady gaze, meeting each eye. Many of the faces were red-eyed and drawn with grief, but every one was burdened with some unspoken need or want to be met. Liked a peddler laying out his wares on a blanket, the storyteller served up a world removed from sorrow and farther still from the drudgery of that stark winter.

'Long ago and far away . . .'

How could the day have brought such mixed pain and pleasure? Gandulf could not face his father's cold hall, so he paid a visit to his mother. Even she could not soothe his sorrow or ease his restlessness. In the parlor, Sister Emma watched her son pace across the room. 'Gandulf, please sit down; it makes me dizzy just to watch you.'

'I'm sorry, Mother,' he said, sitting beside her. But almost immediately he was up again and pacing.

'You seem so agitated, Son,' said Sister Emma. 'Is it spring fever? Perhaps you need a purge or a change of scene?' She hesitated, then ventured, 'The abbess has given me permission to go on pilgrimage in June, Gandulf. 'Tis to fulfill a vow to Saint Austin, my patron saint. I was wondering if you'd like to accompany me.'

'What vow?'

She smiled shyly. 'When they took you away, I never thought to see you again. I promised God that I would go to Saint Austin in Canterbury if He brought you back to me. This has been the happiest year of my life, and 'tis time to show God my gratitude.'

Touched, Gandulf took her hands and kissed her cheek. 'Of course I'll come.'

'Gandulf,' she said, suddenly fearful, 'look at the circles under your eyes. Are you ill? Or mistreated? Something is wrong, I can tell.'

''Tis nothing, Mother,' he said, his eyes dodging her scrutiny.

'Is it the marriage negotiations?'

'What are you talking about?' he asked sharply. 'Whose marriage negotiations?'

'Yours, of course. Surely Ralf has discussed this with you? The negotiations have apparently been going on for some time, although I have only just heard of them myself.'

'No, I'd heard nothing. I would certainly have mentioned it. Where did you hear this?'

'Sister Agnes's niece Catherine de Broadford sent her aunt a letter to ask if she knew of a Gandulf fitzGerald hereabouts. She is heiress to a great estate near Ralf's holdings in Normandy, and she says her parents are negotiating with Ralf for her betrothal. Sister Agatha asked me what I knew of it, which was, of course, nothing.'

'Oh, God!' moaned Gandulf. He sat down heavily and groaned, 'I suppose I should have expected it, but I would have thought he'd at least make mention of it.'

'Gandulf, you're twenty-seven years old; 'tis high time you considered marriage. Your father was in the midst of negotiations for you to be wed when he sent you off to Paris, but that put an end to that, of course. You might have been fifteen years wed by now.'

'Perhaps,' growled her son dubiously, 'but it couldn't have come at a worse time.'

'What do you mean?' she asked apprehensively.

'Oh, nothing,' came his impatient reply.

'If you could explain, I might be of some help, Son.'

'Mother, you wouldn't know a thing about it,' he said in exasperation. Shamed by her hangdog look, he added dispiritedly, ''Tis a girl. But 'tis hopeless. She is Saxon and a peasant as well, and the maiden would care for the pairing even less than Father.'

'A Saxon?' asked his mother, more intrigued than shocked. 'Tell me about it.'

Relieved to have made the admission aloud, he blurted, 'She holds my heart in her hands, and I cannot get it back. If I can't have her, I want no other. How can I explain?'

'I know a little something of love,' said Sister Emma softly, taking his hand.

Gandulf shot her a puzzled look.

'Oh, not Ralf,' she said quickly. ''Twas before your time, dearest. But, yes, even I have loved after a fashion. Come, tell me about this girl of yours.'

'That's just it, Mother. She's not mine and could never be. She tolerates my presence, and I burn. But I'd rather have no one than some dull creature I care nothing for. And no girl raised in Normandy would want a man like me.'

'Have you told this Saxon peasant girl how you feel?'

'Of course not! I've made a fool enough of myself. Were I to declare myself, she might refuse to see me at all.'

'You and I are too much alike in many way . . .'

Gandulf opened his mouth to speak, but she placed a finger over his lips. 'No, Son, I'd not change a thing about you. You are a man of peace and learning, raised in a court of imbeciles who glory in killing, and you have suffered for it. If only I could have protected you; alas, you have learned too well to protect yourself. You try to shut out the pain, but love *is* pain. Without it you can feel no joy, and that is a walking death. Even I, who would seem to have so little, find comfort in the love I once knew. 'Tis all I have to cling to besides you, my sweet. And, of course,' she sighed, 'I still have my honor.'

'Is that so small a thing?' he began.

'Gandulf,' she insisted, 'hear me out. I have no earthly goods to leave you, and as for wisdom, very little. But if I have learned one thing, it is that honor and duty are shallow substitutes for love. Gather what shreds of happiness you can, that they might sustain you through this unfortunate marriage. Go to your girl and tell her what you have told me. If she cannot love you for who you are, she is not worthy of you. If she can love you for all your gentle nature, then together you must do what you can to wring a little happiness out of this life while you may.'

'I can't, Mother. I just can't.' The agony of his frustration and despair was so intense that it seemed to darken the room.

CHAPTER EIGHTEEN

April 1087

At Edwina LongBraid's toft, Gandulf reined in Cathedra and whistled. A silver muzzle poked through the branches of the hedge, and Baldwin eagerly scrambled across the ditch. 'Ready for a run, lad?' said Gandulf, turning his horse toward the open fields. But as he rode past the mill, Mildburh Miller waved him over. Gandulf enjoyed talking to her; she always told him everything he wanted to know without his ever having to ask.

'So you and Baldwin are off,' she said cheerfully. ''Tis a good service you do, for when he's not in the fields with you, he is driving the chickens and herding the children.'

Gandulf laughed. 'He wasn't ready to hang up his crook.'

'He returns from your runs with more wag in his tail. But he misses his master.'

'As do we all,' agreed Gandulf.

'I suppose you've heard that Lufe is paying court to Christine now. She's young, but Lufe says he's willing to wait,' explained Mildburh. 'A shepherd is no small catch for a girl of Christine's prospects. And now that Lufe's grandfather is gone, 'tis a solitary life in the hills. Loneliness nips at his heels and drives him down to her door.'

Gandulf nodded, and she continued, 'I suppose it won't be long before young Leofwine Clerk will be going courting. He's filling out to be a sturdy lad and a good prospect.'

Gandulf was pleased, for he had a personal interest in Leofwine. Once Father Edmund had taught him all that he knew, Gandulf had stepped in to assist in his further education.

Agilbert happened by, hoe in one hand, his son in the other, and Bertha trotting along behind. The lordling called out a greeting. '"The whole family is off to the fields?'

'Aye, my Lord, late as usual. Now that Little Edmund has gruel, feeding and cleaning him take longer, and Bertha never was a quick starter. She watches him when I work, but I liked it better when she could hold a hoe,' he admitted. Baldwin sniffed at Bertha, who squealed indignantly and retreated to safety between Agilbert's feet. 'Poor old Baldwin is confused,' said Agilbert. 'He keeps trying to round Bertha up with the pigs.'

When he had gone, Mildburh said, 'Have you heard the latest about Osgot and Eafa?'

'I heard that she chose the three cows over him.'

'Well, no one would argue with the girl's choice, but it looks doubtful that she'll get the cows either. Osgot has two cows but won't deliver the first two until he has the third and says he cannot get the third without selling property to his detriment.'

'Can he not get the cow from his mother?'

'The old biddy says she didn't get the girl pregnant, so she shouldn't have to pay her off. They're waiting to take it to the next court leet, hoping all the while that Eafa will not press suit for fear of calling Father Odo's attention to her case.'

'Perhaps it need not come to that,' said Gandulf, frowning. 'I'll ride home through Alcester today and pay Osgot and his mother a visit.'

Mildburh nodded approvingly. 'Speaking of Father Odo, 'tis a scandal the way he has treated Helga! 'Tis three court leets he's dodged his summons, and now they say at the abbey he's trying to trump up some charge against Sirona.'

'Sirona can take care of herself,' Gandulf replied, then paused. 'How is . . . Sirona?'

'As full of piss and vinegar as ever, but Aldyth . . .' replied Mildburh. 'That's a different story; she's still plagued by those terrible nightmares.'

Gandulf's heart jumped. 'Nightmares? What nightmares?'

'Aldyth isn't one for talking, but Edith, whose house is one toft over, tells me she sometimes hears Aldyth cry out at night.'

'What does Sirona say?' asked Gandulf, trying to disguise his alarm.

'She says only that Aldyth must deal with this herself.'

'That seems cold of her,' said Gandulf in dismay. 'Is there nothing Sirona can do?'

Mildburh shrugged and Gandulf bade her good day; he had to be alone with his thoughts. Nightmares! If Aldyth would not talk to her best friend, Gandulf knew that she certainly would not confide in him. But he understood the terror she must feel, for he too was haunted by his own dreadful nightmares. He was used to coping with problems alone and in silence, but somehow it seemed wrong that Aldyth should have to face such horror on her own. Deep down Gandulf felt that he was to blame. Could it be that his own nightmares were so powerful that they had forced their way into her dreams?

Aldyth spied Gandulf riding down the lane with Baldwin at his horse's heels and ducked into the shadow of the hedge. She wondered at the ferocity of his frown without realizing the intensity of her own expression. Was he angry, worried, in pain? He was still as unreadable as ever. Her thoughts followed Gandulf even as he disappeared from sight. For the last two Sundays, he had been coming to Father Edmund's after church to tell stories. The first week, Aldyth had sat spinning on a bench outside her door when Edith had hastened by to fetch her to the impromptu gathering.

'Aldyth,' she had said, 'the aethling is at Father Edmund's. He has brought a feast and has promised us a tale as well. If you hurry, you will still find a seat.'

'You go on,' Aldyth had stammered. 'I need to gather my spinning.'

Aldyth's fingers shook so that the distaff slipped from her grasp and rolled under the bench. When Aldyth knelt to retrieve it, she found she was shaking all over. She knew then that she would not be going to that gathering, nor to any other that Gandulf attended.

The following Sunday, while Gandulf gathered Aldyth's friends and neighbors about him, she went alone to gather herbs in the hills. She walked past Melbury Abbas and up Zig-Zag Hill to the old ridgeway, the hilltop highway used in ancient times by the small dark people. Aldyth could look back to Sceapterbyrig, halfway to Sarum, and, as it was a clear day, she could even see the silver shimmer of sunlight reflected by the distant sea.

Between landmarks were the ridges, like the bony spines of winter-starved cattle, their grassy covering stretched thin like a winter-worn hide, lying shoulder deep in the verdant forests of the chase. Beneath the canopy of leaves, the vale teemed with life, swarming and unceasing. Even now, some fox was pouncing upon a hare, a poacher's arrow was being loosed, and the king's foresters were tracking a weary outlaw. She knew that the daffodils stood high amid the tangle of last year's grass and the hedgerows were alive with robins building their nests, laying their eggs, and feeding their tiny hatchlings.

She felt removed from it all, released from the struggles of the everyday world. So high above all human habitation, unlikely to meet even a wandering shepherd, and beckoned by distant prospects, for the first time in her life she understood the compulsion to follow the road to the horizon; it must have been that feeling that made folk think the ridgeways were enchanted, uncanny, even haunted. With no conscious decision, she set off and walked until her feet were blistered, until rumbles of hunger called out from her stomach and died away unheeded. Not until the tolling of curfew, barely audible in the distance, like the tolling of a Fairy bell from the bottom of a lake, did she realize how far she had walked. The spell was broken; the bells were calling her home.

It was near dawn when she stumbled back into Enmore Green. Chilled, hungry, and drained, she crawled into bed. Sirona pulled her into her arms, saying only, 'The distance you would keep cannot be attained on two or even four legs, child,' and Aldyth fell into an exhausted sleep on her godmother's bosom. A week passed, and she dared not return to the ridgeway, for she did not trust her strength to resist its call. She had responded too fervently to the sense of freedom she had felt on the road that stretched out to eternity. But she knew that Sirona spoke truly: a thought can travel any distance in the space of a heartbeat, and she could not keep her thoughts free of him. Yet somehow it was easier to harden her heart against Gandulf when he was not near.

Aldyth looked down the hedge-lined path that Gandulf and Baldwin had just taken. 'My life is as narrow and confined as these little lanes,' she thought bitterly. 'He can go wherever he pleases, yet he comes down here to rob me of my only solace, my friends.'

In her dejection, she focused on the ground. Tiny shoots of green grew up between close-cropped roots of brown. Those who had survived the harsh winter could live on fresh shoots until the early crops came in. Black lovage had been collected as soon as it sprouted, the long stems cut up for soups. Children ran home waving spring-tender burdock stalks, fresh wood mallow shoots, and cucumber-flavored lungwort. Winifred LongCross had spoken for them all when she had said, 'Praise the Lady we need not eat any more stewed sorrel. It got me through the winter but made me piss like a fountain.'

'Only think of Godiva,' Aldyth told herself. Sirona had turned the little cow loose to live off the land or die. But yesterday her pet had wandered home, followed by a small red calf. Then there was the tooth, a small ivory shoot sprung up from Little Edmund's lower gum. His father's joy at his son's clever accomplishment was heartening; the spring thaw had begun to melt the chill of Agilbert's spirit, and he had reestablished his own roots in the land of the living. Even Edith was pregnant again. Spring fever was upon them all. Children hid from their mothers, who sought to dose them with bitter tansy brewed to purge the winter out of their blood. The day before, Aldyth had seen Gandulf carrying a fugitive child on the saddle before him as they sought refuge in the outlying hills.

The hills. How Aldyth longed to have someone sweep her away into the hills! Bedwyn had come only once since his midnight visit in January, expressly to warn them that the two men who had followed Gorm to the fountain last autumn had returned. Bedwyn thought it no coincidence that the head of one of the Weaver twins was rotting on a spike over Ludgate in London, and he feared the other twin had cracked, for how else could they have found the hide north of Sarum? After the smoke had cleared, one of its guides, Edwin LongStaff, was dead. Worse yet, Edwin's cousin and accomplice, Ine Thatcher, had been taken alive; the remaining Weaver twin would soon have company in the tower. Each broken link brought the hunt closer to home, and the closer to home the hunt came, the greater was their danger. Bedwyn had not even stayed to break bread on his way through that night; he was off to repair the link. With a distracted peck on Aldyth's cheek, he had left with nothing more than a promise to keep them informed and a stern reiterance of his warning to guide no one along the Path without first coming for him.

But he had not kept them informed, thought Aldyth as she crossed the green. She still had not heard whether Bedwyn had reached Sarum that night or been able to patch the broken link. Most important, she yearned for reassurance that he had survived his mission. Did he not think she would want to know? She wondered sadly if Bedwyn had meant none of the sweet things he had said to her last Christmas, or if he had tired of playing a game in which there could be no winning and no prize. She set down her pitcher and sat wearily beneath the Wishing Tree. It was still bare, except for a few winter-faded rags tied to its branches. She was leaning against the trunk of the tree, trying to warm herself in the thin April sun, when Aelfric approached with his usual jaunty swagger. His tone as he spoke, though, was studiedly natural.

'I found some acorns in the woods that the pigs seem to have missed,' he said.

Instantly alert, Aldyth answered with the same casual air as she rose and filled her pitcher at the fountain. 'Will I need my basket, Aelfric?'

'I would guess so, for there's a good lot of them.'

'What's going on?' she whispered as they walked across the green toward her toft.

'A friend of yours is waiting at the church. I think she's hurt.'

'Is Father Edmund there?'

'No,' replied the boy. 'He went up to the abbey to find work for Thurgood.'

Aldyth frowned. 'Where's Sirona?'

'In the field with Alcuin. He's helping her with the plowing. Shall I fetch her?'

'No,' said Aldyth quickly, 'I'll see to it.'

She stocked her basket with food, clean bandages, and a skin of fresh springwater, then walked toward Saint Wulfstan's. For appearances' sake, she scooped an armload of daffodils out of a hedgerow bursting with bloom. She spread them over Bertha's grave and entered the church. It was dark as a cave but for the flickering of the votive candles in the chapel. In the stone-dark gloom, a figure peered around the altar. When Aldyth approached and knelt by the crouching shadow, she heard a sigh of relief. A woman in a ragged cloak drew back her hood to reveal a haggard face and said, 'Aldyth Lightfoot!'

'Ricole!'

Ricole was keeper of the hide immediately north of Bedwyn's and just south of the Sarum hide that had been raided. It was thought wiser if guides knew only the hide before and behind, but leakage of intelligence could not be helped, and Aldyth had known for several years that Ricole, a widowed crofter living outside of Gillingham, had served as a guide since the death of her husband, with the help of her grown son.

'What's happened?' asked Aldyth in alarm. 'Are you hurt?'

'They've got Alfred,' she sobbed, pulling back her cloak to reveal a bloodied sleeve. 'I hid in a pile of rubbish; they ran it through with a pitchfork, but I held my tongue and they must not have seen the blood on the tines. Aldyth, what will they do to my son?'

Both women knew what the answer must be, but neither dared speak it aloud.

'Hush, now, mother,' said Aldyth, 'and we will do what we can.'

Aldyth would have heard had any entered, but she peeked over the altar to be sure the church was empty. Then she cut away the shoulder of Ricole's kirtle. The wound was neither deep nor dire; Aldyth cleansed it with springwater and salved it with rue and butter. 'You're certain you were not followed, Ricole?'

'Before they took Alfred away,' Ricole whispered, 'he told

them he worked alone, and I think they believed him. When they torched the rubbish pile, I fainted, and when I woke up, I was alone.' Ricole shook her head. 'I wish it had been me instead of him!'

'I'm so sorry, Ricole,' said Aldyth, 'but his solace will be in knowing that he was able to see you safely away; for Alfred's sake, we must make good your escape.'

It would be hours before night fell, hours before Sirona would return from the fields. 'I must fetch Bedwyn,' thought Aldyth. But that too would take hours. She could not let Ricole wait here to be taken by the king's men; the church would be the first place they would look, for they had no respect for the right of sanctuary. She reasoned that Bedwyn's fear of infiltrators was unfounded in this case, for Aldyth was certain beyond doubt of Ricole's loyalty; this desolate creature, wounded and weeping, was no traitor. If Aldyth could be absolutely certain they were not being followed, she could deliver this runner to Bedwyn before Ricole's danger became acute – and contagious.

'Ricole,' said Aldyth, with firm resolve, 'can you walk?'

'Aye.'

'Good,' said Aldyth. She helped the older woman to her feet and placed her own cloak over Ricole's shoulders, pulling up the hood. Slipping her basket handle over Ricole's good arm, Aldyth led the fugitive to the church door. Peering out, she saw nothing to arouse suspicion. Down in the vale, peasants labored in the fields. A forester's ax rang out, and somewhere a cow lowed to its calf. Turning an ear uphill, she could hear the hum of bees moving from flower to flower and children at play. The only sounds of discord were the French curses of Lord Ralf's foremen drifting down from Castle Hill as they supervised the moving of earth for the castle foundations, but that was not out of the ordinary.

'I want you to walk slowly back toward the Crystal Spring,' said Aldyth to Ricole, 'but don't stop there. Follow that path to a smaller one forking off the left. It will take you safely into the woods. Two furlongs down, you will come to Sula's Stump, the charred oak felled by lightning. Wait inside its hollow trunk for me. If I cannot be there by nightfall, I'll send the lad who summoned me. There is bread if you are hungry.'

Ricole nodded, but at the door she hesitated.

'The Lady walks with you, mother,' Aldyth reminded her.

Ricole nodded again and resolutely stepped out. Through the crack in the door, Aldyth watched her slow, stiff progress up the hill into the village. She waited as long as she thought it would take Ricole to reach the fountain, then stepped out the back door of the church, careful not to walk widdershins, against the direction of the sun, for they had had bad luck enough already. She forced herself to amble along the narrow paths, to observe what was coming into bloom at the foot of the hedgerows or at least appear to do so; that was how she happened to walk into Father Odo's grasp. He was stripping the meager accumulation of rags from the branches of the Wishing Tree. Aldyth glanced up to see him, but before she could retreat, he called out harshly, 'Ho, there, witch spawn!'

Cursing her bad luck and her carelessness, Aldyth answered his summons. 'Yes, Father?'

'Look at this shameful display of Devil worship!'

Aldyth's eyes followed his contemptuous gesture to the gnarled old oak. Father Odo waved a tattered rag at her and asked, 'Do you know what this is?'

Aldyth made no reply; she had a feeling he would tell her.

'This is a slap in the face of God! How many of these are yours?'

Aldyth noted that the rag she had tied among the branches for Bertha had long since been removed, but she recalled Sirona's advice for dealing with Father Odo: 'Save your breath to cool your porridge instead of using it to fan the flames.' Sirona was right; generally Father Odo would rail at her until he had used up his wind, then move on. But that day Aldyth had a feeling that he would not be satisfied with a mere tongue-lashing.

''Tis too late for the witch, but you are young yet. You could confess your wickedness and do penance for your sins. Do not let that hag drag you down to Hell with her.'

Aldyth tried to hide her contempt. 'Sirona is my godmother, as sacred a tie as that of blood in the eyes of the Church. And there is no witchcraft in healing. Would you condemn her for works of charity?'

'Call it what you will, but incantations, potions, and spells are black magic.'

'She does no different than Mother Rowena at the abbey. Would you call her a witch?'

'How dare you slander a woman of the Church! The abbess will hear of this!' He seized her upper arms with a bruising grip. 'You're next!' he cried, flinging her away like one more tainted rag. 'The company you keep will be your downfall! And your Saxon priest only encourages this insolence. By God, he shall hear from me as well!'

Father Odo went storming down the hill toward Saint Wulfstan's. Aldyth quivered with the realization that the flagstones behind the altar were still warm from Ricole's fearful vigil and that Ricole must have barely missed running into the priest at the fountain. Had Father Odo seen her wearing Aldyth's cloak and carrying her basket, it would have been Ricole that he had accosted instead of Aldyth.

When Sirona had not returned by midafternoon, Aldyth considered seeking her out but decided against it rather than chance another clash with Father Odo. She ducked past the fountain into the woods, threading her way along the path. It was dusk when she came to the lightning-blasted oak, but she walked on by. Around the first bend, she dived into the bushes and waited, to be sure she had not been followed. Then she circled back to Sula's Stump to find Ricole huddled within, safe though wretched. They took the longer, less traveled path to the hermit's hut. Between the greater distance and the slow pace set by Ricole, it was fully night when they approached Bedwyn's clearing. As an added precaution, Ricole waited in the woods while Aldyth went to the hut.

The geese announced Aldyth's arrival, but to no one in particular, for the hut was dark and the ashes on the hearth were cold. Aldyth had not counted on this. Bedwyn might be out poaching, wenching, or, worse, on his way to William's tower. A wash of silver along the eastern horizon foretold the rising of the moon. While she stood indecisively in the shadows of the doorway, the moon made a great leap, freeing itself of the clutching branches of the treetops. The meadow shone silver, and the topmost leaves of the trees reflected the moon's brilliance, but between the two strips of brightness, the understory of the forest loomed like a black palisade. Aldyth looked out of the doorway and scanned the surroundings. The slight movement at the edge of the woods was most likely a deer come to lick the salt from the pissing rock where Bedwyn customarily answered nature's call; it was an easy way to attract the yearling deer to within arrow shot of his doorstep.

She could not stay there forever, risking discovery. But as she stepped into the naked moonlight, she spotted two figures cautiously emerging from the woods. They had seen her too, for they instantly jumped back into the gloom. Aldyth rejected her initial impulse to retreat into the hut; she must not be taken. Hiking up her skirts, she darted around the corner. Like a flash of quicksilver, she bolted for the woods, keeping the hut between her and the two shadows, hoping that if they followed, they would not know in which direction she had fled.

King's men! The dreadful certainty flooded through her that they had followed her from Enmore Green. Though blinded by darkness, Aldyth Lightfoot slipped through the underbrush with the skill that had named her. From a distance, she heard them beating the bushes; they must have lost her trail. Then, without warning, she dropped into the gaping entry of a badger's den with the snap of breaking branches and a loud thud.

The crash of Aldyth's fall was immediately echoed in the distance; she had given away her position and could hear her tracker in renewed pursuit. Silence gave way in importance to speed, and, like a flushed deer, Aldyth took to her heels. Neither she nor her pursuer spoke aloud, although by gauging the distance of his angry growls, she knew that he was gaining ground. Aldyth's ear discerned only one man giving chase; her odds of escape were improved, but Ricole's danger had increased considerably, for the other must have gone off to search for her. Ricole's best chance was to stay still as a fawn in hiding, but Aldyth's only hope lay in flight. A light step gave no advantage once her whereabouts were known; this chase required sheer muscle and endurance. Brush whipped at her face, thorns snatched at her skirts and scratched her bare legs. She fought down screams of terror, saving her breath for flight.

It might have been an evil bogle that reached out of the dark to seize Aldyth's ankle, bringing her down to hands and knees. By the time she regained her footing, her stalker was nearly upon her. But Aldyth sensed the sharp drop of the slope just ahead. In midflight she ducked behind a tree, hoping that her tormentor would continue along the same path; just a few steps forward would send him tumbling down the slope. But this hunter was not put off by simple tricks; he came to a halt to get his bearings and listened. The impenetrable gloom was like a blindfold, yet it amplified every sound. It took only a moment for the rasp of Aldyth's labored breathing to give her away. Again she took to her heels, but only steps into her flight, she was nearly jerked her off her feet; it was her pursuer, snatching at her collar. In a frenzied struggle, Aldyth ripped free, leaving a long, narrow strip of her kirtle in his grasp. His snarl of animal fury was bloodcurdling, and his rage must have lent him strength, for he hurled himself against her like a maddened bull. The force of his leap sent them both somersaulting through the brush down the steep ridge that Aldyth had instinctively tried to avoid. They rolled to a stop, stunned. But as Aldyth lay sprawled and panting in the darkness, it dawned on her that her attacker had lost his grip. With exhausted muscles powered by desperation, Aldyth sprang up; with a furious roar, he too was on his feet. In a bold gamble he leapt into the darkness, and his aim was true. He landed on her back like an attacking wildcat, the force of the impact knocking them both to the ground. In a trice, he had straddled her back and was reaching for her throat. Aldyth twisted her head around and bit down on his wrist so hard that she tasted blood. Startled and in pain, he loosened his grip but almost immediately clamped his hands back down on her windpipe.

Aldyth surrendered to her fate. 'My Lady,' she prayed silently, 'make it swift.'

To her surprise he hesitated, as though faltering at his grim task. Driven by instinct as much as by hope, Aldyth again sank her teeth into his bloodied forearm.

'God damn you, bitch!' he snarled. 'You're making this very easy for me!'

'Oh, my Lady!' Aldyth cried, recognizing his voice even through its masking rage. 'Bedwyn!' she screamed. ''Tis me!'

'Jesus Christ!' He leapt aside and quickly flipped Aldyth, limp and trembling, onto her back. As he peered into her face, she could smell his panic, feel the throbbing heat of his exertion. 'My God, Aldyth!' His rasping breath came in sobs as he crushed her to his sweat-dampened chest. The tears that Aldyth had repressed gushed forth, the sobs she had sought to contain forced their way out as stifled squeaks.

'Christ Almighty!' he groaned, pulling her more tightly against him. It was too dark beneath that heavy canopy of leaves to gauge time by the progress of the moon, but their clothes, damp with sweat, grew clammy, and exhausted muscles grew stiff before Aldyth could even attempt to sit up. Bedwyn was shaken out of his trance.

Still barely able to speak for lack of composure, he whispered, 'I thought you were a spy, running off to deliver intelligence.' With an abruptness that caught her off guard, he dropped his arms and snarled, 'Damn you, Aldyth! I told you to stay away from here!'

Even before this ferocious outburst, Aldyth had felt fear creeping into her consciousness, intellectual rather than visceral. She had never seen this feral side of Bedwyn, and it terrified her. Unsteadily, she rose to her feet and backed away from him, too stunned to reply. But her knees shook so uncontrollably that she stumbled backward and fell. Bedwyn leapt to his feet and rushed toward her, but she shrank away.

'Don't touch me!' she said coldly with more command than she felt.

She sensed his anger stabbing at her through the darkness. Both of them stood silent and breathless. She was furious and frightened; he was furious and frightened.

'Well, then,' Bedwyn said at last in a stiff, harsh voice, 'I have somebody in the bushes I need to fetch.'

'Well, so do I,' she retorted in an equally hard tone.

'I'll see you back at my place.' He turned on his heel and stomped off.

Aldyth launched herself back into the sinister woods. 'Once Ricole is delivered into his hands,' Aldyth promised herself, 'I will never see him, never speak to him again.' She would tell Sirona that she was finished with the Starlit Path, then devote herself to her work in the village. 'Trust a man to try to kill you and then be mad at you for it,' she thought bitterly. Damn him anyway! Those thoughts did nothing to speed her along. Finally she heard a rustling among the bracken, and someone snatched at her sleeve. Aldyth was so wrought up that she nearly screamed.

'What happened?' whispered Ricole anxiously. 'I heard shouting.' Aldyth sank down beside her runner in the ferns. 'Aldyth, are you all right?'

'Yes, yes, I'm all right.' Then she hissed, 'I hate men! I hate them all!' After another moment, her limbs stopped quaking and her mind began to work again. 'Poor Ricole!' she cried. 'Forgive me. Soon you'll be safe in Bedwyn's hands.'

Aldyth paused outside his door and steeled herself before entering. Her eyes, unaccustomed to the dim light of the hut, barely distinguished the two men standing by the newly built fire, presumably Bedwyn and the one he had gone to fetch.

Suddenly Aldyth felt her companion tear away. 'My God!' cried Ricole, throwing herself into the arms of Bedwyn's companion. 'Alfred!'

For a long moment, there was no sound but that of inarticulate joy. Aldyth stared, unable to draw her eyes away from such a compelling display of unabashed emotion. Ricole took her son's face in her hands, stroked his hair, and wiped away his tears. As Bedwyn watched, the hard set of his features melted away, and he looked at Aldyth with an unspoken plea that might have been perceived as an apology. But remembering the feel of his hands tightening about her throat, Aldyth refused to acknowledge it.

'I heard them take you away!' exclaimed Ricole when she could speak.

'And I saw them set fire to the rubbish heap you hid in!' said her son.

'We all have some catching up to do tonight,' said Bedwyn. 'Does anyone else need a drink before we sit down and straighten this mess out?' Without waiting for an answer, he filled four mugs with a musty sour ale. He set two on the table before Alfred and Ricole, who sat side by side, still clinging to each other. He set the remaining two on the opposite side of the table and sat down heavily on the other bench, leaving room for Aldyth beside him. To his annoyance, Aldyth chose to sit on the small stool by the fire. He leaned over to hand her the mug, saying sarcastically, 'Do you think I bite?'

Aldyth blushed when she saw the ugly tooth marks on his wrist and arm, but outrage overcame embarrassment. 'You're ready enough to throttle the life out of a person!' she retorted.

Startled, Ricole asked, 'Bedwyn, was it you that she drew away from my hiding place?'

'Why don't we start at the beginning?' said Bedwyn wearily.

'If not for Bedwyn,' said Alfred, 'I'd be halfway to London by now.'

'And if not for his bad aim, you'd be dead,' added Bedwyn bitterly.

''Tis a twisted tale to be sure,' agreed Alfred, 'and I'd as lief let Bedwyn tell it.'

Bedwyn nodded and took a bracing gulp of ale before beginning, 'Garth KnockKnees, harvesting saplings from the abbey coppices, saw some Normans headed toward Gillingham and brought word to me. I suspected a raid, for they were too many and too well armed for anything else. I could only assume that it was your hide they were after, and I made a beeline through the woods to warn you, but I was afoot and they on horse-back. I got there in time to see them take Alf and his runner. Who was he anyway, Alf?'

'I don't know,' responded Alfred. 'He claimed to be Aelfgar of Bedford, yet now that I think of it, when I asked for news of my cousin living in Bedford, he turned me aside.'

'I'll wager he was a plant. I don't feel so bad about killing him now,' said Bedwyn grimly. 'I saw no sign of Ricole and could only hope that she had escaped, but there was no escape for Alf and his runner. Quick death by my arrow was preferable to the attentions of the king's executioners, so I readied two arrows. I took my time with the runner and my aim was true, but made haste with the second shot, for the first one brought the whole pack upon me. I lost them in the woods and returned to look for Ricole and to give Alf a Christian burial. But he had something to say about that.'

'In their zeal to give chase,' chimed in Alfred, 'the king's men left the two of us for dead, but Bedwyn's arrow had struck my holy rock.' He pulled some fragments of stone from his pouch and pieced them together on the table in their original form, a smooth ring of stone whose central hole had been worn by the waves of the sea, not by any human hand. Such stones were said to be sacred to the Goddess and were worn as amulets.

'The Lady is good,' whispered Ricole thankfully.

'Aye,' agreed Alfred, 'for only She could have guided Bedwyn's arrow so truly. When I came to my senses, I was still bound hand and foot, sure that each hare hopping past was a Norman come back for me. Imagine my relief when the first to come was Bedwyn.'

'We might've been followed,' continued Bedwyn, 'and I had no wish to give Alf back into the Bastard's hands; had anyone even a suspicion that Alf was still alive or that I was in any way involved with him . . . and upon our return to find Aldyth lurking about in the shadows . . .' He paused and winced. 'I let my nerves take over like a green recruit.'

'So you still didn't know that Aldyth was guiding me here,' said Ricole.

'How could I,' he snapped, glaring at Aldyth, 'when I specifically told her not to?'

'But, Mother,' persisted Alfred, who was either too tired to notice or too courteous to remark upon Bedwyn's harsh comment, 'you still haven't told us your story.'

As Ricole related her tale, Aldyth dwelt upon Bedwyn's. No wonder he was so angry. He had nearly died that night and had very nearly killed her as well. She watched him wrap a rag around his injured arm, and the taste of blood and terror jumped back at her. She quickly lifted her mug to her lips as though she could wash away the memory.

'Your bridges are burned,' observed Bedwyn. 'The question

now is where to go from here. I dare not send you along the Path—'

'What choices have we?' asked Ricole.

'Not many,' Bedwyn replied. 'If you've no money to buy passage overseas, you can either take to the woods or take to the road. I wouldn't give you two days on the road.'

'I doubt we could last a week in the woods,' said Alf. 'Crofting is all I know.'

'I'll take you to the outlaws' camp in Cranborne Chase. Like you, they're good people whose luck ran out. If you've a willing hand, they'll teach you all you need to know.'

A quick look of understanding passed between mother and son. 'When do we leave?'

'Sooner is better,' said Bedwyn. ''Tis a long walk; I'll take you there tomorrow night. But for now, you would be safer at the lambing hut.'

Aldyth marveled: only Bedwyn would think to take on a dozen armed and mounted soldiers single-handedly. But his mad rescue had taken its toll; never had she seen him so dispirited. He too, she realized, had just lost his place and purpose in the world. Aldyth was overwhelmed by all she had to absorb. She stood up abruptly to leave, and, as he had a hundred times before, Bedwyn rose to see her to the door.

'Don't get up,' she said to Bedwyn, perhaps too quickly. By the set of his jaw she saw that she had offended him. 'So be it,' she thought stubbornly. Turning toward the door, she felt a draft and remembered with chagrin the rip Bedwyn had made in her kirtle. But if she thought to make a quick escape, she had misread him. Bedwyn jumped up so suddenly that he knocked the table over, and he caught Aldyth at the door.

Seizing her shoulders, he roughly turned her around to face him. 'You just can't comprehend, can you?' he raged.

She looked away, not wanting to face the fury that still lurked behind his eyes. But he misread her movement, taking it for a confirmation of his accusation.

'Aldyth, I could have killed you!' he growled. 'How do you think I'd have felt when I returned to bury the body?' Then, pleading: 'Can't you put yourself in my place?'

With their runners looking on in embarrassed silence,

Aldyth shook free of his grasp. She too was embarrassed, and her feelings were hurt. But she recalled his heartfelt reaction when he realized his mistake, and she softened. 'Of course I understand,' she protested.

'I'm sorry I was so rough with you, Aldyth; I hadn't an inkling it was you, and when I discovered that it was, well . . . perhaps I overreacted.'

'I overreacted too,' she conceded. 'But please, Bedwyn, I just want to go home.'

Bedwyn seemed reluctant to release her before he was certain that she understood. 'Aldyth, do you realize what this means? Our closest link is broken, and we'll be next. It's over; even Hereward the Wake is dead. The Normans were gloating about it to Alf.'

'No!' cried Aldyth, denying the doom she had read in Hereward's elfin eyes while guiding him on his last journey. 'They were just saying it to torment him!'

'Would to God I could believe that,' he replied, 'but it has the ring of truth. He would have just returned from his journey along the Path. He was ambushed in his own castle by jealous rivals at court. Even now his head rots on the ramparts.'

That was the final blow; Aldyth buried her face in her hands. Bedwyn took her by the shoulders and looked on helplessly, swearing softly under his breath. At last he said, 'Aldyth, I'm going to see you home tonight. Alf, do you know where the lambing hut is?'

Alfred nodded.

'Good. Take wine, bread, and a blanket. No fire. I'll be along as soon as I can.'

Taking his cloak from a peg on the wall, Bedwyn threw it over Aldyth's shoulders and guided her, quietly weeping, outside. Not knowing if he would be rebuffed, he cautiously put his arms around her. Aldyth relaxed into his embrace, and the Bedwyn she had known for a lifetime brushed her hair back from her brow. How could this gentle man be the same animal who had just tried to kill her with his bare hands? Aldyth shuddered.

'Poor Mouse. Are you still afraid of me?' he asked tenderly.

'Or is it Hereward? I shouldn't have told you – not tonight.' He took her hand and drew her along after him.

'No, Bedwyn, 'tis not your fault,' she answered, sniffing. 'I don't know what is wrong with me.'

'We've been under a lot of pressure, and God knows, we've had a hellish night. I was too hard on you, Mouse; you were right to bring Ricole.'

'I was so afraid that I had led the soldiers to your doorstep.'

'Well, you didn't. I'll see you home, and you'll feel better after a good night's rest.'

'Oh, Bedwyn, I haven't had a good night's rest in months.' Her voice trembled and she stopped walking to stifle a fresh bout of tears. The tension of the night's near calamity and the irrevocable loss of Hereward and the Path took her by storm.

Aldyth was still trying to silence her sobs when she felt Bedwyn's arms slide around her. He kissed her hair and, holding her tight, rested his chin on the top of her head, waiting patiently for her tears to subside. At last she composed herself enough to wipe her eyes upon her sleeve, though she was still wracked by dry sobs. Bedwyn, loosing his embrace, took hold of her hand again, and they recommenced their walk.

'Bedwyn,' she quavered, allowing herself to be drawn in his wake, 'this time it really is the end, isn't it?'

'I'm afraid so, Mouse,' he said grimly. 'I knew before I set out for Gillingham that Hereward was right; it was time to cut our losses and get out.'

'What will you do, Bedwyn? It's dangerous for you here now. Alfred isn't the only one who might be forced into betraying you. Will you move on?'

'I don't know; the truth is that I never really thought this would happen. I'll probably stay on and live off the king's deer until I decide. I could go back to live in the chase again, and there's always the Varangian Guard. What about you, Aldyth?'

She thought she had been dealt the final blow, but now she reeled as it struck her that Bedwyn would be leaving. It had been half a lifetime since Sirona had initiated her into that great network of Saxon endeavor, with Bedwyn as her closest link, and now Bedwyn was cutting her loose. 'I have no choice; I live here,' she said dully.

'That fact makes it all the more important that you keep your nose clean,' he said urgently. He swung around and, giving her a little shake, he chided, 'You're so stubborn, Aldyth; I just know the first hungry beggar that comes to the fountain—' Accusingly, he added, 'Sirona doesn't even know you're here, does she?'

Aldyth wanted neither scolding nor advice. All she wanted was to be comforted; she was still on the brink of hysteria and could not dam up the flood of tears that arose at his rebuke. Bedwyn heaved a sigh. Up ahead, against the inky blackness, slivers of light broke through the trees. He led her down the path like a docile cow and into a brilliant glade. Whisking her into his arms, he carried her to a dry grassy spot beneath the budding branches of a spreading oak. Leaning against its trunk, he settled her on his lap.

'Bedwyn,' she gasped, 'I'm so embarrassed.'

'For being human?'

She smiled gratefully through her tears. His arm reached around her waist, and she felt the rag bandage that had stanched the bleeding from two savage bites. 'I should tend to that,' she began ruefully. Then she gave a start. 'My basket!'

'Don't worry, Mouse,' he assured her. 'It'll wait.'

Aldyth nodded. Leaning her head against his broad chest, she focused on the sound of his heartbeat. Closing her eyes, she remembered the first time she had ever set eye upon this sun-haired lad. 'Oh, my Lady,' she thought, 'he was beautiful to look at.' As Bedwyn had grown into manhood, she had watched him come into his own, and as she had grown into womanhood, she had harbored an intense curiosity about him. To Aldyth, Bedwyn was all men: foreign, fascinating, forbidden. Looking forward to seeing him had been a secret pleasure, though she had never expected anything in return. To her surprise, she had been blessed with his friendship and camaraderie, as much as any woman could expect from him. But soon she would be saying good-bye forever.

Aldyth opened her eyes to find him watching her. A smile tinged with melancholy flitted across his features, and he kissed her forehead. She ran her hand across his scratchy growth of whiskers. He laughed softly, wistfully, and took hold of the hand. 'Dear girl,' he murmured, impulsively leaning down to kiss her gently on the mouth, then pulling her head back against his shoulder. Gradually Aldyth became aware that his breathing had quickened, that his heart had begun to pound.

'Aldyth,' he blurted, 'life doesn't have to begin and end in Enmore Green.'

'What do you mean?'

'Come with me. It wouldn't matter where we went or what we did. Come with me.'

'Please, Bedwyn, don't tease me tonight.'

'But I'm serious.'

Aldyth sat up in surprise. She understood Bedwyn as she understood the unfolding of the seasons. His emotions were close to the surface, and he rarely took the trouble to hide them. She sensed the sincerity in his voice, and she knew he meant what he said.

''Tis impossible,' she replied, laying her head back down against his chest.

'Why?' he persisted.

'You make it sound so easy, Bedwyn.'

'Why make things out to be so hard? We could leave tonight.'

She gasped. She could not deny that she had fantasized about this moment almost since the day she had met him. But that was all it had ever been, a fantasy. If everything had changed for Bedwyn, nothing had changed for her. Still, she could picture herself and Bedwyn traveling hand in hand along the ridgeway. He would help her find her family. He would provide laughter, protection, and adventure. No less than she had been on the ridgetop, Aldyth found herself tempted and terrified, and her own heart began to pound.

Sensing her wishful thinking, Bedwyn threaded his fingers through her hair and pulled her mouth toward his. This was no kiss of peace, but close enough. Even so, her breath quickened and Aldyth knew that she should go. Bedwyn kissed her again, and it was a hungry kiss. Aldyth closed her eyes to keep the rest of the world at bay.

He laid a strong hand along the side of her face and caressed her cheek with his thumb. Gently he pulled the cloak from her shoulders and let it drop, then brushed back long locks of tawny hair, bleached silver by the moon. The back of her gown now in tatters, Bedwyn was able to draw it down to reveal the milky white skin of her neck and shoulders, mottled with bruises, like the dim shadows across the moon.

'God help me, Aldyth, I'm so sorry,' he choked, frowning at the ugly bruises.

Aldyth found the honest emotion in his voice more moving than any practiced kisses. Impetuously he leaned forward to brush each bruise with his lips, as if he might kiss away the hurt; they were like the kisses of an angel, the kisses of a hot wind upon her skin. She leaned back into the crook of his arm and closed her eyes; once again she was on the top of the ridgeway with the breeze ruffling her hair, whispering its siren call into her ear.

With a hand so kindly that it could have gentled a butterfly, Bedwyn drew her kirtle down to expose her breasts. She let him slip her arms out of the sleeves. But when he cupped a full, round breast in his hand, Aldyth shook her head and reached up to push his hand away. Bedwyn rolled her backward into the grass, his weight pinning her to the ground, and the hardness she felt between his legs both repelled and attracted her.

'Bedwyn,' she gasped, 'I can't.'

'Then let me,' he coaxed.

She had to laugh but was not swayed. Bedwyn sighed and withdrew his hand from her bosom to brush the soft golden hair away from her face, but he did not release her.

'What about this?' he asked, kissing her forehead. She saw no harm in that.

'What about this?' He nipped at her ear lobe. She made no protest.

'And this?' Bedwyn reached up and tweaked her nose, saying with a hearty laugh, 'I've owed you that one since last autumn.'

Taken by surprise, Aldyth guffawed, and her laughter brought out his. The tension between them vanished like a mist in sunlight. She playfully shoved him off her, scolding,

'You tease.' She leaned on her side and propped her head on her elbow.

He mirrored her movement. Then his eyes strayed downward, not to her bare bosom but to the bruises encircling her neck. Bedwyn's smile quickly died away, and his brows knit into a pained frown. 'Aldyth,' he said, 'there's much you don't know about me.'

She put her finger to his lips. 'You don't have to tell me anything.'

Refusing her absolution, he said, 'I'm not trying to excuse myself—'

'Hush, now,' she whispered. 'I understand.' Aldyth ran her fingers through his long golden hair, telling herself it was no more than a gesture of comfort. He snatched up her hand, kissed her palm, then drew her arm around his neck.

'Let me please you, Aldyth,' he whispered.

She found the velvet tone of his voice as intriguing as his words but had to decline. 'No, Bedwyn. I'm a virgin and must remain so.'

'I know how to make you feel good, Mouse, and you will still have your maidenhead.'

'I think it's time to go,' she said reluctantly.

She had not actually forbidden him, so he cajoled tenderly, 'Don't be afraid, love. Just say the word, and I'll stop.'

Cradling her head with one arm, his hand traveled down from throat to breast, where it lingered before moving down along the outside of her thigh. Gently he hiked her kirtle up to her hips. She tingled with anticipation, though of what she was not quite sure.

'Kiss me, love,' he instructed, and when she gingerly complied, Aldyth realized that Bedwyn had made her a willing accomplice in her own seduction. It felt so good she kissed him again, and she knew he was pleased when she felt rather than heard his quiet laughter. His breath quickened, and, while he was showing admirable self-restraint, she could not help but notice that he was casting a long shadow in the moonlight where before there had been none. He followed her eyes with his own and chuckled softly at her wide-eyed observation. She blushed and pulled away, but Bedwyn drew her back, kissed

241

her forehead tenderly, then placed her hand on the object of her curiosity.

His voice was husky with rising excitement. 'You see what you do to me, Mouse?'

Aldyth squeaked from sheer surprise and wondered how it all came together between man and woman. It did not occur to her to be afraid, and with Bedwyn it all seemed so natural that she simply could not see the sin in it.

He swallowed hard and shook his head, halting her hand from its tentative exploration. 'Not yet,' he whispered hoarsely. 'That's not what I meant to show you.'

He ran his hand up under her kirtle and in between her thighs. By now the patch of soft, golden curls between her legs was moist, and Aldyth ached for relief. But the instant she felt the touch of his fingers, she jumped and sat up with a start.

Aldyth tugged her skirts back down past her knees and pulled her torn kirtle up to cover her breasts. 'Now I know why Sirona has warned me against you, Bedwyn!'

'And she doesn't know the half of it,' he crooned. 'Aldyth, just imagine it. I have friends throughout England; everywhere we go, there would be food, shelter, a warm welcome. And every night, every morning, any time you wished, I would be there to stir your blood the way you stir mine. Holy Mother of God,' he said with a laugh, 'I can't wait to show you.' He kissed her again until her boiling liver fairly made her cry out.

'Bedwyn, I'm so confused . . . I never dreamed I would ever consider it . . .'

'Just once, Aldyth, just this once, follow your heart instead of your head. I swear I'll do my best to see that you never regret it.'

'Let me think about it,' she pleaded, wavering.

'You can do more than just think about it.'

Bedwyn lifted her onto his lap, and with his lips he brushed aside a lifetime of steadfast resolve. Burying his face in her bosom, he kissed, caressed, and nuzzled her throat. There was an insistence, a desperation that Aldyth had never felt before. His mouth found her nipple; first he teased it with his tongue and then he sucked, like a newborn babe, she thought, deeply moved. How could such an innocent act stir such fire? Hugging him even closer, she stroked his hair. Aldyth had never felt tempted by his flirting and innuendo, not seriously, but she felt herself toppling, ready to collapse against this tender barrage. One of his hands wandered in between her legs once again.

'Aldyth,' he whispered urgently, 'I'll be careful ... I promise ...'

But Aldyth instinctively knew that if she let him do what he wanted, she would soon be begging him to take her maidenhead. 'Please don't make me decide tonight, Bedwyn.'

Bedwyn lifted his head and met her eyes to assure himself that she truly meant what she said. He sighed and laid his cheek against her bare breast, listening to her heart thundering in her chest. 'Very well, Mouse,' he said at last. 'I can wait if you can.'

'I don't know if I can,' she said tearfully. If she was afraid to let Bedwyn have his way, her body cried out for it. She kissed him hungrily; he returned the kiss. With each moment that passed, Aldyth felt that it was she who could not wait.

Just when she knew she had not the strength to pull herself out of his arms, Bedwyn sat up abruptly and said cheekily, 'You were supposed to say the word.' When he pulled her to her feet, Aldyth was so dizzy that Bedwyn had to put his arms out to steady her. Pressing his rough cheek against hers, he murmured, 'I've never taken a woman against her will, Mouse.' Guiding her arms back into her sleeves, he said, 'I can tell you're not quite ready yet, but you will be ... and I'll be waiting.' He wrapped his cloak around her shoulders and, fingers entwined, they walked in a charged silence as he led her homeward. Aldyth's mind was racing; had it been a wild dream? No, she decided, for her breasts still tingled with his touch and there was a warm, wet feeling between her legs.

Before they came to the last of the fields surrounding the village, he slowed his pace and exercised more caution. Even Bedwyn was not so foolhardy as to see Aldyth to her door. They were still in the cover of the outlying woods when he drew her to a halt and bent to kiss her one last time. Aldyth, having had time to regret her folly, meant to resist but instead found herself lifting her lips to meet his, her arms winding their way back around his neck. With a teasing bravado, Bedwyn

243

pulled her hips against his, that she might know his interest was as strong as ever.

'I'll come for my answer on May Eve,' he promised. Like a wraith he was gone, leaving her arms bereft of the warmth and comfort she so desperately craved.

May Eve! That's so far away, thought Aldyth, her heart racing and her loins afire. 'Could I do it?' she wondered. 'Could I throw caution to the wind and go with Bedwyn?'

Then she stopped dead in her tracks. Quite suddenly it occurred to her: 'He never promised to marry me.'

CHAPTER NINETEEN

May Eve 1087

The instant she woke, Aldyth remembered that Bedwyn would be coming for his answer that night. Since their accidental unleashing of passion, every waking moment and most of her dreams had been colored by thoughts of Bedwyn; his lips, his deft hands, the excitement she had felt in his arms. Aldyth had returned home that night to find Sirona waiting up, the old woman's spinning untouched on her lap. Her godmother's relief had been visible. Then one of her eyebrows had shot up as if to say, 'Well?'

Aldyth had told Sirona about guiding Ricole, of Bedwyn's rescue of Alfred, even of the wild night chase, but she had said nothing of Bedwyn's offer. Her withholding had felt like a lie by omission, yet speaking it aloud might give it a meaning she dared not grant it. She must deny the temptation just as she had deafened her ear to the call of the ridge road. The next morning, she had found her forgotten basket, set just inside the door. On top had rested a neatly folded kirtle. A week later, she still wondered where Bedwyn had found a kirtle to replace the rag she had worn home that night, but she could never accept his offering – unless, of course, she were to run away with him. Then who else but herself and Bedwyn would be there to question the propriety of the gift?

Aldyth finished Godiva's morning milking and set the milk aside to let the cream rise. After skimming the cream with a scallop shell, she would give the milk to Godiva's little red calf, Maeve, and save the cream to make butter. Aldyth tethered them both within the toft, where they browsed on fresh buds of the border hedge while she weeded the garden. Godiva's ears pricked up at the lowing of cattle down the lane. Gandulf had seen to it that Eafa collected her settlement from Osgot. Of those three cows, two had calved, and Eafa now had the means to provide for herself and her unborn child. Out of gratitude to the healers, Eafa, now surnamed ThreeCows, took Godiva to graze with her own tiny herd each day.

Aldyth looked at a swallow's nest under the eaves and recalled her sport with Bedwyn by moonlight. Her loins tingled, and she sought to master those feelings. They came at the oddest time, catching her off guard. She forced her thoughts to a higher plane.

The winter fever had abated. Mother Rowena had told Aldyth that when the grippe had seized Sister Emma, Gandulf had stayed at her bedside, holding her head as she retched and wiping her mouth afterward. With the coming of spring Sister Emma, like so many others, had recovered her strength.

Winter had taken its toll on Father Edmund, but he had never mentioned the bishop of Salisbury's investigation of claims that he observed pagan rites, nor the churchmen sent at Father Odo's urging, who subjected him to one useless interrogation after another.

'Don't trouble yourself, Edmund,' Sirona told him, 'for you are a small fish to fry. Up in Northumberland the priests are still sacrificing horses to Odin!'

The milking done, Aldyth was free to go gathering. She wandered farther than her custom and found herself in a beech wood where the leaves sprouted so high overhead that they seemed to have no connection with the earth. Aldyth came to a wall of green undergrowth backlit by the sunny blaze of a clearing. She stepped into a glade where daffodils thronged like a joyous crowd at a festival, like the splash of sunbeams striking the earth. Aldyth sat beside a burbling stream and, raising her face to the sun, shook her hair loose from its confining shawl. Her trained eye noted the profusion of strawberry leaves spangling the meadow; she would come back when the berries were ripe. She had begun rinsing the day's harvest of herbs when an unexpected rustling so startled her that she dropped them into the brook and they drifted unnoticed downstream.

Gandulf was no less surprised than she when he rode into the clearing, Baldwin trailing at his heels, to find Aldyth staring at him, frozen like a startled doe. But it was too late for him to withdraw without looking foolish. After only a slight hesitation, he reined in his little mare and said, 'A lovely spot, is it not?' Baldwin padded up to Aldyth for a scratch, and Gandulf envied the dog's ease of manners. 'Are we disturbing you?'

Aldyth smiled and shook her head. 'I was just startled. I wouldn't have expected to see anyone here at all, unless it were a Fairy or a badger.'

'I come often,' said Gandulf, 'and take my midday meal here. Have you eaten today?'

She shook her head, and Gandulf groaned inwardly at his tactless question; of course not, for what peasant in Dorset could scrounge more than one meal a day after a winter of famine? 'What I meant to say is, would you care to join me in a midday meal?'

It was all coming back to Aldyth, all the reasons she had avoided him for so long: he was too kind, too diffident, too endearing in his awkwardness. He took her silence for reluctance and sat frozen in the saddle while trying to decide what excuse he could make to escape. Aldyth took pity on him. 'I would be pleased,' she replied.

With a smile of mixed relief and gratitude, Gandulf dismounted, dropped Cathedra's reins, and left her cropping the grass. Swinging the saddlebag over his shoulder, he began, 'That big rock over there is sunwarmed, and I often break bread there.'

Gandulf came up from behind to lift Aldyth onto the rock by the waist. She was immediately self-conscious, for she was wearing the ragged kirtle that Bedwyn had torn and that she had mended, but she assured herself that men rarely noticed such things.

'What can possibly have happened to her kirtle?' Gandulf wondered and wished again that he could replace it. Suddenly he knew that he had made a dreadful mistake in stopping. He couldn't say that he had gotten over her, but the pain had grown steady and dull, instead of piercing and cruel. He set a cloth down and took out a rich soft cheese and two large meat pies. Offering her his wineskin, he apologized that he had no cup to give her. Then he watched her drink, fascinated and anticipating the pleasure of drinking from the same flask. He tore his eyes away and tossed a tidbit to Baldwin, who snapped it up in midair.

Aldyth laughed. 'You two have taken to each other like peaches and cream.'

'I feel privileged that he allows me to tag along with him.'

Their conversation was unexpectedly pleasant; immediately the thought made Aldyth shy. Gandulf, initially encouraged, found that their friendly banter had suddenly dried up. He was not skilled enough at the art of small talk to continue without Aldyth's cooperation. In an attempt to break back into the warmth of their earlier rapport, Gandulf ventured, 'You must be very busy these days, Aldyth. I never see you at the gatherings anymore.'

'I've gatherings of my own, herbs to collect this time of year.' It was not quite a lie.

He looked away across the glade. ''Tis not the same without you.'

Studying her bare feet, she replied, 'I've missed going.'

'I haven't heard of any tongues wagging lately . . . if that has anything to do with it.'

'No. At first, perhaps . . .'

'Might I help with your gathering, that you might have time for us on Sunday?'

'I wouldn't dream of troubling you.'

Gandulf knew that the subject was closed. The idea of an unchaperoned maiden accompanying her lord into the woods did smack of impropriety. Yet she had never been a slave to convention; even now she was breaking bread with him. It must be the Saxon. But it had taken an inordinate amount of nerve for Gandulf to have pressed so far, and he dared not probe further. His senses had absorbed all he needed to know; the smell of her hair, the feel of her waist in his hands, the flash of her eyes like mingled emeralds and sunlight. He would ask for no deeper attachment from her than she gave to her fellow villagers, but even that, he knew, was too much to hope for. Leaving her the remains of their meal, he nodded farewell, whistled to the dog, and took his leave.

As Aldyth watched Gandulf ride off, she thought with alarm, 'I am overly affected by his presence. The Goddess guided me here today to show me that 'tis not just one man or the other I must resist, but all men.' As Aldyth rose to go home, she knew that half a lifetime of dreaming must come to an end; she had an answer for Bedwyn.

As Aldyth approached her toft, a small group hurried from the opposite direction, obviously an informal council of elders. With old Elviva and Grimbald Shepherd gone, the group seemed pitifully small. In the lead was Edwin MoonCatcher, the oldest man in the village, holding the hand of his wife, Mildred. On his other side walked Winifred LongCross, now the oldest women in the village – excepting Sirona, of course. 'Is Sirona home?'

Aldyth could see her godmother within. 'Aye, that she is. Do come in.'

Sirona looked up to see the elders and set aside the picnic supper she was packing. 'It would appear that you have business to discuss,' she remarked without preamble.

Mildred whimpered, and Edwin patted his wife's hand absently, saying, 'Sirona, we won't mince words. Last year was a bad one, and all signs point to another poor year.'

Sirona sat silent as a stone, waiting for Edwin to explain himself.

'In the old days,' he continued, 'the land was fed with blood at the festivals each year. It has been a long time since such an offering. Perhaps the earth needs to be fed again.'

Mildred's whimpers intensified into wails.

'Did you have an offering in mind, Edwin?' asked Sirona.

Edwin and Winifred, glaring at each other, answered in unison, 'Yes.'

'And what might that offering be?' asked Sirona.

'Now, Edwin, you hush,' said Winifred quickly.

'I thought the matter was decided,' the old man retorted.

Mildred howled and buried her face in Edwin's neck. Putting an arm around her, he said over his wife's trilling sobs, 'If anyone, it should be me. I'm the oldest, and I've enjoyed the bounty of the Goddess longer than anyone; I stand ready to pay my debt.'

Winifred responded, 'I'm widowed, and even my grand-children are grown. You have a wife who needs you, nephews, nieces, grandchildren. You would be too sorely missed—'

'Do I have no say in this?' Sirona broke in.

The two elders looked surprised and then as chastened as scolded puppies.

'You decide then, Sirona,' said Winifred.

'Very well, hear me out,' said the wisewoman. ''Tis true that in the ancient time, blood was offered, but the druids were weak-kneed, for they could not trust the Goddess to make her own choices in her own time. They hoped to avert the loss of a mighty chief or a beloved son by choosing for her, thereby giving her the unclean blood of unwilling victims. Your offering is made with a good will, but the Goddess values it too highly to accept it. Serve Her, as you always have, and be assured that She will have Her due.'

Mildred burst into a fresh flood of tears and covered Edwin with kisses. 'Save that for tonight, Millie,' he chuckled, 'when I take you into the bushes.'

But Winifred said solemnly, 'I confess that I was not looking forward to tonight's festivities as much as I have in other years.'

'Now you can go and make merry. Your joy is also an offering.' Sirona embraced them and sent them home with a much lighter step than when they had come.

'We live among good folk,' said Aldyth, watching them go. 'Godmother,' she ventured, 'who will the Goddess choose for Her due?'

'I know no more than you, child. We can only put in our requests and pray.' Sirona chuckled wryly. 'But you can be certain that the Goddess *will* take Her tithe. Now let us set aside dark thoughts, at least for a while, and enjoy ourselves.'

For weeks people had scoured the area for firewood and noted where the wildflowers grew. After the bonfire, they would pick them by moonlight to weave into garlands. Hildegarde Brewer had collected the scrapings of everyone's granary to brew a batch of ale for the night; in a prosperous year they would have drunk mead, but the honey was long gone and no more would be harvested until June. On Castle Hill new tunics and gowns of green silk had been ordered for the day. But at the bottom of the hill, people had to be satisfied with a green ribbon tied around a sleeve or a wreath of flowers for their hair.

As the sun, sinking below the horizon, gilded the topmost leaves of the Wishing Tree, Sirona and Aldyth stepped out of their toft and made the walk to the wall, where Enmore Green held its most important celebrations. From there, they looked out over the valley at the fires springing up in the twilight, dotting the vale like orange stars.

'Look,' said Sirona, pointing to a faint twinkle on the horizon, 'in Glastonbury the fire atop the tor already blazes brightly.'

Sirona had already made certain that the woodpiles included the wood of nine different types of trees. On May Eve two fires, one for the rising sun and one for the setting sun, were laid a road's width apart, to be kindled at sunset, and it was always a MoonCatcher to whom the honor fell. That night it was Edwin's turn to wield the fire drill, calling forth a virgin fire from the sacred oak. Edwin grew flushed as he bent over the eastern woodpile, furiously sawing the bow that twirled the stick whose friction would light the tinder. At last the kindling caught, but the rising flames were no match for the joy blazing in the old man's eyes.

By the flicker of firelight, Sirona spoke. 'The Green Man has returned, sent by His mother to make our cows and sheep fat and fertile. The flowers we wear are for Him, and we raise these flames for the Mother.' Sirona displayed a twig broom, or besom, carefully kept since last May Day, and touched it to Edwin's tiny fire. Instantly it burst into flame. Gilded by its glorious blaze, she proclaimed, 'Behold the divine fire at the center of all things, whose spark of life is carried within each of us. Let us ask for Her blessing and give thanks for Her gift by using it well.' She touched the burning besom to the woodpile of the east, and flames leapt out of the dark spaces between branches. Then, turning to the west, she lit that fire also and tossed the blazing besom into the rising flames.

By the light of the May Day fires, they ate potluck. There were custards, fresh greens, even a spring lamb, and the square May cakes of oatmeal. Lufe brought out his pipes, calling up the stars to mirror the many fires spangling the vale below. He played tunes so old that the words were no longer understood, although they had not lost their meaning. While Lufe piped, the animals were herded between the two fires to receive the blessing of the Goddess. Then Sirona led her people from field to field carrying torches lit from the sacred fires to bless their crops. When they reassembled by the bonfires on the green, Sirona withdrew to watch benevolently from the shadows as they obeyed her charge to celebrate and enjoy the gift of the Goddess. That was when the wooing, the singing, and the dancing began in earnest. Aldyth knew how it would go; as the embers sank down, those by the fire would become fewer, until the last drunk lapsed into snoring and the last whispering couple slipped into the darkness.

The dancers formed a ring, and nearly everyone joined in, until it was huge and snaking. As the night progressed, pairs broke off and the circle shrank. Aldyth sat just outside the ring of firelight with the littlest ones and their grandparents. Bertha moved among them, snuffling up to sleeping babies. Older children giggled and ran into and out of the shadows, to be dragged away from the fire before they could scorch themselves. As the evening wore on, they fell asleep and were carried home in blankets. Even Gandulf came, bringing a keg of honey mead undoubtedly filched from the garrison stores. Both he and his offering were received enthusiastically by the villagers. Aldyth bristled when Red Mary from Alcester sidled up to him; the woman obviously thought he was searching for a partner. Reluctantly he let her pull him into the dance. Old Edwin invited Aldyth to dance. When she saw that Mildred was dancing with Agilbert, Little Edmund perched upon his father's shoulders, Aldyth took Edwin's hand and followed him into the dance. She refused even to look at Gandulf; the sight of Red Mary fawning over him, flirting shamelessly, made her angry at them both. Granted, the lordling appeared uncomfortable, but he suffered her attentions nonetheless. If he had any shame, Aldyth silently fumed, he would send the hussy packing –

unless he intended to take her up on her implicit invitation. Intent on putting distance between herself and Gandulf, Aldyth usurped the lead from Edwin and high-stepped to the far side of the circle.

Strong arms seized her by the waist. At first Aldyth thought it might be Gandulf, but when she faced her self-appointed partner, she met a pair of glittering blue eyes. 'Bedwyn!' she whispered. How could she have forgotten he was coming?

Edwin winked at Bedwyn's audacity and gave up his partner with a good will, moving away to steal Mildred back from Agilbert.

'Bedwyn,' scolded Aldyth, 'you shouldn't be here.'

'If you insist,' he teased, dancing her out to the farthest fringes of firelight.

'If you don't care what happens to you, some of us do,' she said in annoyance. 'In case you haven't noticed, there is a Norman present.'

Bedwyn shrugged. 'Do you think I don't know that? I've already scouted the area, and he's alone.' More lightly, 'Aldyth, 'tis the time of the May.' He reached overhead and pulled a branch from one of the willow trees growing in the spring runoff, then wove it into a circlet and set it playfully on her head. 'And I have come to crown you Queen of the May.' Aldyth had to laugh. She let him draw her back into the dance. As a concession, Bedwyn allowed, 'If it will make you easier, we'll stay in the shadows.'

Gandulf, like a dog sensing the presence of a ghost, felt his hackles rise. Turning, he saw the big Saxon for whom he had been scouring the countryside. Gandulf, his expression fiercely dark, followed his progress. The man was well regarded, he could see, for as he passed through the crowd, he was warmly greeted. Gandulf wondered again why he had never seen this Saxon at other gatherings, since he and the villagers were so clearly acquainted. The lordling's fist clenched convulsively when the man swept Aldyth out of Edwin's arms. He lost sight of them, yet couldn't tear his eyes from the gloom that hid them. A tug on Gandulf's sleeve startled him, and he looked at Red Mary. She was waiting for an answer, though Gandulf had no idea what the question had been.

'Have you had your fill of dancing, my Lord?' she repeated. Then she whispered into Gandulf's ear, 'There are better things to do on May Eve.'

'Who is he?' Gandulf asked sharply.

'Who?' said Red Mary with a pout, although there could be no doubt who Gandulf meant, for he had not taken his eyes off Bedwyn since the moment he had arrived.

'What does it matter? They've made their choice,' said Mary with a shrug.

'So it would appear,' replied Gandulf irritably.

Lufe finished his tune, and Bedwyn took the opportunity to greet Aldyth with a warm kiss. Instinctively, she stepped back to escape the force of his compelling charisma.

'I've come for my answer,' said Bedwyn, closing the space between them.

'My answer is "nay," Bedwyn,' said Aldyth wretchedly, avoiding his eyes.

'You did not seem averse to the idea the last time we were together,' he reminded her, gently tugging at the green ribbon tied to her sleeve.

Aldyth blushed at the thought of their last meeting and stammered, 'I had thought to remain a maid, but were I ever to go with a man, 'twould be only as his wedded wife.'

Bedwyn's eyebrows shot up, and an amused smile spread slowly across his face. 'All right, then,' he agreed with only the slightest hesitation. 'If that's all that holds you back, we'll go to Father Edmund tonight and ask him to marry us.'

Aldyth gasped, caught off guard. She had not even considered the possibility that he would agree to marry her.

'What? Isn't that what you wanted?' he snapped.

Breathlessly, in a rush of words, she replied, 'If we were to marry, I – I would want to have children.' She knew that she was hedging.

'Fine,' he said. 'We could have four or five.'

'How would we live? What kind of life could we offer a family?'

'We'll figure it out, Mouse. We don't need all the answers right away. I'm still getting used to the idea of being married.'

'Bedwyn, this seems so sudden.'

'What's going on, Aldyth?' he asked crossly. 'I had to work up my courage to decide to wed you – and you're backing out?'

'Marriage is only the first step . . .'

'How can you call that only the first step? We've known each other for half our lives, and after the other night, what more do you need to know?'

'Do you love me? Or is it simply because I'm the only one who has ever said "no"?'

'I told you once before, 'tis not that at all. As for why, need I spell it out?' He took her by the shoulders, glared into her eyes, then kissed her soundly, leaving her shocked and breathless. Her traitorous body responded to his touch, reawakening visceral memories she had tried to squelch. She wriggled free to stand at a safer distance.

'Oh, no, you don't!' she sputtered. 'You can't just kiss away these concerns.'

'Let me try,' he coaxed, and before she could take another step backward, his hands shot out and prevented her escape. 'Let's go somewhere quiet and talk, love.'

'Talk?' she asked skeptically.

He shrugged, raising his eyebrows disarmingly.

'If you think to get me into the bushes, Bedwyn, you're sadly mistaken.'

'Are you so afraid that you'll succumb?'

She was, but she had no intention of admitting it to him.

'Aldyth,' he demanded, 'did the other night mean nothing to you?'

He gave her a kiss meant to melt away her resistance, but she pulled back and said, 'Have you no shame? Take your hands off me!'

'You heard her,' growled a fierce voice. 'She told you to take your hands off.'

Both Saxons' heads snapped around to face Gandulf. Aldyth was shocked at his ferocity; she had never thought of him as anything but the mildest of men.

'What business is it of yours, Norman?' snarled Bedwyn contemptuously. Releasing Aldyth, he turned to square off with

Gandulf. 'You may be a cockerel strutting the barnyard up on Castle Hill, but down here there are full-grown cocks.'

Gandulf was hardly a stripling; he was like a wiry stallion next to Bedwyn's destrier. Bedwyn was fearsome in his fury, but Gandulf's rage was alarming in its controlled intensity. The copper in his dark eyes glinted hot and cold, like the glare of fire on steel.

As far as Aldyth knew, the two men had never met; she was shocked at the immediate and open hostility between them. How strange to have two such separate parts of her world explode at first contact, and how embarrassing to have it happen so publicly – though neither one of *them* seemed to mind.

Blushing crimson, Aldyth said hastily, 'Gandulf, you needn't involve yourself.'

'You heard her,' echoed Bedwyn. ''Tis none of your damned business.'

''Tis obvious you're forcing yourself upon her,' spat Gandulf.

'Who are you to say, you son of a cast-off runt?' bellowed Bedwyn, and he shoved Gandulf in the chest with a force that nearly knocked the Norman off his feet.

Gandulf, his fury fanned by the insult to his mother, smashed his fist into Bedwyn's jaw, sending him sprawling backward. There was dead silence for the space of a heartbeat, broken by a great roar from Bedwyn as he leapt for Gandulf's throat. But he was caught in midleap by a knot of panicked Saxons. It took Wulfric, Eldred, Agilbert, and Godwin Swineherd to restrain him; were Bedwyn to strike the lordling and bring himself to notice of the law, it would mean losing a hand to most Saxons, and death to a known outlaw. Bedwyn, straining against the hold of his desperate friends, and Gandulf, hard put to restrain himself, glared at each other like a pair of leashed mastiffs.

Aldyth stepped between and scolded, 'Shame on you! You're acting like wild animals!'

Sirona's voice cut through the shocked silence; 'Like a pair of rutting stags.'

Bedwyn testily shrugged off his restrainers. Both men looked embarrassed, but they were still as mad as wet cats. 'Bedwyn,' pleaded Aldyth, 'I think you had better go now.'

'Not until this is finished!' he snapped.

'Please, Bedwyn, you could have your pick of the women.'

'And I picked you.'

'If you were wise,' snarled Gandulf to Bedwyn, 'you would leave.'

'Or what?' growled Bedwyn in challenge.

'Or you will be made to leave,' threatened Gandulf coldly.

Aldyth panicked. 'Gandulf, stay out of this,' she said curtly. 'It doesn't concern you.'

'Don't be so sure,' he retorted, glaring at Bedwyn.

'Aldyth,' cried Bedwyn, 'have you been carrying on with this Norman dog? You swore there was nothing between the two of you.'

'No more than between you and me, or anyone else for that matter. Bedwyn, I've known you for years. Yet all of a sudden you make an offer and you think you own me.'

'I've been pursuing you for years, Aldyth.'

'But never seriously. Always flirting. Always in jest.'

'Well, I'm serious now,' stated Bedwyn flatly.

'So am I,' responded Gandulf between clenched teeth.

Bedwyn was disturbed by this new turn of events; he had not counted the Norman as a serious rival. 'Aldyth, I understand I caught you by surprise tonight. Just think about it.' His eyes burned into Gandulf meaningfully as he said, 'I'm not asking you to be my whore; I'm asking you to be my wife.'

In a cold fury, Gandulf seized her elbow. 'Aldyth, I'm taking you home.'

'Get your hands off her!' thundered Bedwyn, thrusting Gandulf's hand aside.

But when Bedwyn then reached to claim Aldyth, she slapped the Saxon's hand away. 'Do you think I'm a prize pig to be fought over and tossed to the winner?' she exploded. With that she snatched off the leafy wreath that Bedwyn had placed on her head and flung it to the ground. 'I'm old enough to make my own choice. And I choose to be an old maid!'

She stormed off amid a shower of teasing hoots and whistles from the men and cheers from the women, leaving the two bewildered rivals staring dumbly after her.

CHAPTER TWENTY

May Day 1087

The boy clambered into the branches of the Wishing Tree. Seizing the slack-jawed calf's head from the upraised platter, he tied it to the branch overhanging the Crystal Spring. The crowd below cheered, and many hands reached up to lift the boy down. Holding him high above their heads while chanting the ancient song of the may, they hurled him into the spring: the bigger the splash, the better the omen. The boy, chosen by lot for this honor, had been dressed by Sirona in the faded tunic of green kept for this purpose. In former times, the chosen one would not have been allowed to come out of the spring alive, and his own head would have been hung in the tree. Father Odo had tried time and again to halt the proceedings, but country folk clung to their traditions.

At noon every Saxon in Sceapterbyrig had met at the town gate to take part in the Besom Ceremony. The town herald led the procession down Tout Hill, carrying a fresh green besom, the attribute of the Mother. On the herald's right stood the man whose job was to carry the calf's head on a platter. The assembly then piped and danced its way down the hill, to be met by an escort from Enmore Green, led by the boy chosen to represent the Green Man, the symbol of all that was fresh and growing, the son and husband of the Great Mother. He guided them to the village green and led them in a sunwise dance around the Maypole, then to the Crystal Spring, where Sirona awaited them.

When the shivering lad splashed out of the spring, everyone followed him across the green to take up the dance again. Not till the blatantly pagan portion of the celebration was over did Father Edmund and Wulfstan the Reeve join them, for the village priest must respect Pope Gregory's injunction against offering the heads of beasts as sacrifices to trees and wells, and Wulfstan had enough problems as Lord Ralf's overseer without antagonizing Father Odo, however much it went against his MoonCatcher blood to abstain.

The manor lord always provided the fare for the festivities. ''Tis cheaper,' Lord Ralf remarked with a sniff, 'to give them a sheep carcass once a year than to do battle every time we send down our carts for water.' Leaving his steward and reeve to represent him, Lord Ralf had led his own party out hawking; they would have an elegant picnic to mark the day.

As Margaret packed Gandulf's provisions for the day, she said, 'If you find yourself in Enmore Green, would you be so kind as to bring me a cross of rowan wood? A cross made without the use of iron, not cut with a knife, and tied with red yarn?'

'And what is the purpose of such a cross?' Gandulf inquired.

'To keep away evil spirits, of course; they can't enter a house that has one over the door. And get it from Aelfric, if you can.'

'Aelfric?'

'He is a Fairy changeling,' she told him. 'His crosses are more effective.'

'Well, that explains why he gets away with bloody murder around here,' said Gandulf with a laugh. 'I've wondered why he hasn't been stoned out of the village by now.'

'You'd be amazed, my Lord,' said Margaret gravely, 'how useful the lad can be. Everyone hereabouts owes him either fear or favor.'

'Fear?' asked Gandulf in disbelief. 'What is there to fear from the lad, aside from finding a fresh cowpat hidden by darkness on the toft bridge at night?'

'Aelfric knows everything that goes on, no matter how secret or how evil. Were it not for his winning ways, 'twould be enough to give one chills.'

'That such a scamp should hold such power does give one chills,' joked Gandulf.

'Laugh, then,' she admonished, 'but if you'd any sense, you'd buy one for yourself.'

Aelfric did a lively business in Enmore Green. Gandulf observed him accept a dozen eggs, a loaf of bread, a parsnip, and a pot of long-hoarded honey for his crosses. 'Aelfric is the only one here not moon-touched,' thought Gandulf, 'and he's making the most of it too.'

Gandulf spotted Aldyth, a cloud of hawthorn flowers in her hair, but there was no sign of the Saxon. Bedwyn was bold but no fool. Gandulf heaved a sigh. So Bedwyn had offered Aldyth marriage, something he could never do. Gandulf had lost the game even before it had begun.

He came to realize that he was being watched by the villagers, who were also watching Aldyth. Aldyth, aware of Gandulf's watchful eye, drifted to the other side of the green. The nosiest villagers gravitated with her. Gandulf followed the crowd, and the whole party drifted around the May-pole in a slowly milling circle dance.

Finally Agilbert sidled up to Gandulf, trying to be inconspicuous with a pig underfoot and an Edmund under each arm. Agilbert's eyes followed Gandulf's hungry gaze toward Aldyth, and he whispered, 'Speak up if you want her, man.'

Gandulf shifted his eyes to Agilbert, who swarmed with passengers like a dog with fleas. Agilbert gave the Norman an encouraging nudge. Gandulf winced, shaking his head.

''Tis how I won Bertha,' persisted Agilbert. ''Twasn't easy, but 'twas worth it in the end. She might drop into your hand like a ripe plum, but you'll never know till you try.'

'Hardly likely,' scoffed Gandulf. But he thought to himself, 'If she's not willing to fall into my hands, at least she might be willing to forgive me for yesterday's debacle.'

Gandulf nodded to Agilbert and set out. The mass movement sped up as Aldyth saw Gandulf approach, hastily moved away, and was followed. Aldyth was sure that her path was being blocked on purpose, but actually the onlookers were just pressing in for a good view. The effect was the same, for she was unable to escape. At last Gandulf stood before her, his eyes shifting nervously. 'Might we speak privately, Aldyth?'

'Not too privately, I hope,' Aldyth replied, the tone of

her voice as cool as the water that flowed from the Crystal Spring.

'Could we step away from this crowd?'

'Very well,' she said grudgingly. But when they tried to ease through the mob, the mob eased along with them. In exasperation Aldyth exclaimed, 'What's the point?'

'About last night . . .' Was it his imagination, or had the crowd begun to thicken?

'Yes, about last night,' she snapped. 'I've never seen such an outrageous display of strutting and posturing. I might've expected it of Bedwyn, but surely you knew better.'

'Let the poor man speak, Aldyth,' urged Winifred LongCross.

'Aye,' said Edwin MoonCatcher, 'give the lad a chance.'

'Did nothing happen last night more worthy of your attention?' Aldyth sharply asked the onlookers. 'Wasn't there almost a drowning in the spring? Didn't Osgot of Alcester's plowshed disappear? And who among you stole Father Rannulf's toft bridge?'

Her neighbors laughed in good-natured acknowledgement of the thrust as Aldyth forced her way through the mob and stamped off. Gandulf felt his color rise as he watched her go; if he had stood up on the back of a cart to proclaim his business, he could not have done so more effectively. He turned to escape and found the hulking PigWife at his elbow. Agilbert confided, 'It didn't work the first time with Bertha either.'

Disgusted, Gandulf turned on his heels and elbowed his way through the mob. 'What new lows I've sunk to,' he berated himself, 'to be taking advice for the lovelorn from a man who is married to a pig!'

As he broke through the outer ring of people, he could not help but notice Aelfric, leaning against the Wishing Tree. With a quick jerk of his head, the boy beckoned to Gandulf. Gandulf had half a mind to ignore the urchin's imperious summons, but, remembering Margaret's charge to him, he snapped, 'Well, what do you want?'

Aelfric replied, ''Tis a green fisherman who spreads his net in a dusty road.'

Irked by the effrontery, Gandulf asked, 'Where would you spread your net, cleverpuss?'

Aelfric grinned slyly. 'How much is it worth to you?'

'Why you little rogue! Have you sold all your rowan crosses? What makes you think I'd be willing to pay for anything you've got to say?'

'You're certainly not doing very well when left to your own devices.'

Gandulf sputtered with indignation, then sighed. 'True enough, you shameless cutpurse.' Handing the lad a penny, he said, 'I'll have one of your crosses for Margaret.'

Gandulf tucked the talisman into his purse and turned to leave, but Aelfric followed. 'I know the game, I know the trail, and I know where she goes to earth,' he stated baldly.

Gandulf faced Aelfric, and frowned. 'Would you sell her so cheaply?'

'No, not cheaply,' Aelfric assured him. 'But for tuppence I would.'

Gandulf shook his head chidingly but remembered Margaret's words. Aelfric could steer him no further off course than PigWife. Slapping the coins into Aelfric's hand, he said, 'All right. Who's the Saxon? Why doesn't he come to the gatherings? Is he an outlaw?'

'He lives in the vale. He and Aldyth have known each other forever and a day.'

There were so many questions, and Gandulf's thoughts were so jumbled that he did not notice Aelfric's avoidance of any incriminating information. But there was really only one question to which Gandulf really needed an answer. He hesitated. 'Does she love him?'

Aelfric replied earnestly, 'Aye, that she does.' Then the boy shrugged and added impudently, 'She loves me too, but she doesn't want to marry me.'

Gandulf perceived that he was being toyed with and wondered if he had gotten his tuppence worth of humiliation yet or if there was more to come. There was.

'Do you know for certain if he loves her?' Gandulf asked.

'Aye, that he does. In his own way.'

'And what way might that be?'

'Ask half the milkmaids from here to Motcombe,' said the boy cheekily.

Gandulf was outraged. 'She wouldn't throw her honor away for a philanderer.'

'No, that's what makes her different. But half the fun for Bedwyn is in the chase.'

'Would he use her and cast her aside?'

'If he promised to marry her, you'd better believe he means to do it.'

'What of her feelings?'

'Bedwyn could melt butter at a glance and ice with a kiss – so the ladies say,' Aelfric replied primly. 'He swears 'tis just a matter of time before he melts her heart as well.'

Gandulf pursed his lips. 'Well, 'tis no business of mine.'

'You made it your business yesterday,' said Aelfric, 'and quite publicly, too.'

'I was a fool to do so.'

'True enough,' agreed Aelfric, 'but 'tis not too late to take a new tack.'

Gandulf's eyes narrowed. 'And I suppose you're the one to lay it out for me?'

'For a price.'

'Of course,' said Gandulf acidly, slapping another penny into Aelfric's grubby hand.

Leaning toward Gandulf, Aelfric advised in a conspiratorial tone, 'Lay low for a week or so – to let her cool off. Aldyth has a terrible temper, but she's also very forgiving. Catch her in the morning when she's fresh, on her first trip to the well. Be humble; 'twill take her off guard. And apologize, as if she deserved it. She won't stay mad after that. Then make the pitch. Come clean, no nonsense; she'll see through the sweet talk.'

'Is that all?' Gandulf asked coolly.

'If I think of anything else, I'll let you know.'

'For a price,' added Gandulf sourly.

'Of course.'

Gandulf waited a week, as Aelfric had advised. The mist was still rising, and a sleepy cock crowed, as he loitered at the well waiting for Aldyth. He was embarrassed to be taking the advice of a roadside cupid, but it was logical advice. Left to his own devices, he knew he would have surrendered to despair and sunk back into his cloistered, moody ways.

Many of the things Gandulf had been driven to do of late were a surprise to everyone, including himself. He had never before flown off the handle the way he had on May Eve. It was the first time in his memory that he had ever struck out in anger, and that frightened him; he had lost control. His heart had always been subservient to his intellect. But instead of fleeing from the cause, like moth to flame he was even more drawn to Aldyth's forbidden light. It did not help that his father had heard of the altercation and ribbed him mercilessly for tomcatting about the village, and last Sunday Father Odo had preached a pointed sermon on the sin of lust. Gandulf could only plead guilty, but he felt even worse about publicly staking a claim on that to which he had no right.

The dew was still heavy on the grass when Aldyth passed by on her way to the woods. Gandulf leapt to his feet. It was pitiful, she thought, how nervous, even humble, he looked, now that he had declared himself. She was polite if distant.

'Aldyth . . .'

'I thought you were a footpad in the dark, Gandulf, sneaking out of the shadows.'

Only the week before Winifred LongCross and her great-granddaughter had been gathering wildflowers in the woods when two strange Normans had accosted them, doubtless seeking the next hide on the Starlit Path, and questioned them about the comings and goings in the village. Afterward Winifred had come to warn Aldyth.

'Can you describe the two men, Winifred?' Aldyth had asked.

Winifred had shuddered. 'Aye. The little one, I believe, was called Rollo. He had a scar across his mouth and the look of a ferret. The other was big as a bear and none too clever, if you ask me, but ready enough to strike an old woman.'

They fit the description of those who had ruined Alfred and Ricole, as well as the Weaver brothers and Ine Thatcher. Now they were trying to ferret out Bedwyn's hide. It made sense, for only the week before, a stranger had raised a hue and cry after being robbed outside of Enmore Green. He had said that two robbers, Normans, had attacked and held him at arrow point while they questioned him. Being a stranger to the area, he had had no answers, so they had simply beaten him and relieved him of his purse. But just before that, a Norman merchant on a richly caparisoned mule had gone past unmolested. 'A strange robber,' thought Aldyth, 'who lets a rich merchant pass and robs a poor pilgrim.' But, asserted the pilgrim, he had seen the merchant go by as he stopped to rest or dine.

'Are you going gathering?' Gandulf asked, forcing her thoughts back to the present.

'Yes,' she answered curtly.

'Would you mind an escort?'

'As you will,' she replied coolly.

Gandulf fell into step beside her, and he grudgingly congratulated Aelfric for his success so far. But as the silence dragged on, he fretted. He had not Bedwyn's gift with women and had to struggle for an opening. As he had no penchant for small talk, and as Aelfric had recommended frankness, he said at last, 'I apologize for my behavior last week—'

'Accepted. Let that be the end of it.'

'Aldyth, please, if you'll just let me explain—'

'Oh, Gandulf,' she said in exasperation, 'how could you have created such a spectacle? You must know that my position in the community requires an untarnished reputation.'

She walked on briskly. He followed, half a step behind this time. 'I'm sorry, Aldyth, but when I saw him seize you against your will, my only thought was for your safety.'

'Your *only* thought?'

'Well, my primary thought,' he admitted. 'These last months, I had reason to believe that you had given your heart to another, and so I was resigned. But when I realized that you were free—'

'I'm not nearly as free as you think, Gandulf.'

He felt a massive surge of guilt, for he knew that his own freedom would soon end. 'What do you mean, Aldyth? You were free enough to consider the Saxon's offer.'

'It was in a moment of madness, and at least *he* offered marriage. Gandulf, what future do you imagine us sharing? You haven't thought that far ahead, have you?'

'I haven't thought about anything else!' he exclaimed. 'I've cursed the fates that have placed us in such separate spheres and will settle for whatever you can willingly give.'

'That is little enough, Gandulf, for I am a maiden and shall remain so.'

'Have you taken a vow?' he asked anxiously.

'Not yet, but 'twill be necessary.'

'Who would force this vow?'

'It is my duty, and I accept it.'

'Is it some kind of religious commitment?'

'Aye,' she said, 'that it is.'

'I would like to try to change your mind, if you would not forbid me.'

'Can't you understand that it's hopeless? 'Twould only cause grief for us both.' She faced him, and he was taken aback by her intensity. Not unkindly, but with finality, she said, 'I will say this: though it goes against all my instincts, and though I have tried to deny it, I have feelings for you. But even were I free to choose, which I am not, I would not stain my honor to become someone's paramour, not even yours.' She kissed his cheek lightly and said, 'We'll speak no more of it, Gandulf. From here on, I walk alone.'

As she disappeared down the path, he thought, 'I am watching her walk out of my life.'

CHAPTER TWENTY-ONE

June 1087

Aldyth had been unbending with Gandulf that day by the well. But it had taken every ounce of her willpower not to toss her honor aside and throw herself into his arms. Until now, she had had no romance but that of her unspoken fantasies. Suddenly two very compelling men were nipping at her heels, each trying to drive her into his own fold. It never rained but it poured, she thought wryly, and she was left sitting alone in the mud.

Several weeks had passed. Gandulf, respecting Aldyth's wishes, had not approached her, though he continued his Sunday storytelling and paid an occasional visit to Sirona.

Aldyth left the web of paths tying together the tofts of Enmore Green to gather goat's rue before the bloom passed and hyssop flowers to be used for lung ailments. All day, as she collected her herbs, Aldyth mulled over how she had muddled matters with Bedwyn. They had both been vulnerable, and each had sought comfort in the other's arms. She still had her life in Enmore Green, but Bedwyn's life had been the Starlit Path. Yet Bedwyn would surely find someone else to love. Gandulf, too. But Aldyth knew that she never would; the Crystal Fountain seemed a cold life's mate.

In spite of her brooding, she was pleased with her harvest. On her way home that afternoon, however, she had a strange feeling that she was not alone. She tried to shrug it off, but as she stepped out of a sunny glade and into the sun-dappled shadows of the woods, she heard a rustling in the brush and felt, rather than saw, the presence of two figures falling into step on either side of the path. Glancing over her shoulder, she glimpsed movement through the light and shadow and quickened her step; so did the shadows. Feeling like a stalked deer, Aldyth broke into a run, drawing her pursuers out into the open. Like wolves moving in for the kill, they abandoned all stealth and charged their quarry. Aldyth shot forward until she realized she had no hope of outrunning them. Not wanting to be brought to bay like a cornered hart, she turned to face them. Though startled to a halt, her stalkers made a quick recovery. The big one circled behind, while the other approached from the front. Aldyth forced herself not to stare at the scar twisting the smaller one's lip into a perpetual sneer. This had to be the scarred one Gorm had described, who had accosted Winifred in the woods; these men had destroyed Ricole and Alfred, Willibald and Willibrord, and it was their mission to destroy Bedwyn, Sirona, and herself. Aldyth decided that righteous indignation was her best defense. 'Who are you?' she demanded. 'What do you want?'

Ignoring her, the big one asked, 'Is this the one we're after, Rollo?'

'I think so.' Rollo, his breath stinking of garlic, put his face uncomfortably close to Aldyth's. 'We just want to ask a few questions.'

Aldyth's mouth went dry. 'Ask, then, and be done with it.'

'Where have you been today?' demanded the Norman.

'I've been collecting herbs in the woods,' she answered truthfully.

The Norman snatched Aldyth's basket and dumped the contents onto the ground. He kicked at the goat's rue, the blanket weed, and the hart's clover she had gathered; Aldyth leapt forward to save the day's harvest but found her arms pinned from behind. 'Ask your questions and let my herbs alone,' she said. 'You're bruising the leaves.'

'Mayhap that need be the only bruising incurred today. Do you know the penalty for treason?' asked Rollo, lifting a lock of her hair and rolling it between his fingers.

Refusing to appear affected by his insolence, Aldyth answered, 'Who doesn't?'

The one in back yanked her hair. 'We want answers, not more questions, girl.'

'Now, Hugo,' rebuked Rollo. Then he asked Aldyth, 'You're the witch's granddaughter?'

'She's a healer, not a witch, and I'm her goddaughter,' corrected Aldyth, giving her head a toss in an effort to pull her hair free.

Rollo laughed under his breath, but his voice was cold as he continued, 'Do you ever stray out after curfew?'

'Once in a while everyone miscalculates the time it takes to get home from the fields.'

'Do you ever see strangers when you "miscalculate" the time it takes to get home?'

'Of course. Pilgrims, merchants, market goers. Strangers come through every day.'

She did not even see the blow before it hit her cheek.

'Let's try again, shall we?' said the Norman. 'Do you ever speak to strangers when you're out after curfew?'

Aldyth was too stunned to respond.

'Answer me!' he ordered sharply.

'I'm too busy getting home myself,' she stammered.

This time she was braced for the blow.

'Stop playing games. You can flash those green eyes at Ralf fitzGerald, but it won't work on us.' He had dropped all pretense of civility. Gripping her chin, his fingers digging into her cheeks, he growled. 'What of the Hermit of the Blackmore Vale?'

Aldyth tried not to let her panic show; they would not ask after Bedwyn if they had taken him, but they had obviously made a connection between the Hermit of the Blackmore Vale and the Starlit Path. She thought of Ine Thatcher, held in the tower. How much did he know, and how much would he tell? Had they already twisted it out of him?

'Who hasn't heard the stories?' she replied.

'Where does he live?'

'How can I say? No one even knows if there is such a person. The stories have been around longer than any man's natural life span.'

'People around here live longer than is natural – God knows why.'

'Or the Devil,' said Hugo.

'You have heard of the Devil?' asked Rollo. He delivered several more blows in quick succession. Aldyth felt a hot, sticky liquid running down her face; her nose was bleeding.

'I don't think that will work with this one,' said Hugo.

'Perhaps not, but she's hiding something. 'Tis not in her basket; mayhap she's hidden it in her kirtle.' With a crude leer, he grabbed at the front of her gown, roughly snatching at her breasts. Aldyth struggled to pull away but was pinned from behind. 'Only a virgin would struggle so,' smirked Rollo.

'Don't you remember the tailor's wife?' his accomplice reminded him. 'She liked it no better than this one.'

'Still, I'd be willing to wager this one has got her maidenhead.'

'Ask her,' suggested Hugo.

'She's lying about everything else. There's really only one way to find out for sure.'

Rollo began to unlace his trousers, and Aldyth realized with revulsion that they had never intended to release her unharmed. Bedwyn! Gandulf! she cried out in her mind. Why was a man never around when you wanted him? Aldyth's heart pounded as Rollo slipped his weapon of choice out of his trousers.

'No!' shrieked Aldyth. She rent the air with a bloodcurdling scream that startled her attackers. Using Hugo's hold for a brace, she lifted both feet and kicked Rollo in the groin with all her might. Clutching himself, he fell to the ground, groaning and cursing.

'Unhand the maiden!' barked a commanding voice. Rollo, still writhing in pain, paid no heed, but both Aldyth and Hugo turned to see a lay brother rein in the mule he was riding.

'Unhand her!' he ordered again, dismounting.

Uncertainly, Hugo looked to Rollo for orders, but Rollo was in no condition to protest.

'Be quick about it, or I'll have the abbess of Saint Mary's herself deal with you.'

Hugo found his voice at last. 'We're here on the king's business.'

'Is it the business of a king to molest defenseless women? Let go of her, you lout. And you,' he said to Rollo, nudging him roughly with his sandaled foot, 'put your prick back in your trousers and get out of here before I finish what the girl started.'

The beast Aldyth's rescuer rode was the first of two mules bearing a dusty litter between them. Even after he dismounted, the lay brother cut a commanding figure. Hugo backed away from Aldyth. The lay brother, fists clenched, stepped forward and growled, 'I've connections in Sceapterbyrig, but I would settle this here and now.'

A woman parted the curtains of the litter and called, 'What's going on? The abbess will be furious that you've left her in our dust. Call the others here quickly!'

The lay brother blew the horn that hung at his belt. Seizing the opportunity, Hugo lifted Rollo to his feet and dragged him to the woods in a shameless retreat.

Aldyth's knees buckled, and she dropped to the ground, shivering.

'A fright like that chills one to the bones,' said the lay brother, and Aldyth recognized the rolling downs and the tang of salt in his pleasant Wessex drawl. Kneeling beside her, he threw his cloak over her shoulders and gave her a little hug. 'Are you hurt, lass?'

Aldyth shook her head.

With great callused hands, the lay brother tilted up her chin and dabbed at her bloody nose with his sleeve. 'Hold still,' he said, 'and I'll have you cleaned up in a trice. You're sporting a bruise or two, but I reckon that Norman is hurting worse than you.' He chuckled. 'Did he loosen any teeth?'

'No, thank you; I'm fine,' Aldyth assured him.

Two nuns, dusty and disheveled, stepped out of the litter, veils askew. 'Is she hurt?'

The lay brother laughed. 'She gave as good as she got.'

'Good for you,' said the younger of the two. 'We knew something was afoot when Brother Ansgar spurred on his beast until our teeth were fairly rattling.'

'Gunhild,' said the other nun, 'the water flask and a cloth, if you please.'

The nun called Gunhild leaned into the litter and returned with a cloth and a skin. 'When you are finished, Sister Edith, she might like something stronger to settle her nerves.' And she proffered a flask of wine as well.

Sister Edith washed the dust and blood from Aldyth's face. Her touch was gentle and kind as she smoothed the hair back from Aldyth's brow. 'What is your name, child?'

'They call me Aldyth Lightfoot.'

The lay brother guffawed. 'You trod none too lightly a moment ago; the next child that Norman begets will have your footprints on it!'

'Brother Ansgar!' scolded the elder nun, though with little heat.

He grinned and knelt to lift the flagon of wine to Aldyth's lips. 'Drink your fill, child, but slowly. There is nothing to fear now, for you are safe among friends. Another sip,' he urged, 'for you're still shaking like a windswept willow.'

Aldyth drank, hugging herself beneath the borrowed cloak, then wondered at her good fortune. 'What luck that an armed escort should happen by.'

Everyone but Aldyth broke into ironic laughter. Her brow knit in puzzlement, and Brother Ansgar explained, 'Lightly armed, indeed, for I bear only two fists.'

It occurred to Aldyth that the escort Brother Ansgar had summoned had not yet arrived. 'Where are the others?' she asked, looking toward the highway.

'In truth, we are traveling alone. Sister Edith conjured them out of thin air.'

Aldyth shook her head in amazement, then observed. 'Two fists were more than sufficient. How can I ever thank you?'

'You can say a prayer for Brother Ansgar.' Gesturing toward his companions, he added, 'And for Sister Edith and Sister Gunhild. Now, where do you call home, child?'

'The village of Enmore Green, Brother.'

'Tell me, Aldyth Lightfoot, how far might Enmore Green be from here?'

'Perhaps two miles.'

'Good. Then we shall see you safely home.'

Fearful that the Normans might yet be lurking nearby, Aldyth accepted gratefully. 'Though I hope 'twill not carry you far from your own path.'

''Tis a fair exchange, for good company shortens the road.'

Many travelers came to Sceapterbyrig on pilgrimage to see the martyr's bones or do business with the abbey. What was it about these travelers that seemed so uncommon? Like all other lay brothers, Brother Ansgar was clean-shaven and tonsured. His dress was coarse and road-rumpled, but Aldyth noted that there was nothing common about this silver-haired stranger. Even as he knelt to gather her scattered herbs, he carried himself more like an abbot than a lay brother. A jagged scar extended above the collar of his robe, and another protruded from beneath a sleeve. His nose had been broken, but it only added interest to his features, and however harsh a life this man had led, it had not put a chill into his gentle blue eyes; some blue eyes sparkled like jewels, some like ice, but Brother Ansgar's were the soft blue of periwinkles.

The nuns shook the dust off their outer cloaks only to reveal that their habits underneath were just as disheveled. Sister Gunhild was still attractive, though she had seen at least thirty summers, and Sister Edith too would have been a beauty in her day.

''Tis crowded in the litter,' said Brother Ansgar. 'Shall I have Sister Gunhild come up with me, or are you able to ride, Aldyth?'

'I think I can ride.'

'There's a good lass.' Aldyth let him draw her up behind on the mule.

They returned to the king's highway, a pair of muddy ruts cut by cart-wheels interlaced with paths worn by foot travelers. It wound down the middle of a swath cleared from the forest, for King William had decreed that, in the interest of safety, all woodland must be at least a bow shot's distance from the highway.

''Tis sunny here, away from the woods,' said Brother Ansgar, sensing Aldyth's unease, 'and the cleared verges make it difficult to be taken unawares. But a comely lass should keep to well-traveled places or, better yet, travel in good company.'

His straightforward assessment of her recent trauma actually served to settle Aldyth's jangled nerves, for he had drawn a nightmare back into the light of day. Brother Ansgar then deftly changed the subject. His conversation was charming and amusing, and Aldyth was surprised to find herself smiling. Brother Ansgar was either a wizard or a close student of human nature, for half an hour before she had been certain the day's terror would darken her outlook for the rest of her life.

Aldyth too was adept at drawing people out, but by the time the mules had crossed the common, she realized that Brother Ansgar had had from her nearly every bit of news about Sceapterbyrig, Enmore Green, and the turn of local events. With a tingle of apprehension, it occurred to her that she still knew nothing about him.

'I suppose you have business at the abbey?' she asked.

'Aye, lass. Is the road as well traveled as it once was?'

'Though the market has shrunk and the town has lost half its houses since the Normans came. When were you last here?'

'Before your mother ever let you down from her knee.'

She could not get a straight answer from him, not even when she asked directly, yet he put her off so smoothly that she might never have perceived it had not she been on the alert. She even wondered if the situation had been contrived so that an infiltrator in the guise of a charming rescuer might gain her confidence. Could this man be one of King William's spies, or might he be spying for someone else? England was crawling with agents and informers, like a carcass covered with maggots; the king's spies might not know the earl's spies and the earl's spies might not know the sheriff's. Brother Ansgar certainly knew more than he admitted, and Aldyth suspected that he was pretending to be something that he was not. Yet she liked him far too much to want to believe this.

Aldyth directed the brother to her toft. As he lifted her down, Sister Edith parted the curtains and called warmly, 'God bless you, child.'

'Thank you, Sister,' said Aldyth.

With a steadying arm about Aldyth's waist, Brother Ansgar saw her to her door. 'God keep you, lass, but let you try to make his job easier.'

From her doorstep Aldyth watched their mules plod on their way. All three strangers were interesting and attractive, yet amiability was no proof of good intent. However gentle or pious his guise, a rat catcher was still a rat catcher. She resolved to visit Mother Rowena; perhaps the infirmarian could learn more about these strangers than she had, and Aldyth could always rely upon Sister Arlette for gleanings.

Aldyth turned to step inside when, from over the fence, Edith MoonCatcher called out in alarm, 'Aldyth Lightfoot! Sirona's been asking after you all afternoon.' Edith shouted in the other direction, 'Sirona! Come quick! Aldyth's back, looking like falcon bait!' Then she hurried around to Aldyth's gate to follow her friend inside.

'Louder, please, Edith,' said Aldyth, shaking her head in affectionate exasperation. 'I don't think they quite heard you in Alcester.' She reached up to unpin her cloak and realized that she still wore that of Brother Ansgar.

Edith gasped at the sight of Aldyth's blood-spattered kirtle. 'Good Lord, Aldyth!'

''Twas just a nosebleed, Edith.'

Aldyth was madly trying to sort out her thoughts; what could she tell Edith, and which parts of the story were for Sirona's ears alone. To buy time as she got her story straight, Aldyth carefully folded the borrowed cloak and tucked it on the shelf, then reached for her other kirtle. The door flew open with a loud bang. In rushed Sirona and Mildburh, followed by a gaggle of wildly excited children and, worst of all, Gandulf.

'Aldyth, what happened to your dress? Is that your blood?' cried Mildburh in alarm.

''Twas only a nosebleed,' Aldyth asserted with such fervor that she was beginning to believe it herself.

'A good wash is all she needs,' Edith said, winking at the wide-eyed children as she sat Aldyth down on the bench, stirred the embers, and poured water into the cauldron to heat. 'But there's a story here, I'll wager,' she added, plopping down beside Aldyth.

Frustrated by their lack of urgency, Gandulf frowned and started toward Aldyth, but Sirona placed a restraining hand on his arm and threw him a warning look, nodding toward the children. In a tone of forced calm, he said to them, 'Hold out your hands.' He emptied into their upturned palms a pouchful of raisins, which he had gotten into the habit of carrying on his visits, and said, 'Off with you now. 'Tis all I have.'

The children departed, happily distracted, and attention turned back to Aldyth. But before anyone could speak, she said, 'Now, don't make a fuss.' Using humor to mask her terror, she quipped, 'I was set upon in the woods, but Saint Christopher, in the shape of a lay brother leading a litter full of nuns, came along and rescued me.'

Gandulf tipped her bruised face toward the light of the open door. 'Apparently your Saint Christopher didn't come soon enough. It wasn't that Saxon, was it? If it was, I'll—'

'Of course not!' she said, cutting him off irritably. ''Twas two Normans.'

'If they're my father's men, by the head of Saint Denis, they'll pay!' vowed Gandulf.

''Twas none of Lord Ralf's men,' Aldyth said.

'Did you recognize them?' asked Gandulf sternly. 'What did they do to you?'

'I never saw them before,' she replied truthfully, although she knew them by description. 'And my virtue is still intact, if that's what you mean.'

'Thank the Lady,' said Sirona, 'and Saint Christopher too, whoever he proves to be!'

Anxious to deflect inquiry, Aldyth joked, 'He left me his cloak, Gandulf. It seems that you have started a fashion, and I have started a collection.'

''Tis nothing to jest about, Aldyth,' he scolded. 'I don't want you out gathering your herbs in the fields alone . . . or whatever it is you do out there.'

'Who are you to say?' said Aldyth, her hackles rising.

'Let me rephrase that,' he suggested in an effort to appease her. 'The woods hereabouts are no longer safe. Please, if you must go gathering, allow me to escort you.'

''Tis kind of you, Gandulf, but unnecessary.' A plan was already forming in Aldyth's mind, one that could not possibly involve the Norman. She must warn Bedwyn immediately that the rat catchers were at their doorstep.

'You're such an innocent,' said Gandulf impatiently. 'Must

I tell you what violence men are capable of?' Turning to Sirona, he pleaded, 'Can't you make her understand?'

'He makes a good point, child,' agreed the crone. 'Something is afoot in the vale. Best wait until these men are apprehended before setting out alone.'

'You can't be serious, Sirona! This is herb-gathering time; everything will be out of season before this is settled. Besides, I have my dirk and I'm not afraid to use it.'

'A lot of good it did you today!' barked Gandulf.

'Well, I need to collect southernwood leaves. With the warmer weather, the leaves lose their virtue. We'll have need for it this winter to purge the children of gut worms and to keep the moths out of our clothes and the mealworms out of our stores.'

'Surely it can wait until the day after tomorrow,' said Sirona, 'when I can go with you. Tomorrow I owe to Lord Ralf, but the next day—'

'I'll be careful and I'll be quick,' Aldyth assured her, 'and I'll be back before you know I've gone. And after that, I promise to stay close to home.'

Aldyth noted with satisfaction that no one offered any argument. She did not, however, note the meaningful glance exchanged over her head between Gandulf and Sirona.

Gandulf returned to the garrison plagued with worry. He suspected that Aldyth's gathering in the woods was not entirely innocent nor her interests solely botanical. He questioned her connection to the Saxon called Bedwyn, and there, too, he suspected there was more to their relationship than was admitted. Gandulf could not be Aldyth's personal watchdog, but it drove him to distraction to think how cruelly she had been used and how much worse it might have been. He determined to track down her attackers and punish them.

'I must settle this before I leave for Canterbury,' he thought grimly, 'to make the woods safe for Aldyth. The wonder is that she hasn't been assaulted before.' Sirona's protection was a powerful, if invisible shield; thus Gandulf reasoned that her attackers were from outside the area. While it was possible that they were common scoundrels, somehow Gandulf doubted it. He would speak to Sirona, for he needed more information.

Hugh fitzGrip, who had answered a summons from the earl of Gillingham, was taking advantage of Lord Ralf's hospitality on his homeward journey to join them at table. Over whole roast pigeons, glazed custard tarts, and venison pasties, Lord Ralf boasted to his guest of the progress his workmen were making on the castle.

'The motte is done, the timbers cut, and by Lammas we'll lay the stone foundations.'

'How can you afford the cost of construction on the heels of this damnable famine?'

'Labor is the worst problem,' expounded Ralf, 'but I've a good master mason, and I know how to "inspire" the workforce.'

FitzGrip, laughing heartily at the jest, reached for his wine goblet and said, 'My peasants drag their feet and blame it on the weather.'

'Why do you listen? They'll grumble no matter how you treat them.'

'Tell me truly, Ralf,' coaxed fitzGrip, leaning forward with a conspiratorial air, 'how are you managing to finance this pet project of yours? I had understood that you were short of the necessary funds. Did King William grant you assistance?'

Lord Ralf smirked, 'I haven't given up on that yet, but I've found an alternative.' He looked toward Gandulf and said casually, 'I'm leaving for London the day after tomorrow.'

Gandulf's first reaction was relief, for everyone in the garrison was more at ease when Ralf was away.

'Don't look so pleased, Gandulf,' said his father. 'You're coming with me.'

Gandulf's heart sank. It was with little hope that he reminded his father, 'You know I'm promised to escort Mother to Canterbury next week.'

'I've made other plans for you,' said Lord Ralf with a chilling finality.

'Does this have something to do with Catherine de Broadford?' asked Gandulf coolly.

Ralf grinned. 'So you've heard. Be sure to dress up in

your finest; that little chit is going to build my castle with her dowry.'

Gandulf fumed but knew it was useless to argue. If his father had to drag him to London in chains, he would not hesitate to do so. Gandulf looked down at his clenched hands to find that the pasty he had been eating was a mangled clump of mush. Angrily he shook the mess from his fingers, wiped his hands on the tablecloth, and rose to leave.

'Where are you going?' demanded his father.

'To the abbey,' retorted Gandulf, 'to inform Mother of "my" change of plans.'

'You can go to Hell for all I care,' sneered Lord Ralf, 'as long as you're packed to leave the day after tomorrow.'

As Gandulf strode across the hall, his humiliation was compounded by the scornful laughter of his father and Hugh fitzGrip.

CHAPTER TWENTY-TWO

It was still so dark that the first faint light of dawn could not penetrate the flimsy cracked walls of their hut. Aldyth, listening to the steady sound of her godmother's breathing as she slept, felt very clever: in her determination to make an early start, she had drunk as much water as she could hold before retiring for the night, so that nature would surely call her for an early rising.

The night before, she and Sirona had not had a chance to discuss the assault because Mildburh and Edith had stayed so late; then she had retired before Sirona could question her further. There would be time for talk after she returned from Bedwyn's. She was anxious about going out alone but reasoned that she had been caught off her guard the last time; she would be watchful and keep her digging tool at hand. It was imperative that she send Bedwyn away, quickly, forever – but first, they must talk frankly when there were no onlookers Bedwyn would feel compelled to swagger for, so that she might make him understand her reasons in a way that would soothe his wounded pride. He might even be relieved to be released from a rash promise.

From the moment she left the house, Aldyth's exaltation at having escaped changed to apprehension. As she approached the fountain, a shadow emerged from the misty dawn. Brandishing her digging tool, she warned, 'Come no closer! I'm armed!'

'I surrender,' came a familiar voice.

'Gandulf!' she scolded. 'Don't go sneaking up on people!'

'I've never seen you so jumpy, Aldyth,' he said accusingly. ''Tis because you know you shouldn't be out by yourself.'

'How long have you been lying in wait to tell me this?'

'Long enough to be glad for the chance to get my blood moving again.'

Gandulf had not gone home after leaving the abbey the night before. He had still been too angry, and he had wanted to be certain of seeing Aldyth one more time while he was still free. 'Where are we going?' he asked.

Rather than waste time arguing, Aldyth decided to accept his escort, then sneak out to Bedwyn's as soon as they returned. 'Very well, Saint Christopher,' she said irritably, for he had ruined all her carefully laid plans. 'You may see me to the Fairy hill.'

'Gladly,' said Gandulf with relief, though somewhat surprised that she had yielded so readily. He fetched Cathedra from the brush where she waited sleepily, mounted the bay mare, and pulled Aldyth up behind. She was still too annoyed to put her arms around him, but he reached back, took her wrists, and wrapped them about his waist. Testily she withdrew them. Firmly taking hold of them once more, he said, as though patiently explaining to a wayward child, 'I'm not guarding you from the footpads only to drop you on your head, as hard as it may be.' Then he added, 'I'll try not to enjoy it.'

The sun had risen, waking the birds. A chorus of doves purred like mellow thunder, and dewdrops glittered like crystal in grass bejeweled with wild strawberries. 'I'll try not to enjoy it either,' Aldyth told herself primly.

'How good to be with her,' thought Gandulf. His mind carried him back to their first ride out to the Fairy hill, and he mused, 'How much has changed between us since then.'

Aldyth, too, was remembering that ride. 'Nothing has really changed since then,' she thought. Admittedly, she knew Gandulf better now, but familiarity had not dulled her initial attraction to him. She had stopped waiting for this perverse affliction to clear up and tried instead to regard it as a chronic condition that she could learn to live with, like Winifred's rheumatism or, she thought ruefully, Agilbert's delusion. She had not acquired immunity to Bedwyn's charms; why should it be any easier to resist Gandulf's?

'Are we going back for more chicory?' he asked, breaking into her musing.

'No. We're going to gather blue flax.'

'What use will you find for it?'

''Tis a mild laxative, and I sometimes use it to make poultices.'

'I'm impressed with your learning, Aldyth. I spent fifteen years at Saint Denis, but I don't employ my education to any purpose. You use yours daily, to the benefit of many.'

'Don't underestimate the value of knowledge for its own sake, Gandulf. In how many other villages can the peasants quote chansons de geste?'

Gandulf smiled and lapsed into a thoughtful silence before he continued, 'I studied Lucretius in Paris, Aldyth. He laid out on parchment the nature of the world and the universe. My understanding of the world is much like that, all on parchment. Yours is read from life.' He paused, knowing that he would never again be able to speak so openly.

'I know you're angry with me, Aldyth, and I don't blame you. I've been acting the fool since the day we met. It has never been my wish to make your life more difficult, though God knows, I have brought you more than your share of grief. But I want you to know that I am grateful to you for teaching me to read life like a new language.'

'And I shall always be grateful for your warm cloak,' she teased, unable to hold on to her anger any longer. She wondered, however, what had prompted such serious talk.

When they arrived at the Fairy hill, Gandulf reined in Cathedra and dismounted. As he held his arms up to Aldyth, he felt unexpectedly stirred. Her curves had filled out since the depths of winter, her hair had regained its sheen and glistened like beads of honey in the summer sun. But she was not the same woman who had bowled him over in the bailey nearly a year before. Perhaps the winter had taken its toll, for he detected a sadness that had not been there last autumn.

As Aldyth waited for Gandulf to lift her from the saddle, she looked down into his upraised face and saw grief in his eyes of such depth that it frightened her. Then it occurred to her that there was a time when his features might have been carved of stone for all the emotion she could read in them. Was she so much more aware, or had he finally let down his shield? She longed to reach out and comfort him but dared not, for fear of encouraging this mad and fruitless courtship. Instead she focused on the way his dark brown hair caught the light of the sun and turned its gleam to copper. The immaculate cleanliness of his neatly pared fingernails emphasized the graceful strength of his fine, strong hands. Unlike many of the knights in Lord Ralf's court, the only jewelry Gandulf wore was a golden signet ring bearing the seal of his station, his family crest, and he was the only Norman she knew who did not shave the back of his head in the harsh and unbecoming fashion favored by the Normans. Gandulf's nonconformity in the face of stern disapproval was an outward sign of an inward stubbornness she admired.

Gandulf lifted her down but did not release her. 'Aldyth,' he said somberly, 'there is something I must tell you, for you're bound to hear of it sooner rather than later.'

She waited for him to speak, but he could only look down at her helplessly.

'Yes, Gandulf?'

'I'll be leaving tomorrow on a journey. I'll be gone for six weeks, maybe more.'

She waited for him to continue, then finally prompted, 'Where to?'

'To London.'

'For pleasure or business?'

Choking on his words, he whispered, 'Sorrowful business.'

'Gandulf, whatever can it be?' Forgetting her resolutions, she touched his cheek.

'I am going to meet the girl I am to wed,' he blurted, pressing her hand to his cheek.

Aldyth's stomach gave a lurch. 'Is it certain?' she asked, withdrawing her hand awkwardly. 'Has a date been set?'

'The negotiations are nearing an end. I've been told to go and make myself pleasant. If she and her parents find me acceptable, my father will sign the contract.'

'Perhaps she will make you a good wife,' stammered Aldyth, stepping out of reach.

'Aldyth,' he cried in despair, 'she's only thirteen years old and hasn't even begun her monthly flux! The poor child is likely scared unto death at the idea of marrying an old man like me, and I can hardly bear the thought of such a union. Yet if it should come to pass,' he said, reclaiming Aldyth's hands, 'you must know this was not of my choosing.'

'Could you not refuse?'

He shook his head. ''Twould prove useless.'

'And have you no other choice?'

'Were I to renounce my name and heritage, what could I do?' He shrugged in disgust. 'I am trained for nothing but the life of a monk. Though that lot would be preferable to me, entering the monastery requires an endowment. Were I to reject this marriage, I would be disowned, no one's man, no better than an outlaw.'

'I'm afraid you'd make a very poor outlaw, Gandulf,' she said ruefully.

Gandulf laughed in response, but it was a humorless sound. Aldyth brushed the windblown hair from his eyes. 'Poor Gandulf.'

'Aldyth,' he said, his eyes brightening, 'perhaps I could run off to Northumberland or Burgundy. I might get a place as steward on a manor, keeping accounts. You told me once that you had feelings for me; could you learn to love me? Would you be wife to No One's Man? To the clerk of a minor knight on the farthest edges of the kingdom? Were you to come away with me, 'twould be no exile but the answer to all my hopes.'

'Gandulf,' she said in awe, 'you would give up your title and inheritance to wed me?'

''Tis little enough. I would give up my life.'

Her eyes filled with tears, and she shook her head in stunned disbelief. Bedwyn had lost everything and had sought her as consolation. But Gandulf would throw it all away for her sake. And with all her heart, Aldyth knew she wanted to go with him if only she could. This time there was none of the uncertainty, no doubts or question of motives. Neither marriage nor children had the least bearing on her feelings; she knew only that she wanted to be with him. With Gandulf at her side, she would never fear growing old, for she knew he would be there to cherish and protect her. And she would fend off his sorrows, shielding him from hurt and pain with the power of her love.

Her tears spilled over, and Gandulf brushed them aside reverently. Watching her face intently for any sign of resistance, he pulled her into an embrace. As Aldyth laid her head upon his chest and listened to the wild pounding of his heart, she was drawn back to the day they had met, to the first, the only other time Gandulf had held her in his arms. Once again they were on the stone steps outside his father's hall, where he had saved her from a terrible fall. But this time they were both reeling, and there was nothing to stop them, nothing to save them, nothing to cling to but each other.

'Can it be true?' he whispered in disbelief. 'Do you really care for me?'

'More than you will ever know,' she said softly.

At that moment, the joy of knowing that she loved him overshadowed everything else; it made up for every slight, every cruelty that he had ever suffered, and for one shining instant Gandulf was happier than he had ever been in his life. Joy burst over him like waves, and he kissed her with a tender intensity, crying 'My dearest Aldyth!'

'Oh, Gandulf, no,' said Aldyth, recoiling in horror, for he had misunderstood her.

'What?' mumbled Gandulf, half to himself.

'My vow,' Aldyth groaned. 'My life, like yours, is predestined. I cannot go with you, though it be my heart's desire.' She buried her face in her hands and wept.

The agony of comprehension dawned in his eyes. 'God in Heaven, Aldyth, how can this be?' He seized her shoulders and, with a ferocious desperation, cried, 'That I could find someone to love is miracle enough. That she should love me too is beyond believing. That it can never be is beyond bearing!'

A lone tear brimmed up in one of his eyes and spilled over. Aldyth, her fingers wet with her own tears, reached up and touched it. With a gasp Gandulf closed his eyes, sending a rivulet down his cheek. He buried his head in her shoulder, and Aldyth held him close, his body wracked with sobs, which tore at her so fiercely that her own defenses crumbled. The two of them stood there clinging, unimaginable joy mingled with unbearable sorrow.

'Oh, Gandulf, my poor Gandulf,' she whispered through her tears.

'Aldyth, Aldyth, Aldyth,' he kept repeating. Distilled in the name were feelings he could never speak aloud, an intensity of longing, a universe of undiscoverable joy and unholy loneliness.

When all their tears were spent, Gandulf heaved a great sigh and wiped her flushed face with his cuff. Then he ran his sleeve across his own redrimmed eyes. 'Could Tristan's fate compare in cruelty?' He looked down at her and said, 'At the gathering, when I told the story of Tristan and Iseult, was it for us that you wept?'

Aldyth tightened her grip about his neck, and nodded. 'I'm so sorry, love.'

'No one is to blame, sweeting. I never expected to find happiness. Far less did I expect to find love.' They held each other in silence, waiting for the heaving gasps of their dying sobs to fade away. Out of the stillness, Gandulf confided, ''Tis strange, Aldyth, but I've not shed a tear since I was a boy; I thought I had none left to cry.'

He looked away to the distant hills and was surprised to find the birds still sang, oblivious to the wrenching drama played out on the ridge. The whole hillside reflected the blue of the sky as it rippled with breeze-tossed flax blossoms. Yet on that balmy summer morning, their lives had been blasted by a cruel, wintry wind, and he wondered if he would forever feel so bleak and cold inside. But his sorrows would not keep the grass from growing or the sun from shining; he had no choice but to go on.

'Come, love,' he said to Aldyth, taking her hand. ''Tis getting late, and I promised to help you gather flax.' He led her through the flower-spangled grasses of the Fairy hill.

'Gandulf!' cried Aldyth suddenly, pulling him to a stop. 'We can ask the Fairies!'

'The Fairies?'

'The elfin folk who live in the hill.'

'But I thought you said the hill was a burial place for the ancient ones.'

'They're not all dead. They watch us at every moment. If anyone can help, they can.' Pulling him to the base of the Fairy hill, Aldyth solemnly turned him around, and followed suit. 'We must walk backward sunwise around the hill three times,' she said.

Gandulf followed in her wake, caught up like a child in the magic. When they had completed the third circle, Aldyth instructed, 'Cast yourself down upon the hill.' As he did so, she lay down beside him. 'The Fairies will know the question in your heart,' she explained. 'Think upon it, and press your ear to the grass to listen for their answer.'

Fingers entwined, they lay in the grass, each one's face turned toward the other, eyes closed in concentration as they listened for the Fairies' reply. The cool ground, the sweet grass, the good earth reached up to comfort them. Aldyth listened, expecting an oracle or some prophecy, but instead a lilting melody crept into her mind. She recognized it as a song the village children sang at play and tried to shake it loose from her thoughts that she might better concentrate, but it was no use. She opened her swollen eyes to find Gandulf propped on his elbow watching her. He leaned over and kissed her lightly.

'What did the Fairies say to you?' she asked anxiously.

'Nothing,' he replied, not surprised but disappointed. 'Did they speak to you?'

She shook her head sadly.

'Did you really expect an answer, Aldyth?'

Her lower lip began to tremble, and she shook her head. Gandulf pulled her into the crook of his arm, and they lay back amid the sweet grass, her head upon his shoulder.

'Sorry fools, indeed,' he said, 'who have only their own foolish counsel to guide them.'

Riding home, Aldyth clung to his waist and leaned her head against his shoulder, defying the tongues to wag. When next she saw Gandulf, he would be wed to another – or at least betrothed, which was just as binding. Gandulf began to whistle, a slow and sorrowful melody. With a start, Aldyth recognized it as a melancholy version of the same children's ditty running through her mind and wondered briefly at the coincidence.

Gandulf reined in Cathedra before Aldyth's toft and dismounted. Lifting Aldyth from the saddle, he pleaded, 'Aldyth, promise me you won't go gathering until I return.'

She nodded, and he sighed in relief. Holding her wrists for a moment before releasing her, he gave her a dolorous smile that said more than words could convey, then rode off to face the desolate climb up Castle Hill.

In her dingy hut Aldyth threw herself upon her straw pallet, spent and hopeless, with no more tears to cry. It appalled her to think that Gandulf had endured a lifetime of such emptiness. Heartsick, she shuddered with pain, but there was no simple, no potion, no herb to treat this malady – and no comfort in knowing that she was not alone in her agony.

The next morning Aldyth rose late, her eyes still swollen from the sorrows of the previous day. She was thankful that Sirona was not there to see her but out keeping the vigil of the new moon. Aldyth milked Godiva in the little cow's corner of the hut, the only morning task that must be done before she left to warn Bedwyn. From outside came the excited shouting of children on the green. The dust was rising above Tout Hill; it must be a great procession. All the villagers ran to see the fitzGeralds and their retinue. First came the banner bearers, holding aloft the crest of the fitzGerald clan. Their heraldic device was a raven, harking back to their Viking roots, for the Normans had abandoned their Scandinavian home only to seize possession of Normandy's greener fields some two hundred years before. How fitting a symbol, thought Aldyth, for the raven was a battlefield scavenger that lived off the sorrow of others.

Then came the nobles, dressed to impress the peasants; even their horses were richly caparisoned. They would change into their road clothes later, but it was important to put on a good show for the locals. Lord Ralf, decked in a red woolen cloak trimmed with lambskin, followed his banner. A few paces behind, on an impressive black destrier, came Gandulf, who looked alone amid the great company. Someone had found him a new cloak of fine blue worsted, taffeta-lined and embroidered with golden thread. The baron and his son were followed by servants, seneschals, the falconer, men-at-arms to protect the party, and Father Odo to watch over their souls. Even Sheriff fitzGrip and his wife accompanied them with their own lesser entourage, for when fitzGrip had learned of their journey, he had offered to travel in company, as he had property in Kent that required his attention and it was safer to combine forces.

Villagers stood gawking. Younger children lined up on either side of the road, while the older children ran along-side. 'Gandulf!' they cried, each one trying to catch his eye. The peasants waved to him as he passed. Two little girls tossed wildflowers, and Gandulf recognized them as Mildburh's daughters. Agilbert was there with Little Edmund riding on his shoulders, and Leofwine Clerk held a child on his hip and one by the hand. As Gandulf caught his eye, Leofwine bowed his head in respect. Next to the lad, Father Edmund made the sign of the cross, and Gandulf knew that the old man was praying for him. As miserable as he was, some small warmth stole into his heart.

His father, however, was disgusted at the riffraff's familiarity and commented snidely, 'I see you've finally found comrades of the same mettle. What do you do for amusement? Go mousing?' Gandulf stiffened in the saddle but would not be baited.

Aldyth stood in the shadows of her doorway watching the procession, but Gandulf's searching stare drew her out. As she stepped into the sunshine and their eyes met, she saw a flicker of emotion disturb his stonelike mask. Then he was gone. Who would suspect that such passion boiled beneath that cold, impenetrable exterior? Aelfric had told her that Lord Ralf was going to be sure that Gandulf behaved himself enough to negotiate the contract. Aldyth hoped the girl would appreciate him, that his father would not be too harsh, but she knew both were faint hopes with scant chance of coming to pass.

As they paraded by the well, Aelfric stepped out from under the Wishing Tree and caught the lordling's eye. With a flick of his dirt-smudged hand, he sent a small object hurtling through the air toward Gandulf, who caught it instinctively. It was a rowan cross tied with red yarn. When Gandulf met Aelfric's bright blue eyes, the imp was wearing a half smile as he mouthed the words 'For free.' A hint of a smile lit Gandulf's face as he tucked it into his belt; then he turned a wooden gaze back to the road.

People would want to discuss the display, and Aldyth knew that they would want to include her. She could not bear it, so she slipped out of the village before the spectators could disperse into little clumps of fermenting gossip. She was thankful that she would not have to worry about Father Odo's whereabouts, but the Lady only knew where the king's spies might be. Rumors were the currency of the land, and no one stopped to comment on the weather without passing on news. Aldyth had heard that Hugo and Rollo were harassing the folk of Motcombe, no doubt casting about for a scent, having lost the trail in Enmore Green. She was sorry for the people of Motcombe, but that meant that the woods about Enmore Green would be safer, at least for a while.

Her destination was a broad stretch of the downs where the view was unrestricted. She gathered herbs and wildflowers, watching for any signs of disturbance: a sudden flight of birds, the cessation of the insects' hum, a rustling of the underbrush when the breeze was still. At the edge of the woods, Aldyth ducked among the trees and waited to be certain that none had followed. Then she took an indirect route to Bedwyn's, for she knew now who might be lurking out there and what they would do if they caught her.

Aldyth missed the pleasant anticipation she always felt when going to see Bedwyn. Her life seemed cold and dull. As she approached his hut, Aldyth believed at first that it was merely her own perception that made his dwelling seem equally bleak. Then she sensed that something was wrong: the geese were silent. From the cover of the woods, she saw one of Bedwyn's feathered sentries foraging in its fringes and could only wonder why they had scattered. She watched for such long a time that the wild creatures who had gone into hiding at her approach gradually emerged and continued about their business. Summoning her courage, she crossed the clearing to the hut. It was empty, and the hearth was cold. Bedwyn's spare cloak was gone from the peg on the wall, and mice were stirring in the thatch. How long had he been gone? She hoped the decision to depart had been his own. If it were only a move to greener pastures, she wished that he had told her so that she wouldn't worry; but then, she admitted ruefully, he owed her nothing.

'May you rest in the hands of the Goddess, Bedwyn, wherever you are,' she whispered. As she passed his beehives, humming with bees at the height of their busy season, Aldyth stopped to speak, for bees were known to understand the language of humankind. 'If Bedwyn has left, he would have told you,' she said wistfully. Though she knew it was unlikely, she added, 'If he should come back, please tell him I was here.'

Aldyth was desolate. Though her affinity with Bedwyn had paled next to the firestorm of emotion that she had shared with Gandulf, he had been warp and weft in the fabric of her life and as close to kin as she had, next to Sirona. Both of the men who had been the color, the spice, the sparkle of her life were now gone, one on the road to London and the other on the road to Hell for all she knew.

As she plodded across the village green to her hut, Aelfric dashed out to meet her. 'Aldyth!' he cried, 'I thought you'd never get here! Wulfric was in a haying accident, and Sirona is nowhere to be found.'

As Aldyth hurried after Aelfric, she could not help but think, 'I still have a place.'

CHAPTER TWENTY-THREE

There was not much to pack. It was all bundled into Sirona's cloak: the rune sticks and her tiny bronze bowl for divining, a bit of bread and cheese to carry her there, and a few bunches of tender herbs that would not thrive on the downs. Once again Sirona prepared for the journey she made each year to spend Midsummer, the holiest of days, with her own folk. As the wisewoman tucked the last of the rosemary into her bundle, Aldyth confessed to her godmother about her secret trip to Bedwyn's and told of his unexplained absence. She confided her feelings of confusion about Bedwyn but could not bring herself to share her grief over Gandulf. It was too bitter, too deep; nor did Aldyth wish Sirona to think that she begrudged her responsibilities to the Goddess.

'Aldyth, consider how poorly you have fared on these ill-thought excursions of yours,' said Sirona sternly. 'How could you have gone without saying a word to me?'

'You would only have forbidden it.'

'And what does that tell you about the nature of your mission? Do you see these white hairs on my head? There is one there for every foolish chance you have taken.'

'I'm sorry, Sirona.'

Her godmother softened. 'I do not like to leave you, Aldyth. I sense a heavy burden weighing you down. If only you could let me, I would gladly share it, but I understand that matters of the heart are difficult for you to confide. You go to the forest for peace and healing, but for now I must forbid it,' she said, pulling together the corners of her cloak and knotting them into a pack.

She then embraced Aldyth, slung her pack over her shoulder, and walked out across the green. Aldyth watched her godmother stop to kneel in prayer at the fountain. After twenty years, the Keeper of the Crystal Spring was still a mystery to Aldyth; her footsteps would be very difficult to follow. Aldyth knew herself to be no mystic, no saint, only flesh-and-blood human.

Aldyth called on Wulfric, who had sprained a wrist in a haying accident the day before. She bathed his wrist in springwater and bound it with crushed plantain leaves. 'This infusion is willow bark,' she explained, 'for the pain and the swelling.'

'How long will this keep me out of the fields, Aldyth?' asked Wulfric anxiously.

'You are not to fret over this, Wulfric. Garth and Helga are mowing your field; he says he owes you more than a few days' work for putting a roof over his head last winter.'

'I'm grateful that he remembers a good turn, even at the height of the haying season.'

'Aldyth,' said Edith, 'will you break bread with us this morning?'

Aldyth looked at her friend, and observed how wan and fragile she seemed. 'Do you keep your breakfast down these days?' she asked, feeling Edith's swelling belly.

'Yes, the sickness passed with the coming of the new moon, as you predicted.'

'I'm glad. Has the child quickened?'

'I think I felt it move for the first time this morning,' Edith answered, beaming.

'If it had quickened before this,' said her husband, grinning, 'believe me, you'd already have heard about it, along with everyone else in the village.'

Laughing, Aldyth sat down to share a meal before visiting Agilbert. As she approached his toft, he slipped outside, holding his finger to his lips.

'They're not up yet,' he whispered.

Aldyth nodded and tiptoed in. The smell of unwashed wool, unwashed man, and unwashed pig assaulted her nostrils. Curled up in a wild nest of blankets was a small, gently heaving mass, where the baby and the pig slept interwined and snoring.

'I have something to help with the teething. Mother Rowena sent this,' said Aldyth, taking a tiny vial from her basket. ''Tis a rare concoction of clove oil from beyond the Holy Land. Rub a tiny dab on Little Edmund's gums when he cries.'

'He never cries,' said the boy's father, 'but this will keep him from chewing on Bertha's tail. It makes her cross.'

Aldyth nodded and added, 'Use it sparingly. When this is gone, 'tis gone for good. If his gums still bother him, come to me, and I'll give you a mild syrup of poppyseed.'

Agilbert nodded, hesitated, then asked, 'How does Bertha look to you today? She does not have the appetite she once had.'

'She's come into her full growth,' replied Aldyth. 'She won't need as much.'

Agilbert sighed in relief. 'That's all it is; I was worried. 'Tis good to know she'll get no bigger. She doesn't take up much space, but she does kick so in the bed at night.'

A dreadful thought occurred to Aldyth. How seriously did Agilbert take his conjugal duties to his pigwife? If it were merely a matter of a man and his pig, she would not worry, for whatever passed between them, the pig was certainly fond of Agilbert; but Little Edmund would soon be old enough to notice his parents' peculiar relationship.

'Agilbert, I don't like to pry, but—'

'Yes, Aldyth?'

'Do you and Bertha . . . well, do you consider her a wife in all ways? What I mean to say is . . . do you treat her in every way as a wife?'

'Of course I do!' he said. 'Except that she won't wear a kirtle, and I'll not force her.'

Aldyth was alarmed.

Agilbert continued emphatically, 'I feed her, shelter her, and take care of her just as I did when she wore clothes.'

Aldyth blushed. 'Then you and she . . .' Her voice trailed off, for she could think of no delicate way to say it.

A sudden look of comprehension was followed by a flush of outrage, and Agilbert demanded, 'How can you think that of me, Aldyth? Her health is much too frail to permit another pregnancy! I'll not put her through that again.'

Aldyth apologized profusely. 'Naturally, I'd never imagined any such thing. But I feel responsible for her well-being, and I had to be sure.'

'Of course,' he said, nodding. 'You have your job to do, and she is very dear to you. You know as well as any what she suffered for the sake of Little Edmund.'

Aldyth barely had time to feel relief before she realized that the situation still had other possibilities for awkward complications. How would Agilbert cope the first time Bertha went into heat and came home carrying the farrow of another boar? Would he cast her out or take her to court for legerwite? Or would he forgive her and raise as his own a litter of half brothers to Little Edmund?

Aldyth placed a gentle hand upon his arm and ventured, 'Agilbert, now that Bertha has attained womanhood, she will likely attract admirers.'

'Bertha was ever faithful to me, Aldyth,' he rebuked.

'Yes, I know, Agilbert, but she is so very attractive. . . . She might have attentions forced upon her by an amorous boar; they run free in the village, you know.'

'I never considered that possibility,' he said in alarm. ''Tisn't safe for a maid in the woods, as you know too well. I'll take extra care to protect her.' He clasped her hands. 'Ever so wise and thoughtful, Aldyth.'

She stepped outside, relieved and bemused. There was many a maid who would gladly have had Agilbert, for he had proven a faithful husband and a good provider, even if he had bred true to his MoonCatcher blood, but he had made his choice.

Later that morning, as she weeded the toft garden, Aldyth still dwelt upon Agilbert and how he coped with his sorrow and loneliness. 'If only you could talk, Maeve,' said Aldyth, fondling the ears of the little calf browsing on the hedgerow, 'but you're too young to discuss such matters.' She groaned. 'Listen to me! I'm as bad as Agilbert.'

In the forest the strawberries would be ripe, yet she was forbidden to venture out after them. She owed a workday to Lord Ralf – but then a delightful thought came to her. 'It has been a while since I have called on Mother Rowena. Mayhap she has learned something of Brother Ansgar and his nuns.'

She glanced at the garden and decided, with barely a twinge of guilt, that the weeds could wait. But first she must leave word of her whereabouts in case she were needed. She walked to Mildburh's field and found her friend there mowing hay. The two Edmunds played under the watchful eyes of Bertha while Agilbert weeded his toft garden. Jenena and Aethela, Mildburh's four- and three-year-old daughters, were gathering wildflowers at the edge of the Millers' field when they saw Aldyth. Squealing with delight, they tumbled over to her like a pair of puppies, to be coddled and petted. Mildburh smiled indulgently as Aldyth smothered them with hugs, then shooed them off so that she and Aldyth could talk.

As the girls scampered off, Mildburh grabbed bunches of grass in one hand and, with her sickle in the other, slashed them off at the roots. Aldyth followed, laying out the fresh grass to dry into hay. It was tedious and tiring, but the two women worked to the sound of Mildburh's chatter, and the work went quickly. Mildburh was Aldyth's age and had been Aldyth's closest friend since childhood. She was a refreshing foil to Aldyth's more serious and taciturn nature, for she was always cheerful and uncomplicated. They spoke of the harvest, the weather, the children. It was Mildburh who brought up Midsummer.

''Tis coming up so soon!' said Mildburh. 'The honey harvest is in, and there will be a new batch of mead. Of course, I won't be drinking much this year . . .'

'But, Mildburh, you love sweet mead.'

'I fear 'twill make me queasy.' Mildburh stopped her work and smiled with the air of one sharing a delicious secret.

'Mildburh, you're not—'

'Aye, that I am. Since May Eve.'

'A child of the May!' exclaimed Aldyth. She dropped the armful of cut grass to embrace her friend. ''Twill be a lucky child, to be sure.' A child conceived on May Eve was considered a blessing sent by the Fairies. 'How are you managing?'

'All goes well. Eldred is pleased, but he hopes the Fairies will help feed this one.'

'You and Edith will raise your babies together,' Aldyth said with a tinge of envy.

Mildburh, suddenly self-conscious of her own good fortune, said, 'Surely Gandulf will be back by then? He'll jump over the fire for you; he'd throw himself into the fire if only you asked. Oh, Aldyth, would you want to be a fine lady and wear silk and furs?'

'Not outside of wedlock. Mildburh . . .' Aldyth paused. 'He's gone to meet his bride.'

'Oh, Aldyth!' cried Mildburh. 'I knew he'd gone to London, but I didn't know why. Why must I blurt out everything that comes into my head?'

'Because it almost always makes so much sense. But not this time,' said Aldyth.

Mildburh gave Aldyth a hay-strewn, sweaty hug, but Aldyth said stoutly, 'I'm fine. In fact, I'm on my way to see Mother Rowena. I hope to discover more about my Saint Christopher. If anyone should need me, you can send Aelfric up to the abbey to fetch me.'

Mildburh nodded. 'With Sirona gone it must be very quiet in your toft. Come by tonight for supper.' As an incentive, she added, 'We're having frumenty.'

Aldyth could picture herself at Mildburh's hearth, surrounded by the happy din of children. She would pick the nits out of the girls' hair and sing them to sleep, then afterward sit with a cup of warm ale and stay up too late as she and her friend gossiped and teased the eavesdropping Eldred, who pretended to be above such things.

'Thank you, Mildburh,' said Aldyth. 'I'll be there.'

When the children saw her leaving, they cried, 'Don't go, Aldyth! Don't go!'

'I'm off to the abbey, poppets, but I'll be back to sup with you tonight.' They clung to her skirts and thrust their drooping posies into her hands. As she walked up Tout Hill, Aldyth looked down at the stemless handful of wilted flowers and smiled.

'Life will still have its rewards,' thought Aldyth, 'while I have friends like Mildburh.' Yet she would always be on the periphery of others' joy, the affectionate aunt and adoring godmother, never knowing the wonder of mother love. Worse yet, she had tasted another form of love, that shared between man and woman, and she finally understood how great was the sacrifice required of the Keeper of the Crystal Spring.

Once through the town gate, Aldyth was swept into the tide of street hawkers and beggars, merchants and apprentices scurrying about on errands or roaming aimlessly once out of their masters' sight. She passed John Baker's shop, where he stood at the door haggling with a customer; he shouted a greeting and tossed Aldyth a warm bun. Smiling, she caught it and set it in her basket as a supper gift for Mildburh's brood.

Sister Arlette waylaid her at the abbey gate. Aldyth was listening to the latest gleanings when Brother Ansgar came in to sweep the courtyard. He strode over the cobbles to greet her. 'Good day, Sister Arlette. And hail to you, Aldyth Lightfoot. I've been meaning to inquire about your well-being after our meeting last week.'

'I'm fine, thanks to you, and I've brought you your cloak,' she replied, taking it from her basket and handing it to him.

He held the folded cloak to his nose and said, 'Rosemary for remembrance.'

'Rosemary for moths,' she quipped.

Brother Ansgar laughed. 'Nevertheless, I'll think of you when I next wear it.'

Sister Arlette said, 'I heard from Sister Gunhild about your fright in the woods, child. 'Twas by God's grace that Brother Ansgar happened along.'

Adroitly changing the subject, Ansgar asked, 'How go the preparations in Enmore Green for the Midsummer festivities?'

'They gather and stack wood for the fire every day. A new batch of mead has been made. The hobbyhorse has come down from the rafters at Judith Alcester's house, and her husband, Godwin, is replacing the string that snaps the jaws open and shut, for during last year's procession they snapped the jaws so hard that the old string broke.'

'Is that the hobbyhorse of Enmore Green, or does it belong to Sceapterbyrig?'

'We have our own,' said Aldyth proudly, 'but it visits Sceapterbyrig and Long Cross and Alcester as well.' Neighboring villages looked to Enmore Green, an important ritual center with its well and its tree and its wisewoman, for its ancient ties to the old ways.

'And do you look forward to the revels, Aldyth?' he asked.

She shrugged. 'I enjoy it well enough, but I always seem to have a lapful of babies.'

'None of your own?'

'Everyone else's but mine.'

'Mayhap next year 'twill be your own; I've no doubt the young men will be lined up to leap over the fire for you.' More seriously, he asked, 'You are staying out of the woods?'

The porteress leaned forward, her one long eyebrow furrowed, and with the thrill of vicarious danger, she said, 'No roads are safe these days. Just this morning Sister Emma and Sister Agnes left on pilgrimage to Canterbury with only a handful of men for an escort. We will all be praying for her safe return.'

Brother Ansgar drew a sharp breath. 'Emma fitzGerald? Lord Ralf's lady? She has left for Canterbury? How long will she be gone?'

'Not less than a month. And if you think that is a journey, Dame Eulalia is planning to go all the way to Normandy to petition the archbishop in the name of the abbey.'

But Brother Ansgar was no longer listening. With a polite excuse he hurried off. Aldyth wondered what had happened to set the worried look upon his brow. When Sister Aethelswith approached with a message from the abbess, the porteress turned happily toward the novice to repeating the old news to a fresh audience, and Aldyth made her escape. On her way to the infirmary, Aldyth noticed Sister Priscilla with her hard little eyes on Brother Ansgar as he disappeared into the kitchen. She found the nun's perpetual look of discontent disturbing. The nuns who had no positive focus turned sour and looked for anything to add interest to otherwise dull lives. Sister Priscilla's passions and ambitions were inconsistent with the life of the cloister; Aldyth wondered if she might have turned out differently had she been allowed to marry and run a household.

Mother Rowena was not in the infirmary, so Aldyth went to the chapel. The stone walls with their tiny arched windows blocked out the heat and light of the bright June day, but the smell of incense and hot wax was soothing, and flickering candles brightened her spirits. Aldyth walked through the echoing church to the front altar and knelt to pray.

'Our Lady,' she whispered, 'give me strength to keep to my path that I might better serve you and my people. And please . . . watch over them both, wherever they are.'

Aldyth wiped away a silent tear, took a steadying breath, then rose to leave. A soft voice called out to her. Aldyth had not noticed Sister Edith in the shadows, for she had been lying full length on the floor, hands clasped over her head, apparently keeping vigil, a form of prayer reserved for extreme need and sometimes lasting for days.

'Come sit beside me, child,' said the nun, seating herself on the altar steps.

Aldyth complied, surprised at the warmth with which Sister Edith took her hand. 'You're the lass, then, who is paid court by Lord Gandulf?'

'You've heard the stories.'

'Sister Arlette—'

'Of course,' said Aldyth. 'There are rumors.'

'Rumors rarely spring out of thin air.'

Aldyth sensed a compelling goodness about Sister Edith; she *wanted* to trust her. She hesitated a moment, then began, 'In the strictest confidence . . .'

Sister Edith raised her finger to her own lips to indicate complicity.

Aldyth nodded gratefully and continued, 'Nothing has happened between us, and nothing will. Even now he is in London with his bride. They shall wed and I shall weep, but I pray to the Lady to make him happy and to help me bear it graciously.'

'The story is not yet over, my dear.'

'But it is, Sister. Who ever heard of a match between peasant and lord?'

'Stranger things have happened. I was common-born yet wed my lord's son. He too rode off to wed another, but 'twas I who shared his bed and bore his children.'

'I need only say the word and I too could share his bed, but

I'd be sharing his wife's bed as well and bearing his poor bastard children.'

'My husband defied convention and the advice of all his counselors, for at the very last he could not bring himself to wed the one chosen for him. Lord Gandulf seems to be a man not greatly influenced by public opinion but rather by his own conscience.'

'There are complications . . .' began Aldyth, thinking of poor Gandulf's vulnerable nature, his cruel father, and the greatest of obstacles, her own vow of chastity.

'There are always complications,' said Sister Edith.

Aldyth was touched by the nun's good intentions but skeptical of her advice. She wondered about Edith's husband, the lord who had wed his servant's daughter. Perhaps Mother Rowena could tell her more. She found the infirmarian in the garden chatting with Sister Gunhild, who smiled a welcome as Aldyth approached.

'You look three shades less green than the last time I saw you,' said the nun.

'Aye. Thanks to you and your company, Sister.'

Sister Gunhild turned to Mother Rowena and grinned. 'You would have been impressed to see this little wildcat in action. She struck her assailant a blow that most likely changed his voice. Where did you learn to do that, Aldyth?'

Aldyth blushed; she found Gunhild's cheek at once alarming and attractive.

The infirmarian said, 'I could hardly credit my ears when they told me that my Aldyth had felled the great brute who attacked her.'

'I hope you don't think the worse of me, Mother.'

'Nay, child; I shall sleep better at night knowing that you can protect yourself.'

They spoke of the weather, the martyr's recent festival, and, inevitably, Midsummer.

'What sorts of festivities are customary in these parts?' asked Sister Gunhild.

'Well do I remember the high spirits and gay frolics of Midsummer,' said Mother Rowena. 'Do the same wild antics go on just beyond the glow of the bonfires?'

'I couldn't say for sure,' Aldyth replied, 'but in nine months' time we always have more than the usual number of babies born. How do you hear of such things, Mother?'

'I haven't always been a nun,' said Mother Rowena with a wink.

Gunhild guffawed. 'Aldyth,' she said, "'tis you who should have been the nun.'

'Aethelstan and I used to go down to Enmore Green for the fire jumping,' said Mother Rowena. 'He led the revelers carrying torches from fire to field bearing the blessing.'

Aelfric, strolling from the direction of the kitchen, approached the threesome. After nodding a greeting to Sister Gunhild and flashing a grin at Mother Rowena with his mouth full of filched pastry, he said, 'I've come to fetch Aldyth back down to the village to treat a fever. No need to have conniptions, Aldyth, 'tis only that worrywart Elfleda.'

Aldyth nodded in comprehension. Elfleda was as likely to call the healers from their warm beds to treat a hangnail as a broken limb. On the walk home, Aldyth did not have to wonder long why the lad had troubled himself to fetch her. Aelfric, never one to beat about the bush, asked, 'So did you find anything out?'

'Little enough,' she replied. 'I know only that they seem to be good people who chanced to make a very timely appearance when I had need of them.' She looked at him through narrowed eyes. 'Is that what you were up to in the kitchen? Pumping gossip from the scullion?' She hesitated but could not resist. 'What did you discover, Aelfric?'

'They've come from Wilton Abbey in Wiltshire, and they are very well born indeed.'

'How do you know?'

'I have my ways,' he said smugly.

'What else, little know-all?'

'That they've been shut up in the abbey since Hastings.'

'Are they really nuns?' asked Aldyth, feeling a twinge of guilt at gossiping.

'Oh, yes,' Aelfric assured her, 'but I'll reckon he's no monk.'

*　　*　　*

Aldyth stepped out of the tanner's hut in Alcester, where she had gone to stitch up his torn scalp. It was with a sinking feeling that she saw Red Mary flouncing toward her, and she resisted her impulse to duck back inside. She had never cared for Red Mary, and she suspected she would enjoy her company still less that day than in the past.

Before Aldyth could give her good day, the Alcester woman sneered, 'Well, if it isn't Aldyth Lightfoot! Now that Lord Gandulf has done with you, I see you've come down off your high horse to rub elbows with the likes of us in Alcester. How does it feel to be cast off like a bad stitch?'

Aldyth smiled sweetly. 'I wouldn't know, Mary. Why don't you tell me?'

She did not wait for an answer but continued on her way, her chin high and her step steady, but inside she seethed. Mary was not the only one whose gloating eyes she had felt following her through Alcester, and she knew that they took satisfaction from the rumor that Gandulf had cast her aside to marry a noblewoman.

She fared well enough during the days, but with Sirona gone, night-time was harder for her, with only her own thoughts and Godiva and the hens for company. The night before Midsummer Eve, she could not sleep. The drowsy clucking of the roosting hens, which she ordinarily found soothing, kept her awake. The moon, nearly full, called to her through the cracks in the walls. Pulling her blanket about her for a cloak against the night air, Aldyth stepped out into her toft. It was warmer outside than in the dank hut, and the soft breeze was as sweetly scented as a great lady's bath. The hazel hedge cast black shadows, and the apple and pear trees reached up to the moon. It was long past curfew, but the sensual beauty of the night drew Aldyth out. Glancing about to make certain she was unobserved, she slipped out the gate to walk off her restlessness. As she passed Father Edmund's toft, she saw a dim light coming from the cracks in his wattle walls. 'He's up late,' she thought in surprise. She stepped up to his door, never meaning to eavesdrop, yet could not help but hear him talking. It dawned on her that she heard only the priest's voice. 'Of course!' she thought. 'He's talking to Gregory.' She knocked and heard the squeak of a bench as the old priest started.

''Tis just me, Father,' she called softly.

The old priest opened the door. 'Aldyth, is anything wrong? Come in.' He hastily closed the door behind her lest their breaking of curfew be observed by the wrong eyes.

''Tis nothing, Father,' she assured him. 'I was up and saw your light.'

'At this hour?'

'I cannot sleep,' she confessed.

'I know how that is,' he confided. 'God gives us this time for meditation.' He smiled sheepishly. 'But I squander it to keep Gregory abreast of the news.' He filled two mugs with a hot brew made from tender pine buds and the dried heads of chamomile flowers. 'Sirona gives me this to soothe sleeplessness,' he said.

They sat by the low-burning embers of the hearth fire and spoke of the affairs of the village, their hopes for the lambs of their shared flock. Leofwine was not inclined toward the Church but would earn a good wage keeping books for some lord or merchant.

'Such a position would support a family,' noted the priest, 'and that is his wish.'

'He'll be a good father,' said Aldyth. 'See how he cares for his brothers and sisters.'

''Tis Eafa who worries me. Every day her spirits sink,' observed the priest.

'I've noticed,' agreed Aldyth. 'She's never much of a talker, but on my last visit, she said hardly a word. And if she holds her head high, there is a slump to her shoulders.'

'She's not one to look to us for help,' said Father Edmund, 'nor are there many who would take in so headstrong a lass and her fatherless child.'

'Yet she's so frail,' added Aldyth. 'How can they both be sides of the same woman?'

Aldyth glanced up from the fire to see Father Edmund watching her, unaware that he had just been thinking the same thing about her. 'I've been worried about you too, Father,' Aldyth confided. 'What word from the bishop?'

Father Edmund smiled. 'They keep their tally and count up the black marks. If the bishop were to believe Father Odo, I'm the spawn of the Devil himself and teaching you all to worship pagan idols. 'Tis for Sirona that I fear.' He hesitated, unwilling to burden Aldyth with his confidence. She nodded encouragement, and he forged onward.

'The Church has such a reasonable attitude concerning the Devil and the witches who follow him. It has always been Church doctrine that God would not allow such creatures any true power; He permits them to practice witchcraft only so that they can damn or redeem themselves by their own free will. But some, like Father Odo, believe that witches must be hunted down. He has set his sights on Sirona and me, meaning to prove us apostate and witch; I worry that you'll be suspect due to your association with us.'

'I'm too small a fish for him to cast his net for,' Aldyth assured him.

'Last year I might have agreed, but his attention has been drawn your way by Father Rannulf and, I regret to say it, by our Lord Gandulf.'

'Who is no favorite either and surely suffers from his association with all of us.'

'True enough, true enough.'

It was difficult to tear herself away from the old priest's fire, more difficult still to step out of the fragrant silvery blue night and into the black cave of her hut. In spite of the soothing chamomile, she tossed and turned on her straw pallet. It was cool for a June night, and as she lay there, the damp chill seemed to take its place in the bed beside her, sucking the warmth from her bones. Aldyth did not know whether she slept fitfully or not at all, but the atmosphere became very close, and she had difficulty breathing the choking, fetid air. Then it dawned on her that the mound beside her was a corpse. She put out her hand to feel its damp, clammy skin, and it came away sticky. She screamed with all her being, then came to herself to find someone roughly shaking her. She slapped away the hands, fearful that the corpse had sprung to life and come after her.

'Aldyth, wake up!'

'Aelfric!' she cried, her voice shaking with relief. She hugged the boy, and he tolerated it for an unusual length of time before pulling free.

'Oh, Aelfric!' she gasped. 'I don't know what would have happened if you hadn't come.'

'What is it, Aldyth,' asked the boy in dismay, 'that the Mara sends to you at night?'

'I don't know,' she said in despair. 'I only know that it gets worse each time it comes.'

Aelfric laid his tattered blanket beside the fire and stirred the embers to warm away the cold handprints of the Mara still chilling Aldyth's heart. She lay back down, and Aelfric pulled Gandulf's cloak down from the shelf, unfolded it, and tucked it up over her shoulders. After Aldyth had nestled back into the straw, the lad settled down across the fire from her, wrapped in his own blanket. Over the sizzle of the embers, his high, clear voice rose up in a soft sweet melody. It was an unfamiliar tune with words Aldyth could not understand, but it filled the hut, warmed her heart, enfolded her in its calm. And at last it lulled her back into a mercifully dreamless sleep.

As Aldyth drifted off, she thought, 'He is old beyond his years.'

CHAPTER TWENTY-FOUR

Midsummer Eve 1087

''Tis time!' came a child's cry from the branches of the Wishing Tree. Others chimed in as the sun sank beneath the horizon. The bonfire was always lit at sunset. The Midsummer celebration had begun hours before with supper in the graveyard, a gesture of respect to the dead, who were thus included in the festivities. Such goings-on in the churchyard were beginning to be considered a desecration of holy ground by some churchmen, but Father Edmund felt that nothing done with such charitable intent could be taken ill by God. Everyone feasted among the graves, toasting the memory of their ancestors. They ate frumenty from a common pot and new-baked bread with butter. The abbey had sent a sheep and some carp from the stews to be distributed among the parishioners in observance of Saint John's Day, though it was difficult to say how many were observing Saint John's Day and how many the ancient feast of Alban Heruin.

Afterward the revels moved up the hill from the church-yard to the Crystal Spring. The first order of the night was to ensure a roaring fire, for it was said that the year's grain would grow as high as the flames of the bonfire. Lufe took up his pipes and played a tune as wild and high as the breeze over the downs, a tune learned from the Fairies. It whistled and wound and trilled like a nightingale, carrying all of summer's most solemn secrets. The dance circle filled out, and the pitch of the music rose. Oscar Fisher joined Lufe on a skin drum, and the feral throbbing of the drum became the quickening heartbeat of the cosmos. Even the most reserved bystanders found themselves impelled to join in the dancing. Round and round they went, leaping sunwise about the flames.

Aldyth, as she had predicted, sat with the babies and the old women who minded them. Eafa too sat on the fringes, heavy with child, sadness hanging about her shoulders like a damp shawl. Her cows were no comfort to her now; they would not leap over the fire for her. The music flowed through Aldyth like her own life's blood, and she bounced the baby on her knee to its rhythm but refused a string of invitations to join the dance. Eldred approached looking determined, if shy, as he held out his hand to her.

'No, thank you, Eldred. Go dance with your wife, and tell Mildburh that if she sends anyone else over, I won't dance with him either.'

Aldyth had all the entertainment she needed, observing the tales being played out on the fringes of the firelight. There was a continuous buzz of activity around the mead pot while children ran into and out of the firelight, moving constantly in an effort to stay awake. Gradually the number of children declined and the heat of the dance rose higher still. People broke away from the circle and paired off, sharing a mead cup or a kiss as they moved to the music. Edith MoonCatcher's dance was unsurpassed, for she had learned her steps on the Fairy hill. Though she was heavy with child, the result of a previous, more private dance, her sinuous movements set the heat waves themselves gyrating as she and Wulfric reprised their dance of courtship. The Millers, each with a child on one hip and with another balancing in between, were surprisingly unimpeded in their dance.

Well into the evening Aldyth saw the crowd move forward to welcome a newcomer. A full red-gold beard disguised his features, but the swagger was unmistakable. She hastily disengaged from the mob of squirming babies and put a sleeping child into the arms of Winifred LongCross, who winked at her in a way that Aldyth wished she had not. Paying no mind, Aldyth rushed over and threw herself into Bedwyn's arms, nearly bowling him over. He laughed heartily and gave her a hug that lifted her off her feet.

'Bedwyn, where have you been? When I found your hut empty, I feared for your life.'

'I told you once before I'd never leave without saying good-bye,' he chided gently. 'I had six weeks to kill and no wish to be rounded up like a wandering sheep. I'd have gone months ago had I known I'd come home to such a welcome.' He pulled her close and rested his cheek against hers, ostensibly to whisper into her ear, 'I traveled the Path north to Wales to assess the damage for myself. But we'll talk more of that later.'

'Bedwyn,' she said in a hushed voice, drawing him into the shadows, 'you shouldn't be here tonight. Have you heard that the king's men pounced upon gathered revelers in Gillingham on May Eve in search of outlaws and rebels who had come down from the hills for the celebration? And the scarred one came looking for you a fortnight ago; I went to warn you, but you had already gone. You mustn't go back there, Bedwyn.'

'And where would I stay, Mouse? Would you take me in?'

Shocked, she pulled back and said, 'Aelfric will be staying by my hearth tonight.'

'I can deal with Aelfric,' Bedwyn assured her with a wink. When he kissed her soundly, her initial impulse was to push him away, but she was too relieved to scold.

'My offer still stands, Mouse, and I've come for an answer.'

'Bedwyn,' she said, 'my answer stands the same as well.'

Secure in his disbelief, Bedwyn laughed and lifted her off her feet whether she would or no. He whirled her about, setting her skirts flying. Putting her down, he murmured, 'Give me one night in your bed, Aldyth. Then you wouldn't want to send me away.'

'I'll dance with you, Bedwyn, if you promise to place no meaning or hope upon it. You'll not share my bed or lure me into the bushes this night or any other.'

He smiled wickedly. 'The night is young, Aldyth . . .'

He pulled her back into the fringes of firelight. She had made her position abundantly clear and was so happy to see him that she allowed herself to be led into the revels. He pulled her into a tight hug, letting the music guide them in a dance for two. His natural grace showed to good advantage in a slow, sensuous orbit around the fire. Aldyth worried that their dance was too obviously one of courtship.

'Bedwyn,' she said, 'there's Helga dancing with Edwin. Why don't we join them?'

'I'm not your grandfather, nor are you a child.' He tipped her chin up and met her eye. 'Our place is not in the firelight,' he said tenderly, and Aldyth had to remind herself that the dancing flames in those blue eyes were merely a reflection of the bonfire.

There was a hum of voices from across the fire, and Aldyth, welcoming a distraction, tore her gaze away to peek over Bedwyn's shoulder. She was so startled that she jumped, waking Bedwyn's alarm. Quickly he glanced over his shoulder, then stiffened.

Gandulf, still covered with the dust of the road, stepped into the firelight and scanned the gathering.

'What in the name of God's blood is he doing here?' growled Bedwyn.

'He's supposed to be in London,' said Aldyth. It struck her that it was midnight on Saint John's Eve, when girls made magic to conjure the image of their future husband. Both her loves had appeared, but at least one of them must be a ghost or phantom.

'Please excuse me, Bedwyn,' she said, pulling away.

He caught her hands urgently. 'Don't scurry off, Mouse.'

'Bedwyn, please,' she begged, withdrawing her hands, 'you've had your answer.'

He followed her eyes across the fire to the Norman lordling, and he scowled. 'You're not really interested in that worm, are you? The gossip from here to Bath is that he went to London to see his bride. Don't make a fool of yourself for him.'

'Don't stick your nose into things you don't understand. If it makes you feel any better, I can no more run off with him than I can with you. But he's my friend, and I'll not be told by anyone who I can or cannot talk to.'

'I'm not telling you that you can't talk to him, Mouse, though why you would want to escapes me. But I won't be brushed aside like a bothersome gnat.'

Aldyth sensed his upset and said, 'Try to understand that he is my friend and no more than that. We'll talk later, Bedwyn, and lay this matter to rest once and for all.'

'That suits me fine,' he said, appeased.

Aldyth guessed that he too planned to lay the matter to rest once and for all – in his own favor. Let him believe what he would, she thought irritably, so long as it forestalled another humiliating public display. Aldyth nodded and stepped around him. But before she had taken a step, Bedwyn saw Gandulf's face as he caught sight of Aldyth. Whatever Aldyth believed, Bedwyn knew in that instant that no mere friendship could inspire such passion. A towering jealousy overwhelmed him. Seizing Aldyth by the arm, he cried, 'Would he leap over the fire for you or just into your bed?'

'Bedwyn, please, not again!' Aldyth pleaded. 'Let's talk. We'll go for a walk. *Now.*'

Ignoring her invitation, Bedwyn loosed her, and she nearly stumbled backward. She looked on in puzzlement as he unbuckled his belt and tossed it aside, his eyes never straying from her face. He peeled off his tunic, and his muscular torso, gleaming with sweat from the heat of the dance, incited a scattering of whistles from the women. Playing to the crowd, he flexed his muscles and stepped up to the fire. Although the flames had not burned down enough to be safe for the fire jumping, Aldyth suddenly understood what he intended.

'Bedwyn, no!' she cried.

Turning a deaf ear, Bedwyn called, 'Who would win the maiden's heart must dance with the flames, Norman.'

With a toss of his golden mane, Bedwyn wound up his muscles and, graceful as a leaping stag, launched himself through the chest-high swirl of flames. Cries of admiration broke out as Bedwyn landed squarely on the far side of the fire. He swaggered up to his rival and gestured toward the crackling fire in open challenge. Gandulf bridled more at the sight of Bedwyn's handling of Aldyth than at his belittling dare. He did not doubt Aldyth's devotion to himself but could not

315

understand why she tolerated such liberties. His first impulse had been to demand an explanation of her, but Bedwyn's hard stare hooked him as completely as it had Aldyth. The village folk made way as the lordling stepped into the fire circle, where Bedwyn was waiting. From the far side of the fire, Aldyth's eyes found Gandulf's, and she shook her head in warning. The Norman stared mutely, first at Aldyth, then at Bedwyn, then at the raging blaze. Angrily he yanked off his travel-stained cloak and tossed it aside; the omnipresent Aelfric was there to catch it. Gandulf unbuckled his sword belt and stripped down to shirt and hose, escalating the excitement of the crowd. There would be a show that night!

The lordling shot Bedwyn a killing look, then leapt through the swirling bonfire. Landing safely on the other side, he glanced smugly back at his rival. Aldyth, now on the same side of the fire, snatched at his sleeve, but he shrugged her off.

Without missing a beat, Bedwyn strode to the woodpile, gathered an armload of kindling, and tossed it onto the fire. Embers popped and hissed, and the flames blazed higher. With a great bellow, he hurled himself through the fire on a split-second journey that seemed endless to Aldyth as heat waves rose and billowed up around him. He landed heavily but kept his footing. Then he smirked at Gandulf, issuing a fresh challenge.

Gandulf, carried on by the course of events, heaved another log upon the fire.

'Gandulf, no!' cried Aldyth, but the Norman was already hiking up his shirttail. He thrust back his shoulders and bounded not over but through the raging flames. He nearly stumbled upon landing but caught himself before he went sprawling in the dirt. Heedless of the stink of singed boot leather, he turned, and the two rivals stood panting and glaring at each other over the fire.

Attracted by the commotion, people poured out of the bushes to view the spectacle. Not in living memory had there been such sport, such daredevilry on Midsummer Eve. Bedwyn tossed yet another log onto the towering blaze. The spectators cleared a runway, for they knew that he would need a running start to clear the rising flames. Bedwyn sprinted and sprang and, carried over by the force of his leap, went rolling to his knees. When he jumped to his feet, cheers rose like the sparks of the fire, and Bedwyn acknowledged the adulation with a little victory dance. Everyone turned to Gandulf, expectantly, and shouts trailed off into into an even louder silence. Aldyth was fuming at this vainglorious display, her heart jolting with each leap. When Gandulf started toward the woodpile, everyone broke into applause except Aldyth, who stamped her foot and stormed toward him to put an end to the foolishness.

'This has gone far enough!' she raged, snatching Gandulf's cloak from Aelfric to thrust it at the lordling.

But Bedwyn caught her by the waist and held her from behind. 'Let him fight his own battles, Mouse.' When Aldyth resigned herself and stilled her struggles, Bedwyn released her. 'If you must defend him,' he said, 'he can't be a man worth having.'

'This won't change a thing between us!' she snapped.

'It's gone beyond that, Mouse. Now 'tis between the aethling and me.'

Gandulf, bristled to see Bedwyn laying an unwelcome hand upon Aldyth, but he knew that she was in no immediate danger. This battle, he sensed, must be waged according to Saxon custom. The crowd parted for Gandulf, as he backed up for a running start. With a bracing shout, he hurled himself into the flames but landed a foot short of his goal. Heat enveloped him and blurred his vision while he fought desperately to keep his balance. Screams pierced the air as spectators retreated from the tumble and crash of red-hot logs and sparks that shot out in every direction. Gandulf staggered out of the fire amid the stench of scorched leather and burnt hair. Dazed and disoriented, he was further assaulted on all sides by shouts. At first he thought the crowd was jeering him: then he realized that they were calling out an alarm: his shirttail was aflame. He beat at the flaring shirttail, and within seconds buckets of icy water splashed over him.

The shock set him swaying until Wulfric appeared and put out a supporting hand. 'There, my Lord,' he said, 'you'll be all right.' He peered into the Norman's eyes to be certain that Gandulf was alert before releasing his hold. Then he stepped behind to tear away the damp and draggled shirt while the drenched and shivering lordling tried in vain to appear dignified and self-possessed to those who crowded in for a closer look. There was a moment of breathless silence as they waited for a report.

Wulfric looked up with an air of gravity, then announced cheerfully, 'He'll live.'

Everyone, it seemed, wanted to shake Gandulf's hand or share a teasing remark.

'Is Enmore Green rubbing off on you, lad?' asked Edwin merrily.

Agilbert sidled up and whispered, 'That'll catch her eye.'

'So would being tarred and feathered,' mumbled Gandulf in disgust.

Aldyth had just managed to shoulder her way through the crowd to Gandulf's side when the Norman's attention was drawn away by the force of a dark look focused upon him. Gandulf met Bedwyn's eye from across the fire circle, took an instant to gather what dignity he could muster, and pushed his way through the crowd to confront his rival. As they stared wordlessly into each other's faces, the animosity between them crackled like the hissing embers of the bonfire. Then the Norman lordling held out his hand to the Saxon. Bedwyn took the outstretched hand, but not very graciously.

Aldyth caught up to them. 'Bedwyn, don't sulk!' she scolded. 'And you, Gandulf,' she said irritably, 'could you hold still for just one minute while I look at you?'

'Why do I feel as if I had lost when I made the best show?' Bedwyn muttered. A cup of mead was thrust into his hands, and a crowd of well-wishers moved in to congratulate him. With a last sullen glare at Gandulf, Bedwyn let himself be drawn away.

Exasperated, Aldyth could do no more than shrug off Bedwyn's foul mood and attend her patient. She pulled Gandulf, shivering in his wet hose, toward the firelight. His skin glistened, and trickles of water moved through the curly dark hairs of his chest.

'Turn around,' she ordered briskly, 'and we'll have a look at your back.' Feeling foolish, Gandulf, obeyed and watched over his shoulder. 'You've some mild burns, mostly on your lower back, which is better than you deserve,' she chided, though with obvious relief. 'I'll wash them in springwater and apply some of the salve I brought with me; some fool always burns himself at the Midsummer bonfire.'

'You needn't tell me that I'm this year's fool,' he said ruefully. 'Have you anything for my wounded pride?'

'Indeed I have not. Gandulf! What were you thinking?'

He shrugged and sighed. 'I'm afraid I wasn't thinking at all,' he admitted.

Wulfric placed a cup of mead in his hand. 'He let his balls do his thinking for him.'

'The stags are rutting again!' joked Mildburh.

There was more to their teasing than they might know. It was unusual for Gandulf to make even the most inconsequential decision on impulse. The rush of exhilaration had not yet dissipated, and he felt an exuberance that was new to his experience. Bystanders laughed and offered cups of mead. When Gandulf's teeth began to chatter, Aelfric materialized at his elbow to place his cloak about his shoulders.

Agilbert went to clap Gandulf on the back, but Aldyth intercepted. 'Gently, Agilbert. If he's not sore now, he will be. Aelfric, please fetch my basket; I left it with Winifred.'

So Gandulf too was surrounded by well-wishers, and Bedwyn's annoyance only increased at the sight. Gazing over the heads of his followers, Bedwyn nursed a cup of mead and a grudge. It was then that he noticed the stranger. Instantly alert, he observed her over the rim of his cup. He knew everyone who lived in the Blackmore Vale, at least by sight, and her presence put him on his guard; rat catchers came in all shapes and sizes. This one, if that was what she was, was plainly dressed, but the drape of her kirtle emphasized the womanly figure beneath it. From under a simple veil, short golden curls peeked out, and there was a saucy air about her that, at another time, might have aroused more than just his suspicions. She might be a relative of a villager, but that was not likely; they were

319

tolerating her presence but were not making her especially welcome.

'No,' thought Bedwyn to himself, 'she no more belongs here than does the Norman.'

Their eyes met, and the stranger smiled and crossed directly over to him.

'Were you looking for someone?' he asked casually.

'Not anymore,' she answered. 'I thought you were magnificent.'

He shrugged carelessly. With a start, he realized that he'd allowed himself to lose sight of Aldyth. When he spotted her, Bedwyn was annoyed that she was still examining the Norman's injuries, but at least she had not strayed far from his watchful eye.

'I like a man who performs well,' said the stranger meaningfully.

Her insinuation was lost on Bedwyn, who was tracking Gandulf and Aldyth's progress.

'You seem to be the only one who noticed,' he growled absently.

'Won't you fill my cup?' she purred.

Something in her tone made Bedwyn look at her appraisingly. A smile slowly spread across his sullen face. At least there was to be some sort of prize for the night's effort. Bedwyn flashed a grin. 'With pleasure,' he replied. Taking her by the elbow, he escorted her to the mead bucket. But if he had hoped for a reaction from Aldyth, he was disappointed, for she was too absorbed by her ministrations to notice.

When Aldyth led the bemused Norman toward the fountain and settled him under the branches of the ancient oak, Gandulf's following tactfully dropped off. Dipping a cup into the well, Aldyth washed his back. 'Wear nothing abrasive,' she instructed. 'Old linen would be best until it heals.'

The excitement over, Lufe took up his pipe once again, but now the music he played had the sweetness of honeysuckle drifting drowsily on a soft summer night's breeze. Aldyth finished applying a soothing salve and wrapped Gandulf's waist with a bandage. Then, draping his cloak about his shoulders, she sat down beside him and sipped her mead.

'Thank you, Aldyth,' he said. 'That feels better already.'

'I ought to let you suffer,' she scolded. 'Wasn't your performance on May Eve enough? What will you do to top this at Lammastide?'

Gandulf opened his mouth to reply but reconsidered and shut it again.

'I don't want you to think I'm not happy to see you,' said Aldyth warmly, giving his hand a squeeze. 'But aren't you supposed to be in London? Didn't things go well?'

'Oh, all went just as expected. I was polite. She was civil. I was unimpressive. She was unimpressed. But our parents were enthusiastic about the match. Hers want the political tie, and my father is determined to build his castle with her dowry.' He sighed heavily, letting that one sigh tell the whole story.

Aldyth took a sip of mead and surmised, 'Then all will proceed as planned.'

'So it would appear,' he said glumly. 'Unless my sudden departure has spoiled it.'

'I'm so sorry,' said Aldyth.

In the distance, they could hear muted laughter and applause drifting over from the bonfire. At times the murmur of voices passed close by in the darkness, accompanied by an occasional crashing and stumbling in the bushes. The fire had died down far enough for others to step forward to leap over the flames. The last of the revelers gathered to watch the show, although it was far from the spectacle they had all enjoyed earlier.

Aldyth took another sip. 'That's strange,' she said, peering into her cup, 'I thought I'd drunk more than that. But tell me,' she continued, 'what brings you back so soon?'

'I ran away from home,' he said wryly.

'You came without your father's blessing?'

'I came without his knowledge, and there'll be the Devil to pay.'

Aldyth was horrified. 'What will your father do?'

'I don't know, but I refuse to think about it tonight.'

'Oh, my love, why would you do such a thing?' cried Aldyth. Forgetting herself, she reached out to adjust his cloak, then rested her hand on his chest. 'I'm afraid for you.'

Gandulf took her hand and pressed it more firmly into place. 'I came to relieve your fears, not increase them.' He looked up at the canopy of leaves dancing in the night wind, their undersides gilded with the sunset glow of reflected firelight, their rustle like the whisper of elves. Then he turned to her and said quietly, 'Aldyth, I had a strange dream.'

'Tell me,' she urged.

'Three nights ago a man came to me in a dream, a tall, richly garbed Saxon. "Your love needs you," he said. He held out a trinket on a chain. I'm not sure what it was, but when I reached for it, the movement woke me, and I was alone in the dark. I know not whether he was an angel or a saint, but I left immediately, for I feared that Bedwyn meant to come down from the hills to force himself upon you. 'Twas four days' ride, and I had only three days till Midsummer, but perhaps your angel lent me wings, Aldyth.'

'Oh, my dear Gandulf. I know not what danger is foretold in this dream, but Bedwyn would never hurt me. In any case, he seems to have found consolation elsewhere.'

She nodded her head toward Bedwyn and his lady. Bedwyn's hand caressed his companion's rounded backside, and the lady leaned into his embrace.

Gandulf kissed Aldyth lightly on the forehead. 'Does it sadden you, sweeting? Are we both losers tonight?'

Aldyth's head was spinning as she snuggled into the curve of his arm. His nearness, his male scent, the hint of woodruff in the damp wool of his hose were intoxicating.

''Tis a burden lifted from my shoulders, love. In truth, you have rescued me from an awkward entanglement. But 'twas no danger worth placing yourself at such risk.'

Aldyth knew that she was too close to him, for she felt her liver rising. She decided to move to a respectable distance, but her limbs were leaden and would not obey. She lifted her cup (was it still that full?) to sip, then rolled the honey sweetness languidly on her tongue. Her head, heavy with fatigue, fell to rest upon his shoulder, and she closed her eyes, feeling as disconnected as the full moon that hung over them in the night.

'Oh, Gandulf,' she sighed, hardly realizing that she spoke aloud, 'when I saw you tonight, my heart leapt like a salmon in the rapids. You don't realize what a striking figure you cut, do you?' she demanded, lifting her head to gaze dreamily into his eyes. 'You could be the hero of one of the lays you recite, but you view your reflection and see only a broken nose.' He was about to protest, but she placed a finger upon his lips to cut him off. 'I see thick, dark hair, slightly singed,' she teased, 'an intelligent forehead, and that little frown you get when Sirona pokes fun at you.' Running her hand across his cheek, she unconsciously stroked the stubble on his chin. 'Bedwyn is a golden godling, but he overpowers, like too much mead.' Leaning closer, she whispered, 'Your eyes are deep and brown as peat water on a summer day, when the sun is so hot that all one wants to do is lie in the shade with one's lover.'

As soon as the words escaped from her lips, she became aware that Gandulf's jaw was hanging open in astonishment. What had she said, anyway? Wasn't it something about his eyes? She couldn't remember! Her already flushed face grew hotter, even in the cooling evening breeze. To fill the awkward moments, she reached for her cup but noticed a movement at her elbow. It was Aelfric in the shadows, filling her cup from a pitcher.

'Aelfric!' she scolded. 'That's not funny! Sirona will hear about this.'

'I was just being helpful,' he said in injured innocence. He guiltily dropped his pitcher and dodged her wildly swinging palm to disappear into the darkness. Aldyth settled back down with an air of satisfaction and lifted her cup toward her lips.

But Gandulf touched his fingers to the rim and said gently, 'I think you've had enough, Aldyth.'

Bridling, she replied, ''Tis just my first cup.' She applied a stronger upward pressure on her cup and gasped as the mead went spilling down her front.

'Well, it looks like you're done with that cup,' chuckled Gandulf, mopping the front of her kirtle with his cloak while she looked on dumbly. Two silhouettes stumbled over from the fire, and Aldyth glanced up to see Bedwyn and his paramour standing before her.

'Oh, my Lady!' she gasped, for earlier she had been too preoccupied to place the woman. It was Gunhild the nun – or could she be a rat catcher in disguise? 'Bedwyn, Bedwyn!' cried Aldyth. Attempting to scramble to her unsteady feet, she caught her heel in her skirts and fell backward onto her rump.

Bedwyn looked down sternly and slurred, 'Look at yourself, Aldyth. The Norman has made you drunk. 'Tis time you went home.' The reproach in his voice froze her in midmotion. Bedwyn dropped his arm from Gunhild's shoulders and held out a hand to Aldyth.

Gandulf realized with dismay that Bedwyn had not given up his claim upon Aldyth but had merely been biding his time. 'That's exactly what I was saying,' agreed Gandulf, quickly, 'and since you appear to be otherwise occupied, Bedwyn, I volunteer my escort.'

'Your services, you mean?' Bedwyn swayed drunkenly as he leaned forward to pull Aldyth to her feet, but Gunhild hauled him back by the belt. Ignoring her, Bedwyn said, 'He just means to use you. Give me your hand, Mouse; 'tis not over between us.'

But Gunhild said firmly, ''Tis not over between us either, Bedwyn.'

She slapped him hard on the rump, hauled his arm back over her shoulder, and dragged him off. As he stumbled toward the bushes, he had a look of bewildered astonishment on his face.

Gunhild, looking over her shoulder toward Gandulf, called, 'Good hunting, brother.'

Gandulf laughed aloud as he watched them go, but Aldyth stared after them, wide-eyed and dumbfounded. Trailing after the two revelers came the sound of Gunhild's earthy laughter, mingled with Bedwyn's drunken protestations.

'He's finally met a woman who can handle him,' said Gandulf, grinning.

'But . . . but . . . she's no woman,' stammered Aldyth.

'You're drunker than I thought, sweeting,' he said, helping

Aldyth up. Gandulf led her stumbling across the green in a mead-induced haze. Aldyth tripped and would have fallen had he not caught her. She clung to him until her head slowed its dizzying spin, then looked up to find him evaluating her condition with a studied detachment.

'I'm not drunk, you know,' she stated indistinctly. ''Tis just dark and hard to see the path. I only had one cup of mead all evening – or perhaps two, thanks to Aelfric – but I'm not drunk. I never get drunk.' Swaying like a birch in the wind, she clutched the collar of his cloak and said accusingly, 'But you are, Gandulf. You can't even stand up straight.'

'I don't think you've ever been drunk enough to know what drunk is.'

'Exactly my point,' she said emphatically.

Crossing over the little bridge into her toft, Aldyth caught at the wattle gate to keep her balance but leaned too hard, tearing the old leather hinges loose. She and Gandulf went tumbling into the shallow ditch. For a moment, they lay stunned in an awkward tangle of limbs. The fragrance of freshmown hay, honeysuckle and hedge rose, sweet woodruff and rosemary hung pleasantly about them. In the distance, the strains of Lufe's pipe lulled them into a comfortable haze. Gandulf shifted slightly, removing his elbow from her sternum. The one discomfort gone, Aldyth settled cozily against him.

'Oh, Gandulf,' she sighed, 'why couldn't we just stop time and stay here forever?'

'Because we'd catch our death of cold,' he said firmly, admonishing himself as well as Aldyth for having the very same thought. He staggered to his feet, noting that he himself was none too steady as he clumsily tried to haul her out of the ditch.

'Tell me again, Aldyth,' he said with a chuckle, 'why it is they call you "Lightfoot."'

Aelfric stepped out of her hut, his blanket over his shoulder. 'After tonight,' the lad cracked, 'they'll be calling her Mistress Leadfoot.'

'And no thanks to you, you little weasel!' she squawked indignantly.

Aldyth bent to pick up a stick to throw at him; that was

a mistake. The ground jumped up at her, and she saw stars. As she reeled forward, a strong arm came around her belly from behind to catch her. The next thing she knew, she was in Gandulf's arms and sinking into a pleasant oblivion. But just as she was drifting into a dreamy sleep, she had the disturbing sensation of falling. Gasping, she threw her arms around Gandulf's neck before she realized that he was just lowering her onto her pallet.

'There, now, sweeting, I won't drop you,' he murmured.

Her every sense was full of him. His skin, dried by the summer breeze, was cool and smooth. He wore only his damp hose and his cloak slung loosely about his shoulders. She nestled her cheek against his chest and felt the throbbing of his heart. In a moment he would be gone, she thought sadly, and when next she saw him, he would be wed to another. She felt the blanket beneath her and his arms sliding out from under her. Sadness turned to panic. She gave a little cry and clamped her hands behind his neck. Startled, he instinctively pulled back, but she had locked her fingers to prevent his escape.

'Aldyth,' he said in bewilderment, 'what are you doing?'

He reached around and tried to loosen her fingers gently, one by one, but as he pried each one away, she clamped the last one back. He hesitated, then sighed. 'Very well,' he conceded. 'If you'll loose me, I'll stay for a short while.'

Only then did Aldyth release him, and Gandulf stretched his long body beside hers, allowing her to nestle into the crook of his arm. As they lay there in the tumbling darkness. Aldyth tried unsuccessfully to fight back a wave of melancholy. This was the first and last time they would ever be together like this, entwined in the darkness. She tried to blink back tears, but they spilled over. She stifled a sob, but its escape made her tremble. Gandulf mistook it for a shiver.

'Are you cold, sweeting?' When she made no answer, he touched her cheek and found it wet. 'What's this?' he asked in dismay. 'What's this?'

Aldyth did not trust herself to speak but clung to him as

the last leaf of autumn clings to a branch in a winter storm. He stroked her hair and whispered, 'Sweet Aldyth.'

In the darkness, she ran her fingers through his silky hair, traced his lips with her fingertips, and caressed his cheeks, now softly bristled with three days' growth. As the moon calls to the tide, so Aldyth was drawn to that primal lullaby that replays endlessly within the depths of every living creature. She lay her head on Gandulf's chest and listened to the gentle drumming of his heart; that sound alone filled her consciousness, driving away all sadness, all loneliness, all pain. From the void, she gradually became aware of the pleasant sensation of his chest hairs tickling her cheek.

Gandulf became aware that she was nuzzling against him. 'Poor lass,' he thought dolefully. 'Let her find her comfort where she may.' He was exhausted, had eaten little in the last three days, and was feeling his cups. He knew he should go; it was too easy to lie beside her and take his own comfort there. What harm if she laid her cheek against his shoulder or played with the hair on his chest? But when she began drawing little circles around his nipples, he was aroused from his pleasant drowsiness.

'Aldyth, no,' he whispered uncertainly, trying to still the exploration of her roving hands. She pulled them free and found a tumescent resting place. Gandulf started and admonished in a cracking voice, 'Don't do this to me, sweeting.'

Aldyth made no answer but in concession removed her hands to caress his cheeks. If she could kiss him only one more time ... but when she pulled him toward her, he became alarmed and tried to disengage. His throat tightened, his breath shortened, and his heart roared in his ears while they engaged in a silent tug of love and war between an immovable object and an irresistible force. At last, with a little moan, Gandulf conceded defeat. Suddenly his weight was pressing against her breasts, his hips had come down to meet hers, his hands were running through the wild and fragrant tangle of her hair.

'God forgive me,' he murmured. Then, in impassioned tenderness, he rained a flurry of kisses on her cheeks, her eyelids, her lips. His mouth found the soft hollow at the base of her neck, but when he felt the roar of blood racing through the veins in her throat, he looked up guiltily. 'Aldyth, I should go,' he said, his voice trailing off.

She shook her head and whimpered pleadingly. Her lips found his, and she covered them with her own, her tongue gently probing. Then she reached around and, easing her hands inside the back of his hose, placed them firmly on his buttocks and pulled him closer. Through her kirtle, he caressed her soft breasts, his thumbs gently massaging her hardened nipples. He was swiftly reaching the point of no return as he pressed his swollen groin down hard against hers, fearing and yet hoping for resistance. He gasped aloud when she parted her legs for him, nothing but the threadbare fabric of her kirtle and the damp wool of his hose between them and instant relief. He could not repress a guttural moan as she wrapped her legs around his waist and arched her back. He was losing control, and he broke out into a cold sweat.

A rasping sob rose from deep within her throat. 'Oh, oh, oh!' she cried with increasing tone and intensity. Her breath came in short bursts, and her whole body tensed and writhed, her fingers grasping reflexively at his back. Set off by her wild abandon, the passion of her cries, he was unable to control his natural response any longer. With a cry of despair, he quickly tried to wrench free from between her legs and raise himself up on his arms to create distance between them. But it was too late; with a mortified groan Gandulf felt his throbbing passion explode.

Aldyth hovered above the twisting love knot on the pallet below. Then she was rising high into a sapphire sky, heading straight for the sun. On swift strong wings she flew, an eagle soaring to where the air grew thin. Below her stretched the lush, rolling hills of Dorset in all their emerald glory. She heard his cries before she saw him: a magnificent bird, a cock eagle swooping toward her. They looped and hurtled past each other, close enough for the wind of their passage to ruffle each other's feathers. They circled back and went through the ritual display of their love dance high in the sun-fevered heavens, no sound but the rush of the wind through their feathers. Then suddenly in midair they found each other. Like a thunderclap, they imploded.

Clutching each other with sharp talons interlocked, wings outstretched like the vanes of a windmill, locked in tight embrace, they tumbled, fell, plummeted, headfirst down to earth. The landscape whirled madly, first below, then above. All the while they clung to each other, two wild things, fiercely melded by the passion of mating. The ground rose up to swallow them, and then blackness ensued.

CHAPTER TWENTY-FIVE

Midsummer Day

Aldyth woke with a splitting headache and a mouth as dry as dust. She was sick to her stomach and sticky with the passion of the night. She still wore her kirtle, though it was crumpled and mead-stained, but her shawl was folded on the bench, her belt neatly coiled on top of it. She did not remember doing that.

'Gandulf!' cried Aldyth, sitting bolt upright. She groaned, trying desperately to remember what had happened. To her dismay, her memory was as impenetrable as a moonless night. How could he do this? she raged. For that matter, what had he done? She vaguely remembered that she had thrown herself at him and that he had resisted valiantly. Apparently he had succumbed only when she had pulled him into her bed on top of her. What wantonness had possessed her? He had not even waited until morning to leave; he must have been too disgusted. All that rubbish she had spouted about vows and duty!

It was humiliating beyond bearing. She could never face him again. The consequences of one night's indiscretion bombarded her, and she was filled with self-loathing. A life lived with one aim alone was suddenly made meaningless. Worst of all, how could she confess to Sirona that she had betrayed her godmother's trust, betrayed the friends and neighbors who depended upon her, betrayed the Goddess Herself?

'Oh, my Lady,' moaned Aldyth, 'forgive me.' Overcome by nausea, she retched into a bucket. Too drained to cry herself to sleep, she slipped dully into oblivion.

Aldyth woke again to hear scrabbling on the roof; undoubtedly Aelfric was scattering ashes from the Midsummer bonfire to ensure fertility, God forbid, and good luck, which Aldyth would need. If it had not been a feast day, everyone would have been long gone to the fields, but Aldyth could hear her neighbors running between tofts to gossip about the previous night's escapades, and she knew that her part in the revels would not be overlooked. Every time she heard footsteps without, she cringed, but she could not hide in her blanket forever. When the abbey bells rang for Lady mass, she forced herself to rise. She stripped off her filthy kirtle, resisting the impulse to burn it, and tried to scrub away the dim memory of the previous night. She dosed herself with agrimony for headache, then peeked out her door. Most of the villagers had gone to mass, and the few hungover stragglers trod lightly. On their way home, they would be stopping to beg a cure. The day before, Aldyth had prepared tiny bundles of herbs used to treat imprudent revelers. She placed them in a bowl on her door, as was customary on a morning after. Most would not be first-time callers and would know what to do with the simple.

The burden of her guilt was simply too heavy to bear alone; she had to talk to Mother Rowena. She waited until the path was deserted, then slipped out. A carter passing her on the road took pity and offered a ride up the hill, but Aldyth refused, for she knew the bumpy ride would set her stomach churning. It took her twice the usual time, and when she arrived at the abbey, the look of horror she received from Sister Arlette was enough to confirm what she already suspected: she must look like a truant cadaver. As Aldyth shuffled across the courtyard on her way to the infirmary, her head bowed to lessen its throbbing, she almost bumped into a nun. With one eye squinting against the light, Aldyth looked up to beg pardon, but the apology stuck in her throat when she saw that it was Sister Gunhild, back in her austere habit, looking like a sleek, well-fed cat.

'Aldyth, you look terrible; let me take you to the infirmary.'

'I'm not so far gone that I can't make it on my own,' Aldyth said sharply.

Sister Gunhild shrugged and said, too pleasantly, 'As you wish.'

Aldyth was embarrassed at how poorly she herself had fared after her own night of debauchery, and she was more than a little shocked at the nun's behavior.

'I must not be judgmental,' she chided herself, 'nor jealous either.' But she had to admit that she felt twinges of envy, though she had no right, for she had cut Bedwyn loose. Still, she was incredulous that Gunhild the nun, in half an hour, had conquered Bedwyn as completely as he had every maid between Melbury Abbas and Gillingham.

As Aldyth stumbled over the infirmary doorstep, Mother Rowena took one look at her and said, 'My poor Aldyth, you look like a foretaste of Judgment Day!'

'Mother,' groaned Aldyth miserably, ''tis no matter to jest about.'

Sister Rinalda was soaking up sun on a bench in the garden, and the infirmary was empty, save for the infirmarian and the penitent. The nun sat down on a bed and drew Aldyth toward her. Aldyth dropped to her knees and buried her head in Mother Rowena's lap. Mother Rowena stroked her hair, whispering 'Whatever has happened, my child?'

'Oh, Mother,' wailed Aldyth, 'I have sinned.'

'Would you care to be more specific than that, my girl?'

'I'm afraid I can't.' Though she could not confide her destiny as Keeper of the Crystal Spring to her Christian mentor, Aldyth told Mother Rowena of the longing she felt for Gandulf and even confessed her misadventures of the previous evening.

'It doesn't sound like you've enjoyed yourself enough to have sinned,' said Mother Rowena. 'But you say that Gandulf proposed to you? Why don't you accept?'

'Even were he still willing to run away with me, I'm too angry to go. Besides, now that he's gotten what he wanted for free, why should he be willing to pay for it?'

'Have a little more faith in the lad,' chided Mother Rowena gently.

Why had Aldyth thought that Mother Rowena would be able to absolve her? She buried her head in the nun's lap and wept. Mother Rowena raised her and pulled her into an embrace. 'Do nothing until Sirona comes home, child. She will know the answer.'

The infirmarian dosed her with a fresh egg in a cup of milk mixed with honey and cinnamon, followed by two big goblets of water. Aldyth kept it down, but just barely.

She finally girded herself for the trip back to Enmore Green. 'There will be people needing more than a dose of agrimony, and I must be there for them.'

'Very well, but first I'll bathe your face in rose water. 'Twill make you feel better.'

'I will never speak to him again,' said Aldyth firmly as Mother Rowena held a cold cloth to her red, swollen eyes.

'Wait and see how you feel tomorrow or next week, Aldyth. Perhaps another sunrise will change your outlook. Come now, my dear, I'll see you to the gate.'

As they walked across the sunny, herb-scented silence of the cloister, to Aldyth's dismay they saw Gandulf heading for the gate, their paths bound to intersect. The infirmarian whispered, 'If it is any consolation, he looks as wretched as you do, dear.'

'I hope he feels as wretched as he looks; I know I do,' responded Aldyth grumpily.

Her pasty cheeks blushed pink at being caught in such a sorry state, and Gandulf was no less embarrassed. His manner was stiffer than usual and he wore no belt – because of the burns on his back, Aldyth surmised.

'My Lord Gandulf,' said Mother Rowena pleasantly, 'are you coming from mass? The choir has been practicing for weeks for our Saint John's Day service.'

'I'm afraid I was too late for mass. My mother is due back from Canterbury at any time and I – I was hoping to find her here this morning.'

Mother Rowena stifled a tender smile. 'I could offer you

an infusion of mint for upset stomach and perhaps something for headache as well.'

'You needn't trouble yourself.' Bowing slightly, he said, 'Ladies,' then turned abruptly and strode off. But rather than heading for the abbey gate, as he had been, he went to the garden instead. Why the garden instead of the gate? Surely to avoid having to speak to or be seen with a woman of Aldyth's lowly station and questionable character. What would he tell his mother, Aldyth wondered, and who would Sister Emma tell in turn? Aldyth had thought nothing could make her feel worse, but she had been wrong.

Aldyth's notion of what drove Gandulf was wide of the mark; he barely made it to the bushes in the back of the garden before he heaved up what little remained in his stomach. As he retched into the bushes, he thought, 'This isn't the worst of it. I've still got to face my father.' The idea set him heaving again, but at last his stomach was still. He wiped his mouth with leaves plucked off the nearest bush and resolved not to think of his father any sooner than necessary. As he rose unsteadily to his feet, he caught sight of a row of wide-eyed novices peering over the lavender hedge. At his startled glance, they jumped like coneys caught raiding a toft garden. Gathering his tattered dignity about him, Gandulf bowed. 'Good Saint John's Day, Sisters,' he said and made his retreat.

It was the second day after Midsummer that Sirona returned. Although it was noon, she stepped in to find Aldyth still huddled in her blanket. 'What black gloom fills this place?' Sirona raised one eyebrow quizzically at Aldyth's silence. 'Am I to guess?'

'Oh, Godmother,' whispered the girl. 'I cannot bear to tell you.'

'Does this have anything to do with the Midsummer celebrations?'

Aldyth nodded miserably. Sirona dropped her bundles and sat down beside her. The crone had returned refreshed, the years having melted away as they always did after Midsummer. Aldyth, however, looked years older.

'Come, child; 'tis never as bad when said aloud as when it is held deep down within.'

'You wouldn't say that if you knew ...'

'Let me guess. A late night. An excess of mead. And who was it? I know you are drawn to that bullheaded Bedwyn, and he is pretty to look at ... but something tells me not.' She paused. 'Are you trying to tell me that Lord Gandulf saw you home that night?'

Aldyth nodded and buried her face in her hands.

'Never mind; 'tis all over the village about the bonfire antics. Beneath the lordling's well-banked ashes, there are embers that burn surprisingly hot,' she teased.

'How can you make light of this, Sirona? I'm ruined. No longer a maiden. Whatever shall I do?' she wailed, burying her face in her hands.

'There is only one thing to do,' said Sirona, more seriously. 'Get on with your life.'

'But you don't understand. My life is over.'

Sirona studied Aldyth's face for a moment, then said, 'Since you feel so strongly, let us ask the Goddess.' One method of divination was to watch the path of a wandering beast. Even when turned loose, Godiva preferred to linger at home, so Sirona had to employ a more adventurous creature. Father Edmund's donkey had proved most satisfactory. Given half a chance, he would saunter off the moment his halter had been slipped. At first the priest had been astounded at Gregory's ability to escape from every form of restraint, but eventually he had realized the donkey had an accomplice. ''Tis good for Gregory to get out once in a while,' said the crone, 'and Father Edmund can use the exercise.'

So they walked down the hill to Father Edmund's toft. The priest was out, but Gregory was tied to the hedge, browsing on the fresh spring growth. Sirona gathered a handful of fragrant vernal grass growing in the ditch. The little donkey's ears perked up, for he recognized Sirona as friend and liberator. She fed him his treat and slipped the halter over his head. The donkey immediately went wandering along the narrow paths among the houses, stopping to browse on hedges or a luscious section of ditchside growth. But his general direction never changed, and his destination was clear. Gregory made his way to the Crystal Spring and drank his fill. Sirona smiled and scratched his ears.

'Thank you, Gregory. You are dismissed,' she said, with an imperious wave of her hand. Then to Aldyth she said portentously, 'The signs are unmistakable.'

They left Gregory at the fountain and followed the runoff downstream, past the fishponds, past the mill, until they came to a shallow pool running through an oak grove. There the streambed had been widened into a pond to create a shady spot where the women did their laundry. They found it deserted. 'Good,' said Sirona. Turning to Aldyth, she said abruptly, 'Are you prepared to take your medicine?'

Aldyth nodded gravely.

'Very well, child. Strip and dip.'

'What?'

'Take off your clothes and get in.'

Aldyth looked into the cold, clear depths of the pool. With little enthusiasm, she removed her kirtle and her shift, so that she wore only the little ivory pendant around her neck. She held it up questioningly.

'You must be naked as the day you were born,' said her godmother firmly.

Aldyth slipped it off and set it onto the pile of discarded clothing, then stepped into the icy waters up to her knees, looking to Sirona for further instruction.

'Deeper,' said the wisewoman with a wave of her hand. Aldyth waded in up to her crotch. 'Deeper,' came her godmother's relentless demand from the dry bank. Aldyth waded in up to her belly. When she was in up to her neck in the icy waters, Sirona said dryly, 'You wanted to go all the way. What are you waiting for? Go all the way.' Aldyth took the plunge. She came up spluttering, her teeth chattering through blue lips.

'Good girl,' said Sirona. 'Now wash yourself all over with this. Everywhere, including the injured part.' Sirona took a nosegay of vervain, rosemary, and myrtle from her basket and tossed it to Aldyth, who scrubbed herself gently with it.

'Now ask the Goddess for the return of that which you

have lost.' Aldyth's eyes widened. 'Come, child,' said Sirona. 'Nothing is impossible for the Goddess.'

Aldyth closed her eyes and, through chattering teeth, begged the Goddess for another chance. She opened her eyes and saw Sirona looking at her with affection and amusement.

'Now see if your prayer has been answered, child,' said her godmother.

Beneath the water, Aldyth's fingers probed intimately, and she gasped aloud. She was shocked and overjoyed, for her fingers met the resistance of a sound maidenhead. 'Oh, my Lady!' she cried. 'My Lady Gefion!' Splashing out of the pool, Aldyth threw herself into her godmother's arms. 'The Goddess is good! I shall never stray again!'

Sirona wrapped her shawl about her goddaughter's wet shoulders and said smugly, 'The value of a maidenhead is highly overrated, but as it means so much to you . . .'

Two days after Sirona returned, Eafa disappeared. That morning, as usual, she had picked up Godiva and her calf to graze with her own cows. That evening Godiva and Maeve wandered home alone. Eafa's baby was due at any time. Some worried that her birthing had begun on the downs, but Father Edmund feared she had thrown herself into the river. Sirona assured him that Eafa was not one to fall prey to despair but agreed that a search would hurt nothing. The men of the village set aside their work at the height of haying season to seek the missing woman. The whole next day they scoured the woods and the downs. The search party returned that evening without Eafa and without Agilbert and Thurgood.

The healers were sitting on their doorstep, making dandelion wine. They had a basket of freshly washed dandelion heads and were dropping the golden flowers into a kettle to soak. 'A taste of summer sun stored up for next winter,' said Sirona. Both women looked up sharply when Wulfric burst through the gate, nearly pulling it off its hinges.

'Wulfric, we just mended that gate, and we'd like to see it last another fortnight,' chided Sirona. 'What drives you so?'

''Tis Agilbert! The stubborn ass refused to come home; I fear the wolves will get him.'

'Begin at the beginning,' said Sirona calmly. She gave a nod to Aldyth, who fetched a cup of ale for Wulfric, to slow him down enough that they might understand him.

'We got as far as the badger glade by the Fairy hill, with still no sign of Eafa,' he explained, 'so we decided to turn homeward, as the sun was getting low. Agilbert folded his arms and refused to return. He is convinced that Eafa is lost in the woods and bearing her child alone. He says that what happened to Bertha must not happen to Eafa, and he swears he will not return until he has found her. We tried to carry him back, for the man isn't quite right in his head and we feared to lose him as well. But he climbed a tree and threw sticks to drive us away. We left what we had of our lunches with Agilbert's cousin Thurgood, who stayed with him. Has Agilbert finally lost what little sense he had left?'

'You say you left Thurgood there with him?'

'Aye.'

'Well, between the two MoonCatchers, there's one good pottle of brains. They'll have a cold night but be none the worse for it. Wulfric, would you fetch Little Edmund and Bertha from Father Edmund? Then get you to bed. I've said it before and 'tis still true today: morning is wiser than night.'

By midmorning the next day Agilbert and Thurgood had come down from the hills. They went directly to Sirona's. Bertha and Little Edmund both squealed with delight when Agilbert stepped in through the door. He knelt to kiss the pig and apologized, 'You know I wouldn't have stayed away without good cause, Buttercup.' He then picked up his little son, who took hold of his father's sparse young beard in chubby dimpled hands.

'Papapapa!'

'Big boy!' said Agilbert proudly. To the company he bragged, 'See how well he talks already.' He kissed the boy, then set him down next to Bertha.

'Mamamama!' said the baby, reaching for the pig, which nuzzled him affectionately.

Agilbert beamed proudly, then looked up to announce, 'We needn't worry about Eafa.'

'You found her?' asked Sirona, mildly surprised.

'No, but she is in good hands. Thurgood and I found the spot where she must have taken her midday meal, and she was not alone. Someone had brought her lunch, for they left the bones for the foxes. I followed their tracks until they disappeared without a trace. There was never a sign of struggle, so she must have gone peacefully.' He concluded, 'Eafa's gone with the Fairies, and there's no better midwife than a Fairy.'

'Agilbert,' said Sirona, 'how old are you?'

'Eighteen, maybe nineteen summers. Why?'

'You are blessed with an uncommon wisdom,' said the wisewoman.

Agilbert looked surprised but pleased at the unexpected praise. Thurgood guffawed and slapped him on the back, saying, 'Let's go tell Grandfather Edwin what Sirona says.'

'He'll never believe it,' said Agilbert, picking up his son. Bertha followed, and the last thing they heard was Agilbert saying, 'Did you mind your mother while I was gone?'

A week had passed since Midsummer, and Lord Ralf had not returned. Gandulf had called at Aldyth's toft, but she had scurried into the woods. He had waited at the fountain, but she had refused to fetch water. Unsure whether she was angry with him for stealing her virtue or because she was afraid of losing it again, Aldyth stayed clear of both Gandulf and the abbey, for she would chance no meetings there either.

Gandulf could not understand why she refused to speak to him. She had every right to be angry about what had passed between them on Midsummer Eve. But he had believed that she loved him, and it cut him deeply to be cast aside with no explanation. Gandulf had never understood women, and now he was quite certain he never would.

Sitting on the bench by the fire in the great hall, he brooded over the tale of Tristan and Iseult, feeling as star-crossed and ill-fated as they. Absently he held the book in his hand, for the fire no longer afforded enough light to read by; in any case, he knew the story by heart. It was quiet in the manor hall with the lord away. Those who had been left to guard the holding were settling in for the night. Supper had been informal, a common pot over the fire. Some were rolled up in their blankets; others stood talking quietly, blankets over their arms. At the sound of horses in the bailey everyone froze. Within seconds the door crashed open and Lord Ralf stormed in, his angry footsteps echoing through the hall. Heads poked out of blankets, and hushed whispers grew silent.

It was the time of reckoning. Gandulf steeled himself and stood silent as his father ripped the book from his hands and threw it into the fire. The stink of burning parchment filled the air, but Gandulf had no time to rue the loss of a book worth a small fortune before Lord Ralf seized him by the shoulder and drew back his hand in a fist.

'There goes the nose again,' thought Gandulf.

But his father checked himself. 'No, you must look your best next week,' he snarled. He lowered his aim and slammed his fist into his son's gut instead. Gandulf raised his forearms in a clumsy effort to deflect the blows, until he collapsed onto the floor. Lord Ralf growled into his pain-twisted face, 'You almost ruined this marriage, insulting your bride to go tomcatting about in Enmore Green! I'll tell you this once and only once; nothing will prevent this marriage. It took me three days to talk those fools into stopping on the way to their estate on the coast next week. If you can't convince them you'll be a decent husband, I'll kill you with my bare hands.' He turned to leave but stopped and called over his shoulder, 'And if you set foot in Enmore Green before the wedding, I'll make King William's razing of York look like a maying jaunt.'

Lord Ralf stormed up to the solar, barking orders as he went. Gandulf rested his aching head on the cold floor and shut his eyes. His humiliation was complete, his misery absolute. 'Now I cannot speak to Aldyth, even should she permit it. I have nothing left to lose by this wretched marriage.'

* * *

'Stop that bawling!' commanded Lady de Broadford, raising her voice to be heard over the creak of wagons and the chatter of their attendants outside the litter. 'Your eyes will be swollen by the time we get to Scafton, and your skin is already blotched!'

'Why should I care how I look for him? The uglier the better!' wailed Catherine.

'It doesn't matter what he thinks. You must make a good first impression upon the locals. After all, you will be their mistress, and they must respect and obey you.'

'How can they respect me, knowing my husband was beaten into marrying me?'

At the tavern where they had nooned talk was that Gandulf fitzGerald had run away from marriage negotiations to go whoring and had been beaten into submission by his father.

'You don't know how lucky you are,' countered her mother. 'At least you can assume he won't beat you. Look at Lady Joan: if her husband doesn't like what she sets before him on the table, she goes to bed with a black eye. A weak man is easier to manage. Once you get him under control, if you are discreet and clever, you can pick your own lover.'

Catherine looked up with greater interest. She would have been lovely if not for her red-rimmed eyes and sullen mouth. Her budding figure promised to ripen into the voluptuousness of her mother's, and she was learning to use her assets to good advantage.

'How much farther to Scafton, Mother? May I have a cold cloth for my eyes?'

'There's a good girl,' said Lady de Broadford, patting her daughter's hand. 'You will find, my dear, that money and influence are powerful consolations for even the worst match. And he's not bad-looking, you know.'

Grooming Cathedra for the third time that day, Gandulf brooded over the lecture his father had given him the morning after his return. He suspected that it was as close to an apology as his father was capable of. When Lord Ralf had summoned him to the solar, Gandulf had been wary, but grateful for that little bit of privacy.

'Sit down,' his father had ordered, waving to his own chair by the fire. Lord Ralf had thrust the goblet of wine he carried into his son's hand, then paced in silence for several moments before launching into a tirade that Gandulf suspected was rehearsed. 'Do you think I'd have taken your mother to wife if I'd had a choice in the matter? No! I had my eye on a plump and pretty maid.' Lord Ralf stopped in his tracks and glared at his son. 'But I did as I was bid, for that was my duty. And my father would have beaten the shit out of me had I refused.' Reacting to the shock on Gandulf's face, he had laughed bitterly. 'Oh, yes, your grandfather spared not the rod, and your life has been a soft one next to mine, Gandulf.' As much as he hated and feared his father, Gandulf had felt stirrings of pity. Lord Ralf, reading this unwanted response, had curled his lip in distaste. 'Oh, don't be maudlin,' he had growled. 'It made a man of me, which was more than I could do for you. My father, the bastard, married me off to your mother, then spent her dowry ere I came of age. At least you'll have a castle when I'm gone.' He had paused as if deciding whether to go on, then gruffly nodded toward the door. 'Get out of here,' he had said quietly.

Gandulf still could not help but pity his father and, for the first time in years, fought the impulse to try to please him. He had begun making an unnatural effort to participate in table talk or to hold his head higher when his father entered the room, but when he actually found himself contemplating a haircut, he had taken to the stables. Now he spent most of his time grooming the horses and pondering the hound who would forgive a thousand beatings for one pat on the head.

A road-weary servant entered, and Gandulf recognized him as a groom employed at the abbey. 'They said you might be here, my Lord. I bring a message from Sister Emma.'

'Is she unwell?' Gandulf asked in alarm, for he had expected her return by now.

'She was well when I left her, my Lord, and that was just on the Feast of Saint Alban.' The groom handed him a small parchment cylinder with his mother's wax seal upon it.

'Were you instructed to wait for a reply?' asked the lordling.

'No, my Lord.'

Gandulf gave the messenger a coin, and as soon as the groom was gone, he anxiously ripped open the letter. 'Damn it all!' he exclaimed so sharply that the horses started. 'What in the name of Saint Denis is at Battle Abbey? Damn it all!' he swore again.

'Sister Emma,' implored Sister Agnes, Emma's companion and chaperone, 'you must come in out of the weather; if not for your own sake, then for that of the servants.'

'Tell them to seek shelter in the stable, Sister. I won't be long,' answered Sister Emma. With unaccustomed determination, she lifted her damp skirts and headed down the hill toward the edge of the cliff, not even turning to see if her orders had been obeyed.

'But Sister Emma! There's nothing there but windblown chalk.' Sister Agnes's words were lost in the wind, and if Emma had heard them, she made no sign.

Battle Abbey was the great abbey that King William had ordered raised upon the very spot where King Harold was said to have fallen in the Great Battle. When Sister Emma had announced an unexpected visit to Battle Abbey, her escort had assumed that she was going to thank God for the victory that had put England into King William's hands and Scafton into Lord Ralf's. Sister Emma had prayed in the abbey, still under construction, its walls rising jaggedly around her. The stonemasons had retreated to the shelter of their lodge with the onset of the storm, and only the whistle of wind and the spatter of raindrops on the tile floor had interrupted her contemplation. Her escort had taken shelter in the lee of the highest wall; when she emerged from the abbey, with Sister Agnes trailing behind, they rose quickly, anxious to return to a blazing tavern fire. Twenty-one years before, Duke William, playing upon Harold's impulsive nature and soft heart, had destroyed everything in the vicinity to lure the English king into defending the locals before his full defense was assembled. The land was still scarred from the wasting, but the nuns and their escort had found a modest inn nearby. All they wanted was to return to its shelter, yet Sister Emma walked past them, leaving Sister Agnes to pass on her orders.

She stumbled down the muddy hillside until she stood alone before the cold cairn that covered the bones of Harold Godwinson. The wind whistled through the stones of the cairn and pulled at the pitiful offerings strewn about the forlorn tomb. Bunches of wildflowers fluttered, a jug of wine rested in the lee of the rocks, and scraps of cloth were tucked into the cracks, just as at the Wishing Tree. Stones had been carried from all corners of England to add to the cairn. There was red sandstone from Herefordshire, alabaster from Fauld, firestone from Surrey, blue limestone from Worcestershire, ragstone from Kent, flint from Sussex, even limestone all the way from Yorkshire, all offerings for their fallen king. Emma looked into the wind that cut across the Narrow Sea, driving ahead of it a bonechilling rain. Whether William had intended it or not, Sister Emma mused, it was a fitting resting place for the last of the English kings; here, for all time to come, Harold Godwinson could guard the shores of the country he had loved and died for. The wind whipped salt spray into her face to run down cheeks already wet with tears. She gazed over the cliff with unseeing eyes, too well wrapped in her thoughts to feel the chill. Then, with a sigh, she made the sign of the cross and placed her silver crucifix among the stones that covered his grave: so lonely a grave on the barren, wind-scoured cliff, with not even a cross or the blessing of the Church to speed a poor soul on its way.

CHAPTER TWENTY-SIX

Edith MoonCatcher dropped her bag of grain with a puff of dust next to Edwina LongBraid's sack. Edwina was waiting on a bench outside the mill to have her grain ground into flour, and Mildburh was keeping her company. Baldwin sat at their feet, his tail drooping.

'You two look as glum as Good Friday,' said Edith. 'Shove over.'

The two women made room on the bench. Edith plopped herself down and said, 'I've seen wakes more lively than this. Even Baldwin looks down in the mouth.'

'He misses the lordling,' said Edwina. 'I fear he will surely pine away.'

'My children ask after their Lord Gandulf,' said Mildburh. 'What can I tell them?'

'Tell them to look up on the hill,' said Edith, 'for sometimes I see him standing on the palisade, looking down at us as we work.'

'Bless him for keeping his distance,' said Edwina. 'If the stories are true, Lord Ralf will have it out of our hides if he is caught down here before his wedding.'

'If only there were something we could do for him,' said Mildburh.

'Even just to let him know we're thinking of him,' added Edith.

'How could we? None of us knows how to write,' said Edwina dispiritedly.

'There's Father Edmund,' suggested Edith. 'He knows his letters.'

'He's in enough trouble as it is,' said Mildburh. 'If Lord Ralf were to learn of it . . .'

They all nodded and fell back into a glum silence.

Suddenly Edwina sat up straight. 'Baldwin, could you find Gandulf?' At the mention of his friend's name, the dog's tail thumped eagerly.

'Wait,' said Mildburh. She ducked into her herb garden and returned holding a spring of rosemary. Tucking it into Baldwin's rag collar, she explained, 'For remembrance.'

'Baldwin,' commanded Edwina, holding the dog's face and looking into his eyes, 'find Gandulf. Go, laddie. Find Gandulf!'

The dog fidgeted happily, then darted off. They watched him dash off toward Tout Hill, leaving a faint trail of dust to settle back into the road.

'Do you think he understood?' asked Edith.

'Oh, aye. Baldwin is smarter than half the male population here in Enmore Green.'

Aldyth was on her way to the mill to have some early grain ground when she had to jump aside or be bowled over by a furry black streak. 'Was that Baldwin?' she asked her friends as she approached.

'We sent him up to visit Gandulf,' explained Edith.

Aldyth blushed at the mention of his name. Enough time had elapsed that she found herself halfheartedly wishing that Gandulf's theft of her virtue had been permanent. She had even envisioned herself stealing up to the garrison. Margaret would deliver her message to Gandulf, and he would meet her at Saint Wulfstan's. Sometimes she pictured them going by foot, other times a horse. She never got so far as to imagine where they might go or how they might live, but she often wondered if he would heed her summons or if his curiosity had been satisfied on Midsummer's Night.

'Do you think we should let Aldyth join us?' teased Mildburh. 'We don't want such a sourface to dampen our fun.'

'Shove over,' said Aldyth, and she plopped glumly down beside them.

*   *   *

The next morning, sickle in hand, Aldyth was on the way to her field when she saw a company of hawkers; trailing behind were Gandulf and a girl she knew must be Lady Catherine de Broadford, with a groom and a matronly chaperone following at a respectful distance. Baldwin, at Gandulf's heels, was the only one who looked at all cheerful. Both the groom and the chaperone looked bored, the groom because he had ridden this trail so many times, though seldom in such dull company, and the chaperone because there was pitifully little need for her services.

Aldyth ducked down into the brush and waited until they had gone before trudging out to her field. She must get the hay in and had no excuse to put it off. The hills grew lush with healing herbs, but Sirona had forbidden her to go gathering. She, like Gandulf, had been confined to her own tiny sphere. Aldyth thought of the Christmas wren, beating its wings vainly against the basket that imprisoned it.

She was startled at a movement from the hedgerow bordering the field. Like a ripe peach falling from a tree, a man dropped out of the branches. Aldyth did not know which was more surprising, that someone should drop out of the sky in front of her or that it should be Bedwyn. He had not shaved his beard, and he had exchanged his hermit's tunic of blue for drab garb more suited to a peasant.

'Bedwyn, what are you doing here?' she chided. 'And in broad daylight!'

'I've come to help you with the haying.'

'This doesn't change anything. My answer is still no.'

'You're angry about Midsummer, aren't you? She meant nothing to me.'

'Who you spend your nights with is none of my business.'

Ignoring her protests, Bedwyn fell to one knee and pressed her hand to his lips. 'I beg forgiveness, Aldyth; if you cannot grant it, let me bask in the heat of your anger.'

The corners of Aldyth's lips trembled as she fought down contradictory impulses to burst out laughing or take back her hand and slap his face with it. The laughter won out. Bedwyn

349

rose and said, 'I have come to pay tribute with the sweat of my brow.'

'Spare me your nonsense, Bedwyn,' she said, trying in vain to be stern. 'Stay if you wish, though I don't know why you would want to. Just keep your mind out of the gutter.'

He grinned, stripped down to his breeches, and took the sickle from Aldyth's hands. They went down the row, he wielding the sickle and she laying out the hay to dry. To keep the blade steady, Bedwyn kept rhythm with a song. 'Harvest home! Harvest home! We've plowed, we've sown, we've reaped, we've mown. Harvest home! Harvest home!'

His voice, deep and clear, carried them swiftly down the row. At the far end of the field, he stretched like a cat. Looking back at their work, he nodded with satisfaction, then turned to Aldyth. 'Mouse, I've been doing some hard thinking . . .'

'I need to talk to you too, Bedwyn, but not now while we're having such a nice time.'

He shrugged. 'Very well, how about a riddle?' He started down the field, his sickle swinging. 'I am a wonderful help to women, shaggy below and the hope of something to come. The peasant girl grabs me, holds me hard, and claims my head. She who catches me will feel our meeting, and her eye will be wet before we are done.' Bedwyn cast a glance to be certain that his riddle had had the desired effect. He was not disappointed.

'Bedwyn!' chided Aldyth, throwing a handful of new-mown hay at him.

''Tis just an onion!' he said with a chuckle, trying to dodge the shower.

Aldyth laughed as Bedwyn shook bits of grass out of his long hair. 'You look like a hedgehog with green quills,' she teased.

'If I'm a hedgehog, then you're a butterfly.' He took two long stems of grass and set them in her hair to wave and bob like antennae. Glancing at the crows waiting in the nearby hedge for insects stirred up by the mowing, he warned, 'Beware the crows, for they will take a peck if you give them a chance.' With that he leaned forward, gave her a fleeting kiss on the cheek, and turned back to his mowing. Aldyth watched him fondly and shook her head in wonder; she had been so certain that she would never laugh again.

'I told you that hawk could deal death in a trice!' boasted Lord Ralf. The russet hawk had plummeted earthward and disappeared into the unmown hay of the meadow. When its head bobbed back up into view, the hawkers cheered, for its beak was dripping blood.

'A magnificent creature,' agreed Lord William de Broadford as he watched the hawk being lured back to the falconer's wrist and the coney whisked away to the kitchen.

'He shall be yours when Catherine is wed to my son,' promised Lord Ralf.

Lord de Broadford was taken aback by Lord Ralf's generosity, for a good hawk was prized more highly than an honest steward and loved more than many a wife. The offer made Gandulf realize how desperate his father was to seal this union, for he knew how highly he valued his hawks and his reputation as a falconer. Glancing at his future in-laws, Gandulf tried not to let his distaste show. Lady de Broadford was still a handsome woman, but not as handsome as she thought. She reminded him of a beady-eyed ferret on a gold leash, her eyes constantly darting about, calculating prices and possibilities. It would be amusing were it not foretaste of his own future with Catherine. The lady's disregard for her husband was obvious, if well merited. William de Broadford had never been handsome, and his face was marked with all the vices that ruled him. They were social climbers, as grasping as Lord Ralf but more interested in power and connection. Their castle was already built, thought Gandulf dryly. They had little concern for their daughter's happiness, for it was apparent how ill suited he and Catherine were to each other, as epitomized by the fervor with which Catherine enjoyed the hunt, her hawks, the glory of the kill. Gandulf had always been repelled by the hunt, which had put him at a great disadvantage socially, for hawking was the gentry's most popular pastime; society revolved around it. But whenever he saw a powerful hawk ripping down through the air upon a defenseless bird, he shuddered. Once, when he was still trying to please his father, Gandulf had gone hawking and held a young pheasant stunned by a falcon. Its heart had fluttered wildly, its eyes had been frantic, and even as he cradled it, it had died of fright in his hands. For some reason, that memory always made his heart ache for his mother. That was the last time he had gone hawking. Yet here he was, once again at the hunt to please his father.

Catherine rode over to him, holding up a dead coney, one of the rabbits brought over from Normandy and introduced into the forests to improve the hunt. 'The hunting is excellent in Cranborne Chase,' she said demurely. 'It makes me look very good.'

She was fishing for a compliment. He should tell her it was her skill, not the abundance of game, or that she would look good anywhere, but he could not bring himself to utter such an insincerity. He tried to summon the words, but it was too late. Catherine flushed angrily, flung the coney to the ground, and galloped off. One of her grooms gave Gandulf a killing look and retrieved it. Her ill humor would be vented upon her servants, and they would be miserable as well. Gandulf, who had spent a lifetime bending his will to fit his father's demands, noted Lord Ralf's glare and sighed. As well trained as one of his father's vaunted hawks, albeit less valued, Gandulf urged Cathedra into an amble and halfheartedly followed after Catherine to make amends. He looked forward to getting this ordeal over with and the wedding behind him; then these horrid people would go home, and he could lick his wounds in relative privacy.

At noon, Bedwyn and Aldyth stopped to rest in the dappled shade of the tree.

'You must be hungry,' said Aldyth to Bedwyn, and she took her dinner from her basket, a loaf of bread wrapped in a napkin and a hunk of skimmed-milk cheese. She broke the bread into two pieces and handed one to Bedwyn.

As he lounged in the grass, leaning on an elbow, he ate

in thoughtful silence. 'Aldyth,' he said at last, 'I've been here half the day, and no one knows the difference. Why couldn't I live with you here? I could be a long-lost cousin come to help with your holding.'

Aldyth wondered at the simplicity of it. It would not take long for Bedwyn to make a place for himself. His bees and his honey would be welcome, and if the villagers knew who and what he was, they respected him for it and would shield him from scrutiny. She laughed and said, 'You've thought it all out, Bedwyn, except for one thing: you could never settle down. Not in Enmore Green nor anywhere else.'

'I think I could. Without the Starlit Path, I really will be living the life of a hermit. Now there is no longer a reason for you to visit me; I've missed you, Aldyth.'

'Well, how do you think I'd feel, taking you in, knowing that you'd rolled in the hay with every willing maid in the Blackmore Vale?'

'You'd be the envy of the Blackmore Vale,' he said cheekily.

Aldyth sighed; it was probably true. 'But why am I different from any other maid?' she asked, not really expecting an answer.

'Because you're the only one I've ever asked to share my life.'

'Yes, but why? A woman needs to understand why she is loved in order to believe it.'

'I'd sooner show you, Mouse.'

'Do you actually expect to succeed, or are you just hoping for a free sample?'

'Well, at least if I didn't succeed, my time wouldn't have been entirely wasted.' He grew serious and mused, 'I hardly understand myself. Perhaps having watched you grow up and, in a sense, to have grown up with you.' He sought in her face a clue to the argument that would melt her heart but, finding no answer there, stumbled on. 'Aldyth, I've sown my wild oats for warmth, for pleasure, for amusement, to drive away loneliness or simply to cool my blood. But the thought of my child growing in your womb is enough to fill me with – I don't know – a tenderness I've never felt before.' He shrugged. 'I'm making a complete fool of myself.'

Why was it, Aldyth wondered, that a few well-chosen words from Bedwyn could make her wish to forget her vow to the Goddess? Once before she had almost thrown it all away, just because he had asked her to. She was touched to see him risking his pride, baring his heart for her sake. While knowing that she could never love him in the way she loved Gandulf, she wondered if she might find solace with Bedwyn. He was so grounded in her everyday world. She could envision their working side by side, making love, having babies, things she could never imagine herself doing with Gandulf. Gandulf was too serious, too high-minded for her simple nature. Not that Bedwyn did not possess principles, but he bore them lightly, while every aspect of Gandulf's life was governed by his. Gandulf was grounded not in place, as Aldyth was, but in ideas. She directed an appraising glance at Bedwyn and thought, 'He makes his place wherever he is.'

She asked wryly, 'Aren't you going to ask me what happened on Midsummer Night?'

Smiling, he shook his head. 'I won't ask you if you won't ask me.' His grin vanished like the sun behind a cloud, and he said soberly, 'I've never tried to hide the sort of man I am, and I make no apologies. Nor will I make promises I don't know I can keep. But if you wed me, Aldyth, I swear to love you and care for you and, if the Goddess grants it, give you strong children. And I will never cast you off.'

Aldyth knew Bedwyn was referring to Gandulf's impending marriage, and she wondered what conclusions he had drawn from the Midsummer gossip. She was deeply touched at his willingness to accept her with all her faults and frailties, no questions asked. Aldyth blushed to think of her intended vow, abandoned for love of Gandulf, but it made her all the more determined not to make the same mistake again. 'Bedwyn,' she began, 'you know I love you dearly, but as a sister might love a brother—'

'Don't tell me you'd kiss a brother the way you kissed me that night in the forest.'

'All right, I love you like a cousin, then,' she conceded,

'but in any case, you must know, however much I cherish your friendship, that I am already promised to the Goddess.'

Bedwyn's eyes widened, and he nodded. 'That would explain things. You've been too careful with me, Aldyth. After that first kiss in the glade, I knew you were inclined—'

'Well, now that you know of my vow you must accept my answer.'

'No, Mouse. I've made a vow of my own. The question is whether you will keep yours or I shall keep mine.' He leaned over and brushed her lips with his. Then, with an earnestness that gave her chills, he said, 'I'm warning you, Aldyth, I respect your vow, and I'll fight fairly, but I'll not give up the game.'

Gandulf had begged forgiveness of Catherine and promised that he would try to learn to love the hunt, a promise not even his father had been able to extract from him. The look she had given him was one of thinly veiled triumph and complete disdain, and it had chilled him to the bone. But Catherine had thereafter allowed him to ride at her side, for appearance's sake. With their parents appeased, they rode in silence. Gandulf wondered how a child of thirteen could have mastered the art of domination and manipulation so fully, but he had only to look at her mother for the answer.

Gandulf still had a sour taste in his mouth as they rode homeward, but it went all the way down to his stomach as they passed the field he knew to be Sirona's holding. To anyone else in the hawking party, a pair of sweaty Saxon peasants dallying at their noonday meal was too commonplace to stand out from the scenery. But Gandulf saw with painful clarity the woman he loved sitting far too close to the rival he could not hope to match. He frowned to note that Bedwyn was stripped to the waist, showing off his muscular torso, and Aldyth's kirtle was unselfconsciously hiked up to her knees. When Bedwyn leaned forward to kiss her, Gandulf felt his gorge rising and quickly turned away. It did not occur to him that the simplest way of removing his rival would be a single command to one of the men-at-arms riding escort. All the way up Castle Hill, Gandulf brooded silently as those around him tossed frivolous small talk back and forth. How could Aldyth allow that randy brute to press his attention upon her? Could she truly be taking Bedwyn's suit seriously? Perhaps, Gandulf conceded, now that he was clearly out of the running. He had known that Bedwyn would not give up on Aldyth but had not expected him to pursue her in broad daylight, almost up to the gates of his own father's stronghold; he had to respect the man's nerve, and maybe Aldyth did, too. It was no longer a matter of which man would win but whether Bedwyn would be able to beat out the Goddess.

The sorrow in his mother's face shocked Gandulf when he first caught sight of her, and he wondered what might have inspired such grief, for the message he had received at breakfast informing him of her return said that the journey had passed without incident. When his mother looked up from her embroidery and saw him, her face brightened and all traces of care disappeared. Gandulf decided his fears were unfounded when she gave a joyful cry and rose, her embroidery falling from her lap. She held out her arms to her son, and he ran forward to embrace her. 'Mother, how I have missed you!'

'How good it is to see you, my son.'

'How was your journey?'

'Oh, it went well,' she said dismissively. 'But I understand that things have not gone so well for you here. Tell me what passed while I was gone.'

'As you know, the de Broadfords are here, Mother. There is a great deal of feasting and hunting, and the negotiations go well.'

'That is just the face of it. What is in your heart?'

He hesitated, then said quietly, 'My life is over.'

'Oh, my poor boy. Can anything be as bad as all that?'

'The lady despises me, and I cannot see past the petty hauteur. The thought of begetting children upon her makes me ill.'

'Why don't you bring her to see me? Surely we can find something to like about her.'

'Very well,' said Gandulf unenthusiastically. 'At least 'twill be an escape from the watchful eye of her parents.'

'I remember at a court banquet many years ago, I sat a trencher away from Lady de Broadford,' said his mother, smiling sadly. 'She couldn't sit down to supper without examining the tablecloth for holes and appraising the value of the silver plate.'

'I fear I do not bear up well under her scrutiny,' said her son wryly.

'King William himself could not measure up to her standards,' Emma assured him, 'but perhaps the daughter will prove a better judge.'

Gandulf was doubtful but took Catherine to the abbey the next day. She was glad to go, for it provided an opportunity for her to state her position on several key matters.

'I will, of course, bring my own servants,' she stated flatly. 'For I won't be served by Saxons. And those ragged cloths in the hall must be replaced by decent tapestries.'

'Your parents will provide for all your needs in the contract,' he replied glumly.

'That's another thing. I want this marriage no more than you, but you might at least respect my station by looking less like a guest at a funeral in front of the servants.'

'I'm sorry, Catherine, you're right. I'll try to keep up appearances, and perhaps in time we shall come to feel as we act.'

She curled her lip at the suggestion, and he suspected that the charade would be difficult to maintain. Before a word had passed between his mother and his bride-to-be, he knew that it would be impossible; Catherine's blatant disdain of Emma was apparent and inexcusable. Catherine must have known how little influence his mother had with his father and how little there was to gain by winning her favor. She obviously regarded Emma as even more pathetic a creature than her spineless son. At least the visit was mercifully short. They took their leave of Emma, and Catherine briskly led the way to the gate in stony silence, as if trying to outpace her destiny, while Gandulf straggled behind. As they crossed the sunny cloister, Gandulf distracted himself with a game he had played as a

357

child to shut out unpleasant realities. Focusing on the hem of Catherine's dress, he noted the way it twitched with each step, then marked the rhythm of her gait in his head. Gandulf followed her into the shade of the colonnade on the far side of the cloister, but before his eyes could adjust, he bumped into an old lay brother. The monk's trowel clattered to the cobbles, and the old man stepped back to make way.

'Watch where you're going!' snapped Catherine to the old monk. Turning on Gandulf, she spat, 'That's another thing! You have to demand respect if you want it, and you won't get it from anyone if you cannot even get it from a clumsy Saxon oaf. Just look at him,' she fumed. 'He must be deaf and dumb, or he would be begging your forgiveness.'

The monk stood staring mutely. Gandulf picked up the old man's tool, recalling ironically that he had feared Catherine might be a frightened child bride. His concern now was whether she would be a husband beater or just a shrew. To the lay brother Gandulf bowed and said, 'Your trowel, sir. Forgive my clumsiness.'

Catherine stamped her foot and stormed off toward the outer gate. Gandulf sighed and followed. Brother Ansgar stared after them with surprising intensity.

The sound of hurried footsteps came from across the cloister. 'Be so good as to call back that gentleman,' begged the hastening nun. 'He's forgotten his gloves.'

Brother Ansgar had only just turned to pass on the message when he was distracted by a cry of distress from the other direction. The nun's knees sagged and her arms splayed as she clutched vainly at the air for support. The monk dashed forward and caught her as she toppled. He pulled back her veil, which had fallen over her face, and his cheeks, still blanched after his collision with Gandulf, now flushed crimson.

'Emma,' he gasped. Scooping her into his arms like a sick child, he rushed the unconscious nun to the infirmary. Mother Rowena's eyes flew to the small limp body he cradled, and the monk explained urgently, 'She collapsed in the cloister.'

'Over here,' said the infirmarian, leading him to a bed in the corner. As soon as he set Sister Emma down, Mother Rowena felt for a pulse, then produced a vial of smelling salts from the pouch at her waist. She held it under Sister Emma's nose, and Sister Emma's eyelids fluttered.

'She'll be all right,' observed the infirmarian. 'She's just fainted.'

The monk breathed a heavy sigh of relief. 'Thank God.'

Mother Rowena turned her full attention to him for the first time. Their eyes locked in sudden silent recognition. The lay brother had arrived at the abbey some weeks before, but he had taken care not to cross paths with the well-known infirmarian.

Mother Rowena said breathlessly, 'And who might you be, Brother?'

'I am called Ansgar.'

'Forgive my surprise, Brother Ansgar. I was startled to see you.'

'Most understandable,' he allowed with a subdued, but grateful smile.

Sister Emma gave a little moan and opened her eyes. 'Mother Rowena,' she whispered, 'might I have a moment alone to thank my brother in Christ?'

'Of course. If you need me, I will be in the stillroom.' Mother Rowena withdrew discreetly, resisting the urge to look over her shoulder or peek out the stillroom door.

'Are you trying to bait me?' Catherine demanded hotly. She turned on Gandulf so abruptly that he almost bumped into her.

'Bait you?' he asked, though he knew full well his offense.

'Treating that churl of a monk like a king!'

Gandulf sighed. To heighten his discomfort, strolling around the corner came Aldyth and Sister Arlette, absorbed in conversation. Gandulf had not been to Enmore Green since his father had threatened to raze it, but he had not given up hope of meeting Aldyth at the abbey. But at the sight of Gandulf, Aldyth quickly ducked back around the corner, leaving Lady Catherine with the impression that the porteress was babbling to herself. Gandulf was seized with an inspiration, and, uncharacteristically, he acted upon it.

'Sister Arlette,' he called, 'allow me to introduce you to Lady Catherine de Broadford. Did you know she is niece to Sister Agnes?' To Catherine, he said, 'Surely while we are here you would like to visit your aunt?'

Sister Arlette brightened, took the girl by the arm, and asked, 'Have you seen our chapel yet? 'Tis on the way. You'll notice the abbey walls are being rebuilt, and you'll never guess where we're getting the money from . . .'

Gandulf slipped away, hoping that he was not too late to catch Aldyth. She had darted from the cloister into the gardens, and he pursued her, heedless of the shocked looks he received. Aldyth cut through the kitchen, dodging the startled cook and scullions as they prepared the noon meal. Over her shoulder she saw Gandulf collide with a scullion carrying a dishpan full of dirty water. Dodging the flying dishpan, Gandulf went slipping and sliding as Aldyth ducked out the far door into the enclosure where firewood was kept. But she found herself trapped, for the gate leading to the outside was locked.

The kitchen door crashed open behind her. 'Aldyth!' demanded Gandulf, griping her elbow to prevent her escape. 'Why don't you speak to me?'

Panting and flushed from the chase, she snapped, 'Gandulf, what's the use?'

He stared at her in hurt silence. 'You're right, of course,' he said at last. 'I don't know what I was thinking; I really have nothing new to say.'

A flicker of sympathy warmed her eyes. She said gently, 'I hear it went badly with your father. I'm so sorry. But if he were to hear that we'd met at the abbey, it would bode ill for you, and who knows what repercussions might fall upon the village?'

'I didn't think . . .'

'You can leave off pawing the trollop,' came Catherine's acidic voice from the doorway. 'Can't you at least wait until after the wedding to take up your wenching?'

Gandulf loosed Aldyth's elbow but replied coolly, 'Pray

forgive Lady Catherine, Aldyth. She has yet to learn of Dorset customs and manners.'

Smiling maliciously, Catherine retorted, 'Perhaps my father can convince your father to teach you some Devon manners.' The young heiress was aware of the power she wielded, at least until her dowry was delivered. Gandulf watched her storm off, then turned to Aldyth. 'I'm sorry, Aldyth,' he told her somberly. 'I'm sorry for you. I'm sorry for me. I'm even sorry for her.'

Aldyth nodded. 'Best hurry, Gandulf, and catch her before she speaks to her father.'

CHAPTER TWENTY-SEVEN

'Are you an angel? Are you a ghost? Or am I finally going mad?' Sister Emma asked of Brother Ansgar as he knelt by her bedside and clasped her hands in his.

'Far from an angel and not quite a ghost. Call me Brother Ansgar, Emma.'

'I thought you were dead,' she choked, weeping unabashedly. 'What are you doing here? 'Tis sheer madness.'

'I came to meet our son. Emma, why didn't you tell me?'

'It would have been the ruin of us all. You gave me a child to love, and I wasn't going to have him labeled a bastard or killed at the hands of my husband. Besides, public acknowledgment was impossible, and it would only have caused hurt for your wife.'

He nodded in understanding. 'Does the lad know?'

She shook her head. 'I thought to tell him after Ralf's death.'

'I have heard it has gone hard with him. What kind of a man has the lad grown into?'

'He takes after his father, and I rejoice in the likeness.' She swallowed back tears at the thought of her son.

'Tell me more,' urged his father.

Across the room Sister Rinalda sat rocking in bed, talking and praying to herself. Mother Rowena brought refreshment to the reunited lovers, and the shadows moved slowly across the wall as they spoke quietly. Sister Emma told of Gandulf's childhood, his love of learning, his solitary nature, his precocious protectiveness of her, and what it had cost him. She told of his youth, his life with the monks, his bent for letters, and his steely resolve to wend his own path. Then she told of the man Gandulf had become, champion of the oppressed, poet and storyteller, devoted son, but luckless in love.

When Sister Priscilla learned from Sister Arlette that the visiting lay brother had not left Sister Emma's side since delivering her to the infirmary, the prying nun arrived on the pretext of visiting Sister Rinalda, but as she spoke to the bedridden nun, Sister Priscilla watched Sister Emma and Brother Ansgar with the piercing gaze of a hawk.

'Do you feel steady enough to walk, Emma?' asked the monk. 'Let us find a more private place before the nun across the aisle wrenches a muscle trying to overhear us.'

'That might be wise, Brother. She is a notorious gossip and a relentless busybody.'

'Worse than Sister Arlette?'

'Much worse,' warned Sister Emma. 'Sister Arlette spreads her news to entertain, but Priscilla does it with malice. She makes me nervous.'

He held out a steadying arm as they took their leave of the infirmary. As they entered the deserted garden, the abbey bells called the nuns to vespers. They found a stone bench, shielded from view by a grape arbor, and were seating themselves when Brother Ansgar looked about sharply. 'Did you hear something?' he asked Sister Emma.

'What could it be?' she replied. 'All the sisters are at evening prayer.'

He scanned the garden to reassure himself that they were alone, then sat by Sister Emma and confessed, 'I've been anxious as a hen whose eggs are pipping, just waiting for your return. I thought to wait a few days after I arrived before seeking you out, to allay suspicion. But my caution proved my undoing, for I learned that the boy had left for London two days after I arrived, and then I missed you by only hours! I'd have gone after you, Emma, but didn't dare leave Gunhild and Edith. There was nothing to do but bide.'

'If only I'd known,' she sighed.

He shrugged. 'What matters now is that I have a son. I want to meet him. He need not know who I am, nor that I am his father. I'll respect your wishes. What say you?'

'First tell me what is in your heart.'

'My children are all dead, save two girls. One is married and settled happily enough; I've been to see her to set my mind at ease. The other I have with me; I'm taking her away, and her mother too, and shall not return. But I could not depart without seeing my son. When Edith told me she was certain the lad was mine, I cannot tell you of my joy. You have found solace in him all these years, Emma. Pray God my turn has come.'

'I understand,' she said, smiling through her tears, for never had she hoped to bring her son together with his father. It was a miracle, a gift from God.

'How soon can you arrange a meeting?' he asked.

'Soon. Very soon,' she said eagerly. 'He comes to see me nearly every day.'

'I will wait for word from you. In the meantime, I have set aside my sword for a broom, and you will likely find me mucking out the stables,' he said with a wry smile.

'Vespers are almost over. We had best not be seen together,' she reminded him.

Their hearts were full, their word hoards empty, and though the path of one led to the dorter and the other's to the stable, their minds dwelt in the same place. But when their footsteps had died away, a stealthy rustling broke the silence. Sister Priscilla stepped from behind the grape arbor, a satisfied smirk twisting her features.

The next morning, Mother Rowena went to the abbess with a list of the supplies she would need for the winter. As she lifted her hand to knock upon the door of the abbess's chambers, it swung open and Sister Priscilla swept out, nearly bowling her over.

Dame Eulalia was the first Norman abbess to govern at the Abbey of Saint Mary and Saint Edward, having come only a handful of years after the conquest. Sister Priscilla was also Norman, and she bitterly resented Mother Rowena's friendship with the abbess. She called the Saxon lady flotsam that the conquest had washed ashore, yet she herself was flotsam washed up from a different shore. Sister Priscilla was only the daughter of a minor knight, and she lacked the ability required to advance in the abbey hierarchy. As a nun, she was denied carnal pleasure, material delights, and sensual satisfaction. One of the few worldly pleasures left to her was her malice. When Mother Rowena saw the vicious smile on Sister Priscilla's face, she wondered whom she had targeted this time.

The last time it had been the cook's assistant: Sister Priscilla had complained about his laziness, implied that he was a thief, and prayed loudly for his worthless soul whenever she had an audience. The abbess's defense of his character had spurred Sister Priscilla on in her mission to destroy him. He had finally gone off to seek a position where he was not the object of such hate. Mother Rowena feared that Sister Priscilla's behavior was growing more extreme and irrational; sometimes she even questioned the nun's sanity, for the austerities of the religious life had broken many a stronger spirit.

Dame Eulalia's age was a mystery, for she was one of those women who seemed never to have been young, yet never appeared to age. She came of a noble family and had not been raised with the humility befitting a nun; she let her habit of command show more than might be thought godly. But in the privacy of her chambers, the abbess addressed Mother Rowena informally: 'Come in, daughter, and sit you down.' After a moment's reflection, she began, 'You must have crossed paths with Sister Priscilla just now.'

'Yes,' said Mother Rowena with distaste.

'She came bearing tales.'

'Again?'

'Yes, but this time the tales could have serious consequences. She has overheard a conversation between our own Sister Emma and the visiting lay brother who escorted the nuns from Wiltshire. It would seem that his pilgrimage has nothing to do with the martyr's bones. Sister Priscilla claims that he begot Sister Emma's son, Gandulf.'

'Even were that true,' said Mother Rowena, trying to

366

mask her shock and alarm, 'it had to have been before she took her vows.'

'Not before she took her wedding vows. Sister Priscilla urges me to go to Ralf fitzGerald and have his son declared a bastard. If she had her way, Sister Emma would be stoned for adultery and the lay brother turned over to Lord Ralf.' She paused and tapped her fingertips together. 'What are your thoughts on this matter, Rowena?'

''Tis a delicate situation,' said Mother Rowena cautiously. 'After all, Lord Ralf has no other heir, and how can we know if there is even a grain of truth to this rumor?'

The abbess nodded. 'I told her to speak to no one and to do nothing until I have considered the matter carefully, and I reminded her of the penalty for the sin of gossip.'

'Perhaps your warning will give the matter enough time to resolve itself,' said Mother Rowena, though in her heart she was doubtful of that.

After their meeting, Mother Rowena hastened to find Sister Emma, who was kneeling in prayer in the chapel. 'I hope you are feeling better, Sister,' said the infirmarian.

'Much better, thank you,' Sister Emma replied.

'Still, I would have you come to the infirmary for a dose of physic.'

'Your concern is appreciated, Sister, but not necessary.'

'I think it is,' insisted Mother Rowena, taking the surprised nun's elbow and guiding her out of the chapel, through the cloister, and into the infirmary. She paused at the doorway to scan the shadows with such care that Sister Emma half expected her to peer under the beds. Mother Rowena then cocked her head to listen, but the only sound was Sister Rinalda's loud snoring, which echoed throughout the hall. Sister Emma felt her discomfort grow into alarm as she was ushered into the stillroom.

Without preamble, the Saxon nun turned to the Norman and stated, 'I trust last night yours was a good visit with Brother Ansgar.'

'Yes. We are old acquaintances, in fact,' replied Sister Emma uneasily.

'Sister, the abbess has confided that certain allegations have been made against you,' said the infirmarian. 'Your reunion with Brother Ansgar was overheard.'

'Sister Priscilla!' hissed Emma.

Mother Rowena nodded in confirmation and continued, 'I do not know or care if the tales are true, but I must warn you that there is mischief afoot.'

'Gandulf!' cried Emma. Wringing her hands, she faced Mother Rowena. 'I'll tell you frankly that what you have heard is true, but what can be done?'

'I don't know,' said Mother Rowena. 'The implications are serious, and you know better than I what Lord Ralf is capable of. We must both watch Sister Priscilla carefully.'

'Thank you, Sister, for coming to me.' More hesitantly: 'Brother Ansgar must be warned immediately. If it is dangerous for my son or me, 'tis even more so for him. Could you seek him out and send him to me here?'

'Of course, Sister,' agreed Mother Rowena, clasping Sister Emma's hands.

Sister Emma recited Pater Nosters and paced nervously until she heard footsteps on the flagstones. Brother Ansgar entered, and she fell to her knees before him. 'There, now, Emma,' he said, lifting her to her feet, 'tell me.'

'You must leave tonight,' she whispered fearfully. 'Our tryst was spied upon.'

'But what of Gandulf?' he asked in dismay. 'I cannot leave before I've seen him.'

'If you will not see to your own safety, what of your wife's and daughter's?'

He made a frustrated, helpless movement with his hands. 'How can this have happened? The story repeats itself: I bring only grief to those I love.'

'My Lord, 'tis not so! One day Gandulf will hear of the danger you braved in coming and know that the very qualities Ralf despises in him are his greatest strengths, gifts from his father, and the sign of a noble house. As for me, all these years I have lived without hope of seeing you again this side of Heaven.' She stood soul-naked before him and, through a blur of tears, stared up into his eyes. They were blue as cornflowers and deep with compassion, just as she had remembered them to be. Her chin trembled as she stammered, 'I have always longed to tell you how much you have meant to me and to ask . . .' She paused and looked away, 'You must have cared a little . . . if you are here.'

'Emma, how could you doubt me?' His voice was as soft as a sigh. 'I never meant for what happened between us to occur, nor could I have expected such far-reaching consequences. But was it real? Was it true? Hardly a day has gone by when I have not thought upon you, my gentle friend, a sleeping lamb who woke to become a lioness.'

'You are the only one to know me.'

'The knowledge was more cherished for that. If things had been different . . . if I had not already given my heart to another, if we two had not been born on opposite sides of the channel . . . and then there was Hastings. But Emma, you have given me a son, I hope for the future when I had only sorrow and defeat. Yes, Emma, I loved you then, and I love you still. But there is danger here for you, sweeting,' he continued, taking her firmly by the shoulders. 'I've just spoken to Edith, and she welcomes you to come away with us.'

Sister Emma shook her head and squelched the quavering sob that rose up in her throat.

He mistook her silence. 'Please come,' he urged, taking her hands. 'Edith is good and giving, and you must allow me to make amends to you for the years of suffering.'

'I would never leave our son. But to be asked, to know that it meant to you a fraction of what it has meant to me, is the fulfillment of my dreams. Oh, my dearest! Go to Edith and carry her to safety with my blessing and my heartfelt love.'

'You have not changed.' He kissed her forehead and promised, 'I shall return.'

'Godspeed,' she whispered.

After twenty-eight years he was there; then, just as suddenly, he was gone, like a phantom from the past conjured up by her longing. He had not merely climbed mountains or crossed over an ocean; he had come back from the dead to be with her.

CHAPTER TWENTY-EIGHT

Brother Ansgar pulled up his hood and slipped out through the back gate in the garden wall of the abbey. It meant skittering down the steep southern slope of Sceapterbyrig's great hill into Alcester. He had considered carefully; it was possible that someone might spot him, but if he left by the front gate it was impossible that Sister Arlette would not. As he skidded down among the scrub, he was aware of the evening breeze, especially pleasant after too long a confinement in the walled air of the abbey. When he reached the path to Alcester at the foot of the hill, the smells began to change. Twilight was deepening, and the scent of wood smoke and supper cooking hung in the air. But this was soon overpowered by the stench of the tanneries. Brother Ansgar wrinkled his nose as he skirted the outlying buildings of Alcester. It would be a short walk around the base of the hill to Enmore Green, where he would seek out Sirona, whom he had known years before and who, he knew, could arrange to spirit Edith and Gunhild away. He wished that Emma was not so determined to stay. He could charm the spots off a leopard, but all she had to do was look at him with her soulful eyes and he was helpless to oppose her will.

His ears discerned furtive scufflings on the wooded path ahead; someone or something was taking care not to be heard. Brother Ansgar could not afford to be sighted, even by a poacher, so he melted into the shadowy brush under the dark shelter of the trees. Quiet, hasty footsteps halted near his hiding place. Had he been seen scrambling down the hill? A voice hissed, 'I can't find a trail, Rollo; he must have gone to ground.'

The brother's skin crawled as he recognized the voice of one of the footpads who had assaulted Aldyth Lightfoot. They must have lain in wait for him to leave the sanctuary of the abbey, he thought, drawing his dagger.

'What are you waiting for, Hugo?' snapped Rollo.

Hugo began probing the bushes with his pike while Rollo slashed at the brush on the opposite side with his sword. They came closer and closer to where the old brother was concealed, and he tightened his grip on his dagger. They were within a pike's length of him when there came a sudden yelp and a mad scrambling nearby. Someone else was fleeing, heedless of the may tree's thorns. It was a different prey, then, that the Normans pursued. As the fugitive fled past him, Brother Ansgar saw that it was only a boy. The Normans nearly stepped on him as they gave chase, cursing the thorns. But with their senses concentrated ahead of them, they bypassed the man crouching silently in the brush. The lad they hunted avoided the pathway, heading instead for the tangled thickets, where his small size would be an advantage over brute strength.

'Clever lad,' thought Brother Ansgar, impulsively leaping to his feet. So that he might not be immediately recognized as the pilgrim brother, he pulled off his robe to follow the hunt dressed only in his knee-length shirt and sandals. A confrontation could be disastrous; Edith and Gunhild tugged at his conscience, yet the boy's need was immediate. He would find a way to cover his tracks once the lad was safe.

Brother Ansgar scrambled through the woods in the deepening twilight, hoping that the Normans would not hear him over their own crashing and bellowing. Suddenly all was silent. He halted immediately, lest the sound of his progress give him away. A sharp cry of pain told Ansgar that they had apprehended the boy. He crept closer to watch as they dragged the lad back onto the path, faintly lit by filtered moonlight. Hugo held the boy in a choke hold from behind while Rollo brandished a knife. The brother could not distinguish the Norman's words, but there was no doubt of his menace when he lifted the knife to the boy's ear and

372

gave it a quick flick. The boy shrieked but quickly regained his composure. Lifting his chin, he stated imperiously, 'I've connections in Sceapterbyrig, you lummox. In fact,' taunted the boy, 'the abbess herself is to meet me here tonight to go poaching, and when she hears of this . . .'

The Normans' eyes locked; the entire village must be laughing behind their hands over the episode with the witch's apprentice and the interfering brother. From the boy's words, Brother Ansgar knew him for the same lad who tagged after Aldyth Lightfoot, and he also knew that the cocky lad had forced Rollo's hand.

'You stupid little whoreson!' snarled Rollo. 'I'll teach you to mock your betters. You've just sealed your fate.'

Brother Ansgar let out a hair-raising bellow and charged. Before the startled Normans could react, he snatched up Hugo's pike from the ground and brought it down with a bone-crunching thud upon Rollo's crown. Rollo dropped like a felled ox, his knife vanishing into the leafy ground cover. Hugo roared like a berserker and, throwing Aelfric aside, drew his sword. Aelfric rolled out of range and stared wide-eyed.

'Get up, boy, and flee!' shouted Brother Ansgar.

Aelfric leapt to his feet and in a flurry, like a panicked sparrow, vanished into the woods. Taking advantage of the monk's distraction, Hugo sprang. The brother leapt back in time to save his skin but not his shirt, for steel slashed through the linen shirtfront, shaving off a few chest hairs. Brother Ansgar recovered his footing and swung the pike, delivering a solid blow to the Norman's side with a sickening thud.

'Idiot!' gasped Hugo, jumping back. 'Lay down your arms or answer to the king!'

Brother Ansgar's response was to lunge forward, aiming a blow at his opponent's sword hand. The skirmish recommenced, neither combatant wasting any more breath on empty words; only the thud of steel against wood echoed through the darkening forest, punctuated by the strained grunts of parry and thrust. The two opponents were well matched in size, although Brother Ansgar's age was beginning to tell. Sensing his opponent's fatigue, Hugo launched a relentless hail of blows. Brother Ansgar, forced backward, tripped over Rollo's body. But before Hugo could strike again, he recovered his grip on Hugo's pike. From the ground where he had fallen, he thrust the pike forward, barring the Norman's advance. But Hugo sent his dagger hurtling through the air. Instinctively, Brother Ansgar threw up his forearm to shield himself from the whistling missile. There was a sharp, searing pain and the ugly sound of steel scraping bone. Brother Ansgar's left arm, numbed to the shoulder, fell useless to his side, and the pike, a two-handed weapon, was also rendered useless.

The Norman brayed bitterly and closed in for the kill. 'By God, you'll pay for what you've done to Rollo.'

Frantically Brother Ansgar groped for anything that might serve as a weapon. His hand fell upon cold steel: Rollo's dagger. Hope flickered. His hand closed around the blade, and he wasted precious seconds fumbling for the handle. But Hugo stamped on the brother's hand, snatched up the dagger, and jerked him to his feet by the shirtfront. Pressing the point of the dagger to the old man's throat, he growled, 'I should've killed you the last time we met, king's business or no. But now you've made it my business, and I'll not make that mistake again.' Choking down a sob, he added, 'This is for Rollo.'

'Edith, forgive me,' the old Saxon thought as the Norman forced him to his knees.

Then came the thwack of wood on bone, and Brother Ansgar was pressed between the two king's men. Before he could even register what had happened, an elfin face peered into his. 'We took care of those shit-eating scumbags, didn't we?' crowed Aelfric.

Stunned by this sudden and unexpected reversal of fate, the brother relaxed into the heap of bodies to catch his breath. 'You could hardly call it a fair fight,' he quipped. 'Two Saxons, an old man and a boy, against only two Normans; they didn't stand a chance.'

Aelfric's wide grin gleamed in the moonlight.

'Be so kind as to get this big ox off me,' said Brother Ansgar.

Aelfric used the pike to roll the Norman aside, then helped Brother Ansgar to his feet. By moonlight, the blood on his white shirt stood out starkly. 'You're hurt,' said Aelfric.

"Tis just a scratch,' lied Ansgar. 'Can you cut me some strips from the hem of my shirt, lad? We'll bind it up in no time.'

'Right you are,' replied the lad, 'but the Normans can better spare the linen.' Aelfric was no stranger to leechcraft; he had grown up watching Sirona and Aldyth practice their art. Efficiently, he cut strips from Hugo's shirt and bound the arm.

'Where did you learn to do that?'

'Here and there. I've seen enough to know 'tis no mere scratch. I'll wager Lord Ralf's dirk that it's cut to the bone. We've got to get you to Sirona's where she can treat you properly. 'Tis not far . . . can you walk, or shall I carry you?'

'Perhaps something between the two,' ventured Brother Ansgar. 'Go find my robe, for I'd rather not parade through Enmore Green with my arse hanging out of my shirttail. I'll finish the business at hand,' he said, nodding toward the fallen Normans sprawled in the path. 'Hand me the dagger, lad, and wait for me up ahead,' he ordered, wishing to spare the boy both the guilt and the horror of Hugo's slaughter.

'Forget the robe,' argued Aelfric. 'We can scrounge you a pair of trousers later. Right now it'll take the both of us to hide the bodies.'

Approaching voices sent them diving for cover, their grim business unfinished. They waited, though without much hope that the passersby would miss the bodies in the gloom and they could finish what they had started. Shouts of alarm sent them scrambling deeper into the woods but covered the sound of their retreat.

Once out of earshot, Aelfric grumbled, 'Another minute was all we needed.'

'We'll be needing much more than that now, lad,' said Brother Ansgar soberly.

Aldyth and Sirona, spinning more by feel than by the dim firelight, were startled by a stealthy knocking. Aldyth opened the door. 'Brother Ansgar!' she gasped. White as a ghost, he stood with one arm hanging bloody and useless, the other arm wrapped around Aelfric's scrawny shoulders for support. Aldyth's assessment was both spontaneous and reflexive: he had suffered a dangerous loss of blood and looked to have incurred the deadly chill. 'Over here by the fire,' she said urgently, leading him by his uninjured arm. Aelfric closed the door with a quick glance behind.

Sirona, hurrying over to assist, saw the man's face and cried, 'Your Highness!'

Brother Ansgar said simply, 'None of that, Sirona.'

The crone, as close to flustered as Aldyth had ever seen her, composed herself and nodded. Noting Aelfric's puzzled expression, she told the boy, 'Hurry, lad, and fetch fresh springwater. Aldyth, we'll need bandages, salve, and a compress of wild pansy and red dead nettle to stanch the bleeding. Let's move him to the pallet.' She poured Brother Ansgar a cup of wine and handed it to him. ''Tis poppy for the pain; you'll be needing it, my Lord.'

Aldyth cut away his shirtsleeve and winced in empathy for the groan he stifled as she lifted the rest of the bloodied rag over his head. His bared body was a mass of long-healed scars, unmistakably inflicted in battle. The two healers lowered him onto their pallet; then Aldyth collected every blanket, cloak, and rag she could find to cover their patient and preserve his precious body warmth. Sirona cut away the drenched make-do dressing that Aelfric had applied in the woods. 'You've lost far too much blood,' she remarked, holding a basin under the injured arm and cleansing it with strong wine.

With fingers that trembled, Aldyth threaded Sirona's bone needle with silken thread. Even as she performed her task, Aldyth's mind was racing. His Highness? This man could not possibly be King William, for he was unmistakably a Saxon.

A knock at the door made them jump until it was followed by Aelfric's whisper, ''Tis just me.' Setting the bucket by Sirona, who was stitching up Brother Ansgar's wound, he asked excitedly, 'Did he tell you what happened? Those Norman dogs fell upon me – the same ones who attacked you, Aldyth. They were asking about you and Sirona too.'

'Aelfric,' said Aldyth, turning his face to the fire, 'what did they do to you?'

'Never mind the ear; this is the one that hurts,' he said, pointing to a small gash in his thigh that had bloodied his ragged trousers. Aldyth unwound the cross garters tying up his pant legs while Aelfric continued, 'They ran me down in the woods by Alcester. That's when Brother Ansgar charged out of nowhere, just like in one of Gandulf's stories.' Aelfric's eyes shone, and he grinned at his champion.

Aldyth had cleansed the boy's thigh wound and was applying a compress, when she wondered aloud, 'Could someone have found them?'

'We were chanced upon,' replied the old man, 'and were forced to flee.'

Sirona and Aldyth exchanged a worried glance. Aldyth bound Aelfric's thigh, gave him a pat on the rump, and treated the injured ear. 'There, elfling. Just don't pick at it.'

'Aelfric,' said Sirona, 'go borrow Agilbert's spare shirt and trousers and scrounge a clean pair for yourself from one of Alcuin's boys; no one must know of your adventure.'

As he ran off to do her bidding, Sirona turned to Brother Ansgar and said grimly, 'Would that your wounds were so easily mended, my Lord. Were both Normans killed?'

'I broke the one's crown; the other may have been merely stunned and could very well have had time to find his way up the hill by now.'

'You shouldn't be moved, but there's no help for it,' said Sirona. 'They'll be down from Castle Hill, searching all the homes, and you must be safely away by then.'

'That's why I was coming to see you in the first place, Sirona – to seek safe passage to the sea for Edith and Gunhild.'

Aelfric returned with Agilbert's Sunday best, his only change of clothing.

'Can you stand?' Sirona asked Brother Ansgar. They raised him up, and Aelfric eased one foot at a time into the legs of Agilbert's trousers and tied them at the waist. Then the fugitive sat down heavily on the bench while the lad tied up the cross garters.

'Blast it all!' exclaimed the injured man. 'I've been drawn from cover. Hugo recognized me and will surely find my robe. Edith and Gunhild will be questioned.'

In alarm, Sirona asked, 'Do the Normans know who you are?'

'I think not, but they know Gandulf is my son. I fear for both his and Emma's safety.'

Aldyth's jaw dropped. 'Gandulf in danger?' she quavered. 'Couldn't he just leave the shire? Surely Lord Ralf's vengeance can stretch only so far.'

'There are factors here beyond your understanding, child,' Sirona told her.

Brother Ansgar enveloped Aldyth's hand in his callused one. 'Aldyth,' he said gently, 'I've heard of your feelings for the lad, but 'tis not so simple as a run to the next shire. If the Normans knew who had sired the lad, there isn't one who wouldn't want him dead.'

She blanched. 'Who are you?' she whispered.

He sighed and hesitated, then looked at Sirona, who nodded acquiescience.

'A lifetime ago,' he confided, 'I was Harold Godwinson.'

Aelfric gasped, and, as he was already on his knees, he bent his head in homage. Young or old, there wasn't a Saxon who did not revere the name of Harold Godwinson. Harold ruffled the boy's sandy hair. 'No, lad,' he said quietly. 'We stand on even ground now.'

'Aelfric,' ordered Sirona, 'take a clump of garlic from the garden and sweep your trail to put off the hounds. Keep watch for signs of activity on Castle Hill.'

The boy nodded and rose, that he might deliberately kneel before Harold to place his hands between his lord's. 'I am your man, my Lord,' he swore before dashing off.

'King Harold?' whispered Aldyth. 'But he's dead, may the Goddess bless his bones.'

'My bones need all the blessings they can get, child, but I am still above ground.'

'Then whose bones are buried beneath the cairn of stones at Hastings?'

'Those of my brother Leofwine, God rest his soul. In the

heat of battle, I took an arrow in the throat. While I was unconscious, Leofwine seized my shield and stood beneath my banner.'

'But why?'

'So that our men would not lose heart knowing their king had fallen. 'Twas he who took those final blows.' His voice choked. 'My brother Garth fell with him and the last of my hearth troops. William's soldiers unwittingly assisted in the masquerade by mutilating the body they thought was mine. When William summoned my wife to identify the body, Edith falsely confirmed Leofwine's body to be mine, ending their search.'

'But where were you?'

'I came to my senses three weeks later, having been spirited away by a handful of faithful followers and taken to the monks at Ely. I wanted to rally the Saxon cause, but by then the pope had declared William's a holy war and had excommunicated me. The monks – my own countrymen – restrained me to prevent further bloodshed.

'Edith fled to Exeter with my mother and the girls, where they were captured the following year. My eldest sons, barely grown to manhood, fled to Ireland to continue the fight.' Harold sighed. 'They were bitter and unforgiving of William and the English who accepted him; they fell in with Danish raiders and were killed pirating their own shores.

'The monks told me that I went mad, and perhaps I did; I remember little of those years. I lost the will to live; why should I be spared when every soul in England had suffered for my cause? I thought God Himself had deserted me.'

'Yet now you seem whole,' said Aldyth gently. 'What changed for you? And when?'

'Just before Ely was taken, the abbot, the same abbot who had betrayed Hereward's rebel force to the Normans, had me sent to another prison.'

'So that you wouldn't fall into Norman hands?' speculated Aldyth.

'Perhaps,' said Harold doubtfully. 'More likely he realized the enormity of the treason he had committed in keeping me, yet still he would not have my death on his conscience, and so he consigned me to a living death. He died several years later. Though I cannot say for sure, I believe the abbot's secret was buried with him.'

'How do you know all this?' asked Aldyth. 'Did the abbot tell you these things?'

Harold shook his head. 'I had time enough to figure it out for myself. For obvious reasons, the abbot had entrusted me to a deaf-mute. By the time my keeper died, there was no one left who knew who I was nor even why I was being held. I persuaded his replacement to aid my escape that I might make a pilgrimage for the salvation of my soul, only that pilgrimage took me not to Rome but to Russ.'

'Why Russ, of all places?' asked Aldyth.

'Only my elder daughter, Gytha, escaped William's vengeance, for she had married a Viking prince of Russ just before the conquest. I went to her. She is alive and well and the mother of kings. So you were right, Sirona, those many years ago,' he said, turning to the wisewoman, 'when you predicted that I would be the grandfather of kings.'

Sirona smiled ruefully. 'The readings are always true, if only we knew how to interpret them. Did you find what you sought from Gytha, my Lord?'

Harold nodded. 'She was blessed with the wisdom of her mother. "Go home," said Gytha, "for you've nothing to lose and aught to gain." I went to Wilton Abbey, where my wife and daughter had been confined since the fall of Exeter. Over the years, security had grown lax. No one looked twice at an old pilgrim, except Edith SwanNeck and her daughter Gunhild. We escaped into the night, and I thought my work in Wessex done – until Edith told me that Emma fitzGerald had come to Wilton years before, accompanied by her son, Gandulf, and that except for his Norman coloring, he was the spitting image of our boy Godwin. Edith counted the years since Lord Ralf's stay at King Edward's court, where I was serving at the king's right hand, and she knew he was mine. But until I came for her, she knew not how to inform me, nor even if I were living or dead.

'When I have made my peace with Gandulf, the only

earthly task remaining to me shall be to buy freedom for my brother Wulfnoth, who is still hostage to William.'

'You can't do that,' said Sirona sharply. 'You have nothing left to bargain with.'

'I have myself.'

'William has no scruples; he would kill you and keep Wulfnoth just the same.'

'As you say, Sirona, I have nothing else to offer.'

Aldyth no longer had to wonder about Sister Edith, for everyone knew Edith SwanNeck's story. She had been only the daughter of Harold's father's steward, but, when barely more than children, the two of them had eloped. Harold had chosen love over connection, wealth, or station, and they had shared a handfast marriage that had bound them through five children, two wars, death and resurrection – and adultery. Now Edith was doing everything in her power to bring her beloved together with his son by another woman. Edith SwanNeck, thought Aldyth, must love Harold very deeply.

'Enough,' said Sirona. 'You are in my keeping, and I mean to see you safely away.'

The door burst open, and Aelfric rushed in. 'They're coming down Castle Hill on horseback, and it sounds like a bloody army.'

'Aldyth,' ordered Sirona quickly, 'take him to Bedwyn.'

'Not without my wife and daughter,' said Harold firmly.

'Aldyth will fetch them from the abbey as soon as the city gates open at dawn.'

'What of Gandulf?' asked Harold.

'Just go!' said Sirona, leading their little cow from her corner. 'You won't be able to walk the distance,' she said, 'but Godiva can.' Sirona helped him lift a leg over the little cow's back. 'May the Goddess go with you,' she said, handing Godiva's halter to Aldyth and slapping the beast on the rump to hurry her out. Before they had crossed over the toft bridge, Sirona had cleaned up and damped the fire. To throw off the dogs, she tucked garlic with Harold's bloodied rags into the underside of the thatched roof.

Aldyth hurried the bewildered cow into the cover of the woods. In the distance, she heard the clank of armed soldiers galloping down the hill. Before ducking into the brush that grew around the spring, she glanced over her shoulder and saw the glow of torches, heard the shouted orders, the villagers' cries of alarm. The Normans had created the diversion she needed to slip away, but her heart quaked for her friends.

When the runaways had gone far enough that the sound of havoc was lost in the gentle hum of crickets, Harold said softly to Aldyth, 'Now it is you who rescue me.'

Walking alongside Godiva, Aldyth kept a steadying arm around his waist. Blood loss had taken its toll, and she could almost feel his strength ebbing. 'Turnabout is fair play,' she replied, marveling that she was bantering with Harold Godwinson, the rightful king of England, as if he were a neighbor. She understood the devotion and affection that his people bore for him, why they still clung to the impossible hope of his return. She compared him to another great man, King William, who now sat upon the throne of England. William was a man of astounding accomplishment, but he was not a good man. 'Please, my Lady,' prayed Aldyth silently, 'do not let Harold die.'

Six miles had never gone so slowly for Aldyth. A cow walked no faster than a human, a heavily laden cow walked more slowly still, and the smell of blood made Godiva uneasy and harder to lead. With each passing minute, it became more difficult to prevent the injured man from sliding off his mount. Aldyth's arms ached from the strain and her head ached with worry, for she had had time to fret over Bedwyn's reaction at her arriving unbidden with another fugitive in tow. Even worse was her fear that he would not be at home, for he had no reason to expect visitors. She was relieved to hear the obnoxious honking of the geese, for at least she knew then that Bedwyn had not decamped.

'Do you hear the call of the sentries, my Lord? This is Bedwyn's place.'

'The fewer people who know who I am, lass, the safer we all will be.'

'Of course,' she agreed. Aldyth debated: should she leave Harold in the woods, as she had with Ricole? She decided against it, for he could never stay astride on his own and, once he had dismounted, could never remount should hasty retreat be required. Aldyth drew Godiva up to Bedwyn's door and knocked softly, then opened the door to glance inside the hut. Aldyth was bracing herself to receive Harold's weight when she felt strong arms come up from behind. She almost cried with relief as Bedwyn lifted Harold down from the cow's back and, helping him inside, settled the injured man on his own pallet. Aldyth hurried after and prepared a new dressing while Bedwyn heated water.

Bedwyn's eyes kept returning to the stranger's face. 'Who is he?' he demanded at last.

'I am called Brother Ansgar,' said Harold weakly.

As Aldyth cut away the old dressing, Bedwyn supported Harold's shoulders and lifted a cup of strong wine to his lips. 'This will do you good,' he said.

Harold took a sip, then said with a half smile, 'I've heard of the Hermit of the Blackmore Vale. 'Twill be good to receive guidance from a fellow religious.'

Bedwyn chuckled. 'I'm not the one to show you the way to Heaven, Brother.'

'The coast will be good enough for now,' replied Harold.

Aldyth gently washed the ugly wound with water from the Crystal Spring, then handed Bedwyn the compress, which he held as she bandaged it in place. When she was finished, she held a cup to Harold's lips. ''Tis poppy,' she explained, 'to help you rest.' As she washed up, she said, 'Bedwyn, trouble is brewing. Brother Ansgar killed a Norman – in Aelfric's defense. I'm sure it was Rollo, and now Hugo will be looking to avenge him.'

'Well done, Brother,' said Bedwyn, 'for sending another deserving sinner off to meet his Maker.'

'Seriously, Bedwyn,' cautioned Aldyth, 'this is the moment Hereward warned us of. Lord Ralf's men will surely be recruited, fitzGrip's too. Take extra care tonight. I'll return soon after dawn with two more runners to be moved on as soon as may be. Brother Ansgar will be better able to travel tomorrow.' Or dead, Aldyth told herself grimly.

Bedwyn could not know that Gunhild was a nun, thought Aldyth, nor yet that she was Harold Godwinson's daughter.

When Gunhild the nun, his cast-off lover, arrived at Bedwyn's doorstep to be placed into his keeping, he would find himself in a very awkward position. Aldyth decided not to worry him with details just yet.

Aldyth emptied the wash water outside, listening to the night sounds: only Godiva's steady cropping of grass and the chirping of crickets. The call of an owl, a lonely, haunting sound, drove her back inside.

She knelt beside Harold and took his hand. 'May the Goddess watch over you, Brother. I'll be back soon with your companions. Now try to get some sleep.'

Harold nodded in agreement. 'I shan't be going out again this evening.'

Bedwyn, smiling appreciatively at the wry humor, saw Aldyth to the door.

'Thank you, Bedwyn,' she said wearily.

Bedwyn brushed a loose strand of hair back from her eyes. 'Take the long way, Mouse,' he advised, 'and be most careful as you near the village; they may have posted guards.'

It was not a brotherly kiss he gave her, but Aldyth hugged him warmly and whispered, 'You'll find there are other fish to fry, Bedwyn, maybe even for breakfast.'

As she turned to leave, Bedwyn took hold of her arm and said, 'There's only one fish I want to land, Aldyth. Slippery as an eel, but I'll catch her yet.'

Harold watched silently as Aldyth slipped out of Bedwyn's grasp and into the night. From the doorway, Bedwyn followed her retreat until she and her cow had blended with the gloom. Then he shut the door and turned back to Harold, who said, 'She's a lovely girl.'

'Aye,' Bedwyn agreed, 'but with a will of her own.'

'It might be rather dull otherwise.'

'True enough; when a woman holds the bit in her mouth, you never know where she'll take you. But how did you become the expert on women, Brother Monk?'

'I learned in the same school you did, Brother Hermit,' said Harold with a wink.

Bedwyn chuckled, thew a branch onto the fire, and settled

down beside his guest. 'I've seen you somewhere, Brother. Were you ever in York . . . a long time ago?'

'I can hear the Yorkshire moors in your voice,' observed Harold.

''Twas my home before my father was imprisoned and his lands given to some thieving Norman.'

'Tell me about it,' said Harold.

They talked as Bedwyn made himself a pallet out of bee skep straw. He gave his ward the infusion Aldyth had left of Saint-John's-wort for inflammation and Madonna lilies for healing, administered the brew, covered his charge with a blanket, and banked the fire to burn low but how. The poppy was taking effect, and the injured man drifted off into drugged oblivion, but Bedwyn could not sleep. He liked Brother Ansgar but found him unsettling. Finally Bedwyn too drifted off.

Once again he was ten years old, standing at his father's side. They had ridden to York to swear fealty to King Harold, the first English king who had ever bothered to journey to the northernmost reaches of the kingdom. Young Bedwyn had felt very important when he knelt and placed his hands between the king's. His eyes, which had been focused on Harold's ruby ring, had surreptitiously darted up to the king's face. He had, unexpectedly met Harold's deep blue eyes, and he had blushed at being caught snatching glance. But the king had smiled warmly, and in that throng of thousands gathered from throughout the shire, no Saxon loved his king more fiercely than that ten-year-old boy.

Bedwyn woke with a start, sweating profusely as he sat bolt upright in bed. The hair was now silvered, the handsome face careworn and scarred by battle, but in his gut he knew, as a bee knows the queen of its hive, that it was none other than Harold Godwinson he sheltered. And he wept for joy.

Sobered by the awesome responsibility, Bedwyn wiped his eyes on his sleeve and composed himself. He strained his ears and listened to his companion's hoarse breathing from across the dying fire. This was no ghost, thought Bedwyn, but a flesh-and-blood man. He stirred the embers on the hearth, then replaced the blanket that the wounded man had kicked aside. Bedwyn covered Harold with his own blanket as well and sat up to keep watch over the sleeping king.

The moon still shone through the cracks in the door when Harold stirred. Bedwyn reached over and felt his charge's forehead; it was burning hot.

'Aldyth left me something for fever,' said Bedwyn. 'I'll brew you a simple.' Bedwyn put water on to heat, then bathed his patient's head with a cold cloth.

'So sorry, lad,' mumbled Harold. 'I'll soon be on my way.'

'The next hide is just a lambing hut,' Bedwyn reassured him. 'You can take your time recovering there, and I'll look after you.'

'After all this time,' said Harold, ''tis gladdening to see Englishmen hang together. You and your like are the backbone of Saxon England.'

Bedwyn placed his hand between Harold's. 'But you could be its head, sire.'

There was a startled silence. At last, Harold spoke: 'How did you know?'

'I was only ten when I swore fealty to you in York, but 'twas the oath of a lifetime. I know not how it can be, but I know I am not mistaken. God has sent you back to pull England out of the mire. I would lay down my life to win back England. There are thousands of us, sire, waiting for a sign, for a leader. All you need is say the word.'

Their eyes interlocked, and the pregnant silence drew out, the air about them crackling with intense but unspoken emotion. The strident honking of excited geese shattered the night, and the two men started as if released from a spell.

'Someone is coming,' hissed Bedwyn, drawing his dagger and peering out through a crack in the door. He swore under his breath. In the faint light of near dawn, he could see a dozen armed soldiers on horseback, though none dismounted out of respect for the pugnacious geese. They were lighting torches to fend off the geese and conduct a search.

''Tis Hugh fitzGrip's lieutenant – so they have brought the sheriff in on the search. I recognize some of fitzGerald's soldiers from the garrison at Sceapterbyrig. And God damn it!'

snarled Bedwyn. ''Tis Osgot of Alcester; he led them straight to our doorstep.'

Bedwyn thrust the handle of his dagger into Harold's hand. 'They can't know who you are,' he whispered. ''Tis just a blind search for Rollo's killer. Be still, and as soon as you can, get out to the cover of the woods.'

'No,' whispered Harold, catching Bedwyn's sleeve. 'Let me surrender myself.'

'Over my dead body!' growled Bedwyn. He slipped outside, and Harold heard the shouts of the men-at-arms, like the baying of hounds, as they sighted Bedwyn. He heard Bedwyn yell at Osgot, 'Traitor!' The shrill whinny of a frightened horse was followed by a man's shriek, more shouting, and the scuffle of horses crashing through the brush. Harold knew that they had given chase. Still gripping Bedwyn's dagger, he crawled to the bench and pulled himself to his feet. Shambling across the room, he pressed himself against the wall behind the door. At last a sweaty soldier burst into the dark and grimy hut, took a brief glance around, then shouted, 'There's nothing in here.'

From without came a harsh voice: 'Torch it.'

The soldier took a firebrand from the hearth and shoved it up into the dry thatch. The flames caught hold immediately, and the soldier ducked out hastily to escape the fierce heat of the blaze and the black, billowing smoke.

CHAPTER TWENTY-NINE

Aldyth ducked back into the bushes and sat trembling in the dark long after the Norman patrol has passed. It was only two foot soldiers, probably assigned to enforce curfew and detain offenders, but she shuddered to think what might have happened had she been taken; so many were depending upon her, and her capture would throw suspicion upon Sirona and Aelfric, who could least bear the scrutiny.

When Aldyth slipped quietly into her hut, she found Sirona awake in the dark, awaiting her. 'Take the warm spot,' said the old woman, moving over. 'All went well?'

'Yes,' replied Aldyth, crawling under the covers, 'except that I had to turn Godiva loose to find her own way home. 'Tis hard to be inconspicous with a cow on your heels.'

There was nothing to add in spite of the worries that plagued them. After all, a plan had been devised and it remained only to wait until they could execute it. Aldyth had looked forward to collapsing onto her pallet for an hour or two until sunrise, when the city gates would open and she could fetch the nuns. But sleep would not come. She felt compelled to give voice to her fears. 'He is in terrible danger,' she whispered.

'We'll move him to the next hide as soon as possible,' came her godmother's reply.

''Tis of Gandulf that I speak.'

'I cannot disagree,' said Sirona with a sigh. 'There are two cups on the hearth. Get up, daughter, and drink the one that smells of honey. Bring me the other.'

Aldyth obeyed. The honeyed fragrance of mead rising from the one cup was unmistakable, and she knew from the bittersweet smell of the other that Sirona intended to drink the Draft of Dreams, in hope that the Goddess would speak to her. Only on the direst occasions did Sirona presume to seek out the Goddess, instead of waiting for the Goddess to come to her. Aldyth drank mead while the wisewoman softly chanted a prayer in the ancient tongue, then slowly sipped the concoction of sacred herbs. Aldyth listened as Sirona's rhythmic breathing grew slow and faint, and she feared for her godmother, for there was always the risk that the Goddess might choose to keep the dreamer. Aldyth fought to stay awake, but, weighed down by exhaustion, she fell into a honey-induced slumber.

Sirona's voice penetrated the depths of her dreamless sleep: 'Wake up, child.'

Consciousness returned with the suddenness of a window opening. With a cry of relief, Aldyth sat up and threw her arms about her godmother. 'Sirona, you came back!'

'Yes, child.' The wisewoman, already dressed, returned her goddaughter's embrace. 'I'm off to fetch the nuns. You've walked enough for one day and will be walking more soon. I just needed to tell you to wait at Sula's Stump until I arrive with our guests.'

Aldyth knew that Sirona wanted to spare her the most dangerous task before them, breaching the city walls and carrying off the fugitive nuns. Choking down the lump of fear in her throat, she asked hesitantly, 'Last night, Godmother, did She come to you?'

In Sirona's obsidian eyes was an exalted distance that Aldyth recognized but could never share, and Aldyth knew that the Goddess had come. 'Later,' said Sirona.

But before Sirona had even reached the door, it banged open with a force that sent the mud daubing of the house walls flying. Breathless and flushed, Aelfric burst in. 'They took Bedwyn!' he cried. 'Now they're on their way here to arrest Sirona.'

'Well, maybe I won't get the nuns just yet,' said Sirona dryly. Noting Aldyth's blanched cheeks, she said, 'Doubtless they are rounding up the usual suspects, and I'm always the first to be questioned. But Aelfric,' she warned, trying to shoo him out the door, 'you should not be seen here. Get you gone, lad, and hurry.'

''Tis too late,' he whispered. 'They're at the toft gate.'

Without conscious thought, Aldyth pushed the boy against the wall and forced him down onto all fours. Then, spreading out her skirts, she sat upon him as upon a stool or a bale of wool. There came a pounding on the door, and a contingent of men-at-arms stormed in, Hugo in the lead. Enlisting the aid of Lord Ralf in the name of the king, he had impressed into his service a dozen of the warlord's foot soldiers.

Sirona met them with a crooked smile. Taking note of the ugly bruises on their hands, she quipped, 'Have you been feeding the geese, lads?'

'No, they've been feeding on us,' countered Gilbert. 'But we bite back.' Sirona and Lord Ralf's men were old adversaries. Over time the Normans had come to respect her and, however grudgingly, to enjoy her wit. 'We're hauling you in again, old woman.'

'This is no invitation; this is an arrest,' spat Hugo to the soldiers. 'Do your job.'

Sirona shrugged and said, 'Let's get this over with, lads.'

'This one too,' growled Hugo with a quick nod at Aldyth.

'Aldyth, stay,' ordered Sirona, adding, 'Her ankle is twisted, and she mustn't walk on it.'

'Then carry her up or drag her by the hair if you have to,' insisted Hugo.

'She's the midwife hereabouts,' said Gilbert uneasily.

'And she's my goddaughter,' said Sirona with the hint of a threat in her voice.

The Normans all shifted nervously. There was not a man in Dorset, Norman or Saxon, who had not heard of Sirona's power. Hugo too had heard the tales but had given them little credit. Yet it was unnerving to see soldiers who knew the crone firsthand squirming like guilty schoolboys at the least sign of her displeasure. He was almost relieved when Gilbert said, 'Leave her be, man. We can always come back for her.'

Hugo gave a curt nod, then stamped off without waiting to see his orders carried out.

'If the ankle needs tending before I return, Aldyth,' said Sirona, 'borrow Father Edmund's donkey to carry you up to the abbey infirmary and see the nuns about it.'

As soon as the soldiers had led off their prisoner, Aldyth sprang up from her squirming footstool. Aelfric collapsed and moaned, 'Christ's blood, Aldyth, another minute and I'd have been squashed as flat as a cow pie in the marketplace.'

'What of Brother Ansgar?' she demanded. 'Have they got him, too?'

'No word of him, so they can't have found him yet,' he replied, picking himself up.

'He can't have gone far. I must find him, Aelfric, before they do.'

'I'm going too,' said the boy.

'No, elfling, you heard Sirona. You must go tell Father Edmund to deliver a message to the abbey. Have him tell Sister Edith that I am still coming, but not until tonight. They must not attend the evening service but instead must wait by the garden gate. Then, as soon as you speak to Father Edmund, make yourself scarce until Sirona returns.'

Aldyth picked up the pitcher and went to the door.

'Where are you going without your basket?' asked the boy uneasily.

'To fetch some springwater for Brother Ansgar.'

Aelfric snatched away the pitcher and ran off to the spring. Aldyth decided that it would not hurt to let him be a hero in this small way, and she used the time he had saved her to collect fresh bandages, salves, and herbs. But when she finished, and the lad still had not returned, she began to fret. She was about to go after him when he slipped into the hut with an empty pitcher.

'There was a guard posted at the spring,' he explained. 'Lord Ralf knows his men; he sent that tight-assed Robert. I figured he was there to keep an eye out for the fugitive, but to be sure, I waited and watched. When Mildburh came for water, he told her he was posted there to prevent all Saxons from drawing water from the Crystal Spring.'

'But what of those who cannot carry water all the way from Alcester?'

'That's what Mildburh said. He told her 'twas no business of his; his only business was to keep the Saxons from drawing water until someone turns in the fugitive.'

'Thank you, Aelfric,' said Aldyth grimly. 'As soon as I've gone, you must find Father Edmund and tell him.'

Aldyth could only trust that Aelfric was slippery enough to stay out of trouble. Carrying her basket, she stepped outside and was startled to see a Norman on the toft path, shrouded by the dawn mist. She froze, and he seized her roughly by the arm. She gasped as the basket tumbled from her hands, spilling its incriminating contents at her feet. She looked up fearfully at her captor and started. She would never have known him at a distance, for he wore the shabby hooded cloak of a stable groom. 'Gandulf, you shouldn't be here!'

'I made certain that I was not seen,' he said simply. They both knelt to gather up the scattered contents of her basket. 'Where are you off to in such a hurry, Aldyth?'

'Picking berries,' she said.

'You're a poor liar.' He picked several blades of grass from the poultice, then looked up and said skeptically, 'I suppose this is for a wounded blackberry bush. Aldyth, the woods are crawling with fitzGrip's men. They took your friend Bedwyn last night, and my father is so outraged by the murder of a Norman on his holdings that he has told his men that they may do whatever they must to catch the killer. 'Tis an ugly situation, and you shouldn't be about.'

Gandulf had just confirmed what Aelfric had only guessed at, that they did *not* have Harold. But they were stepping up the search. She would have to find him before the Normans did. They would return to the hermit's cottage – if they had not already left a sentry there.

'I've got to go. If you'll excuse me—' Aldyth ducked to one side and tried to slip past Gandulf, but he seized her by the wrist.

'Let me go!'

He tightened his grip. 'They brought Osgot's body back this morning. He led them to Bedwyn, and I don't know what else he might have told them. I can't let you go, Aldyth.'

Panic rising, she tried to break free. To complicate matters, the door of Aldyth's hut flew open and a sandy-haired urchin bolted out and launched himself onto Gandulf's back. Aelfric's thin arms tightened around the lordling's neck, and he threatened, 'I don't want to hurt you, Gandulf, but I will if you don't take your hands off her!'

Failing to shrug his puny assailant off his shoulders, Gandulf growled, 'Aelfric, leave it alone.' Then he continued, 'Aldyth, you've got to tell me what's going on here.'

Aelfric began to pound his bony fists against the Norman's head and shoulders.

'Aelfric, no!' cried Aldyth frantically. She had to put a stop to the scene her two defenders were causing before they inadvertently betrayed her. 'He's trying to help. Go, elfling, and take care of your errand.'

'Are you sure, Aldyth?' asked the boy.

She nodded, and Aelfric slid down, shooting Gandulf a look that would curdle milk.

'Thank you, Aelfric,' said Aldyth soothingly, nodding and waving him on his way.

'Aldyth,' Gandulf urged, more gently now, 'how deeply mired are you in this mess?'

Aldyth stifled a sob. Gandulf pulled her into a hug. The wild pounding of her heart against his chest made him think of the falcon-stunned pheasant he'd held long ago.

'Gandulf,' she confided tearfully, 'I'm in over my head. But if it's dangerous for me, 'tis the more so for you. Please stay clear of it. 'Tis none of your affair.'

'I mean to make it so.'

They stared grimly at each, neither one saying a word, neither one yielding.

'Humor me,' Gandulf said at last.

Aldyth conceded defeat and nodded her consent. Visibly relieved, Gandulf lifted her hood to conceal her honey-colored hair and led her down back lanes to the hedgerow where Cathedra was waiting. They mounted, and Gandulf held the little mare to a trot until they were safely away. Then he urged her into a gallop.

CHAPTER THIRTY

An ominous silence greeted Aldyth and Gandulf as they approached Bedwyn's clearing. A scattering of broken geese lay dead on the grass, but their attention was riveted on the ruins of the hut. Charred timbers and a tangle of scorched wattle rose from a heap of smoking ashes, and the acrid stink of damp, charred wood drifted across the clearing.

'No!' whispered Aldyth, sliding off the horse to gaze into the ruins.

'There's no smell of burnt flesh, and there's no sign of a body,' Gandulf assured her. 'He can't have been in the hut when it burned, and we would surely have heard if the soldiers had cut him down when they took Bedwyn.'

Aldyth nodded, a tiny flicker of hope rising. 'He can't have gone far, Gandulf.'

'All the easier to find him, then. Let's fan out in widening circles around the hut.'

'We'll cover more ground if we split up. I'll stay within call,' she promised.

Parting and peering through bush after dew-dampened bush, Gandulf doubted they would find the old monk, but at least he could keep an eye on Aldyth and intervene on her behalf, should they be set upon by a Norman patrol. He was poking at a hawthorn thicket that he considered too thick to give shelter when he saw a foot protruding. It stirred memories of mangled bodies on bloody battlefields, and he recoiled. Drawing up sharply, he signaled Aldyth with a low whistle and began disentangling the injured man's clothing from the thorns. 'While I pull him out,' he told Aldyth, 'you fend off the branches.'

The move roused the injured man, and he began to mumble incoherently. Aldyth felt his forehead. 'He's burning up with fever. Let's get him out of these wet things.'

Aldyth stripped off the old man's borrowed shirt and trousers, while Gandulf removed his own overtunic, then helped her ease it over the fugitive's head. Pulling the corners of his cloak snugly about the injured man, Gandulf fastened it with his own cloak pin, not daring to think of the consequences should the fugitive be found in his cloak.

The bandage on Harold's forearm was stained a noxious yellow-green from the weeping of the infection, while streaks of red shot up the flesh of his arm. Aldyth removed the old dressing to cleanse the wound. She had strong wine to bathe it in but said to Gandulf, 'I would gladly trade this for a flask of the Goddess's springwater.' Then softly, as she worked, she added, 'No wonder Bedwyn gave himself up so readily. He was leading them away from here like a mother bird protecting her chicks.'

Harold's eyes flickered open. 'Aldyth Lightfoot,' he murmured.

'Yes, Brother, you are among friends.'

While she worked, Gandulf washed soot from the old man's face with water from the skin he had fetched from his saddle bag. Harold, dimly aware of their presence, rambled on in his delirium, not realizing that he was speaking aloud. 'Edith . . . I've let you down again . . .'

'Never worry,' said Aldyth tenderly, 'for soon you will be together again.'

Harold's eyes glazed over, and tears of remorse spilled onto his flushed cheeks. Moved by his suffering, Gandulf wiped them away with a cool cloth. The old man turned his eyes to the younger man. There was a spark of recognition; then his eyes glazed over once again. To Aldyth, he said, 'Have you brought me my son?'

'Hush, now,' said Aldyth gently, tying off the last strip of ragged linen. To Gandulf: 'We've got to move him. They could be back at any time.'

But Gandulf did not hear her; he was staring at this stranger, who was obviously hallucinating. Harold rambled on, 'He has his mother's eyes.'

That was true, thought Gandulf, but how would a stranger know that? He recalled his mother's near confession about having had a lover. 'Who are you?' whispered Gandulf.

'We've no time for talk,' said Aldyth quickly, 'and you can see he's not in his right mind. Gandulf, we'll wait for word of Sirona at the lambing pen, one step farther from Bedwyn's trail. But how will we get him into the saddle?' she asked in dismay.

Gandulf's eye fell upon a big rock at the edge of the woods. 'That rock could serve as a mounting block. Do you suppose he could walk – with help, I mean?'

Aldyth followed Gandulf's gaze across the clearing to Bedwyn's pissing stone. It was hardly a fit mounting block for a king, but she nodded. 'We'll have to try.'

'No,' mumbled Harold. 'Leave me.' But they refused, and he was too weak to resist.

Gandulf fetched Cathedra; then they half led, half carried Harold to the rock. With Gandulf supporting him from behind, Aldyth helped Harold swing a leg over the saddle.

'Sit behind him, Aldyth,' said Gandulf. 'I'll tie him in place with strips of my cloak.'

'There goes another cloak,' remarked Aldyth.

Harold drifted into and out of consciousness, and Aldyth's muscles ached from keeping the big Saxon astride. When at last they arrived at the lambing pen, Gandulf unfastened Harold's bingings and caught him as he slid out of the saddle.

'Inside?' asked Gandulf with a nod toward the crude little hut.

'No,' said Aldyth. 'He will need the sun to warm him.'

Gandulf's ragged cloak over a mattress of fresh grass made a fair pallet, while Aldyth's served as a blanket. Gandulf raised Harold up while Aldyth held a wooden cup to his lips. 'This will help him sleep,' said Aldyth. When they had given Harold all he could swallow, Aldyth wiped his chin and Gandulf laid him back down. She felt the injured man's skin; it was cold and clammy. 'Gandulf, lie down beside him,' she said urgently.

After a startled instant, Gandulf obeyed, and Aldyth lay down on Harold's other side, careful not to jar his injured arm. 'We'll share our warmth with him,' she explained.

Each instinctively placed a protective arm over the unconscious man. Aldyth gave Gandulf's hand a squeeze, then released it to stroke Harold's hair back from his brow. 'Sleep, my dear,' she crooned, 'sleep and rest,' until he lapsed into drugged slumber.

'Aldyth,' said Gandulf quietly, 'you always surprise me.'

She looked up at him inquiringly.

'You're so competent, so practical, so deft. You must do this all the time.'

'Not exactly.' As an afterthought she added, 'But more often than I'd choose,'

Gandulf frowned, studying the old man's face. 'Who is he? Why won't you tell me?'

'I have no right to tell you,' she replied, 'although you've every right to know.'

Gandulf looked at her pleadingly. Aldyth hesitated, then blurted, 'This is Harold Godwinson, the rightful king of England, and you are his only living son.'

Gandulf had been ready for a surprise, but nothing could have prepared him for the shock of her announcement. He caught his breath, then felt himself retreating into his old shell, distancing himself from his emotions. 'Harold's dead,' he said flatly.

''Twas his brother Leofwine who died in his place.'

'Then where has he been all these years? Why did my mother never tell me?' Gandulf shot back, trying to build a wall of reason and rhetoric against tidings that threatened the order of his universe. Yet even as Gandulf shook his head in stubborn denial, he saw his own face reflected in the features of the sleeping man.

'Gandulf, you were a helpless baby at Lord Ralf's mercy. One misspoken word would have been fatal. And your father was a prisoner, wounded in spirit as well as in body.'

Gandulf felt the foundations beneath his citadel of reason crumbling, and he lashed out, 'If he has denied me all these years, why should I care for him now?'

'He just learned of your existence and came back for you, in spite of the danger.'

Demons that Gandulf thought had been exorcised circled like vultures, and he tried to beat them off with indignation. Was there not enough anguish in his life already? What had loving Aldyth gained for him but misery? Once he opened his heart, was there never to be an end to it? The air in his lungs thinned, and he struggled for breath. Demons fluttered about his face like bats, and his eyes dimmed like a dying torch. His head went spinning, and ghouls howled savagely in his ears. In a sudden flash of insight he understood that all he had to do to satisfy the goblins was to snatch back his heart and lock it away forever, to give them the key and cease the struggle. It would be so easy. But from a distance, he heard someone calling his name.

'Gandulf . . . Gandulf, are you ill?'

Gandulf gradually became aware of Aldyth's touch as she brushed the damp hair from his forehead. He was drenched with sweat, and, as his eyes regained their focus, he found her peering into them. To his amazement, he realized that throughout the brutal internal battle that had just been waged, he had not changed position, had not even closed his eyes – and that it was Aldyth's loving voice that had exorcised the monsters as the sun dispatches darkness.

By the returning intelligence in his eyes, Aldyth knew he had come to himself, though she could feel him trembling even yet. 'Gandulf,' she whispered, 'please speak to me.' Her eyes searched his face for some clue as to where he had just been.

Aldyth, realized Gandulf, had just pulled him away from the edge of an abyss that he dared not look back at, but one that he somehow knew he would never return to. He reached for her hand and, fervently kissing her palm, held it to his flushed cheek.

'I'm sorry, Gandulf. I shouldn't have told you.'

He shook his head and smiled thinly. She returned the smile, obviously relieved, and Gandulf felt his heart swell with love for her. He wondered if he would ever have the words to tell her how he felt, but for now it was enough just to let it be so. He took a deep breath, and when he looked down at his father, it was with an open heart.

'No wonder I was such a cuckoo's child,' he whispered, 'born of a Saxon swan and a Norman goose.' His mind boggled at the implications. He could imagine Lord Ralf's fury when he found out, yet his overwhelming reaction was relief at not being fitzGerald's son. He marveled at his mother's audacity and could not wait to discuss with her all that had happened, all that it meant. And he determined, above all, to ensure Harold's escape.

'He is so good, Gandulf. I could never understand how you had sprung from the loins of Lord Ralf, but now it all fits: you are a Godwinson.'

'A bastard,' he observed.

'The son of a king,' she countered.

'Are you properly impressed? Now will you run away with me?'

'You dare bring that up again after the way you treated me on Midsummer Eve?'

'For obvious reasons I haven't come calling, and you did refuse to see me. After the way you glowered at me the morning after—'

'I'm not really angry, Gandulf. You're only human, and I did throw myself at you like some wanton. So much has happened since then; I can't begin to tell you . . .'

'Try,' he urged.

'It was a miracle,' she stammered. 'Gandulf,' she added, 'Sirona gave me back my maidenhead, and the Goddess has given me another chance to serve.'

Gandulf's expression changed from intense puzzlement to total confusion. 'What? Sirona restored your maidenhead? Who took it?' Scowling fiercely, he demanded, 'Was it Bedwyn? Did he come back that night, or was it later? I've seen you with him in the fields.'

'Of course not! Don't you remember? You must have been drunker than you realized.' Aldyth blushed furiously and looked away.

He started in sudden comprehension. 'You think I—'

'Well, who else?' she cried.

A look of enlightenment came over Gandulf's face. 'You must have been drunker than you thought, Aldyth! Do you think I would ravage you in your sleep?'

'My Lady!' exclaimed Aldyth. Forgetting herself, she leaned across her unconscious charge and, cheeks painted scarlet by embarrassment, whispered awkwardly, 'But Gandulf, the fire of life coursed through my veins. I thought 'twas the ecstasy of love.'

'My dear Aldyth, it was; I felt it too. But—' It was his turn to blush. Averting his eyes, he confessed, 'I launched my arrow while it was yet in the quiver.'

Aldyth's eyes widened as his meaning registered. Hardly knowing whether to laugh or cry, she pondered aloud, 'Which is worse? That you went as far as you did or that you had a chance to have me willing and eager and refused to take it? Didn't you want me?'

'Not that way. I knew you'd never forgive me or yourself.'

She shook her head in wonder. 'You're always a better man than I give you credit for.'

'You always give me credit for being a better man than I am.'

As Gandulf leaned over his father and kissed her, a shadow fell over them. Aldyth and Gandulf stared up in shocked silence to see Lufe eyeing them warily, his dog, Aethling, at his heels. Aethling growled and bared his teeth.

'There's a b-b-big reward offered for him, N-Norman,' Lufe stated baldly with a nod toward the unconscious man.

Gandulf's guts tightened. He knew the shepherd hated him as he hated all Normans. If Gandulf were caught aiding the fugitive, he would be punished as a traitor and his father – or rather, Lord Ralf – would be there to tighten the thumbscrews. Lufe must know that the fugitive was Saxon, but that had not stopped Osgot; a reward compounded with revenge upon a hated enemy might be too great a temptation.

The tense silence drew out until at last Lufe spoke again. 'The N-Normans are everywhere. 'Tisn't s-s-safe around here. We'll have to g-g-get him into b-b-better c-c-cover,' he said, nodding again toward Harold.

Gandulf hoped that his relief was not too apparent. 'Where would you suggest, Lufe? If we must move him, could you get word to Sirona when she's freed?'

'Christine s-s-says she's already b-b-been released.' Turning to Aldyth in preference to the Norman, Lufe said, 'Aldyth, shall I f-f-fetch her?'

'That would be a great help, Lufe,' she answered.

Lufe turned and strode off, his dog following on his heels.

The sun was at its zenith when Harold finally stirred. Aldyth, who had dozed off, immediately sat up to attend him. Harold's eyes flickered open. Aldyth placed a hand gently upon his brow and said, 'You're safe, my Lord. How are you feeling?'

Gandulf too had dozed but awakened at the sound of her voice. Immediately alert, he scanned the horizon for intruders. Once satisfied that they were alone, Gandulf turned to watch Aldyth and the stranger, his father. He felt suddenly shy: it was one thing to drive off the demons who meant to lock up his heart, quite another to open it himself and invite someone in. Harold looked from Aldyth to Gandulf and smiled weakly.

'Are you thirsty, my Lord?' Gandulf asked stiffly.

'No one's lord and no one's man. Do you know who I am, lad?'

'I know what Aldyth tells me . . .' replied Gandulf, his voice trailing off.

'Do you believe it?'

'I don't know what to believe.'

'If only you could have seen my boy Godwin – your brother – you could have been his dark-haired twin.' Harold held his hand out to Gandulf, who hesitated only an instant before taking it. 'Your mother tells me you have grown into a man I can be proud of. No son of hers could have done otherwise.' Noting Gandulf's look of perplexity, Harold said, 'I know this comes as a shock. You must understand that what happened between your mother and me was an accident, though neither one of us has any regrets. Whatever you think of me, you must not think ill of your mother.'

'Why did you come?' asked Gandulf. 'What did you want from me?'

'I hardly knew that myself. As for what I sought, you have already given it. My son, I sense in you a goodness that goes against every example set for you in fitzGerald's court; harsh words and beatings rarely foster a gentle heart.' Harold's words touched the quick of Gandulf's soul, and he opened his mouth to brush them off to a safer distance.

'No,' said Harold firmly, 'I will have my say, lad. God help me, boy, if only I could take back those years. Yet if I could there would be no Gandulf, for any known son of mine would be dead or rotting in a Norman prison, as my brother Wulfnoth is to this day. For that reason alone, I rejoice that I knew not of your existence.

'You'd no hint of your Saxon blood, yet you risked your life to spirit away an old Saxon lay brother; Emma has told me how you champion the people in their oppression. Dear boy, you are a sign from God that I am not forsaken.'

Gandulf felt dizzy. Could it be true? God's love, he wanted it to be so. In the space of a conversation, Gandulf felt himself washed as clean as a slate; not only had he been absolved, but his sins had been transformed into virtue. Yet his proud and loving father, who had delivered him from a lifetime of deprivation, would likely die of his wounds, if not at the hands of the Normans. Gandulf shuddered to think that Harold might go to his grave never knowing he had held Gandulf's heart in his hands like a captive wren and tossed it up to fly free. Gandulf's tears spilled over, and his father brushed them aside.

Gandulf's voice nearly failed him as he stammered, 'There can be no greater honor . . . nor greater joy . . . I will try to make you proud . . .' Harold need not have been a king, nor worshiped by throngs of devoted subjects. Gandulf would have been satisfied had the old man been a lay brother or even a beggar, for Harold was a father who loved his son and, for the first time in his life, Gandulf had a father he would be able to make proud of him.

Harold opened his mouth to speak, but no words came. Gandulf leaned forward, the better to hear, but his father's eyes grew dull and flickered shut, and his breath grew suddenly shallow. Gandulf gasped and looked up at Aldyth in a panic.

'He's exhausted, Gandulf,' she said. 'Sleep is the medicine he needs now. Could you fetch some fresh bracken for him to lie on?'

Gandulf gazed upon his newfound father, none of the love, the longing, the fear he felt showing upon his face, then solemnly walked off. Aldyth had given him make-work, but he was grateful, for he too was exhausted by the force of emotions ravaging his heart.

Gandulf stumbled down the hillside, not so far that he could not keep a watchful eye on the others but far enough to be alone with his thoughts. Once he had believed that no pain could match that of unrequited love, but now he was nearly crazed with fear – not for himself but for Harold and Aldyth. If Aldyth were implicated, if Brother Ansgar's true identity were even suspected . . . the thought made him nauseous, and his eyes stung with helpless tears.

'Gandulf?'

He whirled to face Aldyth, blushing to be caught once gain with wet lashes.

'He's asleep now.' Taking his hands, she said, 'This must be difficult for you.'

Gandulf shook his head. 'Not in the way it might seem, and yet a total stranger has walked into my life – and has made me a stranger to myself.' He gazed out at the sage-green downs melting into the dark hills of Cranborne Chase. 'They would have us believe that Harold Godwinson was the Devil incarnate, a liar, a blasphemer, forsworn to God.'

'To justify the theft of his throne!' replied Aldyth hotly.

'The Normans say he swore on holy relics that he would put Duke William on the throne after King Edward's death. Is that not true?'

''Tis absurd!' seethed Aldyth. 'He swore only to present Duke William's claim to the Great Council and, should the council choose to crown him, to support him as long as he worked for the good of England. Even so, the pope has ruled that a forced vow is not binding.'

'Yet the pope made Duke William's invasion a holy war,'

observed Gandulf, 'based on Harold's forswearing of that forced vow.' A look of disgust came over his face. 'I'd wager it had more to do with the gold Duke William sent the pope than with the judgement of God.'

'Sirona says the pope has always been willing to sell his banner to the highest bidder,' said Aldyth, 'but there is more to it than that. She says they do things differently in Normandy. King Edward was raised in Normandy and did not understand that England was a nation and not a property. To be lawful king of Saxon England, a man would have to be chosen by the Council and accepted by the people. It was only after King Edward had promised England to Duke William, as if it were a country manor to be bestowed at his pleasure, that he came to understand this. Realizing that England would never accept Duke William, on his deathbed, King Edward appointed Harold his successor.'

'Why would Harold have made such a vow, Aldyth, that could so easily be used against him by the Normans and by the Church?'

'You heard him speak of his brother Wulfnoth, even now a prisoner in King William's dungeons. Earl Harold was away from court when King Edward's distant cousin William, duke of Normandy, visited him in England and extracted the promise of the throne. King Edward gave Harold's younger brother to Duke William as a pledge. When Harold went to Normandy to gain Wulfnoth's freedom, he too was held against his will as a "guest" of Duke William. Months went by, and England was falling to ruin in the hands of King Edward; Harold was desperate to return to put things to rights. So he made the vow and kept it as he had sworn it. Sirona says he took Duke William's claim to the Council, but they would not hear of a Norman king on the English throne. Duke William had bragged to all of Christendom that he would be king of England, so when King Edward died and Harold was crowned, Duke William crossed the channel to save face as much as to fight for what he thought was his own.'

'So it was all a gross miscarriage of justice, a tragic misunderstanding between two peoples who think so differently that they couldn't even comprehend the gulf that separated them. 'Tis no small wonder we Normans can make neither head nor tail of you Saxons.' Shaking his head, he added quietly, 'And no wonder you hate us so fiercely.' Half in jest he added, 'And I am caught in the middle. How do I tell Lord Ralf that I am no heir of his?'

Aldyth gasped. 'Don't be a fool, Gandulf! He would kill you, not even knowing who your father is, and revenge himself upon your mother.'

'My God! Of course you're right. What am I to do?'

'Oh, Gandulf, I don't know. If King William were to have the slightest suspicion that you are Harold's son, he would surely have your head! He has suffered none of Harold's other sons to live, and no one knows better than he that bastardy is no bar to a throne.'

'I care nothing for the throne.'

'I know, but a grasping man like King William could never understand or believe it.'

Gandulf put his arms around her waist and pulled her close. Pressing his cheek against hers, he sighed, 'Aldyth, whatever will become of us?'

'It gets more complicated all the time. Sirona might advise you to marry Catherine, for until Lord Ralf dies, your life is not secure, and I suspect she will want you to inherit.'

Did Aldyth think Gandulf was going to let an ancient midwife dictate the course of his life? Shrugging, he conceded, 'It can't hurt to hear what she has to say.' He looked down at Aldyth fondly. 'And to think you loved me even as the despised brat of Lord Ralf!' Before he knew what he intended, he had covered her lips with his. Like a candle melting in the blaze of passion, she leaned into his embrace. Drawing back, she looked breathlessly up into his flushed face and saw his eyes glittering with a feverish love. She closed her eyes to keep from being overcome, and he covered her eyelids with tender kisses.

'Leave a wolf to guard the sheep!' came Sirona's stern voice.

Aldyth and Gandulf sprang apart like cat-startled mice.

Lufe Piper, at the old woman's heels, wore a smirk that nettled Gandulf every bit as much as it was meant to. Disregarding the deflating effect she had had upon them,

Sirona walked past the blushing couple to where Harold lay sleeping fitfully. The crone set down her basket and her bundle, then knelt to examine the wound.

'I've bathed it in wine and given him sage and Saint-John's-wort for fever and a compress of marjoram, Madonna lily, and feverfew,' said Aldyth. ''Tis still putrid, but at least he's been sleeping more soundly since taking a draft of poppied wine.'

Harold stirred at the sound of their voices. 'Sirona,' he mumbled, 'good to see you.' Then he drifted back into his drugged and fevered oblivion.

Sirona looked up and said, 'He's doing well enough, considering.' With deft fingers she applied a poultice to the wound and re-dressed it. Tucking Aldyth's cloak up under his chin, she chanted a blessing over him, then ushered the three onlookers out of earshot.

'They're searching every hut and outhouse for the Saxon fugitive, who will be hanged for murder, but not before he's questioned thoroughly. Thank the Lady it was Rollo who died; he was the brains of the operation, but what Hugo lacks in brains he makes up for in tenacity. The Blackmore Vale is crawling with soldiers – Lord Ralf's, fitzHugh's – and Hugo is threatening to send for reinforcements if the murderer isn't apprehended soon.' To Aldyth, Sirona said, 'You've done well, but we need springwater, and we must move him to a safer place. 'Twill be dangerous not only for his health but for ours.'

'A guard has been posted at the spring,' Aldyth told her. 'We have only the runoff.'

'Not good enough,' said Sirona brusquely. 'The spring runs purest at its source.'

'I can fetch some for you and be back by vespers,' offered Gandulf. Then he recalled a complication. 'You know that Lord Ralf has threatened to raze the village if I'm seen there?'

'What if I told you he has no chance at all without it?' Sirona countered.

He nodded. 'Somehow I'll get it for you.'

Lufe startled them all by saying sharply, 'W-w-wait!'

'Yes, Lufe?'

'W-w-we need your horse.'

Gandulf glanced at Sirona, who raised her eyebrows in question at Lufe.

'S-s-search parties here any t-t-time.'

'Is it more urgent than getting springwater, Lufe?' Sirona asked the lad.

'W-w-won't do him any g-g-good if they c-c-catch him first.'

'True enough.' the old woman conceded, 'but let us be quick about it.'

Using two poles tied to one of the hurdles from the sheepfold fence, Gandulf and Lufe constructed a litter and lifted Harold onto it. They secured the front ends of the poles to Cathedra's saddle, then each man shouldered the other ends. Sirona led Cathedra while Aldyth walked alongside. They stayed low on the hillsides and in the ravines, keeping careful watch for horsemen. As they descended to lower elevations, the woods closed in. Aldyth fended off low-hanging branches and they followed narrow game paths. At last they came to a beech forest with more clearings and less brush. They could smell wood smoke before they saw the camp, and soon they came upon a series of black mounds. Among them was a small conical tent made of grimy hides.

'At last,' said Sirona with relief.

The camp appeared to be deserted, but its paths were well trodden. A woman stepped from behind a tree to greet them. Gandulf recognized her from the Christmas gathering as Rhiannon CharcoalBurner. Her skin was pale, her eyes clear blue, and long ginger hair tumbled down her back. Aldyth had explained that Rhiannon was one of Sirona's people. Especially outside the villages, there were still families of pure-blooded Welsh who had resisted the pounding waves of invaders. Five hundred years before, this had been their land. With unwitting irony, the Saxons had called them 'Welsh,' meaning 'foreigners,' even though it was the Saxons themselves who had come from foreign shores. The lonely life of charcoal burners isolated them, as did their habit of marrying among themselves. The charcoal burners lived deep with the chase, where fuel was at hand. Their work required close supervision of the kilns for days at a time, and they came into town only to sell their wares, to celebrate the high holidays, or to purchase salt and iron.

'This man needs a secure place to bide, daughter,' said Sirona without preamble.

Rhiannon nodded. 'Have you eaten?'

Neither Aldyth nor Gandulf had eaten since dawn, and already the shadows were growing long. 'A bite of bread would sit well,' Aldyth replied gratefully.

Rhiannon called out orders in a language that Gandulf assumed was Welsh, and a mob of children swarmed from hiding among the trees, like soot-smudged wood elves. A scrawny, ginger-haired girl ran into the tent and returned with a pitcher of buttermilk and bread. Another child followed, festooned in blankets. At a nod from his mother, an older boy walked with Lufe to one of the black mounds. Lufe and the charcoal burner's boy pulled back the wet hides that covered it, revealing a carefully stacked circle of logs.

Charcoal was wood-heated to drive out the smoky gases, and it burned hotter and cleaner than even seasoned wood. Wet hides covering the stacks of carefully monitored burning wood kept the air supply low to prevent the wood from bursting into flame. After days of smoldering, the wood was reduced to small black chunks that were carted off to the towns to be sold to smiths who needed the intense heat of a charcoal fire and wealthy lords who could afford the luxury of hot, smokeless fires.

The kiln looked like all the others, until they pulled off the first layer of logs in one place to reveal a cavelike hollow in the center; the kiln was only a shell. 'Ingenious!' thought Gandulf. 'So this is how so many poachers vanish into the chase without a trace.' Lufe, who was obviously familiar with the arrangement, directed Gandulf as they slid Harold's litter inside. A small fire had been laid directly under the smoke hole. Little light filtered through the opening. For added light and warmth, and to give the appearance of an actively burning kiln, Lufe touched an ember to the unlit fire and fanned it up to a smoky flame.

The healers crawled inside and settled down beside Harold.

411

Rhiannon handed in bread, cheese, a jug of ale, and a small chamber pot. Gandulf knelt at the opening; he felt uneasy and was made even more so by Lufe and the Welsh boy, who hovered, impatiently waiting to close Aldyth into the dark, close chamber.

'I'll be off now,' he said stiffly. Such a cold leave-taking, he thought ruefully, constrained by the dampening presence of Lufe, Sirona, and the host of wood elves.

'Make it fast,' said Sirona to Gandulf. 'We must leave immediately after dark.'

'Where to?' asked Aldyth.

'To the only place where they will never find him,' stated the wisewoman.

Gandulf was too flustered to question her. 'I don't like leaving you this way . . .' This place was vaguely ominous and familiar to him. 'Aldyth, will you be all right in there?'

'Of course, Gandulf. You just worry about yourself.'

'We're in good hands,' Sirona assured him. 'May the Goddess go with you, lad.'

He looked longingly at Aldyth, wishing he dared kiss her, but his nerve failed him. He ducked out, not daring to look back as they were closed into the tiny log prison.

Margaret had just stepped into the pantry when she heard a whisper in her ear.

'Shhh. Not a word.' Gandulf, dressed in his undertunic and covered with soot, herded her to the darkest corner of the pantry, which could not be seen from the door. In hushed tones, he said, 'Margaret, I need fresh springwater. Can you get it for me?'

'When do you need it, lad?'

'As soon as may be.'

They heard footsteps in the hall. Margaret pressed her fingers to her lips, went to the pantry door, and looked to see who it was. 'Gilbert,' she called.

'Aye, Margaret.'

'My bad tooth is acting up. Can you fetch me some springwater to ease the pain?'

'Not now,' he said gruffly. 'I just got off my watch, and I need to put my feet up.'

Margaret had never been a beauty, and she had lost the last bloom of youth many years before, but she knew each soldier's weakness. 'Would you like to be helping yourself to hot apple tarts while putting your feet up?'

'Well, that paints a prettier picture,' said Gilbert, brightening.

'Off with you, then, and be quick, for I'm beside myself!' she said. 'You'll not be sorry for your trouble when you find what's awaiting you upon your return!'

Back in the pantry, Gandulf said, 'Margaret, you're a wonder!' and kissed her plump, rosy cheek. 'Now tell me quickly, what have they said about my absence?'

'As far as I can tell, you've not been missed, lad. They've spent the whole morning going over the books, counting up the number of eggs you'll be worth at Easter. When they summoned me to fetch hazelnuts and wine, I heard them planning to tour the manor farm and take supper there tonight. I could tell them you've been called to the abbey.'

'That should do it. They'll be glad not to have me underfoot. But while we wait for the springwater, can you find me something decent to wear?'

'I might have expected you to lose another cloak, lad, but an overtunic!'

''Tis a long story . . .'

'Aren't they all?' said Margaret, chuckling.

'I'll need you to pack some provisions for a journey.'

'How long a journey? How many people?'

'I don't know.'

Aldyth heard the approach of horses and drew her dagger. The two healers listened apprehensively but relaxed at the sound of friendly voices outside their refuge. It seemed an eternity before Aldyth heard the scraping of heavy hides being lifted, the thudding of the outmost layer of logs being removed. Then a dark, crouching figure, silhouetted in the doorway, moved into the tiny circle of dim firelight.

413

'Gandulf!' said Aldyth, her heart leaping into her throat. She crept on hands and knees to throw her arms around him. Gandulf closed his eyes for a moment, shutting out everything else. 'How is he?' he said at last.

'Much the same. He asked for you.'

Gandulf nodded. 'May we step outside?'

Sirona waved them off. Outside, Aldyth shook the kinks out of her cramped muscles and breathed deeply of the fresh air. Gandulf led her to where Cathedra and an old nag on a lead rope waited. Both were laden with sacks of provisions, a skin of springwater, and several skins of wine. Gandulf shook out a warm cloak, which he wrapped about Aldyth's shoulders, adjusting the clasp and pinning it in place. 'The night is chill,' he explained.

'Aldyth,' he said, 'they made a wreck of Alcester and Long Cross, even got as far as Motcombe, but the search parties are drifting back up the hill; you should be safe tonight.'

'What news of Bedwyn? What have they done to him, Gandulf?'

'Nothing yet,' he replied. 'But after the excitement of the manhunt dies down, they'll turn their attention back to him. If they haven't turned up the fugitive, they'll try to get leads out of Bedwyn before he's executed for Osgot's murder. Aldyth,' he asked, 'could he get you into trouble . . . with what he knows about whatever it is you two do out here?'

'He knows enough to see me hanged for treason, but he would never betray me.'

'Even after you've rejected his suit?'

'He would rather die than betray a Saxon hen to a Norman pig.'

Gandulf nodded, keeping his doubts to himself. When Sirona emerged from the false kiln, Gandulf discreetly stepped away from the wisewoman's goddaughter, but not before catching the raised eyebrows and the knowing look on the old crone's face.

Aldyth reached for the nag's reins.

'No,' said Gandulf. 'Take Cathedra; she'll be quicker and more sure-footed. Please take good care of her for me, sweeting. She's not used to stranger's hands.'

'Gandulf,' demanded Aldyth, fear edging into her voice, 'how could you part with Cathedra? What do you mean to do?'

'God's truth, I don't know, Aldyth.'

Gandulf transferred the bundles from the nag's back to Cathedra's, and Sirona said brusquely, 'Kiss her quickly and get it over with. We don't have time to moon about.'

Aldyth gave him her hands and proffered her cheek, but Gandulf, heedless of onlookers, swept her fervently into his arms and kissed her. He pressed his cheek against hers and breathed deeply of the rosemary scent that clung to her hair even through the smell of wood smoke. 'God keep you,' he whispered and was gone. Aldyth sensed that Gandulf was saying good-bye for the last time; her tear-blurred eyes barely made out his shape as he mounted the nag and turned its head toward Sceapterbyrig.

Gandulf hoped that no one had noticed him leave the garrison with an extra horse loaded down with provisions. Would anyone question his returning without Cathedra? There was some advantage in being considered absurd and inconsequential; perhaps in the excitement of the manhunt and Lord Ralf's preoccupation with his future in-laws, no one would have noticed. He turned his thoughts back to what his heart would dwell upon. Aldyth! He could hardly bear to leave her. Aldyth! He wanted to cry out her name to the heavens. Sweet Aldyth! And he gripped the reins until his knuckles turned white.

As Sirona watched Gandulf depart, she said soberly, 'He will be sorely tried.'

With the help of many hands, they were able to lift Harold into the saddle. A rope tied about his waist anchored him to the pommel, a precaution he meekly accepted. But when Aldyth mounted up behind him, he said in no uncertain tone, 'Young woman, you're not coming.'

'Of course I am, my Lord. You are in no condition to ride unaided.'

Sirona, who had been blessing the children, cut short the

benediction, seized the lead rope, and departed at a brisk gait, hoping to forestall any argument. But Harold would have his say. 'Sirona, leave Aldyth with the charcoal burners,' he repeated. 'You are a hardened warrior, but she is just a slip of a girl; there is no need to bring her into this.'

'Appearances can be deceiving, my Lord, as you well know.'

'I'll háve no more blood on my conscience.' In his most regal voice, Harold ordered, 'I command you to leave me.'

Awed by his tone of authority, Aldyth reflexively prepared to slide off the saddle.

But Sirona retorted, 'You abdicated; I'm in charge here. Now be quiet and sit still.'

Both Aldyth and Harold let their jaws drop. As she watched Harold submit to Sirona's iron will, Aldyth knew that she would never again question the authority the Goddess had vested in her godmother. It seemed like a good time to change the subject, so Aldyth asked Sirona, 'What happened when you were up at the garrison, Godmother?'

'The same as usual,' said Sirona dismissively. 'They asked questions, and I gave answers – not necessarily the ones they wanted – and then I made them take me home.'

'I'm surprised you haven't taken Lord Ralf over your knee and put him in his proper place,' said Harold dryly.

Sirona chortled, then said more seriously, 'I can handle Lord Ralf, but 'tis that hateful Norman priest that concerns me at the moment. He is thirsting for blood.'

'Whose?' asked Aldyth anxiously.

'He'd like a taste of mine, but he's after the heart's blood of Father Edmund. Our old friend is not suited to match wits with Father Odo. Edmund is a simple man and a good Christian but not a very good churchman, and he cannot be bothered with the intrigues of Church politics. The Church has more to do with power on earth than with the spirit of God, and the spirit of God is the only thing Father Edmund understands. Wait and see,' predicted Sirona. 'Father Odo will use the current confusion to advance his own purposes.'

They lapsed into silence and continued into the ever-thickening woods. The shadows had long since blended into the darkness, but the pictures playing in Aldyth's mind were as vivid and bright as a garland of ribbons and far more precious. She thought back on the revelations of the day, each more astounding than the last. Had she and Gandulf truly displayed their feelings for each other openly, even before Sirona? Was Gandulf actually the son of Harold Godwinson? Most incredible of all, had King Harold truly returned?

The canopy overhead was as dense as any Aldyth had seen, and it blocked out the night sky, yet Sirona never once wavered in her gait. Aldyth grew stiff as hour followed hour, without pause to rest, and she would never have believed that Harold might be able to sit ahorse this long. But as she hugged him from behind, she could almost feel the strength flowing back into his limbs, the beat of his heart growing more steady; the spring-water was working its wonder, and Aldyth said a silent prayer of thanksgiving to the Goddess.

The steady rhythm of the horse lulled Aldyth into a doze. Through the fog of fatigue, she gradually became aware of a peaceful stillness that settled over them like a warm cloak. She was not sure when she realized that they were not alone. The stillness was so intense she could almost hear the Fairy bells ringing on the night air. At first she thought she was dreaming, but when she shook herself awake and peered into the darkness, the sensation was just as strong. She could compare it only to the feeling she got when a curious fox trailed her, and it increased with each step until she had the impression that they were moving in the midst of a silent crowd. She could not shrug off the feeling and decided to bring it to Sirona's attention, but before she could speak, she began to distinguish shapes in the intense gloom. She told herself that they were the shadows one sees against the darkness when nothing is truly there, but Harold too had roused himself and was watching intently. They came to a spot where a great tree had fallen, opening the forest to the night sky, and she realized that they were surrounded by a host of silent beings. Had they been there the whole time? One approached Sirona and wordlessly relieved her of the lead rope. Two more stationed themselves at either stirrup. No taller than youths at the threshold of manhood, their slender hands reached up to support Harold by the waist; he dwarfed them with his big Saxon bulk as much as Cathedra did. But the mare, skittish since parting company with her loving master, calmed immediately and even nickered a friendly greeting to the one who led her.

Sirona spoke softly to their escort in a tongue that was foreign to Aldyth, resembling neither the musical lilt of Sirona's Welsh language nor the drawled vowels of Norman French. The relief in the wisewoman's voice was audible as she turned to her companions and said simply, 'We're going home.'

CHAPTER THIRTY-ONE

Lammas Day, Day of the Dead
August 1087

Lord Ralf peered in through the tiny window on the cell door. He had anticipated this moment since he had seen the prisoner dragged into the bailey, for there was something about the Saxon's cocksure arrogance that both intrigued and annoyed him.

Lord Ralf had spent the day going over accounts and touring his lands with the de Broadfords. He despised them as much as they did him, and curbing his acerbic tongue was a great strain on one used to speaking his mind with neither forethought nor diplomacy. When Lord Ralf hunted, the exhilaration of the chase and the thrill of the kill loosed his tensions. He had brought to bay a worthy prey in the Saxon captive and was finally free to go to the undercroft and do whatever was required to bend him to his will. To a Saxon, the odds in such a contest would appear to favor Lord Ralf, but in the Norman's mind, the object was not merely to kill; the triumph would lie in the breaking of the prisoner's spirit. Deep down, he feared that Bedwyn might yet emerge the winner in this battle of wills.

With a clanking of keys, the sentry admitted his lord. The Norman was annoyed that the prisoner did not rise at his entrance. 'Get up!' he ordered. 'And bow before me!'

Bedwyn rose, as if humoring a sulky child, and gave a cursory bow. Outraged at his insolence, Lord Ralf sent an iron fist flying full force into Bedwyn's face.

*　　*　　*

'What of the Saxon brought in yesterday?' asked William de Broadford over supper.

'He knows something, of that I am certain, but I beat the pulp out of him and he's still not talking. He's got balls,' said Ralf in grudging praise.

'Balls, you say?' said fitzGrip with a smirk. 'We could do something about that. I've a man in Wiltshire who could carve them, roast them, and make him eat them.'

'That's very inventive,' said Ralf caustically, 'but a dead man provides no challenge.'

FitzGrip grinned. 'My man Gauter can skin a man alive and do it so skillfully that he will live to see his own guts twisted on a stick. Trust me, he'll keep the Saxon alive long enough to tell you whatever you need to know. Ralf, don't be stubborn,' fitzGrip persisted. 'Amateurs always over-estimate their abilities, and King William would not be pleased if you allowed him to take his information to the grave.'

Breaking Bedwyn had become Lord Ralf's paramount concern; he had almost forgotten that his object was to extract information. 'Very well,' he grumbled. 'How long would it take your man to get here?'

'Two days at most. He was working on a treason case in Devon. He'll be done by now.'

'All right, send for the bloody fool, and we'll see how good he really is.'

Everyone at the high table laughed at Lord Ralf's grudging consent, except Gandulf, who stared blank-faced at his trencher. He could not even pretend to pick at his food.

'I've been to hangings,' commented Catherine, 'but I've never seen a man tortured.'

'Were you hoping for an invitation?' asked Gandulf in revulsion.

She stiffened at his tone, but he was too repulsed to care. The discussion of Bedwyn's ordeal over the dainties before them made him sick. The moment fitzGrip's man stepped through the door, Bedwyn's fate would be sealed. Once again, Gandulf considered the possibilities. He could offer Bedwyn quick release through poison, which was risky, for Lord Ralf would be furious. But if Bedwyn must die, Gandulf wanted it to happen before he was destroyed completely. He owed the Saxon more than Bedwyn could ever know, for he had sacrificed himself that Gandulf's blood father might live. Yet the force that truly drove Gandulf was the fear that if Bedwyn were to give up his secrets, he would take Aldyth with him.

The clang of keys alerted Bedwyn that the night's ordeal was not over. He had been stripped and tied belly down to a bench. His back and buttocks were welted and bleeding from the whip. Both eyes had been blackened, and one of them was nearly swollen shut. Dried blood from a broken nose heightened the effect of the carnage. Forcing pained muscles to obey, Bedwyn lifted his head to see a cowled priest walk in with the guard.

'I'm here for his confession,' the priest told the guard, 'and I would speak privately with him.'

'Where is Father Odo?' asked the sentry.

'In light of Father Odo's failure with the prisoner, the bishop of Salisbury has sent me to persuade the Saxon to be more forthcoming and to save his soul while he can.'

'I'll have no more to say to you than to the last one, Priest,' growled Bedwyn. 'You can take my confession in Hell, for I'm sure to see you there.'

'That is your anger speaking, my son,' the priest replied sanctimoniously, adding to the guard, 'Leave us.'

The guard hesitated. 'But Lord Ralf said—'

'The prisoner is not going anywhere,' the priest assured him.

Uneasily, the guard agreed. 'Very well, Father. Perhaps you'll have more success than Lord Ralf did at extracting a confession. I'll be right outside if you need me.'

'Thank you, my son.'

The door closed behind the guard, and the priest made the sign of the cross. '*In nomine Patri et Filii et Spiritu Sanctu*,' he intoned.

'Normans are all murdering scoundrels,' spat Bedwyn, 'and you priests are the worst of all, because you do it in God's name.'

The priest knelt and whispered, 'Then let's see if you can make a better priest.'

He pulled back the hood just far enough for Bedwyn to see his face. He was already cutting the ropes from around the prisoner's chafed wrists before Bedwyn could collect himself and respond, 'Harold's bones! What are you doing here, fitzGerald?'

'I'm saving your soul,' replied Gandulf, helping Bedwyn to his feet, then removing a small flask from his sleeve. 'Springwater,' he explained. 'Take it with you; they've barred all Saxons from the fountain, and you look as though you could use it.'

Gandulf slipped off his robe and tunic, then stepped out of his hose so that the two men stood naked in the dark shadows of the flickering torchlight. 'Brace yourself,' warned Gandulf. 'This is going to hurt.' With that, he turned around and pressed his bare back against Bedwyn's, which was still oozing blood from his open wounds and weeping welts. When Gandulf pulled away, his back was covered with Bedwyn's blood. 'Will I pass for a mangy, hog-tied Saxon dog?' he whispered.

'In the dark and from a distance, perhaps,' said Bedwyn doubtfully. 'Although you're scrawnier and not nearly so good-looking.'

'You obviously haven't caught a glimpse of yourself lately,' retorted Gandulf.

Bedwyn was surprised at how gently the Norman lowered the priest's robe over him. Pulling the hood forward over Bedwyn's face, Gandulf inquired, 'Do you speak French? No? Never mind, I'll summon the guard. But first listen carefully. By the head of Saint Denis, I charge you to see Aldyth through this nightmare. I know that in your own clumsy way you love her and she loves you. But if you ever lay a hand on her against her will, I swear to God by all that is holy, I swear by the Devil himself, I shall rise up from Hell and drag you back down with me. Is that clear?'

Bedwyn nodded, then impulsively said, 'There are two of us; we can overpower the guard when you call him in. You come too, and we can worry about who gets Aldyth later.'

Gandulf shook his head. 'There are four sentries in the guardroom down the hall, and the bailey is alive with soldiers. Now for God's sake, give me your word and get out.'

'You have it.'

Visibly relieved, Gandulf said, 'Aldyth and Sirona were at the charcoal burners' camp. Tonight they're taking the Saxon into deeper hiding, I'm not sure where, but Aldyth knows the king's men are searching the village; she's bound to come rushing back into the hornets' nest. Get her out of here, do you understand?'

They clasped hands, at last of the same mind where Aldyth was concerned.

Gandulf positioned himself on the bench, then called out, 'Guard, release me.'

Bedwyn, hood pulled forward over his face, waited by the door. The guard unlocked the door and, nodding toward the prisoner, asked, 'Any luck, Father?'

Bedwyn shook his head and left. From his dark corner on the bench, Gandulf listened to the door slam shut and Bedwyn's footsteps receding down the hall. After the time he figured it would take Bedwyn to reach the town walls, he rose and dressed. He heard the squeak of a rat and saw a movement in the mucky straw. He watched in morbid fascination as a bony rat crept out of hiding. Its beady eyes fell upon him, and it froze. After sizing Gandulf up as an empty threat, it sidled directly toward him. Gandulf started, and the rat jumped but did not retreat. The mangy rodent eyed the prisoner for the space of one of Gandulf's desperate Pater Nosters, then resumed its progress. Gandulf heaved a sigh of relief when he realized that it had set its sights on Bedwyn's slop bowl. Finding slim pickings there, it reared up on its hind legs for a last backward glance.

'Thank you for your patience,' said Gandulf with grim humor. 'I shan't keep you waiting long.' It seemed to him that the rat flashed a toothy grin before slipping through a crack gnawed into the door by its forefathers.

Gandulf was glad that this final plan had occurred to him. His life was only misery anyway. This way, at least his death would have some meaning. He wished he had had a chance to bid his mother farewell and prayed that she would understand. He smiled wryly and wondered if they had found Father Odo yet. He had Aelfric to thank for the priest's robe, for he had covered a pile of dog shit with dry leaves and set it afire on the church porch, as he had seen Aelfric do on New Year's Eve. The priest had not fallen for the same trick twice but had come rushing out to give chase. While Gandulf's plan had not worked exactly as anticipated, he had still been able to drag the priest back into the chapel unseen. There he had stripped him, bound him with his belt, and hidden him behind the altar. In this garrison full of sinners, mused Gandulf, Father Odo might not be discovered for weeks.

Gandulf had no expectation of mercy after Lord Ralf discovered that he had engineered Bedwyn's escape. A traitor in the family could cause strained relations with the king, which Lord Ralf could not afford when he was hoping to fund his castle with King William's help. But the final die had not yet been cast. Gandulf would wait until the changing of the guard, then tell the turnkey that he had been overpowered by the Saxon. If he could persuade the guard to release him before Ralf discovered him there, he might yet escape.

Gandulf was unsure whether he had actually slept or even dozed, when he was startled by the sound of the bolt in the door and jerked himself into a sitting position. He heard the guard stammer a salute and Lord Ralf's voice cutting him off to say, 'I'll have one more crack at him before Gauter arrives. Get out, and don't come back until I call you.'

Gandulf's heart sank. He sprang to his feet, but his knees almost buckled when he saw the cold, unbridled fury in Ralf fitzGerald's face. Once again he was seven years old and helpless, but he took courage in the secret knowledge that this monster was no kin of his. Whatever power this evil stranger had over him, it could not compare to the capacity for injury that a father held over his son.

With a strange detachment Gandulf listened to the deep, bestial growl that rose up from Lord Ralf's throat. He watched the hammy, ringed fist fly toward him until it crashed into his face with a force that sent him slamming against the wall. He collapsed into the already bloodied rushes and was amazed to discover that he scarcely felt the pain. Strangely euphoric, he marveled, 'He has lost the power to harm me.'

From a faraway place, he heard Lord Ralf roar, 'How could you do this to me?'

A booted foot connected with Gandulf's ribs, and he felt a dull crack. Another kick struck him full in the gut. He doubled up and retched onto the floor. One last blow to the side of his head sent him sprawling. 'Kill me and get it over with,' he groaned.

The sight of blood streaming from Gandulf's nose, ears, and mouth brought Ralf to himself. In dismay he realized that he had probably already killed Gandulf; so he too would have to make an escape. Storming to the darkest corner of the cell, he kicked away the straw and shoved aside a heavy wooden lid to uncover a deep pit: The oubliette, the Place of the Forgotten. He dragged Gandulf, half conscious, across the cell to the edge of the pit. 'Let the rats finish you off,' he hissed, and with a nudge of his boot he sent Gandulf hurtling over the edge. There was a loud thud as he hit bottom, then a deathly silence.

When Lord Ralf peered down into the darkness to ascertain whether Gandulf still lived, from the depths rose a hoarse whisper: 'My apologies to fitzGrip's man.'

Lord Ralf thundered with rage. Dragging the wooden cover back over the pit, Lord Ralf bellowed to the guard to release him.

Gandulf lay in the darkness at the bottom of the pit. Blood streamed into his eyes, but he could not lift a hand to wipe it away. His ribs clicked with each ragged breath, and he guessed that a broken rib must have pierced his lung. 'Aldyth,' he whispered, as if speaking the name aloud might give him strength. 'Aldyth . . .'

'There's someone who would like to talk to you, Aldyth.'

Aldyth looked up from bandaging the leg of Jenena, Mildburh's four-year-old daughter, to see Aelfric standing in the doorway of the Millers' house. The night before, when Jenena had heard Lord Ralf's knights pound into the village, she had dashed into the lane for a better look. No one could say if the horseman had seen the child before running her down, but Aldyth doubted whether it would have made a difference. Jenena was only one of the casualties that Aldyth had found waiting upon her return.

She had stayed with Sirona long enough the night before to help settle Harold among the Silent Ones. One of them, communicating by hand signs, had helped Aldyth onto Cathedra, then climbed into the saddle before her. Drawing her arms about his slender waist, he had reached around to pull her head gently down upon his shoulder. She remembered nothing else until she heard a low whistle and drowsily looked up to discover that they were at the edge of the woods overlooking the Crystal Spring. Her escort twisted around in the saddle to meet her eye questioningly. She nodded, and he lowered her down. By the early-dawn light, she saw that he was clean-shaven and his long hair, black as a crow's wing, was bound by a leather headband. He wore a sleeveless tunic of mossy brown, adorned by a leather belt with a gold buckle. Adorning his neck was a twisted gold torque and above each elbow a golden armlet. Aldyth had never seen a face like his, except at his encampment, where everyone had the same delicate bone structure, high cheekbones, and pale skin. His eyes, like Sirona's, were as black as obsidian and seemed to hold the same mystery. He spoke to Aldyth in his own language, his words soft and spare and musical, reminding Aldyth of a mother's whisper to her newborn. She could not understand what he was saying, but she grasped his meaning.

'Thank you,' Aldyth answered gratefully. 'May the Lady go with you also.'

He leaned down from his mount and touched her forehead with his first two fingers. Then he turned Cathedra and melted into the woods. Reluctantly Aldyth hurried on, loath to step out of the serenity of his world and back into the toil and trouble of her own.

The nuns had been told to expect her the night before, but her unplanned night trek had kept her away, with no possibility of sending word. She believed that Edith and Gunhild were in no immediate danger while under the protection of the abbess but hoped that they had not been upset by her nonappearance. Upon her return to Enmore Green, she had found Father Edmund desperately picking up the pieces wherever the wreckage was strewn most thickly. Aldyth had taken over his duties and sent him directly to the abbey with instructions to the nuns to await her in the garden that night.

426

In the meantime, Norman soldiers patrolled Enmore Green, Alcester, and Long Cross, and an ultimatum had been issued by the Normans: surrender the outlaw, or suffer the penalty.

Aldyth's day had disappeared in a haze of fatigue and hurry. Darkness was upon them, there was no word of Sirona, and Father Edmund had not reported back from his morning mission. Aldyth was concerned for the priest, as well as the nuns, yet her people had no one else to turn to, nor could she afford to draw suspicion to herself by a conspicuous absence, so she stayed to bind broken crowns and soothe frightened children.

'Aldyth,' repeated Aelfric, 'I said there's someone who wishes to speak to you.'

She nodded and tied off the bandage. 'Aelfric, have you seen Father Edmund?'

'Yes, and he wants to talk to you also.' Something in his tone made the hairs on her neck rise. 'And bring your basket,' he said ominously. Aldyth tucked a blanket up to Jenena's chin and kissed her on the forehead before hurrying off with Aelfric.

Father Edmund stood at the door of Saint Wulfstan's, trying very hard to appear nonchalant. Aldyth forced herself not to run to him, but when she got to him she clasped his hands tightly. 'Father, I was worried when you didn't return.'

'The soldiers picked me up on my way to the abbey, took me up to the garrison for questioning, and held me there most of the day.'

Even in the dark, Aldyth could see the bruise on his cheek. 'It was Father Odo, wasn't it?'

He shrugged dismissively, then said gravely, 'Aldyth, I never had a chance to deliver your message, for I have only just been released. You go inside; I'll keep watch, and you can tell me in a moment whether you still want me to go up to the abbey.'

Aldyth nodded and, assailed by faceless fears, hurried into the church with Aelfric at her heels. She scanned the dark interior, hardly knowing what she sought. Then a priest stepped out of the shadows cast by a few guttering votive candles and started toward her. When she was close enough to distinguish his features, he pulled back the hood to reveal a face so bruised and swollen that she stifled a cry.

427

'What has happened to this poor man?' she asked Aelfric.

'Aldyth, don't you know me?'

'Bedwyn! Oh, my Lady! What have they done to you?' she sobbed.

''Tis not as bad as it looks.' He motioned her into the sacristy, the small chamber off to the side of the altar where the communal wine and clerical vestments were kept. It was evident from his hobble that Bedwyn had suffered more than a broken nose.

'Aelfric, help me,' she said. It took them both to ease the robe over Bedwyn's head, for it clung to sores on his back that had long since clotted. Aldyth was too absorbed in her role as healer to blush at his nakedness, and he was in too much pain to swagger. She cleared the communion vessels off the bench. 'Bedwyn, can you lie down here?'

'I hope you're gentler than the last one.'

'Aelfric, hand me that vessel,' said Aldyth, pointing to a stoneware jug.

'Communion wine?' asked Aelfric, glancing nervously toward the door.

But Bedwyn quipped, 'Can't you see, lad? I am the body and the blood.'

Aelfric grinned and gave her the jug, then held a torch aloft so that she could see to work. 'This is going to hurt,' she warned.

'People keep telling me that today,' Bedwyn said with a grim smile. Wincing as she cleansed the cuts on his buttocks with the communal wine, Bedwyn said, 'Before you waste any more of that, I know a better use for it.'

Aldyth handed Bedwyn the jug, and he lifted it to swollen lips and drank deeply. Returning it, he explained, 'It works faster that way.'

As she treated the patchwork of cuts, Bedwyn said bitterly, 'The game's up, Aldyth.'

'What do you mean?'

'You know what I mean. The Starlit Path is gone, and its ruin will crush us all. After today, I can never again show my face in Enmore Green.' He stopped for a moment and grimaced while she swabbed the grit out of one of the deeper cuts. 'Come with me, Aldyth,' he urged. ''Tis the chance of a lifetime. We'll join Harold and fight the good fight. You could be the mother of a horde of proud Saxon warriors.'

'You should know me better than that, Bedwyn,' she told him. 'I'm a healer. I'll not shed blood, English or Norman, nor raise sons to kill other mothers' sons.'

'Very well,' he conceded. 'Consider this, then: I've a few coins tucked away, enough to buy two passages to Byzantium. We'll get married, and I'll join the Varangian Guard.'

'Bedwyn,' she said in exasperation, 'you know I am sworn to the fountain.' More gently she added, 'I have no springwater to bathe your wounds; the Normans have it under guard.'

'There's a flask of springwater by the altar,' he replied.

While Aelfric ran to fetch it, Aldyth asked in surprise, 'Where did you get that?' Then, suddenly suspicious, she demanded, 'How did you make your escape?'

Bedwyn knew that the moment Gandulf's name was spoken aloud, his charge was doomed to failure. He sighed. He was many things but never a liar. 'It was the lordling,' he confessed. 'He came to my cell dressed as a priest, and we traded places.'

'Oh, my Lady!' cried Aldyth in horror. 'Lord Ralf will kill him!'

That possibility had never occurred to Bedwyn. 'Surely not his own son?'

'Especially Gandulf. I must go to him.'

Aelfric piped up, 'Aldyth, Margaret says you're not to come up to the garrison until after the second watch is well begun.'

Bedwyn shot him a withering glance. 'Aldyth,' he said urgently, 'fitzGerald made me swear to take you away from here; he gave you into my charge.'

'I was no charge of his to be thus disposed of. I release you from your promise.'

'There's nothing you can do for him,' said Bedwyn impatiently. 'You can't just stroll up to the garrison and demand his release.'

She set her jaw and gave him a stubborn look.

'Then if you insist upon this fool's errand, Aldyth, let me be your fool,' offered Bedwyn. 'I'm familiar with the layout of the dungeon.'

'Bedwyn, you dear, sweet, big oaf. Don't you see, you'd stand out like a broken nose? But they know me up there and have no reason to do me harm.'

He saw the logic of her argument and knew that she had made up her mind. Aldyth applied a balm to his wounds and helped him to his feet so that she could wrap his back.

'He's a fool,' said Bedwyn softly, looking down at her as she worked.

'Who?'

'The lordling.'

'Aye, that he is.'

'Unschooled in the wiles of men and the ways of war; green as a willow branch.'

'Aye.'

'But I think I understand what you see in him now.'

Aldyth had never known Bedwyn to lose, in contests or at love, and it warmed her heart to know that he was graceful even in defeat. She smiled gratefully at him through a shimmering rainbow of tears. All three of them had taken their chances and lost, but Aldyth hoped that at least for Bedwyn there would be other games, other loves. 'Bedwyn, you know that I have loved you dearly, and I think that you have loved me.'

He nodded and took her hands.

'For the sake of our friendship,' she continued, 'I now place one last charge upon you. I was to fetch two nuns from the abbey tonight. Please go in my stead and ask for Sisters Edith and Gunhild. You must keep them safely in hiding until Sirona comes for them. Father Edmund will help you,' she said, tying off the last of the bandages.

'Aldyth, you can't mean to go up there and die with the Norman.'

She made no reply.

'Aldyth,' he whispered, 'I've never in my life begged for anything from anyone. But I'm begging you now, please . . . don't go.'

'Swear to me by the milk of the Goddess that you will fulfill my charge,' she said, laying a hand gently upon his arm.

'I swear,' he muttered, then added fiercely, 'and I swear by the prick of Thunor that if Ralf fitzGerald lays a hand on you I'll rip out his heart with my bare hands!'

'Take it back, Bedwyn!' she cried.

'You know I can't do that. I will not be forsworn.'

'Then may the Goddess protect you.'

The back door of the church creaked open, and Wulfric slipped in carrying a change of clothing. 'Edwin says the soldiers are swinging back this way,' he warned, helping Bedwyn into a pair of trousers. 'You had best hurry!'

Bedwyn nodded. 'Give the MoonCatcher and his gaggle of sentries my thanks.'

'Off to the woods now?' asked Wulfric.

'Off to the abbey,' growled Bedwyn, 'to fulfill a vow.'

Wulfric raised his eyebrows in surprise.

'Don't ask,' said Bedwyn disgustedly.

Bedwyn waited in the abbey garden, cursing his bad luck and wondering how he, hitherto the master of his own fate, had become such a pawn. Who would be the next to extract an oath and lay a charge upon him? Must he really throw away his life for a pair of hairy-faced nuns? At the sound of approaching footsteps, Bedwyn pressed himself against the wall behind the grape arbor and drew his dagger. He noted warily that it was one set of footsteps and not two, and whoever it was moved through the darkness with deliberate stealth, stopping to listen not three feet from where Bedwyn was concealed.

'Aldyth?' came the tentative whisper.

'Cousin?' asked Bedwyn.

'Bedwyn, is that you?' whispered Mother Rowena, peering among the grape leaves. In dismay she cried, 'What have you done to your face? You must come to the infirmary at once.'

Bedwyn let out his long-held breath in one rush of relief. 'No time for that, my Lady,' he replied. 'But tell me, what are you doing here?'

'I was about to ask you the same question, lad. Where is Aldyth?'

Bedwyn hesitated; he knew of the infirmarian's attachment to the girl. 'She has gone to the garrison,' he groaned at last.

Mother Rowena gasped and sat down hard on the garden bench. Bedwyn slipped out of hiding to take her hands. Lady Rowena and her husband, Lord Aethelstan, had given refuge to Bedwyn and his mother after they had been driven from York. But soon after they had taken him in, Sceapterbyrig had fallen to Lord Ralf. Bedwyn, only ten at the time, had escaped into Cranborne Chase. Since that time, the Saxon outlaw's path had seldom led to the abbey, but Mother Rowena was the only living kin Bedwyn knew of. He often asked after her, had Aldyth deliver gifts of honey and goose quills, and someday would mourn her passing.

'I'm sorry, my Lady,' he said. 'I tried to talk some sense into her. She is as stubborn as they come! But where are the nuns, Cousin? I'm here to fetch them for Aldyth.'

Mother Rowena replied fretfully, 'They've gone, Bedwyn. When Aldyth didn't come at evensong, they insisted upon going alone, for fear of bringing ruin upon the abbey.'

'For the love of God!' swore Bedwyn. 'Now I must seek them out among swarms of Norman men-at-arms, or I'll be forsworn to Aldyth. Where did they go, Cousin?'

'I sent them to your cottage.'

'But it's burned to the ground.'

'I had no idea. God help us all, Bedwyn,' she said quietly. 'God help us all.'

Bedwyn placed a gentle hand upon her shoulder and replied dismally, 'No one else could untangle this mess.'

Margaret nervously popped yet another raisin into her mouth and swallowed it without tasting it. If Aldyth Lightfoot did not come soon, she would finish the summer's supply and make herself sick at the same time. When Aldyth finally appeared at her elbow without so much as the sound of a footfall, Margaret nearly choked on a raisin. The big woman recovered herself, rose from her bench, and hurriedly picked up a large wineskin from beneath it. 'Springwater,' she whispered to Aldyth.

'How did you get that?' asked Aldyth incredulously.

'Gilbert is partial to apple tarts and brings me springwater whenever I ask, for toothache and rheumatism. He'd get fat from all the tarts he's been eating lately, except that he works it off on the trip down the hill and back.' Handing Aldyth the skin, she led her into the courtyard and around to the small door of the undercroft. She knocked softly, and when there was no answer, they tiptoed in onto a long corridor. On the right were several locked doors, to which Margaret had the keys. 'Storerooms,' she told Aldyth. On the left, torchlight streamed from the guardroom. Around the table the night watch slumped, empty flagons and tankards lying every which way. 'I gave them their fill of highly salted stew, then let them quench their thirst with Lord Ralf's good wine, which I "forgot" to water down,' explained Margaret. 'Their heads will be pounding tomorrow.' Nodding down the hall, she said, 'The last door on the left is the one where Gandulf is kept. There's only one guard down there, Jehanne's husband, Roland.'

Margaret would know that it was Roland's wife and baby that Aldyth had saved during a difficult birthing the previous autumn. 'God go with you, child,' she whispered. She gave Aldyth a quick hug, then hurried back to her kitchen before she was missed.

Aldyth hurried down the dark corridor. Roland, looking pale, let her into the cell and whispered, 'Go to the far corner and lift the wooden cover off the oubliette while I keep watch. He's in there. And hurry!' he said his eyes darting anxiously to the far end of the hall. Aldyth nodded and went over to the corner, but the lid was so heavy that she was barely able to shift it. Roland barked impatiently, 'Be quick about it, girl!'

''Tis too heavy,' she groaned.

He swore under his breath and hurried over. Together they pulled it aside. By the flickering torchlight, Aldyth could barely make out the crumpled heap at the foot of the pit. 'Gandulf?' she whispered.

'Aldyth?' he mumbled weakly. Then he cried, 'My God! Get out . . . quickly!'

Roland's sweaty hand shook her shoulder. 'Give him the water, damn it, and get out.'

Aldyth knelt to drop the water skin into the pit. 'I'm coming down,' she said.

'No!' came a cry of startling strength from within the pit.

It was echoed by another cry from behind her. In confusion, Aldyth looked up to see Roland's eyes, wide and staring. A trickle of blood escaped from the corner of his mouth, and he fell to his knees. As the soldier toppled, Lord Ralf stepped forward holding a bloodied knife.

'You goddamned slut!' he roared, his eyes burning with hatred. 'Is it you who have bewitched my son and turned him into a traitor? You've ruined *me* into the bargain!' He grabbed a fistful of Aldyth's hair and wrenched her to her feet.

'No!' screamed Gandulf from below. Lord Ralf sucked in a deep breath of triumph. His son was not beyond reach after all, and he had just revealed the chink in his armor.

Lord Ralf flung Aldyth against the wall and drew back a fist to break the girl's nose, but he caught a glint in the dim torchlight; she had drawn a dagger. Her flushed cheeks, the fire, and the fury in her eyes sent his mind flashing back to a day more than twenty years before, when he had faced another Saxon tigress. He felt a stirring in his groin such as he had not known since the witch Sirona had cursed him. Then he was struck suddenly by a thought so wicked that he surprised even himself: with one simple act, he would repay the witch for years of humiliation and hurt his son beyond bearing.

'You never told me your whore was such a beauty, Gandulf,' Lord Ralf called into the pit.

The Norman warrior lunged, and Aldyth feinted at him with her knife. Surprisingly agile for one of his bulk, Lord Ralf ducked to one side and hooked his leg behind her knee, throwing her to the floor. Before she could regain her footing, he was upon her, nearly breaking her wrist as he wrestled the knife from her hand. He sneered and tossed it to one side. Grasping the collar of her kirtle, he gave it a violent jerk, tearing away the front of her dress, then crowed as she clutched defensively at the neck of her shift. He seized Aldyth's hands and, gripping both wrists in one of his hard fists, used the other to rip open her shift, revealing her soft, white curves. Straddling her waist, he pinned her hands to the floor. 'Now, Gandulf, you may listen to the wench's delight,' he gloated, 'when a real man buries his sword in her sheath.'

'No!' screamed Aldyth, lifting her head to bury her teeth in his wrist.

'You bitch!' he yelled. With each act of resistance, his passion grew. His breath came in hard gasps as he frantically began to hike Aldyth's kirtle up to her waist. His eyes glinted at the sight of her vulnerable innocence unveiled and open to his assault, and he grunted with pleasure. Locking his knees on either side of her slender frame, he pulled his tunic up over his head and tossed it impatiently to one side, then peeled down his hose. His excitement was only increased by the pleading of the broken man who lay helpless at the bottom of the pit. Lord Ralf forced Aldyth's legs open with his knees and pressed his face close to hers. 'Do you know how long I've waited for this?' Turning to the pit, he shouted, 'This time the right of the First Night will be that of the last night.'

But when he turned back to Aldyth, chills ran up his spine. Her trembling, which had sent shivers of lust coursing through his veins, was not from fear, as he had thought, but from fury, born of rage to match his own. She stared up at him with a piercing, chilling composure, and an uncanny fear crept over him. It immediately became apparent that even had he wanted to continue his assault, he was no longer able to.

'Not you too, witch,' he snarled, his voice edged with panic. 'I won't let you do this to me.' He clutched at his groin and tried desperately to revive his shriveled passion.

Even as he realized that his efforts would be futile, Aldyth hissed, 'I curse you. In the name of the Goddess to whom I belong and She whom I serve, I curse you! Steal my maiden-head, and you steal it from Her. I defy you to spill one drop of my blood, that you might know the wrath of Sula!' Then Aldyth spit into his face and opened her legs to him.

Beads of sweat broke out on her attacker's upper lip. The silence dragged on; even the cries from the pit had ceased. Springing to his feet, Lord Ralf pulled up his hose to hide his pathetic defeat. 'Very well, bitch. Not a drop of your virgin's blood shall I spill.'

With that, he wrapped Aldyth's long hair around his fist and wrenched her to her feet. Hurling her down into the oubliette, he called after her, 'You can watch each other die. And to protect your cursed maidenhead,' he growled, 'a chaperon.' Lord Ralf heaved Roland's body after her and pulled the heavy cover back over the oubliette, shutting out all light, and life, and hope.

CHAPTER THIRTY-TWO

'I always figured I'd die for a woman,' thought Bedwyn in disgust as he scouted the perimeter of his clearing. 'At the hands of some jealous husband or outraged father,' he fumed silently, 'But at least I'd imagined getting some gratification for my pains.'

His entire body ached as he stealthily parted a curtain of branches. His search was slow work, and dangerous, as his peripheral vision was obscured by his facial swelling. 'What am I doing here?' he silently raged. 'I ought to be on the road to Byzantium.'

Scrambling down the steep hillside from the abbey into Alcester, he had nearly walked into a Norman patrol lying in wait. When Hugo had recognized Brother Ansgar as Aelfric's rescuer, he had demanded that the abbess surrender the lay brother and his traveling companions. But the nuns had left that morning, so the abbess could truthfully say they were gone; she did, however, in admonition that she would not have violated sanctuary and that no good Christian would have expected it. Outraged, Hugo had dispatched a messenger to the king, asking for permission to search the abbey, then stormed off to appropriate some of Ralf fitzGerald's men to keep watch in case Brother Ansgar or the nuns should attempt to escape. It was not Brother Ansgar but Bedwyn whom he had nearly snared.

When Bedwyn came upon the first of his geese lying dead and broken in the clearing, he felt a surprising depth of sorrow. He had grown fond of the nasty-tempered creatures, and, of course, it was easier to mourn their passing than to think of Aldyth.

The hut was in ruins; he kicked at the charred timbers, but as he stood staring into the darkness, he heard a furtive rustling. Instinct impelled him to draw the dagger Father Edmund had scrounged for him. Taking cover behind the ruined wall, he listened. Hearing nothing, he crept toward the thicket from which the sound had originated, every movement shooting an ache through his battered body. Most likely a sentry had been posted to watch for his return. He circled on hands and knees, then froze at another stirring in the undergrowth. He proceeded at a pace that would have tried the patience of a snail until he could hear people breathing.

Tensing his muscles, he sprang over the last curtain of brush, unable to stifle the groan of pain caused by his movement. His prey made no attempt to stifle their screams. Cowering at his feet, where they crouched in hiding, were two cloaked women. One rose to her knees protectively before the other, her puny table knife drawn defensively. Her face was an oval blur framed by darkness, the frightened face of a veiled nun. After a moment of mutual consternation, a voice he recognized spoke. 'Bedwyn?' she said, appalled. 'You look like gallows bait.'

'Gunhild?' he said, equally appalled. 'Jesus Christ, you never said you were a nun!'

'You'd never have slept with me if I had,' she replied. 'Besides, you never asked.'

As Bedwyn waited for the jealous husband of this bride of Christ to strike him down, an even more horrifying thought occurred to him: all Gunhild had told him was that she had come on pilgrimage to the abbey with her father, a Brother Ansgar. For the first time, he made the connection. Even in his state of shock, it became clear to Bedwyn that he had seduced and cast off the daughter of his king, his hero, Harold Godwinson, to whom he had only that morning sworn life, limb, and fealty.

'Jesus Christ!' he repeated. 'Does your father know?'

'I don't know,' said Gunhild with a shrug. She turned to the other nun and said, 'Mother, did you mention it to him?'

'Jesus Christ!' swore Bedwyn again.

*   *   *

Harold walked down a long, dark corridor closed by a heavy timber door at the far end. It swung open, and, after all those years, he and William stood face to face. William was older, but there was a hardness in his eyes that time could not temper. It was with disdain and, worse, with a gesture of dismissal that William slammed the door shut in his face – but not before Harold had glimpsed Gandulf, bleeding on the floor, and his younger brother Wulfnoth, bound in chains, which rattled as he reached out in vain to aid his nephew. Harold flung himself against the door, which still rang with the force of its closure. He beat against it with his fists and shouted, 'It's not over! It's not over!'

Harold felt hands pull him away from the door. A quiet voice said, 'Peace, my Lord.'

He looked up into a pair of obsidian eyes set in granite. 'Sirona,' he groaned and let her push him back onto his blanket and bathe his forehead and neck with a cool cloth.

'How long?' he asked weakly.

'Three days,' she replied. 'If not for the water of the Crystal Spring fetched for you by your son, my Lord, I'm sure you would have been three days dead.'

'So I've returned from the dead again? Where am I this time?'

'Where they will never find you.'

He nodded, then frowned. 'What of Gandulf? I've had a dream that bodes ill for him.'

'That I cannot tell you.'

'And Edith and Gunhild?'

'Safely in hiding by now.'

'Thank God!' he cried. 'At least they have not been destroyed by my foolish impulse. All my life I have brought ruin upon those I love.'

'You made one mistake twenty years ago. Who would ever have expected the loss of one battle to seal the fate of a nation? Can you not forgive yourself?'

'One mistake?' he refuted. ''Twas a disastrous chain of errors, each one compounding the last. I picked one straw out of the fire when I stole back my wife and daughter, but my brother still calls to me from Normandy.'

'No man can transcend his destiny,' Sirona warned. 'Not you, nor Wulfnoth either.'

'You can say that, but you did not know my little brother. When I fell into William's hands in that ill-fated attempt to rescue him, he was only fifteen, Sirona, yet he had the courage of a man grown as he urged me to make that damned vow to leave him behind, that I might go home to set England to rights. When we parted, I wept, but Wulfnoth held his head high, never wavering in his faith in me. He knew I'd be back for him, and by God, I shall. I have sworn to bring him home or die trying, and I shall not be forsworn.' .

Sirona, understanding the futility of argument, laid her gnarled hand upon his shoulder in a gesture of comfort, then went to the door of the hut. 'Eafa,' she called to a red-haired woman with a baby in a sling, 'have your husband fetch a litter. Our guest will require a strengthening broth. Give him his refreshment within Gelfion's Grove.' To Harold, she added, 'There is a council of elders I must attend. Eafa will see to your needs.'

Eafa bowed and signaled to two small dark men, both dressed in sleeveless moss-colored tunics, with golden torques and armlets. Gently they lifted Harold onto a litter and covered him with a blanket. In an easy, fluid rhythm, they carried him through a small, mossy courtyard walled with sod. A bright-eyed calf peered curiously from a doorway as they stepped through a gate overgrown with brambles. It opened onto a sod-walled common around which all of the houses were grouped. Over every doorway there were sprigs of rowan, ash, and hawthorn bunched with a bit of red yarn. Running down the middle of the sloping street in a stone-lined channel was a small brook that brought fresh water to everyone's doorstep, then flowed out beneath the village gate. Grouped around the brook was a trio of small naked children with little boats, each made of a leaf with another leaf for a sail. The delight on their faces made an eerie contrast to the silence in which they played. Two slight, dark women smiled indulgently as they watched, one grinding acorns in a bowl-shaped rock, the other woman spinning. Up the lane several more women stood beside a young mother, singing to the child in her arms in such harmony that it could have been taken for the humming of bees. They watched, their faces impassive but their eyes warm, as Harold was borne by. He dwarfed them all with his big Saxon frame, but these secretive folk seemed to have strength beyond their size. The encampment's walls were of sod as well but grew as green as the surrounding hills beneath a brushy cover of brambles. When they passed through the settlement gate, Harold looked back but saw only a briar-covered hill and Eafa following along behind.

The settlement was at the edge of an impenetrable forest. A steep bluff fell away on one side of the ridge, making approach impossible from that direction. The other side gradually descended to the bare rolling hills of the downs, so that no arrival came unseen. Above all, the settlement was far from highways, roads, or even straggling paths leading to the lonely hut of an isolated charcoal burner or beekeeper. The likelihood of anyone's stumbling upon this encampment, even had he known of its presence, was virtually nil. It was invisible to anyone not actually within its walls, for the turf that grew on the roofs merged with the hillsides into which the huts were dug.

Here on the edge of the Blackmore Vale, thick woods nestled in the folds of the hills and spread to cover the rich river valleys. Higher up toward the crest of the ridges, the woodland thinned into chalky uplands mantled with grass. On the ridge crest rose a huge mound crowned by a grove of great, twisted trees, visible from the entire valley. Harold recognized the Fairy Grove as a landmark he had seen far across the downs from the heights of Sceapterbyrig, but, like almost everyone else, he had never been to it; it was not on the road to any Saxon destination, it was in barren, unsettled land, and, above all, he had always understood that, even if someone were stubborn enough to fight through miles of wilderness, he would find it haunted, jealously protected by the Fairies.

As the tiny procession left the settlement, one of his escorts whistled like a hawk. There was an answer from above, where a small boy kept watch in the upper branches of a great oak. The boy scanned the countryside for intruders, then waved them on.

They followed a steep path until the forest thinned to scrub, and then, rising up to the sky, they came to the great ridge of the Neolithic roadway. They continued to the top, where the countryside spread out beneath them like God's view from Heaven.

The litter bearers assumed an attitude of reverence as they approached the grove. A wreath of ancient trees formed a circle around a lawn of rich green grass, kept short by the tread of many feet dancing. The litter bearers set Harold down in the shade of the oaks, where he could look out over the valley, then retired to the far side of the grove.

Eafa arranged a backrest of pillows for Harold. He expected that she would speak no more than the others, but she asked, 'Are you comfortable? Or hungry, my Lord?'

'Now that I think of it, I'm famished,' he replied.

Eafa took a wooden bowl and a skin jug from a sack. She poured a steaming liquid into the bowl, then lifted it to Harold's lips. ''Tis a broth of beef for strength,' she told him.

He drank his fill and settled back with a sigh. 'Thank you, lass.'

Eafa refilled the bowl with rich, creamy milk, still warm from the cow. Again Harold drank. Then he wiped the milk from his whiskers, and settled back among his pillows.

'Thank you,' he said again, his hunger satisfied but his curiosity only whetted. 'You weren't born here, were you, lass?'

'No. I'm Saxon, like yourself, my Lord.'

'Sit down beside me, and tell me how you come to be here.'

Eafa blushed but sat on the spot he patted with his hand. The baby in the sling mewed, and the young mother slipped her dress off her shoulder to give it her breast.

'I was Eafa AtWood, living at the edge of the wood between Enmore Green and Long Cross. Just like my cottage, I was neither here nor there, and I found my cows better company than most of my neighbors. So Sirona sent my husband to find me and woo me if he would. At the edge of the woods, he found me, grazing my cows and heavy with child.'

'And you went with him?'

'He loves me and my child. These folk cherish children above all and treat women with at least as much respect as they do their men. The head of this village is a woman. Bloodlines go through the women, you see, and 'tis the man who leaves home to marry. My husband, Grann, was an only child. To have your only child a male is a great misfortune, for he will leave you when he marries, unless he marries a woman with no family of her own. My mother-in-law welcomed me as her adopted daughter, and I am all the more valued because I bring a child as a dowry, and a girl child at that.'

'I'm glad for you,' Harold said sincerely. 'Would that we could all find our place in the world as you have, Eafa. But tell me more of these people.'

'I don't speak the language very well. 'Tis a strange and ancient tongue, and the people speak so seldom that there is little opportunity to practice. So I know only what Sirona has told me. She says these people grew out of the land long before any others walked on English soil. When the first outsiders came, they brought treasures that these people coveted: copper cauldrons, bronze daggers, and ax heads. To get these goods, the small dark ones violated the earth, their mother, destroying forests to sell the wood, overgrazing the land, exhausting the soil to pay for the luxuries that had become necessities. Then Sirona – not this Sirona, but an earlier one – told them that if they wished to retain the favor of the Goddess and their freedom, they must return to their stone arrowheads and their wood-and-antler hoes and abandon the unclean goods of the traders, or they would end up not owning but being owned by these possessions. The temptation of iron was so great that Sirona said they mustn't even touch the metal, so these folk will not even allow a piece of iron in their camp. They make their own pottery and baskets, weave their own cloth, and do without what they can't make themselves. For centuries after that they lived in peace, tilling their gardens and growing their crops. But then came settlers who wanted to take the fields and enslave their owners to labor in them. A family that stays in its hut by its fields can easily be found, but one that follows its herds must be hunted. So Sirona – yet another Sirona – advised them to abandon their fields and move far from the invading foreigners who would destroy them.'

'How long ago was all this?' asked Harold, astonished. 'The Saxons have been here five hundred years, and it was the Welsh we displaced. I've never heard of these people.'

'Oh, but you have,' said Eafa. 'Surely you have heard of the Fairies. They know the secrets of the Goddess. A few, like Sirona, stayed behind to watch over the sacred wells and groves and to keep the Lady's festivals. Over the centuries, as Romans and Saxons and Danes and Normans, each in their turn, swept over the holy hills of the Goddess, Her Folk have grown few and retiring, but they survive because they live as they did when the Lady walked among them. So long as the Folk follow Her ways, for just that long and no longer, the sun will rise at dawn, the fountains will flow, and spring will blossom.'

Eafa burped the child, then gave it the other breast. She turned back to Harold and said earnestly, 'They are a strong, stubborn folk, and so surely do they believe it is their ancient, sacred ways that bring up the sun and send out the spring that I have come to believe it myself. They speak the language of the beasts. They can disappear in the blink of an eye. You have heard of their power to heal or to harm, both by magic and by lore. They worship the Goddess at their sacred sites, and the Goddess protects them.'

'Are these the last of their kind, or are there others?' asked Harold doubtfully.

'Sirona knows of other Fairy settlements scattered throughout Wessex. They reunite to worship each Midsummer, traveling the ridgeways to assemble near Sarum, where the Queen of the Fairies lives. But at all other seasons they make themselves scarce, even to each other, and for the sake of secrecy they shun large gatherings.'

'Astounding!' said Harold. 'Please go on.'

'You are weary, my Lord, and Sirona would be ill pleased were I to wear you out with my ramblings. In any case, she can tell you more than I.'

Harold let her lower him back onto his pillows and tuck the blanket under his chin. He drifted off, feeling a serenity that he had not felt since England was at peace and he had slept in Edith's arms shriven by a night of love. When he woke, he felt the cool of the afternoon shadows upon his face. He felt so far from all his cares that he could not bring himself to stir. When at last he opened his eyes, he found that he was not alone.

'Feeling better, my Lord?' said Sirona, laying her hand upon his chest to feel the beat of his heart.

'As contented as a cow in a new meadow. Was the broth drugged?'

'Nay, my Lord,' smiled the old woman. 'One needs no herbs in Gefion's Grove.'

'What is this place?' he asked in wonderment.

''Tis a holy site, a gift from the Goddess. We come here to renew ourselves.'

'Or to ease an aching heart,' he said softly.

'Aye, my Lord. That, too.'

'Your council meeting is over?'

Sirona nodded. 'The headwoman welcomes you. You may stay as long as you wish.'

'Nothing would please me more,' he said. Then he added reluctantly, 'But I must go.'

'You're not fit to go anywhere,' admonished Sirona.

'Whether it be the springwater or Fairy magic, I feel strong enough for a journey. I must go to William for Wulfnoth's sake; I saw it in my dream, Sirona.'

'The Conqueror is ruthless; he would kill you both, and were he to have it out of you that you had a son still living, he would track the lad down and destroy him as well.'

Harold got to his feet and, testing his muscles, said, 'I shan't be needing the litter.'

Sirona pursed her lips in exasperation and signaled Eafa, who sat watching one of the litter bearers playing with a child while the other kept a lookout on the far side of the grove. Eafa answered her summons, bowing her head to both Harold and the crone.

'Is that your baby awake now and playing with her father?' Harold asked Eafa.

'Aye, my Lord,' said Eafa proudly.

445

'She is as pretty as her mother. Might I dandle her on my knee?'

'Of course, my Lord,' said Eafa.

As Harold crossed the grove, Sirona said grimly to Eafa, 'We must watch him closely.'

CHAPTER THIRTY-THREE

Aldyth marveled at the continuing survival of her virginity even as she was hurled into the pit of Hell. Frantically she tried to break her fall by clawing at the earthen walls of the pit. She landed with a thud at Gandulf's feet. Before she could gather her wits, Roland's body came flying after, and she ducked the flailing limbs of the falling corpse. Lord Ralf's curses scarcely penetrated Aldyth's consciousness as she was assailed by the stench of the charnel house. Then came the scraping of the heavy cover over the pit, the slamming of the cell door. And darkness.

Aldyth forced herself to quell her panic while she tried to sort out the quick from the dead in the impenetrable blackness. 'Gandulf,' she pleaded, 'speak to me, if you can.'

'Aldyth,' he rasped, the despair thick in his voice, 'why did you come?'

'What else could I have done?' she asked simply. Following his voice, she found him in the darkness. His skin was as cold as a corpse's, and he smelled of death. From above she had glimpsed by torchlight the battered face, the telltale signs of bleeding from the ears, nose, and mouth. All she could hope to do was to make him more comfortable.

'My basket is only feet away,' she moaned. 'if only I could get to it—'

'There is nothing in your basket for me, sweeting,' he whispered hoarsely. 'But the rats will surely find good use for it.' The sound of raspy wheezing sputtered into a cough; Aldyth realized that he was laughing. Lung damage, she thought in despair. She ran her fingers over his face to see if the bones were sound, and his hand caught at hers.

'Where there is breath there is hope, love,' she said, struggling to believe it herself.

She squeezed his hand gently, then continued her examination. She heard him suck his breath in sharply, setting off another painful round of hacking. 'Your ribs—' she began.

'I know. Broken. Lungs, too. Don't waste your time on me. What about Roland?'

'He's dead,' she whispered.

'Poor Jehanne,' he murmured.

Aldyth found his pulse feeble but steady. 'Gandulf,' she warned, 'I'm going to sit you up so that your lungs don't fill and drown you in your sleep.'

'No, Aldyth,' he pleaded, ''twill only make it worse.' Ignoring his protests, she put her hands under his armpits and slowly lifted him into a sitting position. He cried out, and Aldyth felt him shudder and go limp.

'Gandulf?' Her voice echoed in the silence; he had lost consciousness. ''Tis for the best,' she thought grimly. Sirona would advise her to pray for quick death, the best ending she could expect. 'Please, my Lady,' Aldyth prayed fervently, 'don't let him die.'

She could do nothing but wait, and there was nothing to wait for but his death. Aldyth hugged her knees to her chest and cried into the heedless darkness. With Gandulf mercifully unconscious, there was no one to be brave for, only a lifeless corpse to watch her keen and only the rats to listen. She must have slept but had no idea how long, for there was no sun, no moon, no dawn breeze, no cockcrow to mark the passage of time.

Shifting to relieve her stiff joints, Aldyth felt a hand plop into her lap and woke with a start. 'Gandulf?' She reached for the hand; it was icy cold. Suppressing a scream, she forced herself to feel the face that the hand belonged to. She came to the shaven nape and knew the hand was Roland's. In dismay, she realized that she must do something before he stiffened; he was already taking up more than his share of space.

Aldyth stood on wobbly legs and stretched her arms as

high as she could. The pit was too deep – at least seven feet – to attempt that route of escape. Stretching her arms out to gauge the size of her prison, she jammed her fingers against the walls on either side and guessed that it was three feet by six feet. The dimensions of a grave, she thought morbidly, and in it there were one corpse, one near corpse, and herself; she could only wish she were dead.

'Forgive me, Roland,' she whispered, dragging his body to the corner opposite Gandulf's, an unnerving task in the pitch dark. Her footing was slick and uncertain; she could not see what she was stepping in, and it made her flesh crawl. She had intended merely to prop his corpse up out of the way, but on second thought she decided to strip his body. It was chill and damp; Gandulf would need whatever he could get to ward off the cold, even a dead man's tunic. When she unbuckled Roland's belt, she was surprised to feel his dagger still in its sheath. The poor man had never had the chance to draw it, a fact Lord Ralf had obviously overlooked. Aldyth fingered it thoughtfully, then tucked it behind his body. She would be glad for a quick release after Gandulf no longer needed her.

As she took inventory by feel, she came across something cool and yielding. With a squeak of alarm, then a cry of joy, she recalled the skin of springwater that she had dropped into the pit. That gave her something to work with – if she still had a patient. She felt Gandulf's neck for a pulse. It was still there, though much weaker than before.

With a new sense of purpose, Aldyth stripped Roland of his tunic and undertunic. First she would wash Gandulf, who was lying in his own filth; both his stomach and his bowels had emptied in the assault. She removed his over- and undertunics, then his soiled hose. Making rags of the clean ends of his hose, sparingly and carefully she dampened the rags and gently bathed him in the waters of the Crystal Spring. How like laying out a body for burial, she thought sadly. Storing the soiled bundle behind Roland's body, she was morbidly amused at her efforts at housekeeping. She covered Gandulf with Roland's tunic and wrapped him in the dead man's cloak. She stripped down to her torn shift and tucked her kirtle over Gandulf for added warmth.

Now there was nothing left to do but squeeze in beside Gandulf with the large skin of water. She took a sip, pressed her lips to Gandulf's, and, forcing his mouth open with her tongue, transferred the water from her mouth into his. She lost track of how many times she did this, but suddenly she became aware that his breathing had changed.

'Gandulf?'

'You don't give up,' he mumbled.

''Tis water from the Crystal Spring,' she explained. 'Can you drink, or shall I help?'

'Not now, Aldyth. It would just ... prolong the suffering.'

'Humor me,' she said, lifting the skin to his lips.

'Where is he?' grumbled Catherine, scowling.

'Wipe that look off your face,' scolded her mother. ''Tis most unbecoming.' As an afterthought, Lady de Broadford mused, 'I didn't see him break his fast this morning.'

'If Gandulf wants to start the day hungry, 'tis no concern of mine, but 'tis outrageous that he should keep us waiting like this. I won't have it!' snapped Catherine.

William de Broadford muttered, 'He knew we were to go hawking today.'

Lord Ralf adjusted his horse's cinch strap for the third time and was uncustomarily silent as the de Broadfords vented their anger. Once again he regretted the rash act with which he had placed himself in such an awkward position. 'Sometimes Gandulf forgets himself,' he said with uncharacteristic understatement.

'Beg your pardon, my Lord,' one of the grooms said hesitantly, 'but this morning I noticed that his horse was missing. He does like an early-morning ride.'

'So there!' said Lord Ralf with obvious relief, 'He has gone riding and will doubtless be waiting for us upon our return.'

Lord Ralf found the hawking a poor distraction, and the complications of his indiscretion the night before preoccupied him. Cathedra's disappearance was so very convenient, offering such a plausible explanation of Gandulf's absence, that he did not pause to wonder how she had come to be missing. She was not very valuable and was a small price to pay for even a minor reprieve. Even more convenient would be for the mare to show up in the possession of some minor brigand, whom he could blame for the death of his son. Should the horse chance to wander home, he decided, he would see that the beast was placed in the hands of some troublesome peasant, perhaps even the witch woman, and he could kill two birds with one well-aimed stone. Sirona had plagued him once too often, he decided, and even her power could not reach out from the grave.

When Gandulf had not presented himself by dinnertime, de Broadford requested a private audience with Lord Ralf. 'It's over, fitzGerald,' said de Broadford disgustedly. 'You and I both know that neither of our children is enthusiastic about this match, but I will tolerate only so much effrontery on behalf of the good name of de Broadford. Catherine swears she will go to a nunnery before she marries your son. I might still beat her into submission, but if he doesn't turn up by morning, I shan't bother.'

Lord Ralf opened his mouth to spew out an angry retort, then closed it again. He dared not admit that he had as good as killed his own son; he raged in bilious silence. Without a dowry, his castle would never be built, and without a son to marry off, there would be no hope of a dowry. As he brooded by the fire in the solar, he thought bitterly of Gandulf.

''Tis all Emma's fault,' he fumed. He had agreed to marry her only because of her lands. If he had been looking for a brood mare, he certainly would have chosen a different mate and sired sons of a better ilk. But Gandulf had bred true to his worthless dam. Things might have gone differently, thought Ralf sourly, had she shown the least bit of spirit for then she might have won his respect, if not his love. Even in bed, she would not respond to him; the less she responded, the more he lashed out, and the more he lashed out, the less she responded, until the only way he could move her was by violence. Most effective was violence wrought upon her son, but Gandulf was beyond his reach now. Then a smile twisted his features: Gandulf, dead or alive, could yet be used against her. News of his disappearance would breach even the abbey's cloistered walls. Emma would be frantic with worry and powerless to act.

'At least,' he thought, 'I will have some small satisfaction from this mess.'

Father Edmund roused himself from a troubled sleep to answer the summons rapped upon his door. As he stumbled through the dark, he assumed that it was Father Odo with the bishop's men or Lord Ralf with more questions about the Saxon fugitive. The last time he had been detained, the priest had been certain he would never again see the light of day, and then who would be left to speak out for his flock?

But when he opened the door a crack, he saw no torches, no horses, no soldiers; only one lone, lean figure, who whispered, 'You took your time answering.'

'Sirona!' he cried. The priest was so relieved to see the wisewoman that he forgot himself and embraced her, then quickly drew her inside. 'Sirona, where have you been? We feared never to see you again . . . you cannot imagine all that has come to pass.'

'Edmund,' she interrupted, 'you look hag-ridden. I want to hear all about it. But first, I must know: Is Brother Ansgar here?'

'No. We've had no word of him since he disappeared from the abbey.'

'Confound it!' she swore. 'He's gone to Rouen.'

'What's in Rouen?' asked Father Edmund, in puzzlement.

'King William.'

'What has Brother Ansgar to do with the king?' asked the bewildered priest.

'I'll tell you, Edmund,' she replied, 'but you'd best sit down first.'

Father Edmund sat and gasped at Sirona's revelations, shaking his head and crossing himself again and again. 'God guide him,' he said repeatedly, 'and protect him.'

After a sigh of resignation, Sirona too sat down heavily. 'Well, what has been happening around here, Edmund?'

'I hardly know where to begin,' he said, still thunderstruck by Sirona's confidence.

'Every day since you've gone, Mother Rowena has sent down a runner from the abbey to ask after you. It seems the de Broadfords have left in a tiff.'

'Is that not a blessing?'

'In itself it would be, but they left because Gandulf is missing. The two nuns Aldyth sent me to fetch are missing.' The priest paused and said grimly, 'And Aldyth is missing.' He shook his head. 'Now Brother Ansgar is missing as well?'

'How long missing?' she asked anxiously.

'Which one?' asked Father Edmund in dismay.

'Aldyth, of course.'

'They all seemed to disappear about the same time, the day before yesterday.'

The two old friends speculated over the mysterious comings and goings. The night was nearly gone when Sirona took her leave. As she reached her door, an owl hooted, its call out of place so far into dawn. The wisewoman froze, for the owl was the messenger of the Goddess, and she sensed it was a warning. Steeling herself, she stepped into the cold, dark hut. Something moved in the gloom.

'Aldyth?' she whispered doubtfully.

She was seized from behind with an iron grip that nearly lifted her off her feet, and Father Odo's gloating voice pierced the darkness: 'This time there will be no escape, witch. Your arrest is by order of Lord Ralf. And don't think that you can frighten these men with your tricks; they were handpicked by the bishop.' To one of the soldiers he commanded, 'Throw a blanket over her head.'

Sirona was trussed up and carried like a sack of grain to the outskirts of the village, where the blanket was removed. By the sullen light of predawn, she could see half a dozen men standing at their horses' bridles, covering their mounts' noses to keep them quiet. Seeing them, Sirona knew the whole episode had been too well planned to allow hope that someone might have seen her stolen away. She was lifted onto a horse and tied into place. As she was led off into the thinning darkness, she thought ironically, 'And now *I'm* missing.'

Sirona was surprised when her captors turned away from Castle Hill, until she realized that their destination must be Lord Ralf's hunting lodge. 'A well-laid plan,' she mused. 'The bishop's men will have no qualms about the "Witch of Enmore Green," and in the chase Father Odo need fear no interference from Dame Eulalia or Father Edmund.'

As they reined in their mounts before the lodge, Father Odo gloated, 'I'm not one of those Saxon pig boys you can frighten with your cheap tricks. Lord Ralf has finally given me a free hand to do what I will with you. I've waited years for this, and now you and the Saxon priest are playing into my hands. I know you're both involved with the murder of the king's man, or at least in hiding the fugitive, and one way or another I'll prove it. FitzGrip is loaning us his man Gauter, an expert at extracting information. When he's done at the garrison, he'll find work here. You can make it swift or draw it out, witch, but however it goes, we shall twist and turn a confession out of you.'

As the priest dismounted, his foot caught in the stirrup and he took a misstep, then fell to the ground, groaning in pain and clutching at his foot.

'Twist it, did you?' asked Sirona. 'Or turn it? I could give you something for that.'

The bishop's men, though strangers to both the area and the old woman, looked nervously at the fallen priest and then at each other. One of them crossed himself.

'Well, lads,' said Sirona, smiling crookedly, 'aren't you going to ask me in?'

Harold Godwinson stared at King William and wondered, 'Is it just another dream?' But it was no dream, for he had been stalking the man for a week. He had stolen a horse from a Norman manor near Ansty, ridden it to the coast, then sold it to pay his passage to France. Learning at an inn that William was on campaign in Mantes, he had gone there directly. He should have known what to expect; as an unwilling 'guest' at William's court twenty-three years before, Harold had gone to war with William against the count of Brittany and three years later against William in the fight for England. Age had not mellowed William, and he was making war no less cruelly than he had in his youth. One of the minor nobility in the Vexin, a province bordering on Normandy, had jested that William had grown too fat to sit ahorse. William had set out to prove him wrong by leading an army to the town of Mantes. He had burned the harvest in the fields and torched the town, including a church filled with unarmed peasants who had sought sanctuary there. Harold had arrived in time to be an unwilling witness to this holocaust, horrified and helpless, as he watched from the cover of the adjacent woods.

Harold knew that he could expect no mercy or even fair play from the engineer of this madness. Still he delayed indecisively, shadowing the king at a distance and passing for one of the unsavory scavengers and opportunists who followed the army. There were the pimps and whores, the cut-purses and beggars, and, most distasteful of all, the human vultures who hovered about the battlefield, preying upon the dead and dying. Harold spoke to no one and kept to the shadows, berating himself for his ill-advised impulse. Yet still he waited and still he watched.

At last his moment came. William rode his destrier through the rubble, still smoldering in the aftermath of the town's razing. Harold followed the cortege on foot, lurking in ash-strewn alleyways. Up ahead he heard a tumult as William flew into one of his notorious rages, turned upon his attendants, and screamed at them to disperse and leave him. They scuttled off, and there was only a haunting silence broken by the occasional crackling of embers. Harold slipped around the corner to see William staring sullenly after his departing retainers. Then the Conqueror looked back upon the destruction he had wrought and frowned. Harold guessed that he must be feeling remorse – if not for the suffering, then for the waste.

'There will never be a better time, and there may never be another chance,' Harold told himself. He stepped out of the shell of a burnt building, and his movement drew William's attention. Their eyes locked, and each man stared at the other. Harold's waist had thickened, his hair had silvered, and he bore many more scars, yet there was still a king's carriage beneath it all. But time had not been so kind to the duke of Normandy. He had grown fat and jowly. Though five years younger than Harold, he looked two decades older. The years and, perhaps, the weight of his sins had slumped his shoulders.

'Do you know me, William?' asked Harold quietly.

William's eyes bulged in horror. He put out a hand to ward off the apparition.

'No, William,' insisted Harold. 'There is something that must be settled between us.'

To Harold's consternation, William began to shout, his voice shrill with terror. 'Stay back! By Christ's blood, stay back!' he screamed, flailing wildly at Harold with his whip. William's destrier, unnerved by his master's frenzied panic, reared and plunged. William lurched forward, clutching desperately to keep his seat. 'I am dead!' he cried. 'He has come for me!'

At the king's cries, a horde of retainers rushed from the nearby alley where they been skulking until their master should recover from his fit of temper and recall them. While the king's attendants fought to seize the reins of his startled horse, a dozen gawking camp followers gathered like cockroaches scrambling out of the woodwork to view the commotion. Too stunned to run, Harold gaped dumbly, jostled by curious onlookers. By the time he could collect himself, he realized that flight would have made him conspicuous. His only hope lay in losing himself in the crowd.

William moaned and pointed directly at him. 'There, you fools!' he screamed. 'Can't you see? 'Tis Harold Godwinson!'

Once of his attendant knights said, 'But, sire, you see him everywhere.'

'No,' insisted William, 'this time he is real.' William's eyes rolled and, grasping in vain for the pommel of his saddle, he tumbled from his horse and landed in the dirt.

'My God!' said the knight, kneeling over the writhing king. Frowning, he scanned the milling spectators until his eye fell upon Harold. 'You there!' he commanded. 'Come here!'

Hemmed in by the crowd, Harold could only go forward to face his fate.

CHAPTER THIRTY-FOUR

If Aldyth strained her ears, she could distinguish the sound of footsteps in the hallway, and it occurred to her that this must be the changing of the guard. If she could recall how many times she had heard it, she could calculate how long they had been imprisoned. But all was a black and formless blur, and it seemed irrelevant in any case. Because hunger no longer gnawed away at her, she guessed that a week had passed. There was still some carefully rationed water in spite of Gandulf's insistence that she take a sip whenever she made him drink. That it had lasted this long was a gift of the Goddess. Hardly a waking moment went by when she did not thank the Lady for Her mercy. At first she had simply waited for Gandulf to die, wrapping herself in the cold comfort of the hidden dagger. Gradually she had realized that his pulse was stronger, his breathing less labored. Fearful of jarring his pain-racked body, she had merely kept a light hand on his leg, that he might feel her presence and to reassure herself that he had not grown stiff. Then he had awakened and bidden her lie beside him.

Hesitating, she had said, 'I fear I would jostle your poor broken ribs.'

'Come, sweeting,' he had insisted, 'and warm me.'

As she had slid in beside him, she was surprised to find his skin had lost its sickly clamminess. 'Tell me truly, Gandulf,' she said, 'you must be suffering terrible pain.'

'Not like before you came.'

''Tis the water of the Crystal Spring,' she declared. 'The

Goddess has spared you so that She might give us one last gift, this time together before we die. There is nothing to hold back for now,' she mused, 'no one else to consider, nothing to hide. Birth, blood, nationality: they mean nothing to me, Gandulf.'

'Death and darkness make equals of us all,' he agreed. 'Aldyth, I have wanted to hear you say that almost since the first time I saw you, but not at this cost.' Angrily he blurted, 'Bedwyn promised that he would take you away.'

'Oh, ho! So that's why he tried to whisk me away to Byzantium. Did you think you could just hand my bridle over to Bedwyn the way you gave Cathedra over to me?'

She heard him laugh softly. 'I must have been a fool to try. Will Bedwyn recover?'

'For all that he has suffered, Bedwyn will have only a broken nose and some scars, and he always said that a good scar impresses the ladies. As long as they don't catch up with him, that is; I sent him to the abbey to fetch your sister and stepmother.'

Bemused, Gandulf marveled, 'I have a sister ...' He imagined growing up with a sister. Why stop there? With a whole family of brothers and sisters, a father like Harold ...

As quiet descended, Aldyth listened to the drip of moisture on the cold, damp walls, felt the darkness seeping into her pores. The corpse, the blackness, the smothering closeness: suddenly it all connected, and she exclaimed, 'Oh, my Lady!'

'What?' asked Gandulf, his voice sharp with alarm.

'I just realized that I'm living the nightmare that has been haunting me for months.'

'Mildburh told me of your nightmares, but I didn't dare ask, matters being what they were between us. But, Aldyth, 'tis stranger than you think. I too have been haunted by the same nightmare. Sometimes you were with me, but then you were in all my dreams.'

'After all is said and done, our fates are inextricably entwined as our bones will be.'

'Like the ivy and the rose of Tristan and Iseult,' mused Gandulf. 'I'd have preferred a different ending, love. But though all may be done, perhaps all is not yet said.'

'What do you mean, Gandulf?'

He drew her into a warm embrace. 'Aldyth,' he said, 'marry me.'

'What?'

'Marry me. Grant the last wish of a dying man. What have we to lose? It will have to be a handfast wedding, seeing as how there is no priest and only one witness.'

'Poor Roland,' sighed Aldyth. 'Poor Jehanne. At least she has their baby to love.'

Gandulf kissed her forehead tenderly. 'That is more than I can give you, sweeting. But please say that you'll be my wife. And,' he added ironically, 'I will pledge to honor, cherish, love, and protect you for as long as we both shall live.'

'For whatever that's worth,' added Aldyth wryly.

The black humor of their situation struck them, and they laughed aloud. But when their laughter faded, an expectant silence filled the tiny chamber.

'Gandulf, you're serious, aren't you?'

'More serious than I have ever been about anything in my life.'

Aldyth, intrigued, replied at last, 'And I had always thought to die an old maid!'

'Now you shall die a young married maid!' he teased.

Up above the cockroaches ceased their scuttling and the rats their scavenging to listen to the unaccustomed sound of laughter drifting up from under the heavy oak planks.

In the nuns' parlor, Father Edmund fidgeted as he listened to the nuns at their morning prayers. He usually took pleasure in the music but today wished only for the service to end and Mother Rowena to come. The old priest did not know Mother Rowena very well, for Aldyth was the one who carried news between Enmore Green and the abbey, yet he had known her long.

At last she entered. 'Forgive the wait, Father,' she apologized. 'Your message did not come until after our service was begun.'

Father Edmund looked nervously at his hands. 'Sister, there

461

is a matter of great importance, a very delicate matter, and I do not know who else I can trust.'

Mother Rowena was often called upon to champion the causes of the peasants. 'Tell me, Father,' she said kindly.

'Aldyth Lightfoot has been missing for seven days now,' he blurted.

Mother Rowena started. 'Is there no clue to her whereabouts? What says Sirona?'

'Sirona has been missing for four days.'

The color drained from the nun's face as she considered aloud. 'That would explain why she hasn't answered my messages. I assumed she was gathering her herbs or attending a birth, but for four days?' Almost pleading, she continued, 'You are certain neither left word of her whereabouts? Perhaps with Aldyth's friends at the mill?'

'The night Sirona disappeared, we had made plans to meet the next day.'

'I was afraid of this,' whispered Mother Rowena, her trembling hands clutching at her rosary. Glancing sharply at the priest, she ventured, 'Lord Ralf?'

'Aldyth did go up to the garrison the night she disappeared, and Margaret tells me Gandulf is missing, too. When inquiring after Aldyth, I spoke with the wife of a Norman soldier, who has also disappeared. Even Gregory has vanished, and this time it can't be Sirona who has taken him, for he didn't go missing until yesterday.'

'Gregory?' asked Mother Rowena.

'My donkey,' explained the old priest. Visibly struck by a thought, he said, 'Could there could be any connection between Aldyth's disappearance and that of Gandulf?'

'Sit down, Father. Let me think.' Mother Rowena's mind was racing. Of course there was a connection. She wished she could believe that Aldyth and Gandulf had eloped, but she knew that Aldyth would never have deserted the village in such a time of need. The question was whether Lord Ralf had discovered the secret of Gandulf's parentage. If so, Gandulf was already dead. They were probably both dead in any case, victims to Lord Ralf's fury over the de Broadford affair. Abbess Eulalia and Sister Priscilla were the only ones who could have revealed Gandulf's secret, presuming that Sisters Gunhild and Edith had not fallen into Lord Ralf's hands. But if they had, the abbess would surely have heard of it. More likely, the nuns were lost in the depths of Cranborne Chase. She shook off that disturbing thought to focus on the immediate problem: Had Priscilla gone to Lord Ralf?

'Father, I will look into this and send word as soon as I know anything.'

She must act quickly. Could she trust the abbess? Mother Rowena's heart echoed the pounding of her footsteps on the flagstones as she hastened to seek out the abbess. Knocking on the door of the solar, where the abbess conducted her business, she was greeted by a clerk.

'Sister Rombolda,' said Mother Rowena, 'I must speak to Dame Eulalia immediately.'

'I'm sorry, but the abbess is going over her monthly accounts.'

'Please, Sister. It is very urgent.'

'The abbess is quite firm about her hours—' began the officious clerk.

'Sister Rombolda, what is it?' came the stern voice of the abbess. She stepped into the antechamber and saw Mother Rowena. Taking in the infirmarian's flustered appearance, the abbess said to her clerk, 'Sister Rombolda, go fetch a pitcher of ale.'

'Yes, my Lady Abbess,' said the nun in surprise. She curtsied and hurried to obey.

'Come in, child, and tell me what burdens you,' said the abbess to the infirmarian.

There was no time for formalities, and even as she settled herself on a bench across the table from Dame Eulalia, Mother Rowena launched into her story. The abbess sat silently frowning and drumming the tips of her fingers on the tabletop. Chilling doubt assailed Mother Rowena: perhaps she had misjudged the sympathies of the abbess.

Sister Rombolda returned. 'Thank you, Sister,' said the abbess. 'Now be so good as to summon Sister Priscilla. Rowena, you will wait in the solar.'

When Sister Priscilla arrived, her face was so sullen that the abbess had to disguise her distaste. 'Sister, do you remember our discussion about the evils of gossip?'

'Yes, my Lady Abbess,' Sister Priscilla admitted grudgingly.

'Then your aspersions against Sister Emma have spread no farther than this office?'

'Why is my silence so crucial?' Sister Priscilla's eyes narrowed. 'Unless you mean to do nothing to address this outrage.'

''Tis not for you to question my orders, nor to judge the sins of others.' In a tone that brooked no disobedience, Dame Eulalia added, 'I will hear no more of this, do you understand?'

'Yes, my Lady Abbess,' muttered Sister Priscilla bitterly.

'You may return to your duties now,' said Dame Eulalia sternly.

Sister Priscilla paused outside the abbess's apartments, her brow as dark as a lowering thundercloud, for she realized that the abbess meant to let all her carefully snared birds fly away free. Pursing her lips, she determined to go to Ralf fitzGerald. Perhaps he would put in a good word for her with the bishop and have her transferred to a house where Saxon upstarts were not favored at the expense of Normans. Once the decision was made, the exuberance of daring and righteousness propelled her. She stormed down the corridor, oblivious of the figure lurking in the deep shadow of a doorway. Her footsteps had hardly died away, and dust motes still danced in her wake, when Sister Emma emerged and hurried after.

Sister Arlette came out of the gatehouse when Sister Priscilla approached, but the irate nun pushed past the porter, snarling, 'Get out of my way, you fat fool.'

'Wait!' cried Sister Arlette, shaken by the venom in Sister Priscilla's voice. 'Where are you going? Have you permission to leave without an escort?'

Sister Priscilla never wavered from her course. After this act of disobedience, there would be no returning, but that knowledge spurred her on with a perverse exhilaration.

Moments later Sister Arlette, still flustered, saw a hooded man slip through the courtyard. He was small and stringy and dressed in castoffs. She wondered how he had gotten into the abbey and guessed that he had slipped in while she was gossiping with the scullion; she prayed that the stranger had done no mischief. Hastily she shooed him out, vowing to herself that it would not happen again. But, recalling the grim stance of the stranger, she was struck with a feeling of foreboding, and she crossed herself.

Aldyth drifted into and out of consciousness; it was difficult to tell the difference in that absolute darkness. There was only one constant that she was aware of, aside from the unchanging void of blind obscurity, and that was the comfort Gandulf provided.

'Are you awake, love?' asked Gandulf, feeling her stir.

'Aye.'

'Have you had time enough to think it over? Will you have me as your husband?'

'With all my heart,' she whispered ardently.

He chuckled softly and said, ''Tis bad luck for the groom to see the bride before the wedding, but we need not worry about that here.'

'At this point a little more bad luck won't make much of a difference,' she said.

'Then shall we pledge our troth?'

'Aye, my love.'

Gandulf felt for the leather thong that secured his boot around his ankle. With it he bound their wrists together. When he spoke, it was with a quiet intensity that mirrored the depth of his feelings. 'My dearest Aldyth, I love you more than life itself and look ahead to eternity by your side. May God bless our union and take us swiftly.' Fumbling in the dark, he added, 'A token. 'Tis far too big, but will you wear my ring?' So saying, he placed his gold signet ring upon her finger.

'Oh, Gandulf,' said Aldyth, her voice breaking under the weight of her emotion, 'I never thought to make such a vow, nor could I have in any other circumstances, yet I'd not change a thing. I've never concerned myself with Heaven or Hell, for the Lady has neither, but now I pray that God and the Goddess find a special place for us to bide. I've no ring, but' – she removed her pendant – 'this is my most valued possession; 'tis who I am, and I bestow it upon you, for today you become my flesh and blood.'

The silvery jingle of bells cut through the sinister blackness as she placed the trinket on its thong around his neck, then kissed him on the lips. They toasted each other with a sip of springwater. Gandulf, intertwining their fingers, began to whistle the song that had haunted Aldyth since that day on the Fairy hill. The sweet melody filled the chamber with light and warmth and colors. Aldyth's eyes grew teary, and she began to sing, her words and his whistled melody mingling, even as the ivy and the rose grew up from the graves of Tristan and Iseult to become one. She wondered at how fitting the song's words were. It was just a child's ditty, so she had never considered the meaning behind them.

> 'Rosy apple, lemon, pear,
> Bunch of roses she shall wear,
> Gold and silver by his side,
> I know who will be the bride.
>
> 'Take her by the lily-white hand,
> Lead her to the altar,
> Give her kisses one, two, three,
> Her heart will never falter.'

After the last notes had died away, Gandulf said, 'I'd never heard the words before.' Then he ventured, 'Do you suppose this is what the Fairies meant us to do?'

'Sirona says the signs are always there if only we know how to interpret them.'

'We depend too much upon our eyes. I see more clearly down here than ever before.'

She reached up and stroked his newly bearded chin. 'And I too, love.'

They were too weak to consider consummation, and even if Roland's presence had not been an inhibiting factor, he would have been a distraction, for he had begun to stink. But again Gandulf surprised Aldyth. Softly he kissed her lips, her eyes, her neck. Then, gently, he opened her shift and laid his head upon her chest, cupping one breast tenderly. Aldyth felt his tears run down her chest. Her own dropped to meet them as she ran her fingers through his hair. A strange wedding night, indeed.

Aldyth woke with a start and cried out. Immediately, Gandulf was holding her, rocking her, whispering soothingly. ''Tis all right, sweeting. Was it a nightmare?'

'Oh, no, Gandulf, it was the most beautiful dream. I dreamed we had been for some time married. We had a dark-haired daughter, and, oh, she had your copper eyes and your long dark lashes. They were wet with tears, for she had fallen and hurt herself. But you sat her on your lap and kissed each little fingertip. You tickled her chin and made her laugh, and her laughter was like the sound of Fairy bells in the breeze.' Aldyth had to stop to force back the sob that formed unwilled in her throat.

''Twas a fine dream, sweeting,' said Gandulf gently, pulling her head against his shoulder and smoothing her hair. 'Go back to sleep, and perhaps you can recapture it.'

As he pulled the cloak up around her shoulders, Aldyth snuggled into the crook of his arm. 'Can't you sleep, love?' she asked.

'I don't want to sleep, Aldyth. Holding my wife in my arms, loving her and being loved in return, I am at this moment living my dearest dream.'

CHAPTER THIRTY-FIVE

'I'd always feared to die alone,' Aldyth confessed. ''Tis a comfort to have you by my side, Gandulf. Your great fear, I know, has been of small spaces.'

'True enough,' he said thoughtfully. 'Even the garderobe seemed too close, but from the moment I faced Lord Ralf, all fear seems to have dropped away. Yet even had I known it would free me of my shackles, I don't think I'd have had the courage to confront him. Aldyth, how dared you curse him to his face, as I had always longed to do? How different my mother's life might have been had she been so daring. Or mine.'

'Sirona taught me that I had that power, but poor Emma had no one to teach her. You have a different kind of courage, Gandulf, harder to fathom and harder to muster. You walked through the front gates of Hell for a man you barely knew and could hardly stand.'

'I did it only so that I might charge Bedwyn to carry you to safety.' Chuckling, he added, 'As if you'd let anyone take charge of you! I can still see you storming into the bailey like a lioness, hair flying, eyes afire. From the first, you took my breath away.'

'You mean I knocked it right out of you, don't you?' she said, laughing weakly.

'That too,' he acknowledged. 'Sometimes here in the darkness,' he mused, 'I picture you sitting by Father Edmund's fire at the Christmas gathering, children in your lap and at your feet. You were not a lioness then but a contented cat.'

'If I had to choose a moment, Gandulf . . . oh, there are so many! I almost believed you were one of God's angels riding out of the storm on Christmas Eve, when I was like to lie down and die there in the street.'

'You must have been mad, Aldyth: What drove you out into that storm?'

'The same thing that drove you. I had to be alone to make sense out of my shifting world. Suddenly you had appeared in my life and drawn me out of my customary paths—'

'—and you called me away from my one well-traveled road.' It grew very quiet. 'I'm glad it is so dark in here, Aldyth, for I'd much rather you remember me as I was.'

'And you shall not have to see me withering away, Gandulf.' Hesitating, Aldyth ventured, 'It wouldn't have to happen that way; it could be very quick.'

'What are you saying?' Fear edged into his voice.

'Roland's knife. I was saving it to use after you were gone.'

'Suicide is a sin.'

'We're both going to die; we might as well go hand in hand.'

'I don't know, Aldyth,' he said doubtfully. Then he crushed her against his chest, as if to shelter her from such dangerous thoughts.

Aldyth had suspected that he might be reluctant, but more and more she felt the need to be master of her own fate, if only with this last pathetic gesture.

Sister Priscilla leaned back into Lord Ralf's chair, impatient to impart her ruinous knowledge. He had ridden to one of his outlying properties, but she had been told that he would be back at noon for his dinner, and she refused to leave until she had seen him. She had nowhere else to go; returning to the abbey was no longer an option. When the door opened, she rose to greet Lord Ralf but saw only a peasant, probably a servant come to prepare for his lord's arrival. She was resettling herself when the creature drew back its hood and she recognized Sister Emma, whose cold anger swept toward her like an icy wind off a frozen lake. Sister Emma glanced fleetingly about the solar that had once been her home but saw only that there was no one there to thwart her.

'Why have you cast off your habit?' asked Sister Priscilla in alarm.

'Why do you think?' asked Sister Emma coldly.

The sound of horses echoed up from the bailey, and Sister Priscilla taunted, ''Tis no matter. Lord Ralf is come home, you whore, and will be glad to hear the news I have brought.'

'Do you think I would allow you to tell him?'

'How can you stop me? 'Tis too late,' said Sister Priscilla, inching toward the door.

With surprising agility, Sister Emma darted between Sister Priscilla and the door, then advanced. 'I would spend the rest of eternity burning in Hell for my boy,' she said quietly.

Sister Priscilla's face grew ashen. She opened her mouth to scream, but her cries were choked off as Sister Emma lunged forward and her hands circled the informer's throat. Roughly Sister Emma slammed the other nun against the wall and, with the strength of desperation, throttled the life breath out of her. She stepped back, and Sister Priscilla dropped to the floor. Sister Emma looked down at the corpse, unable to believe herself capable of such a heinous act, yet so detached that she felt only grim satisfaction.

The hollow tread of footsteps coming up the stairs jolted her into action. She hurriedly dragged the other nun's limp body behind the curtained bed and hid there herself. Like Sister Priscilla, she had burnt her last bridge. Yet even as it collapsed beneath her, there was one final task to execute. She felt behind the headboard. It had been fifteen years; did Ralf still keep a knife hidden there for fear of assassins?

The door flew open with a resounding bang, and Lord Ralf tramped in to find himself confronted by a ragged little man holding his own knife. 'What the bloody Hell?' he shouted. 'Guard!' It took only a quick lunge and a snatch at the knife for him to subdue the weak creature. By the time his page and a man-at-arms came rushing in, the warlord had his odd little assailant in a choke hold.

'My Lord,' cried the soldier, 'we heard your summons.'

'Did you let this miserable creature into my room?'

'I let in no one but a nun who said she was here on very private, urgent business.'

Keeping a firm hold on his assailant's wrists, Lord Ralf turned the captive around for a better look. He had not laid eyes upon her since she had been packed off to the abbey; the hair that framed her face had grown wispy and gray, but there was no mistaking her identity. The nun they had admitted, he reasoned, had been his wife, though what she was doing in this outlandish costume eluded him. Still he relished the possibilities of the situation. 'Never mind,' he told his attendants. 'Leave us.'

As his men withdrew, Lord Ralf flung the knife to the floor. 'This is amusing, Emma,' he mocked. 'What are you doing here? Never mind, I'm glad you've come; there's something I'd like to show you. Shall we take a walk to the undercroft?'

He turned his back, never suspecting that the lamb might bite. Emma snatched up the discarded knife and, with all her strength, plunged it into his back. Groaning, he fell to the floor, then heaved himself onto his side to stare up at her, incredulous. Panicked that he might yet live, Emma jerked the knife back out and began to slash at him wildly. He fought to pry the knife from her fingers but, weakened by his wounds, found her strength nearly equal to his. When she leaned over to bite the hand that held her, Ralf seized her tunic with his other hand and gave it a jerk, upsetting her balance. Caught off guard, she loosened her grip, and before she could recover herself, Ralf twisted her wrist to turn the knife against her, driving the blade between her ribs. Then he rolled over and gasped, 'You've killed me, you silly bitch.'

Her head fell back onto the floor, and a trickle of blood ran down from the corner of her mouth. 'Yes,' she choked. 'I only wish I'd thought of it sooner.'

'Why?' he cried, knowing that she could not know what he had done to Gandulf. He seized her by the collar and pulled her face close to his. 'Why?' he demanded again.

'To protect my son,' she whispered.

'You stole him away from me in the cradle. He could have been mine,' spat Ralf.

'No, Ralf, he was never yours,' she said hoarsely, the words rattling in her throat.

He looked down and saw his lifeblood slowly pooling on the floor with hers, and he thought how ironic it would be if it were only in death that their blood had truly blended, rather than in their lineage, as he had always supposed. Emma's eyelids drooped, and her head sagged. He had to know for certain. He gave her a vicious shake to rouse her.

'What do you mean?' he insisted, a long-suppressed doubt creeping into his voice.

Her eyes flicked open. When she spoke, her voice was faint, but it carried a note of triumph. 'Do you recall the summer we spent at the English court? The next spring ... Gandulf was born, the son of a man whose boots you aren't fit to lick.'

'I don't believe it,' he said, though without conviction.

''Tis true,' she gasped. 'And do you know who the boy's father is?'

He pulled himself up onto his elbow and stared down at her.

'Harold Godwinson,' she gloated. But she had only an instant of satisfaction.

'He'll be joining us soon, Emma,' he rasped. 'I've killed your bastard. He lies dying in the oubliette, and not a soul knows it. He'll die unshriven and go straight to Hell.'

Her eyes widened in horror. Weakly she screamed, 'Help! Gandulf!'

She summoned her last reserves in an attempt to drag herself to the door. But Ralf snatched the knife from between her ribs. She shrieked in agony as he plunged it into her side again. The exertion was too much; he fell upon her in a tangle of bleeding limbs.

The page posted outside knocked at the door. Receiving

473

no response, he opened it a crack. 'Sweet Jesus!' cried the lad. 'Robert! Come quickly!'

The guard burst past him into the room and stared incredulously. Kneeling beside his master, he turned Lord Ralf over to see his glazed eyes staring blankly at the ceiling.

'He's dead,' said Robert, and he seized the ragged intruder by the collar. 'Who are you?' he demanded. 'Why did you do this?'

The assassin whispered, 'My son . . .' and slumped lifeless in the soldier's grip.

'We won't get any answers from him,' said Robert to the page, releasing his hold on the small corpse and letting it drop to the floor.

'What did he say?' asked the boy, distastefully stepping way from the spreading pool of blood.

'I don't know,' replied the guard, wiping his bloodied hands on the peasant's tunic. 'It must be some crazed rogue with a grievance against Lord Ralf.'

'Well, each one is as dead as the other,' said the page without a hint of sorrow in his voice. No one would mourn for Ralf fitzGerald except, perhaps, King William, who would spare a moment's regret for the loss of a good warrior.

Robert went to wash the blood from his hands in the basin on the side table. 'Oh, my God!' he cried, catching sight of the nun's goggle-eyed corpse on the floor beside the bed. He backed away in horror, crossing himself. 'Lord Ralf has killed a nun!'

'God forgive him,' gasped the page, also making the sign of the cross.

Aldyth lay in Gandulf's arms, fingering Roland's sheathed knife. She waited grim-faced but determined for Gandulf to rouse himself and inform her of his decision. She would not attempt to sway him, for this was clearly a choice he must make for himself. But she knew she was losing the ability to think clearly. She simply could not bear the thought of going mad here, with Gandulf to witness and suffer through it.

Staring vacantly into the unremitting blackness, Aldyth was

surprised to see what seemed to be color, until she decided that it must be spots and dizziness brought on by hunger. But the blur grew brighter and took on shape, like the light of a candle – no, not a candle, but a flickering flame, and it was growing, filling the tiny chamber with a pale blue light, like a will-o'-the-wisp. Aldyth watched with interest as the light slowly took form. Madness had finally descended, she thought clinically, but what a fascinating hallucination. The shimmering light condensed to assume the form of a man, a Saxon and a nobleman by his dress. Aldyth studied her vision with a curious detachment, then jumped in surprise when he actually spoke to her. 'Daughter,' he said quietly.

'Father?'

He nodded and held out his hand to Aldyth. Had he come for her?

'Give me the knife,' he ordered.

'I need it,' she told him, hugging it to her breast. If only she could think; there were so many questions she wanted to ask. Who was he? What had happened to him? Where was her mother? But Aldyth could only stare, held captive by his kindly gaze.

'Give me the knife,' he repeated, his voice gentle but commanding obedience.

Aldyth tore her eyes away to look at the knife, the blade glinting blue in the specter's light. Stubbornly she refused, unwilling to surrender her only means of escape.

'Come, child,' he coaxed. It was the compassion in his eyes that compelled her to relinquish the knife. As he took it, his fingers touched hers, and Aldyth felt a wave of warmth wash over her. 'Brave girl,' he whispered. 'Hold fast.'

Before she could react, the light was fading, the darkness closing in. 'Wait!' she screamed. 'Father, don't leave me! Please take me with you!'

Arms of flesh and bone encircled her. Gandulf crooned, 'Hush, now, love. 'Tis over.'

'Not yet!' Aldyth pleaded. 'Come back!'

She wailed bitterly and clung to Gandulf, her only link to a world of sunlight and humanity, her steadfast anchor to sanity. 'I have gone mad at last,' she mumbled.

'Then we are both gone mad,' said Gandulf.

'You saw him too?'

Gandulf's awed whisper resonated across the tomblike silence. 'Aye,' he said softly. 'When I was in London, he was the angel who came to me in my dream.'

A thunderstorm raged. Within Ralf fitzGerald's hunting lodge, the bishop's men waited for Sheriff fitzGrip and Gauter, anxious for them to get on with their business and be done with it, for the crone made them nervous. She was their prisoner, yet she smiled at them like a cat toying with a mouse. A savage gust of wind rattled the shutters and whistled through the cracks in the door, setting the hearth fire leaping wildly.

'Do you hear horses?' asked the sergeant. 'Guillaume,' he ordered the one sitting closest to the door, 'see if anyone is coming.'

Guillaume cracked open the door, then forced it shut against the screeching wind and rain. ''Tisn't horses,' he replied, shivering. ''Tis the hounds of Hell at their wild hunt.'

'It must have been thunder,' replied Roger, who sat toasting a bit of hard cheese over the hearth fire. 'You're letting the witch make a fool of you. Don't listen to her tales.'

'I've an uneasy feeling is all,' said Guillaume, who had begun to pace.

'You and your old mother,' scoffed the sergeant. 'Go check on the witch.'

Guillaume turned his back to conceal his disgruntled scowl but could not hide his hesitation at starting up the dark, narrow staircase to the room where Sirona was kept. He unlocked the door at the top of the stairs, and the sight that met his eyes was hackle-raising. The hag was standing with her craggy face to the tiny window. In a flash of blue lightning, he could see her arms upraised, as if she herself were directing the storm. Her silver hair, blue in the storm light, flew back in the ever-rising wind like the waves of

476

the sea, and she chanted words in a language Guillaume had
never heard. He was backing out of the room when thunder
boomed and set the floorboards shaking. He screamed and
fled and, in his panic, tripped over his own feet and went
tumbling down the narrow stairs.

'Thank God you're here!' said Gilbert to Mother Rowena and
Sister Aethelswith. 'No one knows what to do. Lord Gandulf
is missing, and when we sent for the sheriff, his wife said that
he'd gone with Gauter to meet Father Odo, but no one has
seen Father Odo either. At least now we've someone to say
a prayer for the dead, God help them.'

As the nuns hurried across the bailey after Gilbert, Sister
Aethelswith whispered to Mother Rowena, 'I am glad 'tis not
only Saxons who are vanishing.'

Up the stone steps they went and into the great hall. No
one seemed to be mourning; on the contrary, there was an air
of suppressed festivity, as on one of the more solemn holidays.
William CloseFist looked up to see them enter and broke away
from a knot of rumormongers to pounce upon them. 'At last!'
he said, as if they had dallied along the way and arrived with
wreaths of flowers in their hair. 'The bodies are upstairs.'

'Have they been laid out?' asked the infirmarian.

'No, they are just as we found them. Circumstances
being what they are,' explained the steward, 'we thought a
representative from the abbey should bear witness.'

Mother Rowena nodded. 'We brought a winding sheet
for each of them, but we'll require warm water and linens,
and we'll need our wax warmed to close up their bodies.'

'Margaret!' bellowed the steward. Margaret hurried out of
the pantry and curtsied to the nuns. 'See that the sisters are
furnished with whatever they require,' he ordered.

Sister Aethelswith followed Margaret into the pantry, and
Mother Rowena followed William CloseFist up the stairs. As
the steward had warned, the grisly scene had been left largely
untouched. At a glance Mother Rowena's unspoken fears
were confirmed: one of the bodies was that of Sister Priscilla.
From the moment word of her flight had been spread by the

scandalized porteress, the infirmarian had worried and waited. She prayed briefly for the renegade nun's soul and at greater length that she had died before doing any harm.

The nun's body had been respectfully laid on the bed. But crumpled on the floor was the body of Lord Ralf, still slumped over a third body, which had not even been mentioned in the dispatch to the abbey. The third corpse wore the rags of a Saxon peasant. Mother Rowena leaned over for a closer look, then gasped as she realized that it was no stranger. Mistaking her cry of surprise for revulsion, the steward observed, ''Tisn't pretty.'

'What happened here?' asked Mother Rowena.

'No one knows for certain. But Lord Ralf seems to have killed the nun. She had some news that she made a pretty mystery of, and perhaps it was not to Lord Ralf's liking. His temper has been getting worse, especially these last weeks. This fellow must have heard the ruckus. How he got in we don't know, but he seems to have died defending her.'

'Yes,' Mother Rowena quickly agreed. 'He is one of ours and deserves a Christian burial. Let me take the body back to the abbey, and we'll bury it there.'

William CloseFist was glad to release the body into her custody, thereby saving himself the trouble of procuring a third winding sheet and the expense of a pauper's burial. Mother Rowena's next concern was to return Sister Emma's body to the abbey unidentified, both to spare Gandulf and to preserve the abbey's good name. To accomplish that, she alone must be the one to wind her body into its grave cloth.

'William, would you be so good as to tell Sister Aethelswith to have the water and wax brought up by a page? She is young, and I would spare her the sight of the carnage.'

The steward nodded and left, leaving Mother Rowena to her grim task.

Margaret settled Sister Aethelswith by the fire and retired to the pantry. As soon as she had heard the dreadful news about Lord Ralf, she had taken advantage of the confusion to sneak down into the undercroft. The disappearance of the Saxon prisoner had been rumored; it was believed that Lord Ralf had accidentally slain him in an overzealous interrogation. No one knew why Lord Ralf had continued to post guards, but the suspicion was that the Norman lord was fearful of the king's wrath should William learn he had done away with a valuable witness. Margaret had her own suspicions. With Lord Ralf dead, and as there seemed no sense in guarding an empty cell, the sentries had abandoned their duty to gossip in the great hall. But she was certain that Aldyth and Gandulf were imprisoned below. Picking up a footstool and a candle, she tiptoed down to the deserted undercroft. Her candle fluttered as she hurried down the long, vaulted hallway to the three cramped cells at the end. She checked them all. Standing on her footstool, she held her candle up to the peephole in the door and peered into the darkness. She whispered their names and waited for an answer. The rats scurried among the rushes, but no answer came to her, except her own conclusion; if Aldyth and Gandulf were shackled in a dark corner of one of those cells, they were beyond help. She returned to the pantry in despair.

She wiped her eyes and tried to concentrate long enough to plan a funeral feast. Normally there would have been a new lord to give orders. The steward, who was always an unpleasant fellow, and more so now that he had assumed command, was busy with the bodies. She should lay on provisions to feed the court of inquest that would likely follow, but she could think only of Gandulf and Aldyth, and she buried her flushed face in her hands.

'Got anything good to eat?' came a cheeky voice.

With a cry of delight, Margaret looked up to see Aelfric, dirty-faced and white with fatigue. 'Where have you been these many days?' she scolded, sweeping him into her arms, 'and me half out of my wits worrying after you?'

'You needn't look so distraught, Margaret,' he said, wriggling like a minnow to squirm out of her embrace. 'I always turn up sooner or later.'

'Oh, lad, if only you knew! I fear the worst for Lord Gandulf and Aldyth.'

'We can mend all that,' said Aelfric, 'but there's no time

479

to waste if we're to find them alive. Down to the dungeons,' he said, grabbing her hand and dragging her along.

"'Tis no use, lad,' she wailed. 'I've already been down there. I could find neither hide nor hair of them. Besides, even if they were down there, the cells are all locked.'

Aelfric reached into the pouch that hung from his waist and pulled out an iron ring jingling with massive keys. 'Then let's use these before they're missed,' he suggested.

'That's the last of the springwater,' said Aldyth, tossing aside the empty skin.

'Another dead soldier,' joked Gandulf.

'It won't be long now,' said Aldyth.

They drifted into and out of light sleep, but the sound of approaching footsteps startled them out of their stupor. Up above they heard the clank of keys. Had Lord Ralf come to finish them off? Or perhaps Gauter had finally arrived. They tightened their embrace.

A thin line of orange light shot through a crack over-head. Then came the sound of rats scurrying for cover. Finally they heard the heavy wooden lid scraping against the top edges of the pit, accompanied by the grunts of those wrestling with its great weight. They heard Aelfric's voice. 'Look, there's her basket.' Then, warily, 'I smell carrion.'

A woman's sob followed.

'One of them might yet be alive,' said Aelfric. 'Let's give it another try.'

The sound of wood scraping on the flagstones echoed into the depths, and torchlight flooded in at the foot of the pit. Margaret's piercing scream drove the prisoners into the darkest corner of their cell. "'Tis Roland,' she sobbed, 'and he's dead as a doornail. Tell Gilbert to fetch a ladder, and we'll fish the poor man out.'

'Elfling,' called Aldyth weakly from her dark corner. 'Over here.'

A pair of startled gasps was followed by an instant of shocked silence. Then came an eager response, accompanied by frenzied efforts to remove the heavy cover. A sudden,

more blinding light shone down as Aelfric passed the torch
directly over them.

'Aldyth! Gandulf! They're alive!'

CHAPTER THIRTY-SIX

'God's mercy!' came a cry of horror and disgust. Faces peered over the brink of the pit, backlit by torches.

'Don't stand there gawking,' came Aelfric's sharp rebuke. 'Get them out of there.'

From the moment the ladder arrived, everything was a blur. Margaret called down words of comfort as Roland's body was passed up to make room for another rescuer to descend. Aldyth felt Gandulf's arms peeled from her as he was carried away. She heard him calling out her name, but it was Gilbert who hoisted Aldyth half over his shoulder and made his wobbly way up the ladder. She was too dazed to register the pity on his face, but not so dazed that she could bear the sight of the living hell from which they emerged; she screwed her eyes shut until she felt flagstones beneath her feet.

'There, you can see she's all right,' said William CloseFist to Gandulf, barely masking his impatience. He tried to hurry his master away, but Gandulf shrugged off the steward's grip, elbowed his way to Aldyth, and put his arms around her.

'Get Lord Gandulf a cloak,' snapped the steward. 'He's naked as a new-hatched chick.'

A cloak was draped over Gandulf's shoulders. Aldyth, dressed only in her torn shift, felt like Eve emerging naked from the Garden of Eden, and she pulled away from Gandulf.

'Cover her,' came Gandulf's imperious command, and another cloak was produced. Gandulf snatched the cloak and laid it around Aldyth's shoulders himself.

She blushed and averted her gaze. 'We must look a sight!' she whispered.

Gandulf lifted her chin and told her, 'You look beautiful.'

Servants circled like vultures, awaiting orders from their new master. Gandulf, his arm protectively about Aldyth's shoulders, tried to shield her against the tide of demanding humanity and unrelenting stares. After unbroken silence and unending darkness, the echoing voices and blaze of light were overwhelming.

'We sent for fitzGrip,' said William CloseFist.

'You know about Lord Ralf, of course,' said Wulfstan the Reeve.

'What about Lord Ralf?' asked Gandulf sharply.

'I'm getting your father's papers in order,' the steward assured him. 'As if things weren't bad enough, we have just received word that King William is dying. We'll have to deal with his son Red William, and he'll be in an even greater muddle than we.'

'We've sent to the abbey,' said Margaret, 'and they're laying out your father's body.'

'Lord Ralf is dead?' asked the heir apparent. 'How? Does my mother know?'

Before Gandulf could question further, he was awash in a babble of counterquestions: 'Can you stand up?' 'Do you want a bath?' 'Are you hungry?'

Gandulf shrugged off the barrage of queries, and William Closefist took it upon himself to call, 'Hugh! Some caudle for his lordship.'

The page pushed ahead to order the thin but nourishing honey pottage to be prepared.

Then came the inevitable tumble of prying questions, more difficult to answer. How had Gandulf gotten into the oubliette? Why was the peasant girl in there? And Roland?

No answers could be had from the dazed and shaken pair, confused by the chaos after having been so long in the dark, the quiet, the solitude. But clearly Lord Ralf had snapped, killing a nun and torturing his own son, as well as the gentle healer of Enmore Green. It was whispered that Sirona had driven the Norman warlord mad with her magic.

Aldyth felt Gandulf wrenched away from her, but Margaret was there to take her under her wing. Into the bailey went the straggling procession, where even the cloud-filtered sunlight of early afternoon dazzled the newly released prisoners' dark-weakened eyes. Then they proceeded up the stairs to the great hall.

Now in her own province, Margaret was torn between her duty to her lord and her affection for Aldyth, as she was surrounded by a horde of demanding servants.

'A towel and hot water, Margaret!' 'Bread for my lord!' 'A razor to shave him!'

Aelfric ushered Aldyth into the pantry and sat her down on a stool. On his face there was no smirk, no grin, only compassion. 'Oh, elfling!' she cried. Flinging her arms around his skinny waist, she laid her head upon his chest and sobbed the bitter tears that she had hoarded throughout her dreadful confinement. Awkwardly, the lad patted her shoulder and looked about, daring anyone to say a word.

Aeliva, the maidservant on duty, told Margaret, 'Take care of the girl; I'll send these people off.' Aeliva filled the orders and satisfied their demands, and at last they were gone.

Wulfwynn, the scullery maid, said to Aldyth, 'Aeliva and I will carry the water up for Lord Gandulf's bath, but I've left some for you; you'll be wanting a wash.'

Aldyth stood naked in a big basin as Margaret scrubbed away the filth of the oubliette, while Aelfric held up a towel to protect her from prying eyes. When Aldyth was dressed in a borrowed shift and kirtle and bundled into a blanket, Aelfric spooned strengthening caudle into her while Margaret crumbled bread crusts into a bowl.

'Sirona!' exclaimed Aldyth like one waking from a dream.

'How can I tell you, lass?' cried Margaret. 'She's not been seen for days.' The buxom cook leaned forward and whispered, 'I fear Lord Ralf had her done away with.'

'I know where she is,' said Aelfric smugly. ''Tis Sirona who sent me to find Aldyth.'

'You've spoken to her? Where is she? When did you see her? Is she safe?'

'When Sirona disappeared a week ago,' the lad explained, 'I suspected Father Odo had something to do with it. I kept watch, and when I saw him going to Sceapterbyrig by way of Enmore Green, I followed him into the bailey, where I heard him send for fitzGrip and Gauter. With Bedwyn gone, who else but Sirona would he need them for? I couldn't find Father Edmund, so when Father Odo left the garrison, I pinched Gregory and followed.'

'Where to?

'To Lord Ralf's hunting lodge.'

'How did you manage to speak with her? Wasn't she under guard?'

'The soldiers were all camped in the undercroft. I found Sirona trying to squeeze out of a small window upstairs in the back of the house, and she waved me over. She told me to go home and get you out of the oubliette, then come back for her.'

'How did she know we were in the oubliette?' asked Aldyth.

'She knows everything,' whispered Margaret in awe.

'Then she should've known that she wouldn't fit through that tiny window.'

'What do you mean, Aelfric?'

'When I left, the king's men were trying to pull her back inside, but she was pretty well wedged. She knows curses that would make me blush.'

The horses pounded out a steady rhythm at a ground-eating pace. It was a comfort, for the sound made it difficult for Aldyth to think. The caudle had been strengthening, and so had the water from the Crystal Spring, but she was still terribly weak; it was only at her stubborn insistence that Margaret and Aelfric had allowed her to accompany the lad on his rescue. CloseFist would never have permitted them to petition Gandulf at this time, nor could they in good conscience have requested that Gandulf involve himself in a mission verging on treason. So they had taken the horses – stolen them, actually – but Aldyth was certain that the new lord would grant them pardon.

Aldyth had always been skeptical of Sirona's claim that her week-long fasts increased her energy and sharpened her thoughts, but after her emergence from the oubliette, if she was light-headed, never had she felt so clear-minded. ''Tis over between us,' she thought, 'and as much a crumbled ruin as the Starlit Path.' Gandulf was a Norman lord now, and she was still just a Saxon peasant. Their fantasy had carried them through their ordeal, but there would be no place for her in his life now. And she could still serve the Goddess. Was it not the water of the Crystal Spring, the goodness of the Goddess, that had seen them back into the light of day after ten days in the oubliette? She reasoned that the Goddess had kept her alive to serve and spared Gandulf to be a good lord to Her people. Nothing had happened in the oubliette that could not be undone, and she would save herself the humiliation and Gandulf the discomfort of having to dismiss her from his life. No matter what Gandulf wanted or thought he wanted, he was obligated to obtain the king's permission to marry. The old king had built his army and his fortune through the advantageous marriages of his nobles and would never allow one of his barons to marry a penniless, landless Saxon peasant. She did not even have a name to add legitimacy to his bloody claim of ownership. Why should the son be any less shrewd than his father?

Aldyth dwelt on such thoughts until she could think no more. By the time they arrived at the clearing surrounding the hunting lodge, her only thought was to keep her seat. Aelfric exclaimed under his breath, and Aldyth gasped at the sight of a pair of legs dangling out of the second-floor window at the back side of the lodge.

'Wait here!' said Aelfric to Aldyth. Kicking his mount into a gallop, the lad thundered across the clearing to rein in his horse beneath the window. By the time he had reached the lodge. Sirona was hanging from the window ledge by both hands.

'Good,' she called over her shoulder to Aelfric, 'you brought horses.'

Reaching up, Aelfric grasped first one ankle and then the

other to guide her feet to a firm footing on the horse's back. The wisewoman slid down to sit pillion behind him. When she was settled, Aelfric started toward cover of the wood. But the guards had heard his approach. Father Odo and his men rushed around the corner of the undercroft in time to see their prisoner fly. 'See you in church!' called Sirona over the rising winds.

The priest shouted after her, 'I'll see you in Hell first!'

Even as Father Odo watched them gallop off, the overcast skies blackened. His face darkened to match the thunderheads, his fury raged like the roiling clouds. He yelled to the bewildered soldiers, 'Don't just stand there; go after them!'

They hesitated, looking first at the enraged priest, then back at the tumultuous sky.

''Tis the witch,' said Guillaume anxiously. 'She's calling up another storm.'

'We told you she sent him flying down the stairs with her magic,' said Roger, another guard.

''Twas a miracle my neck wasn't broken,' Guillaume added.

'Come with me, or you'll answer to the king as well as the bishop before I've done with you!'

Guillaume limped back into the lodge. Roger was the first to follow; the others trailed after.

'She has bewitched you!' cried the priest. 'As God is my witness, I shall not rest so long as she lives!' He seized the last of the retreating guards by the sleeve and shouted, 'If you aren't man enough to come with me, then saddle the fastest horse!' And he gave the man a cuff on the ear to hurry him along. Even as he leapt into the saddle, he felt the first bone-chilling raindrops splash against his face.

'Jehanne is here,' announced William CloseFist, clearly disdainful of the way in which Gandulf was conducting his affairs. He had already chided Gandulf for allowing the servants too much latitude, explaining 'It encourages insolence.'

'Jehanne,' said Gandulf, rising from a table spread with

documents to greet her in this, the last of his most pressing business.

Jehanne, her eyes red-rimmed and her face blotched and puffy, entered and curtsied. It had been only a few chaotic hours since their release, but it would have taken merely minutes for news of Roland's fate to travel across the bailey to the servants' quarters. Gandulf took the widow's elbow and ushered her to a seat by the fire.

'Jehanne, you've heard about Roland.'

She nodded and raised her hands to her face, unable to control her tears.

'He conducted himself bravely to the very last. I owe him my life, yet can never repay him for his loyalty. I shall do my best to make amends to his widow and child.'

Jehanne ran her sleeve under her nose and looked up.

'A perpetual candle will be lit for him and prayers said for the repose of his soul.'

'Thank you, my Lord. 'Tis very good of you.' Jehanne rose to leave.

'Wait, Jehanne, I'm not finished,' he said. 'I intend to arrange, if you wish it, for you to have a position with Margaret, who has been promoted to head of the kitchen.'

'Oh, my Lord.' It was a better living and a more prestigious job than that of laundress.

'As for your child,' he continued, 'how is she called?'

'Genevieve, my Lord.'

'Genevieve,' he repeated, nodding. 'When she is of a proper age, she will become one of my wife's ladies-in-waiting.'

Jehanne gasped. In her eyes, that was almost the same as being ennobled. 'Oh, my Lord. To Lady Catherine?'

'No,' said Gandulf, taken aback. 'To Lady Aldyth.'

Gandulf caught CloseFist's look of disgust, and he shot a quelling glance at his steward over Jehanne's head. 'Thank you, that will be all, Jehanne. Please see Margaret about being fitted for clothing suited to your new station.'

'Aye, my Lord, and God bless you!' she said, curtsying and hurrying off.

'Now that you've shown yourself for an easy mark,'

commented the steward dryly when she had gone, 'every-one with a hard-luck story will be up here looking for a handout.'

'Perhaps you're right, William,' said Gandulf thoughtfully. 'I ought to keep the servants in their place. What would you recommend for an insolent thief of a servant?'

William smiled. He would soon have this whelp totally dependent on him and would be able to line his own pockets with more than a few silver spoons. 'Make an example,' he urged. 'A good beating and a boot down the road.'

'Don't you think that's harsh?' asked Gandulf.

''Tis the only way they will learn,' said the steward firmly.

'Hmmm,' said Gandulf. 'Perhaps you're right, but I think I'll spare you the beating and show you only my boot. You may go to the kitchen and ask Margaret for some provisions for travel. Then get out of my sight and off my land and never show your face here again. If you do, I will assume that you have come to claim the beating owed you.'

William's face flushed crimson. This was not the same man who had gone down into the pit. The steward took Gandulf at his word, bowing his grudging respect and leaving.

'Aldyth,' mumbled Gandulf wearily, wincing from the pain in his side as he sat down. He longed to know how she was faring after her ordeal. He had seen Margaret lead her off, needful of the care only another woman could give. But now he needed her. He called in a crop-haired page. 'Hugh, find Aldyth Lightfoot and bring her to me at once.'

It was an age before the boy returned to report. 'My Lord,' he said, 'Mistress Lightfoot is nowhere to be found.' In a flash, Gandulf seized his cloak and pushed past the bewildered boy, tearing down the solar stairs and into the great hall.

The storm's fury picked up. They stopped to calm their terrified horses, but dared not bide, for Father Odo and his men would not be far behind. Lightning seared the sky so close they could smell the brimstone. Aldyth, who had begun her errand on the brink of exhaustion, swayed in the saddle. 'Set me down,' she pleaded. 'I'm holding you back.'

'Nonsense,' said Sirona. 'Aelfric, ride pillion with Aldyth and give my horse a rest.'

Aelfric leapt like a squirrel to the other horse's back and seated himself behind Aldyth, that he might steady her or save her from a fall if need be. Branches torn loose from the trees whipped the path. The horses' wet manes slapped at their riders' faces, and the riders were barely able to keep their frantic mounts under control.

Aelfric shouted, 'Sirona, the last time I saw you, you were wedged in the window like a pig in a hedge. How did you manage to get out?'

'Last night I found a knife hidden in the straw of my pallet,' replied Sirona over the whistling wind. ''Twas just what I needed to pry off that cursed window frame and widen the opening enough to slip out. Surely it was a gift of the Goddess,' added the wisewoman.

'Or an angel,' whispered Aldyth.

Wild-eyed, Gandulf tore into the pantry and whirled Margaret around to face him.

'Where is she?' he roared.

For the first time in her life, Margaret was afraid of him. 'You won't be angry?'

'I shall be very angry if you don't tell me where she is,' came his heated reply.

'She has gone to your father's hunting lodge with Aelfric to rescue Sirona.'

'How could you let her go?' he bellowed. 'What could she be thinking of?'

'She says to tell you—' Margaret burst into tears, flinging her apron over her head.

Tearing the apron away from her face, Gandulf shouted, 'What? Out with it!'

'She said not to come after her, that she'd return the horses by Aelfric. She told me to give you this.' Margaret held out the golden signet ring, his wedding token to Aldyth.

Groaning, he released Margaret and stormed out through the doorway at a run. Rounding the corner outside the pantry, he crashed into a warm body. Even as he went flying, Gandulf was certain he had found Aldyth in the same way he always seemed to. But to his horror, he discovered that he had floored a matronly nun.

'Mother Rowena, forgive me,' he stammered. He tried to rise to his feet but found the thong around his neck entangled with the crucifix that the nun wore around her neck.

'Gandulf!' exclaimed Mother Rowena frantically. 'Sister Aethelswith just told me you'd been found, thank God! But where is Aldyth?'

'That's a good question,' he muttered, kneeling before her as he tried to disentangle their pendants. But haste made him clumsy, and he fumbled with the knotted cords.

'Is she all right? What are they doing for her? I must see her!' she insisted anxiously. But the nun's tumble of words died in midphrase as she stopped short to stare at the pendant that Gandulf removed from around his neck in order to untangle it from her crucifix. He replaced the amulet and would have tucked it into his tunic, but she snatched at his hand to prevent him. 'Where did you get that?' she asked sharply.

Surprised at her tone, he replied, 'From Aldyth Lightfoot.' Helping her to her feet, he apologized, 'Excuse me, but I'm in great haste. Shall I call a servant to assist you?'

But Mother Rowena seized his arm and said urgently, 'We must speak privately.'

'Can't this wait?'

'I don't believe so,' she said meaningfully. 'It concerns Aldyth – and you.'

Gandulf tried unsuccessfully to mask his impatience, for each moment carried Aldyth farther away from him. 'Later, Mother, later.'

'Why did she give that to you?' persisted the nun, maintaining her grip on his arm.

'For a wedding gift,' he said flatly, as though daring her to object. 'She is my wife.'

Mother Rowena's hands flew to her mouth, and she stared at him wordlessly.

''Twas a handfast marriage in the oubliette,' he admitted.

'Then you did not have benefit of a priest or receive permission of the king?'

'No,' he said crisply, his manner stiffening. 'But we are married nevertheless, and I am not going to unmarry her. As soon as I find her, I will have Father Edmund marry us in the eyes of the Church, and as for the king, if he doesn't like it, he can go to Hell.'

'The king would never permit you to marry a landless peasant. He will have the marriage annulled. I need to talk to you about Aldyth . . . there is much you don't know.'

Gandulf's voice hardened. 'I know that she is my wife. The only thing I don't know about Aldyth that matters to me right now is her whereabouts.' He exhaled in frustration. 'I don't mean to be rude, but my business won't wait. If you still wish to talk, I'll come and see you at the abbey as soon as I am free.' Softening, he added, 'And please tell my mother that I'll come to fetch her soon; her ordeal is over.'

Before the nun could reply, he was racing across the great hall, his cloak billowing behind, his left arm cradling his broken ribs. As the infirmarian watched him fly, she realized that no one had informed him that Sister Emma's ordeal was already over.

Gandulf galloped hell-bent-for-leather on Lord Ralf's fastest steed, splashing through puddles, heedless of the pelting rain. It did not take him long to realize that, though the Goddess had spared his life, he was presuming upon Her mercy to expect Her to keep him through this trial as well. He must have jarred his ribs, for he felt their pain anew with every breath. He knew that he should turn back, for even had he been hale and well, it would have been difficult to find his way to the lodge in this storm, and he was not certain how long he could stay ahorse. Stubbornly he urged his steed on.

Without warning, his mount reared up with a terrified scream. It took all of Gandulf's strength to stay in the saddle. What had alarmed the beast so? Peering through the rain, he saw two horses emerging like ghosts from the curtaining downpour. He could just discern the drenched figures of Aldyth and Sirona, clinging to their saddles. Aldyth's frightened horse came sliding to an abrupt halt before him, then reared into the air. Aldyth nearly went flying, and it was only then that Gandulf saw Aelfric behind her, his white-knuckled hands clinging to her waist as he tried to keep them both in the saddle. The new lord spurred his mount forward and snatched up the reins of Aldyth's horse, trembling to think that he might have found her, only to lose her again beneath the hooves of a bolting horse. That fear laid to rest, he raged that she should have left him and held tight to her horse's bridle, for he had no intention of leting her escape again.

Aldyth and Gandulf stared at each other in stony silence, the air crackling between them as if a lightning bolt had just struck the ground they stood upon. Even Aelfric and Sirona were stunned by the tension they exuded.

At last Aldyth said evenly, 'I told you not to follow.'

'You are my wife,' he retorted.

'That's all changed.'

'Nothing has changed!' he roared. 'We exchanged vows. What of our pledges? Does this mean nothing to you?' he shouted, snatching up her pendant from under his tunic.

'Of course it does!' wailed Aldyth, her thin veneer of composure shattering. 'Can't you see that I'm trying to make this easy for you? Wasn't it clear from the moment we were rescued that it was hopeless, that there was no place for me in your life?'

'Didn't you say the Goddess brought us together?' he argued.

'I was wrong,' she said, weeping. 'I'm still a virgin and could still fulfill my vow.'

'Goddamn your virginity! You've made no vows to the Goddess as yet. But you made one to me, and I'll not release you from it. Go to the Goddess now, and you go forsworn!'

'I wish I had died in the oubliette!' Aldyth sobbed.

'I'd have chosen to die there too,' he shot back, 'had I known I'd lose you this way.'

Aldyth buried her face in her hands and wept.

At the sight of her distress, Gandulf's anger turned to despair and his face crumpled in grief. 'You can't do this to me, Aldyth,' he pleaded. 'You can't do this to us.' His voice caught in his throat. 'Please,' he begged, 'not now. Not again.'

For a moment there was only the sound of the cold rain beating down upon them.

'By the teats of the Goddess,' said Sirona slowly, 'I think I'm beginning to understand.' She looked at Aldyth tenderly and shook her head. 'Aldyth, my poor child, if only you were not so tight-lipped. Did you believe that you were to serve the Goddess as the Maiden of the Fountain? That you must remain a virgin in her service?'

Aldyth nodded miserably.

'Why didn't you just come to me and ask? You are most unsuited for the position.'

Gandulf and Aldyth gaped at her.

'My foolish child,' said Sirona fondly, 'the Goddess has prepared another destiny for you. If only I had known, how much heartache I could have spared you. Yes, you are to serve the Goddess, but not as Maiden of the Fountain. Dear child, I am the Maiden and shall remain Keeper of the Crystal Spring for yet some time.' The wisewoman reached over and squeezed Aldyth's hand. 'Silly girl, the love of a man is more pain than it is worth, but you will discover this for yourself. It is now and always has been your destiny to unite two races, two bloodlines, and from your womb a new race shall be born. From your union with Gandulf shall spring the next Maiden of the Fountain.'

Gandulf shook his head in bewilderment, unable to grasp the meaning of her words.

Sirona shrugged. 'All you need to know, my son, is that she is yours and you are hers. But treat her well . . . or you will answer to me!'

'And me!' piped up Aelfric fiercely, peeking from behind Aldyth's shoulder.

If Aldyth was stunned by Sirona's revelation, Gandulf was spurred into action. He leaned over and, nearly pulling Aldyth out of the saddle, crushed her to his chest.

Interrupting, Sirona said, 'I am wet and cold, and if I am not mistaken, Father Odo is not far behind.'

'I shall deal with him,' said Gandulf grimly, looking up and wiping his wet eyes on his wetter sleeve. 'But we'd best get out of this storm. It looks to be gaining in force.'

In one swift movement that set his ribs popping, Gandulf lifted Aldyth off her horse and settled her onto his lap. Snatching a look over his shoulder to be certain that Sirona and Aelfric were following, he turned his steed and led the way back toward Castle Hill.

'Watch out!' screamed Aelfric, but his warning was carried away by a vicious gust of wind. An ash tree swayed and toppled, missing Gandulf and Aldyth by a nose. Their horse screamed and reared back into Sirona's. Both beasts would have bolted had Gandulf not seized Sirona's reins and soothed the horse in the Norman tongue that it was used to.

By the time they neared Scafton, the storm had reached its full fury. They came home by a rougher road than they had ridden out on, for on their return, the way was blocked by toppled trees and freshets that rushed across the road, cutting gullies into the trail. Gandulf pressed his mount harder than he knew he ought. Each crash of thunder set off another battle for control between riders and mounts. It would have been a difficult ride for a fit horseman, and it was sheer willpower that kept Gandulf in the saddle.

At last they came to the fountain. Sirona shouted over the wind, 'I leave you here.'

'Come to the garrison with us,' urged Gandulf. 'I can give you protection from Odo.'

'No, I must go to Father Edmund and set his mind to rest.'

'Then let Aelfric see you safely there.'

She shook her head. 'Aelfric will accompany you and see to Aldyth's needs.'

Gandulf could not spare the strength to argue, so he let her go and turned his mount toward the steep, muddy climb up Tout Hill. It was well into the evening when they rode through the garrison gates and right up to the stairs of the great hall. Gandulf dismounted stiffly and, unmindful of his injuries, lifted Aldyth down.

'Aelfric, take the horses to the stable and hand them over to a groom,' he said, almost inaudible with exhaustion. 'Then have Margaret find you some dry clothes and a hot meal, and send linens and something hot to drink up to the solar.'

Gandulf scooped Aldyth into his arms and carried her up the stone staircase into the great hall, leaving a trail of wet footprints. Some people were already abed, while others were warming themselves by the fire. When Gandulf entered the hall, those still awake rose, as much to get a better view of the spectacle as out of respect for their new lord. One man-at-arms stepped forward. 'May I help with the lass, my Lord?'

Gandulf, though obviously overburdened, answered with unaccustomed sharpness, 'I can manage.' He felt self-conscious under such scrutiny and bitter that their solicitude should come only after his coming into power and position.

'The solar has been made ready for you, my Lord Gandulf,' said an officious page, bowing too quickly and too low in an attempt to ingratiate himself with the new lord. Ignoring him, Gandulf climbed the stairs to his new quarters, the lord's chamber.

At Gandulf's approach, another page leapt to his feet and opened the door for his master. He would have followed, but Gandulf waved him back. 'That will be all, Hugh.'

'Aye, my Lord,' said the boy, unable to hide his disappointment.

The bed curtains had been drawn back to reveal fresh linens on the feather bed. Lord Ralf's big carved chair and side table had been placed before the fire. The small windows were shuttered against the storm, but the wind whistled eerily through the cracks, and sharp gusts lifted the skirts of the wall hangings and set the candle flames to guttering.

Gandulf set Aldyth down beside the fire. She had not spoken on their long ride home, instead pressing her face against his chest to shield it from the pelting rain. And, he admitted, he had been afraid to speak, for fear of disturbing what seemed a precarious balance of fates. He had yet to question her about Sirona's rescue or Harold's fate; time enough for that later. He removed her cloak and tossed it in a damp heap onto the floor, but when he reached down to pull the dripping kirtle over her head, she jumped back, leaving Gandulf almost as startled as she.

'What are you doing?' she asked in wide-eyed alarm.

'I'm getting you out of those wet things.'

'I can do it myself,' she said curtly.

'As you wish,' he answered, dropping his hands to his sides. Shrugging, he threw off his own sodden cloak and turned down the bedcovers for her, then discreetly turned his back to build up the fire. But when he turned to face her, she was standing in the middle of a spreading puddle of rainwater, still dressed in her dripping kirtle.

'Aldyth,' he said, 'you did not survive the oubliette to catch your death of cold.'

She frowned slightly and pursed her lips.

'Sweeting, you understand that you have been released from your obligation to the Goddess and that Sirona has given us her blessing?'

She nodded, then blew upward to reroute a trickle of water dripping down her nose.

'Do you accept me for your husband?'

Aldyth nodded again.

He sighed, uncertain how to proceed, until a new thought occurred to him. 'Sweeting, do you understand what naturally occurs between husband and wife?'

'Of course I do,' she snapped, blushing. Then she added quickly, 'For the most part.'

'Are you afraid that I will not be gentle or kind?'

'No,' she answered, chewing her lip anxiously.

There was a knock at the door. Gandulf answered it to find Aelfric, in a dry, well-mended suit of clothes, holding a stack of towels. Beside him stood a kitchen boy with two steaming goblets of strong mulled wine and some white-bread manchets and cheese on a tray.

'Thank you,' said Gandulf wearily, taking the tray from the turnspit. 'Aelfric, you can lay the towels on the bed. Margaret will find you a warm place to sleep tonight.'

If Aelfric noticed the tension in the air or Aldyth's hangdog look, for once he was too tactful to tease. When he had gone, Gandulf turned his attention back to Aldyth and stifled a groan of frustration, for she had stepped behind the high-backed chair and was watching him warily. Perplexed, he sighed; he had begun to feel the weight of his own exhaustion, as well as the chill of his damp clothing. Worst of all, he had been unwillingly placed in the role of cat against her mouse. He sought to meet her eye, but she stared into the fire. As he bent to set down the tray, he was seized with a sudden pain in his side. Crying out, he dropped the tray onto the table with such a clatter that wine slopped out of the goblets. Half swooning, he clutched at the chair for support.

'Gandulf, what is it?' Aldyth darted around the chair to steady him.

Through gritted teeth, he groaned, 'I fear I have reinjured my ribs.'

Aldyth eased him into the chair. 'Oh, my poor Gandulf. If only I had been thinking, I would never have let you carry me up those stairs.'

'I wasn't willing to let you out of my hands,' he gasped, trying to manage a smile.

She knelt at his feet to pull off his boots. By the time she had wrestled off the wet, clinging leather, the color had returned to his wan face. 'Can you stand?' she asked.

He nodded, and she helped him up. Lifting the wet tunic and under-tunic over his head, she dropped them to one side. Then, averting her gaze, she unfastened the drawstring of his hose and peeled the wet wool from his skin, until he stood naked but for the love token around his neck. Gandulf, watching her fetch the linens, was as bewildered by this change of mood as he had been by the last. Aldyth wrapped a towel about his waist and threw one over his shoulders and another over his dripping hair.

Refusing to submit to his weakness, Gandulf knelt stiffly at her feet and took hold of the hem of her kirtle, then looked up for her assent. She nodded bashfully and closed her eyes as he lifted the gown over her head. Her wet shift clung like a second skin to her every curve, and, in spite of his pain,

Gandulf felt the tautening of his loins. He kissed Aldyth's forehead before pulling the damp shift over her head and quickly wrapped her in towels, as much to cloak temptation as to serve the lady. Drawing her to the chair, he sat and looked at Aldyth, who was nervously hugging herself beneath the towels.

'Aldyth,' he said softly, 'come to me, please.'

Uncertainly, she took a step forward, and he pulled her into his lap. He rubbed her icy hands in his and toweled off her dripping hair. Then he lifted a silver goblet of warm wine from the spill on the tray and reached for a folded napkin to wipe the base of the goblet. Something fell out of its folds and onto the tray with a clink. The gleam of firelit gold caught his eye. Recognizing his own ring, he blessed Margaret and slipped it onto his finger. With his hands guiding Aldyth's, he lifted the cup to her lips and said, 'Drink, sweeting. 'Twill warm you from within.' Never letting go of her hands, he lifted the same goblet to his own lips and drank.

'Aldyth,' he said gently, 'please help me understand what it is that you fear, for until this marriage is consummated, someone might yet come between us. I cannot chance losing you again; not to the king, not to the Church, not even to Sirona.'

Her lower lip trembled. A tear slid silently down her cheek, and still she could not meet his eyes. He lifted her chin and forced her to look at him. 'What is it, dearest?'

'The king will never consent to this marriage,' she sniffed. 'You could lose everything, and who would your lands be given to? Perhaps another Lord Ralf. More likely they will force you to annul the marriage and I'll be cast off, no longer a maiden, the laughingstock of the vale. I couldn't bear to face Red Mary's gloating, and even if Father Rannulf doesn't preach openly against me, they will all talk behind their hands.'

'Aldyth,' said Gandulf, frowning. 'I'll not lie to you; the king will be unhappy about this marriage. And as you know, I am not even the legal heir. If that secret should come out, it could, along with a dozen other things, prevent my inheriting the fief. But once before I offered to throw it all away if only you would wed me. Did you think I was merely saying that for effect or that having my inheritance at hand would make me reconsider? Of all the uncertainties in this world, there is one truth you can be sure of: I love you. Now. Forever. Always. Is there anything else we need talk about?'

She smiled through her tears and shook her head.

'Then hereafter, if you refuse my advances, I can assume that it is only force of habit and can disregard your refusal?'

She laughed and nodded.

Gandulf removed his ring and placed it on her finger, as he had done once before. 'This time it stays,' he said firmly. 'Now give me your maidenhead, and if you are not satisfied, we can get it back from Sirona in the morning,' he teased.

'You're as bad as she is!' scolded Aldyth. 'Will I ever hear the end of that?'

Laughing, he shoved her off his lap and onto her feet. 'Come, let's to bed now,' he said. But when he reached to sweep her into his arms, he grunted and clutched at his side.

'Gandulf,' said Aldyth in alarm, 'that is quite enough gallantry for one night. Springwater or no, ten days is not time enough to heal a broken bone.'

'There's only one thing you can do for me to effect a cure . . .' He peeled away the wet towels that covered her and instead wrapped her in his arms. Her wet hair smelled of the rosemary water Margaret had rinsed it in, and Gandulf found himself swept back to that warm night at Midsummer, when he had first plunged his face into the honey-colored maelstrom of her hair. Spurred on by the wine and carried away by his emotions, he lifted her up and set her down on the bed, just a bit heavily, offering a prayer of thanksgiving to Saint Denis that he had not dropped his bride. Aldyth, caught by surprise at his overambitious gesture, did not know whether to laugh or to scold.

When he slid in between the sheets beside her, Aldyth reflexively clutched a handful of covers to her breast. As gentle, as patient as her husband was, this moment was a contradiction to all her visions of the future. And it was so irreversible. Her thoughts whirled as wildly as the storm that raged without. Sometime, somehow, she must let go of her fears and trust him fully, with all her heart. When had he ever given her reason to doubt him? Or, thought Aldyth, struck by a sudden insight, was it herself that she doubted? Could she love him so deeply, so completely, so truly?

Aldyth met his eyes and found Gandulf watching her with such trepidation that her overriding impulse was to set his fears, and her own, to rest. She opened her arms to him, and when his searching face peered into hers, she rose up to meet his lips. The warmth of his touch spread through her body like the summer sun. At her surrender, Aldyth came into a state of peace such as she had never known. She felt the elation of one returning home after a desperate journey and knew that this was what the Goddess had made men and women for, this was what she and Gandulf had been destined for. Like countless generations before them and countless generations to follow, Aldyth and Gandulf danced the dance of life, celebrated the cosmic circle, and received the gift of the Goddess no less than when the hills bloomed in the springtime and the apples swelled in the fall.

Father Odo spurred on his horse mercilessly; now that the witch had been given into his power, he was not about to let her slip out of his grasp. At last he came to the outskirts of Scafton, but it was not until he was within sight of the Crystal Spring that he considered his next move. Should he bring back an armed guard to collect the witch or go directly to her house? She was only an old woman, but God only knew what tricks she might be capable of. Hadn't she bewitched four men-at-arms thought to be invulnerable to her wiles?

He reined in his exhausted horse beneath the Wishing Tree. The wind tore leaves and twigs off the branches and hurled them at him. The Norman priest felt an irrational fear rising up in his gut like last night's dinner. He looked deliberately at the tree and berated himself; such fear was unbecoming in a man of God. He shook his fist at the ancient oak and shouted, 'I'll be back for you when I've done with the crone!'

The wishing rags tied in strips to the tree snapped at him in the gale like cracking whips. A bolt of lightning struck the hillside just above the Wishing Tree and set it rocking like a ship at sea. Father Odo's horse, dancing with white-eyed terror, screamed shrilly and reared up on its hind legs. At the same time that his horse carried him upward, a sudden gust of wind sent the branches whipping downward. The priest gasped in horror to see a great forked limb snatch at him with its gnarled fingers.

CHAPTER THIRTY-SEVEN

Aldyth could not remember where she was until the steady sound of Gandulf's breathing beside her brought everything back. She pulled open the bed curtains and, by the early morning light which squeezed through the cracks in the shutters, lay back down beside Gandulf and watched him sleep. She longed for him to open his eyes that she might gaze into their coppery depths once more.

The night before had been unimaginable. Aldyth had felt the fire run in her blood only once before, on Midsummer's Eve; had she known that physical love could bring such ecstasy, she would never have considered chastity. As the storm had raged, she and Gandulf had explored each other's bodies by the glow of the hearth. He had been gentle and reverent, and when at last he had parted her legs and entered her, the pain she had felt as he had come up against her maidenhead had been lost in sheer excitement. Even the thunder could not drown his cries, which Aldyth likened to the cry of an eagle as it plunged downward to meet its mate. When it was over, Gandulf had laid his head upon her chest and, as her pounding heart slowed its beat, had shed tears of joy and wonder. They had lain quietly, shriven, in each other's arms, listening to the storm move off across the vale.

Long after his breathing had slowed to a deep, regular rhythm and Aldyth knew that Gandulf slept, she had lain awake. She felt blessed, even as she was burdened by the responsibility. She loved truly and broadly, but was she capable of loving with the single-mindedness with which

Gandulf loved her? She felt too ordinary for this intense man, and she hoped that he would not be disappointed, in time, to find her only human.

Idly she picked up her keepsake where it rested in the dark curly hairs of Gandulf's chest. His hand closed over hers. 'Oh, no, you don't,' he teased languidly. 'This is mine now. Were you going to take it and run?' Suddenly serious, he said, 'Aldyth, you won't run away from me again, will you?'

'You'd ask me that after last night?'

He kissed her, and she pillowed her head on his shoulder. Picking up her love token, he asked curiously, 'What is this?'

'A baby's rattle. 'Twas once my plaything; now 'tis a keepsake of a forgotten life.'

'There's writing on it,' he observed. 'What does it say?'

'Gandulf, I don't know how to read.'

'I'll teach you, sweeting. We can start with this. 'Tis written in Latin.' He held it closer and translated the worn inscription, '"I was made by Lord Aethelstan for his firstborn child."' Their eyes jumped from the rattle to meet in astonishment.

'Aldyth,' said Gandulf at last, 'this can mean only one thing. You are the daughter of Lord Aethelstan. You, not I, are the true heir to this fief.'

'But the child died, Gandulf. Father Edmund swore he had buried her himself.'

'He would not be the first good man to be forsworn for a worthy cause.'

'But then Mother Rowena would be my natural mother!' she cried. 'Why would she have kept that secret from me all these years?' Aldyth pulled away, hurt and angry.

'Perhaps for the same reason my mother hid the secret of my parentage from me,' Gandulf reasoned. 'Surely for your protection. You might have been killed or given away as a war prize to the highest bidder. With my mother conveniently disposed of, Ralf fitzGerald might have taken you to wife; infants younger than you were married off to legitimize a claim. Your mother knew that you were in good hands with Sirona, and she watched over you from a safe distance.' Aldyth allowed Gandulf to pull her back into his arms. 'We'll ride over to see her this morning; she'll have better answers for you than I. In fact,' he mused, 'I'd not be surprised if that was what she wanted to discuss yesterday.' With a bright smile, he added, 'And you can meet my mother. We'll bring her home with us to live and give her grandchildren, Aldyth. 'Tis high time she had something joyful to look forward to.'

'We must talk to Sirona, too, Gandulf. Perhaps she'll know what has become of your father, and only the Lady knows what has happened to Bedwyn and Gunhild and Edith! As long as Hugo remains to stir up the hornets' nest, they're not safe.'

'CloseFist said that fitzGrip and Gauter went to meet Odo at the hunting lodge, just before the storm broke night before last, probably to interrogate Sirona. Not trusting his quarry to the locals, Hugo insisted upon going too. We'll have the Devil to pay when those three turn up, but the first nasty medicine will be doled out by Father Odo. The last time we met, I left burning dog shit on his doorstep and crowned him for his robe.'

Aldyth was horrified. 'Could he get you into trouble?'

'I suppose he could,' said Gandulf, pushing her back down into the pillows. 'But let's not think about that just yet.'

Their lovemaking was more playful than the night before but no less satisfying. They drifted in and out of slumber until they were awakened by bells tolling for tierce.

'That can't be the ninth hour of the morning already?' said Gandulf groggily.

'I'm afraid so,' said Aldyth. 'I heard them ring for prime long ago.'

Gandulf sighed, kissed his wife, and sat up slowly.

'Can't we just stay here forever?' Aldyth pleaded, only half in jest.

'Ah, love, we can no more hold back the rest of the world than King Canute could stop the tides; 'tis a wonder someone hasn't come beating down the door by now. I'll get you a maidservant to help with your morning toilette,' he said, fetching a basin, 'but I would have that honor today.' He washed her face and hands, but when he went to wash the virgin's blood from between her legs, she blushed and tried to push his hands away.

'Modesty seems misplaced after what we shared in the oubliette,' he teased.

He lifted the sleeve of her borrowed kirtle, still in a damp heap on the floor. 'This will never do. You must have clothing suited to a lady. Margaret will know what to do.'

Gandulf went to summon a page, but when he opened the door, Aelfric, wrapped in a blanket, tumbled in backward and blinked himself awake.

''Tis about time you rose, Gandulf,' grumbled the boy. 'The servants have been wild to get at you all morning.' It was clear that Aelfric did not consider himself a servant.

Gandulf laughed and said, 'If you want to speed things along, Aelfric, you can ask Margaret if we have anything fitting to dress Lady Aldyth in.'

'Elfling,' called Aldyth over Gandulf's shoulder, 'please bring linen to bind his ribs.'

'And I suppose you'll you be wanting some hot water to shave that stubbly chin of yours?' said Aelfric to Gandulf as he straightened his tunic and sauntered downstairs.

Gandulf brushed Aldyth's tangled locks, and she had a revelation that heroics were all very well, but it was the exchange of such small kindnesses that made her feel most loved. Margaret appeared, carrying a pile of folded woolens in richly dyed colors and putting an end to their quiet idyll. Aelfric followed with fresh linens and a jug of steaming water. Margaret beamed at the newlyweds. Then, with the air of a magician conjuring up silken scarves, she shook out an elegant daffodil-green kirtle trimmed with gold braid. Aldyth had never seen anything so lovely, let alone been asked to wear it.

'Aldyth,' exclaimed Gandulf, ''twas made for you!'

'Nay, but for her mother,' said Margaret, her eyes growing misty. 'After the sacking, I was told to cut up Lady Rowena's gowns to make standards for Lord Ralf and tunics for his son, but I tucked this one away for this moment.'

'You knew too?' cried Aldyth in consternation. 'Did everyone know who I was but me?'

'Nay, child,' Margaret said soothingly, 'though many have guessed at the truth. But 'twas I who lowered you over the palisade in a basket to the waiting arms of Sirona.'

'Oh, Margaret!' cried Aldyth, throwing her arms around the buxom cook. 'You could have been killed for my sake. How can I ever thank you?'

'By putting on this shift,' replied Margaret flatly, though the color in her cheeks betrayed her pleasure. 'Here are some stockings and kid slippers for your dainty feet.'

'I have gone barefoot so long, I fear they are hardly dainty,' said Aldyth ruefully.

'Nonsense,' scoffed Margaret. ''Tis nothing that a few good soaks in a tub won't fix. Aelfric, for modesty's sake, you wait in the hall while I dress the Lady Aldyth.'

'Hah!' teased Aelfric. 'I used to know a girl named Aldyth Lightfoot who was not above dancing amid the cowpats on the green, but now that Lady Aldyth has usurped her place, I suppose we'll all be expected to wash our faces every day.'

'You'd best be on your way, you little cowpat, or I'll give you your first face washing,' Gandulf threatened with a grin.

Aelfric snorted and ambled leisurely to the door, but just before he closed it, he shot back, 'And that's another thing! Aren't we grand now that we're a proper lord? Next thing you know, you'll be walking six inches above the ground.'

As the door slammed shut, Gandulf said, 'Well, at least Aelfric hasn't changed.'

'Aye,' chuckled Aldyth. 'He still manages to get the last word in.'

'He's a scamp,' admitted Margaret, 'but you'll have to allow he has his good points.'

'God only knows,' agreed Gandulf. 'If not for that cunning little puppy, Aldyth and I would still be rotting in the oubliette. Today I'd not be so quick to deny his Fairy blood.'

'Well, even Aelfric can't bring back the morning,' said Margaret, slipping a shift over Aldyth's head, then helping her into the kirtle. 'The coup de grâce,' beamed Margaret as she reached around to gild the lily with a girdle of gold. 'You could be your mother standing before me,' said Margaret, misty-eyed. 'She was such a fine lady!'

Aldyth shook her head. 'I cannot imagine Mother Rowena dressed in green and gold and attended by her women. Margaret,' said Aldyth abruptly, 'I'm afraid I won't even know her anymore. How shall I call her? What shall I say?'

Margaret scooped her new mistress to her ample bosom and clucked. 'There, lass. When the time comes, the words will come too. And the sooner the better, I always say. As for you, my Lord,' she said to Gandulf, 'let's see what we can do to speed you along.'

'We must bind his ribs, Margaret,' said Aldyth. 'Just look at the bruising.'

Gandulf squirmed under their ministrations. Being the center of attention was not nearly as comfortable as quietly watching from the periphery.

'Get used to it,' warned Margaret. To Aldyth she said, 'Since he was small enough to walk under a horse's belly, he's been like a spider, hanging in the rafters, watching all and saying nothing.' Margaret tossed Gandulf a sheet. 'Up, lad. 'Tis time to face the world.'

Gandulf wrapped the sheet around his waist, and Aldyth gently probed to determine the extent of the damage. 'I'd guess that two ribs were broken. Gandulf, you should be dead.' Overcome, she threw her arms around him. 'How close I came to losing you!'

'Too much of this,' he quipped, 'and you'll spoil me.'

Before going downstairs, Gandulf stripped the First Night sheets, with their small but significant bloodstains, from the bed. ''Tis a crude custom,' he said, 'but in this case, it cannot hurt.' Gandulf gave them to Aelfric. 'Hang them from the gallery for all to see.'

Gandulf and Aldyth stepped onto the landing above the great hall and looked down at their servants and followers gathered for the day's business, waiting for the appearance of their lord. Aeliva was plucking a chicken, and Wulfwyn was peeling parsnips and carrots and dropping them into the cauldron over the fire. Pages were scattering fresh rushes on the floor, and Lord Ralf's hounds prowled restlessly, their forage gone out with the old rushes. But when Aldyth stepped into view, all activity ceased, and silence fell upon the company.

Aldyth had not realized until that moment how daunting her new role would be. Amid the stillness, a black streak came bounding up the stairs. Baldwin thrust his cold, wet nose into her hand, then fidgeted joyously at Gandulf's feet. Gandulf, ruffling the dog's ears, said, 'Baldwin would be the first to welcome his new mistress.'

The older servants gasped at the sight of Aldyth descending the stairs in Lady Rowena's favorite gown. What many had suspected was suddenly obvious, rendering the announcement Gandulf was about to make unnecessary. 'This is Lady Aldyth,' he proclaimed, 'my wedded wife and daughter to Lord Aethelstan. He who wishes to show me his loyalty will obey her as he would me.'

They lined up in order of precedence to kneel before Aldyth and place their hands between hers. First came the few knights Gandulf had retained; then the butler, the reeve, the men-at-arms, the menservants, all the way down to the little turnspit. Throughout this ritual Gandulf stood behind her, his hand on her shoulder. She needed reassurance that he was not embarrassed by her lowly upbringing; he needed to assure himself that she was not a vision of his fevered brain. Gandulf told the servants, 'You may return to your duties now. Those of you with messages to impart will remain.'

One of the men-at-arms stepped forward and bowed. 'My Lord, I regret to say that Father Odo is no longer missing.'

'Yes, Henry,' prompted Gandulf.

'His body was found this morning, tangled in the branches of the great oak tree in Enmore Green. His horse returned riderless last night at the peak of the storm. We tried to get word to you earlier,' he said, glaring at Aelfric.

'We must hold an inquest,' began Gandulf. 'Hugh fitzGrip—'

'There has been no word of him since he rode out the day before yesterday. Lady fitzGrip says he set out for Lord Ralf's hunting lodge with Gauter and Hugo of Rouen.'

'Perhaps they took shelter from the storm,' said Gandulf. 'Dispatch a search party to the lodge, and be so good as to send a litter down to Enmore Green to fetch Sirona.'

'She sent word this morning that she'll be waiting for you at the abbey,' said Aelfric.

'Even better. Thank you, Henry. Please keep me abreast of the tidings.'

When the crowd had dispersed, Aelfric, Aldyth, and Gandulf retired to the privacy of the solar. 'Aelfric,' said Gandulf, 'if anyone knows where Bedwyn might be, 'tis you.'

'Lufe says they have sheltered with the outlaws in Cranborne Chase.'

'Thank the Lady!' exclaimed Aldyth. 'Then Edith and Gunhild are safe in his keeping.'

Gandulf heaved a sigh of relief, then asked Aelfric, 'Could you get word to Bedwyn?'

The boy nodded.

'Good. Tell him that until fitzGrip and Hugo are found, we cannot chance having him seen and recognized. FitzGrip makes me more nervous than Odo ever did. At least Odo was driven by a genuine passion, while fitzGrip would sell his own mother for sixpence.'

Gandulf called to the page posted on the landing, 'Please have my horse saddled, Hugh.'

When the lad had gone, Aldyth asked, 'Am I not to come? Would you rather go alone?'

'I want very much for you to come but would rather feel your arms about my waist than see you riding at a distance. Unless,' Gandulf teased, 'it would demean your dignity to appear so in public now that you are a great lady.'

'Not at all,' replied Aldyth, laughing. ''Tis just a pity we can't go by way of Alcester.'

On the ride to the abbey, Gandulf chattered cheerfully. Catching Aldyth's eye over his shoulder, he smiled. 'Don't be nervous about meeting my mother, love. You can only compare favorably with the last girl I brought.'

'At least I can thank Catherine for that,' said Aldyth.

Upon arriving, they found Sister Arlette somberly speaking to Sister Aethelswith, who fingered her rosary nervously.

'I'm here to see Sister Emma,' Gandulf declared, tying the reins to a ring in the wall.

'We were expecting you, my Lord,' said Sister Arlette. A snap and a loud clatter made the porteress jump. Sister Aethelswith fell to her knees with a profusion of apologies and began to collect her scattered rosary beads with feverish concentration.

'Gandulf,' said Aldyth uncertainly, 'perhaps we should speak to Mother Rowena first.'

'No,' he insisted, 'I want to see my mother now.'

Aldyth said to Sister Aethelswith, 'Could you fetch Mother Rowena right away?'

'Of course,' said the red-faced nun, relieved to be dismissed. As she stood up, another cascade of beads rattled onto the flagstones of the courtyard.

Gandulf was expecting to be led to the parlor, but the nun guided them to the chapel. 'I'll leave you here,' she said, opening the door and standing aside. Inside two nuns kept vigil over a body on a bier in front of the altar, a host of candles lit for the soul of the dead. Upon seeing them enter, the nuns fluttered off, like bats disturbed in the daytime.

Gandulf stopped short and whispered, 'Aldyth, please leave me.'

Aldyth knew that he had always coped with grief by walling people out when he needed them most. She considered disregarding his command but wavered. Giving his hand a squeeze, Aldyth followed the nuns. Outside the chapel, Mother Rowena and Sirona hurried across the courtyard. Aldyth rushed forward and threw an arm about each.

'Oh, dear,' said Mother Rowena, 'we wanted to prepare him.'

'Then it is his mother?' asked Aldyth, no longer daring to hope otherwise.

Mother Rowena nodded. 'This must come as a terrible shock,' she said.

Suddenly Aldyth knew what she must do. 'Please excuse me, Mother.'

'He is used to keeping his pain to himself—' began Mother Rowena.

'We vowed to share the sorrow along with the joy,' said Aldyth.

Gandulf was kneeling before the coffin, clasping his mother's lifeless hand. When Aldyth approached, he looked up and said simply, 'How can she be grown so cold?'

513

Aldyth's tears were for both mother and son as she held out her arms to him. To her relief, he leaned into them, and she rocked him like the motherless child he was. It began with a ragged sigh, barely distinguishable from his pained shallow breathing. When she stroked his hair and whispered to him of her love and her sorrow, his composure crumbled, and he wept. When at last he lifted his head from from her shoulder and met her eyes, she wiped his face with her kerchief and helped him to his feet. He allowed himself to be led a few paces, then stopped abruptly. Slipping out of Aldyth's encircling arm, Gandulf returned to the coffin to whisper words that Aldyth could not distinguish, then kissed his mother's pale cheek for the last time.

As they stepped out of the chapel, Sirona came forward to meet them. She placed a hand on Aldyth's belly. 'There is a girl child growing within your womb even now,' she said. 'She will be small and dark and strong of spirit.'

'And her name will be Emma,' said Aldyth softly.

In the privacy of the stillroom, Mother Rowena assured Gandulf that no one save herself and the abbess knew the circumstances of Emma's death, and she was fairly certain that Sister Priscilla had been silenced before revealing his secret. As for Harold, Sirona regretted having no news to tell. Preoccupied by the dramatic events of the morning, it had only just occurred to Aldyth that she was sitting beside her birth mother. She felt none of the drama, none of the trauma, none of the tension she had expected to feel. Shaking her head in wonder, Aldyth whispered, 'Nothing has changed.'

'What did you say, dear?' asked Mother Rowena, leaning forward in concern.

'This morning Gandulf read to me the inscription upon the little silver rattle. It told me who I am and who you are to me, Mother.'

Mother Rowena closed her eyes and clasped Aldyth to her. 'Oh, child of my heart!' she cried, her voice shaking with the intensity of her feelings. 'How I have longed to tell you, but as long as Lord Ralf lived, your life was in jeopardy. He was an evil man—'

'You needn't explain, Mother,' said Aldyth. 'In my heart I think I knew all along.'

Sirona accompanied them home from the abbey, for there were plans to be made. But it was a strange and silent ride for Aldyth and Gandulf, for in the space of a morning, one had lost a mother and the other had found one. Though both were absorbed in thought, they clung to each other, each the still center of life's whirlwind for the other.

Upon returning they learned that fitzGrip and his escort had been found. 'We found their horses first,' reported Henry. 'The poor dumb beasts were trembling, frothing, and, strangest of all, scorched. The bodies we found on the open downs, twisted and charred, the clothes burned off their backs. We knew fitzGrip by the rings he wore and could tell Hugo from Gauter by his size. FitzGrip's wife is sending her reeve to claim the jewels – and the body,' Henry added quickly.

Gandulf, trying not to appear too relieved, said, 'I've no doubt an inquest will determine that the king's sheriff with his man Gauter, and Hugo of Rouen, also in service of the king, were caught in a storm on the downs and struck by lightning.'

'Aye,' agreed Sirona. 'Let the records show that they were struck by lightning; 'tis neither the first nor the last time that such has come to pass. But know for a fact,' she declaimed eerily, 'that they were all three victims of the wild hunt.'

'But is that not the Devil with his hounds of Hell out hunting through the skies?'

'So the Church would have it, but 'tis the Goddess who rides as the Horned One. She is not above vengeance and has claimed Her prize on Lammas, the Day of the Dead.'

Several servants crossed themselves, and Gandulf dismissed them with instructions to go pray for the souls of the dead. Then he said to Margaret, 'When Aelfric returns, will you have him recall Bedwyn and his charges? Doubtless he'll be feeling road-weary and ill used; give him this to speed him on his way.' And he handed Margaret a small gold coin.

Margaret tucked the coin into her ample bosom. 'A few

more of those, and *he'll* be the one too grand to keep company with the likes of us!'

Once settled by the hearth in the solar, Sirona said, 'One by one the mysteries are resolved. Only one remains: Where is Harold?' Shrugging, she said, 'The last order of business for today is to send for official permission to marry.'

'It shall be done,' Gandulf assured her.

'Then go and mourn,' said the old healer, laying a gentle hand upon his shoulder.

'I shall proceed with the wedding first. I will request Father Edmund to perform the ceremony tomorrow. If there is a child growing in Aldyth's womb, I shall have no one counting backward on his fingers, ready to claim my child a bastard. And Aldyth shall have the respect due my lawfully wedded wife.'

Sirona nodded approvingly. 'You will make a good lord, my son.'

CHAPTER THIRTY-EIGHT

September 1087

'What was that?' Gandulf looked up from the book he had been reading aloud to the small gathering of loafers and fire huggers.

'It sounded like horses,' said Aldyth eagerly.

The door swung open, and a familiar voice called out, 'A bad penny always turns up.'

'Bedwyn!' cried Aldyth.

Into the great hall he swaggered with Gunhild on one arm and Edith SwanNeck on the other. He bore only traces of the bruising and blackened eyes that he had left with two weeks before. Aldyth rushed into Bedwyn's arms, nearly tumbling him over. Laughing aloud, he hugged her with equal enthusiasm, then set her down and kissed both cheeks.

'I never thought to see you again!' she exclaimed. 'But I forget my manners,' she added, pulling away from Bedwyn to take Sister Edith's hands. 'Welcome!' she said. Turning to her husband, Aldyth cried happily, 'Gandulf, look who has come home to us!'

Gandulf nodded stiffly to Bedwyn and bowed to the ladies. 'Hugh,' he called to a page, 'please have Margaret send supper and wine up to the solar for our guests.'

Unasked but not unexpected, Aelfric trailed after them. As soon as the door closed behind them, Aldyth smiled broadly at Bedwyn and exclaimed, 'Cousin!'

'Sister,' corrected Bedwyn, putting his arm around Gunhild's shoulders. 'My wife, Gunhild. We have married ourselves and plan to be married again before God.'

'Oh!' said Aldyth in surprise. She fought down an irrational pang of jealousy to add warmly, 'My congratulations! You make a handsome pair!'

'Brother!' said Bedwyn to Gandulf mischievously. Gandulf warily held out a hand, but Bedwyn clasped him warmly by the shoulders and pulled him into a hearty embrace.

Blushing, Gandulf retreated a pace but said earnestly, 'I am indebted to you for saving my father's life.' Then more lightly he added, 'And for taking such good care of my sister.'

'No easy task, Brother, for she follows directions no better than your wife.'

Edith smiled with the others but could not hide the pain behind her smile. 'Mother,' said Gandulf, seating her by the fire, 'you must be tired after your journey.'

A knock announced Hugh's arrival with wine, cheese, and cold pheasant. When he had gone, Aldyth said, 'Bedwyn, don't keep us waiting. What happened after you left us?'

'As you can see, I fulfilled my charge to you, Mouse. I found the ladies waiting in the woods near my hut, though who took charge of whom is open to debate. But Aelfric has kept us mightily entertained on the way here with his version of your adventures; now we would like to hear what really happened.'

Aelfric, who had stationed himself by the food, retorted with a mouthful of pasty, 'They might tell you a different version, but nobody will tell you a better one.'

'No one can alter the fact that you are a great lady, Aldyth,' said Bedwyn fondly, adding with a nod toward Gandulf, 'and 'tis good of you to raise this lout to your station.'

'A long-suffering lout at that,' Gandulf shot back. He sighed and said, almost straight-faced, 'Now that he is family, I suppose I shall have to get used to him.'

Once all were settled by the fire with a goblet of warm wine in their hands, Gandulf announced self-consciously, 'You should know that Aldyth is with child.' Gandulf watched Bedwyn's eyes shoot across the room to meet Aldyth's. He raised his eyebrows and his cup to Aldyth, causing her to blush and avert her eyes. Gandulf privately chided himself for bristling at this innocent exchange and continued, 'Under the circumstances, I would not delay making the bond between Aldyth and myself official in the eyes of the Church. Of course, in light of Harold's absence, there will be no question of feasting or celebration.'

'He would give you his wholehearted blessing,' said Edith.

'Perhaps you would not object to a double wedding,' said Gunhild shyly, tucking her arm through Bedwyn's, 'for I would snare this bird before he flies.'

'It would take more than a priest to clip my wings,' quipped Bedwyn, 'but I shall no longer fly alone.'

'To Bedwyn and Gunhild,' said Gandulf, raising his goblet in a toast.

'And to you and your bride, Little Brother,' toasted Gunhild.

'To wedded bliss, my children,' said Edith. 'May you know the joy that I have known.'

Later that evening Gandulf returned from escorting Sister Edith to the abbey, where she preferred to stay and pray. The stable men had all gone to bed, but Gandulf was content to groom Cathedra himself. He had sensed a change in the little mare since Sirona had brought her back from the Fairies. Gandulf knew that Cathedra preferred her Fairy keepers to the stable grooms, and at first he had feared that she might pine for them. But her pleasure in his company was as great as ever, and he sensed that she was glad to come home to him. Still he took pains to rain care and affection upon her, that she might not miss her Fairy friends too much. He gave her one last pat on the rump and walked across the moonlit bailey toward the great hall, anxious to find Aldyth.

'Is Mother settled in?' came a woman's voice from the darkness. Stepping out of the shadows cast by the stone staircase leading up to the hall was Gunhild. In the moonlight, her short golden curls shone silver. Just as a nun's habit seemed a statement of grace when she wore it, a secondhand kirtle on Gunhild was the embodiment of sensuous style.

'Aye,' replied Gandulf. 'I left her with Mother Rowena, who will see to her comfort.'

''Tis a difficult time for her,' said Gunhild, 'though she would hide her fears.'

Gandulf nodded. 'How could it be otherwise, until Harold's fate is known?'

'Whatever happens, Little Brother, you should know how much you mean to Father.'

However confidently Gandulf managed his affairs, his newfound self-assurance did not extend to this sphere. Gandulf wanted to tell Gunhild of his desperately lonely childhood, of his longing for family to share it with. His childhood dream was no less important now that he was grown, and all the more cherished for its unexpectedness. But he could say only, 'I am . . . grateful . . . for the warmth with which I am received into your family.'

Gunhild laughed and took his hand. 'We Godwinsons must stick together, little brother. After all, there aren't that many of us left.'

From across the bailey, they heard the sharp call of the sentry: 'Who goes there?'

'Just us,' came Aldyth's reply, cutting through the night as cleanly as a moonbeam.

'Forgive me, my Lady,' came the watchman's reply. 'On nights like tonight, the spell of the moon is especially strong. It draws many out of the dark hall. Enjoy your walk.'

Brother and sister looked up to see two figures on the palisade silhouetted against the moon-bright sky. Below, two pairs of eyes watched Bedwyn come up behind Aldyth and wrap his arms about her waist. The soft murmur of their voices carried across the bailey, though the silent observers could not distinguish their words.

High up on the palisade, Bedwyn wondered aloud, 'Who would have thought our lives would take such wild turns? I'm still reeling.'

'And I too,' agreed Aldyth. 'But I'm pleased that we can still be friends, Bedwyn.'

'Now we have common blood to seal the bond.' Suddenly earnest, he said, 'Aldyth, I'm not one to cry sour grapes. Cousin or no, I've always thought we'd make a good match, and I still

520

do. But neither am I one to pine away. Gunhild and I will do well together.'

'I haven't the fire to keep you true to me, Bedwyn, but I sense that Gunhild does.'

'If that child you're carrying were mine, Aldyth—' Bedwyn paused, then shrugged. 'But 'tis not, and I feel only . . . well, mostly joy for you and fitzGerald.'

'What will you and Gunhild do now?' asked Aldyth. 'Gandulf says he would gladly knight you and give you a rich manor of your own in the Blackmore Vale.'

'And serve a Norman king?' The scorn in his voice turned to excitement: 'Aldyth, do you recall the new world that Hereward spoke of, beyond Iceland, beyond even Greenland? He called it "Vinland." I've a mind to see it for myself, and Gunhild is willing to come with me.'

'I shall never see you again,' said Aldyth, looking out across the black-and-silver vale.

'Don't be so sure, Mouse. I'm not so easily gotten rid of. I'll always leave word of my whereabouts. If ever you need me, you can send for me, and I'll come to you.'

'Oh, Bedwyn,' she said, turning to face him. How could she help but love him?

Smoothing her hair back from her eyes, Bedwyn said, 'The kiss of peace,' and he bent down to brush her lips with his, then pulled her into a warm embrace.

Far below, Gunhild and Gandulf watched in silence as two silhouettes melted into one.

'Does such a sight chill your heart and raise green envy?' Gunhild asked Gandulf.

Gandulf shook his head. 'Perhaps at one time it might have. Now I no longer doubt my lady's love but only wonder at it. What about you, Sister?'

'Bedwyn I cannot be so sure of. But I like a challenge,' she said with a grin. 'Come, Brother,' she invited, taking his arm, 'let's go addle our brains with too much mead.'

'I can see that life in the convent would never have suited you, Gunhild.'

'Aldyth might say the same of you and your monastery, Gandulf. Once my father met my mother, he never looked back. We Godwinsons were meant to love as well as pray.'

Father Edmund looked up from his tattered psalter, placed Aldyth's hand in Gandulf's, and announced, 'I now pronounce you man and wife.'

Aldyth and Gandulf were still looking at each other in a daze when Bedwyn pushed past the groom, chiding, 'If you're not going to kiss her, fitzGerald, I will.'

Gunhild raised an eyebrow at the warm kiss he bestowed upon the bride. 'Give her some air, Bedwyn, lest the poor girl faint.'

Bedwyn winked at Gunhild and said, 'That kiss must serve as a farewell too, since I leave for Bristol this morning.'

'I hope you haven't any long-lost cousins in Bristol,' said Gunhild wryly.

Bedwyn grinned and took his own wife into his arms. Then Edith SwanNeck embraced her new daughter but had hardly time to offer congratulations when the first petitioner, who had been waiting at the far end of the hall, pushed forward. Leofwine Clerk tried to hold back the tide of reeves and bailiffs waiting to render their accounts to their new lord, but the lad was only thirteen and had not yet acquired the experience and stature needed to manage such affairs. Gandulf allowed himself to be appropriated, for he did need to know what his holdings were worth in order to pass the information on to the king. Aldyth stood by his side, absorbing as much information as Gandulf, for, illiterate as she was, she had been trained to retain amazing amounts of information by heart.

King William had not believed it prudent to give one man dominion over a vast holding but scattered a man's holdings about the country, making it difficult for any man to have too much influence in one area. That kept his underlings moving from manor to manor instead of sitting at home conspiring. Consequently, over the coming weeks reeves would continue to report from estates all over the south of England.

Gandulf told Aldyth, 'When things settle down, we shall make a tour of all our properties and see how the reeves conduct themselves. I have released my father's mercenary knights; I'll not have such unscrupulous rogues as Sir Godfroi in my employ. Instead we shall fill their places with younger sons from our own holdings. On our journey, we shall seek out the sort of man we would wish to represent us.'

Aldyth was too overwhelmed to reply. Her walk on the ridgeway was the farthest she had ever ventured from her own little toft. Once it had been an adventure just to hear of London and Gloucester and the Cinque Ports, but now she would see them for herself.

Still no word came from Harold; Gandulf privately confessed to Aldyth that he expected none. He was delaying their wedding feast, mainly out of respect for his stepmother, though it was assumed by his tenants that the feast had been postponed out of respect for Lord Ralf and the dying king, which Gandulf found ironic but convenient.

During the last week of September a message arrived from the new king. At first they feared it was an order for an inquest into the recent spate of deaths, but it was merely a reminder that King William I was dead, that his son William Rufus had succeeded him, and that a coronation gift of gold was in order. It would be no easy task to come up with enough funds both to satisfy the king and to finance Bedwyn's trip to Bristol. Bristol was a huge seaport with ships and merchants coming and going from throughout the continent, and Bedwyn intended to seek out a shipowner and persuade him to sponsor an expedition to Vinland.

'Do you really think he'll be able to convince anyone to sail off the map or even to finance such a scheme?' Gandulf asked Aldyth doubtfully.

'The man's marrying a nun!' she replied. 'Bedwyn could charm the tide into rising.'

'And yet,' thought Gandulf smugly, 'he couldn't charm Aldyth out of her maidenhead.'

Aldyth was glad of the opportunity to spend time with Gunhild, for if Gandulf enjoyed acquiring new relatives, so did Aldyth. She delighted in having a sister for the first time in her life, and Gunhild's saucy sense of humor constantly shocked and amused her.

Aldyth purchased wedding gifts for Gunhild's trousseau. Gandulf urged them to spend freely, and they took him at his word. As they stepped out of Thorbald Turner's shop, where they had selected wooden bowls, mugs, and plates, Aldyth confessed to Gunhild, 'I've been in Thorbald's shop before, but never with a penny in my purse.'

'Enjoy it,' said Gunhild wryly. ''Tis easier to move up in the world than down.'

'You are probably used to eating from plates of gold,' surmised Aldyth.

'Perhaps, but there will be little call for gold plate when Bedwyn and I go a-Viking.'

Gunhild spent hours teaching Aldyth to manage her household; it was no mean task. It was Aldyth's province to keep her cupboards stocked with the herbs and medicines needed to dose and purge her people, and that in itself was undaunting. But there were also linens from field to loom to bed, and woolens from sheep to loom to clothing chest, to be stored, cleaned, and replaced in their time. The furnishings of kitchen and hall – wooden trenchers, clay bowls, iron cauldrons, and silver plate – all came under her hands. The care and education of each page and maid-in-waiting were also the responsibility of the lady of the manor. She must plan for food and drink for master and man, mistress and maid, for breakfast, dinner, and supper, for festivals and holidays through all the seasons of the year. The household budget too was her dominion, and from that must come funds to purchase salt from the salt driers, needles from itinerant peddlers, and charcoal from the charcoal burners. She must also learn to stretch the budget to allow a few pennies for traveling minstrels, church tithes, hospitality for pilgrims, and alms for the poor.

'And never forget,' warned Aldyth's new mentor, 'that sooner or later the king is bound to descend upon you with all his court. 'Tis less an honor than a form of taxation, for it will cost you dearly and tax your food stores, your patience, and your nerves.'

'How can anyone keep track of it all?' exclaimed Aldyth in despair. 'I considered it good management to make the crab apples last the winter. Gandulf would have been wiser to marry

Catherine, for she has spent a lifetime learning to manage her own household.'

'I suspect,' said Gunhild slyly, 'that it may have been some quality other than your housekeeping that attracted my brother to you.'

At the end of a long day spent training at Gunhild's elbow, Aldyth put on her cloak and picked up her basket. Gandulf looked up from his document-strewn table in the solar. 'You're going out this late?' he asked in surprise. ''Twill be dark in an hour.'

'I haven't had a chance to make my rounds in the village lately,' she explained.

'Do you think it appropriate to go traipsing about after dark without proper escort?'

'I always have before.'

'But you weren't a lady then,' he remonstrated.

All the frustrations and anxiety that had been building up throughout Aldyth's short tenure as mistress of the fitzGerald domain spilled out. 'I'll never be a lady!' she cried. She strode over to his table and leaned across it to glare at him. 'You can't know how hard I have tried. The accounts, the numbers, the letters, the tallies: I'll never learn, and I don't want to!' She picked up a handful of parchments and waved them under his nose. 'This is not who I am!' she cried. 'And it will never be!'

Initially stunned by the force of his wife's outburst, Gandulf rose and hurried around the table that separated them. He placed his hands on her shoulders to soothe her. 'Aldyth, please remember the child you carry; you mustn't upset yourself. We have a steward; we can hire a housekeeper. Do you think that's why I married you?'

Aldyth caught her breath and blinked back tears of relief and gratitude. 'Forgive me, Gandulf. I have felt overwhelmed, like a captive bear too stupid to learn how to dance.'

'Aldyth, your knowledge is staggering. Not knowing your letters is no proof of lack of wit; some of the most foolish men I know are scholars.'

'You're right,' said Aldyth, smiling sheepishly. She kissed him lightly on the cheek and said, 'Well, I'll be going. I wouldn't be surprised if Edwin's rheumatism is acting up from the damp, and I haven't checked on the state of Edith's pregnancy, nor Mildburh's either, since before the oubliette.' Their shared imprisonment had become the signal event by which every other event in their lives was measured; they found themselves categorizing their experiences as either before or after that life-changing ordeal.

'The villagers have Sirona,' Gandulf observed.

'She is old and tires easily,' Aldyth countered.

Gandulf laughed and predicted, 'She'll outlive us all.'

Aldyth lifted her chin stubbornly. It had been a while since Gandulf had seen that look, but he remembered well what it meant. Rashly he pressed on, 'We can see that our people are well cared for, but you do not have to be the one to dose and mend them.'

'Who would you send in my place?' she asked hotly.

'What about your condition?' he countered.

'You never worried about Mildburh, who has always worked in the fields up to the time of the birthing and three days later was back in the fields with a baby at her breast! Why don't you just come out and say what's really troubling you?' she snapped. 'Are you trying to tell me that I am allowed no life apart from you?'

'That is customary.'

'So get a haircut!' she retorted. 'A nice customary Norman one.' Taking a step back, Aldyth cried, 'I pledged to share my life with you, not to give it up entirely!'

Gandulf was alarmed. He could feel as much as see Aldyth distancing herself. She had run away from him before, and he could not bear the thought of losing her again. 'Perhaps you're right,' he conceded quickly. 'You'd not be the woman I fell in love with were you content to stay at home and rest. Nor are you one to turn your back on your people, and I knew that from the first. But will you allow me to see you down to the village?'

'Gladly,' said Aldyth, relieved. Marriage could make a tyrant of the gentlest of loves.

'Perhaps we could even strike a bargain,' suggested Gandulf. 'I'll make you a stillroom of the buttery if you will teach me more about the healing lore.'

'Would you really?' she asked excitedly.

Once again Gandulf was struck by the way she wore her passions, so lightly and fiercely, assuming and discarding them like a cloak. At the moment the glow of her enthusiasm reassured Gandulf that he was redeemed, and her pleasure was reward enough for the effort it would take to redefine attitudes shaped over a lifetime.

'Of course I would,' he said, smiling. 'I'll speak to Margaret about it, and we'll see if we can't find a carpenter to lay out the plans. Now let me carry your basket, sweeting.'

Gandulf reined in Cathedra at the village green.

'It seems like an age since I've been here,' Aldyth told him.

'It was a lifetime ago, Aldyth,' he replied solemnly.

'I've missed them,' she said. Not so much by the words Aldyth uttered, but by the tone of her voice and all the love and longing it conveyed, did Gandulf understand the significance of her simple statement. He realized at that moment that all his love, however true and strong and deep, would not in itself be enough to sustain her. He likened Aldyth to a sunflower that turns its face toward the heat of the sun but still cannot survive without its roots sunk deep in the moist, rich soil where it sprouted. He vowed to himself that he would take greater care to see that Aldyth's roots were nurtured. He was different from her; he had never put down roots – not in Normandy, nor Paris, nor London, nor even Scafton.

Dusk came early to Enmore Green, for it rested in the shadow of Castle Hill. Gandulf knew that the town's yellow walls were still bathed in the orange glow of sunset, and down in the vale, beyond the reach of the outcrop's long shadow, the hills and the rooftops were still gilded with the sun's final benediction. But here in Enmore Green the Goddess had cast a lavender veil over her spring, her tree, and her people. In the cool of the dusk sweet fragrances ascended, like the essence of the Goddess: a late mowing of hay, honeysuckle in the hedgerow, the warm, musky scent of rich, fertile earth. A choir of crickets sang the praise of the Goddess, accompanied by a descent of swallows, whistling and twittering as they darted about at their night feeding, and Gandulf heard the voice of the Goddess Herself in the murmur of Her spring spilling out to feed the valley. He looked up at the Wishing Tree, caressed by a warm breeze, the soft breath of the Great Mother, and detected the whisper of Her Fairy messengers in its rustling leaves. His ears were already attuned to the mystical when he heard the melody, but then he began to distinguish the words.

> *'Rosy apple, lemon, pear,*
> *Bunch of roses she shall wear . . .'*

Were the elves singing to him?

> *'Gold and silver by his side,*
> *I know who will be the bride . . .'*

Elfin laughter wove itself into and out of the song, and Gandulf felt a shiver of wonder.

> *'Take her by the lily-white hand,*
> *Lead her to the altar . . .'*

A pair of barefooted urchins burst onto the green. The boy caught the girl by the hand to lead her blushing, but not unwilling, toward the children who followed close behind.

> *'Give her kisses one, two, three,*
> *Her heart will never falter.'*

As the little boy gave the little girl three quick kisses, the circle of ragtag waifs who looked on squealed with delight, and Gandulf thought, ''Twas only children at play.'

But then he recalled Sirona's words: 'The Goddess speaks in many ways.'

A white-haired grandmother came onto the green along the path the children had taken. The little 'bride' cried out and raced into the old woman's arms. As they turned to go back up the path, the old woman noticed Gandulf and Aldyth and waved a welcome. Gandulf recognized her as Winifred LongCross, and a wash of fond memories swept over him. It was for the sake of Winifred, a lifetime ago, that he and Aldyth had made their first trip to the Fairy hill, and on a cold December night, as he had stood outside Aldyth's hut agonizing over that first impossible step, it had been Winifred's arrival that had impelled him forward; indeed, that night they had stepped into Aldyth's house linked arm in arm. It dawned on him all over again that the Goddess spoke through many people.

'Little Edmund! Bertha!' Agilbert was calling his family in to supper.

Mildburh Miller, Big Edmund on one hip and a small sack of flour thrown over the opposite shoulder, stepped out of a narrow lane onto the green. In the swiftly falling darkness, she took no notice of the couple on horseback but went directly to the little hut on Edith and Wulfric's toft where Garth and Hildegarde were staying. Gandulf knew that Mildburh took flour to the destitute couple whenever she could, for the same reason that Wulfric and Edith had given them use of the hut until they could rebuild.

An image appeared in Gandulf's mind of the common as the heart of Enmore Green, the many paths that converged there as a connecting system of arteries and veins, and the life's blood of the village as a constant flow of humanity, charity, and goodwill. Gandulf felt the old familiar tug that he had come to associate with Enmore Green and was struck by the realization that he too had finally put down roots of his own: tender new rootlets, not nearly so deep nor so strong as Aldyth's, but they had proved strong enough to anchor him during the storm and were growing deeper by the day.

'I've missed them too,' he told Aldyth. Not so much by the words he uttered but by the tone of his voice and all the love and longing it conveyed did Aldyth understand the significance of his simple statement, and they smiled in wordless communion.

'Where shall I take you first?' he asked.

'Take me home.'

When they arrived at Sirona's toft, they knew that something was afoot by the scramble of hens that milled outside the door, waiting to be recalled from exile. The callers exchanged a quick, curious look, then stepped forward to tap softly on the door, to the indignation of the hens, who had been there first. Over their reproachful clucks, Sirona called, 'You're here!' as if she had been expecting them. The crone greeted them, broom in hand to whisk away the feathered flood that would come home to roost.

'Come in, children, but step softly, for I prepare an offering to the Goddess.'

Gandulf stepped in after Aldyth, ducking beneath the lintel and weaving between the festoons of bunched herbs strung up from the rafters. On the hearth bubbled a pot of ale fragrant with herbs, yet such a small amount of ale that it would barely fill a cup, and a greater quantity of herbs than the ale could contain: tips of rosemary, tiny fresh sage leaves, and sprigs of mint rose up from the surface of the simmering concoction.

'There is much yet to do before moonrise,' Sirona said without preamble. 'Gandulf, take this lavender to Edith MoonCatcher. At the full of the moon, the baby in her womb will try to dance like the Fairies. An infusion of this before bed will soothe the child.'

'Am I being gotten rid of?' Gandulf inquired with good humor.

'Say rather that you are being made useful,' replied Sirona with a crooked smile, 'but don't make me use my broom on you too.'

Raising his hands in surrender, Gandulf backed toward the door with the lavender. 'We'll come for you at moonrise,' said the wisewoman, closing the door behind him. The two women laughed to hear him clucking like a hen as he retreated down the path.

The abbey bells had tolled curfew before Aldyth and Sirona, carrying a bowl of the sacred brew, arrived. The house was brightly lit and as noisy as a crowded tavern.

Aelfric, greeting them at the door, said, 'I hope you brought more ale.'

Aelfric of the hundred eyes had seen Gandulf arrive and had followed him in. Agilbert, hearing laughter from across the lane, had come over with a jug of ale, Bertha and Little Edmund in tow. Edwin MoonCatcher, always one of the first to join in on any jollity, had invited himself and brought Mildred too, as well as a loaf of bread and more ale. When Wulfric realized that there was a full-blown party in progress, he had sent for the Millers. By the time Aldyth and Sirona arrived, Edith had summoned Lufe Piper and Christine Smithsdaughter, and of course wherever Lufe went, there would be music. Father Edmund, his cheeks flushed with pleasure – and exertion – dandled pudgy Little Edmund on his knee. And Gandulf, already mellowed by sour ale and sweet company, Big Edmund in his lap, grinned happily and tapped his toes to the tune.

'I might've known we'd find you keeping these good folks from their sleep, Gandulf,' said Sirona in mock sternness. 'Edmund, can't you put this ne'er-do-well in his place?'

Father Edmund smiled and shook his head. 'He seems to have found his place very well with no help at all from me.'

Sirona winked at Gandulf and said, 'And a perfect fit it is, too.'

Cups of ale were thrust into the hands of the newest arrivals, and Lufe played a spritely tune. In the midst of the merriment, from across the green, there came the sound of pounding hoofbeats that stopped outside the toft. Hurried footsteps thudded across the toft bridge, followed by an urgent knocking at the door, which was unlatched and swung open without any help from within. Leofwine Clerk, red-faced and panting, stepped inside, scanned the faces of the crowd, and went to kneel at his lord's feet.

'Our messenger has returned with an answer from the king, my Lord; I thought you would want to know right away.' So saying, Leofwine held out a scroll of parchment, rolled and stamped with the royal seal.

'Thank you,' said Gandulf nervously, handing the child in his lap to Mildburh. There were many unresolved matters between himself and the new king. Gandulf had confided to no one his concern that the deaths of fitzGrip, Gauter, and Hugo, as well as Lord Ralf's murder, might be called into question by William Rufus. And what if the bishop of Salisbury decided to investigate Father Odo's demise? Gandulf's succession could be decided only by the king, and he prayed that the secret of his parentage had gone to the grave with Sister Priscilla. But the ultimate concern was the matter of his marriage.

Years of habit dictated Gandulf's impulse to tuck the message away until he might read it privately. But he looked at his friends, whose eyes were anxiously trained on him and, shrugging, said, 'We might as well get it over with.' He slit the wax seal and unrolled the document. Aldyth waited with all the others as he read the dispatch to himself.

Gandulf rolled up the parchment, tucked it into his tunic, and announced, 'It seems that the king is too busy to concern himself with our small corner of the world. He makes no mention of the inquest, he grants me seisin to all of Lord Ralf's properties – upon payment of the standard fees and taxes, of course – and he thanks me for my generous coronation gift. And,' he added, smiling broadly at Aldyth, 'he graciously gives me permission to proceed with the wedding.'

'And not a moment too soon,' cracked Aelfric. 'Another week, and she'll be showing.' Laughter shook the rafters and drove the mice from the thatch as Aldyth flung herself into his arms.

Sirona stood up and announced, ''Tis time to go to the Crystal Spring – for a rite of thanksgiving. We have much to be thankful for, and I invite you to add your voices to our prayers. Edmund,' she added gently, 'we will understand if you choose not to come.'

'There is no blasphemy in thanksgiving,' he replied. 'God will hear my prayer.'

Sirona led the procession across the green to the Crystal Spring. The full moon cast a silvery benediction upon them, and the Wishing Tree stretched forth its branches in silent blessing. From the shadows beneath the tree, a small figure stepped forward into the brilliant moonlight. The effect was uncanny, as if she had stepped out of a moonbeam.

"'Tis the Goddess herself!' cried Agilbert, falling to his knees. Everyone froze.

Until the old woman cackled and slapped her knee. 'Moonstruck, the lot of you!' she said, and the moment she spoke, they all knew it was Winifred LongCross.

Sheepish laughter rippled through the crowd. Someone said, 'Get up, Agilbert, you silly ass.'

But Sirona gently rebuked them: 'Agilbert is the wisest among you. The tree is not the Goddess any more than Father Edmund's church is God. The spring is not the Goddess any more than the crucifix is Jesus Christ. The Lady speaks in many ways, and tonight Winifred serves as Her messenger.'

'But Sirona,' objected the old woman, 'it just happened that the great-grandchildren were asleep, so I came out to enjoy the moonlight.'

'Why this night and this place? And whose lantern, do you suppose,' asked Sirona, gesturing toward Winifred, 'called this fish into Her net?'

Gandulf, who had consciously missed Winifred's presence after his revelation on the green earlier that evening, marveled at her timely appearance. If he had had any doubts that the Great Mother had been guiding him, they were dispelled once and for all.

'We come to give thanks to Modron for seeing us through this difficult time,' began Sirona, and when the wisewoman spoke, even the crickets fell silent.

'Gandulf and Aldyth step forward,' she commanded.

The couple emerged from the crowd, still holding hands.

'On Lammas, the Day of the Dead, you offered your lives to the Goddess in exchange for the life of another. The Lady accepted your worthy offerings and then returned them to you. Your lives have passed into the keeping of the Goddess, and She has given you to each other as well as to us. Aldyth, as our Lord Aethelstan's rightful heir, the people look to you now, as they have always. Gandulf, as her partner in this charge, your strengths will complement your lady's. We trust you bear your responsibilities nobly and well.'

She gave the wooden bowl to Winifred. 'It is for you to honor us by partaking first.'

Winifred solemnly lifted the bowl to her lips and took a sip, then gave the bowl back to Sirona. The wisewoman presented the bowl to Aldyth, who sipped the heady nectar.

'And you, my son.' Gandulf too partook of the libation.

Sirona touched the bowl to her own lips, then passed it into Father Edmund's hands. He sipped and passed it on to Edith, who passed it to Wulfric, who passed it to Lufe, and so it traveled through the crowd. The last to be given the bowl was Agilbert, who gave a sip to Little Edmund, took a sip himself, and then offered it to Bertha, who drained it so dry that she nearly swallowed the bent silver penny in the bottom of the bowl. Agilbert returned the bowl to Sirona, who tossed the penny into the well, along with the last drop of the herb-laden mead, accompanied by a prayer in a language Gandulf did not recognize.

Sirona, her silver hair transformed into a blue halo by moonlight, gazed at her flock in eloquent silence, then concluded, 'As the moon shines upon you, so does the love of the Lady. Each kindness you do is done in Her name, each act of charity is a gift to Her. Go home now, beloved, and dream sweet dreams, rocked in the bosom of the Great Mother.'

Gandulf was deeply moved as his friends came to place their hands between his and Aldyth's in a solemn gesture of homage. First came Leofwine, then Wulfric and Edith. Mildburh, tears in her eyes, was trailed by her husband and their brood. Agilbert was next with Bertha under his arm and little Edmund on his hip. A quick glance at the thinning crowd told Gandulf that Aelfric had vanished at the first hint of oath giving. Gandulf's wry smile faded when he noticed Lufe Piper hovering in the shadows beneath the Wishing Tree. He had already decided not to insist upon an oath of loyalty from Lufe, for he knew him to be faithful if not to his lord, then to his lady. The last in line was Christine, and Gandulf was surprised when she started homeward without Lufe. Uneasily, Gandulf approached the shepherd to let him know indirectly that he did not mean to extract a hollow oath. He met Lufe's glance, and the intensity in the shepherd's eyes scattered the words Gandulf had silently rehearsed. Before he could gather them up and speak them aloud, Lufe knelt and held up his hands to be enclosed in his lord's.

Gandulf stammered, 'Lufe, I had not thought to require this of you.'

Lufe Piper smiled wryly at Gandulf. 'Even a d-d-dog knows his friends, my Lord.'

As Gandulf looked into the lad's uplifted eyes, he knew with his heart as well as his mind that he was lord and protector of this boy and many more good folk. He understood that the night's fleeting rite, with all that it symbolized, had more depth and power than any bestowal of spurs by a king. This was his true inauguration, and it gave a greater legitimacy to his rule than either royal proclamation or right of inheritance. Silently, Gandulf swore to the Goddess, to Whom he now belonged, to live up to the faith and responsibility that his wife, his people, and his king, as well as this boy, had placed in him.

'And I swear to you, Lufe,' said Gandulf, 'that I shall prove worthy of your trust.'

At Sirona's approach, Lufe rose, touched his forelock in salute to the wisewoman, then took his leave. Gandulf watched in wonder as the lad melted into the shadows, then glanced at Aldyth, who beamed with pleasure.

Sirona linked an arm with each. 'Come, children,' she said, leading them homeward for a mug of hot spiced ale. As they crossed the green, Gandulf had never felt so much at the heart of good things. Unwilling to bring the magic of the night to a close, he carried a bench outside into the toft garden that they might bask in the light of Modron's lantern. Fingers entwined, the couple leaned lazily against the outside wall of Sirona's hut, while inside the old woman prepared her hospitality. There was a hint of chill in the air, a portent of the coming season. Soon it would be time to harvest the apples and gather the acorns and hazelnuts, to turn the sheep loose in the wheat stubble, and to look ahead to the new year. Gandulf slipped his arm around Aldyth's shoulders, and she leaned into him, amazed that a single year could have brought such change and confident that the next year could only be better. She felt only one regret tugging at her.

As Sirona handed them each a mug of hot ale, Aldyth

said, 'Godmother, why did the Starlit Path have to crumble now that we are finally in a position to do so much?'

'Don't you see, my child, that it is no longer needed? Gandulf has more power to do good, and in greater safety, than dozens of peasants working in secret. More important,' she said, 'your good example will set a standard to be followed, that eventually we may have one united country, stronger than that of former days, for it will have the strength and tenacity of the Normans, as well as the Saxons' love of liberty and learning. It will be a long, hard struggle, as every such struggle has been. The last wave has passed over the British shore, and the sand is still awash. But the time will come when there are no longer Normans and Saxons and Welsh, but all British.'

'I am but one lord, and no great one at that,' said Gandulf uncertainly.

'By the melding of your bloodlines, you begin the long task of forging the nation. Your children and your children's children will carry on in the name of the Goddess.' The old woman's eyes blazed with the glory of a distant vision. 'One tiny star shining over one corner of England shall be joined by more and brighter stars, until glorious constellations shall spread across her expanse and not a Starlit Path, but a Starlit Nation, shall shine for all the world to see.'

CHAPTER THIRTY-NINE

October 1087

The bells had already tolled for curfew when Aldyth laid her offering of late-blooming asters before the fountain. She had made her rounds in the village, then dallied to sup with the Millers before walking back up the hill. Violating curfew inspired neither the terror nor the caution that it once had, as the new king had not yet appointed a sheriff to replace fitzGrip. Kneeling in prayer, she was startled by the rustle of a pebble falling into the grass beside her. She looked up into the gloom to locate the source, almost certain that Aelfric was the perpetrator. But the lad was nowhere to be seen. Aldyth's heart began to race. Could it be a runner? How could it be? she puzzled.

Abbess Eulalia, who was ranked as a baron of the realm and who corresponded with churchmen, earls, and barons at court, had told Mother Rowena that William Rufus was a very different man from his father. The new king was not governed by the same obsession with control that had ruled the Conqueror, and what had been a point of pride and paranoia to the father was hardly worth the son's notice; his priorities were to win over his major barons and to squelch his brother Robert's traitorous conspiracies. In a general amnesty, William Rufus had released scores of minor offenders, including two petty rabble-rousers, Ine Thatcher and Willibald Weaver. Even a bird in hand seemed more trouble than it was worth to the new king. A runner had not come through since Ricole's appearance last April; Aldyth assured herself that what she had heard was merely an acorn dropping from the Wishing

Tree. But then another missile landed at her feet, followed by a furtive but deliberate rustling. 'Aldyth Lightfoot,' came the whisper.

It had to be a runner, Aldyth decided, perhaps one who had been in deep hiding since the political climate had changed or one whose crime exceeded even the tolerance of the new king. Should she have him wait here until she could speak to Sirona or take him directly to Sula's Stump? Before Aldyth could decide, a cloaked figure stepped out from the bushes, and he was laughing heartily. 'You bad girl,' he chided. 'You were actually contemplating guiding a runner, weren't you, Mouse?'

'Bedwyn, how could you!' began Aldyth, stamping her foot.

Before she could go on, he swept her into a crushing embrace. 'My God, Aldyth, 'tis good to see you again! And wait until you hear what passed in Bristol!'

Bedwyn took her basket, and she was swept up Castle Hill by the energy and excitement he exuded. Not only had he found an adventurous Icelander with a stout little dragon ship, but he had enlisted a score of good men prepared to set sail as soon as he could return with Gunhild. 'And you'll never guess where I got them!' he crowed.

'Don't keep me waiting,' she wheedled, giddy with relief. 'Out with it, Bedwyn.'

'Aldyth, I returned from Bristol along the Starlit Path. My intention was no more than to disband what was left of it; we owed our comrades that much. But I'll be damned if I didn't recruit a crew from among the displaced guides.'

Grabbing his sleeve, she demanded, 'Who, Bedwyn, who? Would I know any of them?'

Bedwyn made a great show of considering her question. 'Mmmm. I don't suppose you know a young fellow named Alfred Ricoleson?'

'Alf! How perfect!' Then frowning, Aldyth said, 'But what of his mother?'

'I was going to tell you about that,' Bedwyn chuckled. 'I promised Ricole that if she allowed Alf to come away with me, I know a lady in Sceapterbyrig who might find her a

538

place. A good woman, really, although she's fallen into bad company of late.'

Aldyth hooted but then added warmly, 'Of course she's welcome. Now, who else?'

Bedwyn grew serious. 'Willibald Weaver.'

'Willibald Weaver?' she repeated, not crediting her ears. 'But they took his hand.'

'He's still got the dexterity of a weaver,' countered Bedwyn, 'and with one hand and most of his teeth, he can tie a knot almost as well as any of the Icelander's men.'

Aldyth knew that Bedwyn was stretching the truth to make a place for the remaining Weaver twin. But why not? There was really no way to repay the few who had served the many so faithfully and at such risk, but at least he had contrived to share what good fortune he was able to. Best of all was the change Aldyth saw in him. This was the Bedwyn she had always known, who could see a silk purse in a sow's ear and in no time have a tailor sew it, a miser fill it, and then use it to build castles in the air.

Bedwyn had already bagged his sow, commissioned a tailor, and chosen the cloud on which to build. As to filling his purse, he had his eye on if not a miser, then a skeptic.

Bedwyn was up most of the night poring over sea charts while Gandulf studied accounts with his steward. The last of the candles was guttering when a sudden draft blew Bedwyn's map off the table, and a chilling thought occurred to Gandulf as he watched his brother-in-law retrieve it. 'Bedwyn, you'll be setting sail in the stormy season. How many of your men know how to sail or have even seen the ocean?'

Bedwyn shrugged. 'The Icelander has a handful of experienced sailors, but not so many with the guts to sail to the ends of the earth. I've a crew of men willing to lay down their lives in a game of chance – against the odds. That a man is born with; the rest he can learn as he goes.'

Leofwine Clerk looked up from the disarray of parchment rolls littering his end of the table. 'A year ago, who would have imagined me as steward of the fitzGerald fief?'

Gandulf nodded. 'You've proved yourself in these last weeks, lad. You've a knack that William CloseFist never had – and we can finance this expedition on the income that scurvy thief would have skimmed off the top. But tell us, what have you found?'

'We might manage it,' said Leofwine, 'by giving Bedwyn our stores of ready funds, then making up the difference by selling the manor outside Caen. 'Twould mean scraping and pinching until the land was sold, but we could then get by without borrowing.'

'That holding borders the de Broadford lands; 'tis where I grew up,' mused Gandulf.

'I couldn't ask you to sell your childhood home, fitzGerald,' objected Bedwyn.

'Good riddance to it,' answered Gandulf. 'Perhaps de Broadford might like first chance at it. He'd want me for a neighbor no more than I'd want him.' He chuckled. 'Leofwine, you can draft a proposal to de Broadford in the morning, but first get some sleep. Well done, lad,' he added, clapping him on the shoulder. Leofwine blushed at his lord's praise, then went down to the hall in search of a corner to spread out his blanket.

Outside a cock crowed. Bedwyn stretched and yawned. 'Where has the night gone?'

Gandulf opened the shutters to look out across the vale, already brightening from its nighttime obscurity. He saw Enmore Green nestled against the hill like a chick beneath a hen's wing; soon wisps of smoke would rise up from little hearth fires and people would be stirring to meet the new day. But when Bedwyn looked out over Gandulf's shoulder, he saw the road to the sea, winding to the north and the west toward the bustling seaport of Bristol, with its wharves and its ships and, just beyond, endless uncharted waters.

'FitzGerald,' said Bedwyn, 'I was ten when I was dispossessed, old enough to know that even great estates do most business in kind. I don't want to leave you hard pressed.'

'We would not ordinarily have much silver on hand, but Ralf had been squeezing the peasants and selling his assets to build his castle.' Copper eyes locked on sapphire as Gandulf told Bedwyn, 'Sirona was right; that castle will never be completed.'

'What would William Rufus say if he knew that you didn't intend to finish his castle?'

'He has two scheming brothers to contend with, a kingdom seething with unrest, and an empty treasury. I need only ask the king to help finance it, and 'twill end the matter.'

'I can see there will be some welcome changes in the Blackmore Vale,' said Bedwyn.

'You could be a part of them,' offered Gandulf. 'I'd welcome the services of a good knight and reward you well. There's still time to change your mind about Vinland.'

'I might bring myself to serve you, fitzGerald, but I could never swear fealty to a Norman king. I'll make a place for myself in the new world.'

Gandulf nodded. 'I've just found my place, and nothing could tear me away.'

'I can hardly wait to be on my way,' said Bedwyn, his eyes sparkling with excitement, 'and I can scarcely believe that I've found a woman who'll go with me.'

Both men looked toward the bed, where their wives had nodded off while waiting – and waiting – for their husbands to finish their plans. Gunhild still held her packing list, while Aldyth had drifted off sorting remedies for the seafarers' medicine chest. Bunches of herbs lay scattered on the covers, and Baldwin had bedded down among her skirts.

'We were both lucky,' said Gandulf softly.

'Aldyth is quite a catch,' said Bedwyn, 'but your sister is a remarkable woman too.'

'Yes, I know,' Gandulf assured him, 'and you must treat her well.'

'Or what?' asked Bedwyn, bridling. 'You're going to make me?'

'No,' replied Gandulf with a chuckle. 'She will.'

'I've no doubt you're right,' Bedwyn said, grinning.

'Everyone we would want in attendance at your wedding and at our wedding feast is here, Bedwyn, with the obvious exception of Harold. I see no reason to wait. If you do not object,' said Gandulf, 'one feast will serve to celebrate both occasions.'

'Of course I have no objections, Brother, since you're footing the bill. And besides,' Bedwyn added, with a nod toward the women, ''twould be just the thing to win our way back into their good graces after the way we've neglected them tonight.'

The gathering was held in the solar, with only Sirona, Edith SwanNeck, Aelfric, Mother Rowena, and Dame Eulalia attending – besides, of course, Father Edmund, who was to perform the ceremony. The company stood by the fire conversing while awaiting the arrival of the two nuns from the abbey. Hoping to afford his stepmother some solace, Gandulf confided to Edith, 'I intend to go to Normandy to pay my respects to William Rufus in person, and I will use the opportunity to make discreet inquiries after Harold.'

Aldyth was discussing the voyage with Gunhild and Bedwyn. But overhearing her husband's statement, she turned to stare at him in wordless shock. No one noticed the nuns' arrival, for all eyes were fastened on Gandulf.

'You can't go!' cried Aldyth.

'She's right, fitzGerald,' warned Bedwyn. 'You mustn't draw any suspicion to yourself, and you shouldn't be drawing attention to Harold's case either.'

'Could they be holding him without realizing who he is?' asked Gunhild.

'No,' said Mother Rowena firmly, removing her cloak. 'He was months at William's court. If they have him, someone has recognized him; he is not a man easily forgotten.'

'This is all speculation,' said Gandulf flatly. 'We'll never learn anything by staying at home, and who among us has a better reason for going?'

'If you must go, then I will come with you,' stated Aldyth.

'In your condition? I think it best if I go alone, sweeting,' he said, in a tone he hoped would permit no argument.

'Well, I don't,' retorted Aldyth. 'Your father insisted on

going alone, and now there is no one who can say what has befallen him.'

'Then I'll take Gilbert and Henry and Hugh,' Gandulf conceded.

'No need to rush blindly into the lion's den,' Sirona cautioned. 'I'll ask my hens.'

'Very well,' said Gandulf agreeably, 'take your reading, Sirona.'

Aldyth noted that her husband made no promises. His determination to leave her could only mean that it was too dangerous a mission to risk taking her. Gandulf never disputed her arguments or insisted upon the correctness of his own; he simply plowed forward along his chosen path. Aldyth said nothing, but Gandulf could see that the dispute was not over. Unhappily, he recognized the familiar set of her jaw. His fears were realized when Aldyth coolly withdrew her hand from his and refused to meet his eye.

It was no coincidence that Father Edmund chose that moment to bless the marriage of Aldyth and Gandulf. 'How fortunate that Love has found a place at this hearth,' he said.

Aelfric snorted.

Father Edmund shot him what he hoped was a quelling glance and continued, 'Aldyth and Gandulf have passed through the tempest to sail into a safe harbor, yet even the stoutest ship must be caulked and painted, scraped and maintained. There will be storms ahead, yet they will weather the gales and sit out the calms, with Faith as their guiding star, Hope as their anchor, and, above all, Charity for their powering wind.'

Tentatively, Gandulf held out his hand to Aldyth. The pleading look on his face was too comical to resist, and her frown melted. 'Promise me at least,' she insisted, 'that you will not go unless you can first convince me that you must.'

'I promise,' he conceded, 'if you promise to keep your mind open to my arguments.' Aldyth smiled and placed her hand in his.

Father Edmund then asked Bedwyn and Gunhild to come forth. The bride was radiant; the groom looked nervous. Aldyth wondered if Gunhild knew how many hearts she would be breaking and what a legend she was laying to rest.

Father Edmund asked, 'If any present knows of any reason that these two should not be joined in lawful wedlock, let them speak now or forever hold their peace.'

Dame Eulalia stepped forward. 'Is it not true that this woman took a vow to be the bride of Christ, chaste and faithful unto death?'

When Gunhild saw that her accuser was the abbess herself, she grew pale. Bedwyn placed an arm around her and glowered at the abbess. Gandulf would have spoken out in his sister's defense had Aldyth not gently placed a restraining hand upon his arm.

The abbess continued, 'And is it not true that this vow was taken under duress?'

'Aye, my Lady Abbess, 'twas a forced vow, and I a prisoner of war,' said Gunhild.

'The Church holds that a forced vow is not binding. Let it be known that this vow was unlawful, and let it never be mentioned again.' She then declared, 'God bless you, my child, and this union. Go forward with a clear conscience, and let the wedding proceed.'

Leofwine Clerk hastened in to consult with Gandulf in low whispers, then made a hurried exit. Father Edmund wiped his brow and picked up his psalter to resume the ceremony. 'If there are no other objections—'

'Here!' came a commanding voice as the door to the solar swung open. 'I object!'

In came two road-stained men wearing the hooded robes of Benedictine monks.

'Oh, no!' growled Bedwyn, stepping forward threateningly. 'If you've been sent by the bishop, speak to the abbess, for this woman has been absolved of her vow.'

The door shut behind the brothers. One of them threw back his cowl, and everyone gasped; it was the father of the bride. 'Are we too late to kiss the bride?' he asked.

Gunhild broke away from Bedwyn and flung herself into Harold's arms. Edith SwanNeck tottered, clutching at her rosary. Not trusting her trembling legs to carry her across the room to her husband, she simply stood where she was gripping the table. Gandulf stepped quickly to his stepmother's side and took her elbow.

Harold hugged Gunhild and kissed her on both cheeks. 'My little lamb,' he crooned. Bedwyn fell to his knees, but Harold raised him up and embraced him. Clasping his hands, Harold said, 'I cannot repay you for all you have done, but I can give you both my sincerest blessing. I rest easy knowing my daughter goes to a man with a hero's heart. Keep her well, lad.' Chuckling, he added, 'I hope you'll find her easier to manage than I did.'

Bedwyn nodded, then stepped back. Harold went to take Edith's hands, saying tenderly. 'This old man has found his way home to you once again. Will you have me back?'

Edith SwanNeck laid a trembling hand upon his cheek, assuring herself that he was no ghost, then threw her arms around him. As Gandulf watched the old man kiss his wife, he hoped that he and Aldyth would still know such ardor after so many years. Reluctantly Edith released her husband. 'There are others who would greet you, my dear.'

Gandulf's joy at Harold's safe return quickly changed to discomfort, for as much as he loved his newfound father, they were still strangers to each other. In the weeks since their parting, Gandulf had wondered if their heartfelt exchange had been a fiction of his mind. But when Harold turned to Gandulf, his blue eyes were swimming with tears.

'My son,' he said, taking Grandulf's hands, 'the word in every tavern along the king's highway is that both Ralf fitzGerald and Lady Emma are dead.'

Gandulf's eyes closed in pain, and he shook his head, unable to speak.

Harold pulled his son into his arms. 'I am so sorry,' he whispered. 'I loved her well. Tomorrow let you and I go to the chapel and pray for the soul of our beloved Emma. You, Gandulf, are all the more dear to me now, for I shall see her in your eyes.' Placing an arm about his shoulders, Harold said to Aldyth, 'Thank God he has you, lass, to see him through this. From the very first, I had hoped that my son would not let you slip away. I can swear to

545

you both that love is the balm that can soothe, if not heal, a broken heart.

'Now, children,' said Harold, 'there is someone I would have you meet.' Harold held out his hand to his silent traveling companion, who pulled back his hood to reveal the features of a handsome man, just graying at the temples and bearing so striking a resemblance to Harold that he seemed almost a younger version of the man.

'This is your Uncle Wulfnoth,' said Harold.

Edith and Gunhild burst into tears and threw themselves into Wulfnoth's arms. He whispered endearments and assured them that he had truly come home. They withdrew, shaking their heads in wonder. Wulfnoth wiped his eyes upon his sleeve, then held out his arms to Aldyth and Gandulf. 'On our journey home,' said their uncle warmly, 'my brother had much to say about you. I feel I know enough already to love you both well.'

Sirona wryly observed, 'I thought I was coming up the hill to attend a wedding, but this is better entertainment than a Christmas mystery play!'

Then came a clamor of eager voices demanding news and explanations. 'All in good time,' said Harold, 'but first I have a bride to give away.'

By this time, Father Edmund was so flustered that he dropped his prayer book and had to ruffle through it nervously before he could recommence the ceremony for the third time. But at last the vows were spoken, and Bedwyn and Gandulf called for wine to toast the newlyweds while servants set up a trestle table. Then the guests took their seats, and the feast was carried in by a long train of attendants.

Aelfric seated himself at the foot of the table, where he could help himself to the dishes once they had been served. But there was no high table, for here alone, in all of England, was a refuge from the rigid framework of rank and hierarchy, place and status. Where else might abbess and outlaw, lord and liege, saint and scapegrace be found breaking bread, rubbing shoulders, and toasting one another's health?

When the door closed behind the last servant, with instructions to leave until summoned, and the wedding party was again alone, Gunhild demanded, 'Now, Father, you must tell us everything!'

Harold nodded and complied. 'I followed William from Normandy to Mantes, but he was too well guarded to approach, so I shadowed him until my opportunity arose. But he panicked at the sight of me; I believe he actually thought I was a ghost. In his fear, he spooked his horse, it threw him, and he ruptured his gut on the pommel of his saddle. There was a great commotion, with attendants and onlookers rushing in and blocking my escape. His aide-de-camp signaled me out of the crowd, and I was certain that he had taken William's accusation to heart. But I was collared to serve as one of William's litter bearers because of my size. Thank God the knight was a young fellow who must have come to serve at William's court after my time there. I helped deliver William to his headquarters, then was given a silver penny and dismissed.

'That left me in a quandary. William was in no condition to receive petitioners, and there were too many about who might have recognized me. I waited, and when William was moved to Rouen to die, I followed. For days he lingered. 'Twas a hideous death I'd not have wished upon my worst enemy. He slipped into and out of delirium, crying like a child in remorse for his destruction of England, and begging for God's forgiveness for his sins.'

'As well he might!' exclaimed Gunhild.

'Believe me, the wretch suffered for his crimes,' said Harold. 'But it must have been God Himself who gave this thought to the king's confessor: that if William were to empty his dungeons, 'twould be a sign to God of his change of heart.'

Father Edmund crossed himself. 'May God have mercy on his soul.'

'Poor devil,' agreed Harold. 'As soon as they knew he lay dying, every one of his lords-in-waiting raced off to his dominions to guard against uprising, leaving William's own servants to strip the rings from his fingers and the linen from his bed. They even took the candles and left him lying naked on the floor in the darkness.'

'He had three sons. How could they let this happen?' asked Edith in horror.

'Robert, the eldest, had spent years in prison for treason, and his feelings for his father were less than solicitous. The youngest, Henry, fearful of being cheated out of a farthing by his brothers, was already in the treasury counting out his inheritance. And William Rufus was halfway to England to lay claim to his dying father's throne.'

'The judgement of God was clearly revealed at his funeral,' spoke up the abbess.

At their urging, she explained, 'According to the dispatch from Normandy, his body was rotting by the time a Church burial could be arranged, and his corpse was forced into a coffin too small for his corpulent body. In the midst of the service, his coffin burst and his body sprawled on the floor, filling the church with so foul a stench that those few in attendance were driven out of doors. But his same was not over, for in the midst of the funeral mass a man announced that William could not rightfully be buried in that church, for in his lifetime he had stolen the land the church had been built on from this man's father. A hasty settlement had to be cobbled together before the burial could proceed. A shameful day for Normandy, such goings-on before all the world!'

'He was paid in his own coin,' growled Bedwyn.

'Learn from his example, Cousin,' begged Mother Rowena. 'Let go of your ill will.'

'Alas, my lady,' said Bedwyn, 'your nature is gentler than mine. I cannot help but be bitter. And yet,' added Bedwyn, taking Gunhild's hand and gazing at her fondly, 'it is also my nature to look to the future, and I see much there to look forward to.'

'We all do,' agreed Edith, smiling at Harold. 'Dame Eulalia, would you kindly release me from the vows forced upon me, as you did for my daughter?'

'Gladly,' said the abbess. 'How many times must the Church make the ruling that a forced vow is not binding, only to disregard it when it suits its convenience? Until this practice is discontinued, a stain shall remain upon the honor of Holy Mother Church.' Then the abbess asked, 'Rowena, were your vows not also forced?'

'At the time they were, my Lady,' replied Mother Rowena, 'but I keep them freely, for I have found my peace within the abbey walls.'

The abbess smiled fondly, then grew solemn. 'There is one other who must be absolved,' she said. She met Harold's blue eyes; he flinched and looked away.

'Hear me out,' said the abbess sternly. 'This is medicine to purge your soul. The vows forced upon you were no more binding than those forced upon your daughter and wife. And 'twas a heinous sin for William to bribe the pope to justify his conquest in God's name; I daresay William is not the only one who will burn for that blasphemy.'

When Harold lifted his eyes to meet hers, they were glittering with unshed tears.

'You have paid your penance and confessed your sins,' said the abbess. 'I do not hold the keys to God's Kingdom, but I have no small knowledge of Church law and can tell you that, politics of war and conquest aside, you committed no sin legally or morally. When God's Kingdom is come, you will sit among the chosen, as surely as William will not.'

Harold nodded solemnly, crossed himself, then wiped his eyes upon his sleeve.

Bedwyn, addressing the abbess, said, 'You speak of the kingdom to come in Heaven, my lady. But what about here on earth? As you have admitted, the maneuverings among abbots, bishops, and even the pope are no more scrupulous than the politics of court and country. I'm a hopeless sinner, but I recognize you as one governed only by what is right and what is wrong. So I speak freely in your presence, my Lady, and it is with respect that I point out the great miscarriage of justice that has befallen England. My concern at this moment is of our earthly kingdom and what will become of it.'

He turned to Harold and added, 'The Normans are facing rebellion, empty coffers, and quarrel among themselves. If ever there were a time to rise and regain your throne, 'twould be now. I'd gladly raise an army of men willing to die for you.'

'No, Bedwyn,' said Harold firmly. 'I have neither the heart nor the stomach for more bloodshed.' He gestured toward Gendulf and Aldyth. 'Just as you see with this young couple, there will someday be a peaceful blending of peoples, God willing. Sirona tells me that it will be so, and so it shall. As for me,' he said, smiling warmly at his wife, 'I have finally found my place.'

''Tis a good place,' said Sirona, 'where a man can find peace and as good as disappear like a stone in a pond. Harold will not be the first to make his home among the Fairies.'

'Tell me about this place, Harold,' said Wulfnoth.

'Better yet, little brother,' said Harold, reaching over to clasp Wulfnoth's hand, 'I will take you there myself.'

'What a waste!' cried Bedwyn in anguish. 'What of England? What of your people?'

'When the wild geese fly,' said Sirona, 'one goose leads the way to soften the journey for others. When that leader tires, another steps forward to serve.'

'All I would ask,' said Harold softly, 'is that when tales are told round the hearth fire, people will not think too harshly of Harold Godwinson.'

CHAPTER FORTY

New Year's Eve 1097

Gandulf stood behind Aldyth, smoothing her hair with a brush. Her hair was tangled and her cheeks rosy, for she had just returned from visiting Mother Rowena at the abbey. She had removed her everyday kirtle and sat on the bed in her shift. Gandulf parted the cascade of honey-colored hair like a silken curtain and kissed the back of her neck. Reaching around, he unfastened her shift and slipped his hands inside to cup her breasts. A sigh escaped Aldyth as she melted against him. Gently he lowered her onto the bed, and Aldyth, smiling like a contented cat, reached up to unfasten the belt of his tunic.

A drumroll of footsteps up the stairs, followed by a series of thuds at the door, sent Aldyth and Gandulf flying apart guiltily. Two little voices called, 'Mama! Papa!'

'We don't really have time for this,' said Aldyth to Gandulf ruefully.

Gandulf sighed. Straightening his tunic, he opened the door and was nearly bowled over by a pair of overexcited boys who fell upon him like playful puppies. Laughing, he lifted one by the waist and the other by the belt to carry them across the room. They squealed with delight as their father heaved them onto the bed.

'You're as bad as the little ones, Gandulf,' Aldyth chided.

His chastened expression was only a ploy, for he reached past her to seize a pillow.

'Oh, no, you don't,' she said, pulling him into the heap of giggling bodies. 'The last time you started a pillow fight, the bed looked like an eiderducks' nest, the pillows were half the size they'd been, and feathers were turning up for weeks afterward.'

'As I recall,' he replied, 'you were the one who whirled pillows about like flails.'

She laughed and conceded, ''Tis not much of a pillow fight if the feathers don't fly.'

Giggling, they fell back upon the pillows in a heap. Nestled between Gandulf and Aldyth were their six-year-old twins, who could have been mirror images of each other.

'Mama,' asked young Harold, 'when will the company get here?'

'Very soon, love, so you had both better go change into your good tunics.'

'Will Cousin Bedwyn be coming?' asked Aethelstan eagerly.

Aldyth laughed. ''Tis unlikely, poppet. Your cousin is probably snug over his own Yuletide fire on the far side of the sea.' It had been three years before they had heard from Bedwyn and Gunhild, by way of Alf Ricoleson, on his way to Byzantium in Bedwyn's service. On his last trip, Alf had said that Gunhild, now the mother of four golden wolf cubs, was ready to come home to England. Bedwyn, now the owner of three stout little dragon ships, had agreed, for he had already made his fortune and worked only to please himself.

'Bedwyn could return any day,' said young Aethelstan excitedly.

'Well, I hope he does,' said Gandulf. 'He can pay off the rest of his loan. Emma is mine and will be needing a dowry. Then 'twill be Rowena's turn, for she's only a year behind.'

'Perhaps we shall need only one dowry,' said Aldyth. 'After all, 'tis through one of those girls that the fountain will be served.' She frowned. 'It saddens me to think that one of my daughters might never know the joy that we have known as husband and wife.'

'No daughter of mine shall go into a marriage, or even serve the Goddess, if it be not her choice,' said Gandulf firmly.

'Which one will it be?' Aldyth pondered. 'Emma is serious and quiet and eager to learn, but Rowena cannot sit still long enough to listen. She runs wild and barefoot with Mildburh's and Edith's girls, and already she winks at the boys. It has to be Emma.'

'Don't jump to conclusions, sweeting. Remember what trouble it got us into in your case? Just ask Sirona,' said Gandulf, 'instead of working yourself into a state of worry.'

'Do you think I haven't asked her time and time again?' said Aldyth. 'She just smiles that crooked smile of hers and says that time must take its course.'

'Where are the girls now?' Gandulf wondered aloud.

'Emma is helping Margaret in the kitchen,' said Harold, 'and the last time I saw Rowena, she was running down Tout Hill.'

'I suppose we should locate your sister,' said Gandulf, peeling the boys from the bed like wet winter leaves and sending them off with a quick kiss and a smack on the rump.

With Gandulf's help, Aldyth managed to get dressed in just under twice the usual time. When they got down to the hall, Rowena was still nowhere to be found. Gandulf sighed and called for his cloak. He loved his younger daughter with all his heart; she had her mother's honey-gold hair and emerald eyes, but she was just as difficult to fathom. The child took the same joy in living that her mother did but had been born without a scrap of prudence and had not acquired any in the eight years since. As Gandulf was asking Aldyth where he might begin the search for his errant daughter, Aelfric staggered into the hall, apparently unaware of the wet, muddy girl wrapped around his leg.

Aelfric's sandy-colored hair had deepened to a burnished brown, but his eyes were still the same unnerving ice blue until warmed by the smile that he reserved only for his friends. They were not selected by rank or power, so Aldyth and Gandulf felt privileged to be included among his chosen circle. Aelfric was still slipping through the cracks, still living by his wits, and still his own man, for Gandulf had understood that by requiring an oath of fealty from the lad, he would have lost a faithful if erratic retainer. They fed and clothed him, and he did their bidding when it suited him, but he also came and went as he wished, like a cat. And like a tomcat, Aelfric had captured the affections of many a pretty maid. He had been known to dally, but never for long. The only girl he had not been able to disengage at will was young Rowena, who had the tenacity of a bulldog. Aldyth and Gandulf hurried over to the entwined pair.

'Rowena,' chided Aldyth, 'where have you been?'

'I was with Aelfric, Mama,' she answered sweetly.

The corners of Aldyth's mouth quivered. Who could resist such an imp? 'Very well, sweeting. Go to the pantry and clean yourself up. Then change into your good gown.'

The little girl grinned up at Aelfric but made no move to comply. Aelfric frowned and gave his leg a shake as if to dislodge her, but she clung all the more tightly.

Aldyth looked pleadingly at Aelfric.

Aelfric sighed. 'The size of the ticks in this part of the shire is frightful,' he quipped as he staggered off toward the pantry with his passenger still firmly attached.

As Rowena's parents watched them go, Aldyth said to Gandulf, 'Where will we ever find a man willing to take on such a strong-willed little hellion?'

'She'll find someone,' Gandulf assured her. 'You found a husband, didn't you?'

The hall bustled as servants carried platters of pasties, roast apples, sweetmeats, and dried fruits to the sideboard. The trestle tables were set up, linens laid, and saltcellars set into place. Torches burned brightly, greenery hung from the rafters, and Lufe Piper and his family were already in the gallery, warming the cold, drafty hall with their music.

Lord Gandulf often hosted traveling minstrels and bards, especially during the high holidays, but never on New Year's Eve. Over the twelve days of Christmas, the lord and lady of Scafton feasted their lieges of the neighboring villages, each in turn, and the poor were never turned away, except on New Year's Eve, when they received their alms at the kitchen door; that night was for reserved for Enmore Green.

When the Millers arrived, the twins swept the Miller children off, leaving their parents a moment's peace to talk. Mildburh said, 'We are planning a church ale for the Sunday after Plow Monday. 'Twill put a few new slates on the church roof and a bit of fun into the January thaw. Can you come?

Gandulf,' she added, 'the children are already begging for a tale to keep them entertained while their parents addle their brains.'

'We'll be there,' he promised.

Agilbert arrived, carrying Bertha solicitously, his son, Little Edmund, at his side. At eleven, Little Edmund already showed promise of growing up to be as big as his father.

'Did I tell you, Aldyth,' said Agilbert proudly, 'that Father Edmund has offered to make a priest of Little Edmund?'

Aldyth smiled. 'Maybe once or twice.'

Big Edmund ran up and seized his milk brother's hand to drag him off to join the other children. Rarely were the two Edmunds seen apart, and they were still as ill matched a pair as ever. Little Edmund, as good-natured a child as he had promised to be, towered over Big Edmund, as rascally a lad as had ever fished the abbey stews by moonlight.

Bertha struggled to break free of Agilbert's hold. He set her down and fondly watched as the little pig trotted off after the boys with a stiff gait. 'Aldyth,' confided Agilbert, 'I'm concerned about Bertha. Have you anything for the stiffness in her joints?'

'Yes, Agilbert, I'll give you some violet leaves for her gruel. How is her appetite?'

'Much better, thank you. You were right about the parsley,' he said earnestly.

When Agilbert went to warm himself by the hearthfire, Aldyth whispered to Gandulf, 'Bertha is getting old. No herbs will keep her alive forever.'

'I've already sent to every village within two days' travel,' said Gandulf, 'offering a good price for any harelipped pigs, dogs, or even chickens they can deliver. One must eventually turn up, and we can only hope that it does so in a timely fashion.'

Guests arrived in droves, but this would be the first New Year rung in without the aid of Edwin MoonCatcher. Old age and a fever had carried him away, and his fat wife, Mildred, had pined herself haggard for six weeks and then followed. A draft sent the torches guttering in their sconces and announced the arrival of the next group of revelers. It was Sirona in the company of Osfrith Outlaw, Seaxburh MoonCatcher, and their four lusty girls. It was a long walk from the depths of Cranborne Chase, but they came every year and stayed on as guests. Their children were parceled out among the lofts and odd corners of MoonCatchers' cottages throughout Enmore Green, building bridges between generations and extending the precious net of family ties.

'Good Yule, godmother!' said Aldyth, embracing Sirona. Sirona had borne the last ten years most lightly of all. She had not changed a bit, though she liked finding her firewood stacked outside her door and used it more freely than had once been her custom.

Aldyth led the wisewoman to her accustomed place of honor by their hearth fire. 'Genevieve,' said Aldyth to a young dark-haired girl, 'would you please bring wine?'

Genevieve, just turned eleven, was the daughter of Jehanne and Roland. To Aldyth's delight, Genevieve had become deeply attached to her other serving maid, Mildburh's oldest daughter, Jenena. The Saxon girl and the Norman girl could be seen running about their errands hand in hand; it was in these children that Aldyth read hope for the future.

Just then, the sound of horses clattering in the bailey drew their attention. The twins, their mouths full of filched sweetmeats, rushed out of the pantry, where they had been playing hide-and-seek. As they caught sight of the ancient woman seated by the hearth, their rowdy manner changed with a comical abruptness.

'Oh, Grandmother,' said Aethelstan respectfully, 'we didn't hear you come in. Good Yule and Happy New Year.' The boys stood in line to kiss her dry, wrinkled cheek.

As they stepped back, Sirona said with mock severity, 'Did no one ever teach you not to kiss with your mouth full? And don't think that slipping me one stolen sweetmeat will excuse your scapegrace manners.' Taking a bite of the boys' offering, she chuckled, 'I can't be bought off for less than a handful.' The boys broke into silly grins.

A clamor of greeting broke out as into the hall came two men and a distinguished-looking silver-haired woman, all three dressed in mossy brown.

'Grandfather! Grandmother! Uncle Wulfnoth!' cried the children.

Life with the Fairies agreed with them, for the years seemed to have dropped away from them. An elusive sadness still dwelt behind Harold's gentle blue eyes, but the crushing sorrow had lifted. Harold held his arms open to little Emma, who flew into them for a hug, while Edith SwanNeck scooped a little boy into each arm.

'Where's Aunt Sula?' asked Rowena, hugging her uncle.

Wulfnoth patted her cheek and said, 'She's seven months heavy with child and at this moment is snug and warm by our hearthfire. She does send you this, angel.' From his pouch Wulfnoth took a handful of honeyed hawberries. Immediately all of the children opened their mouths wide, like baby birds, and he popped a sweet into each one.

'There will be more after dinner,' he promised.

'When is dinner?' asked young Harold.

'There are the bells chiming,' noted Aldyth. 'Mass is over at the abbey, and 'twill be so at Saint Wulfstan's too. Father Edmund should be here soon.'

'I've a horseman waiting to bring him up to us,' said Gandulf.

'And then we can eat!' exclaimed young Harold.

Midnight was approaching when Sirona announced, 'The wheel of time returns once more to the place where time and eternity mingle. That which was laid to rest may rise, and that which is restless may find peace.'

The wisewoman gazed at all the earnest faces turned toward her. Gandulf was thinking of his mother and hoping that she had found peace. Aldyth pictured the noble face that had come to her in the oubliette and thanked the Goddess for allowing her to feel her father's enduring love. Wulfric hugged the little girl in his lap and dropped a tear for Elviva, while Edith prayed to the Lady to take old Edwin and Mildred under Her wing as they adjusted to their new life. Lufe raised his pipe to his lips and silently played the notes of his grandfather Grimbald's favourite tune. Agilbert crossed himself for the souls of his parents, then tenderly kissed his pig. And Harold Godwinson felt his chest tighten at the thought of his faithful brothers and beloved children, dead and scattered. Wulfnoth, standing behind Harold, rested his hands upon his brother's shoulders in a gesture of silent comfort. Placing a grateful hand over Wulfnoth's, Harold looked around him at the gathering of children and grandchildren and thanked God for them all. He even spared a thought for William, pitying the man who had conquered his world and died alone.

'And now 'tis time,' said Sirona with a twinkle, 'to go home to greet the New Year.'

Like a Fairy hill at cockcrow, the hall was aboil with leave-takers scrambling to collect their cloaks and babies, for it was time for the First Footers to make their rounds.

The men swallowed down a last cup of spiced wine to keep them warm as bread, wine, and kindling were gathered into small bundles for the First Footer. Gandulf, as always, played the part of First Footer in Enmore Green. Several years in a row, he had tried to decline the honor, saying that someone else should have a turn. But as Aelfric had pointed out, 'No one else can afford a whole loaf for each household, and white bread at that.'

'Mama! Mama!' hounded the twins. 'Can't we go with Papa this year?'

'What did your father say?'

'He said to ask you.'

Aldyth said to Gandulf, 'Only if you promise to have them sent home when they fall asleep, instead of carrying them about on the backs of your drunken company all night.'

The boys crowed triumphantly as Aldyth checked to see that their cloaks were fastened against the winter wind, then did the same for their father. 'Rowena, Emma, are you ready?' With an arm about each girl, Aldyth followed Sirona to the wagon that would carry them to the wisewoman's cottage. Aldyth always left Margaret to greet the First Footer on Castle Hill, while she and the girls awaited him with Sirona. 'Enmore Green will always be my home,' Aldyth explained, 'so 'tis fitting we greet the New Year there.'

The wagon rattled as it jolted over the frozen ruts. Before

long, they caught sight of the last stragglers scuttling down the hill, like the dry leaves of autumn. Soon there were tittering, chattering shadows on all sides as the village women made way for the wagon. Rowena leaned perilously over the sideboard to wave at her friends. Emma smiled indulgently but held tight to the corner of her little sister's cloak.

Before long, the First Footer could be heard making his rounds from house to house with his riotous companions, but even the sound of their father's progress was not enough to keep the girls awake. Aldyth looked at her daughters, curled up against each other on Sirona's feather bed. Rowena's head was pillowed in the crook of her sister's arm, and even in her sleep Emma had a protective hand resting on her little sister's shoulder. Aldyth pulled the fur coverlet more closely about them. The girls were as different as night and day, as mist and sunlight, as Norman and Saxon, yet each was as dear as the other. The simple sound of their breathing was more miraculous to Aldyth than angel song. Sirona rose from her bench by the fire to stand quietly at Aldyth's side. Moved by the same impulse, they watched the sleeping girls in shared silence.

'The Lady has made us stewards of a great treasure,' observed the wisewoman, 'one that can never be stolen, though it can be lost through carelessness. A child is like a stone. Lovingly polished, it becomes a gem beyond price. If not valued, it is nothing more than a pebble underfoot.' Sirona took Aldyth's hand. 'My precious jewel, you have made an old woman proud, and now you gift me with yet more priceless gems.'

'Which one will it be, Godmother?' whispered Aldyth. 'Who could take your place?'

'Who can know the heart of the Goddess, child? I can only promise you that from your line will come the next Maiden, the Keeper of the Crystal Spring.'

Wrapped in their thoughts, the two women were surprised by a boisterous knocking at the door. Sirona smiled, nodded toward the door, and told Aldyth, 'Go.'

Aldyth might have opened a door into the past, onto a night eleven years gone, for Gandulf stood drunk on the doorstep, a foolish grin on his face. He still wore his hair longer than was fashionable, his copper eyes still shone with a brightness that defied their depth, and Aldyth still felt a tugging at her heart and her loins when she looked at him. Next to Gandulf stood Aelfric and Wulfric, Agilbert and Thurgood, Leofwine and Alcuin, Garth and Godwin. But the litter of boys who had accompanied them eleven years before were grown, and the first of the new litter followed at their heels. Harold and Wulfnoth Godwinson stood shivering with the rest, each with a sleeping boy lovingly wrapped in his cloak and held in his arms. Time goes on and time stands still, she thought; she could hold it back no more than she could the tears that welled up in her eyes, nor would she have wanted to.

Struck by her stillness, Gandulf paused uncertainly, his grin replaced by concern.

Thurgood cried out, 'What's the delay? 'Tis cold out here!'

Friendly hands pushed Gandulf forward, while someone else cautioned, 'Careful now. Right foot first!'

With the meticulous attention of a man who knows he is drunk, Gandulf placed his right foot over the threshold and stepped inside, followed by the frost-numbed crowd. They stamped their frozen feet and gravitated toward the warmth of the hearth, but no one dared say a word before the First Footer had broken the silence with the traditional greeting. Gandulf looked down at Aldyth and saw the tears in her emerald eyes glittering like crystal by firelight. Suddenly Gandulf saw her as she had been on that night eleven years before, when she had been so close and yet so unreachable. The pain of that time wrenched him anew. He felt a surge of desire and a desperate longing to sweep her into his arms, then realized with a joy so intense it brought tears to his eyes that there were no more barriers between them. He caught Aldyth in his arms and kissed her with a passion born of love, gratitude, and unbridled happiness. There was nothing in Gandulf's world but Aldyth, sweet Aldyth. How long they embraced, he could not say, but the thunder in his ears resolved itself into the pounding beat of two hearts.

He looked up to see the others watching, bemused but

impatient, bursting to send out a barrage of wisecracks yet muzzled, for they might not speak before the First Footer.

Harold's belly laugh filled the tiny hut with the auspicious sound of merriment, while Wulfric hastily shoved a loaf of bread and a stick of kindling into Gandulf's hand, which the remiss First Footer gave to Aldyth. Gandulf was handed a cup with which he made the toast, the traditional good wishes that he had rained upon the inhabitants of every other house he had visited that night. 'I wish you a prosperous and happy New Year,' he said, then added with a fierce, soft fervor, 'God grant that it be so, and God grant that it may always be so.'

'And if He falls short of the job,' chuckled Sirona, 'you may be sure that the Goddess will do Her part.'

AUTHORS' NOTES

The lovely hilltop of Sceapterbyrig did then and still does exist, although now it is known as Shaftesbury. The spring at the base of the hill also existed and was filled in only a few years ago; a small, smoky pub called 'The Fountain' still marks the site. However, we have taken artistic liberties with the facts. For example, half the town of Shaftesbury was indeed held by the abbey, but the other half belonged not to the fictional baron Ralf fitzGerald, but directly to the Crown.

We have used, wherever possible, actual historical names and dates. Sheriff Hugh fitzGrip, Hereward the Wake, and Abbess Eulalia were real people about whom very little is known, and we have made free with their character development. More information is available about the lives of William the Conqueror, Edith SwanNeck, and all the Godwinsons, and we have tried to be consistent with their characters. Rumors of Harold's survival after the Battle of Hastings circulated for centuries, and his last resting places were pointed out to us at Canterbury, Chester, and Waltham, as well as at Hastings. We have not tampered with the facts concerning William's death, nor with Edith SwanNeck's battlefield search for Harold's body or the touching love story lived out between Earl Harold and his steward's daughter. The Besom Ceremony, later called the Byzant Ceremony, has continued to be celebrated regularly until 1830 and sporadically thereafter, up until the present day.

The Abbey of Saint Mary, later renamed the Abbey of Saint Mary and Saint Edward, was founded by King Alfred the Great and was at one time the most powerful religious establishment for women in England. During the Dissolution, King Henry VIII authorized the dismantling of the Roman Catholic Church established in England, packing off the last few of Shaftesbury's nuns to genteel retirement. The abbey fell into ruin, but its excavated foundations may still be visited between Easter and September. Castle Hill is still there; excavations show that the motte of a Norman castle was under construction, but for unknown reasons its foundations were never laid. The view from Castle Hill is magnificent, and on a clear day Glastonbury Tor may still be seen.

We would like to apologize to the good folk of Long Cross, Alcester, Enmore Green, and Shaftesbury; on no occasion did we experience any instances of narrow-minded, moonstruck or puritanical behavior from any of the population of Dorset, who were uniformly kind and generous and helpful. In particular, we would like to thank the librarians at Shaftesbury Public Library; Brenda Innes, a local author and historian; and Sheila Clarke, a heritage farm breeder who opened her private library to us. Most of all, we would like to thank Jane Houghton, a member of the Abbey Foundation and an expert on Anglo-Saxon history, herbs and herbal medicine, and, in particular, the abbey. She shared generously of her time and knowledge and gave us permission to throw a little romance into the mix and take a few artistic liberties with our story.

There are also those at home we wish to thank. This book could not have been written without Marjorie, also known as Grammy, who lovingly and generously took care of Naomi's children, her grandchildren. We thank our sister Lee and Deb's husband, Richard, for their support, and our sister Constance for the suggestions she made while reading and rereading this manuscript. We also thank Naomi's Thom for his faith in this, his wife's seemingly endless and impossible endeavor, for his computer expertise, and for the patience he exercised when called upon to share it at any and all hours.

There is one other we must thank. In looking for a site in which to set our story, we traveled all over the West Country, knowing only that we needed a town that was pre-Norman, had a Saxon abbey and a Norman castle, and was not so far from London as to be out of the flow of historical events. We were on our way to Exeter and, although we had planned to avoid Shaftesbury because it had already been used as a setting in several well-known novels, at the last minute we decided to drive through the town instead of skirting it. It was the road sign outside of Shaftesbury, nearly obscured by twining vines, proclaiming it to be a Saxon hilltop fortress town, that prompted us to stop the car in spite of the driving rain. With each corner we turned, we found ourselves more enchanted. It must have been the Goddess who gave us a gentle push toward Tout Hill; as we walked through a magnificent tunnel of trees, with a stunning view of Dorset's emerald hills to the right of us, we noticed a passerby coming up the hill. It was an elderly woman with an umbrella as big as she was. Again on impulse, and as shy as we were feeling, we approached her and asked, 'Were you born here in Shaftesbury?'

After an initial wariness, she decided that we were harmless and replied, 'I was born in Enmore Green, at the foot of the hill.' She was a retired schoolteacher who had taught in the little one-room school in Enmore Green for twenty-five years. It was she who fired our imaginations with tales of the Byzant Ceremony and the area's unique history, then directed us to the Fountain pub for a pint. Before we had reached the foot of the hill, we had invented the ancient English legend of the Crystal Spring. We have looked upon our unknown guide as a Fairy godmother, or perhaps as an earthly manifestation of the Goddess Herself. We close with special thanks to our unknown benefactress and to the Goddess, whose benevolent hand we have felt guiding us all along the way.

DERYN LAKE

DEATH ON THE ROMNEY MARSH

Summoned to attend a patient in a house near the lonely Romney Marsh, Rawlings does not suspect that he is walking into a web of conspiracy, intrigue and mystery. Until he discovers a body near a deserted church, bearing a coded document.

Rawlings reports the case to London's famous blind magistrate John Fielding who identifies the victim as a French spy master. And Rawlings returns to the marshes to investigate who, amongst the colourful local characters, could be harbouring politically explosive secrets . . .

Don't miss *Death in the Dark Walk, Death at the Beggar's Opera* and *Death at the Devil's Tavern,* all available from Hodder and Stoughton in paperback.

HODDER AND STOUGHTON PAPERBACKS

KAGE BAKER

IN THE GARDEN OF IDEN

She is Doña Rosa Anzolabejar: seventeen year old, Spanish, aristocratic. She has come to England in the wake of Mary Tudor's marriage to King Philip of Spain, and she has lied about her past . . .

He is Nicholas Harpole: an idealistic young Englishman who believes profoundly in a faith that has suddenly become a dangerous luxury. He never expected that a girl who was Catholic and Spanish could touch his heart. It is only much later that he discovers that she is something even more strange and terrifying.

For she is a woman from another world. Her name is Mendoza, and she is really seventeen and Spanish. But she is also the product of a twenty-fourth-century experiment in immortality that has given her staggering intelligence and a virtually indestructible body. Her masters have sent her to Sir Walter Iden's garden in Kent to collect extinct plants, not to fall in love. And by the time they realize what has happened to Mendoza and Nicholas, it is too late . . .

HODDER AND STOUGHTON PAPERBACKS

JOANNA HINES

THE PURITAN'S WIFE

To her neighbours in the small Cotswold town of Tilsbury she is a respectable wife and mother; to her husband Josiah she will always be his 'Doll', the child-bride he brought home from the German wars; to the painter of the family's portrait she is an enigma, remote and unknowable, a mystery perhaps even to herself.

When Royalist soldiers arrive to garrison Tilsbury the tranquil rhythm of country life is shattered. Mistress Doll Taverner is more affected than anyone by the impact of the Civil War, which revives all the half-forgotten nightmares of a childhood tragedy. Then a Cornish officer, Captain Stephen Sutton, begins to pose a threat of a subtler kind; as affection grows between them, she is compelled to question all the certainties by which she has lived her life.

Rich and evocative, steeped in the detail of seventeenth-century life, THE PURITAN'S WIFE is a tender, unusual love story played out against a dark background of murder and betrayal.

Don't miss Joanna Hines's other novels, also available from Coronet: THE CORNISH GIRL, a novel of seventeenth-century Cornwall, and her two contemporary suspense novels: DORA'S ROOM and THE FIFTH SECRET.

HODDER AND STOUGHTON PAPERBACKS